The Norton Introduction to

FICTION

FOURTH EDITION

Maureen Maxine Lewis
@131 Tomphins
NCSU
515-3855

The Norton Introduction to
FICTION

FOURTH EDITION

Jerome Beaty

Emory University

W · W · NORTON & COMPANY · NEW YORK · LONDON

Copyright © 1991, 1985, 1981, 1973 by W. W. Norton & Company, Inc.
All rights reserved. Printed in the United States of America.

The text of this book is composed in Electra,
with the display set in Kabel Book.
Composition by Vail-Ballou.
Manufacturing by Courier-Westford.
Book design by Jack Meserole.

Library of Congress Cataloging-in-Publication Data
The Norton introduction to fiction / [compiled by] Jerome Beaty. —
4th ed.
p.   cm.
ISBN 0-393-95936-8
1. Fiction—Collections.   I. Beaty, Jerome, 1924–
PN6120.2.N6   1991
808.3—dc20   90-21621
CIP

W.W. Norton & Company, Inc., 500 Fifth Avenue, New York, N.Y. 10110
W.W. Norton & Company, Ltd., 10 Coptic Street, London WC1A 1PU
1 2 3 4 5 6 7 8 9 0

WOODY ALLEN: "The Kugelmass Episode" from *Side Effects*. Copyright © 1977 by Woody Allen.
Reprinted by permission of Random House, Inc.
MARGARET ATWOOD: "The Whirlpool Rapids" from *Bluebeard's Egg*. Copyright © 1983, 1986 by
O. W. Toad, Ltd. Reprinted by permission of Houghton Mifflin Co. and the Canadian Publishers, McClelland and Stewart, Toronto.
JAMES BALDWIN: "Sonny's Blues" from *Going to Meet the Man*. Copyright © 1948, 1951, 1957,
1958, 1960, 1965 by James Baldwin. Reprinted by permission of Doubleday, a Division of
Bantam, Doubleday, Dell Publishing Group, Inc.
TONI CADE BAMBARA: "My Man Bovanne" from *Gorilla, My Love*. Copyright © 1972 by Toni
Cade Bambara. Reprinted by permission of Random House, Inc.
ANN BEATTIE: "Janus" from *Where You'll Find Me*. Copyright © 1986 by Irony and Pity, Inc.
Reprinted by permission of Linden Press, a division of Simon & Schuster, Inc.
JORGE LUIS BORGES: "The Garden of Forking Paths" from *Labyrinths*. Copyright © 1962, 1964 by
New Directions Publishing Corporation. Reprinted by permission of New Directions Publishing
Corporation.
JOHN CHEEVER: "The Country Husband" from *The Stories of John Cheever*. Copyright 1954 by John
Cheever. Reprinted by permission of Alfred A. Knopf, Inc.
RICHARD CONNELL: "The Most Dangerous Game." Copyright 1924 by Richard Connell; copyright
renewed 1952 by Louise Fox Connell. Reprinted by permission of Brandt & Brandt Literary
Agents, Inc.
LOUISE ERDRICH: "Love Medicine" from *Love Medicine*. Copyright © 1984 by Louise Erdrich.
Reprinted by permission of Henry Holt and Company, Inc.
WILLIAM FAULKNER: "Barn Burning" and "The Old People" from *The Collected Stories of William
Faulkner*. Copyright 1939 and renewed 1967 by Estelle Faulkner and Jill Faulkner Summers.
Copyright 1930 and renewed 1958 by William Faulkner. "The Old People" from *Go Down,
Moses*. Copyright 1940, 1942 and renewed 1968, 1970 by Estelle Faulkner and Jill Faulkner
Summers. Reprinted by permission of Random House, Inc.
RICHARD FORD: "Great Falls" from *Rock Springs*. Copyright © 1987 by Richard Ford. Reprinted
by permission of Atlantic Monthly Press.

CONTENTS

Exploring Contexts   295

Evaluating Fiction   438

Reading More Fiction   492

Writing about Fiction   611

FOREWORD TO THE FOURTH EDITION

Reading is action. Even though it is often done quietly and alone, reading is a profoundly social activity, and a vigorous and demanding one. There is nothing passive about reading; it requires attention, energy, an act of will. Texts have potential for meaning, implication, response, and result; but the reader must activate them, give them life, and turn them from quiet print into a lively interplay of ideas and feelings. Reading makes things happen, usually in the mind and imagination, but sometimes in the larger world as well, for the process of reading involves not just the consciousness of the self but an awareness of the other—what is beyond the self. Reading doesn't just happen to you; you have to **do** it, and doing it involves decision, reaching out, discovery, awareness. Reading is an act of power, and learning how to get the most out of its possibilities can be an invigorating activity. For all its association with quietness, solitude, and the sedentary life, reading involves—at its deepest level—action and interaction.

Through four editions, *The Norton Introduction to Fiction* has been committed to these principles. This edition, like those before it, offers many different ways of building and reinforcing the skills of reading; it emphasizes the power and importance of historical and cultural contexts. In this edition, I have added an introductory chapter on reading fiction, and I have also added chapters on evaluating fiction and on how the many different elements in any text add up to a whole. And I have retained the popular section on writing about fiction, added paper topics and analytical questions, and provided many, many new selections.

The Norton Introduction to Fiction offers in a single volume a complete course in reading and writing about fiction. It is both an anthology and a textbook—a "teaching anthology"—for the indispensable course in which college student and college teacher begin to read fiction seriously together.

But *The Norton Introduction to Fiction* remains more than a grab-bag of good things to read. The works are arranged in order to introduce a reader to the serious study of fiction. The genre is approached in three logical steps. *Reading Fiction* treats the purpose and nature of fiction and the reading experience generally. This is followed by the seven-chapter section called *Understanding the Text*, in which stories are analyzed by questions of craft, the so-called elements of fiction; this section ends with a chapter entitled *The Whole Text*, which makes use of all or most of the analytical aids offered in the previous chapters, putting them together to see the work as a whole. *Exploring Contexts* suggests some ways of seeing a work of fiction, interacting with its temporal and cultural contexts, and reaching out beyond the page.

The sections on reading, analyzing, and placing the work in context are followed by guidance in taking that final and extremely difficult step—evaluation. *Evaluating Fiction* discusses how one would go about assessing the merits of three stories, not to offer definitive judgments, a litmus test, or even a checklist or formula, but to show how one goes about bringing to consciousness, defining, modifying, articulating, and negotiating one's judgments about a work of fiction.

Reading More Fiction is a reservoir of additional examples, for independent study or a different approach. The book's arrangement seeks to facilitate the reader's movement from narrower to broader questions, mirroring the way people read—wanting to learn more as they experience more.

The Norton Introduction to Fiction offers a full section on *Writing about Fiction*. In it I deal both with the writing process as applied to literary works—choosing a topic, gathering evidence, developing an argument, and so forth—and with the varieties of a reader's written responses, from copying and paraphrasing to analysis and interpretation: I explore not merely the hows, but the whats and whys as well.

In the 90s it is no longer enough, either for reading or writing about literature, to be familiar only with the methods of formal analysis. New to this edition is a discussion of critical approaches, designed to provide the student with a basic overview of contemporary critical theory, as well as an introduction to its terminology.

The Fourth Edition includes 48 stories, 16 of which are new. I have added stories by Margaret Atwood, Ann Beattie, Louise Erdrich, Richard Ford, Charlotte Perkins Gilman, Nadine Gordimer, Ernest Hemingway, Jamaica Kincaid, Bharati Mukherjee, Flannery O'Connor, Katherine Anne Porter, Elizabeth Tallent, Amy Tan, Leo Tolstoy, and Luisa Valenzuela.

Certain editorial procedures that proved their usefulness in earlier editions have been retained. First of all, the works are annotated, as is customary in Norton anthologies; the notes are informational and not interpretative, for the aim is to help readers understand and appreciate the work, not to dictate a meaning or a response. In order to avoid giving the impression that all fiction was written at the same time, I have noted for each selection the date of first book publication (or, when preceded by *p*, first periodical publication).

In all my work on this edition I have been guided by teachers in other English departments and in my own, by students who wrote me as the author of the textbook they were using, and by those who were able to approach me after class as their teacher: I hope that with such help I have been able to offer you a solid and stimulating introduction to the experience of fiction.

Acknowledgments

I would like to thank my teachers, for their example in the love of fiction and in the art of sharing that love; my students, for their patience as I am learning from them to be a better teacher of fiction; my wife and children, for their understanding when the work of preparing this text made me seem less than a perfectly loving husband and father.

I would also like to thank my colleagues, many of whom have taught this book and evaluated my efforts, for their constant encouragement and enlightenment. Of my colleagues at Emory University, I would like especially to thank Michaelyn Burnette, William B. Dillingham, Ron Schuchard, John Sitter, Floyd C. Watkins, and Sally Wolff. I thank also Clark Blaise (University of Iowa); T. E. Blom (University of British Columbia); Norman Feltes (York University); Frederick Goldberg (Clayton Junior College); Christopher Hudgins (University of Nevada); Kristin Hunter (University of Pennsylvania); Kathy King (Montevallo College); Stuart Kurland (Muhlenberg College); Michael Lund (Longwood College); Gayla McGlamery (Loyola College in Maryland); William Morgan (Illinois State University); Nils Peteson (San José State University); Linda Ray Pratt (University of Nebraska); Ronald Schleifer (University of Oklahoma); Dennis Todd (Georgetown University); Richard Turner (Indiana University-Purdue University at Indianapolis); and Melissa Walker.

I would like to thank my friends at W. W. Norton & Company, especially the late John Benedict, to whom I dedicate this revision, and also John Mardirosian, Fred McFarland, Diane O'Connor, Nancy Palmquist, Candace Watt, and last (and most) Barry Wade.

J.B.

The Norton Introduction to

FICTION

FOURTH EDITION

∇ ∇ ∇

FICTION

FICTION

∇ ∇ ∇

Reading Fiction

SPENCER HOLST

The Zebra Storyteller

Once upon a time there was a Siamese cat who pretended to be a a lion and spoke inappropriate Zebraic.

That language is whinnied by the race of striped horses in Africa.

Here now: An innocent zebra is walking in a jungle and approaching from another direction is the little cat; they meet.

"Hello there!" says the Siamese cat in perfectly pronounced Zebraic. "It certainly is a pleasant day, isn't it? The sun is shining, the birds are singing, isn't the world a lovely place to live today!"

The zebra is so astonished at hearing a Siamese cat speaking like a zebra, why—he's just fit to be tied.

So the little cat quickly ties him up, kills him, and drags the better parts of the carcass back to his den.

The cat successfully hunted zebras many months in this manner, dining on filet mignon of zebra every night, and from the better hides he made bow neckties and wide belts after the fashion of the decadent princes of the Old Siamese court.

He began boasting to his friends he was a lion, and he gave them as proof the fact that he hunted zebras.

The delicate noses of the zebras told them there was really no lion in the neighborhood. The zebra deaths caused many to avoid the region. Superstitious, they decided the woods were haunted by the ghost of a lion.

One day the storyteller of the zebras was ambling, and through his mind ran plots for stories to amuse the other zebras, when suddenly his eyes brightened, and he said, "That's it! I'll tell a story about a Siamese cat who learns to speak our language! What an idea! That'll make 'em laugh!"

Just then the Siamese cat appeared before him, and said, "Hello there! Pleasant day today, isn't it!"

The zebra storyteller wasn't fit to be tied at hearing a cat speaking his language, because he'd been thinking about that very thing.

He took a good look at the cat, and he didn't know why, but there was

3

something about his looks he didn't like, so he kicked him with a hoof and killed him.

That is the function of the storyteller.

1971

The Zebra Storyteller" suggests that the <u>purpose of stories is to prepare</u> us for the unexpected. Though the storyteller thinks he is just spinning stories out of his own imagination, in order to amuse, his stories prove to be practical. When the extraordinary occurs—like a Siamese cat speaking Zebraic—the storyteller is prepared because he has already imagined it, and he alone is able to protect his tribe against the unheard-of.

Other storytellers make the function of fiction less extraordinary. According to them, <u>fiction enables readers to avoid projecting false hopes and fears</u> (such as the zebras' superstitious belief that they are being preyed on by the ghost of a lion) and shows <u>them what they can actually expect in their everyday lives, so</u> that they can prepare themselves. In George Eliot's novel *Adam Bede*, Hetty Sorrel is being paid admiring attention by the young squire, and she dreams of elopement, marriage, all sorts of vague pleasures. She does not dream that she will be seduced, made pregnant, abandoned. Her imagination has not been trained to project any "narrative" other than her dreams: "Hetty had never read a novel," George Eliot tells us, "[so] how could she find a shape for her expectations?"

 We are all storytellers, then, of one stripe or another. <u>Whenever we plan the future or ponder a decision, we are telling stories</u>—projecting expectations through narrative. <u>Whether</u> we tell stories or read them, we are educating our imaginations, either extending our mental experience in the actual, as Hetty might have done by reading novels, or preparing ourselves for the extraordinary and unexpected, like the zebra storyteller.

The actual and the extraordinary suggest <u>two different</u> uses readers make of fiction. <u>Sometimes we want to read about people like ourselves,</u> or about places, experiences, and ideas that are familiar and agreeable. Most of us initially prefer American literature and twentieth-century literature to literature remote in time or place. Indeed, stories must somehow be related to our own lives before we can find them intellectually or emotionally meaningful. No matter what our literary experience and taste, most of us relate in a special way to stories about people like us, experiences like our own, and especially to a story that mentions our hometown or neighborhood or the name of the street that we used to walk along on our way to school. <u>No one would deny that one</u>

③ of the many things that fiction may be "for" is learning about ourselves and the world around us.

But at other times the last thing we want is a story about people like ourselves, experiences like those of our everyday lives, and places and times like here and now. At such times we want (or are accused of wanting) to escape. If fiction must be relevant enough to relate meaningfully to us, it must also be "irrelevant," different, strange—as strange, perhaps, as a Siamese cat speaking Zebraic. It must take us out of ourselves, out of the confining vision of our own eyes, which is conditioned by our own background and experience, and show us that there are ways of looking at the world other than our own. So, in addition to many stories about approximately our own time and place, this collection includes a sprinkling of stories written in the last century, a few written in vastly different cultures, and a fair number written about worlds that have not existed or do not (yet) exist.

What a story shows us or teaches us we may call its **message**—an objective, universal truth that we were unaware of before reading the story. We gradually learn, however, that stories tell us not so much what life means as what it's like. Rather than abstract or "objective" truths, stories deal with perceptions. These perceptions may be translated into messages, but we soon discover that the messages boil down to things like "There's good and bad in everybody," "Hurting people is wrong," and "Everything is not what it seems"—messages that Western Union, much less Western literature, might not find too urgent or startlingly illuminating. Indeed, we do not have to agree with what a story says or shows so long as we are convinced that if we had *those* eyes and were *there*, this is what we might see.

Whenever we can say yes, we are convinced, then we have been able to go beyond the limitations of our own vision, our own past and conditions. We are able to see a new world, or the same old world in a new way. And by recognizing that we can see things differently, we realize that things we used to think were fixed, objective entities "out there" were fixed only in our perceptions. Or, as is too often the case, we realize that we have been accepting things at face value; we have been perceiving what habit and convention have told us is "really there." This, then, may awaken us to look at things for ourselves. For example, we "know" a table top is square, but in a story we may be told it is diamond-shaped. We understand that if we were to look at the table top from a certain angle it would look diamond-shaped. But doesn't that mean that the table top is square only when we look from a certain angle? How often do we look at it from that angle? We look again, and we recognize that though we've always "known" a table top is a square, we've never really *seen* it as one. The story has not only allowed us to see reality from another angle, but it has helped us to sharpen our own vision, our own experience.

In the story that follows, both the eighteen-year-old narrator and Jack are storytellers: each projects a future. The story, however, remains in the present, so we cannot tell which projection is right. Like the characters, we are more or less in the same position as we are in the middle of our own lives. Though they may not get to know the future, both Jack and the narrator learn through their storytelling that more than one scenario of the future can be projected. Even if we think the narrator as naive as George Eliot's Hetty, projecting a dream rather than a possible reality, she has now at least "read Jack's novel," so she knows there are alternative futures. And so do we.

Since Jack and the narrator are not zebras but people, people you might think of as real, maybe even people somewhat like yourself, you may feel in a position to take sides. You may be surprised to find that some of your classmates do not agree with you. But in discussion or argument you may discover not only that there are reasonable differences of opinion, but that what one believes about the future of the story tells you something about that person (and that what they believe about their future tells you something about the characters of Jack and the narrator). And it tells you more, perhaps, than just what they think about love. If the storytelling of others tells you something about them, then your own storytelling (opinions, expectations, guesses) tells them and yourself something about you. You may realize too that you, your classmates, Jack, and the narrator may all become increasingly aware of differences and possibilities.

ELIZABETH TALLENT

No One's a Mystery

For my eighteenth birthday Jack gave me a five-year diary with a latch and a little key, light as a dime. I was sitting beside him scratching at the lock, which didn't seem to want to work, when he thought he saw his wife's Cadillac in the distance, coming toward us. He pushed me down onto the dirty floor of the pickup and kept one hand on my head while I inhaled the musk of his cigarettes in the dashboard ashtray and sang along with Rosanne Cash on the tape deck. We'd been drinking tequila and the bottle was between his legs, resting up against his crotch, where the seam of his Levi's was bleached linen-white, though the Levi's were nearly new. I don't know why his Levi's always bleached like that, along the seams and at the knees. In a curve of cloth his zipper glinted, gold.

"It's her," he said. "She keeps the lights on in the daytime. I can't think of a single habit in a woman that irritates me more than that." When he saw that I was going to stay still he took his hand from my head and ran it through his own dark hair.

"Why does she?" I said.

"She thinks it's safer. Why does she need to be safer? She's driving exactly fifty-five miles an hour. She believes in those signs: 'Speed Monitored by Aircraft.' It doesn't matter that you can look up and see that the sky is empty."

"She'll see your lips move, Jack. She'll know you're talking to someone."

"She'll think I'm singing along with the radio."

He didn't lift his head, just raised the fingers in salute while the pressure of his palm steadied the wheel, and I heard the Cadillac honk twice, musically; he was driving easily eighty miles an hour. I studied his boots. The elk heads stitched into the leather were bearded with frayed thread, the toes were scuffed, and there was a compact wedge of muddy manure between the heel and the sole—the same boots he'd been wearing for the two years I'd known him. On the tape deck Rosanne Cash sang, "Nobody's into me, no one's a mystery."

"Do you think she's getting famous because of who her daddy is or for herself?" Jack said.

"There are about a hundred pop tops on the floor, did you know that? Some little kid could cut a bare foot on one of these, Jack."

"No little kids get into this truck except for you."

"How come you let it get so dirty?"

" 'How come,' " he mocked. "You even sound like a kid. You can get back into the seat now, if you want. She's not going to look over her shoulder and see you."

"How do you know?"

"I just know," he said. "Like I know I'm going to get meat loaf for supper. It's in the air. Like I know what you'll be writing in that diary."

"What will I be writing?" I knelt on my side of the seat and craned around to look at the butterfly of dust printed on my jeans. Outside the window Wyoming was dazzling in the heat. The wheat was fawn and yellow and parted smoothly by the thin dirt road. I could smell the water in the irrigation ditches hidden in the wheat.

"Tonight you'll write, 'I love Jack. This is my birthday present from him. I can't imagine anybody loving anybody more than I love Jack.' "

"I can't."

"In a year you'll write, 'I wonder what I ever really saw in Jack. I wonder why I spent so many days just riding around in his pickup. It's true he taught me something about sex. It's true there wasn't ever much else to do in Cheyenne.' "

"I won't write that."

"In two years you'll write, 'I wonder what that old guy's name was, the one with the curly hair and the filthy dirty pickup truck and time on his hands.' "

"I won't write that."

"No?"

"Tonight I'll write, 'I love Jack. This is my birthday present from him. I can't imagine anybody loving anybody more than I love Jack.' "

"No, you can't," he said. "You can't imagine it."

25 "In a year I'll write, 'Jack should be home any minute now. The table's set—my grandmother's linen and her old silver and the yellow candles left over from the wedding—but I don't know if I can wait until after the trout à la Navarra to make love to him.' "

"It must have been a fast divorce."

"In two years I'll write, 'Jack should be home by now. Little Jack is hungry for his supper. He said his first word today besides "Mama" and "Papa." He said "kaka." ' "

Jack laughed. "He was probably trying to finger-paint with kaka on the bathroom wall when you heard him say it."

"In three years I'll write, 'My nipples are a little sore from nursing Eliza Rosamund.' "

30 "Rosamund. Every little girl should have a middle name she hates."

" 'Her breath smells like vanilla and her eyes are just Jack's color of blue.' "

"That's nice," Jack said.

"So, which one do you like?"

"I like yours," he said. "But I believe mine."

"It doesn't matter. I believe mine."

"Not in your heart of hearts, you don't."

35 "You're wrong."

'I'm not wrong," he said. "And her breath would smell like your milk, and it's kind of a bittersweet smell, if you want to know the truth."

1985

Reading fiction may ultimately contribute significantly to the way we understand and experience our own lives, but what kind of an experience is reading fiction itself? What is going on inside us while we are reading? What are we thinking? What are we feeling?

One way to find out is by an act of mental contortion: try looking over your own shoulder while you read. Try it with the next story, Guy de Maupassant's "The Jewelry," paying more attention than you usually do not just to the story but to your own thoughts and responses while you are reading it. You may want to pause a few extra heartbeats after each sentence, fifteen to thirty extra seconds after each paragraph, and two or three minutes after you finish reading the whole thing.

Consider the title first. "The Jewelry"—Will it be lost? Will it be stolen? Inherited? Something else? What will happen? What kind of story will it be? Read the one-sentence first paragraph: nothing about jewelry! But we have a young man and a young woman and love. M. (for Monsieur) Lantin is "enveloped in love as in a net." This does not sound very promising, does it? What are these people like? What is their situation? As you read along how do your expectations change? How does your view of the characters change? As you get into the story notice what you remember of the early portions and any details in mid-story that remind you of earlier ones. There are other questions, but they can wait until after you have watched yourself read the story.

GUY DE MAUPASSANT

The Jewelry[1]

Having met the girl one evening, at the house of the office-superintendent, M. Lantin became enveloped in love as in a net.

She was the daughter of a country-tutor, who had been dead for several years. Afterward she had come to Paris with her mother, who made regular visits to several bourgeois families of the neighborhood, in hopes of being able to get her daughter married. They were poor and respectable, quiet and gentle. The young girl seemed to be the very ideal of that pure good woman to whom every young man dreams of entrusting his future. Her modest beauty had a charm of angelic shyness; and the slight smile that always dwelt about her lips seemed a reflection of her heart.

Everybody sang her praises; all who knew her kept saying: "The man who gets her will be lucky. No one could find a nicer girl than that."

M. Lantin, who was then chief clerk in the office of the Minister of the Interior, with a salary of 3,500 francs a year,[2] demanded her hand, and married her.

He was unutterably happy with her. She ruled his home with an economy so adroit that they really seemed to live in luxury. It would be impossible to conceive of any attentions, tendernesses, playful caresses which she did not lavish upon her husband; and such was the charm of her person that, six years after he married her, he loved her even more than he did the first day.

There were only two points upon which he ever found fault with her—her love of the theater, and her passion for false jewelry.

Her lady-friends (she was acquainted with the wives of several small office holders) were always bringing her tickets for the theaters; whenever there was a performance that made a sensation, she always had her *loge* secured, even for first performances; and she would drag her husband with her to all these entertainments, which used to tire him horribly after his day's work. So at last he begged her to go to the theater with some lady-acquaintances who would consent to see her home afterward. She refused for quite a while—thinking it would not look very well to go out thus unaccompanied by her husband. But finally she yielded, just to please him; and he felt infinitely grateful to her therefor.

Now this passion for the theater at last evoked in her the desire of dress. It was true that her toilette remained simple, always in good taste, but modest; and

5

---

1. Translated by Lafcadio Hearn.   2. A mid-level bureaucratic wage, perhaps about $25,000– $30,000 today.

her sweet grace, her irresistible grace, ever smiling and shy, seemed to take fresh charm from the simplicity of her robes. But she got into the habit of suspending in her pretty ears two big cut pebbles, fashioned in imitation of diamonds; and she wore necklaces of false pearls, bracelets of false gold, and haircombs studded with paste-imitations of precious stones.

Her husband, who felt shocked by this love of tinsel and show, would often say—"My dear, when one has not the means to afford real jewelry, one should appear adorned with one's natural beauty and grace only—and these gifts are the rarest of jewels."

But she would smile sweetly and answer: "What does it matter? I like those things—that is my little whim. I know you are right; but one can't make oneself over again. I've always loved jewelry so much!"

And then she would roll the pearls of the necklaces between her fingers, and make the facets of the cut crystals flash in the light, repeating: "Now look at them—see how well the work is done. You would swear it was real jewelry."

He would then smile in his turn, and declare to her: "You have the tastes of a regular Gypsy."

Sometimes, in the evening, when they were having a chat by the fire, she would rise and fetch the morocco box in which she kept her "stock" (as M. Lantin called it)—would put it on the tea-table, and begin to examine the false jewelry with passionate delight, as if she experienced some secret and mysterious sensations of pleasure in their contemplation; and she would insist on putting one of the necklaces round her husband's neck, and laugh till she couldn't laugh any more, crying out: "Oh! how funny you look!" Then she would rush into his arms, and kiss him furiously.

One winter's night, after she had been to the Opera, she came home chilled through, and trembling. Next day she had a bad cough. Eight days after that, she died of pneumonia.

Lantin was very nearly following her into the tomb. His despair was so frightful that in one single month his hair turned white. He wept from morning till night, feeling his heart torn by inexpressible suffering—ever haunted by the memory of her, by the smile, by the voice, by all the charm of the dead woman.

Time did not assuage his grief. Often during office hours his fellow-clerks went off to a corner to chat about this or that topic of the day—his cheeks might have been seen to swell up all of a sudden, his nose wrinkle, his eyes fill with water—he would pull a frightful face, and begin to sob.

He had kept his dead companion's room just in the order she had left it, and he used to lock himself up in it every evening to think about her—all the furniture, and even all her dresses, remained in the same place they had been on the last day of her life.

But life became hard for him. His salary, which, in his wife's hands, had amply sufficed for all household needs, now proved scarcely sufficient to supply his own few wants. And he asked himself in astonishment how she had managed always to furnish him with excellent wines and with delicate eating which he could not now afford at all with his scanty means.

He got a little into debt, like men obliged to live by their wits. At last one morning that he happened to find himself without a cent in his pocket, and a whole week to wait before he could draw his monthly salary, he thought of selling something; and almost immediately it occurred to him to sell his wife's "stock"—for he had always borne a secret grudge against the flash-jewelry that used to annoy him so much in former days. The mere sight of it, day after day, somewhat spoiled the sad pleasure of thinking of his darling.

He tried a long time to make a choice among the heap of trinkets she had left behind her—for up to the very last day of her life she had kept obstinately buying them, bringing home some new thing almost every night—and finally he resolved to take the big pearl necklace which she used to like the best of all, and which he thought ought certainly to be worth six or eight francs, as it was really very nicely mounted for an imitation necklace.

He put it in his pocket, and walked toward the office, following the boulevards, and looking for some jewelry-store on the way, where he could enter with confidence.

Finally he saw a place and went in; feeling a little ashamed of thus exposing his misery, and of trying to sell such a trifling object.

"Sir," he said to the jeweler, "please tell me what this is worth."

The jeweler took the necklace, examined it, weighed it, took up a magnifying glass, called his clerk, talked to him in whispers, put down the necklace on the counter, and drew back a little bit to judge of its effect at a distance.

M. Lantin, feeling very much embarrassed by all these ceremonies, opened his mouth and began to declare—"Oh! I know it can't be worth much" . . . when the jeweler interrupted him saying:

"Well, sir, that is worth between twelve and fifteen thousand francs; but I cannot buy it unless you can let me know exactly how you came by it."

The widower's eyes opened enormously, and he stood gaping—unable to understand. Then after a while he stammered out: "You said? . . . Are you sure?" The jeweler, misconstruing the cause of this astonishment, replied in a dry tone—"Go elsewhere if you like, and see if you can get any more for it. The very most I would give for it is fifteen thousand. Come back and see me again, if you can't do better."

M. Lantin, feeling perfectly idiotic, took his necklace and departed; obeying a confused desire to find himself alone and to get a chance to think.

But the moment he found himself in the street again, he began to laugh, and he muttered to himself: "The fool!—oh! what a fool; If I had only taken him at his word. Well, well!—a jeweler who can't tell paste from real jewelry!"

And he entered another jewelry-store, at the corner of the Rue de la Paix. The moment the jeweler set eyes on the necklace, he examined—"Hello! I know that necklace well—it was sold here!"

M. Lantin, very nervous, asked:

"What's it worth?"

"Sir, I sold it for twenty-five thousand francs. I am willing to buy it back again for eighteen thousand—if you can prove to me satisfactorily, according to legal presciptions, how you came into possession of it"—This time, M. Lantin was simply paralyzed with astonishment. He said: "Well . . . but please look at it again, sir. I always thought until now that it was . . . was false."

The jeweler said:

"Will you give me your name, sir?"

"Certainly. My name is Lantin; I am employed at the office of the Minister of the Interior. I live at No. 16, Rue des Martyrs."

The merchant opened the register, looked, and said: "Yes; this necklace was sent to the address of Madame Lantin, 16 Rue des Martyrs, on July 20th, 1876."

And the two men looked into each other's eyes—the clerk wild with surprise; the jeweler suspecting he had a thief before him.

The jeweler resumed:

"Will you be kind enough to leave this article here for twenty-four hours only—I'll give you a receipt."

M. Lantin stuttered: "Yes-ah! certainly." And he went out folding up the receipt, which he put in his pocket.

Then he crossed the street, went the wrong way, found out his mistake, returned by way of the Tuileries, crossed the Seine, found out he had taken the wrong road again, and went back to the Champs-Elysées without being able to get one clear idea into his head. He tried to reason, to understand. His wife could never have bought so valuable an object as that. Certainly not. But then, it must have been a present! . . . A present from whom? What for?

He stopped and stood stock-still in the middle of the avenue.

A horrible suspicion swept across his mind. . . . She? . . . But then all those other pieces of jewelry must have been presents also! . . . Then it seemed to him that the ground was heaving under his feet; that a tree, right in front of him, was falling toward him; he thrust out his arms instinctively, and fell senseless.

He recovered his consciousness again in a drug-store to which some bystanders had carried him. He had them lead him home, and he locked himself into his room.

Until nightfall he cried without stopping, biting his handkerchief to keep himself from screaming out. Then, completely worn out with grief and fatigue, he went to bed, and slept a leaden sleep.

A ray of sunshine awakened him, and he rose and dressed himself slowly to go to the office. It was hard to have to work after such a shock. Then he reflected that he might be able to excuse himself to the superintendent, and he wrote to him. Then he remembered he would have to go back to the jeweler's; and shame made his face purple. He remained thinking a long time. Still he could not leave the necklace there; he put on his coat and went out.

It was a fine day; the sky extended all blue over the city, and seemed to make it smile. Strollers were walking aimlessly about, with their hands in their pockets.

Lantin thought as he watched them passing: "How lucky the men are who have fortunes! With money a man can even shake off grief—you can go where you please—travel—amuse yourself! Oh! if I were only rich!"

He suddenly discovered he was hungry—not having eaten anything since the evening before. But his pockets were empty; and he remembered the necklace. Eighteen thousand francs! Eighteen thousand francs!—that was a sum—that was!

He made his way to the Rue de la Paix and began to walk backward and forward on the sidewalk in front of the store. Eighteen thousand francs! Twenty times he started to go in; but shame always kept him back.

Still he was hungry—very hungry—and had not a cent. He made one brusque resolve, and crossed the street almost at a run, so as not to let himself have time to think over the matter; and he rushed into the jeweler's.

As soon as he saw him, the merchant hurried forward, and offered him a chair with smiling politeness. Even the clerks came forward to stare at Lantin, with gaiety in their eyes and smiles about their lips.

The jeweler said: "Sir, I made inquiries; and if you are still so disposed, I am ready to pay you down the price I offered you."

The clerk stammered: "Why, yes—sir, certainly."

The jeweler took from a drawer eighteen big bills,[3] counted them, and held them out to Lantin, who signed a little receipt, and thrust the money feverishly into his pocket.

Then, as he was on the point of leaving, he turned to the ever-smiling merchant, and said, lowering his eyes: "I have some—I have some other jewelry, which came to me in the same—from the same inheritance. Would you purchase them also from me?"

The merchant bowed, and answered: "Why, certainly, sir—certainly. . . ." One of the clerks rushed out to laugh at his ease; another kept blowing his nose as hard as he could.

Lantin, impassive, flushed and serious, said: "I will bring them to you."

And he hired a cab to get the jewelry.

When he returned to the store, an hour later, he had not yet breakfasted. They examined the jewelry—piece by piece—putting a value on each. Nearly all had been purchased from that very house.

Lantin, now, disputed estimates made, got angry, insisted on seeing the books, and talked louder and louder the higher the estimates grew.

The big diamond earrings were worth 20,000 francs; the bracelets, 35,000; the brooches, rings and medallions, 16,000; a set of emeralds and sapphires, 14,000; solitaire, suspended to a gold neckchain, 40,000; the total value being estimated at 196,000 francs.

The merchant observed with mischievous good nature: "The person who owned these must have put all her savings into jewelry."

Lantin answered with gravity: "Perhaps that is as good a way of saving money as any other." And he went off, after having agreed with the merchant that an expert should make a counter-estimate for him the next day.

When he found himself in the street again, he looked at the Column Vendôme[4] with the desire to climb it, as if it were a May pole. He felt jolly enough to play leapfrog over the Emperor's head—up there in the blue sky.

He breakfasted at Voisin's[5] restaurant, and ordered wine at 20 francs a bottle.

Then he hired a cab and drove out to the Bois.[6] He looked at the carriages

---

3. French paper money varies in size; the larger the bill, the larger the denomination.   4. Famous column with a statue of Napoleon at the top.   5. Like the Café Anglais below, a well-known and high-priced restaurant.   6. Large Parisian park where the rich took their outings.

passing with a sort of contempt, and a wild desire to yell out to the passers-by: "I am rich, too—I am! I have 200,000 francs!"

The recollection of the office suddenly came back to him. He drove there, walked right into the superintendent's private room, and said: "Sir, I come to give you my resignation. I have just come into a fortune of *three* hundred thousand francs." Then he shook hands all round with his fellow-clerks; and told them all about his plans for a new career. Then he went to dinner at the Café Anglais.

Finding himself seated at the same table with a man who seemed to him quite genteel, he could not resist the itching desire to tell him, with a certain air of coquetry, that he had just inherited a fortune of *four* hundred thousand francs.

For the first time in his life he went to the theater without feeling bored by the performance; and he passed the night in revelry and debauch.

Six months after he married again. His second wife was the most upright of spouses, but had a terrible temper. She made his life very miserable.

1883

QUESTIONS

1. What specific words or phrases in the first two paragraphs of "The Jewelry" alert you to the possibility that all may not be as it seems? How are these expectations or fears allayed in the next few paragraphs? What new fears or expectations are aroused very soon thereafter?

2. Since the story is called "The Jewelry" and life does not come wrapped in such convenient titles, you may come to suspect the truth before M. Lantin. How does your attitude toward him change?

WRITING SUGGESTIONS

1. Copy "The Zebra Storyteller." Exchange papers with a classmate. Carefully proofread each other's papers. Can you believe you could have made errors in simple copying?

2. Write a parody or imitation of "No One's a Mystery" using "I'm Bad" or a more recent song as the title.

Understanding the Text

1 PLOT

In "The Zebra Storyteller" you can see the skeleton of the typical short story **plot** or **plot structure.** Plot simply means the arrangement of the **action,** an imagined event or a series of such events.

Action usually involves **conflict,** a struggle between opposing forces, and it often falls into something like the same five parts that we find in a play: exposition, rising action, turning point (or climax), falling action, conclusion. The conflict in this little tale is between the Siamese cat and the zebras, especially the zebra storyteller. The first part of the action, called the **exposition,** introduces the characters, situation, and, usually, time and place. The exposition here is achieved in three sentences: the time is "once upon a," the place Africa, the characters a Siamese cat who speaks Zebraic and an innocent zebra, and the situation their meeting. We then enter the second part of the plot, the **rising action**: events that complicate the situation and intensify or complicate the conflict or introduce new ones. The first event here is the meeting between an innocent zebra and the Zebraic-speaking cat. That initial conflict of zebra and cat is over in a hurry—the zebra who is "fit to be tied" is tied up and eaten. Complications build with the cat's continuing success in killing zebras, and the zebras' growing fears and consequent superstitious belief that the ghost of a lion haunts the region preying on zebras. The **turning point** or **climax** of the action is the third part of the story, the appearance of the zebra storyteller: until now the cat has had it all his way, but his luck is about to change. From this point on the complications that grew in the first part of the story are untangled—the zebra storyteller, for example, is not surprised when he meets a Siamese cat speaking Zebraic, "because he'd been thinking about that very thing"; this is the fourth part of the story, the reverse movement or **falling action.** The story ends at the fifth part, the **conclusion**: the point at which the situation that was destablized at the beginning of the story (when the Zebraic-speaking cat appeared) becomes stable once more: Africa is once again free of cats speaking the language of zebras.

Before an author can arrange the parts of the action he or she must select them. Writers leave out some things that seem at first to be important to the story and include others that do not seem very important. **Selection** of events and details is a significant element of storytelling.

But what do we mean when we say an author selects events? Selects from where? It is not as if these events exist somewhere, as historical events do. Like scientists with their hypotheses and philosophers with their premises, many of us who talk or write about fiction begin with a fiction: we speak as if the people and places exist and the events of a story take place in a world of the author's imagination, a world from which he or she chooses the story elements, a world we can understand and almost re-create in terms of our own. We call this world the **history** behind the story.

The opening passage of "The Cask of Amontillado" suggests some of the issues involved in selection. "The thousand injuries of Fortunato I had borne as I best could, but when he ventured upon insult I vowed revenge." What kind of injuries? Were there actually so many? Were they real injuries or is the narrator overly sensitive or paranoid and the injuries exaggerated or merely imagined? What was the insult? How could an insult be worse than a thousand injuries? Poe could have invented answers for these questions—perhaps he did—but he chose not to present them to the reader. He chose or selected what he was to present.

The exciting action of Margaret Atwood's "The Whirlpool Rapids" takes place in just four paragraphs in the middle of the story and the details of the event itself are rather vague, filtered through Emma's rather uninformed recollection. The exposition and rising action leading up to the main event, beginning with the fifth paragraph of the story, seem functional and justified. But why are the first four paragraphs here? How about the final six paragraphs?

Once events have been selected, they must be connected. In the history behind the story, events take place in simple chronological sequence: "The king died and then the queen died," to use one critic's example. This sequential narrative of events, the critic says, is not a plot, for it has not been "tampered with" by an author. But if we connect the events, if we structure the history—"The king died and then the queen died of grief"—we have a plot, a **structuring** of the action.

Many of us are used to thinking of cause and effect as a natural part of an event, as somehow *in* the event, rather than as an interpretation of a relationship between two sequential events, so a simple statement of a cause-effect relationship ("died of grief") may not seem like authorial structuring. Many authors seem to like to hide their structuring, to make it seem as if the events in a story are just naturally or inevitably *there*. Montresor's scheme of revenge against Fortunato in "The Cask of Amontillado" is not the author's plot, Poe leads us to believe, but Montresor's; and, while reading, we probably accept that it is Montresor who, interpreting Fortunato's insult as cause for revenge, generates the events that follow. Only later, putting the story down, do we bother to realize that it is Poe who invented and arranged the events, created the plot.

Sometimes, when the characters do not turn sequence into cause or make any of the connections that turn history into plot, the author makes the reader do it. Though the first-person narrator of "Sonny's Blues" seems to be interpreting all the events for us, making the connections, he says he does not know why he always gives money to the young addict who is a friend of Sonny's (par. 9). It is up to us to make the connection. Some readers will conclude that it is because the boy reminds the narrator of Sonny, so in "helping" him, he is helping Sonny. Other readers will see a different connection.

In the history, events exist in chronological sequence, and they can be reported that way in the story: "The king died and then the queen died." But the events in the story can be ordered differently: "The queen died after the King died" recounts the same history, but the order in which the events are reported has been changed. The history has been structured. The reader of the first sentence focuses on the king first, the reader of the second sentence on the queen. The "same thing" has been said, but the structure has been changed, and the difference in focus, emphasis, effect, and thus in the full meaning of the statement can be significant.

In some stories, such as "The Cask of Amontillado," the events seem to come unstructured from the history: Montresor meets Fortunato, tempts him into the vaults, they walk to the end, and so on. The events are presented one after another in the same order as in the history. The reader finds out moment by moment what happens next. In other stories—detective stories, for example—the major action (the crime) has taken place before the story begins, and the forward action of the story is the detective's attempt to re-create the past and figure out what happened. The reader does not ask, "What will happen?" but "What has happened?" In some other stories, like Faulkner's "A Rose for Emily" in the next chapter, readers may not feel compelled to ask what has happened until the end, when a sudden revelation from the fictional past forces them to reconsider all that has gone before. In such stories it is obvious that the author has created a plot, ordered the events in the story in a sequence different from that in which they occurred. But just as Poe disguised his plot as his narrator's, so Faulkner disguises his reordering of events as the order of the narrator's recollections followed by that narrator's learning a new fact about the past at the end of the story.

Though the sequence of events in the detective story is reordered in terms of the reader's knowledge of events—we learn "who done it" in the past only long after the story begins—the past is not usually replayed: we do not "see" the crime reenacted before us (although detectives often describe the crime when they give their solutions). The story simply begins in the middle of the history—after the crime—and moves forward as the detective figures out what happened. In "Sonny's Blues," however, there is a replay or **flashback** (or rather a series of flashbacks). There is a very brief scene from the past triggered by the word "safe" (par. 79), the narrator recalling his father's words, which then leads to a specific dramatized scene—the last time the narrator talked to his mother. This is followed by another scene—the narrator's conversation with Sonny after their mother's funeral. This scene of course follows the previous one but in terms of where the story began (the fictional present) it is in the past, and therefore is in fact a flashback. Nor does the story return to the fictional present for some time—"I read about Sonny's trouble in the spring. Little Grace died in the fall . . ." (par. 177)—when Sonny has been living with the narrator for two weeks, and it proceeds from that point to the end.

One reason for structuring the history into plot is to engage the reader's attention, to make the reader read on. This can be done not only by arousing the reader's expectations of what will happen next but also by generating **curiosity**—the desire to know what is happening or has happened. It is the sheer power of curiosity, for example, that keeps us reading intensely when we know as little as Watson or Sherlock Holmes himself at the beginning of a story or "case." Nor is it only the detective story that plays upon our curiosity. "Sonny's Blues" begins, "I read about it in the paper . . . ," and that "it" without antecedent is repeated seven times in the first paragraph and first two sentences of the second paragraph. Read those first two paragraphs and stop. If you try at this point to examine what is going on in your mind, you more than likely will find that you are asking yourself what "it" might refer to, and you will more than likely have framed for yourself several possible answers. It may be in part for this reason that Baldwin begins how and where he does, getting you engaged in the story, so that you will read on. Even a title, such as "The Zebra Storyteller," "A Very Old Man with Enormous Wings," or "The Rocking

Horse Winner," can make us curious enough to pick up a story; after that, it's up to the story to keep us engaged.

Perhaps stronger than curiosity is **suspense**—that particular kind of expectation involving anticipation of and doubt about what is going to happen next (as differentiated from expectations about what a character is like, what the theme is or how it will develop, and so on). Even in reading a little fable like "The Zebra Storyteller" our minds are—or should be—at work: a cat speaking Zebraic is killing zebras; the zebra storyteller thinking of plots comes up with the idea of a story in which a cat speaking Zebraic is killing zebras: "What an idea! That'll make 'em laugh!" he tells himself. Then he meets the cat—what will happen next? How many possibilities did you or can you anticipate?

Sometimes the suspense is generated and defined not so much by what happens within the story as it is by what we expect from stories. In "The Jewelry," for example, when Lantin's wife dies so early in the story, we know this is not the end; something is going to happen or be revealed because there are several pages left and stories do not go on unless something is going to happen. But what? Lantin grieves so intensely, locks himself in her room . . . will her ghost return? He is going bankrupt, he looks over his wife's jewelry, and when he goes to sell a piece he finds it is not mere costume jewelry, but real. How much sooner than Lantin himself do you realize the source of the jewelry? There is a certain satisfaction in seeing the truth before he does. But *then* what do you expect to happen next? Do you anticipate his debauching? How did you expect the story to end?

If you were to pause just before reading the final paragraph of the Maupassant story and consciously explore your expectations, you would see that these are based on fictional and actual conventions—indeed, most of us would probably assume the story could have ended with the word "debauch," without the final brief paragraph, and that the story would end with the irony of Lantin's getting pleasure out of his having been betrayed. We can accept this even within our conventional moral terms—he may get bitter pleasures for a time, but he will soon tire of such pleasures or be undone by them.

The final paragraph, however, if it does not contradict, deepens the irony: now he has a truly "upright" wife—and he is miserable. Our conventional expectations that morality brings happiness, that infidelity and debauchery lead to various kinds of ruin, are wrenched into question. He has tired of debauchery, but is he better off leading a moral life? Is the world amoral—or even immoral? Do good guys finish last? We do not have to believe this, but to read the story fully we need to call our perhaps more optimistic and conventional views into question.

In order to keep you engaged and alert, a story must make you ask questions about what will happen or what will be revealed next. To respond fully to a story you must be alert to the signals and guess along with the author. One way of seeing whether and how your mind is engaged in your reading is to pause at crucial points in your reading and consciously explore what you think is coming. In "No One's a Mystery" the story does the pausing and the conscious specification of what might happen next for you—it gives two versions of what might happen and then the story ends, without resolution. (Though not without point; for to suggest that both naivete and cynicism are merely attitudes, and that neither is an infallible clue to the future, is an insight and a challenge, even if it is not, strictly speaking, a resolution.) At least in one aspect, fiction is a guessing game.

Like all guessing games, from quiz show to philosophy, the plot game in fiction has certain guidelines. A well-structured plot will play fair with you, offering at appropriate points all the necessary indications or clues to what will happen next, not just springing new and essential information on you at the last minute ("Meanwhile, unknown to our hero, the Marines were just on the other side of the hill . . ."). It is this playing fair that makes the ending of a well-structured story satisfying or, when you look back on it, inevitable. Most stories also offer a number of reasonable but false signals (red herrings) to get you off the scent, so that in a well-structured story the ending, though inevitable, is also surprising. And though there is usually an overarching action from beginning to end, in many stories there are layers of expectation or suspense, so that as soon as one question is answered another comes forth to replace it, keeping you in doubt and suspense as to the final outcome.

Unlike most guessing games, however, the reward is not for the right guess—anticipating the outcome before the final paragraph—but for the number of guesses, right *and* wrong, that you make, the number of signals you respond to. If you are misled by none of the false signals in the early pages of a story—by Sonny's friend saying, " 'Listen. They'll let him out and then it'll just start all over again' " (par. 36), for example—you may be closer to being "right," but you have missed many of the implications of the story. But, more important, you have missed the pleasure of learning the "truth" offered by the story for yourself, and you know how much less meaningful it is to be told something than it is to learn it for yourself, through your own experience. Fiction is a way of transmitting not just perception but experience.

Though plot is the structuring of events, an event can be an outcome or consequence as well as a happening, and the expectation, surprise, and perception surrounding plot structure can involve meaning as well as action. So, in

"The Whirlpool Rapids," the results of Emma's adventure are somewhat surprising, modifying our conventional expectations of what it means to survive death and become fearless. Though such conventional expectations are not so consciously aroused as are those aroused by action and adventure—the kind of expectation described by the term "suspense"—their fulfillment, modification, or contradiction is a significant aim and effect of many stories. For though fiction is in part a guessing game, it is not merely a game. Many stories seek to give new insights into human perception, experience, meaning, or at least to challenge our more or less unconsciously held beliefs. They strive to tell truths—new, subjective truths, but truths—even though they "lie" about the actuality of the people and events represented. But first they have to get your attention, and one way is by arousing your curiosity and exciting your anticipation. That is one of the primary functions of plot.

Alertness to signals, anticipating what is to come next, and remembering what has been said and signaled earlier are essential to fully appreciating and understanding stories and their structures. How, for example, do you react in "The Cask of Amontillado" to Montresor's concern for Fortunato's coughing? What do you anticipate? What is it that you later discover? By the time you finish the Poe story, you may know why insult is more important to Montresor than injury; you may even be able to suggest why Poe did not recount the thousand injuries or the fatal insult.

PLOT A Glossary

action: an imagined event or series of events (an event may be verbal as well as physical, so that saying something or telling a story within the story may be an event)

climax: see *turning point*

conclusion: the fifth part of the structure, the point at which the situation that was destabilized at the beginning of the story becomes stable once more

conflict: a struggle between opposing forces, such as between two people, a person and something in nature or society, or even between two drives, impulses, or parts of the self

curiosity: the desire to know what is happening or has happened

expectation: the anticipation of what is to happen next (see *suspense*), what a character is like or how he or she will develop, what the theme or meaning of the story will prove to be, and so on

exposition: that part of the structure which sets the scene, introduces and identifies characters, establishes the situation at the beginning of the narrative, though additional exposition is often scattered throughout the story

flashback: that structuring device whereby a scene from the fictional past is inserted into the fictional present or dramatized out of order

history: the imaginary people, places, chronologically arranged events that we assume exist in the world of the author's imagination, a world from which he or she chooses and arranges or re-arranges the story elements

plot/plot structure: the arrangement of the action

red herring: a false lead, something that misdirects expectations

rising action: the second of the five parts of plot structure, in which events are introduced complicating the situation that existed at the beginning of a work and intensifying or complicating the conflict or introducing new ones

selection: the process by which authors leave out some things that seem to be important to the story and include some things that do not seem very important

structuring: the arrangement or rearrangement of the elements in the history

suspense: the expectation of and doubt about what is going to happen next

turning point or **climax:** the third part of plot structure, the point at which the action stops rising and begins falling or reversing

EDGAR ALLAN POE

The Cask of Amontillado

The thousand injuries of Fortunato I had borne as I best could, but when he ventured upon insult I vowed revenge. You, who so well know the nature of my soul, will not suppose, however, that I gave utterance to a threat. At *length* I would be avenged; this was a point definitively settled—but the very definitiveness with which it was resolved precluded the idea of risk. I must not only punish but punish with impunity. A wrong is unredressed when retribution overtakes its redresser. It is equally unredressed when the avenger fails to make himself felt as such to him who has done the wrong.

It must be understood that neither by word nor deed had I given Fortunato cause to doubt my good will. I continued, as was my wont, to smile in his face, and he did not perceive that my smile *now* was at the thought of his immolation.

He had a weak point—this Fortunato—although in other regards he was a man to be respected and even feared. He prided himself upon his connoisseurship in wine. Few Italians have the true virtuoso spirit. For the most part their enthusiasm is adopted to suit the time and opportunity, to practice imposture upon the British and Austrian *millionaires*. In painting and gemmary, Fortunato, like his countrymen, was a quack, but in the matter of old wines he was sincere. In this respect I did not differ from him materially;—I was skilful in the Italian vintages myself, and bought largely whenever I could.

It was about dusk, one evening during the supreme madness of the carnival season, that I encountered my friend. He accosted me with excessive warmth, for he had been drinking much. The man wore motley. He had on a tight-fitting parti-striped dress, and his head was surmounted by the conical cap and bells. I was so pleased to see him that I should never have done wringing his hand.

I said to him—"My dear Fortunato, you are luckily met. How remarkably well you are looking to-day. But I have received a pipe[1] of what passes for Amontillado, and I have my doubts." $\qquad$ 5

"How?" said he. "Amontillado? A pipe? Impossible! And in the middle of the carnival!"

"I have my doubts," I replied; "and I was silly enough to pay the full Amontillado price without consulting you in the matter. You were not to be found, and I was fearful of losing a bargain."

"Amontillado!"

"I have my doubts."

"Amontillado!" $\qquad$ 10

"And I must satisfy them."

"Amontillado!"

"As you are engaged, I am on my way to Luchresi. If any one has a critical turn it is he. He will tell me——"

---

1. A cask holding 126 gallons.

"Luchresi cannot tell Amontillado from Sherry."

"And yet some fools will have it that his taste is a match for your own."

"Come, let us go."

"Whither?"

"To your vaults."

"My friend, no; I will not impose upon your good nature. I perceive you have an engagement. Luchresi——"

"I have no engagement;—come."

"My friend, no. It is not the engagement, but the severe cold with which I perceive you are afflicted. The vaults are insufferably damp. They are encrusted with nitre."

"Let us go, nevertheless. The cold is merely nothing. Amontillado! You have been imposed upon. And as for Luchresi, he cannot distinguish Sherry from Amontillado."

Thus speaking, Fortunato possessed himself of my arm; and putting on a mask of black silk and drawing a *roquelaire*[2] closely about my person, I suffered him to hurry me to my palazzo.

There were no attendants at home; they had absconded to make merry in honour of the time. I had told them that I should not return until the morning, and had given them explicit orders not to stir from the house. These orders were sufficient, I well knew, to insure their immediate disappearance, one and all, as soon as my back was turned.

I took from their sconces two flambeaux, and giving one to Fortunato, bowed him through several suites of rooms to the archway that led into the vaults. I passed down a long and winding staircase, requesting him to be cautious as he followed. We came at length to the foot of the descent, and stood together upon the damp ground of the catacombs of the Montresors.

The gait of my friend was unsteady, and the bells upon his cap jingled as he strode.

"The pipe," said he.

"It is farther on," said I; "but observe the white web-work which gleams from these cavern walls."

He turned towards me, and looked into my eyes with two filmy orbs that distilled the rheum of intoxication.

"Nitre?" he asked, at length.

"Nitre," I replied. "How long have you had that cough?"

"Ugh! ugh! ugh!—ugh! ugh! ugh!—ugh! ugh! ugh!—ugh! ugh! ugh!—ugh! ugh! ugh!"

My poor friend found it impossible to reply for many minutes.

"It is nothing," he said, at last.

"Come," I said, with decision, "we will go back; your health is precious. You are rich, respected, admired, beloved; you are happy, as once I was. You are a man to be missed. For me it is no matter. We will go back; you will be ill, and I cannot be responsible. Besides, there is Luchresi——"

2. Roquelaure: man's heavy, knee-length cloak.

"Enough," he said; "the cough is a mere nothing; it will not kill me. I shall not die of a cough."

"True—true," I replied; "and, indeed, I had no intention of alarming you unneccessarily—but you should use all proper caution. A draught of this Medoc[3] will defend us from the damps."

Here I knocked off the neck of a bottle which I drew from a long row of its fellows that lay upon the mould.

"Drink," I said, presenting him the wine.

He raised it to his lips with a leer. He paused and nodded to me familiarly, while his bells jingled.   40

"I drink," he said, "to the buried that repose around us."

"And I to your long life."

He again took my arm, and we proceeded.

"These vaults," he said, "are extensive."

"The Montresors," I replied, "were a great and numerous family."   45

"I forget your arms."

"A huge human foot d'or,[4] in a field azure; the foot crushes a serpent rampant whose fangs are imbedded in the heel."

"And the motto?"

"*Nemo me impune lacessit.*"[5]

"Good!" he said.   50

The wine sparkled in his eyes and the bells jingled. My own fancy grew warm with the Medoc. We had passed through long walls of piled skeletons, with casks and puncheons intermingling, into the inmost recesses of the catacombs. I paused again, and this time I made bold to seize Fortunato by an arm above the elbow.

"The nitre!" I said; "see, it increases. It hangs like moss upon the vaults. We are below the river's bed. The drops of moisture trickle among the bones. Come, we will go back ere it is too late. Your cough——"

"It is nothing," he said; "let us go on. But first, another draught of the Medoc."

I broke and reached him a flaçon of De Grâve. He emptied it at a breath. His eyes flashed with a fierce light. He laughed and threw the bottle upwards with a gesticulation I did not understand.

I looked at him in surprise. He repeated the movement—a grotesque one.   55

"You do not comprehend?" he said.

"Not I," I replied.

"Then you are not of the brotherhood."

"How?"

"You are not of the masons."[6]   60

"Yes, yes," I said; "yes, yes."

"You? Impossible! A mason?"

"A mason," I replied.

"A sign," he said, "a sign."

3. Like De Grâve (below), a French wine.   4. Of gold.   5. No one provokes me with impunity.   6. Masons or Freemasons, an international secret society condemned by the Catholic Church. Montresor means by mason one who builds with stone, brick, etc.

65 "It is this," I answered producing from beneath the folds of my *roquelaire* a trowel.

"You jest," he exclaimed, recoiling a few paces. "But let us proceed to the Amontillado."

"Be it so," I said, replacing the tool beneath the cloak and again offering him my arm. He leaned upon it heavily. We continued our route in search of the Amontillado. We passed through a range of low arches, descended, passed on, and descending again, arrived at a deep crypt, in which the foulness of the air caused our flambeaux rather to glow than flame.

At the most remote end of the crypt there appeared another less spacious. Its walls had been lined with human remains, piled to the vault overhead, in the fashion of the great catacombs of Paris. Three sides of this interior crypt were still ornamented in this manner. From the fourth side the bones had been thrown down, and lay promiscuously upon the earth, forming at one point a mound of some size. Within the wall thus exposed by the displacing of the bones, we perceived a still interior crypt or recess, in depth about four feet, in width three, in height six or seven. It seemed to have been constructed for no especial use within itself, but formed merely the interval between two of the colossal supports of the roof of the catacombs, and was backed by one of their circumscribing walls of solid granite.

It was in vain that Fortunato, uplifting his dull torch, endeavoured to pry into the depth of the recess. Its termination the feeble light did not enable us to see.

70 "Proceed," I said; "herein is the Amontillado. As for Luchresi——"

"He is an ignoramus," interrupted my friend, as he stepped unsteadily forward, while I followed immediately at his heels. In an instant he had reached the extremity of the niche, and finding his progress arrested by the rock, stood stupidly bewildered. A moment more and I had fettered him to the granite. In its surface were two iron staples, distant from each other about two feet, horizontally. From one of these depended a short chain, from the other a padlock. Throwing the links about his waist, it was but the work of a few seconds to secure it. He was too much astounded to resist. Withdrawing the key I stepped back from the recess.

"Pass your hand," I said, "over the wall; you cannot help feeling the nitre. Indeed, it is *very* damp. Once more let me *implore* you to return. No? Then I must positively leave you. But I will first render you all the little attentions in my power."

"The Amontillado!" ejaculated my friend, not yet recovered from his astonishment.

"True," I replied; "the Amontillado."

75 As I said these words I busied myself among the pile of bones of which I have before spoken. Throwing them aside, I soon uncovered a quantity of building stone and mortar. With these materials and with the aid of my trowel, I began vigorously to wall up the entrance of the niche.

I had scarcely laid the first tier of the masonry when I discovered that the intoxication of Fortunato had in great measure worn off. The earliest indication I had of this was a low moaning cry from the depth of the recess. It was *not* the cry of a drunken man. There was then a long and obstinate silence. I laid the second tier, and the third, and the fourth; and then I heard the furious vibration of the chain. The noise lasted for several minutes, during which, that I might hearken to it with the more satisfaction, I ceased my labours and sat down upon the bones. When at last the clanking subsided, I resumed the trowel, and finished without interruption the fifth, the sixth, and the seventh tier. The wall was now nearly upon a level with my breast. I again paused, and holding the flambeaux over the mason-work, threw a few feeble rays upon the figure within.

A succession of loud and shrill screams, bursting suddenly from the throat of the chained form, seemed to thrust me violently back. For a brief moment I hesitated, I trembled. Unsheathing my rapier, I began to grope with it about the recess; but the thought of an instant reassured me. I placed my hand upon the solid fabric of the catacombs and felt satisfied. I reapproached the wall. I replied to the yells of him who clamoured. I reechoed, I aided, I surpassed them in volume and in strength. I did this, and the clamourer grew still.

It was now midnight, and my task was drawing to a close. I had completed the eighth, the ninth and the tenth tier. I had finished a portion of the last and the eleventh; there remained but a single stone to be fitted and plastered in. I struggled with its weight; I placed it partially in its destined position. But now there came from out the niche a low laugh that erected the hairs upon my head. It was succeeded by a sad voice, which I had difficulty in recognizing as that of the noble Fortunato. The voice said—

"Ha! ha! ha!—he! he! he!—a very good joke, indeed—an excellent jest. We will have many a rich laugh about it at the palazzo—he! he! he!—over our wine—he! he! he!"

"The Amontillado!" I said.

"He! he! he!—he! he! he!—yes, the Amontillado. But is it not getting late? Will not they be awaiting us at the palazzo—the Lady Fortunato and the rest? Let us be gone."

"Yes," I said, "let us be gone."

"For the love of God, Montresor!"

"Yes," I said, "for the love of God!"

But to these words I hearkened in vain for a reply. I grew impatient. I called aloud—

"Fortunato!"

No answer. I called again—

"Fortunato!"

No answer still. I thrust a torch through the remaining aperture and let it fall within. There came forth in return only a jingling of the bells. My heart grew sick; it was the dampness of the catacombs that made it so. I hastened to make an end of my labour. I forced the last stone into its position; I plastered it up. Against the new masonry I re-erected the old rampart of bones. For the half of a century no mortal has disturbed them. *In pace requiescat!*[7]

1846

7. May he rest in peace.

JAMES BALDWIN

Sonny's Blues

I read about it in the paper, in the subway, on my way to work. I read it, and I couldn't believe it, and I read it again. Then perhaps I just stared at it, at the newsprint spelling out his name, spelling out the story. I stared at it in the swinging lights of the subway car, and in the faces and bodies of the people, and in my own face, trapped in the darkness which roared outside.

It was not to be believed and I kept telling myself that, as I walked from the subway station to the high school. And at the same time I couldn't doubt it. I was scared, scared for Sonny. He became real to me again. A great block of ice got settled in my belly and kept melting there slowly all day long, while I taught my classes algebra. It was a special kind of ice. It kept melting, sending trickles of ice water all up and down my veins, but it never got less. Sometimes it hardened and seemed to expand until I felt my guts were going to come spilling out or that I was going to choke or scream. This would always be at a moment when I was remembering some specific thing Sonny had once said or done.

When he was about as old as the boys in my classes his face had been bright and open, there was a lot of copper in it; and he'd had wonderfully direct brown eyes, and great gentleness and privacy. I wondered what he looked like now. He had been picked up, the evening before, in a raid on an apartment downtown, for peddling and using heroin.

I couldn't believe it: but what I mean by that is that I couldn't find any room for it anywhere inside me. I had kept it outside me for a long time. I hadn't wanted to know. I had had suspicions, but I didn't name them, I kept putting them away. I told myself that Sonny was wild, but he wasn't crazy. And he'd always been a good boy, he hadn't ever turned hard or evil or disrespectful, the way kids can, so quick, so quick, especially in Harlem. I didn't want to believe that I'd ever see my brother going down, coming to nothing, all that light in his face gone out, in the condition I'd already seen so many others. Yet it had happened and here I was, talking about algebra to a lot of boys who might, every one of them for all I knew, be popping off needles every time they went to the head.[1] Maybe it did more for them than algebra could.

I was sure that the first time Sonny had ever had horse,[2] he couldn't have been much older than these boys were now. These boys, now, were living as we'd been living then, they were growing up with a rush and their heads bumped abruptly against the low ceiling of their actual possibilities. They were filled with rage. All they really knew were two darknesses, the darkness of their lives, which was now closing in on them, and the darkness of the movies, which had blinded them to that other darkness, and in which they now, vindictively, dreamed, at once more together than they were at any other time, and more alone.

When the last bell rang, the last class ended, I let out my breath. It seemed

1. Lavatory.   2. Heroin.

I'd been holding it for all that time. My clothes were wet—I may have looked as though I'd been sitting in a steam bath, all dressed up, all afternoon. I sat alone in the classroom a long time. I listened to the boys outside, downstairs, shouting and cursing and laughing. Their laughter struck me for perhaps the first time. It was not the joyous laughter which—God knows why—one associates with children. It was mocking and insular, its intent was to denigrate. It was disenchanted, and in this, also, lay the authority of their curses. Perhaps I was listening to them because I was thinking about my brother and in them I heard my brother. And myself.

One boy was whistling a tune, at once very complicated and very simple, it seemed to be pouring out of him as though he were a bird, and it sounded very cool and moving through all that harsh, bright air, only just holding its own through all those other sounds.

I stood up and walked over to the window and looked down into the courtyard. It was the beginning of the spring and the sap was rising in the boys. A teacher passed through them every now and again, quickly, as though he or she couldn't wait to get out of that courtyard, to get those boys out of their sight and off their minds. I started collecting my stuff. I thought I'd better get home and talk to Isabel.

The courtyard was almost deserted by the time I got downstairs. I saw this boy standing in the shadow of a doorway, looking just like Sonny. I almost called his name. Then I saw that it wasn't Sonny, but somebody we used to know, a boy from around our block. He'd been Sonny's friend. He'd never been mine, having been too young for me, and, anyway, I'd never liked him. And now, even though he was a grown-up man, he still hung around that block, still spent hours on the street corners, was always high and raggy. I used to run into him from time to time and he'd often work around to asking me for a quarter or fifty cents. He always had some real good excuse, too, and I always gave it to him. I don't know why.

But now, abruptly, I hated him. I couldn't stand the way he looked at me, partly like a dog, partly like a cunning child. I wanted to ask him what the hell he was doing in the school courtyard.

He sort of shuffled over to me, and he said, "I see you got the papers. So you already know about it."

"You mean about Sonny? Yes, I already know about it. How come they didn't get you?"

He grinned. It made him repulsive and it also brought to mind what he'd looked like as a kid. "I wasn't there. I stay away from them people."

"Good for you." I offered him a cigarette and I watched him through the smoke. "You come all the way down here just to tell me about Sonny?"

"That's right." He was sort of shaking his head and his eyes looked strange, as though they were about to cross. The bright sun deadened his damp dark brown skin and it made his eyes look yellow and showed up the dirt in his kinked hair. He smelled funky. I moved a little away from him and I said, "Well, thanks. But I already know about it and I got to get home."

"I'll walk you a little ways," he said. We started walking. There were a couple of kids still loitering in the courtyard and one of them said goodnight to me and looked strangely at the boy beside me.

"What're you going to do?" he asked me. "I mean, about Sonny?"

"Look. I haven't seen Sonny for over a year, I'm not sure I'm going to do anything. Anyway, what the hell *can* I do?"

"That's right," he said quickly, "ain't nothing you can do. Can't much help old Sonny no more, I guess."

It was what I was thinking and so it seemed to me he had no right to say it.

"I'm surprised at Sonny, though," he went on—he had a funny way of talking, he looked straight ahead as though he were talking to himself—"I thought Sonny was a smart boy, I thought he was too smart to get hung."

"I guess he thought so too," I said sharply, "and that's how he got hung. And how about you? You're pretty goddamn smart, I bet."

Then he looked directly at me, just for a minute. "I ain't smart," he said. "If I was smart, I'd have reached for a pistol a long time ago."

"Look. Don't tell *me* your sad story, if it was up to me, I'd give you one." Then I felt guilty—guilty, probably, for never having supposed that the poor bastard *had* a story of his own, much less a sad one, and I asked, quickly, "What's going to happen to him now?"

He didn't answer this. He was off by himself some place.

"Funny thing," he said, and from his tone we might have been discussing the quickest way to get to Brooklyn, "when I saw the papers this morning, the first thing I asked myself was if I had anything to do with it. I felt sort of responsible."

I began to listen more carefully. The subway station was on the corner, just before us, and I stopped. He stopped, too. We were in front of a bar and he ducked slightly, peering in, but whoever he was looking for didn't seem to be there. The juke box was blasting away with something black and bouncy and I half watched the barmaid as she danced her way from the juke box to her place behind the bar. And I watched her face as she laughingly responded to something someone said to her, still keeping time to the music. When she smiled one saw the little girl, one sensed the doomed, still-struggling woman beneath the battered face of the semi-whore.

"I never *give* Sonny nothing," the boy said finally, "but a long time ago I come to school high and Sonny asked me how it felt." He paused, I couldn't bear to watch him, I watched the barmaid, and I listened to the music which seemed to be causing the pavement to shake. "I told him it felt great." The music stopped, the barmaid paused and watched the juke box until the music began again. "It did."

All this was carrying me some place I didn't want to go. I certainly didn't want to know how it felt. It filled everything, the people, the houses, the music, the dark, quicksilver barmaid, with menace; and this menace was their reality.

"What's going to happen to him now?" I asked again.

"They'll send him away some place and they'll try to cure him." He shook his head. "Maybe he'll even think he's kicked the habit. Then they'll let him loose"—he gestured, throwing his cigarette into the gutter. "That's all."

"What do you mean, that's *all*?"

But I knew what he meant.

"I *mean*, that's *all*." He turned his head and looked at me, pulling down the corners of his mouth. "Don't you know what I mean?" he asked, softly.

"How the hell *would* I know what you mean?" I almost whispered it, I don't know why. 35

"That's right," he said to the air, "how would *he* know what I mean?" He turned toward me again, patient and calm, and yet I somehow felt him shaking, shaking as though he were going to fall apart. I felt that ice in my guts again, the dread I'd felt all afternoon; and again I watched the barmaid, moving about the bar, washing glasses, and singing. "Listen. They'll let him out and then it'll just start all over again. That's what I mean."

"You mean—they'll let him out. And then he'll just start working his way back in again. You mean he'll never kick the habit. Is that what you mean?"

"That's right," he said, cheerfully. "*You* see what I mean."

"Tell me," I said at last, "why does he want to die? He must want to die, he's killing himself, why does he want to die?"

He looked at me in surprise. He licked his lips. "He don't want to die. He 40 wants to live. Don't nobody want to die, ever."

Then I wanted to ask him—too many things. He could not have answered, or if he had, I could not have borne the answers. I started walking. "Well, I guess it's none of my business."

"It's going to be rough on old Sonny," he said. We reached the subway station. "This is your station?" he asked. I nodded. I took one step down. "Damn!" he said, suddenly. I looked up at him. He grinned again. "Damn it if I didn't leave all my money home. You ain't got a dollar on you, have you? Just for a couple of days, is all."

All at once something inside gave and threatened to come pouring out of me. I didn't hate him any more. I felt that in another moment I'd start crying like a child.

"Sure," I said. "Don't sweat." I looked in my wallet and didn't have a dollar, I only had a five. "Here," I said. "That hold you?"

He didn't look at it—he didn't want to look at it. A terrible, closed look came 45 over his face, as though he were keeping the number on the bill a secret from him and me. "Thanks," he said, and now he was dying to see me go. "Don't worry about Sonny. Maybe I'll write him or something."

"Sure," I said. "You do that. So long."

"Be seeing you," he said. I went on down the steps.

And I didn't write Sonny or send him anything for a long time. When I finally did, it was just after my little girl died, and he wrote me back a letter which made me feel like a bastard.

Here's what he said:

Dear brother,

You don't know how much I needed to hear from you. I wanted to write you 50 many a time but I dug how much I must have hurt you and so I didn't write. But now I feel like a man who's been trying to climb up out of some deep, real deep and funky hole and just saw the sun up there, outside. I got to get outside.

I can't tell you much about how I got here. I mean I don't know how to tell you. I guess I was afraid of something or I was trying to escape from something and you know I have never been very strong in the head (smile). I'm glad Mama and Daddy are dead and can't see what's happened to their son and I swear if I'd known what I was doing I would never have hurt you so, you and a lot of other fine people who were nice to me and who believed in me.

I don't want you to think it had anything to do with me being a musician. It's more than that. Or maybe less than that. I can't get anything straight in my head down here and I try not to think about what's going to happen to me when I get outside again. Sometime I think I'm going to flip and *never* get outside and sometime I think I'll come straight back. I tell you one thing, though, I'd rather blow my brains out than go through this again. But that's what they all say, so they tell me. If I tell you when I'm coming to New York and if you could meet me, I sure would appreciate it. Give my love to Isabel and the kids and I was sure sorry to hear about little Gracie. I wish I could be like Mama and say the Lord's will be done, but I don't know it seems to me that trouble is the one thing that never does get stopped and I don't know what good it does to blame it on the Lord. But maybe it does some good if you believe it.

Your brother,
Sonny

Then I kept in constant touch with him and I sent him whatever I could and I went to meet him when he came back to New York. When I saw him many things I thought I had forgotten came flooding back to me. This was because I had begun, finally, to wonder about Sonny, about the life that Sonny lived inside. This life, whatever it was, had made him older and thinner and it had deepened the distant stillness in which he had always moved. He looked very unlike my baby brother. Yet, when he smiled, when we shook hands, the baby brother I'd never known looked out from the depths of his private life, like an animal waiting to be coaxed into the light.

"How you been keeping?" he asked me.

55 "All right. And you?"

"Just fine." He was smiling all over his face. "It's good to see you again."

"It's good to see you."

The seven years' difference in our ages lay between us like a chasm: I wondered if these years would ever operate between us as a bridge. I was remembering, and it made it hard to catch my breath, that I had been there when he was born; and I had heard the first words he had ever spoken. When he started to walk, he walked from our mother straight to me. I caught him just before he fell when he took the first steps he ever took in this world.

"How's Isabel?"

60 "Just fine. She's dying to see you."

"And the boys?"

"They're fine, too. They're anxious to see their uncle."

"Oh, come on. You know they don't remember me."

"Are you kidding? Of course they remember you."

65 He grinned again. We got into a taxi. We had a lot to say to each other, far too much to know how to begin.

As the taxi began to move, I asked, "You still want to go to India?"

He laughed. "You still remember that. Hell, no. This place is Indian enough for me."

"It used to belong to them," I said.

And he laughed again. "They damn sure knew what they were doing when they got rid of it."

Years ago, when he was around fourteen, he'd been all hipped on the idea of going to India. He read books about people sitting on rocks, naked, in all kinds of weather, but mostly bad, naturally, and walking barefoot through hot coals and arriving at wisdom. I used to say that it sounded to me as though they were getting away from wisdom as fast as they could. I think he sort of looked down on me for that.

"Do you mind," he asked, "if we have the driver drive alongside the park? On the west side—I haven't seen the city in so long."

"Of course not," I said. I was afraid that I might sound as though I were humoring him, but I hoped he wouldn't take it that way.

So we drove along, between the green of the park and the stony, lifeless elegance of hotels and apartment buildings, toward the vivid, killing streets of our childhood. These streets hadn't changed, though housing projects jutted up out of them now like rocks in the middle of a boiling sea. Most of the houses in which we had grown up had vanished, as had the stores from which we had stolen, the basements in which we had first tried sex, the rooftops from which we had hurled tin cans and bricks. But houses exactly like the houses of our past yet dominated the landscape, boys exactly like the boys we once had been found themselves smothering in these houses, came down into the streets for light and air and found themselves encircled by disaster. Some escaped the trap, most didn't. Those who got out always left something of themselves behind, as some animals amputate a leg and leave it in the trap. It might be said, perhaps, that I had escaped, after all, I was a school teacher; or that Sonny had, he hadn't lived in Harlem for years. Yet, as the cab moved uptown through streets which seemed, with a rush, to darken with dark people, and as I covertly studied Sonny's face, it came to me that what we both were seeking through our separate cab windows was that part of ourselves which had been left behind. It's always at the hour of trouble and confrontation that the missing member aches.

We hit 110th Street and started rolling up Lenox Avenue. And I'd known this avenue all my life, but it seemed to me again, as it had seemed on the day I'd first heard about Sonny's trouble, filled with a hidden menace which was its very breath of life.

"We almost there," said Sonny.

"Almost." We were both too nervous to say anything more.

We live in a housing project. It hasn't been up long. A few days after it was up it seemed uninhabitably new, now, of course, it's already rundown. It looks like a parody of the good, clean, faceless life—God knows the people who live in it do their best to make it a parody. The beat-looking grass lying around isn't enough to make their lives green, the hedges will never hold out the streets, and they know it. The big windows fool no one, they aren't big enough to make space out of no space. They don't bother with the windows, they watch the TV screen instead. The playground is most popular with the children who don't play at jacks, or skip rope, or roller skate, or swing, and they can be found in it after dark. We moved in partly because it's not too far from where I teach, and partly for the kids; but it's really just like the houses in which Sonny and I grew up. The same things happen, they'll have the same things to remember. The moment Sonny and I started into the house I had the feeling that I was simply bringing him back into the danger he had almost died trying to escape.

Sonny has never been talkative. So I don't know why I was sure he'd be dying to talk to me when supper was over the first night. Everything went fine, the oldest boy remembered him, and the youngest boy liked him, and Sonny had remembered to bring something for each of them; and Isabel, who is really much nicer than I am, more open and giving, had gone to a lot of trouble about dinner and was genuinely glad to see him. And she's always been able to tease Sonny in a way that I haven't. It was nice to see her face so vivid again and to hear her laugh and watch her make Sonny laugh. She wasn't, or, anyway, she didn't seem to be, at all uneasy or embarrassed. She chatted as though there were no subject which had to be avoided and she got Sonny past his first, faint stiffness. And thank God she was there, for I was filled with that icy dread again. Everything I did seemed awkward to me, and everything I said sounded freighted with hidden meaning. I was trying to remember everything I'd heard about dope addiction and I couldn't help watching Sonny for signs. I wasn't doing it out of malice. I was trying to find out something about my brother. I was dying to hear him tell me he was safe.

"Safe!" my father grunted, whenever Mama suggested trying to move to a neighborhood which might be safer for children. "Safe, hell! Ain't no place safe for kids, nor nobody."

He always went on like this, but he wasn't, ever, really as bad as he sounded, not even on weekends, when he got drunk. As a matter of fact, he was always on the lookout for "something a little better," but he died before he found it. He died suddenly, during a drunken weekend in the middle of the war, when Sonny was fifteen. He and Sonny hadn't ever got on too well. And this was partly because Sonny was the apple of his father's eye. It was because he loved Sonny so much and was frightened for him, that he was always fighting with him. It doesn't do any good to fight with Sonny. Sonny just moves back, inside himself, where he can't be reached. But the principal reason that they never hit it off is that they were so much alike. Daddy was big and rough and loud-talking, just the opposite of Sonny, but they both had—that same privacy.

Mama tried to tell me something about this, just after Daddy died. I was home on leave from the army.

This was the last time I ever saw my mother alive. Just the same, this picture gets all mixed up in my mind with pictures I had of her when she was younger. The way I always see her is the way she used to be on a Sunday afternoon, say, when the old folks were talking after the big Sunday dinner. I always see her

[handwritten margin note: narr.'s memory of Sun. afternoons at home and room full of church people]

wearing pale blue. She'd be sitting on the sofa. And my father would be sitting in the easy chair, not far from her. And the living room would be full of church folks and relatives. There they sit, in chairs all around the living room, and the night is creeping up outside, but nobody knows it yet. You can see the darkness growing against the windowpanes and you hear the street noises every now and again, or maybe the jangling beat of a tambourine from one of the churches close by, but it's real quiet in the room. For a moment nobody's talking, but every face looks darkening, like the sky outside. And my mother rocks a little from the waist, and my father's eyes are closed. Everyone is looking at something a child can't see. For a minute they've forgotten the children. Maybe a kid is lying on the rug, half asleep. Maybe somebody's got a kid in his lap and is absent-mindedly stroking the kid's head. Maybe there's a kid, quiet and big-eyed, curled up in a big chair in the corner. The silence, the darkness coming, and the darkness in the faces frighten the child obscurely. He hopes that the hand which strokes his forehead will never stop—will never die. He hopes that there will never come a time when the old folks won't be sitting around the living room, talking about where they've come from, and what they've seen, and what's happened to them and their kinfolk.

[handwritten margin note: darkness motif]

But something deep and watchful in the child knows that this is bound to end, is already ending. In a moment someone will get up and turn on the light. Then the old folks will remember the children and they won't talk any more that day. And when light fills the room, the child is filled with darkness. He knows that every time this happens he's moved just a little closer to that darkness outside. The darkness outside is what the old folks have been talking about. It's what they've come from. It's what they endure. The child knows that they won't talk any more because if he knows too much about what's happened to *them,* he'll know too much too soon, about what's going to happen to *him.*

The last time I talked to my mother, I remember I was restless. I wanted to get out and see Isabel. We weren't married then and we had a lot to straighten out between us.

There Mama sat, in black, by the window. She was humming an old church song, *Lord, you brought me from a long ways off.* Sonny was out somewhere. Mama kept watching the streets.

"I don't know," she said, "if I'll ever see you again, after you go off from here. But I hope you'll remember the things I tried to teach you."

"Don't talk like that," I said, and smiled. "You'll be here a long time yet."

She smiled, too, but she said nothing. She was quiet for a long time. And I said, "Mama, don't you worry about nothing. I'll be writing all the time, and you be getting the checks. . . ."

"I want to talk to you about your brother," she said, suddenly. "If anything happens to me he ain't going to have nobody to look out for him."

"Mama," I said, "ain't nothing going to happen to you *or* Sonny. Sonny's all right. He's a good boy and he's got good sense."

"It ain't a question of his being a good boy," Mama said, "nor of his having good sense. It ain't only the bad ones, nor yet the dumb ones that gets sucked

*[margin: 85]*

[margin: 90]

under." She stopped, looking at me. "Your Daddy once had a brother," she said, and she smiled in a way that made me feel she was in pain. "You didn't never know that, did you?"

"No," I said, "I never knew that," and I watched her face.

"Oh, yes," she said, "your Daddy had a brother." She looked out of the window again. "I know you never saw your Daddy cry. But I did—many a time, through all these years."

I asked her, "What happened to his brother? How come nobody's ever talked about him?"

This was the first time I ever saw my mother look old.

"His brother got killed," she said, "when he was just a little younger than you are now. I knew him. He was a fine boy. He was maybe a little full of the devil, but he didn't mean nobody no harm."

Then she stopped and the room was silent, exactly as it had sometimes been on those Sunday afternoons. Mama kept looking out into the streets.

"He used to have a job in the mill," she said, "and, like all young folks, he just liked to perform on Saturday nights. Saturday nights, him and your father would drift around to different places, go to dances and things like that, or just sit around with people they knew, and your father's brother would sing, he had a fine voice, and play along with himself on his guitar. Well, this particular Saturday night, him and your father was coming home from some place, and they were both a little drunk and there was a moon that night, it was bright like day. Your father's brother was feeling kind of good, and he was whistling to himself, and he had his guitar slung over his shoulder. They was coming down a hill and beneath them was a road that turned off from the highway. Well, your father's brother, being always kind of frisky, decided to run down this hill, and he did, with that guitar banging and clanging behind him, and he ran across the road, and he was making water behind a tree. And your father was sort of amused at him and he was still coming down the hill, kind of slow. Then he heard a car motor and that same minute his brother stepped from behind the tree, into the road, in the moonlight. And he started to cross the road. And your father started to run down the hill, he says he don't know why. This car was full of white men. They was all drunk, and when they seen your father's brother they let out a great whoop and holler and they aimed the car straight at him. They was having fun, they just wanted to scare him, the way they do sometimes, you know. But they was drunk. And I guess the boy, being drunk, too, and scared, kind of lost his head. By the time he jumped it was too late. Your father says he heard his brother scream when the car rolled over him, and he heard the wood of that guitar when it give, and he heard them strings go flying, and he heard them white men shouting, and the car kept on a-going and it ain't stopped till this day. And, time your father got down the hill, his brother weren't nothing but blood and pulp."

Tears were gleaming on my mother's face. There wasn't anything I could say.

"He never mentioned it," she said, "because I never let him mention it before you children. Your Daddy was like a crazy man that night and for many a night thereafter. He says he never in his life seen anything as dark as that road after the lights of that car had gone away. Weren't nothing, weren't nobody on that road, just your Daddy and his brother and that busted guitar. Oh, yes. Your Daddy never did really get right again. Till the day he died he weren't sure but that every white man he saw was the man that killed his brother."

She stopped and took out her handkerchief and dried her eyes and looked at me.

"I ain't telling you all this," she said, "to make you scared or bitter or to make you hate nobody. I'm telling you this because you got a brother. And the world ain't changed."

I guess I didn't want to believe this. I guess she saw this in my face. She turned away from me, toward the window again, searching those streets.

"But I praise my Redeemer," she said at last, "that He called your Daddy home before me. I ain't saying it to throw no flowers at myself, but, I declare, it keeps me from feeling too cast down to know I helped your father get safely through this world. Your father always acted like he was the roughest, strongest man on earth. And everybody took him to be like that. But if he hadn't had me there—to see his tears!"

She was crying again. Still, I couldn't move. I said, "Lord, Lord, Mama, I didn't know it was like that." 105

"Oh, honey," she said, "there's a lot that you don't know. But you are going to find out." She stood up from the window and came over to me. "You got to hold on to your brother," she said, "and don't let him fall, no matter what it looks like is happening to him and no matter how evil you gets with him. You going to be evil with him many a time. But don't you forget what I told you, you hear?"

"I won't forget," I said. "Don't you worry, I won't forget. I won't let nothing happen to Sonny."

My mother smiled as though she was amused at something she saw in my face. Then, "You may not be able to stop nothing from happening. But you got to let him know you's *there*."

Two days later I was married, and then I was gone. And I had a lot of things on my mind and I pretty well forgot my promise to Mama until I got shipped home on a special furlough for her funeral.

And, after the funeral, with just Sonny and me alone in the empty kitchen, I tried to find out something about him.

"What do you want to do?" I asked him.

"I'm going to be a musician," he said.

For he had graduated, in the time I had been away, from dancing to the juke box to finding out who was playing what, and what they were doing with it, and he had bought himself a set of drums.

"You mean, you want to be a drummer?" I somehow had the feeling that being a drummer might be all right for other people but not for my brother Sonny.

"I don't think," he said, looking at me very gravely, "that I'll ever be a good drummer. But I think I can play a piano." 115

I frowned. I'd never played the role of the oldest brother quite so seriously before, had scarcely ever, in fact, *asked* Sonny a damn thing. I sensed myself in the presence of something I didn't really know how to handle, didn't understand. So I made my frown a little deeper as I asked: "What kind of musician do you want to be?"

He grinned. "How many kinds do you think there are?"

"Be *serious*," I said.

He laughed, throwing his head back, and then looked at me. "I *am* serious."

"Well, then, for Christ's sake, stop kidding around and answer a serious question. I mean, do you want to be a concert pianist, you want to play classical music and all that, or—or what?" Long before I finished he was laughing again. "For Christ's *sake*, Sonny!"

He sobered, but with difficulty. "I'm sorry. But you sound so—*scared!*" and he was off again.

"Well, you may think it's funny now, baby, but it's not going to be so funny when you have to make your living at it, let me tell you *that*." I was furious because I knew he was laughing at me and I didn't know why.

"No," he said, very sober now, and afraid, perhaps, that he'd hurt me, "I don't want to be a classical pianist. That isn't what interests me. I mean"—he paused, looking hard at me, as though his eyes would help me to understand, and then gestured helplessly, as though perhaps his hand would help—"I mean, I'll have a lot of studying to do, and I'll have to study *everything*, but, I mean, I want to play *with*—jazz musicians." He stopped. "I want to play jazz," he said.

Well, the word had never before sounded as heavy, as real, as it sounded that afternoon in Sonny's mouth. I just looked at him and I was probably frowning a real frown by this time. I simply couldn't see why on earth he'd want to spend his time hanging around nightclubs, clowning around on bandstands, while people pushed each other around a dance floor. It seemed—beneath him, somehow. I had never thought about it before, had never been forced to, but I suppose I had always put jazz musicians in a class with what Daddy called "good-time people."

"Are you *serious*?"

"Hell, *yes*, I'm serious."

He looked more helpless than ever, and annoyed, and deeply hurt.

I suggested, helpfully: "You mean—like Louis Armstrong?"

His face closed as though I'd struck him. "No. I'm not talking about none of that old-time, down home crap."

"Well, look, Sonny, I'm sorry, don't get mad. I just don't altogether get it, that's all. Name somebody—you know, a jazz musician you admire."

"Bird."

"Who?"

"Bird! Charlie Parker![3] Don't they teach you nothing in the goddamn army?"

---

3. Charlie ("Bird") Parker (1920–1955), perhaps the greatest saxophonist and innovator of jazz; cofounder, with Dizzy Gillespie, of the new jazz, once called "bebop." He was a narcotics addict.

I lit a cigarette. I was surprised and then a little amused to discover that I was trembling. "I've been out of touch," I said. "You'll have to be patient with me. Now. Who's this Parker character?"

"He's just one of the greatest jazz musicians alive," said Sonny, sullenly, his hands in his pockets, his back to me. "Maybe *the* greatest," he added, bitterly, "that's probably why *you* never heard of him."

"All right," I said, "I'm ignorant. I'm sorry. I'll go out and buy all the cat's records right away, all right?"

"It don't," said Sonny, with dignity, "make any difference to me. I don't care what you listen to. Don't do me no favors."

I was beginning to realize that I'd never seen him so upset before. With another part of my mind I was thinking that this would probably turn out to be one of those things kids go through and that I shouldn't make it seem important by pushing it too hard. Still, I didn't think it would do any harm to ask: "Doesn't all this take a lot of time? Can you make a living at it?"

He turned back to me and half leaned, half sat, on the kitchen table. "Everything takes time," he said, "and—well, yes, sure, I can make a living at it. But what I don't seem to be able to make you understand is that it's the only thing I want to do."

"Well, Sonny," I said gently, "you know people can't always do exactly what they *want* to do—"

"No, I don't know that," said Sonny, surprising me. "I think people *ought* to do what they want to do, what else are they alive for?"

"You getting to be a big boy," I said desperately, "it's time you started thinking about your future."

"I'm thinking about my future," said Sonny, grimly. "I think about it all the time."

I gave up. I decided, if he didn't change his mind, that we could always talk about it later. "In the meantime," I said, "you got to finish school." We had already decided that he'd have to move in with Isabel and her folks. I knew this wasn't the ideal arrangement because Isabel's folks are inclined to be dicty[4] and they hadn't especially wanted Isabel to marry me. But I didn't know what else to do. "And we have to get you fixed up at Isabel's."

There was a long silence. He moved from the kitchen table to the window. "That's a terrible idea. You know it yourself."

"Do you have a *better* idea?"

He just walked up and down the kitchen for a minute. He was as tall as I was. He had started to shave. I suddenly had the feeling that I didn't know him at all.

He stopped at the kitchen table and picked up my cigarettes. Looking at me with a kind of mocking, amused defiance, he put one between his lips. "You mind?"

"You smoking already?"

He lit the cigarette and nodded, watching me through the smoke. "I just

4. Snobbish, bossy.

wanted to see if I'd have the courage to smoke in front of you." He grinned and blew a great cloud of smoke to the ceiling. "It was easy." He looked at my face. "Come on, now. I bet you was smoking at my age, tell the truth."

I didn't say anything but the truth was on my face, and he laughed. But now there was something very strained in his laugh. "Sure. And I bet that ain't all you was doing."

He was frightening me a little. "Cut the crap," I said. "We already decided that you was going to go and live at Isabel's. Now what's got into you all of a sudden?"

"You decided it," he pointed out. "I didn't decide nothing." He stopped in front of me, leaning against the stove, arms loosely folded. "Look, brother. I don't want to stay in Harlem no more, I really don't." He was very earnest. He looked at me, then over toward the kitchen window. There was something in his eyes I'd never seen before, some thoughtfulness, some worry all his own. He rubbed the muscle of one arm. "It's time I was getting out of here."

"Where do you want to go, Sonny?"

"I want to join the army. Or the navy, I don't care. If I say I'm old enough, they'll believe me."

Then I got mad. It was because I was so scared. "You must be crazy. You goddamn fool, what the hell do you want to go and join the army for?"

"I just told you. To get out of Harlem."

"Sonny, you haven't even finished school. And if you really want to be a musician, how do you expect to study if you're in the army?"

He looked at me, trapped, and in anguish. "There's ways. I might be able to work out some kind of deal. Anyway, I'll have the G.I. Bill when I come out."

"If you come out." We stared at each other. "Sonny, please. Be reasonable. I know the setup is far from perfect. But we got to do the best we can."

"I ain't learning nothing in school," he said. "Even when I go." He turned away from me and opened the window and threw his cigarette out into the narrow alley. I watched his back. "At least, I ain't learning nothing you'd want me to learn." He slammed the window so hard I thought the glass would fly out, and turned back to me. "And I'm sick of the stink of these garbage cans!"

"Sonny," I said, "I know how you feel. But if you don't finish school now, you're going to be sorry later that you didn't." I grabbed him by the shoulders. "And you only got another year. It ain't so bad. And I'll come back and I swear I'll help you do whatever you want to do. Just try to put up with it till I come back. Will you please do that? For me?"

He didn't answer and he wouldn't look at me.

"Sonny. You hear me?"

He pulled away. "I hear you. But you never hear anything I say."

I didn't know what to say to that. He looked out of the window and then back at me. "OK," he said, and sighed. "I'll try."

Then I said, trying to cheer him up a little, "They got a piano at Isabel's. You can practice on it."

And as a matter of fact, it did cheer him up for a minute. "That's right," he said to himself. "I forgot that." His face relaxed a little. But the worry, the thoughtfulness, played on it still, the way shadows play on a face which is staring into the fire.

But I thought I'd never hear the end of that piano. At first, Isabel would write me, saying how nice it was that Sonny was so serious about his music and how, as soon as he came in from school, or wherever he had been when he was supposed to be at school, he went straight to that piano and stayed there until suppertime. And, after supper, he went back to that piano and stayed there until everybody went to bed. He was at the piano all day Saturday and all day Sunday. Then he bought a record player and started playing records. He'd play one record over and over again, all day long sometimes, and he'd improvise along with it on the piano. Or he'd play one section of the record, one chord, one change, one progression, then he'd do it on the piano. Then back to the record. Then back to the piano.

Well, I really don't know how they stood it. Isabel finally confessed that it wasn't like living with a person at all, it was like living with sound. And the sound didn't make any sense to her, didn't make any sense to any of them—naturally. They began, in a way, to be afflicted by this presence that was living in their home. It was as though Sonny were some sort of god, or monster. He moved in an atmosphere which wasn't like theirs at all. They fed him and he ate, he washed himself, he walked in and out of their door; he certainly wasn't nasty or unpleasant or rude, Sonny isn't any of those things; but it was as though he were all wrapped up in some cloud, some fire, some vision all his own; and there wasn't any way to reach him.

At the same time, he wasn't really a man yet, he was still a child, and they had to watch out for him in all kinds of ways. They certainly couldn't throw him out. Neither did they dare to make a great scene about that piano because even they dimly sensed, as I sensed, from so many thousands of miles away, that Sonny was at that piano playing for his life.

But he hadn't been going to school. One day a letter came from the school board and Isabel's mother got it—there had, apparently, been other letters but Sonny had torn them up. This day, when Sonny came in, Isabel's mother showed him the letter and asked where he'd been spending his time. And she finally got it out of him that he'd been down in Greenwich Village, with musicians and other characters, in a white girl's apartment. And this scared her and she started to scream at him and what came up, once she began—though she denies it to this day—was what sacrifices they were making to give Sonny a decent home and how little he appreciated it.

Sonny didn't play the piano that day. By evening, Isabel's mother had calmed down but then there was the old man to deal with, and Isabel herself. Isabel says she did her best to be calm but she broke down and started crying. She says she just watched Sonny's face. She could tell, by watching him, what was happening with him. And what was happening was that they penetrated his cloud, they had reached him. Even if their fingers had been a thousand times more gentle than human fingers ever are, he could hardly help feeling that they had stripped him naked and were spitting on that nakedness. For he also had to see that his pres-

170

ence, that music, which was life or death to him, had been torture for them and that they had endured it, not at all for his sake, but only for mine. And Sonny couldn't take that. He can take it a little better today than he could then but he's still not very good at it and, frankly, I don't know anybody who is.

The silence of the next few days must have been louder than the sound of all the music ever played since time began. One morning, before she went to work, Isabel was in his room for something and she suddenly realized that all of his records were gone. And she knew for certain that he was gone. And he was. He went as far as the navy would carry him. He finally sent me a postcard from some place in Greece and that was the first I knew that Sonny was still alive. I didn't see him any more until we were both back in New York and the war had long been over.

He was a man by then, of course, but I wasn't willing to see it. He came by the house from time to time, but we fought almost every time we met. I didn't like the way he carried himself, loose and dreamlike all the time, and I didn't like his friends, and his music seemed to be merely an excuse for the life he led. It sounded just that weird and disordered.

Then we had a fight, a pretty awful fight, and I didn't see him for months. By and by I looked him up, where he was living, in a furnished room in the Village, and I tried to make it up. But there were lots of other people in the room and Sonny just lay on his bed, and he wouldn't come downstairs with me, and he treated these other people as though they were his family and I weren't. So I got mad and then he got mad, and then I told him that he might just as well be dead as live the way he was living. Then he stood up and he told me not to worry about him any more in life, that he *was* dead as far as I was concerned. Then he pushed me to the door and the other people looked on as though nothing were happening, and he slammed the door behind me. I stood in the hallway, staring at the door. I heard somebody laugh in the room and then the tears came to my eyes. I started down the steps, whistling to keep from crying, I kept whistling to myself, *You going to need me, baby, one of these cold, rainy days.*

I read about Sonny's trouble in the spring. Little Grace died in the fall. She was a beautiful little girl. But she only lived a little over two years. She died of polio and she suffered. She had a slight fever for a couple of days, but it didn't seem like anything and we just kept her in bed. And we would certainly have called the doctor, but the fever dropped, she seemed to be all right. So we thought it had just been a cold. Then, one day, she was up, playing, Isabel was in the kitchen fixing lunch for the two boys when they'd come in from school, and she heard Grace fall down in the living room. When you have a lot of children you don't always start running when one of them falls, unless they start screaming or something. And, this time, Gracie was quiet. Yet, Isabel says that when she heard that *thump* and then that silence, something happened to her to make her afraid. And she ran to the living room and there was little Grace on the floor, all twisted up, and the reason she hadn't screamed was that she couldn't get her breath. And when she did scream, it was the worst sound, Isabel says, that she'd ever heard in all her life, and she still hears it sometimes in her dreams. Isabel will sometimes wake me up with a low, moaning, strangling sound and I have to be quick to awaken her and hold her to me and where Isabel is weeping against me seems a mortal wound.

I think I may have written Sonny the very day that little Grace was buried. I was sitting in the living room in the dark, by myself, and I suddenly thought of Sonny. My trouble made his real. *his daughter's death bridges the chasm w/ Sonny)*

One Saturday afternoon, when Sonny had been living with us, or anyway, been in our house, for nearly two weeks, I found myself wandering aimlessly about the living room, drinking from a can of beer, and trying to work up courage to search Sonny's room. He was out, he was usually out whenever I was home, and Isabel had taken the children to see their grandparents. Suddenly I was standing still in front of the living room window, watching Seventh Avenue. The idea of searching Sonny's room made me still. I scarcely dared to admit to myself what I'd be searching for. I didn't know what I'd do if I found it. Or if I didn't.

On the sidewalk across from me, near the entrance to a barbecue joint, some people were holding an old-fashioned revival meeting. The barbecue cook, wearing a dirty white apron, his conked[5] hair reddish and metallic in the pale sun, and a cigarette between his lips, stood in the doorway, watching them. Kids and older people paused in their errands and stood there, along with some older men and a couple of very tough-looking women who watched everything that happened on the avenue, as though they owned it, or were maybe owned by it. Well, they were watching this, too. The revival was being carried on by three sisters in black, and a brother. All they had were their voices and their Bibles and a tambourine. The brother was testifying[6] and while he testified two of the sisters stood together, seeming to say, amen, and the third sister walked around with the tambourine outstretched and a couple of people dropped coins into it. Then the brother's testimony ended and the sister who had been taking up the collection dumped the coins into her palm and transferred them to the pocket of her long black robe. Then she raised both hands, striking the tambourine against the air, and then against one hand, and she started to sing. And the two other sisters and the brother joined in.

It was strange, suddenly, to watch, though I had been seeing these meetings all my life. So, of course, had everybody else down there. Yet, they paused and watched and listened and I stood still at the window. " *'Tis the old ship of Zion,*" they sang, and the sister with the tambourine kept a steady, jangling beat, "*it has rescued many a thousand!*" Not a soul under the sound of their voices was hearing this song for the first time, not one of them had been rescued. Nor had they seen much in the way of rescue work being done around them. Neither did they especially believe in the holiness of the three sisters and the brother, they knew too much about them, knew where they lived, and how. The woman with the tambourine, whose voice dominated the air, whose face was bright with joy, was divided by very little from the woman who stood watching her, a cigarette between her heavy, chapped lips, her hair a cuckoo's nest, her face scarred and swollen

180

5. Processed: straightened and greased.   6. Publicly professing belief.

from many beatings, and her black eyes glittering like coal. Perhaps they both knew this, which was why, when, as rarely, they addressed each other, they addressed each other as Sister. As the singing filled the air the watching, listening faces underwent a change, the eyes focusing on something within; the music seemed to soothe a poison out of them; and time seemed, nearly, to fall away from the sullen, belligerent, battered faces, as though they were fleeing back to their first condition, while dreaming of their last. The barbecue cook half shook his head and smiled, and dropped his cigarette and disappeared into his joint. A man fumbled in his pockets for change and stood holding it in his hand impatiently, as though he had just remembered a pressing appointment further up the avenue. He looked furious. Then I saw Sonny, standing on the edge of the crowd. He was carrying a wide, flat notebook with a green cover, and it made him look, from where I was standing, almost like a schoolboy. The coppery sun brought out the copper in his skin, he was very faintly smiling, standing very still. Then the singing stopped, the tambourine turned into a collection plate again. The furious man dropped in his coins and vanished, so did a couple of the women, and Sonny dropped some change in the plate, looking directly at the woman with a little smile. He started across the avenue, toward the house. He has a slow, loping walk, something like the way Harlem hipsters walk, only he's imposed on this his own half-beat. I had never really noticed it before.

I stayed at the window, both relieved and apprehensive. As Sonny disappeared from my sight, they began singing again. And they were still singing when his key turned in the lock.

"Hey," he said.

"Hey, yourself. You want some beer?"

"No. Well, maybe." But he came up to the window and stood beside me, looking out. "What a warm voice," he said.

They were singing *If I could only hear my mother pray again!*

"Yes," I said, "and she can sure beat that tambourine."

"But what a terrible song," he said, and laughed. He dropped his notebook on the sofa and disappeared into the kitchen. "Where's Isabel and the kids?"

"I think they went to see their grandparents. You hungry?"

"No." He came back into the living room with his can of beer. "You want to come some place with me tonight?"

I sensed, I don't know how, that I couldn't possibly say no. "Sure. Where?"

He sat down on the sofa and picked up his notebook and started leafing through it. "I'm going to sit in with some fellows in a joint in the Village."

"You mean, you're going to play, tonight?"

"That's right." He took a swallow of his beer and moved back to the window. He gave me a sidelong look. "If you can stand it."

"I'll try," I said.

He smiled to himself and we both watched as the meeting across the way broke up. The three sisters and the brother, heads bowed, were singing *God be with you till we meet again.* The faces around them were very quiet. Then the song ended. The small crowd dispersed. We watched the three women and the lone man walk slowly up the avenue.

music is like → soothing, warm.

heroin

"When she was singing before," said Sonny, abruptly, "her voice reminded me for a minute of what heroin feels like sometimes—when it's in your veins. It makes you feel sort of warm and cool at the same time. And distant. And—and sure." He sipped his beer, very deliberately not looking at me. I watched his face. "It makes you feel—in control. Sometimes you've got to have that feeling."

"Do you?" I sat down slowly in the easy chair.

"Sometimes." He went to the sofa and picked up his notebook again. "Some people do."

"In order," I asked, "to play?" And my voice was very ugly, full of contempt and anger.   200

"Well"—he looked at me with great, troubled eyes, as though, in fact, he hoped his eyes would tell me things he could never otherwise say—"they *think* so. And *if* they think so—!"

"And what do *you* think?" I asked.

He sat on the sofa and put his can of beer on the floor. "I don't know," he said, and I couldn't be sure if he were answering my question or pursuing his thoughts. His face didn't tell me. "It's not so much to *play*. It's to stand it, to be able to make it at all. On any level." He frowned and smiled: "In order to keep from shaking to pieces."

why Sonny plays

"But these friends of yours," I said, "they seem to shake themselves to pieces pretty goddamn fast."

"Maybe." He played with the notebook. And something told me that I should   205
curb my tongue, that Sonny was doing his best to talk, that I should listen. "But of course you only know the ones that've gone to pieces. Some don't—or at least they haven't *yet* and that's just about all *any* of us can say." He paused. "And then there are some who just live, really, in hell, and they know it and they see what's happening and they go right on. I don't know." He sighed, dropped the notebook, folded his arms. "Some guys, you can tell from the way they play, they on something *all* the time. And you can see that, well, it makes something real for them. But of course," he picked up his beer from the floor and sipped it and put the can down again, "they *want* to, too, you've got to see that. Even some of them that say they don't—*some*, not all."

"And what about you?" I asked—I couldn't help it. "What about you? Do *you* want to?"

suffering

He stood up and walked to the window and I remained silent for a long time. Then he sighed. "Me," he said. Then: "While I was downstairs before, on my way here, listening to that woman sing, it struck me all of a sudden how much suffering she must have had to go through—to sing like that. It's *repulsive* to think you have to suffer that much."

I said: "But there's no way not to suffer—is there, Sonny?"

"I believe not," he said and smiled, "but that's never stopped anyone from trying." He looked at me. "Has it?" I realized, with this mocking look, that there stood between us, forever, beyond the power of time or forgiveness, the fact that I had held silence—so long!—when he had needed human speech to help him. He turned back to the window. "No, there's no way not to suffer. But you try all kinds of ways to keep from drowning in it, to keep on top of it, and to make it

Sonny needs human speech to help him

seem—well, like *you*. Like you did something, all right, and now you're suffer—ing for it. You know?" I said nothing. "Well you know," he said, impatiently, "why *do* people suffer? Maybe it's better to do something to give it a reason, *any* reason."

210   "But we just agreed," I said, "that there's no way not to suffer. Isn't it better, then, just to—take it?"

        "But nobody just takes it," Sonny cried, "that's what I'm telling you! *Everybody* tries not to. You're just hung up on the *way* some people try—it's not *your* way!"

        The hair on my face began to itch, my face felt wet. "That's not true," I said, "that's not true. I don't give a damn what other people do, I don't even care how they suffer. I just care how *you* suffer." And he looked at me. "Please believe me," I said, "I don't want to see you—die—trying not to suffer."

        "I won't," he said flatly, "die trying not to suffer. At least, not any faster than anybody else."

        "But there's no need," I said, trying to laugh, "is there? in killing yourself."

215   I wanted to say more, but I couldn't. I wanted to talk about will power and how life could be—well, beautiful. I wanted to say that it was all within; but was it? or, rather, wasn't that exactly the trouble? And I wanted to promise that I would never fail him again. But it would all have sounded—empty words and lies.

        So I made the promise to myself and prayed that I would keep it.

        "It's terrible sometimes, inside," he said, "that's what's the trouble. You walk these streets, black and funky and cold, and there's not really a living ass to talk to, and there's nothing shaking, and there's no way of getting it out—that storm inside. You can't talk it and you can't make love with it, and when you finally try to get with it and play it, you realize *nobody's* listening. So *you've* got to listen. You got to find a way to listen."

        And then he walked away from the window and sat on the sofa again, as though all the wind had suddenly been knocked out of him. "Sometimes you'll do *anything* to play, even cut your mother's throat." He laughed and looked at me. "Or your brother's." Then he sobered. "Or your own." Then: "Don't worry. I'm all right now and I think I'll *be* all right. But I can't forget—where I've been. I don't mean just the physical place I've been, I mean where I've *been*. And *what* I've been."

        "What have you been, Sonny?" I asked.

220   He smiled—but sat sideways on the sofa, his elbow resting on the back, his fingers playing with his mouth and chin, not looking at me. "I've been something I didn't recognize, didn't know I could be. Didn't know anybody could be." He stopped, looking inward, looking helplessly young, looking old. "I'm not talking about it now because I feel *guilty* or anything like that—maybe it would be better if I did, I don't know. Anyway, I can't really talk about it. Not to you, not to anybody," and now he turned and faced me. "Sometimes, you know, and it was actually when I was most *out* of the world, I felt that I was in it, that I was *with* it, really, and I could play or I didn't really have to *play*, it just came out of me, it was there. And I don't know how I played, thinking about

it now, but I know I did awful things, those times, sometimes, to people. Or it wasn't that I *did* anything to them—it was that they weren't real." He picked up the beer can; it was empty; he rolled it between his palms: "And other times— well, I needed a fix, I needed to find a place to lean, I needed to clear a space to *listen*—and I couldn't find it, and I—went crazy, I did terrible things to *me*, I was terrible *for* me." He began pressing the beer can between his hands, I watched the metal begin to give. It glittered, as he played with it like a knife, and I was afraid he would cut himself, but I said nothing. "Oh well. I can never tell you. I was all by myself at the bottom of something, stinking and sweating and crying and shaking, and I smelled it, you know? *my* stink, and I thought I'd die if I couldn't get away from it and yet, all the same, I knew that everything I was doing was just locking me in with it. And I didn't know," he paused, still flatten- ing the beer can, "I didn't know, I still *don't* know, something kept telling me that maybe it was good to smell your own stink, but I didn't think that *that* was what I'd been trying to do—and—who can stand it?" and he abruptly dropped the ruined beer can, looking at me with a small, still smile, and then rose, walking to the window as though it were the lodestone rock. I watched his face, he watched the avenue. "I couldn't tell you when Mama died—but the reason I wanted to leave Harlem so bad was to get away from drugs. And then, when I ran away, that's what I was running from—really. When I came back, nothing had changed, *I* hadn't changed, I was just—older." And he stopped, drumming with his fingers on the windowpane. The sun had vanished, soon darkness would fall. I watched his face. "It can come again," he said, almost as though speaking to himself. Then he turned to me. "It can come again," he repeated. "I just want you to know that."

"All right," I said, at last. "So it can come again. All right."

He smiled, but the smile was sorrowful. "I had to try to tell you," he said.

"Yes," I said. "I understand that."

"You're my brother," he said, looking straight at me, and not smiling at all.

"Yes," I repeated, "yes. I understand that."

He turned back to the window, looking out. "All that hatred down there," he said, "all that hatred and misery and love. It's a wonder it doesn't blow the avenue apart." darkness

We went to the only nightclub on a short, dark street, downtown. We squeezed through the narrow, chattering, jampacked bar to the entrance of the big room, where the bandstand was. And we stood there for a moment, for the lights were very dim in this room and we couldn't see. Then, "Hello, boy," said the voice and an enormous black man, much older than Sonny or myself, erupted out of all that atmospheric lighting and put an arm around Sonny's shoulder. "I been sitting right here," he said, "waiting for you."

He had a big voice, too, and heads in the darkness turned toward us.

Sonny grinned and pulled a little away, and said, "Creole, this is my brother. I told you about him."

Creole shook my hand. "I'm glad to meet you, son," he said, and it was clear that he was glad to meet me *there*, for Sonny's sake. And he smiled, "You got a

this is a diff. kind of darkness

real musician in *your* family," and he took his arm from Sonny's shoulder and slapped him, lightly, affectionately, with the back of his hand.

"Well. Now I've heard it all," said a voice behind us. This was another musician, and a friend of Sonny's, a coal-black, cheerful-looking man, built close to the ground. He immediately began confiding to me, at the top of his lungs, the most terrible things about Sonny, his teeth gleaming like a lighthouse and his laugh coming up out of him like the beginning of an earthquake. And it turned out that everyone at the bar knew Sonny, or almost everyone; some were musicians, working there, or nearby, or not working, some were simply hangers-on, and some were there to hear Sonny play. I was introduced to all of them and they were all very polite to me. Yet, it was clear that, for them, I was only Sonny's brother. Here, I was in Sonny's world. Or, rather: his kingdom. Here, it was not even a question that his veins bore royal blood.

They were going to play soon and Creole installed me, by myself, at a table in a dark corner. Then I watched them, Creole, and the little black man, and Sonny, and the others, while they horsed around, standing just below the bandstand. The light from the bandstand spilled just a little short of them and, watching them laughing and gesturing and moving about, I had the feeling that they, nevertheless, were being most careful not to step into that circle of light too suddenly; that if they moved into the light too suddenly, without thinking, they would perish in flame. Then, while I watched, one of them, the small black man, moved into the light and crossed the bandstand and started fooling around with his drums. Then—being funny and being, also, extremely ceremonious—Creole took Sonny by the arm and led him to the piano. A woman's voice called Sonny's name and a few hands started clapping. And Sonny, also being funny and being ceremonious, and so touched, I think, that he could have cried, but neither hiding it nor showing it, riding it like a man, grinned, and put both hands to his heart and bowed from the waist.

Creole then went to the bass fiddle and a lean, very bright-skinned brown man jumped up on the bandstand and picked up his horn. So there they were, and the atmosphere on the bandstand and in the room began to change and tighten. Someone stepped up to the microphone and announced them. Then there were all kinds of murmurs. Some people at the bar shushed others. The waitress ran around, frantically getting in the last orders, guys and chicks got closer to each other, and the lights on the bandstand, on the quartet, turned to a kind of indigo. Then they all looked different there. Creole looked about him for the last time, as though he were making certain that all his chickens were in the coop, and then he—jumped and struck the fiddle. And there they were.

All I know about music is that not many people ever really hear it. And even then, on the rare occasions when something opens within, and the music enters, what we mainly hear, or hear corroborated, are personal, private, vanishing evocations. But the man who creates the music is hearing something else, is dealing with the roar rising from the void and imposing order on it as it hits the air. What is evoked in him, then, is of another order, more terrible because it has no words, and triumphant, too, for that same reason. And his triumph, when he triumphs, is ours. I just watched Sonny's face. His face was troubled, he was working hard, but he wasn't with it. And I had the feeling that, in a way,

everyone on the bandstand was waiting for him, both waiting for him and pushing him along. But as I began to watch Creole, I realized that it was Creole who
held them all back. He had them on a short rein. Up there, keeping the beat
with his whole body, wailing on the fiddle, with his eyes half closed, he was
listening to everything, but he was listening to Sonny. He was having a dialogue
with Sonny. He wanted Sonny to leave the shoreline and strike out for the deep
water. He was Sonny's witness that deep water and drowning were not the same
thing—he had been there, and he knew. And he wanted Sonny to know. He
was waiting for Sonny to do the things on the keys which would let Creole know
that Sonny was in the water.

And, while Creole listened, Sonny moved, deep within, exactly like some-   235
one in torment. I had never before thought of how awful the relationship must
be between the musician and his instrument. He has to fill it, this instrument,
with the breath of life, his own. He has to make it do what he wants it to do.
And a piano is just a piano. It's made out of so much wood and wires and little
hammers and big ones, and ivory. While there's only so much you can do with
it, the only way to find this out is to try; to try and make it do everything.

And Sonny hadn't been near a piano for over a year. And he wasn't on much
better terms with his life, not the life that stretched before him now. He and the
piano stammered, started one way, got scared, stopped; started another way,
panicked, marked time, started again; then seemed to have found a direction,
panicked again, got stuck. And the face I saw on Sonny I'd never seen before.
Everything had been burned out of it, and, at the same time, things usually
hidden were being burned in, by the fire and fury of the battle which was occurring in him up there.

Yet, watching Creole's face as they neared the end of the first set, I had the
feeling that something had happened, something I hadn't heard. Then they finished, there was scattered applause, and then, without an instant's warning, Creole started into something else, it was almost sardonic, it was *Am I Blue.*[7] And,
as though he commanded, Sonny began to play. Something began to happen.
And Creole let out the reins. The dry, low, black man said something awful on
the drums, Creole answered, and the drums talked back. Then the horn insisted,
sweet and high, slightly detached perhaps, and Creole listened, commenting
now and then, dry, and driving, beautiful and calm and old. Then they all came
together again, and Sonny was part of the family again. I could tell this from his
face. He seemed to have found, right there beneath his fingers, a damn brand-
new piano. It seemed that he couldn't get over it. Then, for a while, just being
happy with Sonny, they seemed to be agreeing with him that brand-new pianos
certainly were a gas.

Then Creole stepped forward to remind them that what they were playing
was the blues. He hit something in all of them, he hit something in me, myself,
and the music tightened and deepened, apprehension began to beat the air.
Creole began to tell us what the blues were all about. They were not about
anything very new. He and his boys up there were keeping it new, at the risk of
ruin, destruction, madness, and death, in order to find new ways to make us

---

7. A favorite blues piece, brilliantly recorded by Billie Holiday.

listen. For, while the tale of how we suffer, and how we are delighted, and how we may triumph is never new, it always must be heard. There isn't any other tale to tell, it's the only light we've got in all this darkness.

And this tale, according to that face, that body, those strong hands on those strings, has another aspect in every country, and a new depth in every generation. Listen, Creole seemed to be saying, listen. Now these are Sonny's blues. He made the little black man on the drums know it, and the bright, brown man on the horn. Creole wasn't trying any longer to get Sonny in the water. He was wishing him Godspeed. Then he stepped back, very slowly, filling the air with the immense suggestion that Sonny speak for himself.

240   Then they all gathered around Sonny and Sonny played. Every now and again one of them seemed to say, amen. Sonny's fingers filled the air with life, his life. But that life contained so many others. And Sonny went all the way back, he really began with the spare, flat statement of the opening phrase of the song. Then he began to make it his. It was very beautiful because it wasn't hurried and it was no longer a lament. I seemed to hear with what burning he had made it his, and what burning we had yet to make it ours, how we could cease lamenting. Freedom lurked around us and I understood, at last, that he could help us to be free if we would listen, that he would never be free until we did. Yet, there was no battle in his face now, I heard what he had gone through, and would continue to go through until he came to rest in earth. He had made it his: that long line, of which we knew only Mama and Daddy. And he was giving it back, as everything must be given back, so that, passing through death, it can live forever. I saw my mother's face again, and felt, for the first time, how the stones of the road she had walked on must have bruised her feet. I saw the moonlit road where my father's brother died. And it brought something else back to me, and carried me past it, I saw my little girl again and felt Isabel's tears again, and I felt my own tears begin to rise. And I was yet aware that this was only a moment, that the world waited outside, as hungry as a tiger, and that trouble stretched above us, longer than the sky.

Then it was over. Creole and Sonny let out their breath, both soaking wet, and grinning. There was a lot of applause and some of it was real. In the dark, the girl came by and I asked her to take drinks to the bandstand. There was a long pause, while they talked up there in the indigo light and after awhile I saw the girl put a Scotch and milk on top of the piano for Sonny. He didn't seem to notice it, but just before they started playing again, he sipped from it and looked toward me, and nodded. Then he put it back on top of the piano. For me, then, as they began to play again, it glowed and shook above my brother's head like the very cup of trembling.[8]

1957

8. See Isaiah 51:17, 22–23: "Awake, awake, stand up, O Jerusalem, which hast drunk at the hand of the Lord the cup of his fury; thou hast drunken the dregs of the cup of trembling, and wrung them out. . . . Behold, I have taken out of thine hand the cup of trembling, even the dregs of the cup of my fury; thou shalt no more drink it again: But I will put it into the hands of them that afflict thee; . . ."

MARGARET ATWOOD

The Whirlpool Rapids

There are some women who seem to be born without fear, just as there are people who are born without the ability to feel pain. The painless ones go around putting their hands on hot stoves, freezing their feet to the point of gangrene, scalding the lining from their throats with boiling coffee, because there is no warning anguish. Evolution does not favor them. So too perhaps with the fearless women, because there aren't very many of them around. I myself have known only two. One was a maker of television documentaries, and was one of the first to shoot footage in Vietnam. There would be the beach and then the line of jungle with the soldiers advancing toward it, and in front of them, walking backward, would be this woman. Providence appears to protect such women, maybe out of astonishment. Or else, sooner or later, it doesn't.

I'm told the fearlessness goes away when these women have babies. Then they become cowards, like the rest of us. If the baby is threatened they become ferocious, of course, but that is not out of the ordinary.

The other woman I knew, and still know—her luck has held—is Emma, who has always intrigued me. I think of Emma as a woman who will do anything, though that isn't how she thinks of herself. The truly fearless think of themselves as normal.

This, as far as I've been able to tell, is how she got like that.

When she was twenty-one, Emma nearly died. Or so she was told, and since four of those with her actually did die, she had to believe it. At the time she hadn't felt anywhere near dead.

It was a freak accident, and the fact that she was there at all was an accident too, the result of a whim and of knowing someone. Emma always knows a lot of people. The person she knew for this occasion was a man, a boy really, about her own age. He didn't qualify as a boyfriend; he was just one of the group she'd hung out with the previous year, at the university. In the summers he worked for a travel agency, a good one that specialized in organizing out-of-the-ordinary tours: bicycle trips through France, African game parks, that sort of thing. This boy, whose name was Bill, was one of the tour leaders. Because of his prowess with bicycles he had well-developed leg muscles, clearly visible that day, as he was wearing shorts and a T-shirt. It may have been these bicycle muscles that saved him, in the event.

Emma did not have bicycle muscles. At that time she had good biceps, though, the result of lifting heavy trays. She was working as a waitress in the coffee shop of a tourist motel in Niagara Falls. The motel had a neon sign outside that showed two entwined hearts, and even had a bridal suite, wallpapered in red.

This place reflected the vulgarity of the town itself, its transience, its tinsel-and-waxworks tawdriness, fitting contrast to the notion of Eternal Love, which,

5

the abstract ideas: Evolution / Providence Eternal Love /

despite the jokes she's made about it at various times in her life, Emma has never ceased to believe in.

At that point she wasn't thinking of love, but of making enough money to get her through her last year at the university. Niagara Falls was a good place for that: The satiated tip well. If she had been elsewhere, none of this would have happened.

There was nothing remarkable about Bill; he was merely one of those agents of Fate who have intruded on Emma's life from time to time and then departed from it, mission accomplished. Like many fearless people, Emma believes in Fate.

Bill was a nice boy; nice enough so that when he ambled into Emma's coffee shop one day and told her that he wanted her body, Emma took it as a joke and did not resent it. Really he wanted her to come on a test run, he said. The travel agency he was working for was doing a pilot project on a new kind of tour: down the Whirlpool Rapids below Niagara Falls, on a big rubber raft. They'd done the run nine times so far, and it was perfectly safe, but they weren't ready to open the tour to the public until they'd had one more test. It was only travel agency people and their friends going, he said, and they were short of bodies: There had to be a full contingent for the thing to work; they needed forty people for the weight and balance. It struck him as the kind of thing that might appeal to Emma.

Emma was flattered by this image of herself, and readily accepted it as a true one: a physically brave young woman, a bit of a daredevil, willing to put on a life jacket at a moment's notice and sit on a large inflated platform of rubber and swirl down the dangerous Niagara Whirlpool Rapids. It would be like roller coasters, which she'd always found compelling. She would join the ranks of those who had, in the past, wished to challenge Niagara Falls: the tightrope walkers, and those who'd had themselves bolted into padded barrels and flung into the river above the drop; even the suicides, whom Emma lumped in with the challengers, because if you were not in some way gambling, why not just use a gun? In all of these attempts, it seemed to Emma, there was an element of religious trial. All of these people were flinging themselves on the mercy of something or other. Certainly not just a river. *Save me, Lord; show me I'm important enough to deserve it.* This, Emma thought, looking back on it afterward, was what had prompted her: a desire to risk the self that was really a form of arrogance.

Emma said yes at once, and arranged for her next day off to coincide with the tenth rubber-raft test run. On the morning of the day, which was a Monday, Bill picked her up from the run-down frame house she rented with three other girls and drove her across the Rainbow Bridge to the launching site which was on the American side. It turned out afterward—some reporter dug it up—that the Canadian officials had refused permission to launch the raft on their side, considering the enterprise too hazardous. But even if Emma had known this it probably wouldn't have stopped her.

The raft was black and enormous, and seemed, resting at its moorings, very stable. Emma was given an orange life jacket, and buckled herself into it, helped by Bill. Then they scrambled on board and found seats at the front end. They were among the first to arrive, and had to wait for the others. Emma began to feel slightly let down and to wonder why she'd come. The raft was too big, too solid; it was like a floating parking lot.

But once they'd moved out into the current, the rubber surface under her began to ripple, in large waves of contraction, like a giant throat swallowing, and spray came in upon them; and Emma knew that the rapids, which had looked so decorative, so much like cake frosting from a distance, were actual after all. There were some dutiful thrilled noises from the other passengers, and then some genuine noises, less thrilled. Emma found herself clutching Bill's arm, a thing she wouldn't ordinarily have done. The sky was an unnatural blue, and the shore—dotted with the white-clad or pastel figures of tourists, which appeared static and painted, like a design on wallpaper—was very far away.

15

There was a lot of talk later about why the tenth run should have failed so badly, after the other nine had gone without a hitch. Some attempts were made to pin it on the design of the raft; others said that, owing to an unseasonable amount of rain during the preceding week, the water level had been too high and the current far swifter than usual. Emma could not remember wondering why, at the time. All she saw was the front of the raft tipping down into a trough deeper than any they'd yet hit, while a foaming wall of water rose above them. The raft should have curved sinuously, sliding up the wave. Instead it buckled across the middle, the front half snapping toward the back, like the beak of a bird closing. Emma and Bill and the other people in the front row shot backward over the heads of the rest who were jumbling in a heap at the bottom of the V, now submerging. (Emma didn't exactly see this at the time; she deduced it later. Her impressions were of her own movement only, and of course it was all very fast.)

Something struck her on the side of the head—a foot in a boot, perhaps—and she was underwater. Later she learned that the raft had flipped and a man had been trapped underneath it and drowned, so it was just as well that she had been flung clear. But underwater she did not think. Something else made her hold her breath and struggle toward the surface, which she could see above her, white and silver—so her eyes must have been open. Her head rose up, she gasped air and was sucked under.

The water tumbled and boiled and Emma fought it. She was filled almost to bursting with an energy that came from anger: *I refuse to die in such a stupid way* was how she formulated this afterward. She thinks she shouted, at least once: *No.* Which was a waste of breath, as there was nobody around to hear her. There were rocks, and she collided with several and was bruised and scraped, but nothing more hit her head. After what seemed like an hour but was really only ten minutes, the current slowed and she found she could keep her head above the water and actually swim. It was hard to move her arms. She propelled herself toward the shore, and, finally, dragged herself up onto a a small rocky beach. Her running shoes were gone. She must have kicked them off, though she couldn't remember doing it; or maybe they had been torn off. She wondered how she was going to get over the rocks without shoes.

The sky was even bluer than it had been before. There were some blue flowers also, weeds of some kind, cornflowers, growing among the rocks. Emma looked at them and did not feel anything. She must have been cut; her clothes were certainly ripped and there was a lump on the side of her forehead, but she didn't notice any of this at the time. Two people, a man and a woman, in summery clothes, came sauntering toward her along a path.

"What country am I in?" Emma asked them.

"Canada," said the man.

They walked past her and continued their stroll, as if they did not notice anything unusual about her. Probably they didn't. The news of the accident had not yet reached them, so they didn't realize there had been one.

Emma, in her turn, did not find their behavior out of place. That's good then, she thought to herself. She wouldn't have to go back over the bridge and through Immigration, which was lucky, because her purse had been swept away. She began to walk upstream, slowly, because of her bare feet. There was an unusual number of helicopters around. She thumbed a lift to the motel—she doesn't know why she elected to go there instead of to her house—and by the time she got there, the accident had been on the news and everyone thought she was dead.

She was taken to the hospital and treated for shock, and interviewed on television. Her picture was, briefly, in the papers. Bill came to see her and described his own experience to her. He had reached a point, under the water, at which he had given up, and the water had become very peaceful and very beautiful. This was how Emma realized that she herself hadn't been at all close to death. But Bill's bicycle-muscled legs had kicked by themselves, like a wounded frog's, and brought him back.

For a while Emma felt closer to Bill than she did to anyone, but this feeling passed, although they still send each other Christmas cards. There was never any possibility of a romance: They were, after the accident, too much like twins, and then too much like strangers. Intimacy brought about by shared catastrophe can only go so far.

Emma has told me that she learned several things from this experience. One of them was that many more people than she'd thought would have known about her death, had it occurred, and been affected by it in some way; but they wouldn't have been affected very deeply or very long. Soon she would have become just a name, the name of a woman who had died young, in a tragic accident, some years ago. It was for this reason, perhaps, that Emma never had any of those wistful longings for death, those flirtations with the pale horseman, that afflict so many women in their twenties. She never thought to herself, a little hopefully, a little melodramatically, that maybe she wouldn't see thirty, that some unspecified but graceful disease would carry her off. Not her. She was determined to live no matter what.

Nor was she ever tempted, after that, to give up anything—a man, an apartment, a job, even a vacation—in the mistaken conviction that by doing so she would be helping along the happiness of others. Because she found out early how very little difference she makes in the general scheme of things, she has clenched her teeth, ignored whimpers and even threats, and done what she liked, almost always. For instance, none of her friends will go to auctions or bargain sales with Emma anymore: She tends to get what you wanted. And at least four marriages have been trashed by Emma, who has decided in every case that the man wasn't right for her after all. Women who believe in Eternal Love develop such habits.

As you might expect, Emma has frequently been called selfish and unfeeling. I think it has been to her credit that on these occasions she has not trotted out the story of her near-death by drowning as a justification for her dubious behavior.

But the most obvious effect of the accident on Emma was her strong subsequent belief—it amounted to an article of religious faith—that she was invulnerable. She didn't merely feel this, she knew it, as firmly as she knew that her hand was her hand. She had been thrown into the Whirlpool Rapids of Niagara Falls and had lived; therefore nothing could touch her. She walked in a bubble of charmed air, which at times she imagined she could almost see, shimmering around her like mist; like, in fact, the mist that rose from the Falls themselves.

Little by little this belief faded. It was strongest right after the accident, but evaporated year by year, until by now nothing is left of it but a faint phosphorescence. Her friends call it optimism, this conviction of hers that everything will work out for her somehow.

What Emma has become, finally and after many false starts, is an insurance investigator for an airline company, a job that takes her to some strange locales and is more hazardous than you might think. Emma is always getting free cases of champagne, which she returns, or death threats, which she doesn't. I myself keep up with her through the postcards she sends, from places like Zaire. When I see her, once or twice a year, I find myself looking at her skin. The rest of us are beginning to wrinkle, but for some reason Emma is not. It must be that small injection of death, that early dose of mortality, that has rendered her immune.

1983

QUESTIONS

1. Who is the "you" addressed in the first paragraph of "The Cask of Amontillado"? (You may want to wait until you have finished the last sentence in the story before answering this.)

2. Has Emma's experience in "The Whirlpool Rapids" been good or bad for her? made her a better or a worse person?

3. In "Sonny's Blues" how is the first-person narrator, the person telling the story, identified or characterized in the first sentence? in the first paragraph? in the first couple of pages? in the story as a whole?

4. Is Sonny or the narrator the protagonist of "Sonny's Blues"? Why?

WRITING SUGGESTIONS

1. Rearrange the episodes in "Sonny's Blues" as they would appear in the hypothetical history—that is, in chronological order. Pick the three or four changes that seem to you most important. Describe the difference in significance and effect that is achieved by the structuring or rearrangement.

2. Rewrite the action portion of "The Whirlpool Rapids" (pars. 13–20) as if it were the entire story. You may want to add a very brief new beginning and ending. Then write a paragraph of perhaps 250 words explaining the major ways in which your new story differs from the original.

2 POINT OF VIEW

Structuring involves more than plot, more than the ordering of events; selection involves more than the choosing or inventing of incidents. What would "Sonny's Blues" be like seen through the eyes of Sonny? What incidents might he choose to tell? In what order might he arrange them? And what does it do to "The Cask of Amontillado" when we realize, at the end, that it is being told by Montresor fifty years after the event and that his last—probably dying—words, referring to Fortunato, are, "*In pace requiescat*"? Why is he telling the story now? What additional resonance do his final words have?

Who is telling us the story—whose words are we reading? Where does this person stand in relation to what is going on in the story? In drama, events appear before us directly. In narrative, someone is always *between* us and the events—a viewer, a speaker, or both. Narrative, unlike drama, is always mediated. The way a story is mediated is a key element in fictional structure. This mediation involves both the angle of vision—the point from which the people, events, and other details are viewed—and also the words of the story lying between us and the history. The viewing aspect is called the **focus**, and the verbal aspect the **voice**. Both are generally lumped together in the term **point of view**.

Focus acts much as a movie camera does, choosing what we can look at and the angle at which we can view it, framing, proportioning, emphasizing—even distorting. Plot is a structure that places us in a time relationship to the history; focus places us in a spatial relationship.

We must pay careful attention to the focus at any given point in a story. Is it fixed or mobile? Does it stay at more or less the same angle to, and at the same distance from, the characters and action, or does it move around or in and out? In the first three and a half paragraphs of "An Occurrence at Owl Creek Bridge," for example, we seem to be seeing through the lens of a camera that can swing left or right, up or down, but that stays pretty much at the same angle and distance from the bridge. By the middle of the fourth paragraph, however, we're inside the mind of the man who's about to be hanged: "The arrangement commended itself to his judgment . . . He looked a moment . . . A piece of dancing driftwood caught his attention . . . How slowly it appeared to move!" From now on we are inside the condemned man's head. The focus is more limited in scope—for almost all the rest of the story we can see and hear only what he sees and hears. But because the focus is internal as well as limited, we can also know what he thinks. This limited, internal focus is usually called the **centered** or **central consciousness.**

The centered consciousness has been perhaps the most popular focus in fiction for the past hundred years—through most of the history of the modern short story, in fact—and its tightly controlled range and concentration on a single individual seem particularly suited for the short form. During much of this period, fiction, both long and short, has been in one sense realistic—that is, treating the everyday and the natural. It has become increasingly clear, however, that the apparently real is not necessarily what "is" but what is *perceived by* the senses and mind of the individual. (This is sometimes called **psychological realism.**) The centered consciousness, in which things, people, and events are narrated as if they have been perceived through the filter of an individual character's consciousness, has therefore seemed the more realistic way to tell a story. It is a comfortable focus for readers, too. On the one hand, they can identify with someone whose thoughts and perception they share, even if the character is fallible, like Lantin in "The Jewelry," or reprehensible, like Montresor. We can identify with point of view in a story told in the first person ("I"), too, but we are too close at times. We cannot escape. The camera cannot pull back as it can in a third-person story.

First-person stories, like "The Summer My Grandmother Was Supposed to Die," are always limited too, and almost all the time are internal as well (though Montresor in "The Cask of Amontillado" hides his plans from us). While they cannot retract spatially from the narrator, they almost always are withdrawn temporally: that is, the "I" telling the story is older than the "I" experiencing the events of the story, as in "The Summer My Grandmother Was Supposed to Die," where the narrator is clearly older than the boy he was when the action of the story took place.

The psychological realism gained by having a limited narrator exacts a price from the reader. If we don't hold the author (or the story) responsible for the absolute truth, validity, accuracy, and opinions of the focal character—if he or she is just telling us what he or she thinks, feels, sees—we must accept the possibility that the narrator's vision may be **unreliable.** At a significant point in "Owl Creek Bridge," for example, you will find that the camera pulls back from Peyton Farquhar and we are made to recognize to what extent his consciousness is a reliable witness to what has been going on. The history here is only an occurrence; the limited point of view structures the mere occurrence into a story.

When the point of view is limited, whether to a first-person narrator or to a centered consciousness, it is tied to that individual. When he or she leaves the room, the camera must go too, and if we are to know what happens in the room when the focal character is gone, some means of bringing the information to that character must be devised, such as a letter or a report by another character. The camera may pull back out of the character's mind or even, as in "Owl Creek Bridge," above and away from the character, but it does not generally jump around. The somewhat unusual first-person plural point of view of "A Rose for Emily" is not limited to a single individual; anything the town of Jefferson in general can know of past or present, the narrative can know. But neither is it an unlimited focus; "we" could not get into Emily's house before she dies and could never get into her mind.

An unlimited point of view permits such freedom. In "The Zebra Story-teller" we are with the first zebra (who is killed) when he meets a cat speaking Zebraic and are told he is "astonished." We learn that the zebras can smell no lion and so "decided the woods were haunted by the ghost of a lion," and we get inside the mind of the storyteller and "hear" him speaking to himself. Throughout, the story seems free to see matter from one focus or another and even to dip inside a character's mind.

There are no laws governing point of view in fiction, but there is a general feeling that once a point of view is chosen that ought to be the law for that story. The movement of the focus at the beginning of "An Occurrence at Owl Creek Bridge" is not a jump but a narrowing down: the panorama at the beginning of the story, apparently from the point of view and in the voice of a distant observer, is adjusted and then we settle in, which is not an uncommon device (note how many movies used to begin with a panoramic shot of a town and gradually focused on a house or room). When toward the end of the story the "camera" moves back and away from Peyton Farquhar, we find there has been another reason for the panoramic shot at the beginning. There has been no jumping around and the narrowing and widening seem to be justifiable and meaningful. There are stories in this anthology—"The Most Dangerous Game," "Barn Burning," and "The Lame Shall Enter First," for example—in which the point of view does shift—or jump—from a previously established centered consciousness. Whether these are "flaws" must be judged in each case in terms of function: is the shift merely a narrative convenience or manipulation or is it consistent with or does it contribute to the significance or vision of the story?

Focus and voice often coincide; that is why they are commonly lumped together as point of view. There is no discrepancy that I can see (or hear) between the viewing and the telling in "The Cask of Amontillado," for example. But in "The Summer My Grandmother Was Supposed to Die," the

"I" telling the story is older than the "I" experiencing the events of the story, and that is why it is useful to have at hand the terms and concepts of focus and voice as two different aspects of point of view. Notice in the Richler story how many phrases there are like "years later I was shown the telegram" and "in those days . . ." So, too, the language of the story is clearly not that of a young boy: "She arrived punctually at noon"; "I've been told that to study Talmud with him had been a rare pleasure"; "lots of slender volumes of sermons, chassidic tales, and rabbinical commentaries." Such expressions may deal with incidents and information within the boy's perception, but the language in which they are expressed is clearly beyond him.

Like the focus, the voice in "Owl Creek Bridge" at the beginning of the story is not centered in Peyton Farquhar, but even when the focus narrows on him the voice telling the story is not his; note, for example, "As these thoughts, *which have here to be set down in words,* were flashed into the doomed man's brain" (emphasis added). The discrepancy may prepare a careful reader for later developments in the story.

I have used the common term **narrator** in the usual way—to mean the person who tells the story. You will have noticed that often the narrator really is a person in the story, like Muttel, the narrator in "The Summer My Grandmother Was Supposed to Die." But how about the narrator in "Owl Creek Bridge"? Who is it who sets down Farquhar's words and can say things like this: "Death is a dignitary who, when he comes announced, is to be received with formal manifestations of respect, even by those most familiar with him. In the code of military etiquette silence and fixity are forms of deference" (par. 2). Where is he or she standing? What kind of person is this narrator? We might ask the same question of the elusive, unnamed spokesman for the town of Jefferson in "A Rose for Emily." Close attention to the language and chronology of the story, to the references to race and gender, to the use of "they" and "we," reveals that the narrator is an educated white male who at the time of Emily's death is probably a boy or very young man.

Is he Faulkner? Where the narrator plays some role in the story we are less likely to identify him or her with the author; where the narrator is an unidentified voice we often tend to do so. We call the narrator of "Owl Creek Bridge" "Bierce." This is not necessarily wrong, but it can be misleading. We can dig up a few facts about the author's life and read them into the story, or, worse, read the character or detail of the story into the author's life. It is more prudent, therefore, especially on the basis of a single story, not to speak of the author but of the author's **persona,** the voice or figure of the author who tells and structures the story, who may or may not resemble in nature or values the actual person of the author. Mary Anne Evans wrote novels under the name of George Eliot; her first-person narrator speaks of "himself." That male narrator may be a good example of the persona or representative that most authors construct to "write" their stories.

We say *write* the stories. The narrator of "Owl Creek Bridge" has to "set down in words" what Farquhar is thinking. But just as poets write of singing their songs (poems), so we often speak of telling a story, and we speak of a narrator, which means a teller. There are stories, usually with first-person narrators, that make much of the convention of oral storytelling—"My Man Bovanne," for example.

We are used to thinking of a story in terms of its plot, so that to summarize a story usually means giving a plot summary. But if you shift focus and voice you will often find that though the history has not changed, the story has. You might want to test this out by rewriting "The Summer My Grandmother Was Supposed to Die" with the focus and perhaps with the voice of Muttel's mother or "A Rose for Emily" in Emily's voice and focus.

POINT OF VIEW A Glossary

centered (central) consciousness: a limited point of view, one tied to a single character throughout the story, often with access to his or her inner thoughts (but not to the thoughts of others)

focus: the point from which the people, events, and other details in a story are viewed. See *point of view*

limited point of view or **limited focus:** a perspective pinned to a single character, whether first-person or a third-person centered consciousness, so that we cannot know for sure what is going on in the minds of other characters; when the focal character leaves the room in a story we must go too and cannot know what is going on while our "eyes" or "camera" is gone. A variation on this, which generally has no name and is often lumped with the *omniscient point of view*, is the point of view that can wander like a camera from one character to another and close in or move back but cannot (or at least does not) get inside anyone's head, does not present from the inside any character's thoughts.

omniscient point of view: see *unlimited point of view*

point of view: focus; the point from which the people, events, and other details in a story are viewed. This term is sometimes used to include both focus and voice.

psychological realism: a modification of the concept of realism, or telling it like it is, which recognizes that what is real to the individual is that which he or she perceives. It is the ground for the use of the centered consciousness, or the first-person narrator, since both of these present reality only as something perceived by the focal character.

unlimited focus or **omniscient point of view:** a perspective that can be that seen from one character's view, then another's, then another's, or can be moved in or out of any character at any time

unreliable narrator: a speaker or voice whose vision or version of the details of the story are consciously or unconsciously deceiving; such a narrator's version is usually subtly undermined by details in the story or the reader's general knowledge of facts outside the story; if, for example, the narrator were to tell you that Columbus was Spanish, and that he discovered America in the fourteenth century when his ship *The Golden Hind* landed on the coast of Florida near present-day Gainesville, you might not trust other things he tells you.

voice: the acknowledged or unacknowledged source of the words of the story; the "speaker;" the "person" telling the story

AMBROSE BIERCE

An Occurrence at Owl Creek Bridge

I

A man stood upon a railroad bridge in Northern Alabama, looking down into the swift waters twenty feet below. The man's hands were behind his back, the wrists bound with a cord. A rope loosely encircled his neck. It was attached to a stout cross-timber above his head, and the slack fell to the level of his knees. Some loose boards laid upon the sleepers supporting the metals of the railway supplied a footing for him and his executioners—two private soldiers of the Federal army, directed by a sergeant, who in civil life may have been a deputy sheriff. At a short remove upon the same temporary platform was an officer in the uniform of his rank, armed. He was a captain. A sentinel at each end of the bridge stood with his rifle in the position known as "support," that is to say, vertical in front of the left shoulder, the hammer resting on the forearm thrown straight across the chest—a formal and unnatural position, enforcing an erect carriage of the body. It did not appear to be the duty of these two men to know what was occurring at the centre of the bridge; they merely blockaded the two ends of the foot plank which traversed it.

Beyond one of the sentinels nobody was in sight; the railroad ran straight away into a forest for a hundred yards, then, curving, was lost to view. Doubtless there was an outpost further along. The other bank of the stream was open ground—a gentle acclivity crowned with a stockade of vertical tree trunks, loop-holed for rifles, with a single embrasure through which protruded the muzzle of a brass cannon commanding the bridge. Midway of the slope between bridge and fort were the spectators—a single company of infantry in line, at "parade rest," the butts of the rifles on the ground, the barrels inclining slightly backward against the right shoulder, the hands crossed upon the stock. A lieutenant stood at the right of the line, the point of his sword upon the ground, his left hand resting upon his right. Excepting the group of four at the centre of the bridge not a man moved. The company faced the bridge, staring stonily, motionless. The sentinels, facing the banks of the stream, might have been statues to adorn the bridge. The captain stood with folded arms, silent, observing the work of his subordinates but making no sign. Death is a dignitary who, when he comes announced, is to be received with formal manifestations of respect, even by those most familiar with him. In the code of military etiquette silence and fixity are forms of deference.

The man who was engaged in being hanged was apparently about thirty-five years of age. He was a civilian, if one might judge from his dress, which was that of a planter. His features were good—a straight nose, firm mouth, broad forehead, from which his long, dark hair was combed straight back, falling behind his ears to the collar of his well-fitting frock coat. He wore a moustache and pointed beard, but no whiskers; his eyes were large and dark grey and had a kindly expression which one would hardly have expected in one whose neck was in the hemp. Evidently this was no vulgar assassin. The liberal military code makes provision for hanging many kinds of people, and gentlemen are not excluded.

The preparations being complete, the two private soldiers stepped aside and each drew away the plank upon which he had been standing. The sergeant turned to the captain, saluted and placed himself immediately behind that officer, who in turn moved apart one pace. These movements left the condemned man and the sergeant standing on the two ends of the same plank, which spanned three of the cross-ties of the bridge. The end upon which the civilian stood almost, but not quite, reached a fourth. This plank had been held in place by the weight of the captain; it was now held by that of the sergeant. At a signal from the former, the latter would step aside, the plank would tilt and the condemned man go down between two ties. The arrangement commended itself to his judgment as simple and effective. His face had not been covered nor his eyes bandaged. He looked a moment at his "unsteadfast footing," then let his gaze wander to the swirling water of the stream racing madly beneath his feet. A piece of dancing driftwood caught his attention and his eyes followed it down the current. How slowly it appeared to move! What a sluggish stream!

He closed his eyes in order to fix his last thoughts upon his wife and children. The water, touched to gold by the early sun, the brooding mists under the banks at some distance down the stream, the fort, the soldiers, the piece of drift—all had distracted him. And now he became conscious of a new disturbance. Striking through the thought of his dear ones was a sound which he could neither ignore nor understand, a sharp, distinct, metallic percussion like the stroke of a blacksmith's hammer upon the anvil; it had the same ringing quality. He wondered what it was, and whether immeasurably distant or near by—it seemed both. Its recurrence was regular, but as slow as the tolling of a death knell. He awaited each stroke with impatience and—he knew not why—apprehension. The intervals of silence grew progressively longer, the delays became maddening. With their greater infrequency the sounds increased in strength and sharpness. They hurt his ear like the thrust of a knife; he feared he would shriek. What he heard was the ticking of his watch.

He unclosed his eyes and saw again the water below him. "If I could free my hands," he thought, "I might throw off the noose and spring into the stream. By diving I could evade the bullets, and, swimming vigorously, reach the bank, take to the woods, and get away home. My home, thank God, is as yet outside their lines; my wife and little ones are still beyond the invader's farthest advance."

As these thoughts, which have here to be set down in words, were flashed into the doomed man's brain rather than evolved from it, the captain nodded to the sergeant. The sergeant stepped aside.

II

Peyton Farquhar was a well-to-do planter, of an old and highly-respected Alabama family. Being a slave owner, and, like other slave owners, a politician, he

getting us on F.'s side, to cheer him on & to
hope for his escape is, of course, an imp. element
An Occurrence at Owl Creek Bridge ∇ 65
in strategy of story because we want to believe him

was naturally an original secessionist and ardently devoted to the Southern cause. Circumstances of an imperious nature which it is unnecessary to relate here, had prevented him from taking service with the gallant army which had fought the disastrous campaigns ending with the fall of Corinth,[1] and he chafed under the inglorious restraint, longing for the release of his energies, the larger life of the soldier, the opportunity for distinction. That opportunity, he felt, would come, as it comes to all in war time. Meanwhile he did what he could. No service was too humble for him to perform in aid of the South, no adventure too perilous for him to undertake if consistent with the character of a civilian who was at heart a soldier, and who in good faith and without too much qualification assented to at least a part of the frankly villainous dictum that all is fair in love and war.

One evening while Farquhar and his wife were sitting on a rustic bench near the entrance to his grounds, a grey-clad soldier rode up to the gate and asked for a drink of water. Mrs. Farquhar was only too happy to serve him with her own white hands. While she was gone to fetch the water, her husband approached the dusty horseman and inquired eagerly for news from the front.

"The Yanks are repairing the railroads," said the man, "and are getting ready for another advance. They have reached the Owl Creek bridge, put it in order, and built a stockade on the other bank. The commandant has issued an order, which is posted everywhere, declaring that any civilian caught interfering with the railroad, its bridges, tunnels, or trains, will be summarily hanged. I saw the order."

"How far is it to the Owl Creek bridge?" Farquhar asked.

"About thirty miles."

"Is there no force on this side the creek?"

"Only a picket post half a mile out, on the railroad, and a single sentinel at this end of the bridge."

"Suppose a man—a civilian and student of hanging—should elude the picket post and perhaps get the better of the sentinel," said Farquhar, smiling, "what could he accomplish?"

The soldier reflected. "I was there a month ago," he replied. "I observed that the flood of last winter had lodged a great quantity of driftwood against the wooden pier at this end of the bridge. It is now dry and would burn like tow."

The lady had now brought the water, which the soldier drank. He thanked her ceremoniously, bowed to her husband, and rode away. An hour later, after nightfall, he repassed the plantation, going northward in the direction from which he had come. He was a Federal scout.

III

As Peyton Farquhar fell straight downward through the bridge, he lost consciousness and was as one already dead. From this state he was awakened—ages later, it seemed to him—by the pain of a sharp pressure upon his throat, followed by

1. Corinth, Mississippi, captured by General Grant in April 1862.

a sense of suffocation. Keen, poignant agonies seemed to shoot from his neck downward through every fibre of his body and limbs. These pains appeared to flash along well-defined lines of ramification, and to beat with an inconceivably rapid periodicity. They seemed like streams of pulsating fire heating him to an intolerable temperature. As to his head, he was conscious of nothing but a feeling of fullness—of congestion. These sensations were unaccompanied by thought. The intellectual part of his nature was already effaced; he had power only to feel, and feeling was torment. He was conscious of motion. Encompassed in a luminous cloud, of which he was now merely the fiery heart, without material substance, he swung through unthinkable arcs of oscillation, like a vast pendulum. Then all at once, with terrible suddenness, the light about him shot upward with the noise of a loud plash; a frightful roaring was in his ears, and all was cold and dark. The power of thought was restored; he knew that the rope had broken and he had fallen into the stream. There was no additional strangulation; the noose about his neck was already suffocating him, and kept the water from his lungs. To die of hanging at the bottom of a river!—the idea seemed to him ludicrous. He opened his eyes in the blackness and saw above him a gleam of light, but how distant, how inaccessible! He was still sinking, for the light became fainter and fainter until it was a mere glimmer. Then it began to grow and brighten, and he knew that he was rising toward the surface—knew it with reluctance, for he was now very comfortable. "To be hanged and drowned," he thought, "that is not so bad; but I do not wish to be shot. No; I will not be shot; that is not fair."

He was not conscious of an effort, but a sharp pain in his wrist apprised him that he was trying to free his hands. He gave the struggle his attention, as an idler might observe the feat of a juggler, without interest in the outcome. What splendid effort!—what magnificent, what superhuman strength! Ah, that was a fine endeavour! Bravo! The cord fell away; his arms parted and floated upward, the hands dimly seen on each side in the growing light. He watched them with a new interest as first one and then the other pounced upon the noose at his neck. They tore it away and thrust it fiercely aside, its undulations resembling those of a water-snake. "Put it back, put it back!" He thought he shouted these words to his hands, for the undoing of the noose had been succeeded by the direst pang which he had yet experienced. His neck ached horribly; his brain was on fire; his heart, which had been fluttering faintly, gave a great leap, trying to force itself out at his mouth. His whole body was racked and wrenched with an insupportable anguish! But his disobedient hands gave no heed to the command. They beat the water vigorously with quick, downward strokes, forcing him to the surface. He felt his head emerge; his eyes were blinded by the sunlight; his chest expanded convulsively, and with a supreme and crowning agony his lungs engulfed a great draught of air, which instantly he expelled in a shriek!

He was now in full possession of his physical senses. They were, indeed, preternaturally keen and alert. Something in the awful disturbance of his organic system had so exalted and refined them that they made record of things never before perceived. He felt the ripples upon his face and heard their separate sounds as they struck. He looked at the forest on the bank of the stream, saw the individual trees, the leaves and the veining of each leaf—the very insects upon them,

This story was considered "realistic" — is it more than a journalist

most adventure stories + romances ended happily

the locusts, the brilliant-bodied flies, the grey spiders stretching their webs from twig to twig. He noted the prismatic colors in all the dewdrops upon a million blades of grass. The humming of the gnats that danced above the eddies of the stream, the beating of the dragon flies' wings, the strokes of the water spiders' legs, like oars which had lifted their boat—all these made audible music. A fish slid along beneath his eyes and he heard the rush of its body parting the water.

heroes
miracle
escape

He had come to the surface facing down the stream; in a moment the visible world seemed to wheel slowly round, himself the pivotal point, and he saw the bridge, the fort, the soldiers upon the bridge, the captain, the sergeant, the two privates, his executioners. They were in silhouette against the blue sky. They shouted and gesticulated, pointing at him; the captain had drawn his pistol, but did not fire; the others were unarmed. Their movements were grotesque and horrible, their forms gigantic.

here
we
emotion
identify
w/
hero
who
doesn't
make i

Suddenly he heard a sharp report and something struck the water smartly within a few inches of his head, spattering his face with spray. He heard a second report, and saw one of the sentinels with his rifle at his shoulder, a light cloud of blue smoke rising from the muzzle. The man in the water saw the eye of the man on the bridge gazing into his own through the sights of the rifle. He observed that it was a grey eye, and remembered having read that grey eyes were keenest and that all famous marksmen had them. Nevertheless, this one had missed.

A counter swirl had caught Farquhar and turned him half round; he was again looking into the forest on the bank opposite the fort. The sound of a clear, high voice in a monotonous singsong now rang out behind him and came across the water with a distinctness that pierced and subdued all other sounds, even the beating of the ripples in his ears. Although no soldier, he had frequented camps enough to know the dread significance of that deliberate, drawling, aspirated chant; the lieutenant on shore was taking a part in the morning's work. How coldly and pitilessly—with what an even, calm intonation, presaging and enforc-ing tranquillity in the men—with what accurately-measured intervals fell those cruel words:

"Attention, company. . . . Shoulder arms. . . . Ready. . . . Aim. . . . Fire."

Farquhar dived—dived as deeply as he could. The water roared in his ears like the voice of Niagara, yet he heard the dulled thunder of the volley, and rising again toward the surface, met shining bits of metal, singularly flattened, oscillating slowly downward. Some of them touched him on the face and hands, then fell away, continuing their descent. One lodged between his collar and neck; it was uncomfortably warm, and he snatched it out.

25

As he rose to the surface, gasping for breath, he saw that he had been a long time under water; he was perceptibly farther down stream—nearer to safety. The soldiers had almost finished reloading; the metal ramrods flashed all at once in the sunshine as they were drawn from the barrels, turned in the air, and thrust into their sockets. The two sentinels fired again, independently and ineffectually.

The hunted man saw all this over his shoulder; he was now swimming vig-orously with the current. His brain was as energetic as his arms and legs; he thought with the rapidity of lightning.

"The officer," he reasoned, "will not make that martinet's error a second time. It is as easy to dodge a volley as a single shot. He has probably already given the command to fire at will. God help me, I cannot dodge them all!"

An appalling plash within two yards of him, followed by a loud rushing sound, *diminuendo*, which seemed to travel back through the air to the fort and died in an explosion which stirred the very river to its deeps! A rising sheet of water, which curved over him, fell down upon him, blinded him, strangled him! The cannon had taken a hand in the game. As he shook his head free from the commotion of the smitten water, he heard the deflected shot humming through the air ahead, and in an instant it was cracking and smashing the branches in the forest beyond.

"They will not do that again," he thought; "the next time they will use a charge of grape. I must keep my eye upon the gun; the smoke will apprise me— the report arrives too late; it lags behind the missile. It is a good gun."

Suddenly he felt himself whirled round and round—spinning like a top. The water, the banks, the forest, the now distant bridge, fort and men—all were commingled and blurred. Objects were represented by their colors only; circular horizontal streaks of color—that was all he saw. He had been caught in a vortex and was being whirled on with a velocity of advance and gyration which made him giddy and sick. In a few moments he was flung upon the gravel at the foot of the left bank of the stream—the southern bank—and behind a projecting point which concealed him from his enemies. The sudden arrest of his motion, the abrasion of one of his hands on the gravel, restored him and he wept with delight. He dug his fingers into the sand, threw it over himself in handfuls and audibly blessed it. It looked like gold, like diamonds, rubies, emeralds; he could think of nothing beautiful which it did not resemble. The trees upon the bank were giant garden plants; he noted a definite order in their arrangement, inhaled the fragrance of their blooms. A strange, roseate light shone through the spaces among their trunks, and the wind made in their branches the music of æolian harps. He had no wish to perfect his escape, was content to remain in that enchanting spot until retaken.

A whizz and rattle of grapeshot among the branches high above his head roused him from his dream. The baffled cannoneer had fired him a random farewell. He sprang to his feet, rushed up the sloping bank, and plunged into the forest.

All that day he travelled, laying his course by the rounding sun. The forest seemed interminable; nowhere did he discover a break in it, not even a woodman's road. He had not known that he lived in so wild a region. There was something uncanny in the revelation.

By nightfall he was fatigued, footsore, famishing. The thought of his wife and children urged him on. At last he found a road which led him in what he knew to be the right direction. It was as wide and straight as a city street, yet it seemed untravelled. No fields bordered it, no dwelling anywhere. Not so much as the barking of a dog suggested human habitation. The black bodies of the great trees formed a straight wall on both sides, terminating on the horizon in a point, like a diagram in a lesson in perspective. Overhead, as he looked up through this rift in the wood, shone great golden stars looking unfamiliar and grouped in strange constellations. He was sure they were arranged in some order which had a secret and malign significance. The wood on either side was full of singular noises, among which—once, twice, and again—he distinctly heard whispers in an unknown tongue.

His neck was in pain, and, lifting his hand to it, he found it horribly swollen. He knew that it had a circle of black where the rope had bruised it. His eyes felt congested; he could no longer close them. His tongue was swollen with thirst; he relieved its fever by thrusting it forward from between his teeth into the cool air. How softly the turf had carpeted the untravelled avenue! He could no longer feel the roadway beneath his feet!

Doubtless, despite his suffering, he fell asleep while walking, for now he sees another scene—perhaps he has merely recovered from a delirium. He stands at the gate of his own home. All is as he left it, and all bright and beautiful in the morning sunshine. He must have travelled the entire night. As he pushes open the gate and passes up the wide white walk, he sees a flutter of female garments; his wife, looking fresh and cool and sweet, steps down from the verandah to meet him. At the bottom of the steps she stands waiting, with a smile of ineffable joy, an attitude of matchless grace and dignity. Ah, how beautiful she is! He springs forward with extended arms. As he is about to clasp her, he feels a stunning blow upon the back of the neck; a blinding white light blazes all about him, with a sound like the shock of a cannon—then all is darkness and silence!

Peyton Farquhar was dead; his body, with a broken neck, swung gently from side to side beneath the timbers of the Owl Creek bridge.

1891

WILLIAM FAULKNER

A Rose for Emily

I

When Miss Emily Grierson died, our whole town went to her funeral: the men through a sort of respectful affection for a fallen monument, the women mostly out of curiosity to see the inside of her house, which no one save an old man-servant—a combined gardener and cook—had seen in at least ten years.

It was a big, squarish frame house that had once been white, decorated with cupolas and spires and scrolled balconies in the heavily lightsome style of the seventies, set on what had once been our most select street. But garages and cotton gins had encroached and obliterated even the august names of that neighborhood; only Miss Emily's house was left, lifting its stubborn and coquettish decay above the cotton wagons and the gasoline pumps—an eyesore among eyesores. And now Miss Emily had gone to join the representatives of those august names where they lay in the cedar-bemused cemetery among the ranked and anonymous graves of Union and Confederate soldiers who fell at the battle of Jefferson.

Alive, Miss Emily had been a tradition, a duty, and a care; a sort of heredi-tary obligation upon the town, dating from that day in 1894 when Colonel Sar-toris, the mayor—he who fathered the edict that no Negro woman should appear on the streets without an apron—remitted her taxes, the dispensation dating from the death of her father on into perpetuity. Not that Miss Emily would have accepted charity. Colonel Sartoris invented an involved tale to the effect that Miss Emily's father had loaned money to the town, which the town, as a matter of business, preferred this way of repaying. Only a man of Colonel Sartoris' generation and thought could have invented it, and only a woman could have believed it.

When the next generation, with its more modern ideas, became mayors and aldermen, this arrangement created some little dissatisfaction. On the first of the year they mailed her a tax notice. February came, and there was no reply. They wrote her a formal letter, asking her to call at the sheriff's office at her conve-nience. A week later the mayor wrote her himself, offering to call or to send his car for her, and received in reply a note on paper of an archaic shape, in a thin, flowing calligraphy in faded ink, to the effect that she no longer went out at all. The tax notice was also enclosed, without comment.

They called a special meeting of the Board of Aldermen. A deputation waited upon her, knocked at the door through which no visitor had passed since she ceased giving china-painting lessons eight or ten years earlier. They were admit-ted by the old Negro into a dim hall from which a stairway mounted into still more shadow. It smelled of dust and disuse—a close, dank smell. The Negro led them into the parlor. It was furnished in heavy, leather-covered furniture. When the Negro opened the blinds of one window, a faint dust rose sluggishly about their thighs, spinning with slow motes in the single sun-ray. On a tarnished gilt easel before the fireplace stood a crayon portrait of Miss Emily's father.

They rose when she entered—a small, fat woman in black, with a thin gold chain descending to her waist and vanishing into her belt, leaning on an ebony cane with a tarnished gold head. Her skeleton was small and spare; perhaps that was why what would have been merely plumpness in another was obesity in her. She looked bloated, like a body long submerged in motionless water, and of that pallid hue. Her eyes, lost in the fatty ridges of her face, looked like two small pieces of coal pressed into a lump of dough as they moved from one face to another while the visitors stated their errand.

She did not ask them to sit. She just stood in the door and listened quietly until the spokesman came to a stumbling halt. Then they could hear the invisi-ble watch ticking at the end of the gold chain.

Her voice was dry and cold. "I have no taxes in Jefferson. Colonel Sartoris explained it to me. Perhaps one of you can gain access to the city records and satisfy yourselves."

"But we have. We are the city authorities, Miss Emily. Didn't you get a notice from the sheriff, signed by him?"

"I received a paper, yes," Miss Emily said. "Perhaps he considers himself the sheriff. . . . I have no taxes in Jefferson."

"But there is nothing on the books to show that, you see. We must go by the—"

"See Colonel Sartoris. I have no taxes in Jefferson."

"But, Miss Emily—"

"See Colonel Sartoris." (Colonel Sartoris had been dead almost ten years.) "I have no taxes in Jefferson. Tobe!" The Negro appeared. "Show these gentlemen out."

II

So she vanquished them, horse and foot, just as she had vanquished their fathers thirty years before about the smell. That was two years after her father's death and a short time after her sweetheart—the one we believed would marry her—had deserted her. After her father's death she went out very little; after her sweetheart went away, people hardly saw her at all. A few of the ladies had the temerity to call, but were not received, and the only sign of life about the place was the Negro man—a young man then—going in and out with a market basket.

"Just as if a man—any man—could keep a kitchen properly," the ladies said; so they were not surprised when the smell developed. It was another link between the gross, teeming world and the high and mighty Griersons.

A neighbor, a woman, complained to the mayor, Judge Stevens, eighty years old.

"But what will you have me do about it, madam?" he said.

"Why, send her word to stop it," the woman said. "Isn't there a law?"

"I'm sure that won't be necessary," Judge Stevens said. "It's probably just a snake or a rat that nigger of hers killed in the yard. I'll speak to him about it."

The next day he received two more complaints, one from a man who came in diffident deprecation. "We really must do something about it, Judge. I'd be the last one in the world to bother Miss Emily, but we've got to do something." That night the Board of Aldermen met—three gray-beards and one younger man, a member of the rising generation.

"It's simple enough," he said. "Send her word to have her place cleaned up. Give her a certain time to do it in, and if she don't . . ."

"Dammit, sir," Judge Stevens said, "will you accuse a lady to her face of smelling bad?"

So the next night, after midnight, four men crossed Miss Emily's lawn and slunk about the house like burglars, sniffing along the base of the brickwork and at the cellar openings while one of them performed a regular sowing motion with his hand out of a sack slung from his shoulder. They broke open the cellar door and sprinkled lime there, and in all the outbuildings. As they recrossed the lawn, a window that had been dark was lighted and Miss Emily sat in it, the light behind her, and her upright torso motionless as that of an idol. They crept quietly across the lawn and into the shadow of the locusts that lined the street. After a week or two the smell went away.

That was when people had begun to feel really sorry for her. People in our town, remembering how old lady Wyatt, her great-aunt, had gone completely crazy at last, believed that the Griersons held themselves a little too high for

15

20

25

what they really were. None of the young men were quite good enough for Miss Emily and such. We had long thought of them as a tableau; Miss Emily a slender figure in white in the background, her father a spraddled silhouette in the foreground, his back to her and clutching a horsewhip, the two of them framed by the back-flung front door. So when she got to be thirty and was still single, we were not pleased exactly, but vindicated; even with insanity in the family she wouldn't have turned down all of her chances if they had really materialized.

When her father died, it got about that the house was all that was left to her; and in a way, people were glad. At last they could pity Miss Emily. Being left alone, and a pauper, she had become humanized. Now she too would know the old thrill and the old despair of a penny more or less.

The day after his death all the ladies prepared to call at the house and offer condolence and aid, as is our custom. Miss Emily met them at the door, dressed as usual and with no trace of grief on her face. She told them that her father was not dead. She did that for three days, with the ministers calling on her, and the doctors, trying to persuade her to let them dispose of the body. Just as they were about to resort to law and force, she broke down, and they buried her father quickly.

We did not say she was crazy then. We believed she had to do that. We remembered all the young men her father had driven away, and we knew that with nothing left, she would have to cling to that which had robbed her, as people will.

III

She was sick for a long time. When we saw her again, her hair was cut short, making her look like a girl, with a vague resemblance to those angels in colored church windows—sort of tragic and serene.

The town had just let the contracts for paving the sidewalks, and in the summer after her father's death they began to work. The construction company came with niggers and mules and machinery, and a foreman named Homer Barron, a Yankee—a big, dark, ready man, with a big voice and eyes lighter than his face. The little boys would follow in groups to hear him cuss the niggers, and the niggers singing in time to the rise and fall of picks. Pretty soon he knew everybody in town. Whenever you heard a lot of laughing anywhere about the square, Homer Barron would be in the center of the group. Presently we began to see him and Miss Emily on Sunday afternoons driving in the yellow-wheeled buggy and the matched team of bays from the livery stable.

At first we were glad that Miss Emily would have an interest, because the ladies all said, "Of course a Grierson would not think seriously of a Northerner, a day laborer." But there were still others, older people, who said that even grief could not cause a real lady to forget *noblesse oblige*—without calling it *noblesse oblige*. They just said, "Poor Emily. Her kinsfolk should come to her." She had some kin in Alabama; but years ago her father had fallen out with them over the estate of old lady Wyatt, the crazy woman, and there was no communication between the two families. They had not even been represented at the funeral.

And as soon as the old people said, "Poor Emily," the whispering began. "Do you suppose it's really so?" they said to one another. "Of course it is. What else could . . ." This behind their hands; rustling of craned silk and satin behind jalousies closed upon the sun of Sunday afternoon as the thin, swift clop-clop-clop of the matched team passed: "Poor Emily."

She carried her head high enough—even when we believed that she was fallen. It was as if she demanded more than ever the recognition of her dignity as the last Grierson; as if it had wanted that touch of earthiness to reaffirm her imperviousness. Like when she bought the rat poison, the arsenic. That was over a year after they had begun to say "Poor Emily," and while the two female cousins were visiting her.

"I want some poison," she said to the druggist. She was over thirty then, still a slight woman, though thinner than usual, with cold, haughty black eyes in a face the flesh of which was strained across the temples and about the eyesockets as you imagine a lighthouse-keeper's face ought to look. "I want some poison," she said.

"Yes, Miss Emily. What kind? For rats and such? I'd recom—"

"I want the best you have. I don't care what kind."

The druggist named several. "They'll kill anything up to an elephant. But what you want is—"

"Arsenic," Miss Emily said. "Is that a good one?"

"Is . . . arsenic? Yes ma'am. But what you want—"

"I want arsenic."

The druggist looked down at her. She looked back at him, erect, her face like a strained flag. "Why, of course," the druggist said. "If that's what you want. But the law requires you to tell what you are going to use it for."

Miss Emily just stared at him, her head tilted back in order to look him eye for eye, until he looked away and went and got the arsenic and wrapped it up. The Negro delivery boy brought her the package; the druggist didn't come back. When she opened the package at home there was written on the box, under the skull and bones: "For rats."

IV

So the next day we all said, "She will kill herself"; and we said it would be the best thing. When she had first begun to be seen with Homer Barron, we had said, "She will marry him." Then we said, "She will persuade him yet," because Homer himself had remarked—he liked men, and it was known that he drank with the younger men in the Elk's Club—that he was not a marrying man. Later we said, "Poor Emily," behind the jalousies as they passed on Sunday afternoon in the glittering buggy, Miss Emily with her head high and Homer Barron with his hat cocked and a cigar in his teeth, reins and whip in a yellow glove.

Then some of the ladies began to say that it was a disgrace to the town and a bad example to the young people. The men did not want to interfere, but at last the ladies forced the Baptist minister—Miss Emily's people were Episcopal—to call upon her. He would never divulge what happened during that interview, but he refused to go back again. The next Sunday they again drove about the streets, and the following day the minister's wife wrote to Miss Emily's relations in Alabama.

So she had blood-kin under her roof again and we sat back to watch developments. At first nothing happened. Then we were sure that they were to be married. We learned that Miss Emily had been to the jeweler's and ordered a man's toilet set in silver, with the letters H. B. on each piece. Two days later we learned that she had bought a complete outfit of men's clothing, including a nightshirt, and we said, "They are married." We were really glad. We were glad because the two female cousins were even more Grierson than Miss Emily had ever been.

So we were not surprised when Homer Barron—the streets had been finished some time since—was gone. We were a little disappointed that there was not a public blowing-off, but we believed that he had gone on to prepare for Miss Emily's coming, or to give her a chance to get rid of the cousins. (By that time it was a cabal, and we were all Miss Emily's allies to help circumvent the cousins.) Sure enough, after another week they departed. And, as we had expected all along, within three days Homer Barron was back in town. A neighbor saw the Negro man admit him at the kitchen door at dusk one evening.

And that was the last we saw of Homer Barron. And of Miss Emily for some time. The Negro man went in and out with the market basket, but the front door remained closed. Now and then we would see her at a window for a moment, as the men did that night when they sprinkled the lime, but for almost six months she did not appear on the streets. Then we knew that this was to be expected too; as if that quality of her father which had thwarted her woman's life so many times had been too virulent and too furious to die.

When we next saw Miss Emily, she had grown fat and her hair was turning gray. During the next few years it grew grayer and grayer until it attained an even pepper-and-salt iron-gray, when it ceased turning. Up to the day of her death at seventy-four it was still that vigorous iron-gray, like the hair of an active man.

From that time on her front door remained closed, save for a period of six or seven years, when she was about forty, during which she gave lessons in china-painting. She fitted up a studio in one of the downstairs rooms, where the daughters and grand-daughters of Colonel Sartoris' contemporaries were sent to her with the same regularity and in the same spirit that they were sent on Sundays with a twenty-five cent piece for the collection plate. Meanwhile her taxes had been remitted.

Then the newer generation became the backbone and the spirit of the town, and the painting pupils grew up and fell away and did not send their children to her with boxes of color and tedious brushes and pictures cut from the ladies' magazines. The front door closed upon the last one and remained closed for good. When the town got free postal delivery Miss Emily alone refused to let them fasten the metal numbers above her door and attach a mailbox to it. She would not listen to them.

Daily, monthly, yearly we watched the Negro grow grayer and more stooped, going in and out with the market basket. Each December we sent her a tax notice, which would be returned by the post office a week later, unclaimed. Now and then we would see her in one of the downstairs windows—she had evidently shut up the top floor of the house—like the carven torso of an idol in a niche, looking or not looking at us, we could never tell which. Thus she passed from generation to generation—dear, inescapable, impervious, tranquil, and perverse.

And so she died. Fell ill in the house filled with dust and shadows, with only a doddering Negro man to wait on her. We did not even know she was sick; we had long since given up trying to get any information from the Negro. He talked to no one, probably not even to her, for his voice had grown harsh and rusty, as if from disuse.

She died in one of the downstairs rooms, in a heavy walnut bed with a curtain, her gray head propped on a pillow yellow and moldy with age and lack of sunlight.

V

The Negro met the first of the ladies at the front door and let them in, with their hushed, sibilant voices and their quick, curious glances, and then he disappeared. He walked right through the house and out the back and was not seen again.

The two female cousins came at once. They held the funeral on the second day, with the town coming to look at Miss Emily beneath a mass of bought flowers, with the crayon face of her father musing profoundly above the bier and the ladies sibilant and macabre; and the very old men—some in their brushed Confederate uniforms—on the porch and the lawn, talking of Miss Emily as if she had been a contemporary of theirs, believing that they had danced with her and courted her perhaps, confusing time with its mathematical progression, as the old do, to whom all the past is not a diminishing road, but, instead, a huge meadow which no winter ever quite touches, divided from them now by the narrow bottleneck of the most recent decade of years.

Already we knew that there was one room in that region above stairs which no one had seen in forty years, and which would have to be forced. They waited until Miss Emily was decently in the ground before they opened it.

The violence of breaking down the door seemed to fill this room with pervading dust. A thin, acrid pall as of the tomb seemed to lie everywhere upon this room decked and furnished as for a bridal: upon the valance curtains of faded rose color, upon the rose-shaded lights, upon the dressing table, upon the delicate array of crystal and the man's toilet things backed with tarnished silver, silver so tarnished that the monogram was obscured. Among them lay a collar and tie, as if they had just been removed, which, lifted, left upon the surface a pale crescent in the dust. Upon a chair hung the suit, carefully folded; beneath it the two mute shoes and the discarded socks.

The man himself lay in the bed.

For a long while we just stood there, looking down at the profound and fleshless grin. The body had apparently once lain in the attitude of an embrace, but now the long sleep that outlasts love, that conquers even the grimace of love, had cuckolded him. What was left of him, rotted beneath what was left of the nightshirt, had become inextricable from the bed in which he lay; and upon him and upon the pillow beside him lay that even coating of the patient and biding dust.

Then we noticed that in the second pillow was the indentation of a head. One of us lifted something from it, and leaning forward, that faint and invisible dust dry and acrid in the nostrils, we saw a long strand of iron-gray hair.

1931

ironic statement
understatement

MORDECAI RICHLER

The Summer My Grandmother Was Supposed to Die

Dr. Katzman discovered the gangrene on one of his monthly visits. "She won't last a month," he said.

He repeated that the second month, the third, and the fourth, and now she lay dying in the heat of the back bedroom.

"If only she'd die," my mother said. "Oh, God, why doesn't she die? God in heaven, what's she holding on for?"

The summer my grandmother was supposed to die we did not chip in with the Breenbaums to take a cottage in the Laurentians.[1] It wouldn't have been practical. The old lady couldn't be moved, the nurse came daily and the doctor twice a week, and so it seemed best to stay in the city and wait for her to die or, as my mother said, pass away. It was a hot summer, her bedroom was just behind the kitchen, and when we sat down to eat we could smell her. The dressings on my grandmother's left leg had to be changed several times a day and, according to Dr. Katzman, her condition was hopeless. "It's in the hands of the Almighty," he said.

"It won't be long now," my father said, "and she'll be better off, if you know what I mean."

"Please," my mother said.

A nurse came every day from the Royal Victorian Order. She arrived punctually at noon and at five to twelve I'd join the rest of the boys under the outside staircase to look up her dress as she climbed to our second-story flat. Miss Monohan favored lacy pink panties and that was better than waiting under the stairs for Cousin Bessie, for instance. She wore enormous cotton bloomers, rain or shine.

I was sent out to play as often as possible, because my mother felt it was not

---

1. Mountains in eastern Canada between Hudson Bay and the St. Lawrence River.

good for me to see somebody dying. Usually I'd just roam the scorched streets shooting the breeze. There was Arty, Gas sometimes, Hershey, Stan, and me. We talked about everything from A to Z.

"Why is it," Arty wanted to know, "that Tarzan never shits?"

"Dick Tracy too."

"Or Wonder Woman."

"She's a dame."

"So?"

"Jees, wouldn't it be something if Superman crapped in the sky? He could just be flying over Waverly Street when, whamo, Mr. Rabinovitch catches it right in the kisser."

Mr. Rabinovitch was our Hebrew teacher.

"But there's Tarzan," Arty insisted, "in the jungle, week in and week out, and never once does he need to go to the toilet. It's not real, that's all."

Arty told me, "Before your grandma dies she's going to roll her eyes and gurgle. That's what they call the death-rattle."

"Aw, you know everything. Big shot."

"I *read* it, you jerk," Arty said, whacking me one, "in Perry Mason."

Home again I'd find my mother weeping.

"She's dying by inches," she said to my father one stifling night, "and none of them even come to see her. Oh, such children! They should only rot in hell."

"They're not behaving right. It's certainly not according to Hoyle," my father said.

"When I think of all the money and effort that went into making a rabbi out of Israel—the way Mother doted on him—and for what? Oh, what's the world coming to? God."

"It's not right."

Dr. Katzman was amazed. "I never believed she'd last this long. Really, it must be will-power alone that keeps her going. And your excellent care."

"I want her to die, Doctor. That's not my mother in the back room. It's an animal. I want her to please please die."

"Hush. You don't mean it. You're tired." And Dr. Katzman gave my father some pills for my mother to take. "A remarkable woman," he said. "A born nurse."

At night in bed my brother Harvey and I used to talk about our grandmother. "After she dies," I said, "her hair will go on growing for another twenty-four hours."

"Sez who?"

"Arty. It's a scientific fact. Do you think Uncle Lou will come from New York for the funeral?"

"Sure."

"Boy, that means another fiver for me. You too."

"You shouldn't say things like that, kiddo, or *her ghost will come back to haunt you.*"

"Well," I said, "I'll be able to go to her funeral, anyway. I'm not too young any more."

35   I was only six years old when my grandfather died, and I wasn't allowed to go to his funeral.

    I have only one memory of my grandfather. Once he called me into his study, set me down on his lap, and made a drawing of a horse for me. On the horse he drew a rider. While I watched and giggled he gave the rider a beard and the round fur-trimmed cap of a rabbi.

    My grandfather was a Zaddik,[2] one of the Righteous, and I've been told that to study Talmud with him had been a rare pleasure. I wasn't allowed to go to his funeral, but years after I was shown the telegrams of condolence that had come from Eire and Poland and Israel and even Japan. My grandfather had written many books: a translation of the Zohar into modern Hebrew—some twenty years' work—and lots of slender volumes of sermons, chassidic tales, and rabbinical commentaries. His books had been published in Warsaw and later in New York. He had been famous.

    "At the funeral," my mother told me, "they had to have six motorcycle policemen to control the crowds. It was such a heat that twelve women fainted—and I'm *not* counting Mrs. Waxman from upstairs. With her, you know, *anything* to fall into a man's arms. Even Pinsky's. And did I tell you that there was even a French-Canadian priest there?"

    "No kidding?"

40   "The priest was a real big *knacker*.[3] A bishop maybe. He used to study with the *zeyda*.[4] The *zeyda* was some personality, you know. Spiritual and worldly-wise at the same time. Such personalities they don't make any more. Today, rabbis and peanuts are the same size."

    But, according to my father, the *zeyda* (his father-in-law) hadn't been as famous as all that. "There are things I could say," he told me. "There was another side to him."

    My grandfather had come from generations and generations of rabbis, his youngest son was a rabbi, but none of his grandchildren would be one. My brother Harvey was going to be a dentist and at the time, 1937, I was interested in flying and my cousin Jerry was already a communist. I once heard Jerry say, "Our grandpappy wasn't all he was cracked up to be." When the men at the kosher bakeries went out on strike he spoke up against them on the streets where they were picketing and in the *shule*.[5] It was of no consequence to him that they were grossly underpaid. His superstitious followers had to have bread. "Grand-pappy," Jerry said, "was a prize reactionary."

    A week after my grandfather died my grandmother suffered a stroke. Her right side was completely paralyzed. She couldn't speak. At first, it's true, my grandmother could say a few words and move her right hand enough to write her name in Hebrew. Her name was Malka. But her condition soon began to deteriorate.

    My grandmother had six children and seven stepchildren, for my grandfather had been married before. His first wife had died in the old country. Two years

---

2. "Righteous man" in Hebrew.   3. Big shot.   4. Grandfather.   5. Synagogue.

later he had married my grandmother, the only daughter of the richest man in the village, and their marriage had been a singularly happy one. My grandmother had been a beautiful girl. She had also been a wise, resourceful, and patient wife. Qualities, I fear, indispensable to life with a Zaddik. For the synagogue had paid my grandfather no stipulated salary and much of the money he had picked up here and there he had habitually distributed among rabbinical students, needy immigrants, and widows. A vice, and such it was to his hard-pressed family, which made him as unreliable a provider as a drunkard. And indeed, to carry the analogy further, my grandmother had had to make many hurried trips to the pawnbroker with her jewelry. Not all of it had been redeemed, either. But her children had been looked after. The youngest, her favorite, was a rabbi in Boston, the eldest was the actor-manager of a Yiddish theater in New York, and another was a lawyer. One daughter lived in Toronto, two in Montreal. My mother was the youngest daughter, and when my grandmother had her stroke there was a family meeting and it was decided that my mother would take care of her. This was my father's fault. All the other husbands spoke up—they protested their wives had too much work, they could never manage it—but my father detested quarrels, and he was silent. So my grandmother came to stay with us.

Her bedroom, the back bedroom, had actually been promised to me for my seventh birthday. But all that was forgotten now, and I had to go on sharing a bedroom with my brother Harvey. So naturally I was resentful when each morning before I left for school my mother said, "Go in and kiss the *baba*[6] good-bye."

All the same I'd go into the bedroom and kiss my grandmother hastily. She'd say "Bouyo-bouyo," for that was the only sound she could make. And after school it was, "Go in and tell the *baba* you're home."

"I'm home, *baba*."

"Bouyo-bouyo."

During those first hopeful months—"Twenty years ago who would have thought there'd be a cure for diabetes?" my father asked; "where there's life there's hope, you know"—she'd smile at me and try to speak, her eyes charged with effort. And even later there were times when she pressed my head urgently to her bosom with her surprisingly strong left arm. But as her illness dragged on and on and she became a condition in the house, something beyond hope or reproach, like the leaky icebox, there was less recognition and more ritual in those kisses. I came to dread her room. A clutter of sticky medicine bottles and the cracked toilet chair beside the bed; glazed but imploring eyes and a feeble smile, the wet slap of her lips against my cheeks. I flinched from her touch. After two years of it I protested to my mother. "Look what's the use of telling her I'm going or I'm here. She doesn't even recognize me any more."

"Don't be fresh. She's your grandmother."

My uncle who was in the theater in New York sent money regularly to help support my grandmother and, for the first few months, so did the other children. But once the initial and sustaining excitement had passed and it became likely

6. Grandma.

that my grandmother might linger in her invalid condition for two or maybe even three more years, the checks began to drop off, and the children seldom came to our house any more. Anxious weekly visits—"and how is she today, poor lamb?"—quickly dwindled to a dutiful monthly looking in, then a semiannual visit, and these always on the way to somewhere.

"The way they act," my father said, "you'd think that if they stayed long enough to take off their coats we'd make them take the *baba* home with them."

When the children did come to visit, my mother made it difficult for them.

"It's killing me," she said. "I have to lift her onto that chair three times a day maybe. Have you any idea how heavy she is? And what makes you think I always catch her in time? Sometimes I have to change her bed twice a day. That's a job I'd like to see your wife do," she said to my uncle, the rabbi.

"We could sent her to the Old People's Home," the rabbi said.

"Now there's an idea," my father said.

But my mother began to sob. "Not as long as I'm alive," she said. And she gave my father a stony look. "Say something."

"It wouldn't be according to Hoyle."

"You want to be able to complain to everybody in town about all the other children," the rabbi said. "You've got a martyr complex."

"Everybody has a point of view, you know. You know what I mean?" my father said. "So what's the use of fighting?"

Meanwhile, Dr. Katzman came once a month to examine my grandmother. "It's remarkable, astonishing," he'd say each time. "She's as strong as a horse."

"Some life for a person," my father said. "She can't speak—she doesn't recognize anybody—what is there for her?"

The doctor was a cultivated man; he spoke often for women's clubs, sometimes on Yiddish literature and other times, his rubicund face hot with impatience, the voice taking on a doomsday tone, on the cancer threat.

"Who are we to judge?" he asked.

Every evening, during the first months of my grandmother's illness, my mother read her a story by Sholem Aleichem.[7] "Tonight she smiled," my mother would say. "She understood. I can tell." And my father, my brother, and I would not comment. Once a week my mother used to give the old lady a manicure. Sunny afternoons she'd lift her into a wheelchair and put her out in the sun. Somebody always had to stay in the house in case my grandmother called. Often, during the night, she would begin to wail unaccountably, and my mother would get up and rock the old lady in her arms for hours. But in the fourth year of my grandmother's illness the strain and fatigue began to tell on my mother. Besides looking after my grandmother—"and believe you me," the doctor assured her with a clap on the back, "it would be a full-time job for a professional nurse"—she had to keep house for a husband and two sons. She began to quarrel with my father and she became sharp with Harvey and me. My father started to spend his evenings playing pinochle at Tansky's Cigar & Soda. Weekends he took Harvey and

7. "Peace be with you," pen name of Yiddish author and humorist Shalom Rabinovitz (1859–1916).

me to visit his brothers and sisters. And everywhere he went people had little bits of advice for him.

"Sam, you might as well be a bachelor. You're just going to have to put your foot down for once."

"Yeah, in your face maybe."

My cousin Libby, who was at McGill,[8] said, "This could have a very damaging effect on the development of your boys. These are their formative years, Uncle Samuel, and the omnipresence of death in the house . . ."

"What you need," my father said, "is a boy friend. *And how.*"

At Tansky's Cigar & Soda it was, "Come clean, Sam. It's no hardship. If I know you, the old lady's got a big insurance policy and when the time comes . . ."

My mother lost lots of weight. After dinner she'd fall asleep in her chair in the middle of Lux Radio Theater.[9] One minute she'd be sewing a patch on my breeches or be making a list of girls to call for a bingo party (proceeds for the Talmud Torah),[1] and the next she'd be snoring. Then, one morning, she just couldn't get out of bed, and Dr. Katzman came round a week before his regular visit. "Well, well, this won't do, will it?" He sat in the kitchen with my father and the two men drank apricot brandy out of small glasses.

"Your wife is a remarkable woman," Dr. Katzman said.

"You don't say?"

"She's got a gallstone condition."

My father shrugged. "Have another one for the road," he said.

"Thank you, but I have several more calls to make." Dr. Katzman rose, sighing. "There she lies in that back room, poor old woman," he said, "hanging desperately onto life. There's food for thought there."

My grandmother's children met again, and the five of them sat around my mother's bed embarrassed, irritated, and quick to take insult. All except my uncle who was in the theater. He sucked a cigar and drank whisky. He teased my mother, the rabbi, and my aunts, and if not for him I think they would have been at each other's throats. It was decided, over my mother's protests, to send my grandmother to the Old People's Home on Esplanade Street. An ambulance came to take my grandmother away and Dr. Katzman said, "It's for the best." But my father had been in the back bedroom when the old lady had held on tenaciously to the bedpost, not wanting to be moved by the two men in white— "Easy does it, granny," the younger one had said—and afterwards he could not go in to see my mother. He went out for a walk.

"She looked at me with such a funny expression," he told my brother. "Is it my fault?"

My mother stayed in bed for another two weeks. My father cooked for us and we hired a woman to do the housework. My mother put on weight quickly, her cheeks regained their normal pinkish hue and, for the first time in months, she actually joked with Harvey and me. She became increasingly curious about our schools and whether or not we shined our shoes regularly. She began to cook

8. University in Montreal.   9. Weekly radio drama sponsored by Lux soap.   1. Orthodox Jewish school for boys.

again, special dishes for my father, and she resumed old friendships with women on the parochial school board. The change reflected on my father. Not only did his temper improve, but he stopped going to Tansky's every other night, and began to come home early from work. Life at home had never been so rich. But my grandmother's name was never mentioned. The back bedroom remained empty and I continued to share a room with Harvey. I couldn't see the point and so one evening I said, "Look, why don't I move into the back bedroom?"

My father glared at me across the table.

"But it's empty like."

My mother left the table. And the next afternoon she put on her best dress and coat and new spring hat.

"Where are you going?" my father asked.

"To see my mother."

"Don't go looking for trouble."

"It's been a month. Maybe they're not treating her right."

"They're experts."

"Did you think I was never going to visit her? I'm not inhuman, you know."

"All right, go," he said.

But after she'd gone my father went to the window and said, "Son-of-a-bitch."

Harvey and I sat outside on the steps watching the cars go by. My father sat on the balcony above, cracking peanuts. It was six o'clock, maybe later, when the ambulance turned the corner, slowed down, and parked right in front of the house.

"Son-of-a-bitch," my father said. "I knew it."

My mother got out first, her eyes red and swollen, and hurried upstairs to make my grandmother's bed.

"I'm sorry, Sam, I had to do it."

"You'll get sick again, that's what."

"You think she doesn't recognize people. From the moment she saw me she cried and cried. Oh, it was terrible."

"They're experts there. They know how to handle her better than you do."

"Experts? Expert murderers you mean. She's got bedsores, Sam. Those dirty little Irish nurses they don't change her linen often enough, they hate her. She must have lost twenty pounds there."

"Another month and you'll be flat on your back again."

"Sam, what could I do? Please Sam."

"She'll outlive all of us. Even Muttel.[2] I'm going out for a walk."

She was back and I was to blame.

My father became a regular at Tansky's Cigar & Soda again and every morning I had to go in and kiss my grandmother. She began to look like a man. Little hairs had sprouted on her chin, she had a spiky gray mustache and, of course, she was practically bald. This near-baldness, I guess, sprang from the fact that

2. The narrator's Yiddish name; could be the equivalent of Mordecai.

she had been shaving her head ever since she had married my grandfather the rabbi.[3] My grandmother had four different wigs, but she had not worn one since the first year of her illness. She wore a little pink cap instead. And so, as before, she said, "bouyo-bouyo," to everything.

Once more uncles and aunts sent five-dollar bills, though erratically, to help pay for my grandmother's support. Elderly people, former followers of my grandfather, came to inquire after the old lady's health. They sat in the back bedroom with her for hours, leaning on their canes, talking to themselves, rocking, always rocking to and fro. "The Holy Shakers," my father called them, and Harvey and I avoided them, because they always wanted to pinch our cheeks, give us a dash of snuff and laugh when we sneezed, or offer us a sticky old candy from a little brown bag with innumerable creases in it. When the visit was done the old people would unfailingly sit in the kitchen with my mother for another hour, watching her make lockshen[4] or bake bread. My mother always served them lemon tea and they would talk about my grandfather, recalling his books, his sayings, and his charitable deeds.

And so another two years passed, with no significant change in my grand- 105
mother's condition. But fatigue, bed temper, and even morbidity enveloped my mother again. She fought with her brothers and sisters and once, when I stepped into the living room, I found her sitting with her head in her hands, and she looked up at me with such anguish that I was frightened.

"What did I do now?" I asked.

"If, God forbid, I had a stroke, would you send me to the Old People's Home?"

"Don't be a joke. Of course not."

"I hope that never in my life do I have to count on my children for anything."

The summer my grandmother was supposed to die, the seventh year of her 110
illness, my brother took a job as a shipper and he kept me awake at night with stories about the factory. "What we do, see, is clear out the middle of a huge pile of lengths of material. That makes for a kind of secret cave. A hideout. Well, then you coax one of the shiksas[5] inside and hi-diddle-diddle."

One night Harvey waited until I had fallen asleep and then he wrapped himself in a white sheet, crept up to my bed, and shouted, "Bouyo-bouyo."

I hit him. He shouted.

"Children. Children, please," my mother called. "I must get some rest."

As my grandmother's condition worsened—from day to day we didn't know when she'd die—I was often sent out to eat at my aunt's or at my other grandmother's house. I was hardly ever at home. On Saturday mornings I'd get together with the other guys and we'd walk all the way past the mountain to Eaton's, which was our favorite department store for riding up and down escalators and stealing.

3. Married Orthodox Jewish women customarily either shave their heads or cover their hair.
4. Noodles.   5. Gentile girls.

115   In those days they let boys into the left-field bleachers free during the week
and we spent many an afternoon at the ball park. The Montreal Royals, part of
the Dodger farm system, was some ball club too. There was Jackie Robinson
and Roy Campanella, Honest John Gabbard, Chuck Connors, and Kermit Kitman was our hero. It used to kill us to see that crafty little hebe[6] running around
there with all those tall dumb *goyim*.[7] "Hey, Kitman," we'd yell. "Hey, hey,
sho-head,[8] if your father knew you played ball on *shabus*—[9] Kitman, unfortunately, was all field and no hit. He never made the majors. "There goes Kermit
Kitman," we'd yell, after he'd gone down swinging again, "the first Jewish strike-
out king of the International League." This we usually followed up by bellowing
some choice imprecations in Yiddish.

It was after one of these games, on a Friday afternoon, that I came home to
find a small crowd gathered in front of the house.

"That's the grandson."

"Poor kid."

Old people stood silent and expressionless across the street staring at our front
door. A taxi pulled up and my aunt hurried out, hiding her face in her hands.

120   "After so many years," somebody said.

"And probably next year they'll discover a cure. Isn't that *always* the case?"

I took the stairs two at a time. The flat was full. Uncles and aunts from my
father's side of the family, odd old people, Dr. Katzman, Harvey, neighbors,
were all standing around and talking in hushed voices in the living room. I found
my father in the kitchen, getting out the apricot brandy. "Your grandmother's
dead," he said.

"She didn't suffer," somebody said. "She passed away in her sleep."

"A merciful death."

125   "Where's Maw?"

"In the bedroom with . . . you'd better not go in," my father said.

"I want to see her."

My mother's face was long with grief. She wore a black shawl, and glared
down at a knot of handkerchief clutched in a fist that had been cracked by washing soda. "Don't come in here," she said.

Several bearded, round-shouldered men in black shiny coats stood round the
bed. I couldn't see my grandmother.

130   "Your grandmother's dead."

"Daddy told me."

"Go and wash your face and comb your hair. You'll have to get your own
supper."

"O.K."

"One minute. The *baba* left some jewelry. The ring is for Harvey's wife and
the necklace is for yours."

135   "Who's getting married?"

"Better go and wash your face. And remember behind the ears, Muttel."

---

6. Hebrew, Jew.   7. Gentiles.   8. Possibly *shorn-head* (?), referring to short hair or crew cut
of athlete, in contrast to traditional long locks of Orthodox Jews (?).   9. Sabbath.

Telegrams were sent, long-distance calls were made, and all through the evening relatives and neighbors came and went like swarms of fish when crumbs have been dropped into the water.

"When my father died," my mother said, "they had to have *six* motorcycle policemen to control the crowds. Twelve people fainted, such a heat . . ."

The man from the funeral parlor came.

"There goes the only Jewish businessman in town," my Uncle Harry said, "who wishes all his customers were Germans."   140

"This is no time for jokes."

"Listen, life goes on."

My cousin Jerry had begun to use a cigarette holder. "Everyone's going to be sickeningly sentimental," he said. "Soon the religious mumbo-jumbo starts. I can hardly wait."

Tomorrow was the Sabbath and so, according to the law, my grandmother couldn't be buried until Sunday. She would have to lie on the floor all night. Two old grizzly women in white came to move and wash the body and a professional mourner arrived to sit up and pray for her.

"I don't trust his face," my mother said. "He'll fall asleep., You watch him,   145
Sam."

"A fat lot of good prayers will do her now."

"Will you just watch him, please."

"I'll watch him, I'll watch him." My father was livid about my Uncle Harry. "The way he's gone after that apricot brandy you'd think that guy never saw a bottle in his life before."

Harvey and I were sent to bed, but we couldn't sleep. My aunt was sobbing over the body in the living room—"That dirty hypocrite," my mother said— there was the old man praying, coughing, and spitting into his handkerchief each time he woke; and hushed voices and whimpering from the kitchen, where my father and mother sat. Harvey was in a good mood, he let me have a few puffs of his cigarette.

"Well, kiddo, this is our last night together. Tomorrow you can take over   150
the back bedroom."

"*Are you crazy?*"

"You always wanted it for yourself."

"She died in there, bud. You think I'm going to sleep in there?"

"Good night. Happy dreams, kiddo."

"Hey, let's talk some more."   155

Harvey told me a ghost story. "Did you know that when they hang a man," he said, "the last thing that happens is that he has an orgasm?"

"A what?"

"Forget it. I forgot you were still in kindergarten."

"I know plenty. Don't worry."

"At the funeral they're going to open her coffin to throw dirt in her face. It's   160
supposed to be earth from Eretz.[1] They open it and you're going to have to

---

1. Eretz Yisrael, the Land of Israel.

look." Harvey stood up on his bed, holding his hands over his head like claws. He made a hideious face. "Bouyo-bouyo. Who's that sleeping in my bed? Woo-woo."

My uncle who was in the theater, the rabbi, and my aunt from Toronto, all came to Montreal for the funeral. Dr. Katzman came too.

"As long as she was alive," my mother said, "he couldn't even send five dollars a month. Some son! What a rabbi! I don't want him in my house, Sam. I can't bear the sight of him."

"You don't mean a word of that and you know it," Dr. Katzman said.

"Maybe you'd better give her a sedative," the rabbi said.

165 "Sam. Sam, will you say something, please."

My father stepped up to the rabbi, his face flushed. "I'll tell you this straight to your face, Israel," he said. "You've gone down in my estimation."

"Really," the rabbi said, smiling a little.

My father's face burned a deeper red. "Year by year," he said, "your stock has gone down with me."

And my mother began to weep bitterly, helplessly, without control. She was led unwillingly to bed. While my father tried his best to comfort her, as he said consoling things, Dr. Katzman plunged a needle into her arm. "There we are," he said.

170 I went to sit in the sun on the outside stairs with Arty. "I'm going to the funeral," I said.

"I couldn't go anyway."

Arty was descended from the tribe of high priests and so was not allowed to be in the presence of a dead body. I was descended from the Yisroelis.[2]

"The lowest of the low," Arty said.

"Aw."

175 My uncle, the rabbi, and Dr. Katzman stepped into the sun to light cigarettes.

"It's remarkable that she held out for so long," Dr. Katzman said.

"Remarkable?" my uncle said. "It's written that if a man has been married twice he will spend as much time with his first wife in heaven as he did on earth. My father, may he rest in peace, was married to his first wife for seven years and my mother, may she rest in peace, has managed to keep alive for seven years. Today in heaven she will be able to join my father, may he rest in peace."

Dr. Katzman shook his head, he pursed his lips. "It's amazing," he said. "The mysteries of the human heart. Astonishing."

My father hurried outside. "Dr. Katzman, please. It's my wife. Maybe the injection wasn't strong enough? She just doesn't stop crying. It's like a tap. Could you come please?"

180 "Excuse me," Dr. Katzman said to my uncle.

"Of course."

My uncle approached Arty and me.

"Well, boys," he said, "what would you like to be when you grow up?"

1961

2. The lowest of the three categories into which the Jewish people are traditionally divided.

QUESTIONS

1. Looking back over "An Occurrence at Owl Creek Bridge," how many of Peyton Farquhar's sensory perceptions can you reinterpret in terms of what must have really been happening?

2. What are the effects, both emotional and in interpretation, of the manipulation of chronology in "A Rose for Emily"?

3. What is there in the second paragraph of "A Rose for Emily" that suggests that the speaker is not just casually spinning a yarn about a weird lady but sees some more general meaning in the tale?

4. What does "supposed to die" mean in the title of the Richler story?

5. What is the effect of having such details in Richler's story as those involving baseball, Miss Monohan's lacy pink panties, and the humor in this rather serious story?

WRITING SUGGESTIONS

1. Write an outline of "A Rose for Emily" arranging the events in chronological order and dating them as precisely as possible. Then write a three-paragraph analysis of why the story is structured—the chronology rearranged—as it is.

2. Write a brief personal narrative (1000–1500 words), preferably (but not necessarily) based on a real episode, that is in some way comparable to "The Summer My Grandmother Was Supposed to Die."

3 CHARACTERIZATION

In a good many stories the narrator is a disembodied offstage voice, without an identity or a personal history, without influence on the action, without qualities other than those that a voice and style may suggest. So it is in some of the earlier stories in this volume—"The Zebra Storyteller," "No One's a Mystery," "The Jewelry," "An Occurrence at Owl Creek Bridge." Poe's narrator, however, not only tells us the story but acts out the action; without him we not only would not know the story, there just would not be any. Richler's narrator looks back into his past; he is there in the story, speaking, listening, reacting. In addition to being the narrator, he is a **character**: someone who acts, appears, or is referred to in a work.

The most common term for the character with the leading male role is **hero,** the "good guy" who opposes the **villain,** or "bad guy." The leading female character is the **heroine.** Heroes and heroines are usually larger than life, stronger or better than most human beings, almost godlike (and there's even a brand of heroes nowadays so close to being godlike that they are called superheroes). In most modern fiction, however, the leading character is much more ordinary, more like the rest of us. Such a character is called the **antihero,** not because he opposes the hero but because he is not like a hero in stature or perfection. An older and more neutral term than hero for the leading character, a term that does not imply either the presence or absence of outstanding virtue (and with the added advantage of referring equally to male and female), is **protagonist,** whose opponent is the **antagonist.** You might get into long and pointless arguments by calling Lantin or Montresor a hero, but either is his story's protagonist.

The **major characters** are those we see more of over a longer period of time; we learn more about them, and we think of them as more complex and frequently therefore more "realistic" than the **minor characters,** the figures who fill out the story. These major characters can grow and change, as Lantin does and as Judith does in Doris Lessing's "Our Friend Judith"; by the end of these stories both protagonists have acted in a way not predictable from what we learned about them and their past actions earlier in the story. Characters who can thus "surprise convincingly," an influential critic says, are **round characters.** Tallent's and Poe's characters are not very complex and they do not change in surprising ways; they are therefore called **flat.** But we must be careful not to let terms like *flat* and *round* turn into value judgments. Because flat characters are less complex than round ones it is easy to assume they are artistically inferior; we need only to think of the characters of Charles Dickens, almost all of whom are flat, to realize that this is not always true.

The terms *flat* and *round*, like the terms *hero* and *antihero*, are not absolute or precise. They designate extremes or tendencies, not pigeonholes. Is Poe's Montresor entirely flat? Is Shakespeare's Falstaff? Charlie Chaplin's Little Tramp? Little Orphan Annie? Are all these characters equally flat? We will probably agree that Baldwin's Sonny is a round character, but what about Faulkner's Emily? Atwood's Emma? Are they all equally round? Our answers are less important than our looking carefully at these characters to see what we know about each of them, to what degree they can be summed up in a phrase or a sentence; to discover how we learned what we know about them and how our judgment has been controlled by the story; to think about and perhaps judge the assumptions about human motivation, behavior, and nature that underlie the character and his or her characterization. Flat and round are useful as categories but are even more useful as tools of investigation, ways of focusing our attention and sharpening our perception.

Though most of Dickens's flat characters are highly individualized, not to say unique, some, like Fagin, the avaricious Jewish moneylender, are **stereotypes:** characters based on conscious or unconscious cultural assumptions that sex, age, ethnic or national identification, occupation, marital status, and so on are predictably accompanied by certain character traits, actions, even values.

The stereotype may be very useful in creating a round character, one who can surprise convincingly: Judith, according to a Canadian woman, is "one of your typical English spinsters." Judith, however, acts in ways that deny the limitations of the stereotype. A stereotype is, after all, only a quick—and somewhat superficial—form of classification, and classification is a common first step in definitions. One of the chief ways we have of describing or defining is by placing the thing to be defined in a category or class and then distinguishing it from the other members of that class. A good deal of characterization—the art, craft, method of presentation, or creation of fictional personages—involves a similar process. Characters are almost inevitably identified by category—by sex, age, nationality, occupation, and so on. We soon learn that the narrator of "My Man Bovanne" is a middle-aged urban black woman, that Major Monarch is a middle-aged English gentleman, and, as we have seen, that Judith is an English spinster.

You may have noticed something that may seem odd at first: putting a character in more than one general group does not make that character more generalized or stereotyped, but more individual. The category *middle-aged* includes the narrator of "My Man Bovanne," Major and Mrs. Monarch, and Judith.

That Major Monarch is male separates him from the other three; that the narrator of "Bovanne" is American and black separates her from the others, though she is, like Mrs. Monarch and Judith, a woman. So Hazel is to some degree particularized by being identified as a member of three general categories.

Not all generalizations involve cultural stereotypes, of course. Some may involve generalized character traits that the story or narrator defines for us (and that we must accept unless events in the story prove otherwise). Bovanne is said to be "just a nice old gent from the block," the kind of man whose conversation is "comfy and cheery." Physical characteristics also serve as categories. Bovanne is blind. Before we are introduced to him, we are told that blind people hum, and that a blind man called Shakey Bee hums. Only then are we told that there is a blind man named Bovanne who also has the habit of humming. As physical characteristics are multiplied, the result is more and more particularizing or individualizing. The detailed physical description of Judith makes it possible to visualize her rather fully, almost to recognize her as an individual:

> Judith is tall, small-breasted, slender. Her light brown hair is parted in the center and cut straight around her neck. A high straight forehead, straight nose, and full grave mouth are setting for her eyes, which are green, large and prominent. Her lids are very white, fringed with gold, and molded close over the eyeball. . . . (Par. 7)

There are many other ways in which a character is characterized and individualized besides stereotyping and "de-stereotyping," and besides classifying and particularizing by physical description. In most cases we see what characters do and hear what they say; we sometimes learn what they think, and what other people think or say about them; we often know what kind of clothes they wear, what and how much they own, treasure, or covet; we may be told about their childhood, parents, or some parts of their past. We learn a bit about Hazel, the narrator of "My Man Bovanne," from her age, sex, and ethnic identification. We learn a great deal more from the way she talks to her children and they to her, from the fact that men call her "long distance and in the middle of the night for a little Mama comfort," the fact that she carried her baby daughter strapped to her chest until the baby was nearly two years old, and from her short, low-cut dress. We even know what she is thinking.

No matter how many methods of characterization are employed, however, at some point the particularization of the individual stops. No matter how individualized the character may be, he or she remains a member of a number of groups, and we make certain assumptions about the character based on our fixed or stereotyped notions of the groups. To destroy a stereotype, a story must introduce a stereotype to destroy. And somehow the de-stereotyped character, no matter how particularized, remains to some degree representative. If Judith turns out to be not as prudish and prissy as the stereotype of the English spinster has led us to believe, we may well conclude that the stereotype is false and Judith is more representative of the real English spinster than the stereotype is. Indeed, this tendency to generalize from the particulars of a story extends beyond cultural groups, sometimes to human character at large: if Sonny can change his ways after years of habitual conduct, then human character, the story might seem to say, is not permanently fixed at birth, in infancy, childhood, ever.

One of the reasons it is so difficult to discuss character is precisely that the principles of definition and evaluation of fictional characters (not of their characterization, the way they are presented) are the same as those we use for real people, an area of violent controversy and confusion. The very term *character* itself, when it refers not to a fictional personage but to a combination of qualities in a human being, is somewhat ambiguous. It usually has moral overtones, often favorable (a man of character); it is sometimes neutral but evaluative (character reference). Judgment about character (not characterization, remember) usually involves moral terms like *good* and *bad* and *strong* and *weak*. **Personality** usually implies that which distinguishes or individualizes a person, and the judgment called for is not so much moral as social—*pleasing* or *displeasing*. An older term, **nature** (it is his nature to be so or do such), usually implies something inherent or inborn, something fixed and thus predictable. The **existential character** implies the opposite; that is, whatever our past, our conditioning, our pattern or previous behavior, we can, by choice, by free will, change all that right this minute, as Sonny does.

Fictional characters thus frequently seem to be part of the history that lies behind the story or beyond the story as part of our own world, to exist in a reality that is detachable from the words and events of the story in which they appear. We feel we might recognize Tom Jones, Jane Eyre, or Sherlock Holmes on the street, and we might be able to anticipate what they might say or do in *our* world, outside the story. Fictional characters are neither real nor detachable, of course, and they exist only in the words of the works in which they are presented. We must not forget the distinction between the character and the characterization, the method by which he or she is presented; so we must be careful to distinguish the *good character*, meaning someone whom, if real, we would consider virtuous, and the *good characterization*, meaning a fictional person who, no matter what his or her morality or behavior, is well presented.

Henry James's story "The Real Thing" is about the difference between reality and art, character and characterization. Major Monarch is described as a "gentleman, a man of fifty, very high and very straight, with a moustache slightly grizzled and a dark grey walking-coat admirably fitted . . ." (par. 1). He looks like the stereotype of a celebrity. The painter-narrator of "The Real Thing," however, immediately recognizes that because of a "paradoxical law," Major Monarch's appearance means that he is *not* a celebrity: celebrities are not often so "striking." It does not take the narrator long to recognize the Major's real type. Just by the Major's appearance, the painter can "see" the Major's whole gentlemanly life: his hunting, his clothes, his umbrellas, his luggage, his servants, and he can see as well Mrs. Monarch's lady's life, clothes, and so on. They are "the real thing," a real gentleman and a real lady. They are therefore useless as models for the artist. Not only are they so much *one* real thing that they can pose only for that type and no other, but even as a lady and gentleman they are so stereotypical they are useful only for illustrations of bad, stereotyped novels. James seems to be distinguishing *character* and *characterization:* the first is "the real thing" which will not do for art or the *representation* of the real; the second, "the alchemy of art," offers not a copy of reality but an *illusion* of reality, an illusion that seems more real in its representation than the real thing would.

Even if we entirely agree with Henry James—and not all readers do—his distinction between reality and representation does not mean that we cannot learn from one about the other. We must recognize that characters are not finally detachable—that they have roles, functions, limitations, and their very existence in the context of other elements of the story; we must not confuse fictional characters with real people, or character with characterization. This is not to say, however, that we may not learn about real people from characters in fiction or learn to understand fictional characters in part from what we know about real people. For real people too exist in a context of other people and other elements, their history and geography and their "narrator," the one who is representing them—that is, *you.* Indeed, it may be worth paying particular attention to how stories create the images of people and what those images assume about human character precisely because this process and these assumptions are so similar to the way we get to know and understand real people. For we are all artists representing reality to ourselves. If we study the art of characterization we may become better artists, able to enrich both our reading and our lives.

CHARACTERIZATION A Glossary

antagonist: a neutral term for a character who opposes the leading male or female character; see *hero / ine* and *antagonist*

antihero: a leading character who is not, like a "hero," perfect or even outstanding but is rather ordinary and representative of the more or less average person

character: (1) a fictional personage; (2) a combination of a person's qualities, especially moral qualities, so that such terms as "good" and "bad," "strong" and "weak," often apply. See *personality* and *nature*

characterization: the fictional or artistic presentation of a fictional personage; terms like "a good character" can, then, be ambiguous—they may mean that the personage is virtuous, or that he or she is well presented whatever his or her characteristics or moral qualities.

existential character: a person real or fictional who, whatever his or her past or his conditioning, can change by an act of will

flat character: fictional character, often but not always a minor character, who is relatively simple, who is presented as having rather few, though sometimes dominant, traits, and who thus does not change much in the course of a story. See *round character*

hero / heroine: the leading male / female character, usually larger than life, sometimes almost godlike. See *antihero, protagonist,* and *villain*

nature: as it refers to a person—"it is his [or her] nature"—a rather old term suggesting something inborn, inherent, fixed, and thus predictable. See *character, personality*

personality: that which distinguishes or individualizes a person; its qualities are judged not so much in terms of their social or moral value, as in "character," but as to whether they are "pleasing" or "unpleasing."

protagonist: the main character in a work, who may be male or female, heroic or not heroic; thus the most neutral term. See *hero / ine, antihero,* and *antagonist*

round character: a complex character, often a major character, who can grow and change and "surprise convincingly"—that is, act in a way that you did not expect from what had gone before but now accept as possible, even probable, and "realistic."

stereotype: a characterization based on conscious or unconscious assumptions that some one aspect, such as gender, age, ethnic or national identity, religion, occupation, marital status, determines what humans are like, and so is accompanied by certain traits, actions, and even value.

villain: the one who opposes the hero and heroine, the "bad guy"; see *antagonist* and *hero*

TONI CADE BAMBARA

My Man Bovanne

Blind people got a hummin jones[1] if you notice. Which is understandable completely once you been around one and notice what no eyes will force you into to see people, and you get past the first time, which seems to come out of nowhere, and it's like you in church again with fat-chest ladies and old gents gruntin a hum low in the throat to whatever the preacher be saying. Shakey Bee bottom lip all swole up with Sweet Peach[2] and me explaining how come the sweet-potato bread was a dollar-quarter this time stead of dollar regular and he say uh hunh he understand, then he break into this *thizzin* kind of hum which is quiet, but fiercesome just the same, if you ain't ready for it. Which I wasn't. But I got used to it and the onliest time I had to say somethin bout it was when he was playin checkers on the stoop one time and he commenst to hummin quite churchy seem to me. So I says, "Look here Shakey Bee, I can't beat you and Jesus too." He stop.

So that's how come I asked My Man Bovanne to dance. He ain't my man mind you, just a nice ole gent from the block that we all know cause he fixes things and the kids like him. Or used to fore Black Power got hold their minds and mess em around till they can't be civil to ole folks. So we at this benefit for my niece's cousin who's runnin for somethin with this Black party somethin or other behind her. And I press up close to dance with Bovanne who blind and I'm hummin and he hummin, chest to chest like talkin. Not jammin my breasts into the man. Wasn't bout tits. Was bout vibrations. And he dug it and asked me what color dress I had on and how my hair was fixed and how I was doin without a man, not nosy but nice-like, and who was at this affair and was the canapés dainty-stingy or healthy enough to get hold of proper. Comfy and cheery is what I'm tryin to get across. Touch talkin like the heel of the hand on the tambourine or on a drum.

But right away Joe Lee come up on us and frown for dancin so close to the man. My own son who knows what kind of warm I am about; and don't grown men call me long distance and in the middle of the night for a little Mama comfort? But he frown. Which ain't right since Bovanne can't see and defend himself. Just a nice old man who fixes toasters and busted irons and bicycles and things and changes the lock on my door when my men friends get messy. Nice man. Which is not why they invited him. Grass roots you see. Me and Sister Taylor and the woman who does heads at Mamies and the man from the barber shop, we all there on account of we grass roots. And I ain't never been souther than Brooklyn Battery and no more country than the window box on my fire escape. And just yesterday my kids tellin me to take them countrified rags off my head and be cool. And now can't get Black enough to suit em. So everybody passin sayin My Man Bovanne. Big deal, keep steppin and don't even stop a minute to get the man a drink or one of them cute sandwiches or tell him what's

---

1. Compelling need.   2. A brand of dipping snuff.

goin on. And him standin there with a smile ready case someone do speak he want to be ready. So that's how come I pull him on the dance floor and we dance squeezin past the tables and chairs and all them coats and people standin round up in each other face talkin bout this and that but got no use for this blind man who mostly fixed skates and skooters for all these folks when they was just kids. So I'm pressed up close and we touch talkin with the hum. And here come my daughter cuttin her eye[3] at me like she do when she tell me about my "apolitical" self like I got hoof and mouf disease and there ain't no hope at all. And I don't pay her no mind and just look up in Bovanne shadow face and tell him his stomach like a drum and he laugh. Laugh real loud. And here come my youngest, Task, with a tap on my elbow like he the third grade monitor and I'm cuttin up on the line to assembly.

"I was just talkin on the drums," I explained when they hauled me into the kitchen. I figured drums was my best defense. They can get ready for drums what with all this heritage business. And Bovanne stomach just like that drum Task give me when he come back from Africa. You just touch it and it hum thizzm, thizzm. So I stuck to the drum story. "Just drummin that's all."

"Mama, what are you talkin about?"   5

"She had too much to drink," say Elo to Task cause she don't hardly say nuthin to me direct no more since that ugly argument about my wigs.

"Look here Mama," say Task, the gentle one. "We just tryin to pull your coat. You were makin a spectacle of yourself out there dancing like that."

"Dancin like what?"

Task run a hand over his left ear like his father for the world and his father before that.

"Like a bitch in heat," say Elo.   10

"Well uhh, I was goin to say like one of them sex-starved ladies gettin on in years and not too discriminating. Know what I mean?"

I don't answer cause I'll cry. Terrible thing when your own children talk to you like that. Pullin me out the party and hustlin me into some stranger's kitchen in the back of a bar just like the damn police. And ain't like I'm old old. I can still wear me some sleeveless dresses without the meat hangin off my arm. And I keep up with some thangs through my kids. Who ain't kids no more. To hear them tell it. So I don't say nuthin.

"Dancin with that tom," say Elo to Joe Lee, who leanin on the folks' freezer. "His feet can smell a cracker a mile away and go into their shuffle number post haste. And them eyes. He could be a little considerate and put on some shades. Who wants to look into them blown-out fuses that—"

"Is this what they call the generation gap?" I say.

"Generation gap," spits Elo, like I suggested castor oil and fricassee possum   15
in the milk-shakes or somethin. "That's a white concept for a white phenomenon. There's no generation gap among Black people. We are a col—"

"Yeh, well never mind," says Joe Lee. "The point is Mama . . . well, it's pride. You embarrass yourself and us too dancin like that."

"I wasn't shame." Then nobody say nuthin. Them standin there in they

3. Giving a sharp look.

pretty clothes with drinks in they hands and gangin up on me, and me in the third-degree chair and nary a olive to my name. Felt just like the police got hold to me.

"First of all," Task say, holdin up his hand and tickin off the offenses, "the dress. Now that dress is too short, Mama, and too low-cut for a woman your age. And Tamu's going to make a speech tonight to kick off the campaign and will be introducin you and expecting you to organize the council of elders—"

"Me? Didn nobody ask me nuthin. You mean Nisi? She change her name?"

"Well, Norton was supposed to tell you about it. Nisi wants to introduce you and then encourage the older folks to form a Council of the Elders to act as an advisory—"

"And you going to be standing there with your boobs out and that wig on your head and that hem up to your ass. And people'll say, 'Ain't that the horny bitch that was grindin with the blind dude?' "

"Elo, be cool a minute," say Task, gettin to the next finger. "And then there's the drinkin. Mama, you know you can't drink cause next thing you know you be laughin loud and carryin on," and he grab another finger for the loudness. "And then there's the dancin. You been tattooed on the man for four records straight and slow draggin even on the fast numbers. How you think that look for a woman your age?"

"What's my age?"

"What?"

"I'm axin you all a simple question. You keep talkin bout what's proper for a woman my age. How old am I anyhow?" And Joe Lee slams his eyes shut and squinches up his face to figure. And Task run a hand over his ear and stare into his glass like the ice cubes goin calculate for him. And Elo just starin at the top of my head like she goin rip the wig off any minute now.

"Is your hair braided up under that thing? If so, why don't you take it off? You always did do a neat cornroll."[4]

"Uh huh," cause I'm thinkin how she couldn't undo her hair fast enough talking bout cornroll so countrified. None of which was the subject. "How old, I say?"

"Sixtee-one or—"

"You a damn lie Joe Lee Peoples."

"And that's another thing," say Task on the fingers.

"You know what you all can kiss," I say, gettin up and brushin the wrinkles out my lap.

"Oh, Mama," Elo say, puttin a hand on my shoulder like she hasn't done since she left home and the hand landin light and not sure it supposed to be there. Which hurt me to my heart. Cause this was the child in our happiness fore Mr. Peoples die. And I carried that child strapped to my chest till she was nearly two. We was close is what I'm tryin to tell you. Cause it was more me in the child than the others. And even after Task it was the girlchild I covered in the night and wept over for no reason at all less it was she was a chub-chub like

4. Cornrow, a hairstyle in which all the hair is interwoven from the scalp into small braids.

me and not very pretty, but a warm child. And how did things get to this, that she can't put a sure hand on me and say Mama we love you and care about you and you entitled to enjoy yourself cause you a good woman?

"And then there's Reverend Trent," say Task, glancin from left to right like they hatchin a plot and just now lettin me in on it. "You were suppose to be talking with him tonight, Mama, about giving us his basement for campaign headquarters and—"

"Didn nobody tell me nuthin. If grass roots mean you kept in the dark I can't use it. I really can't. And Reven Trent a fool anyway the way he tore into the widow man up there on Edgecomb cause he wouldn't take in three of them foster children and the woman not even comfy in the ground yet and the man's mind messed up and—"

"Look here," say Task. "What we need is a family conference so we can get all this stuff cleared up and laid out on the table. In the meantime I think we better get back into the other room and tend to business. And in the meantime, Mama, see if you can't get to Reverend Trent and—"   35

"You want me to belly rub with the Reven, that it?"

"Oh damn," Elo say and go through the swingin door.

"We'll talk about all this at dinner. How's tomorrow night, Joe Lee?" While Joe Lee being self-important I'm wonderin who's doin the cookin and how come no body ax me if I'm free and do I get a corsage and things like that. Then Joe nod that it's O.K. and he go through the swingin door and just a little hubbub come through from the other room. Then Task smile his smile, lookin just like his daddy and he leave. And it just me in this stranger's kitchen, which was a mess I wouldn't never let my kitchen look like. Poison you just to look at the pots. Then the door swing the other way and it's My Man Bovanne standin there sayin Miss Hazel but lookin at the deep fry and then at the steam table, and most surprised when I come up on him from the other direction and take him on out of there. Pass the folks pushin up towards the stage where Nisi and some other people settin and ready to talk, and folks gettin to the last of the sandwiches and the booze fore they settle down in one spot and listen serious. And I'm thinkin bout tellin Bovanne what a lovely long dress Nisi got on and the earrings and her hair piled up in a cone and the people bout to hear how we all getting screwed and gotta form our own party and everybody there listenin and lookin. But instead I just haul the man on out of there, and Joe Lee and his wife look at me like I'm terrible, but they ain't said boo to the man yet. Cause he blind and old and don't nobody there need him since they grown up and don't need they skates fixed no more.

"Where we goin, Miss Hazel?" Him knowin all the time.

"First we gonna buy you some dark sunglasses. Then you comin with me to   40
the supermarket so I can pick up tomorrow's dinner, which is goin to be a grand thing proper and you invited. Then we goin to my house."

"That be fine. I surely would like to rest my feet." Bein cute, but you got to let men play out they little show, blind or not. So he chat on bout how tired he is and how he appreciate me takin him in hand this way. And I'm thinkin I'll have him change the lock on my door first thing. Then I'll give the man a nice warm bath with jasmine leaves in the water and a little Epsom salt on the sponge to do his back. And then a good rubdown with rose water and olive oil. Then a cup of lemon tea with a taste in it. And a little talcum, some of that fancy stuff Nisi mother sent over last Christmas. And then a massage, a good face massage round the forehead which is the worryin part. Cause you gots to take care of the older folks. And let them know they still needed to run the mimeo machine and keep the spark plugs clean and fix the mailboxes for folks who might help us get the breakfast program goin, and the school for the little kids and the campaign and all. Cause old folks is the nation. That what Nisi was sayin and I mean to do my part.

"I imagine you are a very pretty woman, Miss Hazel."

"I surely am," I say just like the hussy my daughter always say I was.

1972

HENRY JAMES

The Real Thing

I

When the porter's wife, who used to answer the house-bell, announced "A gentleman and a lady, sir" I had, as I often had in those days—the wish being father to the thought—an immediate vision of sitters. Sitters my visitors in this case proved to be; but not in the sense I should have preferred. There was nothing at first however to indicate that they mightn't have come for a portrait. The gentleman, a man of fifty, very high and very straight, with a moustache slightly grizzled and a dark grey walking-coat admirably fitted, both of which I noted professionally—I don't mean as a barber or yet as a tailor—would have struck me as a celebrity if celebrities often were striking. It was a truth of which I had for some time been conscious that a figure with a good deal of frontage was, as one might say, almost never a public institution. A glance at the lady helped to remind me of this paradoxical law: she also looked too distinguished to be a "personality." Moreover one would scarcely come across two variations together.

Neither of the pair immediately spoke—they only prolonged the preliminary gaze suggesting that each wished to give the other a chance. They were visibly shy; they stood there letting me take them in—which, as I afterwards perceived, was the most practical thing they could have done. In this way their embarrassment served their cause. I had seen people painfully reluctant to mention that they desired anything so gross as to be represented on canvas; but the scruples of my new friends appeared almost insurmountable. Yet the gentleman might have said "I should like a portrait of my wife," and the lady might have said "I should like a portrait of my husband." Perhaps they weren't husband and wife—this naturally would make the matter more delicate. Perhaps they wished to be done together—in which case they ought to have brought a third person to break the news.

"We come from Mr. Rivet," the lady finally said with a dim smile that had the effect of a moist sponge passed over a "sunk"[1] piece of painting, as well as of a vague allusion to vanished beauty. She was as tall and straight, in her degree, as her companion, and with ten years less to carry. She looked as sad as a woman could look whose face was not charged with expression; that is her tinted oval mask showed waste as an exposed surface shows friction. The hand of time had played over her freely, but to an effect of elimination. She was slim and stiff, and so well-dressed, in dark blue cloth, with lappets and pockets and buttons, that it was clear she employed the same tailor as her husband. The couple had an indefinable air of prosperous thrift—they evidently got a good deal of luxury for their money. If I was to be one of their luxuries it would behove me to consider my terms.

"Ah, Claude Rivet recommended me?" I echoed; and I added that it was very kind of him, though I could reflect that, as he only painted landscape, this wasn't a sacrifice.

The lady looked very hard at the gentleman, and the gentleman looked round the room. Then staring at the floor a moment and stroking his moustache, he rested his pleasant eyes on me with the remark: "He said you were the right one."   5

"I try to be, when people want to sit."

"Yes, we should like to," said the lady anxiously.

"Do you mean together?"

My visitors exchanged a glance. "If you could do anything with *me* I suppose it would be double," the gentleman stammered.

"Oh yes, there's naturally a higher charge for two figures than for one."   10

"We should like to make it pay," the husband confessed.

"That's very good of you," I returned, appreciating so unwonted a sympathy—for I supposed he meant pay the artist.

A sense of strangeness seemed to draw on the lady.

"We mean for the illustrations—Mr. Rivet said you might put one in."

"Put in—an illustration?" I was equally confused.   15

"Sketch her off, you know," said the gentleman, colouring.

It was only then that I understood the service Claude Rivet had rendered me; he had told them how I worked in black-and-white, for magazines, for storybooks, for sketches of contemporary life, and consequently had copious employment for models. These things were true, but it was not less true—I may confess it now; whether because the aspiration was to lead to everything or to nothing I leave the reader to guess—that I couldn't get the honours, to say nothing of the emoluments, of a great painter of portraits out of my head. My "illustrations" were my pot-boilers; I looked to a different branch of art—far and away the most interesting it had always seemed to me—to perpetuate my fame. There was no shame in looking to it also to make my fortune; but that fortune was by so much further from being made from the moment my visitors wished to be "done" for nothing. I was disappointed; for in the pictorial sense I had immediately *seen* them. I had seized their type—I had already settled what I would do with it.

---

1. When colors lose their brilliance after they have dried on the canvas, they have "sunk in."

Something that wouldn't absolutely have pleased them, I afterwards reflected.

"Ah you're—you're—a—?" I began as soon as I had mastered my surprise. I couldn't bring out the dingy word "models": it seemed so little to fit the case.

"We haven't had much practice," said the lady.

"We've got to *do* something, and we've thought that an artist in your line might perhaps make something of us," her husband threw off. He further mentioned that they didn't know many artists and that they had gone first, on the off-chance—he painted views of course, but sometimes put in figures; perhaps I remembered—to Mr. Rivet, whom they had met a few years before at a place in Norfolk where he was sketching.

"We used to sketch a little ourselves," the lady hinted.

"It's very awkward, but we absolutely *must* do something," her husband went on.

"Of course we're not so *very* young," she admitted with a wan smile.

With the remark that I might as well know something more about them the husband had handed me a card extracted from a neat new pocket-book—their appurtenances were all of the freshest—and inscribed with the words "Major Monarch." Impressive as these words were they didn't carry my knowledge much further; but my visitor presently added: "I've left the army and we've had the misfortune to lose our money. In fact our means are dreadfully small."

'It's awfully trying—a regular strain," said Mrs. Monarch.

They evidently wished to be discreet—to take care not to swagger because they were gentlefolk. I felt them willing to recognise this as something of a draw-back, at the same time that I guessed at an underlying sense—their consolation in adversity—that they *had* their points. They certainly had; but these advantages struck me as preponderantly social; such for instance as would help to make a drawing-room look well. However, a drawing-room was always, or ought to be, a picture.

In consequence of his wife's allusion to their age Major Monarch observed: "Naturally it's more for the figure that we thought of going in. We can still hold ourselves up." On the instant I saw that the figure was indeed their strong point. His "naturally" didn't sound vain, but it lighted up the question. "*She* has the best one," he continued, nodding at his wife with a pleasant after-dinner absence of circumlocution. I could only reply, as if we were in fact sitting over our wine, that this didn't prevent his own from being very good; which led him in turn to make answer: "We thought that if you ever have to do people like us we might be something like it. *She* particularly—for a lady in a book, you know."

I was so amused by them that, to get more of it, I did my best to take their point of view; and though it was an embarrassment to find myself appraising physically, as if they were animals on hire or useful blacks, a pair whom I should have expected to meet only in one of the relations in which criticism is tacit, I looked at Mrs. Monarch judicially enough to be able to exclaim after a moment with conviction: "Oh yes, a lady in a book!" She was singularly like a bad illustration.

"We'll stand up, if you like," said the Major; and he raised himself before me with a really grand air.

I could take his measure at a glance—he was six feet two and a perfect gentle-man. It would have paid any club in process of formation and in want of a stamp to engage him at a salary to stand in the principal window. What struck me at once was that in coming to me they had rather missed their vocation; they could surely have been turned to better account for advertising purposes. I couldn't of course see the thing in detail, but I could see them make somebody's fortune— I don't mean their own. There was something in them for a waistcoat-maker, an hotel-keeper or a soap-vendor. I could imagine "We always use it" pinned on their bosoms with the greatest effect; I had a vision of the brilliancy with which they would launch a table d'hôte.

Mrs. Monarch sat still, not from pride but from shyness, and presently her husband said to her; "Get up, my dear, and show how smart you are." She obeyed, but she had no need to get up to show it. She walked to the end of the studio and then came back blushing, her fluttered eyes on the partner of her appeal. I was reminded of an incident I had accidentally had a glimpse of in Paris being with a friend there, a dramatist about to produce a play, when an actress came to him to ask to be entrusted with a part. She went through her paces before him, walked up and down as Mrs. Monarch was doing. Mrs. Mon-arch did it quite as well, but I abstained from applauding. It was very odd to see such people apply for such poor pay. She looked as if she had ten thousand a year. Her husband had used the word that described her: she was in the London current jargon essentially and typically "smart." Her figure was, in the same order of ideas, conspicuously and irreproachably "good." For a woman of her age her waist was surprisingly small; her elbow moreover had the orthodox crook. She held her head at the conventional angle, but why did she come to *me*? She ought to have tried on jackets at a big shop. I feared my visitors were not only destitute but "artistic"—which would be a great complication. When she sat down again I thanked her, observing that what a draughtsman most valued in his model was the faculty of keeping quiet.

"Oh *she* can keep quiet," said Major Monarch. Then he added jocosely: "I've always kept her quiet."

"I'm not a nasty fidget, am I?" It was going to wring tears from me, I felt, the way she hid her head, ostrich-like, in the other's broad bosom.

The owner of this expanse addressed his answer to me. "Perhaps it isn't out of place to mention—because we ought to be quite business-like, oughtn't we?— that when I married her she was known as the Beautiful Statue."

"Oh dear!" said Mrs. Monarch ruefully.

"Of course I should want a certain amount of expression," I rejoined.

"Of *course*!"—and I had never heard such unanimity.

"And then I suppose you know that you'll get awfully tired."

"Oh we *never* get tired!" they eagerly cried.

"Have you had any kind of practice?"

They hesitated—they looked at each other. "We've been photographed— *immensely*," said Mrs. Monarch.

"She means the fellows have asked us themselves," added the Major.

"I see—because you're so good-looking."

"I don't know what they thought, but they were always after us."

"We always got our photographs for nothing," smiled Mrs. Monarch.

"We might have brought some, my dear," her husband remarked.

"I'm not sure we have any left. We've given quantities away," she explained to me.

"With our autographs and that sort of thing," said the Major.

"Are they to be got in the shops?" I enquired as a harmless pleasantry.

"Oh yes, *hers*—they used to be."

"Not now," said Mrs. Monarch with her eyes on the floor.

II

I could fancy the "sort of thing" they put on the presentation copies of their photographs, and I was sure they wrote a beautiful hand. It was odd how quickly I was sure of everything that concerned them. If they were now so poor as to have to earn shillings and pence they could never have had much of a margin. Their good looks had been their capital, and they had good-humouredly made the most of the career that this resource marked out for them. It was in their faces, the blankness, the deep intellectual repose of the twenty years of country-house visiting that had given them pleasant intonations. I could see the sunny drawing-rooms, sprinkled with periodicals she didn't read, in which Mrs. Monarch had continuously sat; I could see the wet shrubberies in which she had walked, equipped to admiration for either exercise. I could see the rich covers[2] the Major had helped to shoot and the wonderful garments in which, late at night, he repaired to the smoking-room to talk about them. I could imagine their leggings and waterproofs, their knowing tweeds and rugs, their rolls of sticks and cases of tackle and neat umbrellas; and I could evoke the exact appearance of their servants and the compact variety of their luggage on the platforms of country stations.

They gave small tips, but they were liked; they didn't do anything themselves, but they were welcome. They looked so well everywhere; they gratified the general relish for stature, complexion and "form." They knew it without fatuity or vulgarity, and they respected themselves in consequence. They weren't superficial; they were thorough and kept themselves up—it had been their line. People with such a taste for activity had to have some line. I could feel how even in a dull house they could have been counted on for the joy of life. At present something had happened—it didn't matter what, their little income had grown less, it had grown least—and they had to do something for pocket-money. Their friends could like them, I made out, without liking to support them. There was something about them that represented credit—their clothes, their manners, their type; but if credit is a large empty pocket in which an occasional chink reverberates, the chink at least must be audible. What they wanted of me was to help to make it so. Fortunately they had no children—I soon divined that. They would also perhaps wish our relations to be kept secret: this was why it was "for the

2. Flocks of game birds.

figure"— the reproduction of the face would betray them.

I liked them—I felt, quite as their friends must have done—they were so simple; and I had no objection to them if they would suit. But somehow with all their perfections I didn't easily believe in them. After all they were amateurs, and the ruling passion of my life was the detestation of the amateur. Combined with this was another perversity—an innate preference for the represented subject over the real one: the defect of the real one was so apt to be a lack of representation. I liked things that appeared; then one was sure. Whether they *were* or not was a subordinate and almost always a profitless question. There were other considerations, the first of which was that I already had two or three recruits in use, notably a young person with big feet, in alpaca, from Kilburn, who for a couple of years had come to me regularly for my illustrations and with whom I was still—perhaps ignobly—satisfied. I frankly explained to my visitors how the case stood, but they had taken more precautions than I supposed. They had reasoned out their opportunity, for Claude Rivet had told them of the projected *édition de luxe* of one of the writers of our day—the rarest of the novelists—who, long neglected by the multitudinous vulgar and dearly prized by the attentive (need I mention Philip Vincent?) had had the happy fortune of seeing, late in life, the dawn and then the full light of a higher criticism; an estimate in which on the part of the public there was something really of expiation. The edition preparing, planned by a publisher of taste, was practically an act of high reparation; the wood-cuts with which it was to be enriched were the homage of English art to one of the most independent representatives of English letters. Major and Mrs. Monarch confessed to me they had hoped I might be able to work *them* into my branch of the enterprise. They knew I was to do the first of the books, "Rutland Ramsay," but I had to make clear to them that my participation in the rest of the affair—this first book was to be a test—must depend on the satisfaction I should give. If this should be limited my employers would drop me with scarce common forms. It was therefore a crisis for me, and naturally I was making special preparations, looking about for new people, should they be necessary, and securing the best types. I admitted however that I should like to settle down to two or three good models who would do for everything.

"Should we have often to—a—put on special clothes?" Mrs. Monarch timidly demanded. 55

"Dear yes—that's half the business."

"And should we be expected to supply our own costumes?"

"Oh no; I've got a lot of things. A painter's models put on—or put off— anything he likes."

"And you mean—a—the same?"

"The same?"

Mrs. Monarch looked at her husband again. 60

"Oh she was just wondering," he explained, "if the costumes are in *general* use." I had to confess that they were, and I mentioned further that some of them—I had a lot of genuine greasy last-century things—had served their time, a hundred years ago, on living world-stained men and women; on figures not perhaps so far removed, in that vanished world, from *their* type, the Monarchs', *quoi!*[3] of a breeched and bewigged age. "We'll put on anything that *fits*," said the Major.

"Oh I arrange that—they fit in the pictures."

"I'm afraid I should do better for the modern books. I'd come as you like," said Mrs. Monarch.

"She has got a lot of clothes at home: they might do for contemporary life," her husband continued.

"Oh I can fancy scenes in which you'd be quite natural." And indeed I could see the slipshod rearrangements of stale properties—the stories I tried to produce pictures for without the exasperation of reading them—whose sandy tracts the good lady might help to people. But I had to return to the fact that for this sort of work—the daily mechanical grind—I was already equipped: the people I was working with were fully adequate.

"We only thought we might be more like *some* characters," said Mrs. Monarch mildly, getting up.

Her husband also rose; he stood looking at me with a dim wistfulness that was touching in so fine a man.

"Wouldn't it be rather a pull sometimes to have—a—to have—?" He hung fire; he wanted me to help him by phrasing what he meant. But I couldn't—I didn't know. So he brought it out awkwardly: "The *real* thing; a gentleman, you know, or a lady." I was quite ready to give a general assent—I admitted that there was a great deal in that. This encouraged Major Monarch to say, following up his appeal with an unacted gulp: "It's awfully hard—we've tried everything." The gulp was communicative; it proved too much for his wife. Before I knew it Mrs. Monarch had dropped again upon a divan and burst into tears. Her husband sat down beside her, holding one of her hands; whereupon she quickly dried her eyes with the other, while I felt embarrassed as she looked up at me. "There isn't a confounded job I haven't applied for—waited for—prayed for. You can fancy we'd be pretty bad first. Secretaryships and that sort of thing? You might as well ask for a peerage. I'd be *anything*—I'm strong; a messenger or a coalheaver. I'd put on a gold-laced cap and open carriage-doors in front of the haberdasher's; I'd hang about a station to carry portmanteaux; I'd be a postman. But they won't *look* at you; there are thousands as good as yourself already on the ground. *Gentlemen*, poor beggars, who've drunk their wine, who've kept their hunters!"

I was as reassuring as I knew how to be, and my visitors were presently on their feet again while, for the experiment, we agreed on an hour. We were discussing it when the door opened and Miss Churm came in with a wet umbrella. Miss Churm had to take the omnibus to Maida Vale and then walk half a mile. She looked a trifle blowsy and slightly splashed. I scarcely ever saw her come in without thinking fresh how odd it was that, being so little in herself, she should yet be so much in others. She was a meagre little Miss Churm, but was such an ample heroine of romance. She was only a freckled cockney, but she could represent everything, from a fine lady to a shepherdess; she had the faculty as she might have had a fine voice or long hair. She couldn't spell and she loved

3. Whatever.

beer, but she had two or three "points," and practice, and a knack, and mother-wit, and a whimsical sensibility, and a love of the theatre, and seven sisters, and not an ounce of respect, especially for the *h*.[4] The first thing my visitors saw was that her umbrella was wet, and in their spotless perfection they visibly winced at it. The rain had come on since their arrival.

"I'm all in a soak; there *was* a mess of people in the 'bus. I wish you lived near a stytion," said Miss Churm. I requested her to get ready as quickly as possible, and she passed into the room in which she always changed her dress. But before going out she asked me what she was to get into this time.

"It's the Russian princess, don't you know?" I answered; "the one with the 'golden eyes,' in black velvet, for the long thing in the *Cheapside*."

"Golden eyes? I *say*!" cried Miss Churm, while my companions watched her with intensity as she withdrew. She always arranged herself, when she was late, before I could turn around; and I kept my visitors a little on purpose, so that they might get an idea, from seeing her, what would be expected of themselves. I mentioned that she was quite my notion of an excellent model—she was really very clever.

"Do you think she looks like a Russian princess?" Major Monarch asked with lurking alarm.

"When I make her, yes."   75

"Oh if you have to *make* her—!" he reasoned, not without point.

"That's the most you can ask. There are so many who are not makeable."

"Well now, *here*'s a lady"—and with a persuasive smile he passed his arm into his wife's—"who's already made!"

"Oh I'm not a Russian princess," Mrs. Monarch protested a little coldly. I could see she had known some and didn't like them. There at once was a complication of a kind I never had to fear with Miss Churm.

This young lady came back in black velvet—the gown was rather rusty and   80
very low on her lean shoulders—and with a Japanese fan in her red hands. I reminded her that in the scene I was doing she had to look over some one's head. "I forget whose it is; but it doesn't matter. Just look over a head."

"I'd rather look over a stove," said Miss Churm; and she took her station near the fire. She fell into position, settled herself into a tall attitude, gave a certain backward inclination to her head and a certain forward droop to her fan, and looked, at least to my prejudiced sense, distinguished and charming, foreign and dangerous. We left her looking so while I went downstairs with Major and Mrs. Monarch.

"I believe I could come about as near it as that," said Mrs. Monarch.

"Oh, you think she's shabby, but you must allow for the alchemy of art."

However, they went off with an evident increase of comfort founded on their demonstrable advantage in being the real thing. I could fancy them shuddering over Miss Churm. She was very droll about them when I went back, for I told her what they wanted.

"Well, if *she* can sit I'll tyke to bookkeeping," said my model.   85

4. Working-class Londoners, especially in the East End (cockneys), drop *h*'s 'orribly.

"She's very ladylike," I replied as an innocent form of aggravation.

"So much the worse for *you*. That means she can't turn round."

"She'll do for the fashionable novels."

"Oh yes, she'll *do* for them!" my model humorously declared. "Ain't they bad enough without her?" I had often sociably denounced them to Miss Churm.

III

It was for the elucidation of a mystery in one of these works that I first tried Mrs. Monarch. Her husband came with her, to be useful if necessary—it was sufficiently clear that as a general thing he would prefer to come with her. At first I wondered if this were for "propriety's" sake—if he were going to be jealous and meddling. The idea was too tiresome, and if it had been confirmed it would speedily have brought our acquaintance to a close. But I soon saw there was nothing in it and that if he accompanied Mrs. Monarch it was—in addition to the chance of being wanted—simply because he had nothing else to do. When they were separate his occupation was gone and they never *had* been separate. I judged rightly that in their awkward situation their close union was their main comfort and that this union had no weak spot. It was a real marriage, an encouragement to the hesitating, a nut for pessimists to crack. Their address was humble—I remember afterwards thinking it had been the only thing about them that was really professional—and I could fancy the lamentable lodgings in which the Major would have been left alone. He could sit there more or less grimly with his wife—he couldn't sit there anyhow without her.

He had too much tact to try and make himself agreeable when he couldn't be useful; so when I was too absorbed in my work to talk he simply sat and waited. But I liked to hear him talk—it made my work, when not interrupting it, less mechanical, less special. To listen to him was to combine the excitement of going out with the economy of staying at home. There was only one hindrance—that I seemed not to know any of the people this brilliant couple had known. I think he wondered extremely, during the term of our intercourse, whom the deuce I *did* know. He hadn't a stray sixpence of an idea to fumble for, so we didn't spin it very fine; we confined ourselves to questions of leather and even of liquor—saddlers and breeches-makers and how to get excellent claret cheap—and matters like "good trains" and the habits of small game. His lore on these last subjects was astonishing—he managed to interweave the station-master with the ornithologist. When he couldn't talk about greater things he could talk cheerfully about smaller, and since I couldn't accompany him into reminiscences of the fashionable world he could lower the conversation without a visible effort to my level.

So earnest a desire to please was touching in a man who could so easily have knocked one down. He looked after the fire and had an opinion on the draught of the stove without my asking him, and I could see that he thought many of my arrangements not half knowing. I remember telling him that if I were only rich I'd offer him a salary to come and teach me how to live. Sometimes he gave a random sigh of which the essence might have been: "Give me even such a bare old barrack as *this*, and I'd do something with it!" When I wanted to use him he came alone; which was an illustration of the superior courage of women. His wife could bear her solitary second floor, and she was in general more discreet; showing by various small reserves that she was alive to the propriety of keeping our relations markedly professional—not letting them slide into sociability. She wished it to remain clear that she and the Major were employed, not cultivated, and if she approved of me as a superior, who could be kept in his place, she never thought me quite good enough for an equal.

She sat with great intensity, giving the whole of her mind to it, and was capable of remaining for an hour almost as motionless as before a photographer's lens. I could see she had been photographed often, but somehow the very habit that made her good for that purpose unfitted her for mine. At first I was extremely pleased with her ladylike air, and it was a satisfaction, on coming to follow her lines, to see how good they were and how far they could lead the pencil. But after a little skirmishing I began to find her too insurmountably stiff; do what I would with it my drawing looked like a photograph or a copy of a photograph. Her figure had no variety of expression—she herself had no sense of variety. You may say that this was my business and was only a question of placing her. Yet I placed her in every conceivable position and she managed to obliterate their differences. She was always a lady certainly, and into the bargain was always the same lady. She was the real thing, but always the same thing. There were moments when I rather writhed under the serenity of her confidence that she *was* the real thing. All her dealings with me and all her husband's were an implication that this was lucky for *me*. Meanwhile I found myself trying to invent types that approached her own, instead of making her own transform itself—in the clever way that was not impossible for instance to poor Miss Churm. Arrange as I would and take the precautions I would, she always came out, in my pictures, too tall—landing me in the dilemma of having represented a fascinating woman as seven feet high, which (out of respect perhaps to my own very much scantier inches) was far from my idea of such personage.

The case was worse with the Major—nothing I could do would keep *him* down, so that he became useful only for representation of brawny giants. I adored variety and range, I cherished human accidents, the illustrative note; I wanted to characterise closely, and the thing in the world I most hated was the danger of being ridden by a type. I had quarrelled with some of my friends about it; I had parted company with them for maintaining that one *had* to be, and that if the type was beautiful—witness Raphael and Leonardo[5]—the servitude was only a gain. I was neither Leonardo nor Raphael—I might only be a presumptuous young modern searcher; but I held that everything was to be sacrificed sooner than character. When they claimed that the obsessional form could easily *be* character I retorted, perhaps superficially, "Whose?" It couldn't be everybody's—it might end in being nobody's.

After I had drawn Mrs. Monarch a dozen times I felt surer even than before

95

5. Raffaello Sanzio (1483–1520), Leonardo da Vinci (1452–1519), famous Italian Renaissance painters. Leonardo, of course, was also an inventor, military engineer, architect, sculptor, anatomist, etc.

that the value of such a model as Miss Churm resided precisely in the fact that she had no positive stamp, combined of course with the other fact that what she did have was a curious and inexplicable talent for imitation. Her usual appearance was like a curtain which she could draw up at request for a capital performance. This performance was simply suggestive; but it was a word to the wise—it was vivid and pretty. Sometimes even I thought it, though she was plain herself, too insipidly pretty; I made it a reproach to her that the figures drawn from her were monotonously (*bêtement*,[6] as we used to say) graceful. Nothing made her more angry: it was so much of her pride to feel she could sit for characters that had nothing in common with each other. She would accuse me at such moments of taking away her "reputytion."

It suffered a certain shrinkage, this queer quantity, from the repeated visits of my new friends. Miss Churm was greatly in demand, never in want of employment, so I had no scruple in putting her off occasionally, to try them more at my ease. It was certainly amusing at first to do the real thing—it was amusing to do Major Monarch's trousers. They *were* the real thing, even if he did come out colossal. It was amusing to do his wife's back hair—it was so mathematically neat—and the particular "smart" tension of her tight stays. She lent herself especially to positions in which the face was somewhat averted or blurred; she abounded in ladylike back views and *profils perdus*.[7] When she stood erect she took naturally one of the attitudes in which court-painters represent queens and princesses; so that I found myself wondering whether, to draw out this accomplishment, I couldn't get the editor of the *Cheapside* to publish a really royal romance, "A Tale of Buckingham Palace." Sometimes however the real thing and the make-believe came into contact; by which I mean that Miss Churm, keeping an appointment or coming to make one on days when I had much work in hand, encountered her invidious rivals. The encounter was not on their part, for they noticed her no more than if she had been the housemaid; not from intentional loftiness, but simply because as yet, professionally, they didn't know how to fraternise, as I could imagine they would have liked—or at least that the Major would. They couldn't talk about the omnibus—they always walked; and they didn't know what else to try—she wasn't interested in good trains or cheap claret. Besides, they must have felt—in the air—that she was amused at them, secretly derisive of their ever knowing how. She wasn't a person to conceal the limits of her faith if she had had a chance to show them. On the other hand Mrs. Monarch didn't think her tidy; for why else did she take pains to say to me—it was going out of the way, for Mrs. Monarch—that she didn't like dirty women?

One day when my young lady happened to be present with my other sitters—she even dropped in, when it was convenient, for a chat—I asked her to be so good as to lend a hand in getting tea, a service with which she was familiar and which was one of a class that, living as I did in a small way, with slender domestic resources, I often appealed to my models to render. They liked to lay hands on my property, to break the sitting, and sometimes the china—it made them

6. Foolishly.   7. Incomplete profile, showing more of the back of the head and less of the face.

feel Bohemian. The next time I saw Miss Churm after this incident she surprised me greatly by making a scene about it—she accused me of having wished to humiliate her. She hadn't resented the outrage at the time, but had seemed obliging and amused, enjoying the comedy of asking Mrs. Monarch, who sat vague and silent, whether she would have cream and sugar, and putting an exaggerated simper into the question. She had tried intonations—as if she too wished to pass for the real thing—till I was afraid my other visitors would take offence.

Oh they were determined not to do this, and their touching patience was the measure of their great need. They would sit by the hour, uncomplaining, till I was ready to use them; they would come back on the chance of being wanted and would walk away cheerfully if it failed. I used to go to the door with them to see in what magnificent order they retreated. I tried to find other employment for them—I introduced them to several artists. But they didn't "take," for reasons I could appreciate, and I became rather anxiously aware that after such disappointments they fell back upon me with a heavier weight. They did me the honor to think me most *their* form. They weren't romantic enough for the painters, and in those days there were few serious workers in black-and-white. Besides, they had an eye to the great job I had mentioned to them—they had secretly set their hearts on supplying the right essence for my pictorial vindication of our fine novelist. They knew that for this undertaking I should want no costume-effects, none of the frippery of past ages—that it was a case in which everything would be contemporary and satirical and presumably genteel. If I could work them into it their future would be assured, for the labour would of course be long and the occupation steady.

One day Mrs. Monarch came without her husband—she explained his absence by his having had to go to the City.[8] While she sat there in her usual relaxed majesty there came at the door a knock which I immediately recognised as the subdued appeal of a model out of work. It was followed by the entrance of a young man whom I at once saw to be a foreigner and who proved in fact an Italian acquainted with no English word but my name, which he uttered in a way that made it seem to include all others. I hadn't then visited his country, nor was I proficient in his tongue; but as he was not so meanly constituted—what Italian is?—as to depend only on that member for expression he conveyed to me, in familiar but graceful mimicry, that he was in search of exactly the employment in which the lady before me was engaged. I was not struck with him at first, and while I continued to draw I dropped few signs of interest or encouragement. He stood his ground however—not importunately, but with a dumb dog-like fidelity in his eyes that amounted to innocent impudence, the manner of a devoted servant—he might have been in the house for years—unjustly suspected. Suddenly it struck me that this very attitude and expression made a picture; whereupon I told him to sit down and wait till I should be free. There was another picture in the way he obeyed me, and I observed as I worked that there were others still in the way he looked wonderingly, with his head

8. Financial and legal center of London.

thrown back, about the high studio. He might have been crossing himself in Saint Peter's. Before I finished I said to myself "The fellow's a bankrupt orange-monger, but a treasure."

When Mrs. Monarch withdrew he passed across the room like a flash to open the door for her, standing there with the rapt pure gaze of the young Dante spellbound by the young Beatrice.[9] As I never insisted, in such situations, on the blankness of the British domestic, I reflected that he had the making of a servant—and I needed one, but couldn't pay him to be only that—as well as of a model; in short I resolved to adopt my bright adventurer if he would agree to officiate in the double capacity. He jumped at my offer, and in the event my rashness—for I had really known nothing about him—wasn't brought home to me. He proved a sympathetic though a desultory ministrant, and had in a wonderful degree the *sentiment de la pose*.[1] It was uncultivated, instinctive, a part of the happy instinct that had guided him to my door and helped him to spell out my name on the card nailed to it. He had had no other introduction to me than a guess, from the shape of my high north window, seen outside, that my place was a studio and that as a studio it would contain an artist. He had wandered to England in search of fortune, like other itinerants, and had embarked, with a partner and a small green hand-cart, on the sale of penny ices. The ices had melted away and the partner had dissolved in their train. My young man wore tight yellow trousers with reddish stripes and his name was Oronte. He was sallow but fair, and when I put him into some old clothes of my own he looked like an Englishman. He was as good as Miss Churm, who could look, when requested, like an Italian.

IV

I thought Mrs. Monarch's face slightly convulsed when, on her coming back with her husband, she found Oronte installed. It was strange to have to recognise in a scrap of a lazzarone[2] a competitor to her magnificent Major. It was she who scented danger first, for the Major was anecdotally unconscious. But Oronte gave us tea, with a hundred eager confusions—he had never been concerned in so queer a process—and I think she thought better of me for having at last an "establishment." They saw a couple of drawings that I had made of the establishment, and Mrs. Monarch hinted that it never would have struck her he had sat for them. "Now the drawings you make from *us*, they look exactly like us," she reminded me, smiling in triumph; and I recognized that this was indeed just their defect. When I drew the Monarchs I couldn't anyhow get away from them—get into the character I wanted to represent; and I hadn't the least desire my model should be discoverable in my picture. Miss Churm never was, and Mrs. Monarch thought I hid her, very properly, because she was vulgar; whereas if

9. Dante Alighieri (1265–1321), Italian poet, author of *The Divine Comedy*, was inspired for his whole lifetime poetically and spiritually by Beatrice Portinari whom he first saw when they were children and saw only infrequently thereafter.   1. Instinct for striking poses.   2. Street-person.

she was lost it was only as the dead who go to heaven are lost—in the gain of an angel the more.

By this time I had got a certain start with "Rutland Ramsay," the first novel in the great projected series; that is I had produced a dozen drawings, several with the help of the Major and his wife, and I had sent them in for approval. My understanding with the publishers, as I have already hinted, had been that I was to be left to do my work, in this particular case, as I liked, with the whole book committed to me; but my connexion with the rest of the series was only contingent. There were moments when, frankly, it *was* a comfort to have the real thing under one's hand; for there were characters in "Rutland Ramsay" that were very much like it. There were people presumably as erect as the Major and women of as good a fashion as Mrs. Monarch. There was a great deal of country-house life—treated, it is true, in a fine fanciful ironical generalised way—and there was a considerable implication of knickerbockers and kilts. There were certain things I had to settle at the outset; such things for instance as the exact appearance of the hero and the particular bloom and figure of the heroine. The author of course gave me a lead, but there was a margin for interpretation. I took the Monarchs into my confidence, I told them frankly what I was about, I mentioned my embarrassments and alternatives. "Oh take *him!*" Mrs. Monarch murmured sweetly, looking at her husband; and "What could you want better than my wife?" the Major enquired with the comfortable candour that now prevailed between us.

I wasn't obliged to answer these remarks—I was only obliged to place my sitters. I wasn't easy in mind, and I postponed a little timidly perhaps the solving of my question. The book was a large canvas, the other figures were numerous, and I worked off at first some of the episodes in which the hero and the heroine were not concerned. When once I had set *them* up I should have to stick to them—I couldn't make my young man seven feet high in one place and five feet nine in another. I inclined on the whole to the latter measurement, though the Major more than once reminded me that *he* looked about as young as any one. It was indeed quite possible to arrange him, for the figure, so that it would have been difficult to detect his age. After the spontaneous Oronte had been with me a month, and after I had given him to understand several times over that his native exuberance would presently constitute an insurmountable barrier to our further intercourse, I waked to a sense of his heroic capacity. He was only five feet seven, but the remaining inches were latent. I tried him almost secretly at first, for I was really rather afraid of the judgment my other models would pass on such a choice. If they regarded Miss Churm as little better than a snare what would they think of the representation by a person so little the real thing as an Italian street-vendor of a protagonist formed by a public school?

If I went a little in fear of them it wasn't because they bullied me, because they had got an oppressive foothold, but because in their really pathetic decorum and mysteriously permanent newness they counted on me so intensely. I was therefore very glad when Jack Hawley came home: he was always of such good counsel. He painted badly himself, but there was no one like him for putting his finger on the place. He had been absent from England for a year; he had been somewhere—I don't remember where—to get a fresh eye. I was in a good deal of dread of any such organ, but we were old friends; he had been away for months and a sense of emptiness was creeping into my life. I hadn't dodged a missile for a year.

105 He came back with a fresh eye, but with the same old black velvet blouse, and the first evening he spent in my studio we smoked cigarettes till the small hours. He had done no work himself, he had only got the eye; so the field was clear for the production of my little things. He wanted to see what I had produced for the *Cheapside*, but he was disappointed in the exhibition. That at least seemed the meaning of two or three comprehensive groans which, as he lounged on my big divan, his leg folded under him, looking at my latest drawings, issued from his lips with the smoke of the cigarette.

"What's the matter with you?" I asked.

"What's the matter with *you?*"

"Nothing save that I'm mystified."

"You are indeed. You're quite off the hinge. What's the meaning of this new fad?" And he tossed me, with visible irreverence, a drawing in which I happened to have depicted both my elegant models. I asked if he didn't think it good, and he replied that it struck him as execrable, given the sort of thing I had always represented myself to him as wishing to arrive at; but I let that pass—I was so anxious to see exactly what he meant. The two figures in the picture looked colossal, but I supposed this was *not* what he meant, inasmuch as, for aught he knew the contrary, I might have been trying for some such effect. I maintained that I was working exactly in the same way as when he last had done me the honour to tell me I might do something some day. "Well, there's a screw loose somewhere," he answered; "wait a bit and I'll discover it." I depended upon him to do so: where else was the fresh eye? But he produced at last nothing more luminous than "I don't know—I don't like your types." This was lame for a critic who had never consented to discuss with me anything but the question of execution, the direction of strokes and the mystery of values.

110 "In the drawings you've been looking at I think my types are very handsome."

"Oh they won't do!"

"I've been working with new models."

"I see you have. *They* won't do."

"Are you very sure of that?"

115 "Absolutely—they're stupid."

"You mean *I* am—for I ought to get round that."

"You *can't*—with such people. Who are they?"

I told him, so far as was necessary, and he concluded heartlessly: "Ce sont des gens qu'il faut mettre à la porte."[3]

"You've never seen them; they're awfully good"—I flew to their defence.

120 "Not seen them? Why all this recent work of yours drops to pieces with them. It's all I want to see of them."

"No one else has said anything against it—the *Cheapside* people are pleased."

3. That kind of person should be shown the door.

"Everyone else is an ass, and the *Cheapside* people the biggest asses of all. Come, don't pretend at this time of day to have pretty illusions about the public, especially about publishers and editors. It's not for *such* animals you work—it's for those who know, *coloro che sanno;*[4] so keep straight for *me* if you can't keep straight for yourself. There was a certain sort of thing you used to try for—and a very good thing it was. But this twaddle isn't *in* it." When I talked with Hawley later about "Rutland Ramsay" and its possible successors he declared that I must get back into my boat again or I should go to the bottom. His voice in short was the voice of warning.

I noted the warning, but I didn't turn my friends out of doors. They bored me a good deal; but the very fact that they bored me admonished me not to sacrifice them—if there was anything to be done with them—simply to irritation. As I look back at this phase they seem to me to have pervaded my life not a little. I have a vision of them as most of the time in my studio, seated against the wall on an old velvet bench to be out of the way, and resembling the while a pair of patient courtiers in a royal ante-chamber. I'm convinced that during the coldest weeks of the winter they held their ground because it saved them fire. Their newness was losing its gloss, and it was impossible not to feel them objects of charity. Whenever Miss Churm arrived they went away, and after I was fairly launched in "Rutland Ramsay" Miss Churm arrived pretty often. They managed to express to me tacitly that they supposed I wanted her for the low life of the book, and I let them suppose it, since they had attempted to study the work—it was lying about the studio—without discovering that it dealt only with the highest circles. They had dipped into the most brilliant of our novelists without deciphering many passages. I still took an hour from them, now and again, in spite of Jack Hawley's warning: it would be time enough to dismiss them, if dismissal should be necessary, when the rigour of the season was over. Hawley had made their acquaintance—he had met them at my fireside—and thought them a ridiculous pair. Learning that he was a painter they tried to approach him, to show him too that they were the real thing; but he looked at them, across the big room, as if they were miles away: they were a compendium of everything he most objected to in the social system of his country. Such people as that, all convention and patent-leather, with ejaculations that stopped conversation, had no business in a studio. A studio was a place to learn to see, and how could you see through a pair of feather-beds?

The main inconvenience I suffered at their hands was that at first I was shy of letting it break upon them that my artful little servant had begun to sit to me for "Rutland Ramsay." They knew I had been odd enough—they were prepared by this time to allow oddity to artists—to pick a foreign vagabond out of the streets when I might have had a person with whiskers and credentials, but it was some time before they learned how high I rated his accomplishments. They found him in an attitude more than once, but they never doubted I was doing him as an organ-grinder. There were several things they never guessed, and one of them was that for a striking scene in the novel, in which a footman briefly

---

4. Dante, *The Divine Comedy*, "The Inferno," 4:131: actually, *color che sanno*—"those who know."

figured, it occurred to me to make use of Major Monarch as the menial. I kept putting this off, I didn't like to ask him to don the livery—besides the difficulty of finding a livery to fit him. At last, one day late in the winter, when I was at work on the despised Oronte, who caught one's idea on the wing, and was in the glow of feeling myself go very straight, they came in, the Major and his wife, with their society laugh about nothing (there was less and less to laugh at); came on like country-callers—they always reminded me of that—who have walked across the park after church and are presently persuaded to stay to luncheon. Luncheon was over, but they could stay to tea—I knew they wanted it. The fit was on me, however, and I couldn't let my ardour cool and my work wait, with the fading daylight, while my model prepared it. So I asked Mrs. Monarch if she would mind laying it out—a request which for an instant brought all the blood to her face. Her eyes were on her husband's for a second, and some mute telegraphy passed between them. Their folly was over the next instant; his cheerful shrewdness put an end to it. So far from pitying their wounded pride, I must add, I was moved to give it as complete a lesson as I could. They bustled about together and got out the cups and saucers and made the kettle boil. I know they felt as if they were waiting on my servant, and when the tea was prepared I said: "He'll have a cup, please—he's tired." Mrs. Monarch brought him one where he stood, and he took it from her, as if he had been a gentleman at a party squeezing a crush-hat with an elbow.

125   Then it came over me that she had made a great effort for me—made it with a kind of nobleness—and that I owed her a compensation. Each time I saw her after this I wondered what the compensation could be. I couldn't go on doing the wrong thing to oblige them. Oh it *was* the wrong thing, the stamp of the work for which they sat—Hawley was not the only person to say it now. I sent in a large number of the drawings I had made for "Rutland Ramsay," and I received a warning that was more to the point than Hawley's. The artistic adviser of the house for which I was working was of opinion that many of my illustrations were not what had been looked for. Most of these illustrations were the subjects in which the Monarchs had figured. Without going into the question of what *had* been looked for, I had to face the fact that at this rate I shouldn't get the other books to do. I hurled myself in despair on Miss Churm—I put her through all her paces. I not only adopted Oronte publicly as my hero, but one morning when the Major looked in to see if I didn't require him to finish a *Cheapside* figure for which he had begun to sit the week before, I told him I had changed my mind—I'd do the drawing from my man. At this my visitor turned pale and stood looking at me. "Is *he* your idea of an English gentleman?" he asked.

    I was disappointed, I was nervous, I wanted to get on with my work; so I replied with irritation: "Oh my dear Major—I can't be ruined for *you*!" . . .

    It was a horrid speech, but he stood another moment—after which, without a word, he quitted the studio. I drew a long breath, for I said to myself that I shouldn't see him again. I hadn't told him definitely that I was in danger of having my work rejected, but I was vexed at his not having felt the catastrophe in the air, read with me the moral of our fruitless collaboration, the lesson that in the deceptive atmosphere of art even the highest respectability may fail of being plastic.

I didn't owe my friends money, but I did see them again. They reappeared together three days later, and, given all the other facts, there was something tragic in that one. It was a clear proof they could find nothing else in life to do. They had threshed the matter out in a dismal conference—they had digested the bad news that they were not in for the series. If they weren't useful to me even for the *Cheapside* their function seemed difficult to determine, and I could only judge at first that they had come, forgivingly, decorously, to take a last leave. This made me rejoice in secret that I had little leisure for a scene; for I had placed both my other models in position together and I was pegging away at a drawing from which I hoped to derive glory. It had been suggested by the passage in which Rutland Ramsay, drawing up a chair to Artemisia's piano-stool, says extraordinary things to her while she ostensibly fingers out a difficult piece of music. I had done Miss Churm at the piano before—it was an attitude in which she knew how to take on an absolutely poetic grace. I wished the two figures to "compose" together with intensity, and my little Italian had entered perfectly into my conception. The pair were vividly before me, the piano had been pulled out; it was a charming show of blended youth and murmured love, which I had only to catch and keep. My visitors stood and looked at it, and I was friendly to them over my shoulder.

They made no response, but I was used to silent company and went on with my work, only a little disconcerted—even though exhilarated by the sense that *this* was at least the ideal thing—at not having got rid of them after all. Presently I heard Mrs. Monarch's sweet voice beside or rather above me: "I wish her hair were a little better done." I looked up and she was staring with a strange fixedness at Miss Churm, whose back was turned to her. "Do you mind my just touching it?" she went on—a question which made me spring up for an instant as with the instinctive fear that she might do the young lady a harm. But she quieted me with a glance I shall never forget—I confess I should like to have been able to paint *that*—and went for a moment to my model. She spoke to her softly, laying a hand on her shoulder and bending over her; and as the girl, understanding, gratefully assented, she disposed her rough curls, with a few quick passes, in such a way as to make Miss Churm's head twice as charming. It was one of the most heroic personal services I've ever seen rendered. Then Mrs. Monarch turned away with a low sigh and, looking about her as if for something to do, stooped to the floor with a noble humility and picked up a dirty rag that had dropped out of my paint-box.

The Major meanwhile had also been looking for something to do, and, wandering to the other end of the studio, saw before him my breakfast-things neglected, unremoved. "I say, can't I be useful *here?*" he called out to me with an irrepressible quaver. I assented with a laugh that I fear was awkward, and for the next ten minutes, while I worked, I heard the light clatter of china and the tinkle of spoons and glass. Mrs. Monarch assisted her husband—they washed up my crockery, they put it away. They wandered off into my little scullery, and I afterwards found that they had cleaned my knives and that my slender stock of plate had an unprecedented surface. When it came over me, the latent eloquence of what they were doing, I confess that my drawing was blurred for a moment—the picture swam. They had accepted their failure, but they couldn't

130

accept their fate. They had bowed their heads in bewilderment to the perverse and cruel law in virtue of which the real thing could be so much less precious than the unreal; but they didn't want to starve. If my servants were my models; then my models might be my servants. They would reverse the parts—the others would sit for the ladies and gentlemen and *they* would do the work. They would still be in the studio—it was an intense dumb appeal to me not to turn them out. "Take us on," they wanted to say—"we'll do *anything*."

My pencil dropped from my hand; my sitting was spoiled and I got rid of my sitters, who were also evidently rather mystified and awestruck. Then, alone with the Major and his wife I had a most uncomfortable moment. He put their prayer into a single sentence: "I say, you know—just let *us* do for you, can't you?" I couldn't—it was dreadful to see them emptying my slops; but I pretended I could, to oblige them, for about a week. Then I gave them a sum of money to go away, and I never saw them again. I obtained the remaining books, but my friend Hawley repeats that Major and Mrs. Monarch did me a permanent harm, got me into false ways. If it be true I'm content to have paid the price—for the memory.

1892, 1909

DORIS LESSING

Our Friend Judith

I stopped inviting Judith to meet people when a Canadian woman remarked, with the satisfied fervour of one who has at last pinned a label on a rare specimen: "She is, of course, one of your typical English spinsters."

This was a few weeks after an American sociologist, having elicited from Judith the facts that she was fortyish, unmarried, and living alone, had enquired of me: "I suppose she has given up?" "Given up what?" I asked; and the subsequent discussion was unrewarding.

Judith did not easily come to parties. She would come after pressure, not so much—one felt—to do one a favour, but in order to correct what she believed to be a defect in her character. "I really ought to enjoy meeting new people more than I do," she said once. We reverted to an earlier pattern of our friendship: odd evenings together, an occasional visit to the cinema, or she would telephone to say: "I'm on my way past you to the British Museum. Would you care for a cup of coffee with me? I have twenty minutes to spare."

It is characteristic of Judith that the word "spinster," used of her, provoked fascinated speculation about other people. There are my aunts, for instance: aged seventy-odd, both unmarried, one an ex-missionary from China, one a retired matron of a famous London hospital. These two old ladies live together under the shadow of the cathedral in a country town. They devote much time to the Church, to good causes, to letter writing with friends all over the world, to the grandchildren and the great-grandchildren of relatives. It would be a mistake, however, on entering a house in which nothing has been moved for fifty years, to diagnose a condition of fossilised late-Victorian integrity. They read every book review in the *Observer* or the *Times*,[1] so that I recently got a letter from Aunt Rose enquiring whether I did not think that the author of *On the Road*[2] was not—perhaps?—exaggerating his difficulties. They know a good deal about music, and write letters of encouragement to young composers they feel are being neglected—"You must understand that anything new and original takes time to be understood." Well-informed and critical Tories, they are as likely to despatch telegrams of protest to the Home Secretary[3] as letters of support. These ladies, my aunts Emily and Rose, are surely what is meant by the phrase "English spinster." And yet, once the connection has been pointed out, there is no doubt that Judith and they are spiritual cousins, if not sisters. Therefore it follows that one's pitying admiration for women who have supported manless and uncomforted lives needs a certain modification?

One will, of course, never know; and I feel now that it is entirely my fault that I shall never know. I had been Judith's friend for upward of five years before the incident occurred which I involuntarily thought of—stupidly enough—as the first time Judith's mask slipped.

A mutual friend, Betty, had been given a cast-off Dior[4] dress. She was too short for it. Also she said: "It's not a dress for a married woman with three children and a talent for cooking. I don't know why not, but it isn't." Judith was the right build. Therefore one evening the three of us met by appointment in Judith's bedroom, with the dress. Neither Betty nor I was surprised at the renewed discovery that Judith was beautiful. We had both often caught each other, and ourselves, in moments of envy when Judith's calm and severe face, her undemonstratively perfect body, succeeded in making everyone else in a room or a street look cheap.

Judith is tall, small-breasted, slender. Her light brown hair is parted in the centre and cut straight around her neck. A high straight forehead, straight nose, a full grave mouth are setting for her eyes, which are green, large and prominent. Her lids are very white, fringed with gold, and moulded close over the eyeball, so that in profile she has the look of a staring gilded mask. The dress was of dark green glistening stuff, cut straight, with a sort of loose tunic. It opened simply at the throat. In it Judith could of course evoke nothing but classical images. Diana, perhaps, back from the hunt, in a relaxed moment? A rather intellectual wood nymph who had opted for an afternoon in the British Museum Reading Room? Something like that. Neither Betty nor I said a word, since Judith was examining herself in a long mirror, and must know she looked magnificent.

Slowly she drew off the dress and laid it aside. Slowly she put on the old cord skirt and woollen blouse she had taken off. She must have surprised a resigned glance between us, for she then remarked, with the smallest of mocking smiles:

1. Prestigious London newspapers representing roughly the younger more liberal establishment and the Establishment proper respectively.   2. Jack Kerouac (1922–69), leader of the beatniks, 1950s forerunners of the hippies. Kerouac heroes felt themselves completely cut off from and victimized by American society.   3. Head of the British government department responsible for domestic matters.   4. Famous French designer of high fashions.

"One surely ought to stay in character, wouldn't you say?" She added, reading the words out of some invisible book, written not by her, since it was a very vulgar book, but perhaps by one of us: "It does everything *for* me, I must admit."

"After seeing you in it," Betty cried out, defying her, "I can't bear for anyone else to have it. I shall simply put it away." Judith shrugged, rather irritated. In the shapeless skirt and blouse, and without makeup, she stood smiling at us, a woman at whom forty-nine out of fifty people would not look twice.

A second revelatory incident occurred soon after. Betty telephoned me to say that Judith had a kitten. Did I know that Judith adored cats? "No, but of course she would," I said.

Betty lived in the same street as Judith and saw more of her than I did. I was kept posted about the growth and habits of the cat and its effect on Judith's life. She remarked for instance that she felt it was good for her to have a tie and some responsibility. But no sooner was the cat out of kittenhood than all the neighbours complained. It was a tomcat, ungelded, and making every night hideous. Finally the landlord said that either the cat or Judith must go, unless she was prepared to have the cat "fixed."[5] Judith wore herself out trying to find some person, anywhere in Britain, who would be prepared to take the cat. This person would, however, have to sign a written statement not to have the cat "fixed." When Judith took the cat to the vet to be killed, Betty told me she cried for twenty-four hours.

"She didn't think of compromising? After all, perhaps the cat might have preferred to live, if given the choice?"

"Is it likely I'd have the nerve to say anything so sloppy to Judith? It's the nature of a male cat to rampage lustfully about, and therefore it would be morally wrong for Judith to have the cat fixed, simply to suit her own convenience."

"She said that?"

"She wouldn't have to *say* it, surely?"

A third incident was when she allowed a visiting young American, living in Paris, the friend of a friend and scarcely known to her, to use her flat while she visited her parents over Christmas. The young man and his friends lived it up for ten days of alcohol and sex and marijuana, and when Judith came back it took a week to get the place clean again and the furniture mended. She telephoned twice to Paris, the first time to say that he was a disgusting young thug and if he knew what was good for him he would keep out of her way in the future; the second time to apologise for losing her temper. "I had a choice either to let someone use my flat, or to leave it empty. But having chosen that you should have it, it was clearly an unwarrantable infringement of your liberty to make any conditions at all. I do most sincerely ask your pardon." The moral aspects of the matter having been made clear, she was irritated rather than not to receive letters of apology from him—fulsome, embarrassed, but above all, baffled.

It was the note of curiosity in the letters—he even suggested coming over to get to know her better—that irritated her most. "What do you suppose he means?"

---

5. Gelded, castrated.

she said to me. "He lived in my flat for ten days. One would have thought that should be enough, wouldn't you?"

The facts about Judith, then, are all in the open, unconcealed, and plain to anyone who cares to study them; or, as it became plain she feels, to anyone with the intelligence to interpret them.

She has lived for the last twenty years in a small two-roomed flat high over a busy West London street. The flat is shabby and badly heated. The furniture is old, was never anything but ugly, is now frankly rickety and fraying. She has an income of two hundred pounds[6] a year from a dead uncle. She lives on this and what she earns from her poetry, and from lecturing on poetry to night classes and extramural university classes.

She does not smoke or drink, and eats very little, from preference, not self-discipline.

She studied poetry and biology at Oxford, with distinction.

She is a Castlewell. That is, she is a member of one of the academic upper-middleclass families, which have been producing for centuries a steady supply of brilliant but sound men and women who are the backbone of the arts and sciences in Britain. She is on cool good terms with her family, who respect her and leave her alone.

She goes on long walking tours, by herself, in such places as Exmoor or West Scotland.

Every three or four years she publishes a volume of poems.

The walls of her flat are completely lined with books. They are scientific, classical and historical; there is a great deal of poetry and some drama. There is not one novel. When Judith says: "Of course I don't read novels," this does not mean that novels have no place, or a small place, in literature; or that people should not read novels; but that it must be obvious she can't be expected to read novels.

I had been visiting her flat for years before I noticed two long shelves of books, under a window, each shelf filled with the works of a single writer. The two writers are not, to put it at the mildest, the kind one would associate with Judith. They are mild, reminiscent, vague and whimsical. Typical English *belles-lettres*, in fact, and by definition abhorrent to her. Not one of the books in the two shelves has been read; some of the pages are still uncut. Yet each book is inscribed or dedicated to her: gratefully, admiringly, sentimentally and, more than once, amorously. In short, it is open to anyone who cares to examine these two shelves, and to work out dates, to conclude that Judith from the age of fifteen to twenty-five had been the beloved young companion of one elderly literary gentleman, and from twenty-five to thirty-five the inspiration of another.

During all that time she had produced her own poetry, and the sort of poetry, it is quite safe to deduce, not at all likely to be admired by her two admirers. Her poems are always cool and intellectual; that is their form, which is contradicted or supported by a gravely sensuous texture. They are poems to read often; one has to, to understand them.

6. About one-third or even one-half of a subsistence income.

I did not ask Judith a direct question about these two eminent but rather fusty lovers. Not because she would not have answered, or because she would have found the question impertinent, but because such questions are clearly unnecessary. Having those two shelves of books where they are, and books she could not conceivably care for, for their own sake, is publicly giving credit where credit is due. I can imagine her thinking the thing over, and deciding it was only fair, or perhaps honest, to place the books there; and this despite the fact that she would not care at all for the same attention be paid to her. There is something almost contemptuous in it. For she certainly despises people who feel they need attention.

For instance, more than once a new emerging wave of "modern" young poets have discovered her as the only "modern" poet among their despised and well-credited elders. This is because, since she began writing at fifteen, her poems have been full of scientific, mechanical and chemical imagery. This is how she thinks, or feels.

More than once has a young poet hastened to her flat, to claim her as an ally, only to find her totally and by instinct unmoved by words like "modern," "new," "contemporary." He has been outraged and wounded by her principle, so deeply rooted as to be unconscious, and to need no expression but a contemptuous shrug of the shoulders, that publicity seeking or to want critical attention is despicable. It goes without saying that there is perhaps one critic in the world she has any time for. He has sulked off, leaving her on her shelf, which she takes it for granted is her proper place, to be read by an appreciative minority.

Meanwhile she gives her lectures, walks alone through London, writes her poems, and is seen sometimes at a concert or a play with a middleaged professor of Greek, who has a wife and two children.

Betty and I had speculated about this professor, with such remarks as: Surely she must sometimes be lonely? Hasn't she ever wanted to marry? What about that awful moment when one comes in from somewhere at night to an empty flat?

It happened recently that Betty's husband was on a business trip, her children visiting, and she was unable to stand the empty house. She asked Judith for a refuge until her own home filled again.

Afterwards Betty rang me up to report: "Four of the five nights Professor Adams came in about ten or so."

"Was Judith embarrassed?"

"Would you expect her to be?"

"Well, if not embarrassed, at least conscious there was a situation?"

"No, not at all. But I must say I don't think he's good enough for her. He can't possibly understand her. He calls her Judy."

"Good God."

"Yes. But I was wondering. Suppose the other two called her Judy—'little Judy'—imagine it! Isn't it awful? But it does rather throw a light on Judith?"

"It's rather touching."

"I suppose it's touching. But I was embarrassed—oh, not because of the situation. Because of how she was, with him. 'Judy, is there another cup of tea in that pot?' And she, rather daughterly and demure, pouring him one."

"Well yes, I can see how you felt."

"Three of the nights he went to her bedroom with her—very casual about it, because she was being. But he was not there in the mornings. So I asked her. You know how it is when you ask her a question. As if you've been having long conversations on that very subject for years and years, and she is merely contin-uing where you left off last. So when she says something surprising, one feels such a fool to be surprised?"

"Yes. And then?"

"I asked her if she was sorry not to have children. She said yes, but one couldn't have everything."

"One can't have everything, she said?"

"Quite clearly feeling she *has* nearly everything. She said she thought it was a pity, because she would have brought up children very well."

"When you come to think of it, she would, too."

"I asked about marriage, but she said on the whole the role of a mistress suited her better."

"She used the word 'mistress'?"

"You must admit it's the accurate word."

"I suppose so."

"And then she said that while she liked intimacy and sex and everything, she enjoyed waking up in the morning alone and *her own person.*"

"Yes, *of course.*"

"Of course. But now she's bothered because the professor would like to marry her. Or he feels he ought. At least, he's getting all guilty and obsessive about it. She says she doesn't see the point of divorce, and anyway, surely it would be very hard on his poor old wife after all these years, particularly after bringing up two children so satisfactorily. She talks about his wife as if she's a kind of nice old charwoman, and it wouldn't be *fair* to sack her, you know. Anyway. What with one thing and another. Judith's going off to Italy soon in order *to collect herself.*"

"But how's she going to pay for it?"

"Luckily the Third Programme's[7] commissioning her to do some arty pro-grammes. They offered her a choice of The Cid—El Thid[8] you know—and the Borgias. Well, the Borghese, then. And Judith settled for the Borgias."

"The Borgias," I said, "*Judith?*"

"Yes, quite. I said that too, in that tone of voice. She saw my point. She says the epic is right up her street, whereas the Renaissance has never been on her wave length. Obviously it couldn't be, all the magnificence and cruelty and *dirt*. But of course chivalry and a high moral code and all those idiotically noble goings-on are right on her wave length."

"Is the money the same?"

45

50

55

60

7. British Broadcasting Corporation public radio service (and now also television channel) special-izing in classical music, literature and plays, lectures, etc.   8. Castilian, standard Spanish, pro-nunciation of El Cid, the title of an eleventh-century soldier-hero and hero of many works of literature.

"Yes. But is it likely Judith would let money decide? No, she said that one should always choose something new, that isn't up one's street. Well, because it's better for her character, and so on, to get herself unsettled by the Renaissance. She didn't say *that*, of course."

"Of course not."

Judith went to Florence; and for some months postcards informed us tersely of her doings. Then Betty decided she must go by herself for a holiday. She had been appalled by the discovery that if her husband was away for a night she couldn't sleep; and when he went to Australia for three weeks, she stopped living until he came back. She had discussed this with him, and he had agreed that if she really felt the situation to be serious, he would despatch her by air, to Italy, in order to recover her self-respect. As she put it.

65   I got this letter from her: "It's no use, I'm coming home. I might have known. Better face it, once you're really married you're not fit for man nor beast. And if you remember what I used to be like! *Well!* I moped around Milan. I sunbathed in Venice, then I thought my tan was surely worth something, so I was on the point of starting an affair with another lonely soul, but I lost heart, and went to Florence to see Judith. She wasn't there. She'd gone to the Italian Riviera. I had nothing better to do, so I followed her. When I saw the place I wanted to laugh, it's so much not Judith, you know, all those palms and umbrellas and gaiety at all costs and ever such an ornamental blue sea. Judith is in an enormous stone room up on the hillside above the sea, with grape vines all over the place. You should see her, she's got beautiful. It seems for the last fifteen years she's been going to Soho[9] every Saturday morning to buy food at an Italian shop. I must have looked surprised, because she explained she liked Soho. I suppose because all that dreary vice and nudes and prostitutes and everything prove how right she is to be as she is? She told the people in the shop she was going to Italy, and the *signora*[1] said, what a coincidence, she was going back to Italy too, and she did hope an old friend like Miss Castlewell would visit her there. Judith said to me: 'I felt lacking, when she used the word friend. Our relations have always been formal. Can you understand it?' she said to me. 'For fifteen years,' I said to her. She said: 'I think I must feel it's a kind of imposition, don't you know, expecting people to feel friendship for one.' *Well.* I said: 'You ought to understand it, because you're like that yourself.' 'Am I?' she said. 'Well, think about,' I said. But I could see she didn't want to think about it. Anyway, she's here, and I've spent a week with her. The widow Maria Rineiri inherited her mother's house, so she came home, from Soho. On the ground floor is a tatty little *rosticceria*[2] patronised by the neighbours. They are all working people. This isn't tourist country, up on the hill. The widow lives above the shop with her little boy, a nasty little brat of about ten. Say what you like, the English are the only people who know how to bring up children, I don't care if that's insular. Judith's room is at the back, with a balcony. Underneath her room is the barber's shop, and the barber is Luigi Rineiri, the widow's younger brother. Yes, I was keeping him

9. A section of London roughly equivalent to Greenwich Village in New York—foreign restaurants and groceries, haunt of writers, painters, etc.—but in recent years increasingly known for prostitutes and pornography.   1. Proprietress.   2. Grill.

until the last. He is about forty, tall dark handsome, a great *bull*, but rather a sweet fatherly bull. He has cut Judith's hair and made it lighter. Now it looks like a sort of gold helmet. Judith is all brown. The widow Rineiri has made her a white dress and a green dress. They fit, for a change. When Judith walks down the street to the lower town, all the Italian males take one look at the golden girl and melt in their own oil like ice cream. Judith takes all this in her stride. She sort of acknowledges the homage. Then she strolls into the sea and vanishes into the foam. She swims five miles every day. *Naturally*. I haven't asked Judith whether she has collected herself, because you can see she hasn't. The widow Rineiri is matchmaking. When I noticed this I wanted to laugh, but luckily I didn't because Judith asked me, really wanting to know: 'Can you see me married to an Italian barber?' (Not being snobbish, but stating the position, so to speak.) 'Well yes,' I said, 'you're the only women I know who I can see married to an Italian barber.' Because it wouldn't matter who she married, she'd always be her *own person*. 'At any rate, for a time,' I said. At which she said, asperously[3]. 'You can use phrases like for a time in England but not in Italy.' Did you ever see England, at least London, as the home of licence, liberty and free love? No, neither did I, but of course she's right. Married to Luigi it would be the family, the neighbours, the church and the *bambini*.[4] All the same she's thinking about it, believe it or not. Here she's quite different, all relaxed and free. She's melting in the attention she gets. The widow mothers her and makes her coffee all the time, and listens to a lot of good advice about how to bring up that nasty brat of hers. Unluckily she doesn't take it. Luigi is crazy for her. At mealtimes she goes to the *trattoria*[5] in the upper square and all the workmen treat her like a goddess. Well, a film star then. I said to her, you're mad to come home. For one thing her rent is ten bob[6] a week, and you eat *pasta* and drink red wine till you bust for about one and sixpence. No, she said, it would be nothing but self-indulgence to stay. Why? I said. She said, she's got nothing to stay for. (Ho ho.) And besides, she's done her research on the Borghese, though so far she can't see her way to an honest presentation of the facts. What made these people tick? she wants to know. And so she's only staying because of the cat. I forgot to mention the cat. This is a town of cats. The Italians here love their cats. I wanted to feed a stray cat at the table, but the waiter said no; and after lunch, all the waiters came with trays crammed with leftover food and stray cats came from everywhere to eat. And at dark when the tourists go in to feed and the beach is empty—you know how empty and forlorn a beach is at dusk?—well cats appear from everywhere. The beach seems to move, then you see it's cats. They go stalking along the thin inch of grey water at the edge of the sea, shaking their paws crossly at each step, snatching at the dead little fish, and throwing them with their mouths up on to the dry stand. Then they scamper after them. You've never seen such a snarling and fighting. At dawn when the fishing boats come in to the empty beach, the cats are there in dozens. The fisherman throw them bits of fish. The cats snarl and fight over it. Judith gets up early and goes down to watch. Some-

3. Sharply, harshly.   4. Children.   5. Inexpensive restaurant.   6. Shillings. There are twenty shillings to the pound; *one and sixpence* below is one and a half shillings.

times Luigi goes too, being tolerant. Because what he really likes is to join the evening promenade with Judith on his arm around and around the square of the upper town. Showing her off. Can you *see* Judith? But she does it. Being tolerant. But she smiles and enjoys the attention she gets, there's no doubt about it.

"She has a cat in her room. It's a kitten really, but it's pregnant. Judith says she can't leave until the kittens are born. The cat is too young to have kittens. Imagine Judith. She sits on her bed in that great stone room, with her bare feet on the stone floor, and watches the cat, and tries to work out why a healthy uninhibited Italian cat always fed on the best from the *rosticceria* should be neurotic. Because it is. When it sees Judith watching it gets nervous and starts licking at the roots of its tail. But Judith goes on watching, and says about Italy that the reason why the English love the Italians is because the Italians make the English feel superior. They have no discipline. And that's a despicable reason for one nation to love another. Then she talks about Luigi and says he has no sense of guilt, but a sense of sin; whereas she has no sense of sin but she has guilt. I haven't asked her if this has been an insuperable barrier, because judging from how she looks, it hasn't. She says she would rather have a sense of sin, because sin can be atoned for, and if she understood sin, perhaps she would be more at home with the Renaissance. Luigi is very healthy, she says, and not neurotic. He is a Catholic of course. He doesn't mind that she's an atheist. His mother has explained to him that the English are all pagans, but good people at heart. I suppose he thinks a few smart sessions with the local priest would set Judith on the right path for good and all. Meanwhile the cat walks nervously around the room, stopping to lick, and when it can't stand Judith watching it another second, it rolls over on the floor, with its paws tucked up, and rolls up its eyes, and Judith scratches its lumpy pregnant stomach and tells it to relax. It makes *me* nervous to see her, it's not like her, I don't know why. Then Luigi shouts up from the barber's shop, then he comes up and stands at the door laughing, and Judith laughs, and the widow says: Children, enjoy yourselves. And off they go, walking down to the town eating ice cream. The cat follows them. It won't let Judith out of its sight, like a dog. When she swims miles out to sea, the cat hides under a beach hut until she comes back. Then she carries it back up the hill, because that nasty little boy chases it. *Well.* I'm coming home tomorrow thank God, to my dear old Billy, I was mad ever to leave him. There is something about Judith and Italy that has upset me, I don't know what. The point is, what on earth can Judith and Luigi *talk* about? Nothing. How can they? And of course it doesn't matter. So I turn out to be a prude as well. See you next week."

It was my turn for a dose of the sun, so I didn't see Betty. On my way back from Rome I stopped off in Judith's resort and walked up through narrow streets to the upper town, where, in the square with the vine-covered *trattoria* at the corner, was a house with ROSTICCERIA written in black paint on a cracked wooden board over a low door. There was a door curtain of red beads, and flies settled on the beads. I opened the beads with my hands and looked into a small dark room with a stone counter. Loops of salami hung from metal hooks. A glass bell covered some plates of cooked meats. There were flies on the salami and on the glass bell. A few tins on the wooden shelves, a couple of pale loaves, some wine casks and an open case of sticky pale green grapes covered with fruit flies seemed to be the only stock. A single wooden table with two chairs stood in a corner, and two workmen sat there, eating lumps of sausage and bread. Through another bead curtain at the back came a short, smoothly fat, slender-limbed woman with greying hair. I asked for Miss Castlewell, and her face changed. She said in an offended, offhand way: "Miss Castlewell left last week." She took a white cloth from under the counter, and flicked at the flies on the glass bell. "I'm a friend of hers," I said, and she said: *Si,*[7] and put her hands palm down on the counter and looked at me, expressionless. The workmen got up, gulped down the last of their wine, nodded and went. She *ciao*'d[8] them; and looked back at me. Then, since I didn't go, she called: "Luigi!" A shout came from the back room, there was a rattle of beads, and in came first a wiry sharp-faced boy, and then Luigi. He was tall, heavy-shouldered, and his black rough hair was like a cap, pulled low over his brows. He looked good-natured, but at the moment uneasy. His sister said something, and he stood beside her, an ally, and confirmed: "Miss Castlewell went away." I was on the point of giving up, when through the bead curtain that screened off a dazzling light eased a thin tabby cat. It was ugly and it walked uncomfortably, with its back quarters bunched up. The child suddenly let out a "Sssss" through his teeth, and the cat froze. Luigi said something sharp to the child, and something encouraging to the cat, which sat down, looked straight in front of it, then began frantically licking at its flanks. "Miss Castlewell was offended with us," said Mrs. Rineiri suddenly, and with dignity. "She left early one morning. We did not expect her to go." I said: "Perhaps she had to go home and finish some work."

Mrs. Rineiri shrugged, then sighed. Then she exchanged a hard look with her brother. Clearly the subject had been discussed, and closed forever.

"I've known Judith a long time," I said, trying to find the right note. "She's a remarkable woman. She's a poet." But there was no response to this at all. Meanwhile the child, with a fixed bared-teeth grin, was staring at the cat, narrowing his eyes. Suddenly he let out another "Sssssss" and added a short high yelp. The cat shot backwards, hit the wall, tried desperately to claw its way up the wall, came to its senses and again sat down and began its urgent, undirected licking at its fur. This time Luigi cuffed the child, who yelped in earnest, and then ran out into the street past the cat. Now that the way was clear the cat shot across the floor, up onto the counter, and bounded past Luigi's shoulder and straight through the bead curtain into the barber's shop, where it landed with a thud.

"Judith was sorry when she left us," said Mrs. Rineiri uncertainly. "She was crying."

"I'm sure she was."

"And so," said Mrs. Rineiri, with finality, laying her hands down again, and looking past me at the bead curtain. That was the end. Luigi nodded brusquely at me, and went into the back. I said goodbye to Mrs. Rineiri and walked back

70

7. "Yes."   8. Said goodbye to.

to the lower town. In the square I saw the child, sitting on the running board of a lorry[9] parked outside the *trattoria*, drawing in the dust with his bare toes, and directing in front of him a blank, unhappy stare.

I had to go through Florence, so I went to the address Judith had been at. No, Miss Castlewell had not been back. Her papers and books were still here. Would I take them back with me to England? I made a great parcel and brought them back to England.

I telephoned Judith and she said she had already written for the papers to be sent, but it was kind of me to bring them. There had seemed to be no point, she said, in returning to Florence.

"Shall I bring them over?"

"I would be very grateful, of course."

Judith's flat was chilly, and she wore a bunchy sage-green woollen dress. Her hair was still a soft gold helmet, but she looked pale and rather pinched. She stood with her back to a single bar of electric fire—lit because I demanded it— with her legs apart and her arms folded. She contemplated me.

"I went to the Rineiris' house."

"Oh. Did you?"

"They seemed to miss you."

She said nothing.

"I saw the cat too."

"Oh. Oh, I suppose you and Betty discussed it?" This was with a small unfriendly smile.

"Well, Judith, you must see we were likely to?"

She gave this her consideration and said: "I don't understand why people discuss other people. Oh—I'm not criticising you. But I don't see why you are so interested. I don't understand human behaviour and I'm not particularly interested."

"I think you should write to the Rineiris."

"I wrote and thanked them, of course."

"I don't mean that."

"You and Betty have worked it out?"

"Yes, we talked about it. We thought we should talk to you, so you should write to the Rineiris."

"Why?"

"For one thing, they are both very fond of you."

"Fond," she said smiling.

"Judith, I've never in my life felt such an atmosphere of being let down."

Judith considered this. "When something happens that shows one there is really a complete gulf in understanding, what is there to say?"

"It could scarcely have been a complete gulf in understanding. I suppose you are going to say we are being interfering?"

Judith showed distaste. "That is a very stupid word. And it's a stupid idea. No one can interfere with me if I don't let them. No, it's that I don't understand

9. Truck.

people. I don't understand why you or Betty should care. Or why the Rineiris should, for that matter," she added with the small tight smile.

"Judith!"

"If you've behaved stupidly, there's no point in going on. You put an end to it."

"What happened? Was it the cat?"

"Yes, I suppose so. But it's not important." She looked at me, saw my ironical face, and said: "The cat was too young to have kittens. That is all there was to it."

"Have it your way. But that is obviously not all there is to it."

"What upsets me is that I don't understand at all why I was so upset then."

"What happened? Or don't you want to talk about it?"

"I don't give a damn whether I talk about it or not. You really do say the most extraordinary things, you and Betty. If you want to know, I'll tell you. What does it matter?"

"I would like to know, of course."

"*Of course!*" she said. "In your place I wouldn't care. Well, I think the essence of the thing was that I must have had the wrong attitude to that cat. Cats are supposed to be independent. They are supposed to go off by themselves to have their kittens. This one didn't. It was climbing up on to my bed all one night and crying for attention. I don't like cats on my bed. In the morning I saw she was in pain. I stayed with her all that day. Then Luigi—he's the brother, you know."

"Yes."

"Did Betty mention him? Luigi came up to say it was time I went for a swim. He said the cat should look after itself. I blame myself very much. That's what happens when you submerge yourself in somebody else."

Her look at me was now defiant; and her body showed both defensiveness and aggression. "Yes. It's true. I've always been afraid of it. And in the last few weeks I've behaved badly. It's because I let it happen."

"Well, go on."

"I left the cat and swam. It was late, so it was only for a few minutes. When I came out of the sea the cat had followed me and had had a kitten on the beach. That little beast Michele—the son, you know?—well, he always teased the poor thing, and now he had frightened her off the kitten. It was dead, though. He held it up by the tail and waved it at me as I came out of the sea. I told him to bury it. He scooped two inches of sand away and pushed the kitten in—on the beach, where people are all day. So I buried it properly. He had run off. He was chasing the poor cat. She was terrified and running up the town. I ran too. I caught Michele and I was so angry I hit him. I don't believe in hitting children. I've been feeling beastly about it ever since."

"You were angry."

"It's no excuse. I would never have believed myself capable of hitting a child. I hit him very hard. He went off, crying. The poor cat had got under a big lorry parked in the square. Then she screamed. And then a most remarkable thing happened. She screamed just once, and all at once cats just materialised. One minute there was just one cat, lying under a lorry, and the next, dozens of cats.

They sat in a big circle around the lorry, all quite still, and watched my poor cat."

"Rather moving," I said.

"Why?"

"There is no evidence one way or the other," I said in inverted commas, "that the cats were there out of concern for a friend in trouble."

"No," she said energetically. "There isn't. It might have been curiosity. Or anything. How do we know? However, I crawled under the lorry. There were two paws sticking out of the cat's back end. The kitten was the wrong way round. It was stuck. I held the cat down with one hand and I pulled the kitten out with the other." She held out her long white hands. They were still covered with fading scars and scratches. "She bit and yelled, but the kitten was alive. She left the kitten and crawled across the square into the house. Then all the cats got up and walked away. It was the most extraordinary thing I've ever seen. They vanished again. One minute they were all there, and then they had vanished. I went after the cat, with the kitten. Poor little thing, it was covered with dust—being wet, don't you know. The cat was on my bed. There was another kitten coming, but it got stuck too. So when she screamed and screamed I just pulled it out. The kittens began to suck. One kitten was very big. It was a nice fat black kitten. It must have hurt her. But she suddenly bit out—snapped, don't you know, like a reflex action, at the back of the kitten's head. It died, just like that. Extraordinary, isn't it?" she said, blinking hard, her lips quivering. "She was its mother, but she killed it. Then she ran off the bed and went downstairs into the shop under the counter. I called to Luigi. You know, he's Mrs. Rineiri's brother."

"Yes, I know."

"He said she was too young, and she was badly frightened and very hurt. He took the alive kitten to her but she got up and walked away. She didn't want it. Then Luigi told me not to look. But I followed him. He held the kitten by the tail and he banged it against the wall twice. Then he dropped it into the rubbish heap. He moved aside some rubbish with his toe, and put the kitten there and pushed rubbish over it. Then Luigi said the cat should be destroyed. He said she was badly hurt and it would always hurt her to have kittens."

"He hasn't destroyed her. She's still alive. But it looks to me as if he were right."

"Yes, I expect he was."

"What upset you—that he killed the kitten?"

"Oh no, I expect the cat would if he hadn't. But that isn't the point, is it?"

"What is the point?"

"I don't think I really know." She had been speaking breathlessly, and fast. Now she said slowly: "It's not a question of right or wrong, is it? Why should it be? It's a question of what one is. That night Luigi wanted to go promenading with me. For him, that was *that*. Something had to be done, and he'd done it. But I felt ill. He was very nice to me. He's a very good person," she said, defiantly.

"Yes, he looks it."

"That night I couldn't sleep. I was blaming myself. I should never have left the cat to go swimming. Well, and then I decided to leave the next day. And I did. And that's all. The whole thing was a mistake, from start to finish."

"Going to Italy at all?"

"Oh, to go for a holiday would have been all right." 130

"You've done all that work for nothing? You mean you aren't going to make use of all that research?"

"No. It was a mistake."

"Why don't you leave it a few weeks and see how thing are then?"

"Why?"

"You might feel differently about it." 135

"What an extraordinary thing to say. Why should I? Oh, you mean, time passing, healing wounds—that sort of thing? What an extraordinary idea. It's always seemed to me an extraordinary idea. No, right from the beginning I've felt ill at ease with the whole business, not myself at all."

"Rather irrationally, I should have said."

Judith considered this, very seriously. She frowned while she thought it over. Then she said: "But if one cannot rely on what one feels, what can one rely on?"

"On what one thinks, I should have expected you to say."

"Should you? Why? Really, you people are all very strange. I don't under- 140
stand you." She turned off the electric fire, and her face closed up. She smiled, friendly and distant, and said: "I don't really see any point at all in discussing it."

1963

QUESTIONS

1. At the end of "The Real Thing," the narrator says that though it may have done his art some harm, he is glad of his experience with the Monarchs "for the memory." What is so valuable about the memory? Did it not seem a rather painful experience?

2. Because we are told the story of "Our Friend Judith" by a friend, we never get to know Judith from the inside and are never very close to the action. This seems to have the effect of lessening the suspense and perhaps even our interest in or feelings for Judith. What is gained by this focus and voice? How does it change the meaning of the story?

3. The friend says she blundered and lost her opportunity to find out what Judith and her life were really like. How did she lose the opportunity? Was it really a blunder? Could she have found out what she wanted to know if she had not "blundered"?

4. What is the friend "really" like?

WRITING SUGGESTIONS

1. Write a 1000–1500 word scene from "My Man Bovanne" using an omniscient or unlimited point of view or using the focus and voice of one of Hazel's children.

2. Do you agree with Henry James that "real people" do not look like the popular stereotypes of their class, occupation, status, and so on? Write a personal essay describing your own experience of meeting someone who did or did not look like the stereotype: a president, congressman, mayor; an author, a poet; a woman lawyer; a major league baseball / football / basketball player; an actor or actress.

3. Write an analysis of the character of the narrator of "Our Friend Judith." Base your interpretation solidly on specific passages, incidents, and attitudes in the story.

4. Write for or against one of these two interpretations of Judith's character. Or show why neither is satisfactory:

   a. Judith seems to be cool, intellectual, and respectable, but she's really fiery and passionate; she's hypocritical, since she lives one kind of life in the open and another in secret.

   b. Judith is her own woman. She does not need a man to lean on or depend on, but has her own full life, her profession, and does her own thing in her own way, the way men are praised for doing but women often condemned for doing.

4 SETTING

All stories, like all individuals, are embedded in a context or setting—a time, a place, and a culture. The time can be contemporary ("No One's a Mystery") or historical ("The Cask of Amontillado") or even mythically vague ("The Zebra Storyteller"). It can be very limited, only a few minutes elapsing ("No One's a Mystery") or some years ("Sonny's Blues"). The place can be rather fixed and interior ("The Real Thing") or varied ("Our Friend Judith"). It can be foreign ("The Cask of Amontillado") or American ("My Man Bovanne") or tied to a region ("A Rose for Emily" and the South) or a locale ("Sonny's Blues" and Harlem). The individuals in the stories are embedded in the specific context, and the more we know of the setting, and of the relationship of the character to the setting, the more likely we are to understand the character and the story.

Even in a spare story like "No One's a Mystery" the interaction or interrelation of setting, character, and plot are important and revealing. The eighteen-year-old narrator and Jack, her lover, are in his dirty pickup truck on the highway. His wife approaches in her Cadillac—with the lights on even though it's daytime, a habit he hates. The vehicles they drive and their condition tell you a good deal about Jack, his wife, and their relationship. The significance of Jack's driving a pickup (and of the muddy manure on his boots) is modulated by the almost casually dropped information that they are in Wyoming, in or near Cheyenne.

Place or setting is seldom insignificant or unrelated to a larger cultural context. "The Jewelry" is set in Paris in the late 1870s. Quite naturally, you might say, since it was written by a Frenchman in the early 1880s; he's just writing about his own time and place. True enough, but the cynicism, the somewhat bitter irony of the story set among the bourgeoisie and the bureaucracy, owes a good deal of its tone to the recent (1870–71) defeat of France and the siege and occupation of Paris by the Prussian Bismarck. (France paid Germany a billion dollars in reparations, an unheard-of amount in those days, and did so, to the world's astonishment, in just three years; might this have something to do with the emphasis on money in the story?) The interaction of tone and times, setting and situation, are fused in this story in a way that would scarcely be possible in another context. Money, adultery, and high living are not unknown in our society, but try rewriting this story by setting it in New York.

John Cheever's "The Country Husband" is set in the early to middle 1950s, in my time and close enough to yours so that you know the important things about the period—Elvis, Marilyn, all that. World War II seems distant, but not too distant: a man in a mid-life crisis served in the army during that time. It is set in suburban New York, not too remote or exotic a setting, since it has many of the qualities of the suburbs of any medium-sized to large city in the 1990s. Yet the story is still somewhat of a period piece. The myth of the calm, undisturbed, comfortable good life—peace and plenty in the suburbs after the decades of Depression and war, the milieu of "Leave It to Beaver" and "Father Knows Best"—still prevailed. Airplane accidents and alcoholic fathers and memories of war were banned. And it seemed, at certain times, boring, almost unbearably so. All the excitement, all the romance of life, was gone, kept away by rows of white picket fences. Yes, we have suburbs like Shady Hill, but not many of the wives stay at home like Julia Weed and we no longer believe they are fenced off from the problems and promises of the Big City. The setting of this 1958 story makes of Francis a "weed" and though there are still crabgrass and dandelions in some of our finest neighborhoods, he and history would be difficult to transplant.

"The Country Husband" is, despite its relative modernity, an historical story. Its time, place, and cultural setting interact with its narrative. Some stories are more overtly historical, and their cultural milieu—or the stereotypes associated with it—are more obviously significant than those in Cheever's tale. The protagonist and the plot of "The Cask of Amontillado" are Machiavellian (characterized by subtle or unscrupulous cunning; after the Italian Renaissance politician and writer Niccolò Machiavelli, 1460–1527), and the story is set in Italy during the Renaissance. The Puritan Goodman Brown lives in the reign of King William (1689–1702) in Salem, Massachusetts, where in 1692 the famous witch trials were held—what better place and time for a story whose subject is a witches' meeting and whose theme has to do with man's natural depravity? An *English* "spinster" seems (or seemed) much more prudish and virginal than just any old spinster, Italian lovers more sensual than Anglo-Saxon ones, and in "Our Friend Judith" testing that cultural convention is, virtually, the story.

In some stories setting, even when appropriate and natural, can symbolize whole ways of life or value systems. In "The Lady with the Dog," Yalta with its fruit, seashore, and semi-tropical climate exemplifies a more passionate, pleasurable, exciting life than the cold and cloudy, bureaucratic, intellectually rarefied air and routine of Moscow.

Jing-Mei Woo, the narrator of "A Pair of Tickets," explores the relation of place, cultural heritage, and ethnic identity. Living in San Francisco she had, at fifteen, "vigorously denied that I had any Chinese whatsoever below my skin" (par. 2), but at thirty-six, as she crosses the border from Hong Kong into China, she finds that she is "becoming Chinese." In Guangzhou, however, she discovers that within the vast change of place and cultures, in the modern world, at least among the privileged, there is a homogeneity: though men and women are working without safety belts or helmets on a scaffold made of bamboo held together with plastic strips, the hotel she is taken to "looks like a grander version of the Hyatt Regency." There are "shopping arcades and restaurants all encased in granite and glass," and in the rooms color television sets, a wet bar, Coke Classic, M & M's, Johnnie Walker Red, and so on. Her father's family circumvents her plan to have a Chinese feast and they dine on hamburgers, french fries, apple pie à la mode, delivered by room service. In the modern city of Shanghai, meeting her twin half-sisters for the first time, she finds she is Chinese not because of place or face, but because of "blood." But within this story is another story, her mother's story, with another setting in time and conditions. Fleeing from Kweilin and the advance of the Japanese army in 1944, Jing-Mei's mother was forced by overwhelming circumstances to abandon her twin babies. Jing-Mei can now explain a good deal about her own past, about her mother and their relationship, from the story of her actions and the historical circumstances of the war.

If one of the functions of literature is to engender the sympathetic understanding of others and of other subjective visions of the world, setting—the time, place, and culture in which the fictional characters and action are embedded—is an essential element.

JOHN CHEEVER

The Country Husband

To begin at the beginning, the airplane from Minneapolis in which Francis Weed was traveling East ran into heavy weather. The sky had been a hazy blue, with the clouds below the plane lying so close together that nothing could be seen of the earth. The mist began to form outside the windows, and they flew into a white cloud of such density that it reflected the exhaust fires. The color of the cloud darkened to gray, and the plane began to rock. Francis had been in heavy weather before, but he had never been shaken up so much. The man in the seat beside him pulled a flask out of his pocket and took a drink. Francis smiled at his neighbor, but the man looked away; he wasn't sharing his pain killer with anyone. The plane began to drop and flounder wildly. A child was crying. The air in the cabin was overheated and stale, and Francis' left foot went to sleep. He read a little from a paper book that he had bought at the airport, but the violence of the storm divided his attention. It was black outside the ports. The exhaust fires blazed and shed sparks in the dark, and, inside, the shaded lights, the stuffiness, and the window curtains gave the cabin an atmosphere of intense and misplaced domesticity. Then the light flickered and went out. "You know what I've always wanted to do?" the man beside Francis said suddenly. "I've always wanted to buy a farm in New Hampshire and raise beef cattle." The stewardess announced that they were going to make an emergency landing. All but the children saw in their minds the spreading wings of the Angel of Death. The pilot could be heard singing faintly, "I've got sixpence, jolly, jolly sixpence. I've got sixpence to last me all my life . . ."[1] There was no other sound.

The loud groaning of the hydraulic valves swallowed up the pilot's song, and there was a shrieking high in the air, like automobile brakes, and the plane hit flat on its belly in a cornfield and shook them so violently that an old man up forward howled, "Me kidneys! Me kidneys!" The stewardess flung open the door, and someone opened an emergency door at the back, letting in the sweet noise of their continuing mortality—the idle splash and smell of a heavy rain. Anxious for their lives, they filed out of the doors and scattered over the cornfield in all directions, praying that the thread would hold. It did. Nothing happened. When it was clear that the plane would not burn or explode, the crew and the steward-ess gathered the passengers together and led them to the shelter of a barn. They were not far from Philadelphia, and in a little while a string of taxis took them into the city. "It's just like the Marne,"[2] someone said, but there was surprisingly little relaxation of that suspiciousness with which many Americans regard their fellow travelers.

In Philadelphia, Francis Weed got a train to New York. At the end of that journey, he crossed the city and caught just as it was about to pull out the commuting train that he took five nights a week to his home in Shady Hill.

He sat with Trace Bearden. "You know, I was in that plane that just crashed outside Philadelphia," he said. "We came down in a field . . ." He had traveled faster than the newspapers or the rain, and the weather in New York was sunny and mild. It was a day in late September, as fragrant and shapely as an apple. Trace listened to the story, but how could he get excited? Francis had no powers that would let him re-create a brush with death—particularly in the atmosphere of a commuting train, journeying through a sunny countryside where already, in the slum gardens, there were signs of harvest. Trace picked up his newspaper, and Francis was left alone with his thoughts. He said good night to Trace on the platform at Shady Hill and drove in his secondhand Volkswagen up to the Blen-hollow neighborhood, where he lived.

The Weeds' Dutch Colonial house was larger than it appeared to be from the driveway. The living room was spacious and divided like Gaul,[3] into three parts. Around an ell to the left as one entered from the vestibule was the long table, laid for six, with candles and a bowl of fruit in the center. The sounds and

1. Song popular with Allied troops in World War II.   2. On September 8, 1914, over 1000 Paris taxicabs were requisitioned to move troops to the Marne River to halt the encircling Germans.   3. Ancient France (Gaul) is so described by Julius Caesar in *The Gallic War*.

smells that came from the open kitchen door were appetizing, for Julia Weed was a good cook. The largest part of the living room centered on a fireplace. On the right were some bookshelves and a piano. The room was polished and tranquil, and from the windows that opened to the west there was some late-summer sunlight, brilliant and as clear as water. Nothing here was neglected; nothing had not been burnished. It was not the kind of household where, after prying open a stuck cigarette box, you would find an old shirt button and a tarnished nickel. The hearth was swept, the roses on the piano were reflected in the polish of the broad top, and there was an album of Schubert waltzes on the rack. Louisa Weed, a pretty girl of nine, was looking out the western windows. Her young brother Henry was standing beside her. Her still younger brother, Toby, was studying the figures of some tonsured monks drinking beer on the polished brass of the woodbox. Francis, taking off his hat and putting down his paper, was not consciously pleased with the scene; he was not that reflective. It was his element, his creation, and he returned to it with that sense of lightness and strength with which any creature returns to his home. "Hi, everybody," he said. "The plane from Minneapolis . . ."

Nine times out of ten, Francis would be greeted with affection, but tonight the children are absorbed in their own antagonisms. Francis had not finished his sentence about the plane crash before Henry plants a kick in Louisa's behind. Louisa swings around, saying, "*Damn you!*" Francis makes the mistake of scolding Louisa for bad language before he punishes Henry. Now Louisa turns on her father and accuses him of favoritism. Henry is always right; she is persecuted and lonely; her lot is hopeless. Francis turns to his son, but the son has justification for the kick—she hit him first; she hit him on the ear, which is dangerous. Louisa agrees with this passionately. She hit him on the ear, and she *meant* to hit him on the ear, because he messed up her china collection. Henry says that this is a lie. Little Toby turns away from the woodbox to throw in some evidence for Louisa. Henry claps his hand over little Toby's mouth. Francis separates the two boys but accidentally pushes Toby into the woodbox. Toby begins to cry. Louisa is already crying. Just then, Julia Weed comes into that part of the room where the table is laid. She is a pretty, intelligent woman, and the white in her hair is premature. She does not seem to notice the fracas. "Hello, darling," she says serenely to Francis. "Wash your hands, everyone. Dinner is ready." She strikes a match and lights the six candles in this vale of tears.[4]

This simple announcement, like the war cries of the Scottish chieftains, only refreshes the ferocity of the combatants. Louisa gives Henry a blow on the shoulder. Henry, although he seldom cries, has pitched nine innings and is tired. He bursts into tears. Little Toby discovers a splinter in his hand and begins to howl. Francis says loudly that he has been in a plane crash and that he is tired. Julia appears again from the kitchen and, still ignoring the chaos, asks Francis to go upstairs and tell Helen that everything is ready. Francis is happy to go; it is like getting back to headquarters company.[5] He is planning to tell his oldest daughter about the airplane crash, but Helen is lying on her bed reading a *True Romance*

---

4. Common figurative reference to earthly life (vale is valley), though here the tears are literal.
5. That is, like escaping from combat to relative safety behind the lines.

magazine, and the first thing Francis does is to take the magazine from her hand and remind Helen that he has forbidden her to buy it. She did not buy it, Helen replies. It was given to her by her best friend, Bessie Black. Everybody reads *True Romance*. Bessie Black's father reads *True Romance*. There isn't a girl in Helen's class who doesn't read *True Romance*. Francis expresses his detestation of the magazine and then tells her that dinner is ready—although from the sounds downstairs it doesn't seem so. Helen follows him down the stairs. Julia has seated herself in the candlelight and spread a napkin over her lap. Neither Louisa nor Henry has come to the table. Little Toby is still howling, lying face down on the floor. Francis speaks to him gently: "Daddy was in a plane crash this afternoon, Toby. Don't you want to hear about it?" Toby goes on crying. "If you don't come to the table now, Toby," Francis says, "I'll have to send you to bed without any supper." The little boy rises, gives him a cutting look, flies up the stairs to his bedroom, and slams the door. "Oh, dear," Julia says, and starts to go after him. Francis says that she will spoil him. Julia says that Toby is ten pounds underweight and has to be encouraged to eat. Winter is coming, and he will spend the cold months in bed unless he has his dinner. Julia goes upstairs. Francis sits down at the table with Helen. Helen is suffering from the dismal feeling of having read too intently on a fine day, and she gives her father and the room a jaded look. She doesn't understand about the plane crash, because there wasn't a drop of rain in Shady Hill.

Julia returns with Toby, and they all sit down and are served. "Do I have to look at that big, fat slob?" Henry says, of Louisa. Everybody but Toby enters into this skirmish, and it rages up and down the table for five minutes. Toward the end, Henry puts his napkin over his head and, trying to eat that way, spills spinach all over his shirt. Francis asks Julia if the children couldn't have their dinner earlier. Julia's guns are loaded for this. She can't cook two dinners and lay two tables. She paints with lightning strokes that panorama of drudgery in which her youth, her beauty, and her wit have been lost. Francis says that he must be understood; he was nearly killed in an airplane crash, and he doesn't like to come home every night to a battlefield. Now Julia is deeply concerned. Her voice trembles. He doesn't come home every night to a battlefield. The accusation is stupid and mean. Everything was tranquil until he arrived. She stops speaking, puts down her knife and fork, and looks into her plate as if it is a gulf. She begins to cry. "Poor Mummy!" Toby says, and when Julia gets up from the table, drying her tears with a napkin, Toby goes to her side. "Poor Mummy," he says. "Poor Mummy!" And they climb the stairs together. The other children drift away from the battlefield, and Francis goes into the back garden for a cigarette and some air.

It was a pleasant garden, with walks and flower beds and places to sit. The sunset had nearly burned out, but there was still plenty of light. Put into a thoughtful mood by the crash and the battle, Francis listened to the evening sounds of Shady Hill. "Varmints! Rascals!" old Mr. Nixon shouted to the squirrels in his bird-feeding station. "Avaunt and quit my sight!" A door slammed. Someone was cutting grass. Then Donald Goslin, who lived at the corner, began to play the "Moonlight Sonata."[6] He did this nearly every night. He threw the tempo out the window and played it *rubato*[7] from beginning to end, like an outpouring of tearful petulance, lonesomeness, and self-pity—of everything it was Beethoven's greatness not to know. The music rang up and down the street beneath the trees like an appeal for love, for tenderness, aimed at some lovely housemaid—some fresh-faced, homesick girl from Galway, looking at old snapshots in her third-floor room. "Here, Jupiter, here, Jupiter," Francis called to the Mercers' retriever. Jupiter crashed through the tomato vines with the remains of a felt hat in his mouth.

Jupiter was an anomaly. His retrieving instincts and his high spirits were out of place in Shady Hill. He was as black as coal, with a long, alert, intelligent, rakehell face. His eyes gleamed with mischief, and he held his head high. It was the fierce, heavily collared dog's head that appears in heraldry, in tapestry, and that used to appear on umbrella handles and walking sticks. Jupiter went where he pleased, ransacking wastebaskets, clotheslines, garbage pails, and shoe bags. He broke up garden parties and tennis matches, and got mixed up in the processional at Christ Church on Sunday, barking at the men in red dresses.[8] He crashed through old Mr. Nixon's rose garden two or three times a day, cutting a wide swath through the Condesa de Sastagos,[9] and as soon as Donald Goslin lighted his barbecue fire on Thursday nights, Jupiter would get the scent. Nothing the Goslins did could drive him away. Sticks and stones and rude commands only moved him to the edge of the terrace, where he remained, with his gallant and heraldic muzzle, waiting for Donald Goslin to turn his back and reach for the salt. Then he would spring onto the terrace, lift the steak lightly off the fire, and run away with the Goslins' dinner. Jupiter's days were numbered. The Wrightsons' German gardener or the Farquarsons' cook would soon poison him. Even old Mr. Nixon might put some arsenic in the garbage that Jupiter loved. "Here, Jupiter, Jupiter!" Francis called, but the dog pranced off, shaking the hat in his white teeth. Looking at the windows of his house, Francis saw that Julia had come down and was blowing out the candles.

Julia and Francis Weed went out a great deal. Julia was well liked and gregarious, and her love of parties sprang from a most natural dread of chaos and loneliness. She went through the morning mail with real anxiety, looking for invitations, and she usually found some, but she was insatiable, and if she had gone out seven nights a week, it would not have cured her of a reflective look—the look of someone who hears distant music—for she would always suppose that there was a more brilliant party somewhere else. Francis limited her to two week-night parties, putting a flexible interpretation on Friday, and rode through the weekend like a dory in a gale. The day after the airplane crash, the Weeds were to have dinner with the Farquarsons.

Francis got home late from town, and Julia got the sitter while he dressed, and then hurried him out of the house. The party was small and pleasant, and Francis settled down to enjoy himself. A new maid passed the drinks. Her hair

6. Beethoven's *Sonata Quasi una Fantasia* (1802), a famous and frequently sentimentalized piano composition.   7. With intentional deviations from strict tempo.   8. Probably the choir. 9. Rather uncommon yellow and red roses difficult to grow.

was dark, and her face was round and pale and seemed familiar to Francis. He had not developed his memory as a sentimental faculty. Wood smoke, lilac, and other such perfumes did not stir him, and his memory was something like his appendix—a vestigial repository. It was not his limitation at all to be unable to escape the past; it was perhaps his limitation that he had escaped it so successfully. He might have seen the maid at other parties, he might have seen her taking a walk on Sunday afternoons, but in either case he would not be searching his memory now. Her face was, in a wonderful way, a moon face—Norman or Irish—but it was not beautiful enough to account for his feeling that he had seen her before, in circumstances that he ought to be able to remember. He asked Nellie Farquarson who she was. Nellie said that the maid had come through an agency, and that her home was Trénon, in Normandy—a small place with a church and a restaurant that Nellie had once visited. While Nellie talked on about her travels abroad, Francis realized where he had seen the woman before. It had been at the end of the war. He had left a replacement depot with some other men and taken a three-day pass in Trénon. On their second day, they had walked out to a crossroads to see the public chastisement of a young woman who had lived with the German commandant during the Occupation.

It was a cool morning in the fall. The sky was overcast, and poured down onto the dirt crossroads a very discouraging light. They were on high land and could see how like one another the shapes of the clouds and the hills were as they stretched off toward the sea. The prisoner arrived sitting on a three-legged stool in a farm cart. She stood by the cart while the Mayor read the accusation and the sentence. Her head was bent and her face was set in that empty half smile behind which the whipped soul is suspended. When the Mayor was finished, she undid her hair and let it fall across her back. A little man with a gray mustache cut off her hair with shears and dropped it on the ground. Then, with a bowl of soapy water and a straight razor, he shaved her skull clean. A woman approached and began to undo the fastenings of her clothes, but the prisoner pushed her aside and undressed herself. When she pulled her chemise over her head and threw it on the ground, she was naked. The women jeered; the men were still. There was no change in the falseness or the plaintiveness of the prisoner's smile. The cold wind made her white skin rough and hardened the nipples of her breasts. The jeering ended gradually, put down by the recognition of their common humanity. One woman spat on her, but some inviolable grandeur in her nakedness lasted through the ordeal. When the crowd was quiet, she turned— she had begun to cry—and, with nothing on but a pair of worn black shoes and stockings, walked down the dirt road alone away from the village. The round white face had aged a little, but there was no question but that the maid who passed his cocktails and later served Francis his dinner was the woman who had been punished at the crossroads.

The war seemed now so distant and that world where the cost of partisanship had been death or torture so long ago. Francis had lost track of the men who had been with him in Vésey. He could not count on Julia's discretion. He could not tell anyone. And if he had told the story now, at the dinner table, it would have been a social as well as a human error. The people in the Farquarsons' living room seemed united in their tacit claim that there had been no past, no war—that there was no danger or trouble in the world. In the recorded history of human arrangements, this extraordinary meeting would have fallen into place, but the atmosphere of Shady Hill made the memory unseemly and impolite. The prisoner withdrew after passing the coffee, but the encounter left Francis feeling languid; it had opened his memory and his senses, and left them dilated. Julia went into the house. Francis stayed in the car to take the sitter home.

Expecting to see Mrs. Henlein, the old lady who usually stayed with the children, he was surprised when a young girl opened the door and came out onto the lighted stoop. She stayed in the light to count her textbooks. She was frowning and beautiful. Now, the world is full of beautiful young girls, but Francis saw here the difference between beauty and perfection. All those endearing flaws, moles, birthmarks, and healed wounds were missing, and he experienced in his consciousness that moment when music breaks glass, and felt a pang of recognition as strange, deep and wonderful as anything in his life. It hung from her frown, from an impalpable darkness in her face—a look that impressed him as a direct appeal for love. When she had counted her books, she came down the steps and opened the car door. In the light, he saw that her cheeks were wet. She got in and shut the door.

"You're new," Francis said.

"Yes. Mrs. Henlein is sick. I'm Anne Murchison."

"Did the children give you any trouble?"

"Oh, no, no." She turned and smiled at him unhappily in the dim dashboard light. Her light hair caught on the collar of her jacket, and she shook her head to set it loose.

"You've been crying."

"Yes."

"I hope it was nothing that happened in our house."

"No, no, it was nothing that happened in your house." Her voice was bleak. "It's no secret. Everybody in the village knows. Daddy's an alcoholic, and he just called me from some saloon and gave me a piece of his mind. He thinks I'm immoral. He called just before Mrs. Weed came back."

"I'm sorry."

"Oh, *Lord*!" She gasped and began to cry. She turned toward Francis, and he took her in his arms and let her cry on his shoulder. She shook in his embrace, and this movement accentuated his sense of the fineness of her flesh and bone. The layers of their clothing felt thin, and when her shuddering began to diminish, it was so much like a paroxysm of love that Francis lost his head and pulled her roughly against him. She drew away. "I live on Belleview Avenue," she said. "You go down Lansing Street to the railroad bridge."

"All right." He started the car.

"You turn left at that traffic light. . . . Now you turn right here and go straight on toward the tracks."

The road Francis took brought him out of his own neighborhood, across the tracks, and toward the river, to a street where the near-poor lived, in houses whose peaked gables and trimmings of wooden lace conveyed the purest feelings of pride and romance, although the houses themselves could not have offered much privacy or comfort, they were all so small. The street was dark, and, stirred by the grace and beauty of the troubled girl, he seemed, in turning into it, to have come into the deepest part of some submerged memory. In the distance, he saw a porch light burning. It was the only one, and she said that the house with the light was where she lived. When he stopped the car, he could see beyond the porch light into a dimly lighted hallway with an old-fashioned clothes tree. "Well, here we are," he said, conscious that a young man would have said something different.

She did not move her hands from the books, where they were folded, and she turned and faced him. There were tears of lust in his eyes. Determinedly—not sadly—he opened the door on his side and walked around to open hers. He took her free hand, letting his fingers in between hers, climbed at her side the two concrete steps, and went up a narrow walk through a front garden where dahlias, marigolds, and roses—things that had withstood the light frosts—still bloomed, and made a bittersweet smell in the night air. At the steps, she freed her hand and then turned and kissed him swiftly. Then she crossed the porch and shut the door. The porch light went out, then the light in the hall. A second later, a light went on upstairs at the side of the house, shining into a tree that was still covered with leaves. It took her only a few minutes to undress and get into bed, and then the house was dark.

30   Julia was asleep when Francis got home. He opened a second window and got into bed to shut his eyes on that night, but as soon as they were shut—as soon as he had dropped off to sleep—the girl entered his mind, moving with perfect freedom through its shut doors and filling chamber after chamber with her light, her perfume, and the music of her voice. He was crossing the Atlantic with her on the old *Mauretania*[1] and, later, living with her in Paris. When he woke from his dream, he got up and smoked a cigarette at the open window. Getting back into bed, he cast around in his mind for something he desired to do that would injure no one, and he thought of skiing. Up through the dimness in his mind rose the image of a mountain deep in snow. It was late in the day. Wherever his eyes looked, he saw broad and heartening things. Over his shoulder, there was a snow-filled valley, rising into wooded hills where the trees dimmed the whiteness like a sparse coat of hair. The cold deadened all sound but the loud, iron clanking of the lift machinery. The light on the trails was blue, and it was harder than it had been a minute or two earlier to pick the turns, harder to judge—now that the snow was all deep blue—the crust, the ice, the bare spots, and the deep piles of dry powder. Down the mountain he swung, matching his speed against the contours of a slope that had been formed in the first ice age, seeking with ardor some simplicity of feeling and circumstance. Night fell then, and he drank a Martini with some old friend in a dirty country bar.

In the morning, Francis' snow-covered mountain was gone, and he was left with his vivid memories of Paris and the *Mauretania*. He had been bitten gravely.

---

1. The original *Mauretania* (1907–1935), sister ship of the *Lusitania*, which was sunk by the Germans in 1915, was the most famous transatlantic liner of its day.

He washed his body, shaved his jaws, drank his coffee, and missed the seventy-thirty-one. The train pulled out just as he brought his car to the station, and the longing he felt for the coaches as they drew stubbornly away from him reminded him of the humors of love. He waited for the eight-two, on what was now an empty platform. It was a clear morning; the morning seemed thrown like a gleaming bridge of light over his mixed affairs. His spirits were feverish and high. The image of the girl seemed to put him into a relationship to the world that was mysterious and enthralling. Cars were beginning to fill up the parking lot, and he noticed that those that had driven down from the high land above Shady Hill were white with hoarfrost. This first clear sign of autumn thrilled him. An express train—a night train from Buffalo or Albany—came down the tracks between the platforms, and he saw that the roofs of the foremost cars were covered with a skin of ice. Struck by the miraculous physicalness of everything, he smiled at the passengers in the dining car, who could be seen eating eggs and wiping their mouths with napkins as they traveled. The sleeping-car compartments, with their soiled bed linen, trailed through the fresh morning like a string of rooming-house windows. Then he saw an extraordinary thing; at one of the bedroom windows sat an unclothed woman of exceptional beauty, combing her golden hair. She passed like an apparition through Shady Hill, combing and combing her hair, and Francis followed her with his eyes until she was out of sight. Then old Mrs. Wrightson joined him on the platform and began to talk.

"Well, I guess you must be surprised to see me here the third morning in a row," she said, "but because of my window curtains I'm becoming a regular commuter. The curtains I bought on Monday I returned on Tuesday, and the curtains I bought Tuesday I'm returning today. On Monday, I got exactly what I wanted—it's a wool tapestry with roses and birds—but when I got them home, I found they were the wrong length. Well, I exchanged them yesterday, and when I got them home, I found they were still the wrong length. Now I'm praying to high heaven that the decorator will have them in the right length, because you know my house, you *know* my living-room windows, and you can imagine what a problem they present. I don't know what to do with them."

"I know what to do with them," Francis said.

"What?"

"Paint them black on the inside, and shut up."

There was a gasp from Mrs. Wrightson, and Francis looked down at her to be sure that she knew he meant to be rude. She turned and walked away from him, so damaged in spirit that she limped. A wonderful feeling enveloped him, as if light were being shaken about him, and he thought again of Venus combing and combing her hair as she drifted through the Bronx. The realization of how many years had passed since he had enjoyed being deliberately impolite sobered him. Among his friends and neighbors, there were brilliant and gifted people—he saw that—but many of them, also, were bores and fools, and he had made the mistake of listening to them all with equal attention. He had confused a lack of discrimination with Christian love, and the confusion seemed general and destructive. He was grateful to the girl for this bracing sensation of independence. Birds were singing—cardinals and the last of the robins. The sky shone

35

like enamel. Even the smell of ink from his morning paper honed his appetite for life, and the world that was spread out around him was plainly a paradise.

If Francis had believed in some hierarchy of love—in spirits armed with hunting bows, in the capriciousness of Venus and Eros[2]—or even in magical potions, philters, and stews, in scapulae and quarters of the moon,[3] it might have explained his susceptibility and his feverish high spirits. The autumnal loves of middle age are well publicized, and he guessed that he was face to face with one of these, but there was not a trace of autumn in what he felt. He wanted to sport in the green woods, scratch where he itched, and drink from the same cup.

His secretary, Miss Rainey, was late that morning—she went to a psychiatrist three mornings a week—and when she came in, Francis wondered what advice a psychiatrist would have for him. But the girl promised to bring back into his life something like the sound of music. The realization that this music might lead him straight to a trial for statutory rape at the country courthouse collapsed his happiness. The photograph of his four children laughing into the camera on the beach at Gay Head reproached him. On the letterhead of his firm there was a drawing of the Laocoön,[4] and the figure of the priest and his sons in the coils of the snake appeared to him to have the deepest meaning.

He had lunch with Pinky Trabert. At a conversational level, the mores of his friends were robust and elastic, but he knew that the moral card house would come down on them all—on Julia and the children as well—if he got caught taking advantage of a baby-sitter. Looking back over the recent history of Shady Hill for some precedent, he found there was none. There was no turpitude; there had not been a divorce since he lived there; there had not even been a breath of scandal. Things seemed arranged with more propriety even than in the Kingdom of Heaven. After leaving Pinky, Francis went to a jeweler's and bought the girl a bracelet. How happy this clandestine purchase made him, how stuffy and comical the jeweler's clerks seemed, how sweet the women who passed at his back smelled! On Fifth Avenue, passing Atlas with his shoulders bent under the weight of the world,[5] Francis thought of the strenuousness of containing his physicalness within the patterns he had chosen.

40 He did not know when he would see the girl next. He had the bracelet in his inside pocket when he got home. Opening the door of his house, he found her in the hall. Her back was to him, and she turned when she heard the door close. Her smile was open and loving. Her perfection stunned him like a fine day—a day after a thunderstorm. He seized her and covered her lips with his, and she struggled but she did not have to struggle for long, because just then little Gertrude Flannery appeared from somewhere and said, "Oh, Mr. Weed . . ."

Gertrude was a stray. She had been born with a taste for exploration, and she

---

2. The Roman name for the goddess of love (Greek *Aphrodite*) and the Greek name for her son (Roman *Cupid*).   3. Love-inducing and predictive magic; *scapulae* are shoulderblades or bones of the back.   4. Famous Greek statue, described here, now in the Vatican museum; the "meaning" for Weed seems to reside in the physical struggle, not in the legend (in which the priest and his sons were punished for warning the Trojans about the wooden horse).   5. In Greek legend the Titan Atlas supported the heavens on his shoulders but has come to be depicted as bearing the globe; the statue is at Rockefeller Center.

did not have it in her to center her life with her affectionate parents. People who did not know the Flannerys concluded from Gertrude's behavior that she was the child of a bitterly divided family, where drunken quarrels were the rule. This was not true. The fact that little Gertrude's clothing was ragged and thin was her own triumph over her mother's struggle to dress her warmly and neatly. Garrulous, skinny, and unwashed, she drifted from house to house around the Blenhollow neighborhood, forming and breaking alliances based on an attachment to babies, animals, children her own age, adolescents, and sometimes adults. Opening your front door in the morning, you would find Gertrude sitting on your stoop. Going into the bathroom to shave, you would find Gertrude using the toilet. Looking into your son's crib, you would find it empty, and, looking further, you would find that Gertrude had pushed him in his baby carriage into the next village. She was helpful, pervasive, honest, hungry, and loyal. She never went home of her own choice. When the time to go arrived, she was indifferent to all its signs. "Go home, Gertrude," people could be heard saying in one house or another, night after night. "Go home, Gertrude. It's time for you to go home now, Gertrude." "You had better go home and get your supper, Gertrude." "I told you to go home twenty minutes ago, Gertrude." "Your mother will be worrying about you, Gertrude." "Go home, Gertrude, go home."

There are times when the lines around the human eye seem like shelves of eroded stone and when the staring eye itself strikes us with such a wilderness of animal feeling that we are at a loss. The look Francis gave the little girl was ugly and queer, and it frightened her. He reached into his pockets—his hands were shaking—and took out a quarter. "Go home, Gertrude, go home, and don't tell anyone, Gertrude. Don't—" He choked and ran into the living room as Julia called down to him from upstairs to hurry and dress.

The thought that he would drive Anne Murchison home later that night ran like a golden thread through the events of the party that Francis and Julia went to, and he laughed uproariously at dull jokes, dried a tear when Mabel Mercer told him about the death of her kitten, and stretched, yawned, sighed, and grunted like any other man with a rendezvous at the back of his mind. The bracelet was in his pocket. As he sat talking, the smell of grass was in his nose, and he was wondering where he would park the car. Nobody lived in the old Parker mansion, and the driveway was used as a lovers' lane. Townsend Street was a dead end, and he could park there, beyond the last house. The old lane that used to connect Elm Street to the riverbanks was overgrown, but he had walked there with his children, and he could drive his car deep enough into the brushwoods to be concealed.

The Weeds were the last to leave the party, and their host and hostess spoke of their own married happiness while they all four stood in the hallway saying good night. "She's my girl," their host said, squeezing his wife. "She's my blue sky. After sixteen years, I still bite her shoulders. She makes me feel like Hannibal crossing the Alps."[6]

The Weeds drove home in silence. Francis brought the car up the driveway

45

6. The Carthaginian general (274–183 B.C.) attacked the Romans from the rear by crossing the Alps, considered impregnable, with the use of elephants.

and sat still, with the motor running. "You can put the car in the garage," Julia said as she got out. "I told the Murchison girl she could leave at eleven. Someone drove her home." She shut the door, and Francis sat in the dark. He would be spared nothing then, it seemed, that a fool was not spared: ravening lewdness, jealousy, this hurt to his feelings that put tears in his eyes, even scorn—for he could see clearly the image he now presented, his arms spread over the steering wheel and his head buried in them for love.

Francis had been a dedicated Boy Scout when he was young, and, remembering the precepts of his youth, he left his office early the next afternoon and played some round-robin squash, but, with his body toned up by exercise and a shower, he realized that he might better have stayed at his desk. It was a frosty night when he got home. The air smelled sharply of change. When he stepped into the house, he sensed an unusual stir. The children were in their best clothes, and when Julia came down, she was wearing a lavender dress and her diamond sunburst. She explained the stir: Mr. Hubber was coming at seven to take their photograph for the Christmas card. She had put out Francis' blue suit and a tie with some color in it, because the picture was going to be in color this year. Julia was lighthearted at the thought of being photographed for Christmas. It was the kind of ceremony she enjoyed.

Francis went upstairs to change his clothes. He was tired from the day's work and tired with longing, and sitting on the edge of the bed had the effect of deepening his weariness. He thought of Anne Murchison, and the physical need to express himself, instead of being restrained by the pink lamps of Julia's dressing table, engulfed him. He went to Julia's desk, took a piece of writing paper, and began to write on it. "Dear Anne, I love you, I love you, I love you . . ." No one would see the letter, and he used no restraint. He used phrases like "heavenly bliss," and "love nest." He salivated, sighed, and trembled. When Julia called him to come down, the abyss between his fantasy and the practical world opened so wide that he felt it affected the muscles of his heart.

Julia and the children were on the stoop, and the photographer and his assistant had set up a double battery of floodlights to show the family and the architectural beauty of the entrance to their house. People who had come home on a late train slowed their cars to see the Weeds being photographed for their Christmas card. A few waved and called to the family. It took half an hour of smiling and wetting their lips before Mr. Hubber was satisfied. The heat of the lights made an unfresh smell in the frosty air, and when they were turned off, they lingered on the retina of Francis' eyes.

Later that night, while Francis and Julia were drinking their coffee in the living room, the doorbell rang. Julia answered the door and let in Clayton Thomas. He had come to pay for some theatre tickets that she had given his mother some time ago, and that Helen Thomas had scrupulously insisted on paying for, though Julia had asked her not to. Julia invited him in to have a cup of coffee. "I won't have any coffee," Clayton said, "but I will come in for a minute." He followed her into the living room, said good evening to Francis, and sat awkwardly in a chair.

Clayton's father had been killed in the war, and the young man's fatherless- 50
ness surrounded him like an element. This may have been conspicuous in Shady
Hill because the Thomases were the only family that lacked a piece; all the other
marriages were intact and productive. Clayton was in his second or third year of
college, and he and his mother lived alone in a large house, which she hoped to
sell. Clayton had once made some trouble. Years ago, he had stolen some money
and run away; he had got to California before they caught up with him. He was
tall and homely, wore hornrimmed glasses, and spoke in a deep voice.

"When do you go back to college, Clayton?" Francis asked.

"I'm not going back," Clayton said. "Mother doesn't have the money, and
there's no sense in all this pretense. I'm going to get a job, and if we sell the
house, we'll take an apartment in New York."

"Won't you miss Shady Hill?" Julia asked.

"No," Clayton said. "I don't like it."

"Why not?" Francis asked. 55

"Well, there's a lot here I don't approve of," Clayton said gravely. "Things
like the club dances. Last Saturday night, I looked in toward the end and saw
Mr. Granner trying to put Mrs. Minot into the trophy case. They were both
drunk. I disapprove of so much drinking."

"It was Saturday night," Francis said.

"And all the dovecotes are phony," Clayton said. "And the way people clutter up their lives. I've thought about it a lot, and what seems to me to be really
wrong with Shady Hill is that it doesn't have any future. So much energy is spent
in perpetuating the place—in keeping out undesirables, and so forth—that the
only idea of the future anyone has is just more and more commuting trains and
more parties. I don't think that's healthy. I think people ought to be able to
dream big dreams about the future. I think people ought to be able to dream
great dreams."

"It's too bad you couldn't continue with college," Julia said.

"I want to go to divinity school," Clayton said. 60

"What's your church?" Francis asked.

"Unitarian, Theosophist, Transcendentalist, Humanist,"[7] Clayton said.

"Wasn't Emerson a transcendentalist?" Julia asked.

"I mean the English transcendentalists," Clayton said. "All the American
transcendentalists were goops."

"What kind of job do you expect to get?" Francis asked. 65

"Well, I'd like to work for a publisher," Clayton said, "but everyone tells me
there's nothing doing. But it's the kind of thing I'm interested in. I'm writing a
long verse play about good and evil. Uncle Charlie might get me into a bank,
and that would be good for me. I need the discipline. I have a long way to go in
forming my character. I have some terrible habits. I talk too much. I think I
ought to take vows of silence. I ought to try not to speak for a week, and discipline

7. All are deviations from orthodox Christianity and tend to be more man- than God-oriented,
though their differences hardly seem reconcilable; the American Transcendentalists (see below) tended
to change the emphasis from the study of thought to belief in "intuition."

myself. I've thought of making a retreat at one of the Episcopalian monasteries, but I don't like Trinitarianism."

"Do you have any girl friends?" Francis asked.

"I'm engaged to be married," Clayton said. "Of course, I'm not old enough or rich enough to have my engagement observed or respected or anything, but I bought a simulated emerald for Anne Murchison with the money I made cutting lawns this summer. We're going to be married as soon as she finishes school."

Francis recoiled at the mention of the girl's name. Then a dingy light seemed to emanate from his spirit, showing everything—Julia, the boy, the chairs—in their true colorlessness. It was like a bitter turn of the weather.

70   "We're going to have a large family," Clayton said. "Her father's a terrible rummy, and I've had my hard times, and we want to have lots of children. Oh, she's wonderful, Mr. and Mrs. Weed, and we have so much in common. We like all the same things. We sent out the same Christmas card last year without planning it, and we both have an allergy to tomatoes, and our eyebrows grow together in the middle. Well, goodnight."

Julia went to the door with him. When she returned, Francis said that Clayton was lazy, irresponsible, affected, and smelly. Julia said that Francis seemed to be getting intolerant; the Thomas boy was young and should be given a chance. Julia had noticed other cases where Francis had been short-tempered. "Mrs. Wrightson has asked everyone in Shady Hill to her anniversary party but us," she said.

"I'm sorry, Julia."

"Do you know why they didn't ask us?"

"Why?"

75   "Because you insulted Mrs. Wrightson."

"Then you know about it?"

"June Masterson told me. She was standing behind you."

Julia walked in front of the sofa with a small step that expressed, Francis knew, a feeling of anger.

"I did insult Mrs. Wrightson, Julia, and I meant to. I've never liked her parties, and I'm glad she's dropped us."

80   "What about Helen?"

"How does Helen come into this?"

"Mrs. Wrightson's the one who decides who goes to the assemblies."

"You mean she can keep Helen from going to the dances?"

"Yes."

85   "I hadn't thought of that."

"Oh. I knew you hadn't thought of it," Julia cried, thrusting hiltdeep into this chink of his armor. "And it makes me furious to see this kind of stupid thoughtlessness wreck everyone's happiness."

"I don't think I've wrecked anyone's happiness."

"Mrs. Wrightson runs Shady Hill and has run it for the last forty years. I don't know what makes you think that in a community like this you can indulge every impulse you have to be insulting, vulgar, and offensive."

"I have very good manners," Francis said, trying to give the evening a turn toward the light.

"Damn you, Francis Weed!" Julia cried, and the spit of her words struck 90
him in the face. "I've worked hard for the social position we enjoy in this place, and I won't stand by and see you wreck it. You must have understood when you settled here that you couldn't expect to live like a bear in a cave."

"I've got to express my likes and dislikes."

"You can conceal your dislikes. You don't have to meet everything head on, like a child. Unless you're anxious to be a social leper. It's no accident that we get asked out a great deal! It's no accident that Helen has so many friends. How would you like to spend your Saturday nights at the movies? How would you like to spend your Sunday raking up dead leaves? How would you like it if your daughter spent the assembly nights sitting at her window, listening to the music from the club? How would you like it—" He did something then that was, after all, not so unaccountable, since her words seemed to raise up between them a wall so deadening that he gagged. He struck her full in the face. She staggered and then, a moment later, seemed composed. She went up the stairs to their room. She didn't slam the door. When Francis followed, a few minutes later, he found her packing a suitcase.

"Julia, I'm very sorry."

"It doesn't matter," she said. She was crying.

"Where do you think you're going?" 95

"I don't know. I just looked at a timetable. There's an eleven-sixteen into New York. I'll take that."

"You can't go, Julia."

"I can't stay. I know that."

"I'm sorry about Mrs. Wrightson, Julia, and I'm—"

"It doesn't matter about Mrs. Wrightson. That isn't the trouble." 100

"What is the trouble?"

"You don't love me."

"I do love you, Julia."

"No, you don't."

"Julia, I do love you, and I would like to be as we were—sweet and bawdy 105
and dark—but now there are so many people."

"You hate me."

"I don't hate you, Julia."

"You have no idea of how much you hate me. I think it's subconscious. You don't realize the cruel things you've done."

"What cruel things, Julia?"

"The cruel acts your subconscious drives you to in order to express your 110
hatred of me."

"What, Julia?"

"I've never complained."

"Tell me."

"You don't know what you're doing."

115   "Tell me."

"Your clothes."

"What do you mean?"

"I mean the way you leave your dirty clothes around in order to express your subconscious hatred of me."

"I don't understand."

120   "I mean your dirty socks and your dirty pajamas and your dirty underwear and your dirty shirts!" She rose from kneeling by the suitcase and faced him, her eyes blazing and her voice ringing with emotion. "I'm talking about the fact that you've never learned to hang up anything. You just leave your clothes all over the floor where they drop, in order to humiliate me. You do it on purpose!" She fell on the bed, sobbing.

"Julia, darling!" he said, but when she felt his hand on her shoulder she got up.

"Leave me alone," she said. "I have to go." She brushed past him to the closet and came back with a dress. "I'm not taking any of the things you've given me," she said. "I'm leaving my pearls and the fur jacket."

"Oh, Julia!" Her figure, so helpless in its self-deceptions, bent over the suitcase made him nearly sick with pity. She did not understand how desolate her life would be without him. She didn't understand the hours that working women have to keep. She didn't understand that most of her friendships existed within the framework of their marriage, and that without this she would find herself alone. She didn't understand about travel, about hotels, about money. "Julia, I can't let you go! What you don't understand, Julia, is that you've come to be dependent on me."

She tossed her head back and covered her face with her hands. "Did you say that *I* was dependent on *you?*" she asked. "Is that what you said? And who is it that tells you what time to get up in the morning and when to go to bed at night? Who is it that prepares your meals and picks up your dirty clothes and invites your friends to dinner? If it weren't for me, your neckties would be greasy and your clothing would be full of moth holes. You were alone when I met you, Francis Weed, and you'll be alone when I leave. When Mother asked you for a list to send out invitations to our wedding, how many names did you have to give her? Fourteen!"

125   "Cleveland wasn't my home, Julia."

"And how many of your friends came to the church? Two!"

"Cleveland wasn't my home, Julia."

"Since I'm not taking the fur jacket," she said quietly, "you'd better put it back into storage. There's an insurance policy on the pearls that comes due in January. The name of the laundry and maid's telephone number—all those things are in my desk. I hope you won't drink too much, Francis. I hope that nothing bad will happen to you. If you do get into serious trouble, you can call me."

"Oh, my darling, I can't let you go!" Francis said. "I can't let you go, Julia!" He took her in his arms.

130   "I guess I'd better stay and take care of you for a little while longer," she said.

Riding to work in the morning, Francis saw the girl walk down the aisle of the coach. He was surprised; he hadn't realized that the school she went to was in the city, but she was carrying books, she seemed to be going to school. His surprise delayed his reaction, but then he got up clumsily and stepped into the aisle. Several people had come between them, but he could see her ahead of him, waiting for someone to open the car door, and then, as the train swerved, putting out her hand to support herself as she crossed the platform into the next car. He followed her through that car and halfway through another before calling her name—"Anne! Anne!"—but she didn't turn. He followed her into still another car, and she sat down in an aisle seat. Coming up to her, all his feelings warm and bent in her direction, he put his hand on the back of her seat—even this touch warmed him—and leaning down to speak to her, he saw that it was not Anne. It was an older woman wearing glasses. He went on deliberately into another car, his face red with embarrassment and the much deeper feeling of having his good sense challenged; for if he couldn't tell one person from another, what evidence was there that his life with Julia and the children had as much reality as his dreams of iniquity in Paris or the litter, the grass smell, and the cave-shaped trees in Lovers' Lane.

Late that afternoon, Julia called to remind Francis that they were going out for dinner. A few minutes later, Trace Bearden called. "Look, fellar," Trace said. "I'm calling for Mrs. Thomas. You know? Clayton, that boy of hers, doesn't seem able to get a job, and I wondered if you could help. If you'd call Charlie Bell—I know he's indebted to you—and say a good word for the kid, I think Charlie would—"

"Trace, I hate to say this," Francis said, "but I don't feel that I can do anything for that boy. The kid's worthless. I know it's a harsh thing to say, but it's a fact. Any kindness done for him would backfire in everybody's face. He's just a worthless kid, Trace, and there's nothing else to be done about it. Even if we got him a job, he wouldn't be able to keep it for a week. I know that to be a fact. It's an awful thing, Trace, and I know it is, but instead of recommending that kid, I'd feel obligated to warn people against him—people who knew his father and would naturally want to step in and do something. I'd feel obliged to warn them. He's a thief . . ."

The moment this conversation was finished, Miss Rainey came in and stood by his desk. "I'm not going to be able to work for you any more, Mr. Weed," she said. "I can stay until the seventeenth if you need me, but I've been offered a whirlwind of a job, and I'd like to leave as soon as possible."

She went out, leaving him to face alone the wickedness of what he had done to the Thomas boy. His children in their photograph laughed and laughed, glazed with all the bright colors of summer, and he remembered that they had met a bagpiper on the beach that day and he had paid the piper a dollar to play them a battle song of the Black Watch.[8] The girl would be at the house when he got home. He would spend another evening among his kind neighbors, pick-

135

8. Originally a British Highland regiment that became a line regiment and distinguished itself in battle.

ing and choosing dead-end streets, cart tracks, and the driveways of abandoned houses. There was nothing to mitigate his feeling—nothing that laughter or a game of softball with the children would change—and, thinking back over the plane crash, the Farquarsons' new maid, and Anne Murchison's difficulties with her drunken father, he wondered how he could have avoided arriving at just where he was. He was in trouble. He had been lost once in his life, coming back from a trout stream in the north woods, and he had now the same bleak realization that no amount of cheerfulness or hopefulness or valor or perseverance could help him find, in the gathering dark, the path that he'd lost. He smelled the forest. The feeling of bleakness was intolerable, and he saw clearly that he had reached the point where he would have to make a choice.

He could go to a psychiatrist, like Miss Rainey; he could go to church and confess his lusts; he could go to a Danish-massage parlor[9] in the West Seventies that had been recommended by a salesman; he could rape the girl or trust that he would somehow be prevented from doing this; or he could get drunk. It was his life, his boat, and, like every other man, he was made to be the father of thousands, and what harm could there be in a tryst that would make them both feel more kindly toward the world? This was the wrong train of thought, and he came back to the first, the psychiatrist. He had the telephone number of Miss Rainey's doctor, and he called and asked for an immediate appointment. He was insistent with the doctor's secretary—it was his manner in business—and when she said that the doctor's schedule was full for the next few weeks, Francis demanded an appointment that day and was told to come at five.

The psychiatrist's office was in a building that was used mostly by doctors and dentists, and the hallways were filled with the candy smell of mouthwash and memories of pain. Francis' character had been formed upon a series of private resolves—resolves about cleanliness, about going off the high diving board or repeating any other feat that challenged his courage, about punctuality, honesty, and virtue. To abdicate the perfect loneliness in which he had made his most vital decisions shattered his concept of character and left him now in a condition that felt like shock. He was stupefied. The scene for his *miserere mei Deus*[1] was, like the waiting room of so many doctor's offices, a crude token gesture toward the sweets of domestic bliss: a place arranged with antiques, coffee tables, potted plants, and etchings of snow-covered bridges and geese in flight, although there were no children, no marriage bed, no stove, even, in this travesty of a house, where no one had ever spent the night and where the curtained windows looked straight onto a dark air shaft. Francis gave his name and address to a secretary and then saw, at the side of the room, a policeman moving toward him. "Hold it, hold it," the policeman said. "Don't move. Keep your hands where they are."

"I think it's all right, Officer," the secretary began. "I think it will be—"

"Let's make sure," the policeman said, and he began to slap Francis' clothes, looking for what—pistols, knives, an icepick? Finding nothing, he went off and

---

9. Sometimes "fronts" for houses of prosititution.   1. "Have mercy upon me, O God"; first words of 51st Psalm.

the secretary began a nervous apology: "When you called on the telephone, Mr. Weed, you seemed very excited, and one of the doctor's patients has been threatening his life, and we have to be careful. If you want to go in now?" Francis pushed open a door connected to an electrical chime, and in the doctor's lair sat down heavily, blew his nose into a handkerchief, searched in his pockets for cigarettes, for matches, for something, and said hoarsely, with tears in his eyes, "I'm in love, Dr. Herzog."

It is a week or ten days later in Shady Hill. The seven-fourteen has come and gone, and here and there dinner is finished and the dishes are in the dishwashing machine. The village hangs, morally and economically, from a thread; but it hangs by its thread in the evening light. Donald Goslin has begun to worry the "Moonlight Sonata" again. *Marcato ma sempre pianissimo!*[2] He seems to be wringing out a wet bath towel, but the housemaid does not heed him. She is writing a letter to Arthur Godfrey.[3] In the cellar of his house, Francis Weed is building a coffee table. Dr. Herzog recommends woodwork as a therapy, and Francis finds some true consolation in the simple arithmetic involved and in the holy smell of new wood. Francis is happy. Upstairs, little Toby is crying, because he is tired. He puts off his cowboy hat, gloves, and fringed jacket, unbuckles the belt studded with gold and rubies, the silver bullets and holsters, slips off his suspenders, his checked shirt, and Levi's, and sits on the edge of his bed to pull off his high boots. Leaving this equipment in a heap, he goes to the closet and takes his space suit off a nail. It is a struggle for him to get into the long tights, but he succeeds. He loops the magic cape over his shoulders and, climbing onto the footboard of his bed, he spreads his arms and flies the short distance to the floor, landing with a thump that is audible to everyone in the house but himself.

"Go home, Gertrude, go home," Mrs. Masterson says. "I told you to go home an hour ago, Gertrude. It's way past your suppertime, and your mother will be worried. Go home!" A door on the Babcocks' terrace flies open, and out comes Mrs. Babcock without any clothes on, pursued by a naked husband. (Their children are away at boarding school, and their terrace is screened by a hedge.) Over the terrace they go and in at the kitchen door, as passionate and handsome a nymph and satyr as you will find on any wall in Venice. Cutting the last of the roses in her garden, Julia hears old Mr. Nixon shouting at the squirrels in his bird-feeding station. "Rapscallions! Varmints! Avaunt and quit my sight!" A miserable cat wanders into the garden, sunk in spiritual and physical discomfort. Tied to its head is a small straw hat—a doll's hat—and it is securely buttoned into a doll's dress, from the skirts of which protrudes its long, hairy tail. As it walks, it shakes its feet, as if it had fallen into water.

"Here, pussy, pussy, pussy!" Julia calls.

"Here, pussy, here, poor pussy!" But the cat gives her a skeptical look and stumbles away in its skirts. The last to come is Jupiter. He prances through the tomato vines, holding in his generous mouth the remains of an evening slipper.

---

2. "Stressed but always very softly."   3. At the time of the story, host of a daytime radio program especially popular with housewives.

Then it is dark; it is a night where kings in golden suits ride elephants over the mountains.

1958

AMY TAN

[handwritten annotations: narrative here reflects movements of an individual's memory; reports from present — her journey become our journey]

A Pair of Tickets

[handwritten: present] The minute our train leaves the Hong Kong border and enters Shenzhen, China, I feel different. I can feel the skin on my forehead tingling, my blood rushing through a new course, my bones aching with a familiar old pain. And I think, My mother was right. I am becoming Chinese.

[handwritten: past] "Cannot be helped," my mother said when I was fifteen and had vigorously denied that I had any Chinese whatsoever below my skin. I was a sophomore at Galileo High in San Francisco, and all my Caucasian friends agreed: I was about as Chinese as they were. But my mother had studied at a famous nursing school in Shanghai, and she said she knew all about genetics. So there was no doubt in her mind, whether I agreed or not: Once you are born Chinese, you cannot help but feel and think Chinese.

"Someday you will see," said my mother. "It's in your blood, waiting to be let go."

And when she said this, I saw myself transforming like a werewolf, a mutant tag of DNA suddenly triggered, replicating itself insidiously into a *syndrome*, a cluster of telltale Chinese behaviors, all those things my mother did to embarrass me—haggling with store owners, pecking her mouth with a toothpick in public, being color-blind to the fact that lemon yellow and pale pink are not good combinations for winter clothes.

5   But today I realize I've never really known what it means to be Chinese. I *[handwritten: today present]* am thirty-six years old. My mother is dead and I am on a train, carrying with me her dreams of coming home. I am going to China.

We are going to Guangzhou, my seventy-two-year-old father, Canning Woo, and I, where we will visit his aunt, whom he has not seen since he was ten years old. And I don't know whether it's the prospect of seeing his aunt or if it's because he's back in China, but now he looks like he's a young boy, so innocent and happy I want to button his sweater and pat his head. We are sitting across from each other, separated by a little table with two cold cups of tea. For the first time I can ever remember, my father has tears in his eyes, and all he is seeing out the train window is a sectioned field of yellow, green, and brown, a narrow canal flanking the tracks, low rising hills, and three people in blue jackets riding an ox-driven cart on this early October morning. And I can't help myself. I also have misty eyes, as if I had seen this a long, long time ago, and had almost forgotten.

In less than three hours, we will be in Guangzhou, which my guidebook tells me is how one properly refers to Canton these days. It seems all the cities I have heard of, except Shanghai, have changed their spellings. I think they are saying China has changed in other ways as well. Chungking is Chongqing. And Kweilin is Guilin. I have looked these names up, because after we see my father's aunt in Guangzhou, we will catch a plane to Shanghai, where I will meet my two half-sisters for the first time.

They are my mother's twin daughters from her first marriage, little babies she was forced to abandon on a road as she was fleeing Kweilin for Chungking in 1944. That was all my mother had told me about these daughters, so they had remained babies in my mind, all these years, sitting on the side of a road, listening to bombs whistling in the distance while sucking their patient red thumbs.

And it was only this year that someone found them and wrote with this joyful news. A letter came from Shanghai, addressed to my mother. When I first heard about this, that they were alive, I imagined my identical sisters transforming from little babies into six-year-old girls. In my mind, they were seated next to each other at a table, taking turns with the fountain pen. One would write a neat row of characters: *Dearest Mama. We are alive.* She would brush back her wispy bangs and hand the other sister the pen, and she would write: *Come get us. Please hurry.*

Of course they could not know that my mother had died three months before,   10
suddenly, when a blood vessel in her brain burst. One minute she was talking to my father, complaining about the tenants upstairs, scheming how to evict them under the pretense that relatives from China were moving in. The next minute she was holding her head, her eyes squeezed shut, groping for the sofa, and then crumpling softly to the floor with fluttering hands.

So my father had been the first one to open the letter, a long letter it turned out. And they did call her Mama. They said they always revered her as their true mother. They kept a framed picture of her. They told her about their life, from the time my mother last saw them on the road leaving Kweilin to when they were finally found.

And the letter had broken my father's heart so much—these daughters calling my mother from another life he never knew—that he gave the letter to my mother's old friend Auntie Lindo and asked her to write back and tell my sisters, in the gentlest way possible, that my mother was dead.

But instead Auntie Lindo took the letter to the Joy Luck Club and discussed with Auntie Ying and Auntie An-mei what should be done, because they had known for many years about my mother's search for her twin daughters, her endless hope. Auntie Lindo and the others cried over this double tragedy, of losing my mother three months before, and now again. And so they couldn't help but think of some miracle, some possible way of reviving her from the dead, so my mother could fulfill her dream.

So this is what they wrote to my sisters in Shanghai: "Dearest Daughters, I too have never forgotten you in my memory or in my heart. I never gave up hope that we would see each other again in a joyous reunion. I am only sorry it has been too long. I want to tell you everything about my life since I last saw you. I want to tell you this when our family comes to see you in China. . . ." They signed it with my mother's name.

15 It wasn't until all this had been done that they first told me about my sisters, the letter they received, the one they wrote back.

"They'll think she's coming, then," I murmured. And I had imagined my sisters now being ten or eleven, jumping up and down, holding hands, their pigtails bouncing, excited that their mother—*their* mother—was coming, whereas my mother was dead.

"How can you say she is not coming in a letter?" said Auntie Lindo. "She is their mother. She is your mother. You must be the one to tell them. All these years, they have been dreaming of her." And I thought she was right.

But then I started dreaming, too, of my mother and my sisters and how it would be if I arrived in Shanghai. All these years, while they waited to be found, I had lived with my mother and then had lost her. I imagined seeing my sisters at the airport. They would be standing on their tiptoes, looking anxiously, scanning from one dark head to another as we got off the plane. And I would recognize them instantly, their faces with the identical worried look.

"*Jyejye, Jyejye*. Sister, Sister. We are here," I saw myself saying in my poor version of Chinese.

20 "Where is Mama?" they would say, and look around, still smiling, two flushed and eager faces. "Is she hiding?" And this would have been like my mother, to stand behind just a bit, to tease a little and make people's patience pull a little on their hearts. I would shake my head and tell my sisters she was not hiding.

"Oh, that must be Mama, no?" one of my sisters would whisper excitedly, pointing to another small woman completely engulfed in a tower of presents. And that, too, would have been like my mother, to bring mountains of gifts, food, and toys for children—all bought on sale—shunning thanks, saying the gifts were nothing, and later turning the labels over to show my sisters, "Calvin Klein, 100% wool."

I imagined myself starting to say, "Sisters, I am sorry, I have come alone . . ." and before I could tell them—they could see it in my face—they were wailing, pulling their hair, their lips twisted in pain, as they ran away from me. And then I saw myself getting back on the plane and coming home.

After I had dreamed this scene many times—watching their despair turn from horror into anger—I begged Auntie Lindo to write another letter. And at first she refused.

"How can I say she is dead? I cannot write this," said Auntie Lindo with a stubborn look.

25 "But it's cruel to have them believe she's coming on the plane," I said. "When they see it's just me, they'll hate me."

"Hate you? Cannot be." She was scowling. "You are their own sister, their only family."

"You don't understand," I protested.

"What I don't understand?" she said.

And I whispered. "They'll think I'm responsible, that she died because I didn't appreciate her."

30 And Auntie Lindo looked satisfied and sad at the same time, as if this were true and I had finally realized it. She sat down for an hour, and when she stood

up she handed me a two-page letter. She had tears in her eyes. I realized that the very thing I had feared, she had done. So even if she had written the news of my mother's death in English, I wouldn't have had the heart to read it.

"Thank you," I whispered.

The landscape has become gray, filled with low flat cement buildings, old factories, and then tracks and more tracks filled with trains like ours passing by in the opposite direction. I see platforms crowded with people wearing drab Western clothes, with spots of bright colors: little children wearing pink and yellow, red and peach. And there are soldiers in olive green and red, and old ladies in gray tops and pants that stop mid-calf. We are in Guangzhou.

Before the train even comes to a stop, people are bringing down their belongings from above their seats. For a moment there is a dangerous shower of heavy suitcases laden with gifts to relatives, half-broken boxes wrapped in miles of string to keep the contents from spilling out, plastic bags filled with yarn and vegetables and packages of dried mushrooms, and camera cases. And then we are caught in a stream of people rushing, shoving, pushing us along, until we find ourselves in one of a dozen lines waiting to go through customs. I feel as if I were getting on a number 30 Stockton bus in San Francisco. I am in China, I remind myself. And somehow the crowds don't bother me. It feels right. I start pushing too.

I take out the declaration forms and my passport. "Woo," it says at the top, and below that, "June May," who was born in "California, U.S.A.," in 1951. I wonder if the customs people will question whether I'm the same person as in the passport photo. In this picture, my chin-length hair is swept back and artfully styled. I am wearing false eyelashes, eye shadow, and lip liner. My cheeks are hollowed out by bronze blusher. But I had not expected the heat in October. And now my hair hangs limp with the humidity. I wear no makeup; in Hong Kong my mascara had melted into dark circles and everything else had felt like layers of grease. So today my face is plain, unadorned except for a thin mist of shiny sweat on my forehead and nose.

Even without makeup, I could never pass for true Chinese. I stand five-foot-six, and my head pokes above the crowd so that I am eye level only with other tourists. My mother once told me my height came from my grandfather, who was a northerner, and may have even had some Mongol blood. "This is what your grandmother once told me," explained my mother. "But now it is too late to ask her. They are all dead, your grandparents, your uncles, and their wives and children, all killed in the war, when a bomb fell on our house. So many generations in one instant."

She had said this so matter-of-factly that I thought she had long since gotten over any grief she had. And then I wondered how she knew they were all dead.

"Maybe they left the house before the bomb fell," I suggested.

"No," said my mother. "Our whole family is gone. It is just you and I."

"But how do you know? Some of them could have escaped."

"Cannot be," said my mother, this time almost angrily. And then her frown was washed over by a puzzled blank look, and she began to talk as if she were trying to remember where she had misplaced something. "I went back to that house. I kept looking up to where the house used to be. And it wasn't a house, just the sky. And below, underneath my feet, were four stories of burnt bricks and wood, all the life of our house. Then off to the side I saw things blown into the yard, nothing valuable. There was a bed someone used to sleep in, really just a metal frame twisted up at one corner. And a book, I don't know what kind, because every page had turned black. And I saw a teacup which was unbroken but filled with ashes. And then I found my doll, with her hands and legs broken, her hair burned off. . . . When I was a little girl, I had cried for that doll, seeing it all alone in the store window, and my mother had bought it for me. It was an American doll with yellow hair. It could turn its legs and arms. The eyes moved up and down. And when I married and left my family home, I gave the doll to my youngest niece, because she was like me. She cried if that doll was not with her always. Do you see? If she was in the house with that doll, her parents were there, and so everybody was there, waiting together, because that's how our family was."

The woman in the customs booth stares at my documents, then glances at me briefly, and with two quick movements stamps everything and sternly nods me along. And soon my father and I find ourselves in a large area filled with thousands of people and suitcases. I feel lost and my father looks helpless.

"Excuse me," I say to a man who looks like an American. "Can you tell me where I can get a taxi?" He mumbles something that sounds Swedish or Dutch.

"Syau Yen! Syau Yen!" I hear a piercing voice shout from behind me. An old woman in a yellow knit beret is holding up a pink plastic bag filled with wrapped trinkets. I guess she is trying to sell us something. But my father is staring down at this tiny sparrow of a woman, squinting into her eyes. And then his eyes widen, his face opens up and he smiles like a pleased little boy.

"*Aiyi! Aiyi!*"—Auntie Auntie!—he says softly.

"Syau Yen!" coos my great-aunt. I think it's funny she has just called my father "Little Wild Goose." It must be his baby milk name, the name used to discourage ghosts from stealing children.

They clasp each other's hands—they do not hug—and hold on like this, taking turns saying, "Look at you! You are so old. Look how old you've become!" They are both crying openly, laughing at the same time, and I bite my lip, trying not to cry. I'm afraid to feel their joy. Because I am thinking how different our arrival in Shanghai will be tomorrow, how awkward it will feel.

Now Aiyi beams and points to a Polaroid picture of my father. My father had wisely sent pictures when he wrote and said we were coming. See how smart she was, she seems to intone as she compares the picture to my father. In the letter, my father had said we would call her from the hotel once we arrived, so this is a surprise, that they've come to meet us. I wonder if my sisters will be at the airport.

It is only then that I remember the camera. I had meant to take a picture of my father and his aunt the moment they met. It's not too late.

"Here, stand together over here," I say, holding up the Polaroid. The camera flashes and I hand them the snapshot. Aiyi and my father still stand close together,

45

each of them holding a corner of the picture, watching as their images begin to form. They are almost reverentially quiet. Aiyi is only five years older than my father, which makes her around seventy-seven. But she looks ancient, shrunken, a mummified relic. Her thin hair is pure white, her teeth are brown with decay. So much for stories of Chinese women looking young forever, I think to myself.

Now Aiyi is crooning to me: *"Jandale."* So big already. She looks up at me, at my full height, and then peers into her pink plastic bag—her gifts to us, I have figured out—as if she is wondering what she will give to me, now that I am so old and big. And then she grabs my elbow with her sharp pincerlike grasp and turns me around. A man and a woman in their fifties are shaking hands with my father, everybody smiling and saying, "Ah! Ah!" They are Aiyi's oldest son and his wife, and standing next to them are four other people, around my age, and a little girl who's around ten. The introductions go by so fast, all I know is that one of them is Aiyi's grandson, with his wife, and the other is her granddaughter, with her husband. And the little girl is Lili, Aiyi's great-granddaughter. 50

Aiyi and my father speak the Mandarin dialect from their childhood, but the rest of the family speaks only the Cantonese of their village. I understand only Mandarin but can't speak it that well. So Aiyi and my father gossip unrestrained in Mandarin, exchanging news about people from their old village. And they stop only occasionally to talk to the rest of us, sometimes in Cantonese, sometimes in English.

"Oh, it is as I suspected," says my father, turning to me. "He died last summer." And I already understood this. I just don't know who this person, Li Gong, is. I feel as if I were in the United Nations and the translators had run amok.

"Hello," I say to the little girl. "My name is Jing-mei." But the little girl squirms to look away, causing her parents to laugh with embarrassment. I try to think of Cantonese words I can say to her, stuff I learned from friends in Chinatown, but all I can think of are swear words, terms for bodily functions, and short phrases like "tastes good," "tastes like garbage," and "she's really ugly." And then I have another plan: I hold up the Polaroid camera, beckoning Lili with my finger. She immediately jumps forward, places one hand on her hip in the manner of a fashion model, juts out her chest, and flashes me a toothy smile. As soon as I take the picture she is standing next to me, jumping and giggling every few seconds as she watches herself appear on the greenish film.

By the time we hail taxis for the ride to the hotel, Lili is holding tight onto my hand, pulling me along.

In the taxi, Aiyi talks nonstop, so I have no chance to ask her about the different sights we are passing by. 55

"You wrote and said you would come only for one day," says Aiyi to my father in an agitated tone. "One day! How can you see your family in one day! Toishan is many hours' drive from Guangzhou. And this idea to call us when you arrive. This is nonsense. We have no telephone."

My heart races a little. I wonder if Auntie Lindo told my sisters we would call from the hotel in Shanghai?

Aiyi continues to scold my father. "I was so beside myself, ask my son, almost turned heaven and earth upside down trying to think of a way! So we decided the best was for us to take the bus from Toishan and come into Guangzhou—meet you right from the start."

And now I am holding my breath as the taxi driver dodges between trucks and buses, honking his horn constantly. We seem to be on some sort of long freeway overpass, like a bridge above the city. I can see row after row of apartments, each floor cluttered with laundry hanging out to dry on the balcony. We pass a public bus, with people jammed in so tight their faces are nearly wedged against the window. Then I see the skyline of what must be downtown Guangzhou. From a distance, it looks like a major American city, with highrises and construction going on everywhere. As we slow down in the more congested part of the city, I see scores of little shops, dark inside, lined with counters and shelves. And then there is a building, its front laced with scaffolding made of bamboo poles held together with plastic strips. Men and women are standing on narrow platforms, scraping the sides, working without safety straps or helmets. Oh, would OSHA[1] have a field day here, I think.

60   Aiyi's shrill voice rises up again: "So it is a shame you can't see our village, our house. My sons have been quite successful, selling our vegetables in the free market. We had enough these last few years to build a big house, three stories, all of new brick, big enough for our whole family and then some. And every year, the money is even better. You Americans aren't the only ones who know how to get rich!"

The taxi stops and I assume we've arrived, but then I peer out at what looks like a grander version of the Hyatt Regency. "This is communist China?" I wonder out loud. And then I shake my head toward my father. "This must be the wrong hotel." I quickly pull out our itinerary, travel tickets, and reservations. I had explicitly instructed my travel agent to choose something inexpensive, in the thirty-to-forty-dollar range. I'm sure of this. And there it says on our itinerary: Garden Hotel, Huanshi Dong Lu. Well, our travel agent had better be prepared to eat the extra, that's all I have to say.

The hotel is magnificent. A bellboy complete with uniform and sharp-creased cap jumps forward and begins to carry our bags into the lobby. Inside, the hotel looks like an orgy of shopping arcades and restaurants all encased in granite and glass. And rather than be impressed, I am worried about the expense, as well as the appearance it must give Aiyi, that we rich Americans cannot be without our luxuries even for one night.

But when I step up to the reservation desk, ready to haggle over this booking mistake, it is confirmed. Our rooms are prepaid, thirty-four dollars each. I feel sheepish, and Aiyi and the others seem delighted by our temporary surroundings. Lili is looking wide-eyed at an arcade filled with video games.

Our whole family crowds into one elevator, and the bellboy waves, saying he will meet us on the eighteenth floor. As soon as the elevator door shuts, everybody becomes very quiet, and when the door finally opens again, everybody talks at once in what sounds like relieved voices. I have the feeling Aiyi and the others have never been on such a long elevator ride.

---

1. Occupational Safety and Health Administration.

Our rooms are next to each other and are identical. The rugs, drapes, bed- 65
spreads are all in shades of taupe. There's a color television with remote-control
panels built into the lamp table between the two twin beds. The bathroom has
marble walls and floors. I find a built-in wet bar with a small refrigerator stocked
with Heineken beer, Coke Classic, and Seven-Up, mini-bottles of Johnnie Walker
Red, Bacardi rum, and Smirnoff vodka, and packets of M & M's, honey-roasted
cashews, and Cadbury chocolate bars. And again I say out loud, "This is communist China?"

My father comes into my room. "They decided we should just stay here and
visit," he says, shrugging his shoulders. "They say, Less trouble that way. More
time to talk."

"What about dinner?" I ask. I have been envisioning my first real Chinese
feast for many days already, a big banquet with one of those soups steaming out
carved winter melon, chicken wrapped in clay, Peking duck, the works.

My father walks over and picks up a room service book next to a *Travel &
Leisure* magazine. He flips through the pages quickly and then points to the
menu. "This is what they want," says my father.

So it's decided. We are going to dine tonight in our rooms, with our family,
sharing hamburgers, french fries, and apple pie à la mode.

Aiyi and her family are browsing the shops while we clean up. After a hot 70
ride on the train, I'm eager for a shower and cooler clothes.

The hotel has provided little packets of shampoo which, upon opening, I
discover is the consistency and color of hoisin sauce.[2] This is more like it, I
think. This is China. And I rub some in my damp hair.

Standing in the shower, I realize this is the first time I've been by myself in
what seems like days. But instead of feeling relieved, I feel forlorn. I think about
what my mother said, about activating my genes and becoming Chinese. And I
wonder what she meant.

Right after my mother died, I asked myself a lot of things, things that couldn't
be answered, to force myself to grieve more. It seemed as if I wanted to sustain
my grief, to assure myself that I had cared deeply enough.

But now I ask the questions mostly because I want to know the answers.
What was that pork stuff she used to make that had the texture of sawdust? What
were the names of the uncles who died in Shanghai? What had she dreamt all
these years about her other daughters? All the times when she got mad at me,
was she really thinking about them? Did she wish I were they? Did she regret
that I wasn't?

∇   ∇   ∇

At one o'clock in the morning, I awake to tapping sounds on the window. I must 75
have dozed off and now I feel my body uncramping itself. I'm sitting on the
floor, leaning against one of the twin beds. Lili is lying next to me. The others
are asleep, too, sprawled out on the beds and floor. Aiyi is seated at a little table,

2. Sweet brownish-red sauce made from soybeans, flour, sugar, water, spices, garlic, and chili.

looking very sleepy. And my father is staring out the window, tapping his fingers on the glass. The last time I listened my father was telling Aiyi about his life since he last saw her. How he had gone to Yenching University, later got a post with a newspaper in Chungking, met my mother there, a young widow. How they later fled together to Shanghai to try to find my mother's family house, but there was nothing there. And then they traveled eventually to Canton and then to Hong Kong, then Haiphong and finally to San Francisco. . . .

"Suyuan didn't tell me she was trying all these years to find her daughters," he is now saying in a quiet voice. "Naturally, I did not discuss her daughters with her. I thought she was ashamed she had left them behind."

"Where did she leave them?" asks Aiyi. "How were they found?"

I am wide awake now. Although I have heard parts of this story from my mother's friends.

"It happened when the Japanese took over Kweilin," says my father.

"Japanese in Kweilin?" says Aiyi. "That was never the case. Couldn't be. The Japanese never came to Kweilin."

"Yes, that is what the newspapers reported. I know this because I was working for the news bureau at the time. The Kuomintang[3] often told us what we could say and could not say. But we knew the Japanese had come into Kwangsi Province. We had sources who told us how they had captured the Wuchang-Canton railway. How they were coming overland, making very fast progress, marching toward the provincial capital."

Aiyi looks astonished. "If people did not know this, how could Suyuan know the Japanese were coming?"

"An officer of the Kuomintang secretly warned her," explains my father. "Suyuan's husband also was an officer and everybody knew that officers and their families would be the first to be killed. So she gathered a few possessions and, in the middle of the night, she picked up her daughters and fled on foot. The babies were not even one year old."

"How could she give up those babies!" sighs Aiyi. "Twin girls. We have never had such luck in our family." And then she yawns again.

"What were they named?" she asks. I listen carefully. I had been planning on using just the familiar "Sister" to address them both. But now I want to know how to pronounce their names.

"They have their father's surname, Wang," says my father. "And their given names are Chwun Yu and Chwun Hwa."

"What do the names mean?" I ask.

"Ah." My father draws imaginary characters on the window. "One means 'Spring Rain,' the other 'Spring Flower,' " he explains in English, "because they born in the spring, and of course rain come before flower, same order these girls are born. Your mother like a poet, don't you think?"

I nod my head. I see Aiyi nod her head forward, too. But it falls forward and stays there. She is breathing deeply, noisily. She is asleep.

"And what does Ma's name mean?" I whisper.

---

3. "National People's Party" led by General Chiang Kai-shek (1887–1975).

" 'Suyuan,' " he says, writing more invisible characters on the glass. "The way she write it in Chinese, it mean 'Long-Cherished Wish.' Quite a fancy name, not so ordinary like flower name. See this first character, it means something like 'Forever Never Forgotten.' But there is another way to write 'Suyuan.' Sound exactly the same, but the meaning is opposite." His finger creates the brushstrokes of another character. "The first part look the same: 'Never Forgotten.' But the last part add to first part make the whole word mean 'Long-Held Grudge.' Your mother get angry with me, I tell her her name should be Grudge."

My father is looking at me, moist-eyed. "See, I pretty clever, too, hah?"

I nod, wishing I could find some way to comfort him. "And what about my name," I ask, "what does 'Jing-mei' mean?"

"Your name also special," he says. I wonder if any name in Chinese is not something special. " 'Jing' like excellent *jing*. Not just good, it's something pure, essential, the best quality. *Jing* is good leftover stuff when you take impurities out of something like gold, or rice, or salt. So what is left—just pure essence. And 'Mei,' this is common *mei*, as in *meimei*, 'younger sister.' "

I think about this. My mother's long-cherished wish. Me, the younger sister who was supposed to be the essence of the others. I feed myself with the old grief, wondering how disappointed my mother must have been. Tiny Aiyi stirs suddenly, her head rolls and then falls back, her mouth opens as if to answer my question. She grunts in her sleep, tucking her body more closely into the chair.

"So why did she abandon those babies on the road?" I need to know, because now I feel abandoned too.

"Long time I wondered this myself," says my father. "But then I read that letter from her daughters in Shanghai now, and I talk to Auntie Lindo, all the others. And then I knew. No shame in what she done. None."

"What happened?"

"Your mother running away—" begins my father.

"No, tell me in Chinese," I interrupt. "Really, I can understand."

He begins to talk, still standing at the window, looking into the night.

▽   ▽   ▽

After fleeing Kweilin, your mother walked for several days trying to find a main road. Her thought was to catch a ride on a truck or wagon, to catch enough rides until she reached Chungking, where her husband was stationed.

She had sewn money and jewelry into the lining of her dress, enough, she thought, to barter rides all the way. If I am lucky, she thought, I will not have to trade the heavy gold bracelet and jade ring. These were things from her mother, your grandmother.

By the third day, she had traded nothing. The roads were filled with people, everybody running and begging for rides from passing trucks. The trucks rushed by, afraid to stop. So your mother found no rides, only the start of dysentery pains in her stomach.

Her shoulders ached from the two babies swinging from scarf slings. Blisters grew on the palms from holding two leather suitcases. And then the blisters burst and began to bleed. After a while, she left the suitcases behind, keeping only the food and a few clothes. And later she also dropped the bags of wheat flour and rice and kept walking like this for many miles, singing songs to her little girls, until she was delirious with pain and fever.

Finally, there was not one more step left in her body. She didn't have the strength to carry those babies any further. She slumped to the ground. She knew she would die of her sickness, or perhaps from thirst, from starvation, or from the Japanese, who she was sure were marching right behind her.

She took the babies out of the slings and sat them on the side of the road, then lay down next to them. You babies are so good, she said, so quiet. They smiled back, reaching their chubby hands for her, wanting to be picked up again. And then she knew she could not bear to watch her babies die with her.

She saw a family with three young children in a cart going by. "Take my babies, I beg you," she cried to them. But they stared back with empty eyes and never stopped.

She saw another person pass and called out again. This time a man turned around, and he had such a terrible expression—your mother said it looked like death itself—she shivered and looked away.

110 When the road grew quiet, she tore open the lining of her dress, and stuffed jewelry under the shirt of one baby and money under the other. She reached into her pocket and drew out the photos of her family, the picture of her father and mother, the picture of herself and her husband on their wedding day. And she wrote on the back of each the names of the babies and this same message: "Please care for these babies with the money and valuables provided. When it is safe to come, if you bring them to Shanghai, 9 Weichang Lu, the Li family will be glad to give you a generous reward. Li Suyuan and Wang Fuchi."

And then she touched each baby's cheek and told her not to cry. She would go down the road to find them some food and would be back. And without looking back, she walked down the road, stumbling and crying, thinking only of this last hope, that her daughters would be found by a kindhearted person who would care for them. She would not allow herself to imagine anything else.

She did not remember how far she walked, which direction she went, when she fainted, or how she was found. When she awoke, she was in the back of a bouncing truck with several other sick people, all moaning. And she began to scream, thinking she was now on a journey to Buddhist hell. But the face of an American missionary lady bent over her and smiled, talking to her in a soothing language she did not understand. And yet she could somehow understand. She had been saved for no good reason, and it was now too late to go back and save her babies.

When she arrived in Chungking, she learned her husband had died two weeks before. She told me later she laughed when the officers told her this news, she was so delirious with madness and disease. To come so far, to lose so much and to find nothing.

I met her in a hospital. She was lying on a cot, hardly able to move, her dysentery had drained her so thin. I had come in for my foot, my missing toe, which was cut off by a piece of falling rubble. She was talking to herself, mumbling.

"Look at these clothes," she said, and I saw she had on a rather unusual dress for wartime. It was silk satin, quite dirty, but there was no doubt it was a beautiful dress.

"Look at this face," she said, and I saw her dusty face and hollow cheeks, her eyes shining black. "Do you see my foolish hope?"

"I thought I had lost everything, except these two things," she murmured. "And I wondered which I would lose next. Clothes or hope? Hope or clothes?"

"But now, see here, look what is happening," she said, laughing, as if all her prayers had been answered. And she was pulling hair out of her head as easily as one lifts new wheat from wet soil.

It was an old peasant woman who found them. "How could I resist?" the peasant woman later told your sisters when they were older. They were still sitting obediently near where your mother had left them, looking like little fairy queens waiting for their sedan to arrive.

The woman, Mei Ching, and her husband, Mei Han, lived in a stone cave. There were thousands of hidden caves like that in and around Kweilin so secret that the people remained hidden even after the war ended. The Meis would come out of their cave every few days and forage for food supplies left on the road, and sometimes they would see something that they both agreed was a tragedy to leave behind. So one day they took back to their cave a delicately painted set of rice bowls, another day a little footstool with a velvet cushion and two new wedding blankets. And once, it was your sisters.

They were pious people, Muslims, who believed the twin babies were a sign of double luck, and they were sure of this when, later in the evening, they discovered how valuable the babies were. She and her husband had never seen rings and bracelets like those. And while they admired the pictures, knowing the babies came from a good family, neither of them could read or write. It was not until many months later that Mei Ching found someone who could read the writing on the back. By then, she loved these baby girls like her own.

In 1952 Mei Han, the husband, died. The twins were already eight years old, and Mei Ching now decided it was time to find your sisters' true family.

She showed the girls the picture of their mother and told them they had been born into a great family and she would take them back to see their true mother and grandparents. Mei Ching told them about the reward, but she swore she would refuse it. She loved these girls so much, she only wanted them to have what they were entitled to—a better life, a fine house, educated ways. Maybe the family would let her stay on as the girls' amah. Yes, she was certain they would insist.

Of course, when she found the place at 9 Weichang Lu, in the old French Concession, it was something completely different. It was the site of a factory building, recently constructed, and none of the workers knew what had become of the family whose house had burned down on that spot.

Mei Ching could not have known, of course, that your mother and I, her new husband, had already returned to that same place in 1945 in hopes of finding both her family and her daughters.

Your mother and I stayed in China until 1947. We went to many different cities—back to Kweilin, to Changsha, as far south as Kunming. She was always looking out of one corner of her eye for twin babies, then little girls. Later we went to Hong Kong, and when we finally left in 1949 for the United States, I think she was even looking for them on the boat. But when we arrived, she no longer talked about them. I thought, At last, they have died in her heart.

When letters could be openly exchanged between China and the United States, she wrote immediately to old friends in Shanghai and Kweilin. I did not know she did this. Auntie Lindo told me. But of course, by then, all the street names had changed. Some people had died, others had moved away. So it took many years to find a contact. And when she did find an old schoolmate's address and wrote asking her to look for her daughters, her friend wrote back and said this was impossible, like looking for a needle on the bottom of the ocean. How did she know her daughters were in Shanghai and not somewhere else in China? The friend, of course, did not ask, How do you know your daughters are still alive?

So her schoolmate did not look. Finding babies lost during the war was a matter of foolish imagination, and she had no time for that.

But every year, your mother wrote to different people. And this last year, I think she got a big idea in her head, to go to China and find them herself. I remember she told me, "Canning, we should go, before it is too late, before we are too old." And I told her we were already too old, it was already too late.

I just thought she wanted to be a tourist! I didn't know she wanted to go and look for her daughters. So when I said it was too late, that must have put a terrible thought in her head that her daughters might be dead. And I think this possibility grew bigger and bigger in her head, until it killed her.

Maybe it was your mother's dead spirit who guided her Shanghai schoolmate to find her daughters. Because after your mother died, the schoolmate saw your sisters, by chance, while shopping for shoes at the Number One Department Store on Nanjing Dong Road. She said it was like a dream, seeing these two women who looked so much alike, moving down the stairs together. There was something about their facial expressions that reminded the schoolmate of your mother.

She quickly walked over to them and called their names, which of course, they did not recognize at first, because Mei Ching had changed their names. But your mother's friend was so sure, she persisted. "Are you not Wang Chwun Yu and Wang Chwun Hwa?" she asked them. And then these double-image women became very excited, because they remembered the names written on the back of an old photo, a photo of a young man and woman they still honored, as their much-loved first parents, who had died and become spirit ghosts still roaming the earth looking for them.

▽   ▽   ▽

At the airport, I am exhausted. I could not sleep last night. Aiyi had followed me into my room at three in the morning, and she instantly fell asleep on one of the twin beds, snoring with the might of a lumberjack. I lay awake thinking about my mother's story, realizing how much I have never known about her, grieving that my sisters and I had both lost her.

And now at the airport, after shaking hands with everybody, waving good-bye, I think about all the different ways we leave people in this world. Cheerily waving good-bye to some at airports, knowing we'll never see each other again. Leaving others on the side of the road, hoping that we will. Finding my mother in my father's story and saying good-bye before I have a chance to know her better.

Aiyi smiles at me as we wait for our gate to be called. She is so old. I put one arm around her and one arm around Lili. They are the same size, it seems. And then it's time. As we wave good-bye one more time and enter the waiting area, I get the sense I am going from one funeral to another. In my hand I'm clutching a pair of tickets to Shanghai. In two hours we'll be there.

The plane takes off. I close my eyes. How can I describe to them in my broken Chinese about our mother's life? Where should I begin?

"Wake up, we're here," says my father. And I awake with my heart pounding in my throat. I look out the window and we're already on the runway. It's gray outside.

And now I'm walking down the steps of the plane, onto the tarmac and toward the building. If only, I think, if only my mother had lived long enough to be the one walking toward them. I am so nervous I cannot feel my feet. I am just moving somehow.

Somebody shouts, "She's arrived!" And then I see her. Her short hair. Her small body. And that same look on her face. She has the back of her hand pressed hard against her mouth. She is crying as though she had gone through a terrible ordeal and were happy it is over.

And I know it's not my mother, yet it is the same look she had when I was five and had disappeared all afternoon, for such a long time, that she was convinced I was dead. And when I miraculously appeared, sleepy-eyed, crawling from underneath my bed, she wept and laughed, biting the back of her hand to make sure it was true.

And now I see her again, two of her, waving, and in one hand there is a photo, the Polaroid I sent them. As soon as I get beyond the gate, we run toward each other, all three of us embracing, all hesitations and expectations forgotten.

"Mama, Mama," we all murmur, as if she is among us.

My sisters look at me, proudly. "Meimei jandale," says one sister proudly to the other. "Little Sister has grown up." I look at their faces again and I see no trace of my mother in them. Yet they still look familiar. And now I also see what part of me is Chinese. It is so obvious. It is my family. It is in our blood. After all these years, it can finally be let go.

My sisters and I stand, arms around each other, laughing and wiping the tears from each other's eyes. The flash of the Polaroid goes off and my father hands me the snapshot. My sisters and I watch quietly together, eager to see what develops.

145   The gray-green surface changes to the bright colors of our three images, sharpening and deepening all at once. And although we don't speak, I know we all see it: Together we look like our mother. Her same eyes, her same mouth, open in surprise to see, at last, her long-cherished wish.

a lonely story of self-realization

1989

ANTON CHEKHOV

The Lady with the Dog

I

People were telling one another that a newcomer had been seen on the promenade—a lady with a dog. Dmitry Dmitrich Gurov had been a fortnight in Yalta,[1] and was accustomed to its ways, and he, too, had begun to take an interest in fresh arrivals. From his seat in Vernet's outdoor café, he caught sight of a young woman in a toque, passing along the promenade; she was fair and not very tall; after her trotted a white Pomeranian.

Later he encountered her in the municipal park and in the square several times a day. She was always alone, wearing the same toque, and the Pomeranian always trotted at her side. Nobody knew who she was, and people referred to her simply as "the lady with the dog."

"If she's here without her husband, and without any friends," thought Gurov, "it wouldn't be a bad idea to make her acquaintance."

He was not yet forty but had a twelve-year-old daughter and two sons in high school. He had been talked into marrying in his third year at college, and his wife now looked nearly twice as old as he did. She was a tall woman with dark eyebrows, erect, dignified, imposing, and, as she said of herself, a "thinker." She was a great reader, omitted the "hard sign"[2] at the end of words in her letters, and called her husband "Dimitry" instead of Dmitry; and though he secretly considered her shallow, narrow-minded, and dowdy, he stood in awe of her, and disliked being at home. He had first begun deceiving her long ago and he was now constantly unfaithful to her, and this was no doubt why he spoke slightingly of women, to whom he referred as *the lower race*.

5   He considered that the ample lessons he had received from bitter experience entitled him to call them whatever he liked, but without this "lower race" he could not have existed a single day. He was bored and ill-at-ease in the company of men, with whom he was always cold and reserved, but felt quite at home among women, and knew exactly what to say to them, and how to behave; he

---

1. Russian city on the Black Sea; a resort for southern vacations.   2. Conventional sign that was used following consonants; to omit it was then "progressive."

could even be silent in their company without feeling the slightest awkwardness. There was an elusive charm in his appearance and disposition which attracted women and caught their sympathies. He knew this and was himself attracted to them by some invisible force.

Repeated and bitter experience had taught him that every fresh intimacy, while at first introducing such pleasant variety into everyday life, and offering itself as a charming, light adventure, inevitably developed, among decent people (especially in Moscow, where they are so irresolute and slow to move), into a problem of excessive complication leading to an intolerably irksome situation. But every time he encountered an attractive woman he forgot all about this experience, the desire for life surged up in him, and everything suddenly seemed simple and amusing.

One evening, then, while he was dining at the restaurant in the park, the lady in the toque came strolling up and took a seat at a neighboring table. Her expression, gait, dress, coiffure, all told him that she was from the upper classes, that she was married, that she was in Yalta for the first time, alone and bored. . . . The accounts of the laxity of morals among visitors to Yalta are greatly exaggerated, and he paid no heed to them, knowing that for the most part they were invented by people who would gladly have transgressed themselves, had they known how to set about it. But when the lady sat down at a neighboring table a few yards away from him, these stories of easy conquests, of excursions to the mountains, came back to him, and the seductive idea of a brisk transitory liaison, an affair with a woman whose very name he did not know, suddenly took possession of his mind.

He snapped his fingers at the Pomeranian and, when it trotted up to him, shook his forefinger at it. The Pomeranian growled. Gurov shook his finger again.

The lady glanced at him and instantly lowered her eyes.

"He doesn't bite," she said, and blushed.

"May I give him a bone?" he asked, and on her nod of consent added in friendly tones: "Have you been long in Yalta?"

"About five days." 10

"And I am dragging out my second week here."

Neither spoke for a few minutes.

"The days pass quickly, and yet one is so bored here," she said, not looking at him. 15

"It's the thing to say it's boring here. People never complain of boredom in godforsaken holes like Belyev or Zhizdra, but when they get here it's: 'Oh, the dullness! Oh, the dust!' You'd think they'd come from Granada[3] to say the least."

She laughed. Then they both went on eating in silence, like complete strangers. But after dinner they left the restaurant together, and embarked upon the light, jesting talk of people free and contented, for whom it is all the same where they go, or what they talk about. They strolled along, remarking on the strange light over the sea. The water was a warm, tender purple, the moonlight lay on its

3. Romantic city in southern Spain.

surface in a golden strip. They said how close it was, after the hot day. Gurov told her he was from Moscow, had a degree in literature but worked in a bank; that he had at one time trained himself to sing in a private opera company, but had given up the idea; that he owned two houses in Moscow. . . . And from her he learned that she had grown up in Petersburg, but had gotten married in the town of S., where she had been living two years, that she would stay another month in Yalta, and that perhaps her husband, who also needed a rest, would join her. She was quite unable to explain whether her husband was a member of the province council, or on the board of the *zemstvo*,[4] and was greatly amused at herself for this. Further, Gurov learned that her name was Anna Sergeyevna.

Back in his own room he thought about her, and felt sure he would meet her the next day. It was inevitable. As he went to bed he reminded himself that only a very short time ago she had been a schoolgirl, like his own daughter, learning her lessons; he remembered how much there was of shyness and constraint in her laughter, in her way of conversing with a stranger—it was probably the first time in her life that she found herself alone, and in a situation in which men could follow her and watch her, and speak to her, all the time with a secret aim she could not fail to divine. He recalled her slender, delicate neck, her fine gray eyes.

"And yet there's something pathetic about her," he thought to himself as he fell asleep.

II

A week had passed since the beginning of their acquaintance. It was a holiday. Indoors it was stuffy, but the dust rose in clouds out of doors, and people's hats blew off. It was a parching day and Gurov kept going to the outdoor café for fruit drinks and ices to offer Anna Sergeyevna. The heat was overpowering.

In the evening, when the wind had dropped, they walked to the pier to see the steamer come in. There were a great many people strolling about the landing-place; some, bunches of flowers in their hands, were meeting friends. Two peculiarities of the smart Yalta crowd stood out distinctly—the elderly ladies all tried to dress very youthfully, and there seemed to be an inordinate number of generals about.

Owing to the roughness of the sea the steamer arrived late, after the sun had gone down, and it had to maneuver for some time before it could get alongside the pier. Anna Sergeyevna scanned the steamer and passengers through her lorgnette, as if looking for someone she knew, and when she turned to Gurov her eyes were glistening. She talked a great deal, firing off abrupt questions and forgetting immediately what it was she had wanted to know. Then she lost her lorgnette in the crush.

The smart crowd began dispersing, features could no longer be made out, the wind had quite dropped, and Gurov and Anna Sergeyevna stood there as if waiting for someone else to come off the steamer. Anna Sergeyevna had fallen

---

4. An elective provincial council.

silent, every now and then smelling her flowers, but not looking at Gurov.

"It's turning out a fine evening," he said. "What shall we do? We might go for a drive."

She made no reply. 25

He looked steadily at her and suddenly took her in his arms and kissed her lips, and the fragrance and dampness of the flowers closed round him, but the next moment he looked behind him in alarm—had anyone seen them?

"Let's go to your room," he murmured.

And they walked off together, very quickly.

Her room was stuffy and smelt of some scent she had bought in the Japanese shop. Gurov looked at her, thinking to himself: "How full of strange encounters life is!" He could remember carefree, good-natured women who were exhilarated by love-making and grateful to him for the happiness he gave them, however short-lived; and there had been others—his wife among them—whose caresses were insincere, affected, hysterical, mixed up with a great deal of quite unnecessary talk, and whose expression seemed to say that all this was not just love-making or passion, but something much more significant; then there had been two or three beautiful, cold women, over whose features flitted a predatory expression, betraying a determination to wring from life more than it could give, women no longer in their first youth, capricious, irrational, despotic, brainless, and when Gurov had cooled to these, their beauty aroused in him nothing but repulsion, and the lace trimming on their underclothes reminded him of fish-scales.

But here the timidity and awkwardness of youth and inexperience were still 30 apparent; and there was a feeling of embarrassment in the atmosphere, as if someone had just knocked at the door. Anna Sergeyevna, "the lady with the dog," seemed to regard the affair as something very special, very serious, as if she had become a fallen woman, an attitude he found odd and disconcerting. Her features lengthened and drooped, and her long hair hung mournfully on either side of her face. She assumed a pose of dismal meditation, like a repentant sinner in some classical painting.

"It isn't right," she said. "You will never respect me anymore."

On the table was a watermelon. Gurov cut himself a slice from it and began slowly eating it. At least half an hour passed in silence.

Anna Sergeyevna was very touching, revealing the purity of a decent, naïve woman who had seen very little of life. The solitary candle burning on the table scarcely lit up her face, but it was obvious that her heart was heavy.

"Why should I stop respecting you?" asked Gurov. "You don't know what you're saying."

"May God forgive me!" she exclaimed, and her eyes filled with tears. "It's 35 terrible."

"No need to seek to justify yourself."

"How can I justify myself? I'm a wicked, fallen woman, I despise myself and have not the least thought of self-justification. It isn't my husband I have deceived, it's myself. And not only now, I have been deceiving myself for ever so long. My husband is no doubt an honest, worthy man, but he's a flunky. I don't know what it is he does at his office, but I know he's a flunky. I was only twenty when I married him, and I was devoured by curiosity, I wanted something higher. I told myself that there must be a different kind of life I wanted to live, to live. . . . I was burning with curiosity . . . you'll never understand that, but I swear to God I could no longer control myself, nothing could hold me back, I told my husband I was ill, and I came here. . . . And I started going about like one possessed, like a madwoman . . . and now I have become an ordinary, worthless woman, and everyone has a right to despise me."

Gurov listened to her, bored to death. The naïve accents, the remorse, all was so unexpected, so out of place. But for the tears in her eyes, she might have been jesting or play-acting.

"I don't understand," he said gently. "What is it you want?"

She hid her face against his breast and pressed closer to him.

"Do believe me, I implore you to believe me," she said. "I love all that is honest and pure in life, vice is revolting to me, I don't know what I'm doing. The common people say they are snared by the Devil. And now I can say that I have been snared by the Devil, too."

"Come, come," he murmured.

He gazed into her fixed, terrified eyes, kissed her, and soothed her with gentle affectionate words, and gradually she calmed down and regained her cheerfulness. Soon they were laughing together again.

When, a little later, they went out, there was not a soul on the promenade, the town and its cypresses looked dead, but the sea was still roaring as it dashed against the beach. A solitary fishing-boat tossed on the waves, its lamp blinking sleepily.

They found a carriage and drove to Oreanda.

"I discovered your name in the hall, just now," said Gurov, "written up on the board. Von Diederitz. Is your husband a German?"

"No. His grandfather was, I think, but he belongs to the Orthodox Church himself."

When they got out of the carriage at Oreanda they sat down on a bench not far from the church, and looked down at the sea, without talking. Yalta could be dimly discerned through the morning mist, and white clouds rested motion-less on the summits of the mountains. Not a leaf stirred, the grasshoppers chir-ruped, and the monotonous hollow roar of the sea came up to them, speaking of peace, of the eternal sleep lying in wait for us all. The sea had roared like this long before there was any Yalta or Oreanda, it was roaring now, and it would go on roaring, just as indifferently and hollowly, when we had passed away. And it may be that in this continuity, this utter indifference to the life and death of each of us lies hidden the pledge of our eternal salvation, of the continuous movement of life on earth, of the continuous movement toward perfection.

Side by side with a young woman, who looked so exquisite in the early light, soothed and enchanted by the sight of all this magical beauty—sea, mountains, clouds and the vast expanse of the sky—Gurov told himself that, when you came to think of it, everything in the world is beautiful really, everything but our own thoughts and actions, when we lose sight of the higher aims of life, and of our dignity as human beings.

Someone approached them—a watchman, probably—looked at them and went away. And there was something mysterious and beautiful even in this. The steamer from Feodosia could be seen coming towards the pier, lit up by the dawn, its lamps out.

"There's dew on the grass," said Anna Sergeyevna, breaking the silence.

"Yes. Time to go home."

They went back to the town.

After this they met every day at noon on the promenade, lunching and dining together, going for walks, and admiring the sea. She complained of sleeplessness, of palpitations, asked the same questions over and over again, alternately surrendering to jealousy and the fear that he did not really respect her. And often, when there was nobody in sight in the square or the park, he would draw her to him and kiss her passionately. The utter idleness, these kisses in broad daylight, accompanied by furtive glances and the fear of discovery, the heat, the smell of the sea, and the idle, smart, well-fed people continually crossing their field of vision, seemed to have given him a new lease on life. He told Anna Sergeyevna she was beautiful and seductive, made love to her with impetuous passion, and never left her side, while she was always pensive, always trying to force from him the admission that he did not respect her, that he did not love her a bit, and considered her just an ordinary woman. Almost every night they drove out of town, to Oreanda, the waterfall, or some other beauty-spot. And these excursions were invariably a success, each contributing fresh impressions of majestic beauty.

All this time they kept expecting her husband to arrive. But a letter came in which he told his wife that he was having trouble with his eyes, and implored her to come home as soon as possible. Anna Sergeyevna made hasty preparations for leaving.

"It's a good thing I'm going," she said to Gurov. "It's the intervention of fate."

She left Yalta in a carriage, and he went with her as far as the railway station. The drive took nearly a whole day. When she got into the express train, after the second bell had been rung, she said:

"Let me have one more look at you. . . . One last look. That's right."

She did not weep, but was mournful, and seemed ill, the muscles of her cheeks twitching.

"I shall think of you . . . I shall think of you all the time," she said. "God bless you! Think kindly of me. We are parting forever, it must be so, because we ought never to have met. Good-bye—God bless you."

The train steamed rapidly out of the station, its lights soon disappearing, and a minute later even the sound it made was silenced, as if everything were conspiring to bring this sweet oblivion, this madness, to an end as quickly as possible. And Gurov, standing alone on the platform and gazing into the dark distance, listened to the shrilling of the grasshoppers and the humming of the telegraph wires, with a feeling that he had only just awakened. And he told himself that this had been just one more of the many adventures in his life, and that it, too, was over, leaving nothing but a memory. . . . He was moved and sad, and felt a slight remorse. After all, this young woman whom he would never again see had not been really happy with him. He had been friendly and affectionate with her, but in his whole behaviour, in the tones of his voice, in his very caresses, there had been a shade of irony, the insulting indulgence of the fortunate male, who was, moreover, almost twice her age. She had insisted in calling him good, remarkable, high-minded. Evidently he had appeared to her different from his real self, in a word he had involuntarily deceived her. . . .

There was an autumnal feeling in the air, and the evening was chilly.

"It's time for me to be going north, too," thought Gurov, as he walked away from the platform. "High time!"

III

When he got back to Moscow it was beginning to look like winter; the stoves were heated every day, and it was still dark when the children got up to go to school and drank their tea, so that the nurse had to light the lamp for a short time. Frost had set in. When the first snow falls, and one goes for one's first sleigh-ride, it is pleasant to see the white ground, the white roofs; one breathes freely and lightly, and remembers the days of one's youth. The ancient lime-trees and birches, white with hoarfrost, have a good-natured look, they are closer to the heart than cypresses and palms, and beneath their branches one is no longer haunted by the memory of mountains and the sea.

Gurov had always lived in Moscow, and he returned to Moscow on a fine frosty day, and when he put on his fur-lined overcoat and thick gloves, and sauntered down Petrovka Street, and when, on Saturday evening, he heard the church bells ringing, his recent journey and the places he had visited lost their charm for him. He became gradually immersed in Moscow life, reading with avidity three newspapers a day, while declaring he never read Moscow newspapers on principle. Once more he was caught up in a whirl of restaurants, clubs, banquets, and celebrations, once more glowed with the flattering consciousness that well-known lawyers and actors came to his house, that he played cards in the Medical Club opposite a professor. He could once again eat a whole serving of Moscow Fish Stew served in a pan.

He had believed that in a month's time Anna Sergeyevna would be nothing but a vague memory, and that hereafter, with her wistful smile, she would only occasionally appear to him in dreams, like others before her. But the month was now well over and winter was in full swing, and all was as clear in his memory as if he had parted with Anna Sergeyevna only the day before. And his recollections grew ever more insistent. When the voices of his children at their lessons reached him in his study through the evening stillness, when he heard a song, or the sounds of a music-box in a restaurant, when the wind howled in the chimney, it all came back to him: early morning on the pier, the misty mountains, the steamer from Feodosia, the kisses. He would pace up and down his room for a long time, smiling at his memories, and then memory turned into dreaming, and what had happened mingled in his imagination with what was going to happen. Anna Sergeyevna did not come to him in his dreams, she accompanied him everywhere, like his shadow, following him everywhere he went. When he closed his eyes, she seemed to stand before him in the flesh, still lovelier, younger, tenderer than she had really been, and looking back, he saw himself, too, as better than he had been in Yalta. In the evenings she looked out at him from the bookshelves, the fireplace, the corner, he could hear her breathing, the sweet rustle of her skirts. In the streets he followed women with his eyes, to see if there were any like her. . . .

He began to feel an overwhelming desire to share his memories with someone. But he could not speak of his love at home, and outside his home who was there for him to confide in? Not the tenants living in his house, and certainly not his colleagues at the bank. And what was there to tell? Was it love that he had felt? Had there been anything exquisite, poetic, anything instructive or even amusing about his relations with Anna Sergeyevna? He had to content himself with uttering vague generalizations about love and women, and nobody guessed what he meant, though his wife's dark eyebrows twitched as she said:

"The role of a coxcomb doesn't suit you a bit, Dimitry."

One evening, leaving the Medical Club with one of his card-partners, a government official, he could not refrain from remarking:

"If you only knew what a charming woman I met in Yalta!"

The official got into his sleigh, and just before driving off, turned and called out:

"Dmitry Dmitrich!"

"Yes?"

"You were quite right, you know—the sturgeon was just a *leetle* off."

These words, in themselves so commonplace, for some reason infuriated Gurov, seemed to him humiliating, gross. What savage manners, what people! What wasted evenings, what tedious, empty days! Frantic card-playing, gluttony, drunkenness, perpetual talk always about the same thing. The greater part of one's time and energy went on business that was no use to anyone, and on discussing the same thing over and over again, and there was nothing to show for it all but a stunted wingless existence and a round of trivialities, and there was nowhere to escape to, you might as well be in a madhouse or a convict settlement.

Gurov lay awake all night, raging, and went about the whole of the next day with a headache. He slept badly on the succeeding nights, too, sitting up in bed, thinking, or pacing the floor of his room. He was sick of his children, sick of the bank, felt not the slightest desire to go anywhere or talk about anything.

When the Christmas holidays came, he packed his things, telling his wife he had to go to Petersburg in the interests of a certain young man, and set off for the town of S. To what end? He hardly knew himself. He only knew that he must see Anna Sergeyevna, must speak to her, arrange a meeting, if possible.

He arrived at S. in the morning and engaged the best suite in the hotel, which had a carpet of gray military frieze, and a dusty ink-pot on the table, surmounted by a headless rider, holding his hat in his raised hand. The hall porter told him what he wanted to know: von Diederitz had a house of his own in Staro-Goncharnaya Street. It wasn't far from the hotel, he lived on a grand scale, luxuriously, kept carriage-horses, the whole town knew him. The hall porter pronounced the name "Drideritz."

Gurov strolled over to Staro-Goncharnaya Street and discovered the house. In front of it was a long gray fence with inverted nails hammered into the tops of the palings.

80 "A fence like that is enough to make anyone want to run away," thought Gurov, looking at the windows of the house and the fence.

He reasoned that since it was a holiday, Anna's husband would probably be at home. In any case it would be tactless to embarrass her by calling at the house. And a note might fall into the hands of the husband, and bring about catastrophe. The best thing would be to wait about on the chance of seeing her. And he walked up and down the street, hovering in the vicinity of the fence, watching for his chance. A beggar entered the gate, only to be attacked by dogs, then, an hour later, the faint, vague sounds of a piano reached his ears. That would be Anna Sergeyevna playing. Suddenly the front door opened and an old woman came out, followed by a familiar white Pomeranian. Gurov tried to call to it, but his heart beat violently, and in his agitation he could not remember its name.

He walked on, hating the gray fence more and more, and now ready to tell himself irately that Anna Sergeyevna had forgotten him, had already, perhaps, found distraction in another—what could be more natural in a young woman who had to look at this accursed fence from morning to night? He went back to his hotel and sat on the sofa in his suite for some time, not knowing what to do, then he ordered dinner, and after dinner, had a long sleep.

"What a foolish, restless business," he thought, waking up and looking towards the dark windowpanes. It was evening by now. "Well, I've had my sleep out. And what am I to do in the night?"

He sat up in bed, covered by the cheap gray quilt, which reminded him of a hospital blanket, and in his vexation he fell to taunting himself.

85 "You and your lady with a dog . . . there's adventure for you! See what you get for your pains."

On his arrival at the station that morning he had noticed a poster announcing in enormous letters the first performance at the local theatre of *The Geisha*.[5] Remembering this, he got up and made for the theatre.

"It's highly probable that she goes to first nights," he told himself.

The theatre was full. It was a typical provincial theatre, with a mist collecting over the chandeliers, and the crowd in the gallery fidgeting noisily. In the first row of the stalls[6] the local dandies stood waiting for the curtain to go up, their hands clasped behind them. There, in the front seat of the governor's box, sat the governor's daughter, wearing a boa, the governor himself hiding modestly behind the drapes, so that only his hands were visible. The curtain stirred, the

---

5. Operetta by Sidney Jones (1861–1946) which toured Eastern Europe in 1898–99.   6. Seats at the front of a theater, near the stage and separated from nearby seats by a railing.

orchestra took a long time tuning up their instruments. Gurov's eyes roamed eagerly over the audience as they filed in and occupied their seats.

Anna Sergeyevna came in, too. She seated herself in the third row of the stalls, and when Gurov's glance fell on her, his heart seemed to stop, and he knew in a flash that the whole world contained no one nearer or dearer to him, no one more important to his happiness. This little woman, lost in the provincial crowd, in no way remarkable, holding a silly lorgnette in her hand, now filled his whole life, was his grief, his joy, all that he desired. Lulled by the sounds coming from the wretched orchestra, with its feeble, amateurish violinists, he thought how beautiful she was . . . thought and dreamed. . . .

Anna Sergeyevna was accompanied by a tall, round-shouldered young man with small whiskers, who nodded at every step before taking the seat beside her and seemed to be continually bowing to someone. This must be her husband, whom, in a fit of bitterness, at Yalta, she had called a "flunky." And there really was something of a lackey's servility in his lanky figure, his side-whiskers, and the little bald spot on the top of his head. And he smiled sweetly, and the badge of some scientific society gleaming in his buttonhole was like the number on a footman's livery.

The husband went out to smoke in the first interval, and she was left alone in her seat. Gurov, who had taken a seat in the stalls, went up to her and said in a trembling voice, with a forced smile: "How d'you do?"

She glanced up at him and turned pale, then looked at him again in alarm, unable to believe her eyes, squeezing her fan and lorgnette in one hand, evidently struggling to overcome a feeling of faintness. Neither of them said a word. She sat there, and he stood beside her, disconcerted by her embarrassment, and not daring to sit down. The violins and flutes sang out as they were tuned, and there was a tense sensation in the atmosphere, as if they were being watched from all the boxes. At last she got up and moved rapidly towards one of the exits. He followed her and they wandered aimlessly along corridors, up and down stairs; figures flashed by in the uniforms of legal officials, high-school teachers and civil servants, all wearing badges; ladies, coats hanging from pegs flashed by; there was a sharp draft, bringing with it an odor of cigarette butts. And Gurov, whose heart was beating violently, thought:

"What on earth are all these people, this orchestra for? . . ."

The next minute he suddenly remembered how, after seeing Anna Sergeyevna off that evening at the station, he had told himself that all was over, and they would never meet again. And how far away the end seemed to be now!

She stopped on a dark narrow staircase over which was a notice bearing the inscription "To the upper circle."

"How you frightened me!" she said, breathing heavily, still pale and half-stunned. "Oh, how you frightened me! I'm almost dead! Why did you come? Oh, why?"

"But, Anna," he said, in low, hasty tones. "But, Anna. . . . Try to understand . . . do try. . . ."

She cast him a glance of fear, entreaty, love, and then gazed at him steadily, as if to fix his features firmly in her memory.

"I've been so unhappy," she continued, taking no notice of his words. "I could think of nothing but you the whole time, I lived on the thoughts of you. I tried to forget—why, oh, why did you come?"

On the landing above them were two schoolboys, smoking and looking down, but Gurov did not care, and, drawing Anna Sergeyevna towards him, began kissing her face, her lips, her hands.

"What are you doing, oh, what are you doing?" she said in horror, drawing back. "We have both gone mad. Go away this very night, this moment. . . . By all that is sacred, I implore you. . . . Somebody is coming."

Someone was ascending the stairs.

"You must go away," went on Anna Sergeyevna in a whisper. "D'you hear me, Dmitry Dmitrich? I'll come to you in Moscow. I have never been happy, I am unhappy now, and I shall never be happy—never! Do not make me suffer still more! I will come to you in Moscow, I swear it! And now we must part! My dear one, my kind one, my darling, we must part."

She pressed his hand and hurried down the stairs, looking back at him continually, and her eyes showed that she was in truth unhappy. Gurov stood where he was for a short time, listening, and when all was quiet, went to look for his coat, and left the theatre.

IV

And Anna Sergeyevna began going to Moscow to see him. Every two or three months she left the town of S., telling her husband that she was going to consult a specialist on female diseases, and her husband believed her and did not believe her. In Moscow she always stayed at the Slavyanski Bazaar, sending a man in a red cap to Gurov the moment she arrived. Gurov went to her, and no one in Moscow knew anything about it.

One winter morning he went to see her as usual (the messenger had been to him the evening before, but had not found him at home). His daughter was with him, for her school was on the way and he thought he might as well see her to it.

"It is forty degrees," said Gurov to his daughter, "and yet it is snowing. You see it is only above freezing close to the ground, the temperature in the upper layers of the atmosphere is quite different."

"Why doesn't it ever thunder in winter, Papa?"

He explained this, too. As he was speaking, he kept reminding himself that he was going to a rendezvous and that not a living soul knew about it, or, probably, ever would. He led a double life—one in public, in the sight of all whom it concerned, full of conventional truth and conventional deception, exactly like the lives of his friends and acquaintances, and another which flowed in secret. And, owing to some strange, possibly quite accidental chain of circumstances, everything that was important, interesting, essential, everything about which he was sincere and never deceived himself, everything that composed the kernel of his life, went on in secret, while everything that was false in him, everything that composed the husk in which he hid himself and the truth which was in him—his work at the bank, discussions at the club, his "lower race," his attendance at anniversary celebrations with his wife—was on the surface. He began to judge others by himself, no longer believing what he saw, and always assuming that the real, the only interesting life of every individual goes on as under cover of night, secretly. Every individual existence revolves around mystery, and perhaps that is the chief reason that all cultivated individuals insisted so strongly on the respect due to personal secrets.

After leaving his daughter at the door of her school Gurov set off for the Slavyanski Bazaar. Taking off his overcoat in the lobby, he went upstairs and knocked softly on the door. Anna Sergeyevna, wearing the gray dress he liked most, exhausted by her journey and by suspense, had been expecting him since the evening before. She was pale and looked at him without smiling, but was in his arms almost before he was fairly in the room. Their kiss was lingering, prolonged, as if they had not met for years.

"Well, how are you?" he asked. "Anything new?"

"Wait, I'll tell you in a minute. . . . . I can't. . . ."

She could not speak, because she was crying. Turning away, she held her handkerchief to her eyes.

"I'll wait till she's had her cry out," he thought, and sank into a chair.

He rang for tea, and a little later, while he was drinking it, she was still standing there, her face to the window. She wept from emotion, from her bitter consciousness of the sadness of their life; they could only see one another in secret, hiding from people, as if they were thieves. Was not their life a broken one?

"Don't cry," he said.

It was quite obvious to him that this love of theirs would not soon come to an end, and that no one could say when this end would be. Anna Sergeyevna loved him ever more fondly, worshipped him, and there would have been no point in telling her that one day it must end. Indeed, she would not have believed him.

He moved over and took her by the shoulders, intending to caress her, to make a joke, but suddenly he caught sight of himself in the looking-glass.

His hair was already beginning to turn gray. It struck him as strange that he should have aged so much in the last few years, have lost so much of his looks. The shoulders on which his hands lay were warm and quivering. He felt a pity for this life, still so warm and exquisite, but probably soon to fade and droop like his own. Why did she love him so? Women had always believed him different from what he really was, had loved in him not himself but the man their imagination pictured him, a man they had sought for eagerly all their lives. And afterwards when they discovered their mistake, they went on loving him just the same. And not one of them had ever been happy with him. Time had passed, he had met one woman after another, become intimate with each, parted with each, but had never loved. There had been all sorts of things between them, but never love.

And only now, when he was gray-haired, had he fallen in love properly, thoroughly, for the first time in his life.

He and Anna Sergeyevna loved one another as people who are very close and intimate, as husband and wife, as dear friends love one another. It seemd to them that fate had intended them for one another, and they could not understand why she should have a husband, and he a wife. They were like two migrating birds, the male and the female, who had been caught and put into separate cages. They forgave one another all that they were ashamed of in the past and in the present, and felt that this love of theirs had changed them both.

Formerly, in moments of melancholy, he had consoled himself by the first argument that came into his head, but now arguments were nothing to him, he felt profound pity, desired to be sincere, tender.

"Stop crying, my dearest," he said. "You've had your cry, now stop. . . . Now let us have a talk, let us try and think what we are to do."

Then they discussed their situation for a long time, trying to think how they could get rid of the necessity for hiding, deception, living in different towns, being so long without meeting. How were they to shake off these intolerable fetters?

"How? How?" he repeated, clutching his head. "How?"

And it seemed to them that they were within an inch of arriving at a decision, and that then a new, beautiful life would begin. And they both realized that the end was still far, far away, and that the hardest, the most complicated part was only just beginning.

1899

QUESTIONS

1. Describe the location, appearance, and socio-economic make-up of Shady Hill in John Cheever's "The Country Husband." Why is the dog Jupiter "an anomaly" (par. 10)? Why do Clayton Thomas and Anne also not "belong"? You might look at the story as a struggle between Francis Weed (weeds do not belong on suburban lawns) and Shady Hill; who wins? The story begins, "To begin at the beginning . . ." and tells about the near-crash of Francis's plane; why is that the beginning? what is it the beginning of?

2. "The Country Husband" is set in the 1950s; how would the story differ if set in a similar environment but in the 1990s?

3. The mother of Jing-Mei Woo, in "A Pair of Tickets," told her that being Chinese is a matter of genetics and she finds that that is true. What is the role of place and time (history), then, in this story?

4. Yalta, where "The Lady with the Dog" opens, is a resort on the Black Sea; Moscow, where Gurov lives, is described at the beginning of section III. To what extent do the settings relate to the events and emotions of the story? How do other details—such as the watermelon in II (Yalta) and the slightly "off"

sturgeon in III (Moscow)—relate to the settings and the attitudes and feelings associated with the places? Which are conventionally assumed to be more real, the feelings we have on holiday or those in our everyday lives? How is this convention related to our expectations about the outcome of the story? to the meaning of the story?

WRITING SUGGESTIONS

1. Re-tell "The Country Husband," or a portion of it, from Julia Weed's point of view (or from Anne's).

2. Compare the use of episodes from World War II in "The Country Husband" and "A Pair of Tickets."

3. Write a personal narrative about a visit to a place important in your family history that you had never visited before and how you felt about your relation to that place; or about an episode that made you recognize or affirm your ethnic identity or heritage.

4. Compare the treatment of infidelity in Cheever and Chekhov.

5. Write a fifth section of "The Lady with the Dog."

5 SYMBOLS

O ne of the chief devices for bridging the gap between the writer's vision and the reader's is the **symbol,** commonly defined as something that stands for something else: a flower, for example, may be seen as a symbol of a particular state. Symbols are generally **figurative;** that is, they compare or put together two *unlike* things. While a senator may represent a state, he represents it *literally:* the state is a governmental unit, and the senator is a member of the government. But the flower has little to do with governing the state, and so represents it only figuratively.

But why speak of anything in terms of something else? Why should snakes commonly be symbolic of evil? Sure, some snakes are poisonous, but for some people so are bees, and a lot of snakes are not only harmless but actually helpful ecologically. (In Kipling's *The Jungle Book* the python Ka, while frightening, is on the side of Law and Order.) Through repeated use over the centuries, the snake has become a traditional symbol of Evil—not just danger, sneakiness, repulsiveness, but theological, absolute Evil. Had Peyton Farquhar, in "An Occurrence at Owl Creek Bridge," been confronted by a snake when he was thrown ashore, we would not necessarily have said, "Aha—snake, symbol of Evil," though that potential meaning might have hovered around the incident and sent us looking backward and forward in the story for supporting evidence that this snake was being used symbolically. However, when we discover that the stranger in "Young Goodman Brown" has a walking stick upon which is carved the image of a snake, we are much more likely to find it such a symbol because of other, related potential symbols or meanings in the context: the term *Goodman* in the title of the story sets up the distinct possibility that Brown (how common a name) stands for more than a "mere" individual young man. Brown's bride is named Faith—a common name among the early Puritans, but together with *Goodman* suggesting symbolic possibilities. Then, just before the stranger with the walking stick appears, Brown says, "What if the devil himself should be at my very elbow!"

A single item, even something as traditionally fraught with meaning as a snake or a rose, becomes a symbol only when its potentially symbolic meaning is confirmed by something else in the story, just as a point needs a second point to define a line. Multiple symbols, potential symbols, direct and indirect hints such as Brown's mention of the devil: these are among the ways in which details may be identified as symbols (for interpreting symbols is relatively easy once you know what is and what is probably not a symbol).

One form of what may be called an indirect hint is repetition. That an "old maid" like Judith should have a cat seems so ordinary it borders on the trite. But when she chooses to have her male cat put to death rather than neutered, it is likely to make some of us sit up and take notice. This choice may suggest something about the unconventional in her character, but we probably don't think of the cat in itself representing anything. What happens, though, when there appears another cat, a female this time, whose sex life calls forth strange behavior on Judith's part? And when the killing of a kitten interrupts Judith's affair with Luigi? It is difficult to say when or if the literal cats shade off into symbols, for they remain so solidly cats in the story. All we can say for sure is that cats become more important in reading and understanding this story than, say, the cask of Amontillado does in the Poe story. The cask remains a thing pure and simple. Repetition, then, calls attention to details and may alert us to potential symbolic overtones, but it does not necessarily turn a thing into a symbol; so long as we get the suggestions of significance, however, agreeing on exactly what—or when—something can be called a symbol is not important.

Direct hints may take the form of explicit statements. (Authors are not so anxious to hide their meanings as some readers are prone to believe.) We also may be alerted to the fact that something is standing for something else when the something does not seem to make literal sense in itself. It does not take us long to realize that "Young Goodman Brown" is not entirely as realistic a story as "My Man Bovanne" or "The Whirlpool Rapids." When things do not seem explicable in terms of everyday reality, we often look beyond them for some meaning. Roses are real enough, but neither Faulkner's narrator nor anyone else in the story gives Emily a real rose. What, then, does the rose in the title "A Rose for Emily" suggest?

We must remember, however, that symbols do not exist solely for the transmission of a meaning we can paraphrase; they do not disappear from the story, our memory, or our response once their "meaning" has been sucked out of them, any more than Emily ceases to exist as an individual after we recognize her representative or universal nature. Faith's pink ribbons and Judith's cats are objects in their stories, whatever meanings or suggestions of meanings they have given rise to.

As I have often implied and occasionally said, few symbols can be exhausted, translated into an abstract phrase or equivalent: the "something else" that the "something" stands for is ultimately elusive. After you have read Ann Beattie's "Janus" try to paraphrase just what the bowl stands for. Or explain with certainty what Faith's pink ribbon symbolizes in "Young Goodman

Brown." It is not that the bowl and the ribbon mean nothing but that they mean so many things that no single equivalence will do; even an abstract statement seems to reduce rather than fully explain the significance to the reader.

When a figure is expressed as an explicit comparison, often signaled by *like* or *as,* it is called a **simile:** "eyes as blue as the sky"; "the baby brother I'd never known looked out from the depths of his private life, like an animal waiting to be coaxed into the light" ("Sonny's Blues"). An implicit comparison or identification of one thing with another unlike itself, without a verbal signal but just seeming to say "A *is* B," is called a **metaphor:** "the grass was a green carpet"; "there was a boiling wave of dogs about them" ("The Old People"). Sometimes all figures are loosely referred to as metaphors.

An **allegory** is like a metaphor in that one thing (usually non-rational, abstract, religious) is implicitly spoken of in terms of something that is concrete and usually sensuous (perceptible by the senses), but the comparison in allegory is extended to include a whole work or a large portion of a work. *The Pilgrim's Progress* is probably the most famous prose allegory in English; its central character is named Christian; he was born in the City of Destruction and sets out for the Celestial City, passes through the Slough of Despond and Vanity Fair, meets men named Pliable and Obstinate, and so on.

When an entire story, like "Young Goodman Brown," is symbolic, it is sometimes called a **myth.** *Myth* originally meant a story of communal origin that provided an explanation or religious interpretation of man, nature, the universe, and the relation between them. From the vantage point of another culture or set of beliefs, the word usually implied that the story was false: we speak of classical myths, but Christians do not speak of Christian myth. We also apply the term *myth* now to stories by individuals, sophisticated authors, but often there is still the implication that the mythic story relates to a communal or group experience, whereas a symbolic story may be more personal or private. It is hard to draw the line firmly: "Young Goodman Brown" seems to have clearly national, American implications, while "The Rocking-Horse Winner" may be a private Lawrencian symbol or a myth of modern bourgeois society. A plot or character element that recurs in cultural or cross-cultural myths, such as images of the devil, as in "Young Goodman Brown," is now widely called an **archetype.**

A symbol can be as brief and local as a metaphor or as extended as an allegory. Like an allegory it usually speaks in concrete terms of the non- or super-rational, the abstract, that which is not immediately perceived by the senses. Though some allegories can be complex, with paraphrasable equivalences, allegory usually refers to a one-to-one relationship (as the names from *The Pil-*

grim's Progress imply), and literary symbols usually have high complex or even inexpressible equivalences, as in "Janus." "The Termitary" is a rather simple symbolic story. It gets the effect of complexity by masking the symbol until the final sentence, compelling us to think back over the story and construct or reconstruct the parallels, and it gets its power from the surprise and the complex bitterness of the ending. "Janus" is somewhat more complexly symbolic in that there are areas of meaning or implication that cannot be rendered in other terms or conveniently separated from the particulars of the story. The ultimate unparaphrasable nature of most symbolic images or stories is not vagueness but richness, not disorder but complexity.

SYMBOLS A Glossary

allegory: as in *metaphor*, one thing (usually non-rational, abstract, religious) is implicitly spoken of in terms of something concrete, usually sensuous, but in an allegory the comparison is extended to include an entire work or large portion of a work.

archetype: a plot or character element that recurs in cultural or cross-cultural myths

figurative: non-literal; implicitly or explicitly representative of something in terms of some other unlike thing that seems to be similar or analogous

metaphor: an implicit comparison or identification of one thing with another unlike itself without the use of a verbal signal

myth: like allegory, myth usually is symbolic and extensive, including an entire work or story; though it no longer is necessarily specific to a single culture and pervasive in that culture—individual authors may now be said to create myths—there is still a sense that myth is communal or cultural, while the symbolic can often be private or personal.

simile: a figure that explicitly expresses the comparison, often signaled by *like* or *as*

symbol: a person, place, thing, event, or pattern in a literary work that designates itself and at the same time figuratively represents or "stands for" something else. Often the thing or idea represented is more abstract, general, non- or super-rational; the symbol more concrete and particular.

NATHANIEL HAWTHORNE

Young Goodman Brown

Young goodman Brown came forth, at sunset, into the street of Salem village,[1] but put his head back, after crossing the threshold, to exchange a parting kiss with his young wife. And Faith, as the wife was aptly named, thrust her own pretty head into the street, letting the wind play with the pink ribbons of her cap, while she called to goodman Brown.

"Dearest heart," whispered she, softly and rather sadly, when her lips were close to his ear, "pr'y thee, put off your journey until sunrise, and sleep in your own bed to-night. A lone woman is troubled with such dreams and such thoughts, that she's afeard of herself, sometimes. Pray, tarry with me this night, dear husband, of all nights in the year!"

"My love and my Faith," replied young goodman Brown, "of all nights in the year, this one night must I tarry away from thee. My journey, as thou callest it, forth and back again, must needs be done 'twixt now and sunrise. What, my sweet, pretty wife, dost thou doubt me already, and we but three months married!"

"Then, God bless you!" said Faith, with the pink ribbons, "and may you find all well, when you come back."

"Amen!" cried goodman Brown. "Say thy prayers, dear Faith, and go to bed at dusk, and no harm will come to thee."

So they parted; and the young man pursued his way, until, being about to turn the corner by the meeting-house, he looked back, and saw the head of Faith still peeping after him, with a melancholy air, in spite of her pink ribbons.

"Poor little Faith!" thought he, for his heart smote him. "What a wretch am I, to leave her on such an errand! She talks of dreams, too. Methought, as she spoke, there was trouble in her face, as if a dream had warned her what work is to be done to-night. But, no, no! 't would kill her to think it. Well; she's a blessed angel on earth; and after this one night, I'll cling to her skirts and follow her to Heaven."

With this excellent resolve for the future, goodman Brown felt himself justified in making more haste on his present evil purpose. He had taken a dreary road, darkened by all the gloomiest trees of the forest, which barely stood aside to let the narrow path creep through, and closed immediately behind. It was all as lonely as could be; and there is this peculiarity in such a solitude, that the traveler knows not who may be concealed by the innumerable trunks and the thick boughs overhead; so that, with lonely footsteps, he may yet be passing through an unseen multitude.

"There may be a devilish Indian behind every tree," said goodman Brown,

1. Salem, Massachusetts, Hawthorne's birthplace (1804) was the scene of the famous witch trials of 1692; *goodman*: husband, master of household.

to himself; and he glanced fearfully behind him, as he added, "What if the devil himself should be at my very elbow!"

His head being turned back, he passed a crook of the road, and looking forward again, beheld the figure of a man, in grave and decent attire, seated at the foot of an old tree. He arose, at goodman Brown's approach, and walked onward, side by side with him.

"You are late, goodman Brown," said he. "The clock of the Old South was striking as I came through Boston; and that is full fifteen minutes agone."

"Faith kept me back awhile," replied the young man, with a tremor in his voice, caused by the sudden appearance of his companion, though not wholly unexpected.

It was now deep dusk in the forest, and deepest in that part of it where these two were journeying. As nearly as could be discerned, the second traveler was about fifty years old, apparently in the same rank of life as goodman Brown, and bearing a considerable resemblance to him, though perhaps more in expression than features. Still, they might have been taken for father and son. And yet, though the elder person was as simply clad as the younger, and as simple in manner too, he had an indescribable air of one who knew the world, and would not have felt abashed at the governor's dinner-table, or in king William's[2] court, were it possible that his affairs should call him thither. But the only thing about him, that could be fixed upon as remarkable, was his staff, which bore the likeness of a great black snake, so curiously wrought, that it might almost be seen to twist and wriggle itself, like a living serpent. This, of course, must have been an ocular deception, assisted by the uncertain light.

"Come, goodman Brown!" cried his fellow-traveler, "this is a dull pace for the beginning of a journey. Take my staff, if you are so soon weary."

"Friend," said the other, exchanging his slow pace for a full stop, "having kept covenant by meeting thee here, it is my purpose now to return whence I came. I have scruples, touching the matter thou wot'st of."

"Sayest thou so?" replied he of the serpent, smiling apart. "Let us walk on, nevertheless, reasoning as we go, and if I convince thee not, thou shalt turn back. We are but a little way in the forest, yet."

"Too far, too far!" exclaimed the goodman, unconsciously resuming his walk. "My father never went into the woods on such an errand, nor his father before him. We have been a race of honest men and good Christians, since the days of the martyrs. And shall I be the first of the name of Brown, that ever took this path, and kept"—

"Such company, thou wouldst say," observed the elder person, interpreting his pause. "Good, goodman Brown! I have been as well acquainted with your family as with ever a one among the Puritans; and that's no trifle to say. I helped your grandfather, the constable, when he lashed the Quaker woman so smartly through the streets of Salem. And it was I that brought your father a pitch-pine

2. William III 1650–1702, ruled England from 1689 to 1702, until 1694 jointly with his wife, Mary II.

knot, kindled at my own hearth, to set fire to an Indian village, in king Philip's[3] war. They were my good friends, both; and many a pleasant walk have we had along this path, and returned merrily after midnight. I would fain be friends with you, for their sake."

"If it be as thou sayest," replied goodman Brown, "I marvel they never spoke of these matters. Or, verily, I marvel not, seeing that the least rumor of the sort would have driven them from New-England. We are a people of prayer, and good works, to boot, and abide no such wickedness."

20 "Wickedness or not," said the traveler with the twisted staff, "I have a very general acquaintance here in New-England. The deacons of many a church have drunk the communion wine with me; the selectmen, of divers towns, make me their chairman; and a majority of the Great and General Court are firm supporters of my interest. The governor and I, too—but these are state-secrets."

"Can this be so!" cried goodman Brown, with a stare of amazement at his undisturbed companion. "Howbeit, I have nothing to do with the governor and council; they have their own ways, and are no rule for a simple husbandman, like me. But, were I to go on with thee, how should I meet the eye of that good old man, our minister, at Salem village? Oh, his voice would make me tremble, both Sabbath-day and lecture-day!"[4]

Thus far, the elder traveler had listened with due gravity, but now burst into a fit of irrepressible mirth, shaking himself so violently, that his snake-like staff actually seemed to wriggle in sympathy.

"Ha! ha! ha!" shouted he, again and again; then composing himself, "Well, go on, goodman Brown, go on; but, pr'y thee, don't kill me with laughing!"

"Well, then, to end the matter at once," said goodman Brown, considerably nettled, "there is my wife, Faith. It would break her dear little heart; and I'd rather break my own!"

25 "Nay, if that be the case," answered the other, "e'en[5] go thy ways, goodman Brown. I would not, for twenty old women like the one hobbling before us, that Faith should come to any harm."

As he spoke, he pointed his staff at a female figure on the path, in whom goodman Brown recognized a very pious and exemplary dame, who had taught him his catechism, in youth, and was still his moral and spiritual adviser, jointly with the minister and deacon Gookin.

"A marvel, truly, that goody[6] Cloyse should be so far in the wilderness, at night-fall!" said he. "But, with your leave, friend, I shall take a cut through the woods, until we have left this Christian woman behind. Being a stranger to you, she might ask whom I was consorting with, and whither I was going."

"Be it so," said his fellow-traveler. "Betake you to the woods, and let me keep the path."

Accordingly, the young man turned aside, but took care to watch his com-

---

3. Metacom or Metacomet, chief of the Wampanoag Indians, known as King Philip, led a war against the New England colonists in 1675–76 which devastated many frontier communities.
4. The day—in the New England colonies usually a Thursday—appointed for an informal sermon.
5. Just.   6. Short for "goodwife" or housewife.

panion, who advanced softly along the road, until he had come within a staff's length of the old dame. She, meanwhile, was making the best of her way, with singular speed for so aged a woman, and mumbling some indistinct words, a prayer, doubtless, as she went. The traveler put forth his staff, and touched her withered neck with what seemed the serpent's tail.

"The devil!" screamed the pious old lady.

"Then goody Cloyse knows her old friend?" observed the traveler, confronting her, and leaning on his writhing stick.

"Ah, forsooth, and is it your worship, indeed?" cried the good dame. "Yea, truly is it, and in the very image of my old gossip, goodman Brown, the grandfather of the silly fellow that now is. But, would your worship believe it? my broomstick hath strangely disappeared, stolen, as I suspect, by that unhanged witch, goody Cory, and that, too, when I was all anointed with the juice of smallage and cinque-foil and wolf's-bane"—[7]

"Mingled with fine wheat and the fat of a new-born babe," said the shape of old goodman Brown.

"Ah, your worship knows the receipt," cried the old lady, cackling aloud. "So, as I was saying, being all ready for the meeting, and no horse to ride on, I made up my mind to foot it; for they tell me, there is a nice young man to be taken into communion to-night. But now your good worship will lend me your arm, and we shall be there in a twinkling."

"That can hardly be," answered her friend. "I may not spare you my arm, goody Cloyse, but here is my staff, if you will."

So saying, he threw it down at her feet, where, perhaps, it assumed life, being one of the rods which its owner had formerly lent to the Egyptian Magi.[8] Of this fact, however, goodman Brown could not take cognizance. He had cast up his eyes in astonishment, and looking down again, beheld neither goody Cloyse nor the serpentine staff, but his fellow-traveler alone, who waited for him as calmly as if nothing had happened.

"That old woman taught me my catechism!" said the young man; and there was a world of meaning in this simple comment.

They continued to walk onward, while the elder traveler exhorted his companion to make good speed and persevere in the path, discoursing so aptly, that his arguments seemed rather to spring up in the bosom of his auditor, than to be suggested by himself. As they went, he plucked a branch of maple, to serve for a walking-stick, and began to strip it of the twigs and little boughs, which were wet with evening dew. The moment his fingers touched them, they became strangely withered and dried up, as with a week's sunshine. Thus the pair proceeded, at a good free pace, until suddenly, in a gloomy hollow of the road, goodman Brown sat himself down on the stump of a tree, and refused to go any farther.

7. Plants traditionally associated with witchcraft.   8. Exodus 7:9–12. The Lord instructs Moses to have his prophet Aaron throw down his rod before the Pharaoh, whereupon it will be turned into a serpent, and by which miracle the Pharaoh will be persuaded to let the Jews go into the wilderness to sacrifice to God. The Pharaoh has his magicians (Magi) do likewise, "but Aaron's rod swallowed up their rods."

"Friend," said he, stubbornly, "my mind is made up. Not another step will I budge on this errand. What if a wretched old woman do choose to go to the devil, when I thought she was going to Heaven! Is that any reason why I should quit my dear Faith, and go after her?"

40   "You will think better of this, by-and-by," said his acquaintance, composedly. "Sit here and rest yourself awhile; and when you feel like moving again, there is my staff to help you along."

Without more words, he threw his companion the maple stick, and was as speedily out of sight, as if he had vanished into the deepening gloom. The young man sat a few moments, by the roadside, applauding himself greatly, and thinking with how clear a conscience he should meet the minister, in his morning-walk, nor shrink from the eye of good old deacon Gookin. And what calm sleep would be his, that very night, which was to have been spent so wickedly, but purely and sweetly now, in the arms of Faith! Amidst these pleasant and praise-worthy meditations, goodman Brown heard the tramp of horses along the road, and deemed it advisable to conceal himself within the verge of the forest, conscious of the guilty purpose that had brought him thither, though now so happily turned from it.

On came the hoof-tramps and the voices of the riders, two grave old voices, conversing soberly as they drew near. These mingled sounds appeared to pass along the road, within a few yards of the young man's hiding-place; but owing, doubtless, to the depth of the gloom, at that particular spot, neither the travelers nor their steeds were visible. Though their figures brushed the small boughs by the way-side, it could not be seen that they intercepted, even for a moment, the faint gleam from the strip of bright sky, athwart which they must have passed. Goodman Brown alternately crouched and stood on tip-toe, pulling aside the branches, and thrusting forth his head as far as he durst, without discerning so much as a shadow. It vexed him the more, because he could have sworn, were such a thing possible, that he recognized the voices of the minister and deacon Gookin, jogging along quietly, as they were wont to do, when bound to some ordination or ecclesiastical council. While yet within hearing, one of the riders stopped to pluck a switch.

"Of the two, reverend Sir," said the voice like the deacon's, "I had rather miss an ordination-dinner than to-night's meeting. They tell me that some of our community are to be here from Falmouth[9] and beyond, and others from Connecticut and Rhode-Island; besides several of the Indian powows, who, after their fashion, know almost as much deviltry as the best of us. Moreover, there is a goodly young woman to be taken into communion."

"Mighty well, deacon Gookin!" replied the solemn old tones of the minister. "Spur up, or we shall be late. Nothing can be done, you know, until I get on the ground."

45   The hoofs clattered again, and the voices, talking so strangely in the empty air, passed on through the forest, where no church had ever been gathered, nor solitary Christian prayed. Whither, then, could these holy men be journeying,

---

9. A port in extreme southern Massachusetts; Salem is in northern Massachusetts.

so deep into the heathen wilderness? Young goodman Brown caught hold of a tree, for support, being ready to sink down on the ground, faint and overburthened with the heavy sickness of his heart. He looked up to the sky, doubting whether there really was a Heaven above him. Yet, there was the blue arch, and the stars brightening in it.

"With Heaven above, and Faith below, I will yet stand firm against the devil!" cried goodman Brown.

While he still gazed upward, into the deep arch of the firmament, and had lifted his hands to pray, a cloud, though no wind was stirring, hurried across the zenith, and hid the brightening stars. The blue sky was still visible, except directly overhead, where this black mass of cloud was sweeping swiftly northward. Aloft in the air, as if from the depths of the cloud, came a confused and doubtful sound of voices. Once, the listener fancied that he could distinguish the accents of town's-people of his own, men and women, both pious and ungodly, many of whom he had met at the communion-table, and had seen others rioting at the tavern. The next moment, so indistinct were the sounds, he doubted whether he had heard aught but the murmur of the old forest, whispering without a wind. Then came a stronger swell of those familiar tones, heard daily in the sunshine, at Salem village, but never, until now, from a cloud of night. There was one voice, of a young woman, uttering lamentations, yet with an uncertain sorrow, and entreating for some favor, which, perhaps, it would grieve her to obtain. And all the unseen multitude, both saints and sinners, seemed to encourage her onward.

"Faith!" shouted goodman Brown, in a voice of agony and desperation; and the echoes of the forest mocked him, crying—"Faith! Faith!" as if bewildered wretches were seeking her, all through the wilderness.

The cry of grief, rage, and terror, was yet piercing the night, when the unhappy husband held his breath for a response. There was a scream, drowned immediately in a louder murmur of voices, fading into far-off laughter, as the dark cloud swept away, leaving the clear and silent sky above goodman Brown. But something fluttered lightly down through the air, and caught on the branch of a tree. The young man seized it, and beheld a pink ribbon.

"My Faith is gone!" cried he, after one stupefied moment. "There is no good on earth; and sin is but a name. Come, devil! for to thee is this world given." 50

And maddened with despair, so that he laughed loud and long, did goodman Brown grasp his staff and set forth again, at such a rate, that he seemed to fly along the forest-path, rather than to walk or run. The road grew wilder and drearier, and more faintly traced, and vanished at length, leaving him in the heart of the dark wilderness, still rushing onward, with the instinct that guides mortal man to evil. The whole forest was peopled with frightful sounds; the creaking of the trees, the howling of wild beasts, and the yell of Indians; while, sometimes, the wind tolled like a distant church-bell, and sometimes gave a broad roar around the traveler, as if all Nature were laughing him to scorn. But he was himself the chief horror of the scene, and shrank not from its other horrors.

"Ha! ha! ha!" roared goodman Brown, when the wind laughed at him. "Let us hear which will laugh loudest! Think not to frighten me with your deviltry! Come witch, come wizard, come Indian powow, come devil himself! and here come goodman Brown. You may as well fear him as he fear you!"

In truth, all through the haunted forest, there could be nothing more fright-ful than the figure of goodman Brown. On he flew, among the black pines, brandishing his staff with frenzied gestures, now giving vent to an inspiration of horrid blasphemy, and now shouting forth such laughter, as set all the echoes of the forest laughing like demons around him. The fiend in his own shape is less hideous, than when he rages in the breast of man. Thus sped the demoniac on his course, until, quivering among the trees, he saw a red light before him, as when the felled trunks and branches of a clearing have been set on fire, and throw up their lurid blaze against the sky, at the hour of midnight. He paused, in a lull of the tempest that had driven him onward, and heard the swell of what seemed a hymn, rolling solemnly from a distance, with the weight of many voices. He knew the tune; it was a familiar one in the choir of the village meet-ing-house. The verse died heavily away, and was lengthened by a chorus, not of human voices, but of all the sounds of the benighted wilderness, pealing in awful harmony together. Goodman Brown cried out; and his cry was lost to his own ear, by its unison with the cry of the desert.

In the interval of silence, he stole forward, until the light glared full upon his eyes. At one extremity of an open space, hemmed in by the dark wall of the forest, arose a rock, bearing some rude, natural resemblance either to an altar or a pulpit, and surrounded by four blazing pines, their tops a flame, their stems untouched, like candles at an evening meeting. The mass of foliage, that had overgrown the summit of the rock, was all on fire, blazing high into the night, and fitfully illuminating the whole field. Each pendent twig and leafy festoon was in a blaze. As the red light arose and fell, a numerous congregation alter-nately shone forth, then disappeared in shadow, and again grew, as it were, out of the darkness, peopling the heart of the solitary woods at once.

55   "A grave and dark-clad company!" quoth goodman Brown.

In truth, they were such. Among them, quivering to-and-fro, between gloom and splendor, appeared faces that would be seen, next day, at the council-board of the province, and others which, Sabbath after Sabbath, looked devoutly heav-enward, and benignantly over the crowded pews, from the holiest pulpits in the land. Some affirm, that the lady of the governor was there. At least, there were high dames well known to her, and wives of honored husbands, and widows, a great multitude, and ancient maidens, all of excellent repute, and fair young girls, who trembled, lest their mothers should espy them. Either the sudden gleams of light, flashing over the obscure field, bedazzled goodman Brown, or he recognized a score of the church-members of Salem village, famous for their especial sanctity. Good old deacon Gookin had arrived, and waited at the skirts of that venerable saint, his revered pastor. But, irreverently consorting with these grave, reputable, and pious people, these elders of the church, these chaste dames and dewy virgins, there were men of dissolute lives and women of spotted fame, wretches given over to all mean and filthy vice, and suspected even of horrid crimes. It was strange to see, that the good shrank not from the wicked, nor were

the sinners abashed by the saints. Scattered, also, among their pale-faced enemies, were the Indian priests, or powows, who had often scared their native forest
with more hideous incantations than any known to English witchcraft.

"But, where is Faith?" thought goodman Brown; and, as hope came into his
heart, he trembled.

Another verse of the hymn arose, a slow and solemn strain, such as the pious
love, but joined to words which expressed all that our nature can conceive of
sin, and darkly hinted at far more. Unfathomable to mere mortals is the lore of
fiends. Verse after verse was sung, and still the chorus of the desert swelled
between, like the deepest tone of a mighty organ. And, with the final peal of that
dreadful anthem, there came a sound, as if the roaring wind, the rushing streams,
the howling beasts, and every other voice of the unconverted wilderness, were
mingling and according with the voice of guilty man, in homage to the prince
of all. The four blazing pines threw up a loftier flame, and obscurely discovered
shapes and visages of horror on the smoke-wreaths, above the impious assembly.
At the same moment, the fire on the rock shot redly forth, and formed a glowing
arch above its base, where now appeared a figure. With reverence be it spoken,
the apparition bore no slight similitude, both in garb and manner, to some grave
divine of the New-England churches.

"Bring forth the converts!" cried a voice, that echoed through the field and
rolled into the forest.

At the word, goodman Brown stept forth from the shadow of the trees, and
approached the congregation, with whom he felt a loathful brotherhood, by the
sympathy of all that was wicked in his heart. He could have well nigh sworn,
that the shape of his own dead father beckoned him to advance, looking downward from a smoke-wreath, while a woman, with dim features of despair, threw
out her hand to warn him back. Was it his mother? But he had no power to
retreat one step, nor to resist, even in thought, when the minister and good old
deacon Gookin, seized his arms, and led him to the blazing rock. Thither came
also the slender form of a veiled female, led between Goody Cloyse, that pious
teacher of the catechism, and Martha Carrier, who had received the devil's promise
to be queen of hell. A rampant hag was she! And there stood the proselytes,
beneath the canopy of fire.

"Welcome, my children," said the dark figure, "to the communion of your
race! Ye have found, thus young, your nature and your destiny. My children,
look behind you!"

They turned; and flashing forth, as it were, in a sheet of flame, the fiend-
worshippers were seen; the smile of welcome gleamed darkly on every visage.

"There," resumed the sable form, "are all whom ye have reverenced from
youth. Ye deemed them holier than yourselves, and shrank from your own sin,
contrasting it with their lives of righteousness, and prayerful aspirations heaven-
ward. Yet, here are they all, in my worshipping assembly! This night it shall be
granted you to know their secret deeds; how hoary-bearded elders of the church
have whispered wanton words to the young maids of their households; how many
a woman, eager for widow's weeds, has given her husband a drink at bed-time,
and let him sleep his last sleep in her bosom; how beardless youths have made

60

haste to inherit their fathers' wealth; and how fair damsels—blush not, sweet ones!—have dug little graves in the garden, and bidden me, the sole guest, to an infant's funeral. By the sympathy of your human hearts for sin, ye shall scent out all the places—whether in church, bed-chamber, street, field, or forest— where crime has been committed, and shall exult to behold the whole earth one stain of guilt, one mighty blood-spot. Far more than this! It shall be yours to penetrate, in every bosom, the deep mystery of sin, the fountain of all wicked arts, and which, inexhaustibly supplies more evil impulses than human power— than my power, at its utmost!—can make manifest in deeds. And now, my children, look upon each other."

They did so; and, by the blaze of the hell-kindled torches, the wretched man beheld his Faith, and the wife her husband, trembling before that unhallowed altar.

"Lo! there ye stand, my children," said the figure, in a deep and solemn tone, almost sad, with its despairing awfulness, as if his once angelic nature could yet mourn for our miserable race. "Depending upon one another's hearts, ye had still hoped, that virtue were not all a dream. Now are ye undeceived! Evil is the nature of mankind. Evil must be your only happiness. Welcome, again, my children, to the communion of your race!"

"Welcome!" repeated the fiend-worshippers, in one cry of despair and triumph.

And there they stood, the only pair, as it seemed, who were yet hesitating on the verge of wickedness, in this dark world. A basin was hollowed, naturally, in the rock. Did it contain water, reddened by the lurid light? or was it blood? or, perchance, a liquid flame? Herein did the Shape of Evil dip his hand, and prepare to lay the mark of baptism upon their foreheads, that they might be partakers of the mystery of sin, more conscious of the secret guilt of others, both in deed and thought, than they could now be of their own. The husband cast one look at his pale wife, and Faith at him. What polluted wretches would the next glance shew them to each other, shuddering alike at what they disclosed and what they saw!

"Faith! Faith!" cried the husband. "Look up to Heaven, and resist the Wicked One!"

Whether Faith obeyed, he knew not. Hardly had he spoken, when he found himself amid calm night and solitude, listening to a roar of the wind, which died heavily away through the forest. He staggered against the rock and felt it chill and damp, while a hanging twig, that had been all on fire, besprinkled his cheek with the coldest dew.

The next morning, young goodman Brown came slowly into the street of Salem village, staring around him like a bewildered man. The good old minister was taking a walk along the graveyard, to get an appetite for breakfast and meditate his sermon, and bestowed a blessing, as he passed, on goodman Brown. He shrank from the venerable saint, as if to avoid an anathema. Old deacon Gookin was at domestic worship, and the holy words of his prayer were heard through the open window. "What God doth the wizard pray to?" quoth goodman Brown. Goody Cloyse, that excellent old Christian, stood in the early sunshine, at her own lattice, catechising a little girl, who had brought her a pint of morning's milk. Goodman Brown snatched away the child, as from the grasp of the fiend himself. Turning the corner by the meeting-house, he spied the head of Faith, with the pink ribbons, gazing anxiously forth, and bursting into such joy at sight of him, that she skipt along the street, and almost kissed her husband before the whole village. But, goodman Brown looked sternly and sadly into her face, and passed on without a greeting.

Had goodman Brown fallen asleep in the forest, and only dreamed a wild dream of a witch-meeting?

Be it so, if you will. But, alas! it was a dream of evil omen for young good-man Brown. A stern, a sad, a darkly meditative, a distrustful, if not a desperate man, did he become, from the night of that fearful dream. On the Sabbath-day, when the congregation were singing a holy psalm, he could not listen, because an anthem of sin rushed loudly upon his ear, and drowned all the blessed strain. When the minister spoke from the pulpit, with power and fervid eloquence, and, with his hand on the open bible, of the sacred truths of our religion, and of saint-like lives and triumphant deaths, and of future bliss or misery unutterable, then did goodman Brown turn pale, dreading, lest the roof should thunder down upon the gray blasphemer and his hearers. Often, awakening suddenly at midnight, he shrank from the bosom of Faith, and at morning or eventide, when the family knelt down at prayer, he scowled, and muttered to himself, and gazed sternly at his wife, and turned away. And when he had lived long, and was borne to his grave, a hoary corpse, followed by Faith, an aged woman, and children and grandchildren, a goodly procession, besides neighbors, not a few, they carved no hopeful verse upon his tomb-stone; for his dying hour was gloom.

1835

NADINE GORDIMER

The Termitary

When you live in a small town far from the world you read about in municipal library books, the advent of repair men in the house is a festival. Daily life is gaily broken open, improvisation takes over. The living-room masquerades as a bedroom while the smell of paint in the bedroom makes it uninhabitable. The secret backs of confident objects (matchwood draped with cobwebs thickened by dust) are given away when furniture is piled to the centre of the room. Meals are picnics at which table manners are suspended because the first principle of deportment drummed into children by their mother—sitting down at table—is missing: there is nowhere to sit. People are excused eccentricities of dress because no one can find anything in its place.

A doctor is also a kind of repair man. When he is expected the sheets are changed and the dog chased off the patient's bed. If a child is sick, she doesn't have to go to school, she is on holiday, with presents into the bargain—a whole roll of comics tied with newsagent's string, and crayons or card games. The mother is alone in the house, except for the patient out of earshot in the sick-room; the other children are at school. Her husband is away at work. She takes off her apron, combs her hair and puts on a bit of lipstick to make herself decent for the doctor, setting ready a tea-tray for two in the quiet privacy of the deserted living-room as for a secret morning visit from the lover she does not have. After she and the doctor, who smells intoxicating, coldly sweet because he has just come from the operating theatre, have stood together looking down at the patient and making jolly remarks, he is glad to accept a cup of tea in his busy morning round and their voices are a murmur and an occasional rise of laughter from behind the closed living-room door.

Plumber, painter, doctor; with their arrival something has happened where nothing ever happens; at home: a house with a bungalow face made of two bow-window eyes on either side of a front-door mouth, in a street in a gold-mining town of twenty-five thousand people in South Africa in the 1930s.

Once the upright Steinway piano stood alone on the few remaining boards of a room from which the floor had been ripped. I burst in to look at the time on the chiming clock that should have been standing on the mantelpiece and instead flew through the air and found myself jolted down into a subterranean smell of an earth I'd never smelt before, the earth buried by our house. I was nine years old and the drop broke no bones; the shock excited me, the thought of that hollow, earth-breaking dark always beneath our Axminster[1] thrilled me; the importance I gained in my mother's accounts of how I might so easily have injured myself added to the sense of occasion usual in the family when there were workmen in.

This time it was not the painters, Mr. Strydom and his boys, over whom my mother raised a quarrel every few years. *I'm not like any other woman. I haven't got a husband like other women's. The state this house is in. You'd see the place fall to pieces before you'd lift a finger. Too mean to pay for a lick of paint, and then when you do you expect it to last ten years. I haven't got a home like other women.* Workmen were treated as the house-guests we never had; my mother's friends were neighbors, my father had none, and she wouldn't give house-room to a spare bed, anyway, because she didn't want his relatives coming. Mr. Strydom was served sweet strong tea to his taste many times a day, while my mother stood by to chat and I followed his skills with the brush, particularly fascinated when he was doing something he called, in his Afrikaner's English, "pulling the line." This was the free-hand deftness with which he could make a narrow black stripe dividing the lower half of our passage, painted dark against dirty finger-prints, from the cream upper half. *Yust a sec while I first pull the line, ay.*

Then he would drain his cup so completely that the tea leaves swirled up and stuck to the sides. This workmanlike thirst, for me, was a foreign custom, sign of the difference between being Afrikaans and English, as we were, just as I accepted that it must be in accordance with *their* custom that the black "boys" drank their tea from jam tins in the yard. But Mr. Strydom, like the doctor, like deaf dapper Mr. Waite the electrician, who had drinking bouts because he had

---

1. Type of carpet.

been through something called Ypres,[2] and Mr. Hartman who sang to himself in a sad soprano while he tuned the Steinway upright my mother had brought from her own mother's house, was a recurrent event. The state the house was in, this time, was one without precedent; the men who were in were not repair men. They had been sent for to exterminate what we called white ants—termites who were eating our house away under our feet. A million jaws were devouring steadily night and day the timber that supported our unchanging routines: one day (if my mother hadn't done something about it you may be sure no one else would) that heavy Steinway in its real rosewood case would have crashed through the floor-boards.

For years my mother had efficiently kicked apart the finely-granulated earth, forming cones perfect as the shape taken by sand that has trickled through an egg-timer, that was piled in our garden by ordinary black ants. My father never did a hand's turn; she herself poured a tar-smelling disinfectant down the ant-holes and emptied into them kettles of boiling water that made the ground break out in a sweat of gleaming, struggling, pin-head creatures in paroxysm. Yet (it was another event) on certain summer evenings after rain we would rush out into the garden to be in the tropical snowfall of millions of transparent wings from what we called flying ants, who appeared from nowhere. We watched while frogs bold with greed hopped onto the verandah to fill their pouched throats with these apparently harmless insects, and our cat ate steadily but with more self-control, spitting out with a shake of her whiskers any fragment of wing she might have taken up by mistake. We did not know that when these creatures shed their four delicate dragon-fly wings (some seemed to struggle like people getting out of coats) and became drab terrestrials, and some idiotically lifted their hindquarters in the air as if they were reacting to injury, they were enacting a nuptial ceremony that, one summer night or another, had ended in one out of these millions being fertilized and making her way under our house to become queen of a whole colony generated and given birth to by herself. Somewhere under our house she was in an endless parturition that would go on until she was found and killed.

The men had been sent for to search out the queen. No evil-smelling poisons, no opening-up of the tunnels more skilfully constructed than the London Underground, the Paris Metro or the New York subway I'd read about, no fumigation such as might do for cockroaches or moles or wood-borer beetles, could eradicate termites. No matter how many thousands were killed by my mother, as, in the course of the excavations that tore up the floor-boards of her house, the brittle passages made of grains of earth cemented by a secretion carried in the termites' own bodies were broken, and the inhabitants poured out in a pus of white moving droplets with yellow heads—no matter how many she cast into death agony with her Flit spray, the termitary would at once be repopulated so long as the queen remained, alive, hidden in that inner chamber where her subjects who were also her progeny had walled her in and guarded and tended her.

2. Belgian town, site of heavy fighting in World War I.

The three exterminators were one white and two black. All had the red earth of underground clinging to their clothes and skin and hair; their eyes were bloodshot; the nails of their hands, black or white, were outlined in red, their ears rimmed. The long hairs in the nostrils of the white man were coated with red as a bee's legs area yellow with pollen. These men themselves appeared to have been dug up, raw from that clinging earth entombed beneath buildings. Bloodied by their life-long medieval quest, they were ready to take it up once more: the search for a queen. They were said to be very good; my mother was sceptical as she was about the powers of water-diviners with bent twigs or people who got the dead to spell out messages by moving a glass to letters of the alphabet. But what else could she do? My father left it all to her, she had the responsibility.

She didn't like the look of these men. They were so filthy with earth; hands like exposed roots reaching for the tea she brought. She served even the white man with a tin mug.

It was she who insisted they leave a few boards intact under the piano; she knew better than to trust them to move it without damage to the rosewood case. They didn't speak while children watched them at work. The only sound was the pick stopped by the density of the earth under our living-room, and the gasp of the black man who wielded the pick, pulling it free and hurling it back into the earth again. Held off by silence, we children would not go away. We stolidly spent all our free time in witness. Yet in spite of our vigilance, when it happened, when they found her, at last—the queen—we were not there.

My mother was mixing a cake and we had been attracted away to her by that substance of her alchemy that was not the beaten eggs and butter and sugar that went into it; even the lightest stroke of a quick forefinger into the bowl conveyed a coating of fragrant creamy sweetness to the mouth which already had foreknowledge of its utter satisfaction through the scent of vanilla that came not only from the bowl, but from her clothes, her hair, her very skin. Suddenly my mother's dog lifted his twitching lip back over his long teeth and began to bounce towards and back away from the screen door as he did when any stranger approached her. We looked up; the three men had come to the back steps. The white gestured his ochre hand brusquely at one of the blacks, who tramped forward with a child's cardboard shoe-box offered. The lid was on and there were rough air-holes punched in it here and there, just as in the boxes where we had kept silk worms until my mother thought they smelled too musty and threw them away. The white man gestured again; he and my mother for a moment held their hands the same way, his covered with earth, hers with flour. The black man took off the lid.

And there she was, the queen. The smallest child swallowed as if about to retch and ran away to the far end of the kitchen. The rest of us crowded nearer, but my mother made us make way, she wasn't going to be fobbed off with anything but complete satisfaction for her husband's money. We all gazed at an obese, helpless white creature, five inches long, with the tiny, shiny-visored head of an ant at one end. The body was a sort of dropsical sac attached to this head; it had no legs that could be seen, neither could it propel itself by peristaltic action, like a slug or worm. The queen. The queen whose domain, we had seen for ourselves in the galleries and passages that had been uncovered beneath our house, was as big as ours.

The white man spoke, "That's 'er, missus."

"You're sure you've got the queen?"

"We got it. That's it." He gave a professional snigger at ignorance.

Was she alive? —But again the silence of the red-eyed, red-earthed men kept us back; they wouldn't let us daringly put out a finger to touch that body that seemed blown up in sections, like certain party balloons, and that had at once the suggestion of tactile attraction and repugnance—if a finger were to be stroked testingly along that perhaps faintly downy body, sweet creamy stuff might be expected to ooze from it. And in fact, when I found a book in the library called *The Soul of the White Ant*, by Eugène Marais, an Afrikaner like the white man who had found the queen's secret chamber, I read that the children-subjects at certain times draw nourishment from a queen's great body by stroking it so that she exudes her own rich maternal elixir.

"Ughh. Why's she so fat?" The smallest child had come close enough to force himself to look again.

"S'es full of ecks," the white man said. "They lays about a million ecks a day."

"Is it dead?"

But the man only laughed, now that his job was done, and like the showman's helper at the conclusion of an act, the black man knew to clap the lid back on the shoe-box. There was no way for us to tell; the queen cannot move, she is blind; whether she is underground, the tyrannical prisoner of her subjects who would not have been born and cannot live without her, or whether she is captured and borne away in a show-box, she is helpless to evade the consequences of her power.

My mother paid the men out of her housekeeping allowance (but she would have to speak to our father about that) and they nailed back the living-room floor-boards and went away, taking the cardboard box with them. My mother had heard that the whole thing was a hoax; these men went from house to house, made the terrible mess they'd left hers in, and produced the same queen time and again, carrying it around with them.

Yet the termites left our house. We never had to have those particular workmen in again. The Axminster carpet was laid once more, the furniture put back in its place, and I had to do the daily half-hour practice on the Steinway that I had been freed of for a week. I read in the book from the library that when the queen dies or is taken away all the termites leave their posts and desert the termitary; some find their way to other communities, thousands die. The termitary with its fungus-gardens for food, its tunnels for conveying water from as much as forty feet underground, its elaborate defence and communications system, is abandoned.

We lived on, above the ruin. The children grew up and left the town; coming back from the war after 1946 and later from visits to Europe and America and the Far East, it bored them to hear the same old stories, to be asked: "D'you remember Mr. Hartman who used to come in to tune the piano? He was asking after you the other day—poor thing, he's crippled with arthritis." "D'you remember old Strydom, 'pulling the line' . . . how you kids used to laugh, I was quite ashamed . . ." "D'you remember the time the white ant men were in, and you nearly broke your leg?" Were these events the sum of my mother's life? Why should I remember? I, who—shuddering to look back at those five rooms behind the bow-window eyes and the front-door mouth—have oceans, continents, snowed-in capitals, islands where turtles swim, cathedrals, theatres, palace gardens where people kiss and tramps drink wine—all these to remember. My father grew senile and she put him in a home for his last years. She stayed on, although she said she didn't want to; the house was a burden to her, she had carried the whole responsibility for him, for all of us, all her life. Now she is dead and although I suppose someone else lives in her house, the secret passages, the inner chamber in which she was our queen and our prisoner are sealed up, empty.

1980

ANN BEATTIE

Janus

The bowl was perfect. Perhaps it was not what you'd select if you faced a shelf of bowls, and not the sort of thing that would inevitably attract a lot of attention at a crafts fair, yet it had real presence. It was as predictably admired as a mutt who has no reason to suspect he might be funny. Just such a dog, in fact, was often brought out (and in) along with the bowl.

Andrea was a real estate agent, and when she thought that some prospective buyers might be dog lovers, she would drop off her dog at the same time she placed the bowl in the house that was up for sale. She would put a dish of water in the kitchen for Mondo, take his squeaking plastic frog out of her purse and drop it on the floor. He would pounce delightedly, just as he did every day at home, batting around his favorite toy. The bowl usually sat on a coffee table, though recently she had displayed it on top of a pine blanket chest and on a lacquered table. It was once placed on a cherry table beneath a Bonnard[1] still life, where it held its own.

Everyone who has purchased a house or who has wanted to sell a house must be familiar with some of the tricks used to convince a buyer that the house is quite special: a fire in the fireplace in early evening; jonquils in a pitcher on the kitchen counter, where no one ordinarily has space to put flowers; perhaps the slight aroma of spring, made by a single drop of scent vaporizing from a lamp bulb.

The wonderful thing about the bowl, Andrea thought, was that it was both subtle and noticeable—a paradox of a bowl. Its glaze was the color of cream and seemed to glow no matter what light it was placed in. There were a few bits of

---

1. Pierre Bonnard (1867–1947), French painter.

color in it—tiny geometric flashes—and some of these were tinged with flecks of silver. They were as mysterious as cells seen under a microscope; it was difficult not to study them, because they shimmered, flashing for a split second, and then resumed their shape. Something about the colors and their random placement suggested motion. People who liked country furniture always commented on the bowl, but then it turned out that people who felt comfortable with Biedermeier[2] loved it just as much. But the bowl was not at all ostentatious, or even so notice-able that anyone would suspect that it had been put in place deliberately. They might notice the height of the ceiling on first entering a room, and only when their eye moved down from that, or away from the refraction of sunlight on a pale wall, would they see the bowl. Then they would go immediately to it and comment. Yet they always faltered when they tried to say something. Perhaps it was because they were in the house for a serious reason, not to notice some object.

Once, Andrea got a call from a woman who had not put in an offer on a house she had shown her. That bowl, she said—would it be possible to find out where the owners had bought that beautiful bowl? Andrea pretended that she did not know what the woman was referring to. A bowl, somewhere in the house? Oh, on a table under the window. Yes, she would ask, of course. She let a couple of days pass, then called back to say that the bowl had been a present and the people did not know where it had been purchased.

When the bowl was not being taken from house to house, it sat on Andrea's coffee table at home. She didn't keep it carefully wrapped (although she trans-ported it that way, in a box); she kept it on the table, because she liked to see it. It was large enough so that it didn't seem fragile, or particularly vulnerable if anyone sideswiped the table or Mondo blundered into it at play. She had asked her husband to please not drop his house key in it. It was meant to be empty.

When her husband first noticed the bowl, he had peered into it and smiled briefly. He always urged her to buy things she liked. In recent years, both of them had acquired many things to make up for all the lean years when they were graduate students, but now that they had been comfortable for quite a while, the pleasure of new possessions dwindled. Her husband had pronounced the bowl "pretty," and he had turned away without picking it up to examine it. He had no more interest in the bowl than she had in his new Leica.[3]

She was sure that the bowl brought her luck. Bids were often put in on houses where she had displayed the bowl. Sometimes the owners, who were always asked to be away or to step outside when the house was being shown, didn't even know that the bowl had been in their house. Once—she could not imagine how—she left it behind, and then she was so afraid that something might have happened to it that she rushed back to the house and sighed with relief when the woman owner opened the door. The bowl, Andrea explained—she had purchased a bowl and set it on the chest for safekeeping while she toured the house with the prospective buyers, and she . . . She felt like rushing past the frowning woman and seizing her bowl. The owner stepped aside, and it was only

5

2. Mid-19th-century heavy, stuffed German furniture.   3. An expensive German camera.

when Andrea ran to the chest that the lady glanced at her a little strangely. In the few seconds before Andrea picked up the bowl, she realized that the owner must have just seen that it had been perfectly placed, that the sunlight struck the bluer part of it. Her pitcher had been moved to the far side of the chest, and the bowl predominated. All the way home, Andrea wondered how she could have left the bowl behind. It was like leaving a friend at an outing—just walking off. Sometimes there were stories in the paper about families forgetting a child somewhere and driving to the next city. Andrea had only gone a mile down the road before she remembered.

In time, she dreamed of the bowl. Twice, in a waking dream—early in the morning, between sleep and a last nap before rising—she had a clear vision of it. It came into sharp focus and startled her for a moment—the same bowl she looked at every day.

10   She had a very profitable year selling real estate. Word spread, and she had more clients than she felt comfortable with. She had the foolish thought that if only the bowl were an animate object she could thank it. There were times when she wanted to talk to her husband about the bowl. He was a stockbroker, and sometimes told people that he was fortunate to be married to a woman who had such a fine aesthetic sense and yet could also function in the real world. They were a lot alike, really—they had agreed on that. They were both quiet people—reflective, slow to make value judgments, but almost intractable once they had come to a conclusion. They both liked details, but while ironies attracted her, he was more impatient and dismissive when matters became many sided or unclear. But they both knew this; it was the kind of thing they could talk about when they were alone in the car together, coming home from a party or after a weekend with friends. But she never talked to him about the bowl. When they were at dinner, exchanging their news of the day, or while they lay in bed at night listening to the stereo and murmuring sleepy disconnections, she was often tempted to come right out and say that she thought that the bowl in the living room, the cream-colored bowl, was responsible for her success. But she didn't say it. She couldn't begin to explain it. Sometimes in the morning, she would look at him and feel guilty that she had such a constant secret.

Could it be that she had some deeper connection with the bowl—a relationship of some kind? She corrected her thinking: how could she imagine such a thing, when she was a human being and it was a bowl? It was ridiculous. Just think of how people lived together and loved each other . . . But was that always so clear, always a relationship? She was confused by these thoughts, but they remained in her mind. There was something within her now, something real, that she never talked about.

The bowl was a mystery, even to her. It was frustrating, because her involvement with the bowl contained a steady sense of unrequited good fortune; it would have been easier to respond if some sort of demand were made in return. But that only happened in fairy tales. The bowl was just a bowl. She did not believe that for one second. What she believed was that it was something she loved.

In the past, she had sometimes talked to her husband about a new property she was about to buy or sell—confiding some clever strategy she had devised to persuade owners who seemed ready to sell. Now she stopped doing that, for all her strategies involved the bowl. She became more deliberate with the bowl, and more possessive. She put it in houses only when no one was there, and removed it when she left the house. Instead of just moving a pitcher or a dish, she would remove all the other objects from a table. She had to force herself to handle them carefully, because she didn't really care about them. She just wanted them out of sight.

She wondered how the situation would end. As with a lover, there was no exact scenario of how matters would come to a close. Anxiety became the operative force. It would be irrelevant if the lover rushed into someone else's arms, or wrote her a note and departed to another city. The horror was the possibility of the disappearance. That was what mattered.

She would get up at night and look at the bowl. It never occurred to her that she might break it. She washed and dried it without anxiety, and she moved it often, from coffee table to mahogany corner table or wherever, without fearing an accident. It was clear that she would not be the one who would do anything to the bowl. The bowl was only handled by her, set safely on one surface or another; it was not very likely that anyone would break it. A bowl was a poor conductor of electricity: it would not be hit by lightning. Yet the idea of damage persisted. She did not think beyond that—to what her life would be without the bowl. She only continued to fear that some accident would happen. Why not, in a world where people set plants where they did not belong, so that visitors touring a house would be fooled into thinking that dark corners got sunlight—a world full of tricks?

She had first seen the bowl several years earlier, at a crafts fair she had visited half in secret, with her lover. He had urged her to buy the bowl. She didn't *need* any more things, she told him. But she had been drawn to the bowl, and they had lingered near it. Then she went on to the next booth, and he came up behind her, tapping the rim against her shoulder as she ran her fingers over a wood carving. "You're still insisting that I buy that?" she said. "No," he said. "I bought it for you." He had bought her other things before this—things she liked more, at first—the child's ebony-and-turquoise ring that fitted her little finger; the wooden box, long and thin, beautifully dovetailed, that she used to hold paper clips; the soft gray sweater with a pouch pocket. It was his idea that when he could not be there to hold her hand she could hold her own—clasp her hands inside the lone pocket that stretched across the front. But in time she became more attached to the bowl than to any of his other presents. She tried to talk herself out of it. She owned other things that were more striking or valuable. It wasn't an object whose beauty jumped out at you; a lot of people must have passed it by before the two of them saw it that day.

Her lover had said that she was always too slow to know what she really loved. Why continue with her life the way it was? Why be two-faced, he asked her. He had made the first move toward her. When she would not decide in his favor, would not change her life and come to him, he asked her what made her think she could have it both ways. And then he made the last move and left. It was a decision meant to break her will, to shatter her intransigent ideas about honoring previous commitments.

Time passed. Alone in the living room at night, she often looked at the bowl sitting on the table, still and safe, unilluminated. In its way, it was perfect: the world cut in half, deep and smoothly empty. Near the rim, even in dim light, the eye moved toward one small flash of blue, a vanishing point on the horizon.

1986

QUESTIONS

1. Why does goodman Brown go to a witches' meeting?
2. Why does Faith Brown, his wife, wear pink ribbons?
3. Who speaks the first passage of italicized words of "The Termitary" (par. 5)? To whom are they addressed?
4. When do you first begin to anticipate the symbolic function of the termite queen?
5. Why is the centered consciousness, the female protagonist, in "Janus" never referred to by name?

WRITING SUGGESTIONS

1. Write a parody of "Young Goodman Brown" or an imitation, perhaps in the style of Stephen King or Anne Rice.
2. Write an analysis of the symbolism in one of the stories in Reading Fiction or in one of the first three chapters in Text.
3. Write an essay on the characterization of the mother *and father* in "The Termitary" and discuss their function as symbols.
4. Analyze the character of the centered consciousness, the female protagonist, of "Janus."

6 THEME

I f you ask what a story is "about," an author is likely to answer by telling you the **subject.** Indeed, many authors tell you the subject in their titles: "An Occurrence at Owl Creek Bridge," "The Termitary," "Her First Ball." Though a subject is always concrete, it may be stated at somewhat greater length than the few words of a title: "a man's thoughts as he faces execution for spying during the Civil War" ("Owl Creek Bridge"); "a young girl's excitement at her first grown-up dance and an incident that temporarily depresses her" ("Her First Ball").

A friend might be more likely to tell you what a story is about by giving you a summary of the action: "This weird Southern lady is jilted by a Yankee. She kills him and sleeps with his corpse. There's a smell around the house before too long, but nobody knows about the murder until she dies." (We sometimes call this a **plot summary,** but you will notice that this summary is of the history, of the events in more or less chronological order, while the plot is an arrangement or structuring of that history; in "A Rose for Emily," remember, we do not figure out there's been a murder and certainly don't know about Emily's sleeping with him until the end of the story, though of course the jilting, murder, and so on happen in the order described in the summary of the history.)

Your teacher may well tell you what a story is about by summarizing its **theme.** Some refer to the central idea, the thesis, or even the message of the story, and that is roughly what we mean by theme: a generalization or abstraction from the story.

The subject of "Young Goodman Brown" may be said to be a coven (witches' meeting) or, more fully, "a young colonial New England husband is driven mad by finding everyone he thought good and pure attending a witches' meeting." The theme may be "everyone partakes of evil," or, more succinctly, "the Fall." There are, as you can see, degrees of generalization and abstraction; subject (a young man finds that everyone is evil) shades off into theme, which itself can be more or less general and abstract.

Discussions of literature in or out of class sometimes seem to suggest that stories exist for their themes, that we read only to get the "point" or message. But most themes, you must admit, are somewhat less than earth-shattering. That all men and women are evil may be debatable, but it certainly isn't news. That not all unmarried women (even English women) of a certain age are prudish, dried up, and repressed—an apparent theme of "Our Friend Judith"—is rather widely recognized, something we scarcely need a dozen or so pages of fiction to find out. No wonder, then, that some of our more skeptical friends contend that stories are only elaborate ways of "saying something simple," that literature is a game in which authors hide their meanings under shells of words.

Of course, reading a dozen or so pages of a story like "Our Friend Judith" can be enjoyable. Could it be that we really read fiction for fun, and all our talk about themes is just hiding from our Puritan natures the fact that we are goofing off?

I don't believe that articulating the theme of a story is either the purpose of or the excuse for reading fiction, or that authors hide their meanings like Easter eggs. In order to relate his or her unique vision of reality to an absent and unknown reader, a writer must find a way of communicating—some common ground on which to meet the various unique individuals who will read the story. Common experiences, common assumptions, common language, and commonplaces offer such ground. Readers reach out from their own subjective worlds toward that new and different vision of the author with the help of the common elements (the general), and especially through the commonplaces of theme, bringing back the particulars and generalizations of the story to their own reading and living experience. In "Janus," the reader sees a successful suburban real estate agent who is married to a stockbroker but who has lost her lover, a man she truly loved, because she could not or would not decide to leave her husband; a woman whose world is "perfect," but cut in half and empty, like the beloved bowl her lover picked out for her and gave her. Generalizing, the reader may conclude that what the story says (its theme) is that life, or a full or happy life, is more than convention and material success, that love is more important than comfort and "perfection." Though the reader's own situation and choices may be considerably different from those of the protagonist in Beattie's story, he or she may be led by the story to ponder what is truly important and valuable in life, what "the perfect life" consists in, thereby coming to a greater understanding of the story—and, whether he or she agrees with the conclusions of the story or not, to a fuller understanding of the issues and theme of the story.

The significance of any story is modified to some extent by the reader's experience of books and life. You should not reduce every story to the dimensions of what you already know and feel, but you should reach out to the story and bring it back to your own experience as an addition and modification. If you're going to make a story yours, and if you are going to make it more than a yarn about a woman who sells real estate and has been unfaithful to her stock-broker husband and was left by her lover because she would not get a divorce, you will translate it somehow into terms that, while not necessarily psychological or moral precepts, alter or broaden to some degree your own vision of yourself, others, life in general.

When I discussed symbols, I said that even while a symbol suggests the meaning beyond the particulars of the fiction, it remains a detail in the fictional world—the snakelike staff of the stranger in "Young Goodman Brown" remains a staff, Judith's cats remain cats. Some critics would say that this is true also of theme and that theme is related to the story as integrally as symbolic meaning is to detail; that is, rather than "Young Goodman Brown" telling us something we did not know before, its theme and its story modify each other. The theme as I've stated it relates to spiritual evil, the kind of evil suggested by the snake and Satan figures. But this theme is not entirely portable—it cannot be taken out of the story and used as substitute for what the story "means"—nor can it, without qualification, be used to explain all the significant details in the story: the facts that Brown is a newlywed, that Faith wears pink (coquettish?) ribbons, and that she, whom Brown thought so pure and innocent, shows up at the meeting of witches and sinners, suggest a more specific kind of evil than the spiritual or theological evil suggested by the snake and Satan: moral or, even more specifically, sexual evil. This means we must modify our definition of the theme. But how? What does the story imply about the relationship of sex and evil? Is all sex evil? Is original sin sexual? Some details—the snake, the Satanic guide—suggest a theme, other details modify it; still others—Brown's behavior after the night of the witches' meeting—may modify it further, so that the theme, though an approximate version of it may be abstracted from the story, remains embedded in it, ultimately inseparable from the details of plot, character, setting, and symbol.

A statement that can do justice to all the complexity and all the particulars of the story is not likely to take the simple form of a **message**. Indeed, it is the complex particularity of literature, its ultimate irreducibility, that makes critics and teachers reject message (which suggests a simple packaged statement) as a suitable term even for the paraphrasable thematic content of a story.

"Young Goodman Brown" is an allegorical story whose details do function as symbols with paraphrasable meanings, yet even its theme refuses to be reduced to a simple statement. "How Much Land Does a Man Need?" is a **parable,** a short fiction that illustrates an explicit moral lesson. That lesson, the theme, is implied by the title. (And here the devil appears not only, at times, in disguise, but also in his proper person.) Even so, Tolstoy's story is not without complexity. How do you account for the first section of the story? Does your paraphrase of the theme accommodate the conversation between the sisters there?

"Her First Ball" is not allegorical and neither is it parabolic. Though realistic, however, it is a short, rather simple story that seems to have a simple theme overtly enunciated by one of the characters: Leila's elderly partner. But the scene with the elderly partner is not the end of the story. Leila goes on to dance with a young partner and seems to forget the man's "message." What is the story "saying"? Is her forgetting "bad"? Or "sad"? Or "good"? The specifics of the story modify and enrich all the generalizations we can abstract from it, while these themes and questions, if we recognize them, modify and enrich our reading, our experience of the story.

I realize I may have been talking as if a theme or themes spring out at the reader, while to some of you my inference of themes may seem like pulling rabbits out of hats. "How Much Land Does a Man Need?" does not involve much of a trick: the title asks the question that, once answered, suggests the theme. But there isn't even too much conjuring in "Young Goodman Brown": I derived the theme of theological evil from the symbols (the snake-staff, Satan figure, names) and I tested physical details—like pink ribbons and the narrative situation (the three-month marriage)—which had sexual implications against the theme to see if I would have to modify my paraphrase. In "Her First Ball" a character raises a general issue that is tested by subsequent events in the story and modified by them. The title "Beyond the Pale" hints at a theme but too faintly and obliquely to signify until one of the characters brings it to the surface toward the end of the story.

There are, of course, other means by which details suggest generalizations or meaning or by which meaning may be abstracted from detail. Aided by footnotes, perhaps, you likely noticed the historical and biblical **allusions**—references to history, the Bible, sometimes literature, paintings, and so on—in "Young Goodman Brown." The scene is Salem in the time of King William—that is, about the time of the Salem witch trials—and the stranger's serpentine staff is related to Exodus (where the staff of the Egyptian Magi does not turn into a snake). So allusion as well as symbols, plot, focus and voice, and character are elements that contribute to and must be accounted for in paraphrasing a theme. That is why theme is important, and why it comes last in a discussion of the elements of fiction.

But remember, the theme is an inadequate abstraction from the story; the story and its details do not disappear or lose significance once distilled into theme, nor could you reconstruct a story merely from its paraphrased theme.

Indeed, theme and story, history and structure, do not so much interact, are not so much interrelated, as they are fused, inseparable.

THEME A Glossary

allusion: reference in a story to history, the Bible, literature, painting, music, and so on, that suggests the meaning or generalized relevance of details in the story

message: a misleading term for *theme*, or the central idea or statement of a story, misleading because it suggests a simple, packaged statement that pre-exists and for the simple communication of which the story is written

parable: a short fiction that illustrates an explicit moral lesson

plot summary: a description of the arrangement of the action in the order in which it actually appears in a story; the term is popularly used to mean the description of the history, or chronological order, of the action as it would have appeared in reality. It is important to indicate exactly in which sense you are using the term.

subject: the concrete and literal description of what a story is about

theme: a generalized, abstract paraphrase of the inferred central or dominant idea of a story

How Much Land Does a Man Need?[1]

I

An elder sister came to visit her younger sister in the country. The elder was married to a tradesman in town, the younger to a peasant in the village. As the sisters sat over their tea talking, the elder began to boast of the advantages of town life: saying how comfortably they lived there, how well they dressed, what fine clothes her children wore, what good things they ate and drank, and how she went to the theatre, promenades, and entertainments.

The younger sister was piqued, and in turn disparaged the life of a tradesman, and stood up for that of a peasant.

"I would not change my way of life for yours," said she. "We may live roughly, but at least we are free from anxiety. You live in better style than we do, but though you often earn more than you need, you are very likely to lose all you have. You know the proverb, 'Loss and gain are brothers twain.' It often happens that people who are wealthy one day are begging their bread the next. Our way is safer. Though a peasant's life is not a fat one, it is a long one. We shall never grow rich, but we shall always have enough to eat."

The elder sister said sneeringly:

"Enough? Yes, if you like to share with the pigs and the calves! What do you know of elegance or manners! However much your goodman may slave, you will die as you are living—on a dung heap—and your children the same."

"Well, what of that?" replied the younger. "Of course our work is rough and coarse. But, on the other hand, it is sure, and we need not bow to anyone. But you, in your towns, are surrounded by temptations; to-day all may be right, but to-morrow the Evil One may tempt your husband with cards, wine, or women, and all will go to ruin. Don't such things happen often enough?"

Pahóm, the master of the house, was lying on the top of the stove and he listened to the women's chatter.

"It is perfectly true," thought he. "Busy as we are from childhood tilling mother earth, we peasants have no time to let any nonsense settle in our heads. Our only trouble is that we haven't land enough. If I had plenty of land, I shouldn't fear the Devil himself!"

The women finished their tea, chatted a while about dress, and then cleared away the tea-things and lay down to sleep.

But the Devil had been sitting behind the stove, and had heard all that was said. He was pleased that the peasant's wife had led her husband into boasting, and that he had said that if he had plenty of land he would not fear the Devil himself.

1. Translated by Louise and Aylmer Maude.

"All right," thought the Devil. "We will have a tussle. I'll give you land enough; and by means of that land I will get you into my power."

II

Close to the village there lived a lady, a small landowner who had an estate of about three hundred acres. She had always lived on good terms with the peasants until she engaged as her steward an old soldier, who took to burdening the people with fines. However careful Pahóm tried to be, it happened again and again that now a horse of his got among the lady's oats, now a cow strayed into her garden, now his calves found their way into her meadows—and he always had to pay a fine.

Pahóm paid up, but grumbled and, going home in a temper, was rough with his family. All through that summer, Pahóm had much trouble because of this steward, and he was even glad when winter came and the cattle had to be stabled. Though hew grudged the fodder when they could no longer graze on the pasture-land, at least he was free from anxiety about them.

In the winter the news got about that the lady was going to sell her land and that the keeper of the inn on the high road was bargaining for it. When the peasants heard this they were very much alarmed.

"Well," thought they, "if the innkeeper gets the land, he will worry us with fines worse than the lady's steward. We all depend on that estate." 15

So the peasants went on behalf of their Commune, and asked the lady not to sell the land to the innkeeper, offering her a better price for it themselves. The lady agreed to let them have it. Then the peasants tried to arrange for the Commune to buy the whole estate, so that it might be held by them all in common. They met twice to discuss it, but could not settle the matter; the Evil One sowed discord among them and they could not agree. So they decided to buy the land individually, each according to his means; and the lady agreed to this plan as she had to the other.

Presently Pahóm heard that a neighbor of his was buying fifty acres, and that the lady had consented to accept one half in cash and to wait a year for the other half. Pahóm felt envious.

"Look at that," thought he, "the land is all being sold, and I shall get none of it." So he spoke to his wife.

"Other people are buying," said he, "and we must also buy twenty acres or so. Life is becoming impossible. That steward is simply crushing us with his fines."

So they put their heads together and considered how they could manage to buy it. They had one hundred rúbles laid by. They sold a colt and one half of their bees, hired out one of their sons as a laborer and took his wages in advance; borrowed the rest from a brother-in-law, and so scraped together half the purchase money. 20

Having done this, Pahóm chose out a farm of forty acres, some of it wooded, and went to the lady to bargain for it. They came to an agreement, and he shook hands with her upon it and paid her a deposit in advance. Then they went to town and signed the deeds; he paying half the price down, and undertaking to pay the remainder within two years.

So now Pahóm had land of his own. He borrowed seed, and sowed it on the land he had bought. The harvest was a good one, and within a year he had managed to pay off his debts both to the lady and to his brother-in-law. So he became a landowner, ploughing and sowing his own land, making hay on his own land, cutting his own trees, and feeding his cattle on his own pasture. When he went out to plough his fields, or to look at his growing corn, or at his grass-meadows, his heart would fill with joy. The grass that grew and the flowers that bloomed there seemed to him unlike any that grew elsewhere. Formerly, when he had passed by that land, it had appeared the same as any other land, but now it seemed quite different.

III

So Pahóm was well-contented, and everything would have been right if the neighboring peasants would only not have trespassed on his corn-fields and meadows. He appealed to them most civilly, but they still went on: now the Communal herdsmen would let the village cows stray into his meadows, then horses from the night pasture would get among his corn. Pahóm turned them out again, and forgave their owners, and for a long time he forbore to prosecute any one. But at last he lost patience and complained to the District Court. He knew it was the peasants' want of land, and no evil intent on their part, that caused the trouble, but he thought:

"I cannot go on overlooking it or they will destroy all I have. They must be taught a lesson."

So he had them up, gave them one lesson, and then another, and two or three of the peasants were fined. After a time Pahóm's neighbors began to bear him a grudge for this, and would now and then let their cattle on to his land on purpose. One peasant even got into Pahóm's wood at night and cut down five young lime trees for their bark. Pahóm passing through the wood one day noticed something white. He came nearer and saw the stripped trunks lying on the ground, and close by stood the stumps where the trees had been. Pahóm was furious.

"If he had only cut one here and there it would have been bad enough," thought Pahóm, "but the rascal has actually cut down a whole clump. If I could only find out who did this, I would pay him out."

He racked his brain as to who it could be. Finally he decided: "It must be Simon—no one else could have done it." So he went to Simon's homestead to have a look round, but he found nothing, and only had an angry scene. However, he now felt more certain than ever that Simon had done it, and he lodged a complaint. Simon was summoned. The case was tried, and retried, and at the end of it all Simon was acquitted, there being no evidence against him. Pahóm felt still more aggrieved, and let his anger loose upon the Elder and the Judges.

"You let thieves grease your palms," said he. "If you were honest folk yourselves you would not let a thief go free."

So Pahóm quarrelled with the Judges and with his neighbors. Threats to burn his building began to be uttered. So though Pahóm had more land, his place in the Commune was much worse than before.

About this time a rumor got about that many people were moving to new parts.

"There's no need for me to leave my land," thought Pahóm. "But some of the others might leave our village and then there would be more room for us. I would take over their land myself and make my estate a bit bigger. I could then live more at ease. As it is, I am still too cramped to be comfortable."

One day Pahóm was sitting at home when a peasant, passing through the village, happened to call in. He was allowed to stay the night, and supper was given him. Pahóm had a talk with this peasant and asked him where he came from. The stranger answered that he came from beyond the Vólga, where he had been working. One word led to another, and the man went on to say that many people were settling in those parts. He told how some people from his village had settled there. They had joined the Commune, and had had twenty-five acres per man granted them. The land was so good, he said, that the rye sown on it grew as high as a horse, and so thick that five cuts of a sickle made a sheaf. One peasant, he said, had brought nothing with him but his bare hands, and now he had six horses and two cows of his own.

Pahóm's heart kindled with desire. He thought:

"Why should I suffer in this narrow hole, if one can live so well elsewhere? I will sell my land and my homestead here, and with the money I will start afresh over there and get everything new. In this crowded place one is always having trouble. But I must first go and find out all about it myself."

Towards summer he got ready and started. He went down the Vólga on a steamer to Samára, then walked another three hundred miles on foot, and at last reached the place. It was just as the stranger had said. The peasants had plenty of land: every man had twenty-five acres of Communal land given him for his use, and any one who had money could buy, besides, at a rúble an acre as much good freehold land as he wanted.

Having found out all he wished to know, Pahóm returned home as autumn came on, and began selling off his belongings. He sold his land at a profit, sold his homestead and all his cattle, and withdrew from membership in the Commune. He only waited till the spring, and then started with his family for the new settlement.

30

35

IV

As soon as Pahóm and his family reached their new abode, he applied for admission into the Commune of a large village. He stood treat to the Elders and obtained the necessary documents. Five shares of Communal land were given him for his own and his sons' use: that is to say—125 acres (not all together, but in different fields) besides the use of the Communal pasture. Pahóm put up the buildings he needed, and bought cattle. Of the Communal land alone he had three times as much as at his former home, and the land was good corn-land.

He was ten times better off than he had been. He had plenty of arable land and pasturage, and could keep as many head of cattle as he liked.

At first, in the bustle of building and settling down, Pahóm was pleased with it all, but when he got used to it he began to think that even here he had not enough land. The first year, he sowed wheat on his share of the Communal land and had a good crop. He wanted to go on sowing wheat, but had not enough Communal land for the purpose, and what he had already used was not available; for in those parts wheat is only sown on virgin soil or on fallow land. It is sown for one or two years, and then the land lies fallow till it is again overgrown with prairie grass. There were many who wanted such land and there was not enough for all; so that people quarreled about it. Those who were better off wanted it for growing wheat, and those who were poor wanted it to let to dealers, so that they might raise money to pay their taxes. Pahóm wanted to sow more wheat, so he rented land from a dealer for a year. He sowed much wheat and had a fine crop, but the land was too far from the village—the wheat had to be carted more than ten miles. After a time Pahóm noticed that some peasant-dealers were living on separate farms and were growing wealthy; and he thought:

"If I were to buy some freehold land and have a homestead on it, it would be a different thing altogether. Then it would all be nice and compact."

The question of buying freehold land recurred to him again and again.

He went on in the same way for three years, renting land and sowing wheat. The seasons turned out well and the crops were good, so that he began to lay money by. He might have gone on living contentedly, but he grew tired of having to rent other people's land every year, and having to scramble for it. Wherever there was good land to be had, the peasants would rush for it and it was taken up at once, so that unless you were sharp about it you got none. It happened in the third year that he and a dealer together rented a piece of pasture-land from some peasants; and they had already ploughed it up, when there was some dispute and the peasants went to law about it, and things fell out so that the labor was all lost.

"If it were my own land," thought Pahóm, "I should be independent, and there would not be all this unpleasantness."

So Pahóm began looking out for land which he could buy; and he came across a peasant who had bought thirteen hundred acres, but having got into difficulties was willing to sell again cheap. Pahóm bargained and haggled with him, and at last they settled the price at 1,500 rúbles, part in cash and part to be paid later. They had all but clinched the matter when a passing dealer happened to stop at Pahóm's one day to get a feed for his horses. He drank tea with Pahóm and they had a talk. The dealer said that he was just returning from the land of the Bashkírs,[2] far away, where he had bought thirteen thousand acres of land, all for 1,000 rúbles. Pahóm questioned him further, and the tradesman said:

"All one need do is to make friends with the chiefs. I gave away one hundred

2. Extreme eastern European Russia, extending southwest from the Ural mountains; the land is chiefly steppes with fertile meadows in the valleys.

rúbles' worth of silk robes and carpets, besides a case of tea, and I gave wine to those who would drink it; and I got the land for less than a penny an acre." And he showed Pahóm the title-deeds, saying:

"The land lies near a river, and the whole prairie is virgin soil."

Pahóm plied him with questions, and the tradesman said:

"There is more land there than you could cover if you walked a year, and it all belongs to the Bashkírs. They are as simple as sheep, and land can be got almost for nothing."

"There now," thought Pahóm, "with my one thousand rúbles, why should I get only thirteen hundred acres, and saddle myself with a debt besides? If I take it out there, I can get more than ten times as much for the money."

45

V

Pahóm inquired how to get to the place, and as soon as the tradesman had left him, he prepared to go there himself. He left his wife to look after the homestead, and started on his journey taking his man with him. They stopped at a town on their way and bought a case of tea, some wine, and other presents, as the tradesman had advised. On and on they went until they had gone more than three hundred miles, and on the seventh day they came to a place where the Bashkírs had pitched their tents. It was all just as the tradesman had said. The people lived on the steppes, by a river, in felt-covered tents. They neither tilled the ground, nor ate bread. Their cattle and horses grazed in herds on the steppe. The colts were tethered behind the tents, and the mares were driven to them twice a day. The mares were milked, and from the milk kumiss was made. It was the women who prepared kumiss, and they also made cheese. As far as the men were concerned, drinking kumiss and tea, eating mutton, and playing on their pipes, was all they cared about. They were all stout and merry, and all the summer long they never thought of doing any work. They were quite ignorant, and knew no Russian, but were good-natured enough.

As soon as they saw Pahóm, they came out of their tents and gathered round their visitor. An interpreter was found, and Pahóm told them he had come about some land. The Bashkírs seemed very glad; they took Pahóm and led him into one of the best tents, where they made him sit on some down cushions placed on a carpet, while they sat around him. They gave him some tea and kumiss, and had a sheep killed, and gave him mutton to eat. Pahóm took presents out of his cart and distributed them among the Bashkírs, and divided the tea amongst them. The Bashkírs were delighted. They talked a great deal among themselves, and then told the interpreter to translate.

"They wish to tell you," said the interpreter, "that they like you, and that it is our custom to do all we can to please a guest and to repay him for his gifts. You have given us presents, now tell us which of the things we possess please you best, that we may present them to you."

"What pleases me best here," answered Pahóm, "is your land. Our land is

50

crowded and the soil is exhausted; but you have plenty of land and it is good land. I never saw the like of it."

The interpreter translated. The Bashkírs talked among themselves for a while. Pahóm could not understand what they were saying, but saw that they were much amused and that they shouted and laughed. Then they were silent and looked at Pahóm while the interpreter said:

"They wish me to tell you that in return for your presents they will gladly give you as much land as you want. You have only to point it out with your hand and it is yours."

The Bashkírs talked again for a while and began to dispute. Pahóm asked what they were disputing about, and the interpreter told him that some of them thought they ought to ask their Chief about the land and not act in his absence, while others thought there was no need to wait for his return.

VI

While the Bashkírs were disputing, a man in a large fox-fur cap appeared on the scene. They all became silent and rose to their feet. The interpreter said, "This is our Chief himself."

Pahóm immediately fetched the best dressing-gown and five pounds of tea, and offered these to the Chief. The Chief accepted them, and seated himself in the place of honor. The Bashkírs at once began telling him something. The Chief listened for a while, then made a sign with his head for them to be silent, and addressing himself to Pahóm, said in Russian:

"Well, let it be so. Choose whatever piece of land you like; we have plenty of it."

"How can I take as much as I like?" thought Pahóm. "I must get a deed to make it secure, or else they may say, 'It is yours,' and afterwards may take it away again."

"Thank you for your kind words," he said aloud. "You have much land, and I only want a little. But I should like to be sure which bit is mine. Could it not be measured and made over to me? Life and death are in God's hands. You good people give it to me, but your children might wish to take it away again."

"You are quite right," said the Chief. "We will make it over to you."

"I heard that a dealer had been here," continued Pahóm, "and that you gave him a little land, too, and signed title-deeds to that effect. I should like to have it done in the same way."

The Chief understood.

"Yes," replied he, "that can be done quite easily. We have a scribe, and we will go to town with you and have the deed properly sealed."

"And what will be the price?" asked Pahóm.

"Our price is always the same: one thousand rúbles a day."

Pahóm did not understand.

"A day? What measure is that? How many acres would that be?"

"We do not know how to reckon it out," said the Chief. "We sell it by the day. As much as you can go round on your feet in a day is yours, and the price is one thousand rúbles a day."

Pahóm was surprised.

"But in a day you can get round a large tract of land," he said.

The Chief laughed.

"It will all be yours!" said he. "But there is one condition: If you don't return on the same day to the spot whence you started, your money is lost."

"But how am I to mark the way that I have gone?"

"Why, we shall go to any spot you like, and stay there. You must start from that spot and make your round, taking a spade with you. Wherever you think necessary, make a mark. At every turning, dig a hole and pile up the turf; then afterwards we will go round with a plough from hole to hole. You may make as large a circuit as you please, but before the sun sets you must return to the place you started from. All the land you cover will be yours."

Pahóm was delighted. It was decided to start early next morning. They talked a while, and after drinking some more kumiss and eating some more mutton, they had tea again, and then the night came on. They gave Pahóm a feather-bed to sleep on, and the Bashkírs dispersed for the night, promising to assemble the next morning at daybreak and ride out before sunrise to the appointed spot.

VII

Pahóm lay on the feather-bed, but could not sleep. He kept thinking about the land.

"What a large tract I will mark off!" thought he. "I can easily do thirty-five miles in a day. The days are long now, and within a circuit of thirty-five miles what a lot of land there will be! I will sell the poorer land, or let it to peasants, but I'll pick out the best and farm it. I will buy two oxteams, and hire two more laborers. About a hundred and fifty acres shall be plough-land, and I will pasture cattle on the rest."

Pahóm lay awake all night, and dozed off only just before dawn. Hardly were his eyes closed when he had a dream. He thought he was lying in that same tent and heard somebody chuckling outside. He wondered who it could be, and rose and went out, and he saw the Bashkír Chief sitting in front of the tent holding his sides and rolling about with laughter. Going nearer to the Chief, Pahóm asked: "What are you laughing at?" But he saw that it was no longer the Chief, but the dealer who had recently stopped at his house and had told him about the land. Just as Pahóm was going to ask, "Have you been here long?" he saw that it was not the dealer, but the peasant who had come up from the Vólga, long ago, to Pahóm's old home. Then he saw that it was not the peasant either, but the Devil himself with hoofs and horns, sitting there and chuckling, and before him lay a man barefoot, prostrate on the ground, with only trousers and a shirt on. And Pahóm dreamt that he looked more attentively to see what sort of a man it was that was lying there, and he saw that the man was dead, and that it was himself! He awoke horror-struck.

80 "What things one does dream," thought he.

Looking round he saw through the open door that the dawn was breaking.

"It's time to wake them up," thought he. "We ought to be starting."

He got up, roused his man (who was sleeping in his cart), bade him harness; and went to call the Bashkírs.

"It's time to go to the steppe to measure the land," he said.

85 The Bashkírs rose and assembled, and the Chief came too. Then they began drinking kumiss again, and offered Pahóm some tea, but he would not wait.

"If we are to go, let us go. It is high time," said he.

VIII

The Bashkírs got ready and they all started: some mounted on horses, and some in carts. Pahóm drove in his own small cart with his servant and took a spade with him. When they reached the steppe, the morning red was beginning to kindle. They ascended a hillock (called by the Bashkírs a *shikhan*) and dismounting from their carts and their horses, gathered in one spot. The Chief came up to Pahóm and stretching out his arms towards the plain:

"See," said he, "all this, as far as your eye can reach, is ours. You may have any part of it you like."

Pahóm's eyes glistened: it was all virgin soil, as flat as the palm of your hand, as black as the seed of a poppy, and in the hollows different kinds of grasses grew breast high.

90 The Chief took off his fox-fur cap, placed it on the ground and said:

"This will be the mark. Start from here, and return here again. All the land you go round shall be yours."

Pahóm took out his money and put it on the cap. Then he took off his outer coat, remaining in his sleeveless under-coat. He unfastened his girdle and tied it tight below his stomach, put a little bag of bread into the breast of his coat, and tying a flask of water to his girdle, he drew up the tops of his boots, took the spade from his man, and stood ready to start. He considered for some moments which way he had better go—it was tempting everywhere.

"No matter," he concluded, "I will go towards the rising sun."

He turned his face to the east, stretched himself, and waited for the sun to appear above the rim.

95 "I must lose no time," he thought, "and it is easier walking while it is still cool."

The sun's rays had hardly flashed above the horizon, before Pahóm, carrying the spade over his shoulder, went down into the steppe.

Pahóm started walking neither slowly nor quickly. After having gone a thousand yards he stopped, dug a hole, and placed pieces of turf one on another to make it more visible. Then he went on; and now that he had walked off his stiffness he quickened his pace. After a while he dug another hole.

Pahóm looked back. The hillock could be distinctly seen in the sunlight, with the people on it, and the glittering tires of the cart-wheels. At a rough guess Pahóm concluded that he had walked three miles. It was growing warmer; he

took off his under-coat, flung it across his shoulder, and went on again. It had
grown quite warm now; he looked at the sun, it was time to think of breakfast.

"The first shift is done, but there are four in a day, and it is too soon yet to
turn. but I will just take off my boots," said he to himself.

He sat down, took off his boots, stuck them into his girdle, and went on. It   100
was easy walking now.

"I will go on for another three miles," thought he, "and then turn to the left.
This spot is so fine, that it would be a pity to lose it. The further one goes, the
better the land seems."

He went straight on for a while, and when he looked round, the hillock was
scarcely visible and the people on it looked like black ants, and he could just see
something glistening there in the sun.

"Ah," thought Pahóm, "I have gone far enough in this direction, it is time
to turn. Besides I am in a regular sweat, and very thirsty."

He stopped, dug a large hole, and heaped up pieces of turf. Next he untied
his flask, had a drink, and then turned sharply to the left. He went on and on;
the grass was high, and it was very hot.

Pahóm began to grow tired: he looked at the sun and saw that it was noon.   105

"Well," he thought, "I must have a rest."

He sat down, and ate some bread and drank some water; but he did not lie
down, thinking that if he did he might fall asleep. After sitting a little while, he
went on again. At first he walked easily: the food had strengthened him; but it
had become terribly hot and he felt sleepy, still he went on, thinking: "An hour
to suffer, a life-time to live."

He went a long way in this direction also, and was about to turn to the left
again, when he perceived a damp hollow: "It would be a pity to leave that out,"
he thought. "Flax would do well there." So he went on past the hollow, and
dug a hole on the other side of it before he turned the corner. Pahóm looked
towards the hillock. The heat made the air hazy: it seemed to be quivering, and
through the haze the people on the hillock could scarcely be seen.

"Ah!" thought Pahóm, "I have made the sides too long; I must make this
one shorter." And he went along the third side, stepping faster. He looked at the
sun: it was nearly half-way to the horizon, and he had not yet done two miles of
the third side of the square. He was still ten miles from the goal.

"No," he thought, "though it will make my land lop-sided, I must hurry   110
back in a straight line now. I might go too far, and as it is I have a great deal of
land."

So Pahóm hurriedly dug a hole, and turned straight towards the hillock.

IX

Pahóm went straight towards the hillock, but he now walked with difficulty. He
was done up with the heat, his bare feet were cut and bruised, and his legs began
to fail. He longed to rest, but it was impossible if he meant to get back before
sunset. The sun waits for no man, and it was sinking lower and lower.

"Oh dear," he thought, "if only I have not blundered trying for too much! What if I am too late?"

He looked towards the hillock and at the sun. He was still far from his goal, and the sun was already near the rim.

Pahóm walked on and on; it was very hard walking but he went quicker and quicker. He pressed on, but was still far from the place. He began running, threw away his coat, his boots, his flask, and his cap, and kept only the spade which he used as a support.

"What shall I do," he thought again, "I have grasped too much and ruined the whole affair. I can't get there before the sun sets."

And this fear made him still more breathless. Pahóm went on running, his soaking shirt and trousers stuck to him and his mouth was parched. His breast was working like a blacksmith's bellows, his heart was beating like a hammer, and his legs were giving way as if they did not belong to him. Pahóm was seized with terror lest he should die of the strain.

Though afraid of death, he could not stop. "After having run all that way they will call me a fool if I stop now," thought he. And he ran on and on, and drew near and heard the Bashkírs yelling and shouting to him, and their cries inflamed his heart still more. He gathered his last strength and ran on.

The sun was close to the rim, and cloaked in mist looked large, and red as blood. Now, yes now, it was about to set! The sun was quite low, but he was also quite near his aim. Pahóm could already see the people on the hillock waving their arms to hurry him up. He could see the fox-fur cap on the ground and the money on it, and the Chief sitting on the ground holding his sides. And Pahóm remembered his dream.

"There is plenty of land," thought he, "but will God let me live on it? I have lost my life, I have lost my life! I shall never reach that spot!"

Pahóm looked at the sun, which had reached the earth: one side of it had already disappeared. With all his remaining strength he rushed on, bending his body forward so that his legs could hardly follow fast enough to keep him from falling. Just as he reached the hillock it suddenly grew dark. He looked up—the sun had already set! He gave a cry: "All my labor has been in vain," thought he, and was about to stop, but he heard the Bashkírs still shouting, and remembered that though to him, from below, the sun seemed to have set, they on the hillock could still see it. He took a long breath and ran up the hillock. It was still light there. He reached the top and saw the cap. Before it sat the Chief laughing and holding his sides. Again Pahóm remembered his dream, and he uttered a cry: his legs gave way beneath him, he fell forward and reached the cap with his hands.

"Ah, that's a fine fellow!" exclaimed the Chief. "He has gained much land!"

Pahóm's servant came running up and tried to raise him, but he saw that blood was flowing from his mouth. Pahóm was dead!

The Bashkírs clicked their tongues to show their pity.

His servant picked up the spade and dug a grave long enough for Pahóm to lie in, and buried him in it. Six feet from his head to his heels was all he needed.

1886

KATHERINE MANSFIELD

Her First Ball

Exactly when the ball began Leila would have found it hard to say. Perhaps her first real partner was the cab. It did not matter that she shared the cab with the Sheridan girls and their brother. She sat back in her own little corner of it, and the bolster on which her hand rested felt like the sleeve of an unknown young man's dress suit; and away they bowled, past waltzing lampposts and houses and fences and trees.

"Have you really never been to a ball before, Leila? But, my child, how too weird—" cried the Sheridan girls.

"Our nearest neighbor was fifteen miles," said Leila softly, gently opening and shutting her fan.

Oh, dear, how hard it was to be indifferent like the others! She tried not to smile too much; she tried not to care. But every single thing was so new and exciting . . . Meg's tuberoses, Jose's long loop of amber, Laura's little dark head, pushing above her white fur like a flower through snow. She would remember for ever. It even gave her a pang to see her cousin Laurie throw away the wisps of tissue paper he pulled from the fastening of his new gloves. She would like to have kept those wisps as a keepsake, as a remembrance. Laurie leaned forward and put his hand on Laura's knee.

"Look here, darling," he said. "The third and the ninth as usual, Twig?"   5

Oh, how marvellous to have a brother! In her excitement Leila felt that if there had been time, if it hadn't been impossible, she couldn't have helped crying because she was an only child, and no brother had ever said "Twig?" to her; no sister would ever say, as Meg said to Jose that moment, "I've never known your hair go up more successfully than it has tonight!"

But, of course, there was no time. They were at the drill hall already; there were cabs in front of them and cabs behind. The road was bright on either side with moving fan-like lights, and on the pavement gay couples seemed to float through the air; little satin shoes chased each other like birds.

"Hold on to me, Leila; you'll get lost," said Laura.

"Come on, girls, let's make a dash for it," said Laurie.

Leila put two fingers on Laura's pink velvet cloak, and they were somehow   10
lifted past the big gold lantern, carried along the passage, and pushed into the little room marked "Ladies." Here the crowd was so great there was hardly space to take off their things; the noise was deafening. Two benches on either side were stacked high with wraps. Two old women in white aprons ran up and down tossing fresh armfuls. And everybody was pressing forward trying to get at the little dressing table and mirror at the far end.

A great quivering jet of gas lighted the ladies' room. It couldn't wait; it was dancing already. When the door opened again and there came a burst of tuning from the drill hall, it leaped almost to the ceiling.

Dark girls, fair girls were patting their hair, tying ribbons again, tucking handkerchiefs down the front of their bodices, smoothing marble-white gloves. And because they were all laughing it seemed to Leila that they were all lovely.

"Aren't there any invisible hairpins?" cried a voice. "How most extraordinary! I can't see a single invisible hairpin."

"Powder my back, there's a darling," cried some one else.

15 "But I must have a needle and cotton. I've torn simply miles and miles of the frill," wailed a third.

Then, "Pass them along, pass them along!" The straw basket of programs was tossed from arm to arm. Darling little pink-and-silver programs, with pink pencils and fluffy tassels. Leila's fingers shook as she took one out of the basket. She wanted to ask someone, "Am I meant to have one too?" but she had just time to read: "Waltz 3. *Two, Two in a Canoe*. Polka 4. *Making the Feathers Fly*," when Meg cried, "Ready, Leila?" and they pressed their way through the crush in the passage towards the big double doors of the drill hall.

Dancing had not begun yet, but the band had stopped tuning, and the noise was so great it seemed that when it did begin to play it would never be heard. Leila, pressing close to Meg, looking over Meg's shoulder, felt that even the little quivering colored flags strung across the ceiling were talking. She quite forgot to be shy; she forgot how in the middle of dressing she had sat down on the bed with one shoe off and one shoe on and begged her mother to ring up her cousins and say she couldn't go after all. And the rush of longing she had had to be sitting on the veranda of their forsaken upcountry home, listening to the baby owls crying "More pork" in the moonlight, was changed to a rush of joy so sweet that it was hard to bear alone. She clutched her fan, and, gazing at the gleaming, golden floor, the azaleas, the lanterns, the stage at one end with its red carpet and gilt chairs and the band in a corner, she thought breathlessly, "How heavenly; how simply heavenly!"

All the girls stood grouped together at one side of the doors, the men at the other, and the chaperones in dark dresses, smiling rather foolishly, walked with little careful steps over the polished floor towards the stage.

"This is my little country cousin Leila. Be nice to her. Find her partners; she's under my wing," said Meg, going up to one girl after another.

20 Strange faces smiled at Leila—sweetly, vaguely. Strange voices answered, "Of course, my dear." But Leila felt the girls didn't really see her. They were looking towards the men. Why didn't the men begin? What were they waiting for? There they stood, smoothing their gloves, patting their glossy hair and smiling among themselves. Then, quite suddenly, as if they had only just made up their minds that that was what they had to do, the men came gliding over the parquet. There was a joyful flutter among the girls. A tall, fair man flew up to Meg, seized her program, scribbled something; Meg passed him on to Leila. "May I have the pleasure?" He ducked and smiled. There came a dark man wearing an eyeglass, then cousin Laurie with a friend, and Laura with a little freckled fellow whose tie was crooked. Then quite an old man—fat, with a big bald patch on his head—took her program and murmured, "Let me see, let me see!" And he was a long time comparing his program, which looked black with

names, with hers. It seemed to give him so much trouble that Leila was ashamed. "Oh, please don't bother," she said eagerly. But instead of replying the fat man wrote something, glanced at her again. "Do I remember this bright little face?" he said softly. "Is it known to me of yore?" At that moment the band began playing; the fat man disappeared. He was tossed away on a great wave of music that came flying over the gleaming floor, breaking the groups up into couples, scattering them, sending them spinning. . . .

Leila had learned to dance at boarding school. Every Saturday afternoon the boarders were hurried off to a little corrugated iron mission hall where Miss Eccles (of London) held her "select" classes. But the difference between that dusty-smelling hall—with calico texts on the walls, the poor terrified little woman in a brown velvet toque with rabbit's ears thumping the cold piano, Miss Eccles poking the girls' feet with her long white wand—and this was so tremendous that Leila was sure if her partner didn't come and she had to listen to that marvelous music and to watch the others sliding, gliding over the golden floor, she would die at least, or faint, or lift her arms and fly out of one of those dark windows that showed the stars.

"Ours, I think—" Some one bowed, smiled, and offered her his arm; she hadn't to die after all. Some one's hand pressed her waist, and she floated away like a flower that is tossed into a pool.

"Quite a good floor, isn't it?" drawled a faint voice close to her ear.

"I think it's most beautifully slippery," said Leila.

"Pardon!" The faint voice sounded surprised. Leila said it again. And there was a tiny pause before the voice echoed. "Oh, quite!" and she was swung round again.   25

He steered so beautifully. That was the great difference between dancing with girls and men, Leila decided. Girls banged into each other, and stamped on each other's feet; the girl who was gentleman always clutched you so.

The azaleas were separate flowers no longer; they were pink and white flags streaming by.

"Were you at the Bells' last week?" the voice came again. It sounded tired. Leila wondered whether she ought to ask him if he would like to stop.

"No, this is my first dance," said she.

Her partner gave a little gasping laugh. "Oh, I say," he protested.   30

"Yes, it is really the first dance I've ever been to." Leila was most fervent. It was such a relief to be able to tell somebody. "You see, I've lived in the country all my life up until now. . . ."

At that moment the music stopped, and they went to sit on two chairs against the wall. Leila tucked her pink satin feet under and fanned herself, while she blissfully watched the other couples passing and disappearing through the swing doors.

"Enjoying yourself, Leila?" asked Jose, nodding her golden head.

Laura passed and gave her the faintest little wink; it made Leila wonder for a moment whether she was quite grown up after all. Certainly her partner did not say very much. He coughed, tucked his handkerchief away, pulled down his waistcoat, took a minute thread off his sleeve. But it didn't matter. Almost immediately the band started, and her second partner seemed to spring from the ceiling.

"Floor's not bad," said the new voice. Did one always begin with the floor? And then, "Were you at the Neaves' on Tuesday?" And again Leila explained. Perhaps it was a little strange that her partners were not more interested. For it was thrilling. Her first ball! she was only at the beginning of everything. It seemed to her that she had never known what the night was like before. Up till now it had been dark, silent, beautiful very often—oh, yes—but mournful somehow. Solemn. And now it would never be like that again—it had opened dazzling bright.

"Care for an ice?" said her partner. And they went through the swing doors, down the passage, to the supper room. Her cheeks burned, she was fearfully thirsty. How sweet the ices looked on little glass plates, and how cold the frosted spoon was, iced too! And when they came back to the hall there was the fat man waiting for her by the door. It gave her quite a shock again to see how old he was; he ought to have been on the stage with the fathers and mothers. And when Leila compared him with her other partners he looked shabby. His waistcoat was creased, there was a button off his glove, his coat looked as if it was dusty with French chalk.

"Come along, little lady," said the fat man. He scarcely troubled to clasp her, and they moved away so gently, it was more like walking than dancing. But he said not a word about the floor. "Your first dance, isn't it?" he murmured.

"How *did* you know?"

"Ah," said the fat man, "that's what it is to be old!" He wheezed faintly as he steered her past an awkward couple. "You see, I've been doing this kind of thing for the last thirty years."

"Thirty years?" cried Leila. Twelve years before she was born!

"It hardly bears thinking about, does it?" said the fat man gloomily. Leila looked at his bald head, and she felt quite sorry for him.

"I think it's marvelous to be still going on," she said kindly.

"Kind little lady," said the fat man, and he pressed her a little closer, and hummed a bar of the waltz. "Of course," he said, "you can't hope to last anything like as long as that. No-o," said the fat man, "long before that you'll be sitting up there on the stage, looking on, in your nice black velvet. And these pretty arms will have turned into little short fat ones, and you'll beat time with such a different kind of fan—a black bony one." The fat man seemed to shudder. "And you'll smile away like the poor old dears up there, and point to your daughter, and tell the elderly lady next to you how some dreadful man tried to kiss her at the club ball. And your heart will ache, ache"—the fat man squeezed her closer still, as if he really was sorry for that poor heart—"because no one wants to kiss you now. And you'll say how unpleasant these polished floors are to walk on, how dangerous they are. Eh, Mademoiselle Twinkletoes?" said the fat man softly.

Leila gave a light little laugh, but she did not feel like laughing. Was it—could it all be true? It sounded terribly true. Was this first ball only the beginning of her last ball after all? At that the music seemed to change; it sounded sad, sad it rose upon a great sigh. Oh, how quickly things changed! Why didn't happiness last for ever? For ever wasn't a bit too long.

"I want to stop," she said in a breathless voice. The fat man led her to the door.

"No," she said. "I won't go outside. I won't sit down. I'll just stand here, thank you." She leaned against the wall, tapping with her foot, pulling up her gloves and trying to smile. But deep inside her a little girl threw her pinafore over her head and sobbed. Why had he spoiled it all?

"I say, you know," said the fat man, "you mustn't take me seriously, little lady."

"As if I should!" said Leila, tossing her small dark head and sucking her underlip. . . .

Again the couples paraded. The swing doors opened and shut. Now new music was given out by the bandmaster. But Leila didn't want to dance any more. She wanted to be home, or sitting on the veranda listening to those baby owls. When she looked through the dark windows at the stars, they had long beams like wings. . . .

But presently a soft, melting, ravishing tune began, and a young man with curly hair bowed before her. She would have to dance, out of politeness, until she could find Meg. Very stiffly she walked into the middle; very haughtily she put her hand on his sleeve. But in one minute, in one turn, her feet glided, glided. The lights, the azaleas, the dresses, the pink faces, the velvet chairs, all became one beautiful flying wheel. And when her next partner bumped her into the fat man and he said, "Par*don*," she smiled at him more radiantly than ever. She didn't even recognize him again.

1922

WILLIAM TREVOR

Beyond the Pale

We always went to Ireland in June.

Ever since the four of us began to go on holidays together, in 1965 it must have been, we had spent the first fortnight of the month at Glencorn Lodge in Co. Antrim.[1] Perfection, as Dekko put it once, and none of us disagreed. It's a Georgian house by the sea, not far from the village of Ardbeag. It's quite majestic in its rather elegant way, a garden running to the very edge of a cliff, its long rhododendron drive—or avenue, as they say in Ireland. The English couple who bought the house in the early sixties, the Malseeds, have had to build on quite a bit but it's all been discreetly done, the Georgian style preserved throughout. Figs grow in the sheltered gardens, and apricots, and peaches in the greenhouses

---

1. County in Northern Ireland containing the national capital, Belfast.

which old Mr. Saxton presides over. He's Mrs. Malseed's father actually. They brought him with them from Surrey, and their Dalmatians, Charger and Snooze.

It was Strafe who found Glencorn for us. He'd come across an advertisement in the *Lady* in the days when the Malseeds still felt the need to advertise. "How about this?" he said one evening at the end of the second rubber, and then read out the details. We had gone away together the summer before, to a hotel that had been recommended on the Costa del Sol, but it hadn't been a success because the food was so appalling. "We could try this Irish one," Dekko suggested cautiously, which is what eventually we did.

The four of us have been playing bridge together for ages, Dekko, Strafe, Cynthia and myself. They call me Milly, though strictly speaking my name is Dorothy Milson. Dekko picked up his nickname at school, Dekko Deakin sounding rather good, I dare say. He and Strafe were in fact at school together, which must be why we all call Strafe by his surname: Major R. B. Strafe he is, the initials standing for Robert Buchanan. We're of an age, the four of us, all in the early fifties: the prime of life, so Dekko insists. We live quite close to Leatherhead, where the Malseeds were before they decided to make the change from Surrey to Co. Antrim. Quite a coincidence, we always think.

5   "How *very* nice," Mrs. Malseed said, smiling her welcome again this year. Some instinct seems to tell her when guests are about to arrive, for she's rarely not waiting in the large low-ceilinged hall that always smells of flowers. She dresses beautifully, differently every day, and changing of course in the evening. Her blouse on this occasion was scarlet and silver, in stripes, her skirt black. This choice gave her a brisk look, which was fitting because being so busy she often has to be a little on the brisk side. She has smooth grey hair which she once told me she entirely looks after herself, and she almost always wears a black velvet band in it. Her face is well made up, and for one who arranges so many vases of flowers and otherwise has to use her hands she manages to keep them marvellously in condition. Her fingernails are varnished a soft pink, and a small gold bangle always adorns her right wrist, a wedding present from her husband.

"Arthur, take the party's luggage," she commanded the old porter, who doubles as odd-job man. "Rose, Geranium, Hydrangea, Fuchsia." She referred to the titles of the rooms reserved for us: in winter, when no one much comes to Glencorn Lodge, pleasant little details like that are seen to. Mrs Malseed herself painted the flower-plaques that are attached to the doors of the hotel instead of numbers; her husband sees to redecoration and repairs.

"Well, well, well," Mr. Malseed said now, entering the hall through the door that leads to the kitchen regions. "A hundred thousand welcomes," he greeted us in the Irish manner. He's rather shorter than Mrs. Malseed, who's handsomely tall. He wears Donegal[2] tweed suits and is brown as a berry, including his head, which is bald. His dark brown eyes twinkle at you, making you feel rather more than just another hotel guest. They run the place like a country house, really.

2. County in the northern portion of the Irish Republic.

"Good trip?" Mr. Malseed enquired.

"Super," Dekko said. "Not a worry all the way."

"Splendid."

"The wretched boat sailed an hour early one day last week," Mrs. Malseed said. "Quite a little band were left stranded at Stranraer."

Strafe laughed. Typical of that steamship company, he said. "Catching the tide, I dare say?"

"They caught a rocket from me," Mrs. Malseed replied good-humouredly. "A couple of old dears were due with us on Tuesday and had to spend the night in some awful Scottish lodging-house. It nearly finished them."

Everyone laughed, and I could feel the others thinking that our holiday had truly begun. Nothing had changed in Glencorn Lodge, all was well with its Irish world. Kitty from the dining-room came out to greet us, spotless in her uniform. "Ach, you're looking younger," she said, paying the compliment to all four of us, causing everyone in the hall to laugh again. Kitty's a bit of a card.

Arthur led the way to the rooms called Rose, Geranium, Hydrangea and Fuchsia, carrying as much of our luggage as he could manage and returning for the remainder. Arthur has a beaten, fisherman's face and short grey hair. He wears a green baize apron, and a white shirt with an imitation-silk scarf tucked into it at the neck. The scarf, in different swirling greens which blend nicely with the green of his apron, is an idea of Mrs. Malseed's and one appreciates the effort, if not at a uniform, at least at tidiness.

"Thank you very much," I said to Arthur in my room, smiling and finding him a coin.

We played a couple of rubbers after dinner as usual, but not of course going on for as long as we might have because we were still quite tired after the journey. In the lounge there was a French family, two girls and their parents, and a honeymoon couple—or so we had speculated during dinner—and a man on his own. There had been other people at dinner of course, because in June Glencorn Lodge is always full: from where we sat in the window we could see some of them strolling about the lawns, a few taking the cliff path down to the seashore. In the morning we'd do the same: we'd walk along the sands to Ardbeag and have coffee in the hotel there, back in time for lunch. In the afternoon we'd drive somewhere.

I knew all that because over the years this kind of pattern had developed. We had our walks and our drives, tweed to buy in Cushendall, Strafe's and Dekko's fishing day when Cynthia and I just sat on the beach, our visit to the Giant's Causeway[3] and one to Donegal perhaps, though that meant an early start and taking pot-luck for dinner somewhere. We'd come to adore Co. Antrim, its glens and coastline, Rathlin Island and Tievebulliagh. Since first we got to know it, in 1965, we'd all four fallen hopelessly in love with every variation of this

---

3. A formation of basalt cliffs projecting several hundred feet into the sea on the north coast of Antrim.

remarkable landscape. People in England thought us mad of course: they see so much of the troubles[4] on television that it's naturally difficult for them to realize that most places are just as they've always been. Yet coming as we did, taking the road along the coast, dawdling through Ballygally, it was impossible to believe that somewhere else the unpleasantness was going on. We'd never seen a thing, nor even heard people talking about incidents that might have taken place. It's true that after a particularly nasty carry-on a few winters ago we did consider finding somewhere else, in Scotland perhaps, or Wales. But as Strafe put it at the time, we felt we owed a certain loyalty to the Malseeds and indeed to every-one we'd come to know round about, people who'd always been glad to welcome us back. It seemed silly to lose our heads, and when we returned the following summer we knew immediately we'd been right. Dekko said that nothing could be further away from all the violence than Glencorn Lodge, and though his remark could hardly be taken literally I think we all knew what he meant.

"Cynthia's tired," I said because she'd been stifling yawns. "I think we should call it a day."

"Oh, not at all," Cynthia protested. "No, please."

But Dekko agreed with me that she was tired, and Strafe said he didn't mind stopping now. He suggested a nightcap, as he always does, and as we always do also, Cynthia and I declined. Dekko said he'd like a Cointreau.

The conversation drifted about. Dekko told us an Irish joke about a drunk who couldn't find his way out of a telephone box, and then Strafe remembered an incident at school concerning his and Dekko's housemaster, A. D. Cowley-Stubbs, and the house wag, Thrive Major. A. D. Cowley-Stubbs had been known as Cows and often featured in our after-bridge reminiscing. So did Thrive Major.

"Perhaps I *am* sleepy," Cynthia said. "I don't think I closed my eyes once last night."

She never does on a sea crossing. Personally I'm out like a light the moment my head touches the pillow; I often think it must be the salt in the air because normally I'm an uneasy sleeper at the best of times.

"You run along, old girl," Strafe advised.

"Brekky at nine," Dekko said.

Cynthia said good-night and went, and we didn't remark on her tiredness because as a kind of unwritten rule we never comment on one another. We're four people who play bridge. The companionship it offers, and the holidays we have together, are all part of that. We share everything: the cost of petrol, the cups of coffee or drinks we have; we even each make a contribution towards the use of Strafe's car because it's always his we go on holiday in, a Rover it was on this occasion.

"Funny, being here on your own," Strafe said, glancing across what the Malseeds call the After-Dinner Lounge at the man who didn't have a compan-

---

4. Since the 1960s there have been agitation and considerable violence in Northern Ireland. Catholics, led chiefly by the underground Irish Republican Army, want the three counties of Ulster (Northern Ireland) united with the (Catholic) Republic of Ireland.

ion. He was a red-haired man of about thirty, not wearing a tie, his collar open at the neck and folded back over the jacket of his blue serge suit. He was uncouth-looking, though it's a hard thing to say, not at all the kind of person one usually sees at Glencorn Lodge. He sat in the After-Dinner Lounge as he had in the dining-room, lost in some concentration of his own, as if calculating sums in his mind. There had been a folded newspaper on his table in the dining-room. It now reposed tidily on the arm of his chair, still unopened.

"Commercial gent," Dekko said. "Fertilizers."

"Good heavens, never. You wouldn't get a rep in here."   30

I took no part in the argument. The lone man didn't much interest me, but I felt that Strafe was probably right: if there was anything dubious about the man's credentials he might have found it difficult to secure a room. In the hall of Glencorn Lodge there's a notice which reads: *We prefer not to feature in hotel guides, and we would be grateful to our guests if they did not seek to include Glencorn Lodge in the Good Food Guide, the Good Hotel Guide, the Michelin, Egon Ronay or any others. We have not advertised Glencorn since our early days, and prefer our recommendations to be by word of mouth.*

"Ah, thank you," Strafe said when Kitty brought his whisky and Dekko's Cointreau. "Sure you won't have something?" he said to me, although he knew I never did.

Strafe is on the stout side, I suppose you could say, with a gingery moustache and gingery hair, hardly touched at all by grey. He left the Army years ago, I suppose because of me in a sense, because he didn't want to be posted abroad again. He's in the Ministry of Defence now.

I'm still quite pretty in my way, though nothing like as striking as Mrs. Malseed, for I've never been that kind of woman. I've put on weight, and wouldn't have allowed myself to do so if Strafe hadn't kept saying he can't stand a bag of bones. I'm careful about my hair and, unlike Mrs. Malseed, I have it very regularly seen to because if I don't it gets a salt and pepper look, which I hate. My husband, Ralph, who died of food-poisoning when we were still quite young, used to say I wouldn't lose a single look in middle age, and to some extent that's true. We were still putting off having children when he died, which is why I haven't any. Then I met Strafe, which meant I didn't marry again.

Strafe is married himself, to Cynthia. She's small and ineffectual, I suppose   35
you'd say without being untruthful or unkind. Not that Cynthia and I don't get on or anything like that, in fact we get on extremely well. It's Strafe and Cynthia who don't seem quite to hit it off, and I often think how much happier all round it would have been if Cynthia had married someone completely different, some-one like Dekko in a way, except that that mightn't quite have worked out either. The Strafes have two sons, both very like their father, both of them in the Army. And the very sad thing is they think nothing of poor Cynthia.

"Who's that chap?" Dekko asked Mr. Malseed, who'd come over to wish us good-night.

"Awfully sorry about that, Mr. Deakin. My fault entirely, a booking that came over the phone."

"Good heavens, not at all," Strafe protested, and Dekko looked horrified in case it should be thought he was objecting to the locals. "Splendid-looking fellow," he said, overdoing it.

Mr. Malseed murmured that the man had only booked in for a single night, and I smiled the whole thing away, reassuring him with a nod. It's one of the pleasantest of the traditions at Glencorn Lodge that every evening Mr. Malseed makes the rounds of his guests just to say good-night. It's because of little touches like that that I, too, wished Dekko hadn't questioned Mr. Malseed about the man because it's the kind of thing one doesn't do at Glencorn Lodge. But Dekko is a law unto himself, very tall and gangling, always immaculately suited, a beaky face beneath mousy hair in which flecks of grey add a certain distinction. Dekko has money of his own and though he takes out girls who are half his age he has never managed to get around to marriage. The uncharitable might say he has a rather gormless laugh; certainly it's sometimes on the loud side.

We watched while Mr. Malseed bade the lone man good-night. The man didn't respond, but just sat gazing. It was ill-mannered, but this lack of courtesy didn't appear to be intentional: the man was clearly in a mood of some kind, miles away.

"Well, I'll go up," I said. "Good-night, you two."

"Cheery-bye, Milly," Dekko said. "Brekky at nine, remember."

"Good-night, Milly," Strafe said.

The Strafes always occupy different rooms on holidays, and at home also. This time he was in Geranium and she in Fuchsia. I was in Rose, and in a little while Strafe would come to see me. He stays with her out of kindness, because he fears for her on her own. He's a sentimental, good-hearted man, easily moved to tears: he simply cannot bear the thought of Cynthia with no one to talk to in the evenings, with no one to make her life around. "And besides," he often says when he's being jocular, "it would break up our bridge four." Naturally we never discuss her shortcomings or in any way analyse the marriage. The unwritten rule that exists among the four of us seems to extend as far as that.

He slipped into my room after he'd had another drink or two, and I was waiting for him as he likes me to wait, in bed but not quite undressed. He has never said so, but I know that that is something Cynthia would not understand in him, or ever attempt to comply with. Ralph, of course, would not have understood either; poor old Ralph would have been shocked. Actually it's all rather sweet, Strafe and his little ways.

"I love you dear," I whispered to him in the darkness, but just then he didn't wish to speak of love and referred instead to my body.

If Cynthia hadn't decided to remain in the hotel the next morning instead of accompanying us on our walk to Ardbeag everything might have been different. As it happened, when she said at breakfast she thought she'd just potter about the garden and sit with her book out of the wind somewhere, I can't say I was displeased. For a moment I hoped Dekko might say he'd stay with her, allowing Strafe and myself to go off on our own, but Dekko—who doesn't go in for saying what you want him to say—didn't. "Poor old sausage,"[5] he said instead, examining Cynthia with a solicitude that suggested she was close to the grave, rather than just a little lowered by the change of life or whatever it was.

"I'll be perfectly all right," Cynthia assured him. "Honestly."

"Cynthia likes to mooch,[6] you know," Strafe pointed out, which of course is only the truth. She reads too much, I always think. You often see her putting down a book with the most melancholy look in her eyes, which can't be good for her. She's an imaginative woman, I suppose you would say, and of course her habit of reading so much is often useful on our holidays: over the years she has read her way through dozens of Irish guide-books. "That's where the garrison pushed the natives over the cliffs," she once remarked on a drive. "Those rocks are known as the Maidens," she remarked on another occasion. She has led us to places of interest which we had no idea existed: Garron Tower on Garron Point, the mausoleum at Bonamargy, the Devil's Backbone. As well as which, Cynthia is extremely knowledgeable about all matters relating to Irish history. Again she has read endlessly: biographies and autobiographies, long accounts of the centuries of battling and politics there've been. There's hardly a town or village we ever pass through that hasn't some significance for Cynthia, although I'm afraid her impressive fund of information doesn't always receive the attention it deserves. Not that Cynthia ever minds; it doesn't seem to worry her when no one listens. My own opinion is that she'd have made a much better job of her relationship with Strafe and her sons if she could have somehow developed a bit more character.

We left her in the garden and proceeded down the cliff path to the shingle beneath. I was wearing slacks and a blouse, with the arms of a cardigan looped round my neck in case it turned chilly: the outfit was new, specially bought for the holiday, in shades of tangerine. Strafe never cares how he dresses and of course she doesn't keep him up to the mark: that morning, as far as I remember, he wore rather shapeless corduroy trousers, the kind men sometimes garden in, and a navy-blue fisherman's jersey. Dekko as usual was a fashion plate: a pale green linen suit with pleated jacket pockets, a maroon shirt open at the neck, revealing a medallion on a fine gold chain. We didn't converse as we crossed the rather difficult shingle, but when we reached the sand Dekko began to talk about some girl or other, someone called Juliet who had apparently proposed marriage to him just before we'd left Surrey. He'd told her, so he said, that he'd think about it while on holiday and he wondered now about dispatching a telegram from Ardbeag saying, *Still thinking.* Strafe, who has a simple sense of humour, considered this hugely funny and spent most of the walk persuading Dekko that the telegram must certainly be sent, and other telegrams later on, all with the same message. Dekko kept laughing, throwing his head back in a way that always reminds me of an Australian bird I once saw in a nature film on television. I could see this was going to become one of those jokes that would accompany us all through the holiday, a man's thing really, but of course I didn't mind. The

50

5. Soul. (Cockney rhyming slang: "sausage [roll]" = soul.)   6. Wander about.

girl called Juliet was nearly thirty years younger than Dekko. I supposed she knew what she was doing.

Since the subject of telegrams had come up, Strafe recalled the occasion when Thrive Major had sent one to A. D. Cowley-Stubbs: *Darling regret three months gone love Rowena.* Carefully timed, it had arrived during one of Cows' Thursday evening coffee sessions. Rowena was a maid, known as the Bicycle, who had been sacked the previous term, and old Cows had something of a reputation as a misogynist. When he read the message he apparently went white and collapsed into an armchair. Warrington P. J. managed to read it too, and after that the fat was in the fire. The consequences went on rather, but I never minded listening when Strafe and Dekko drifted back to their schooldays. I just wish I'd known Strafe then, before either of us had gone and got married.

We had our coffee at Ardbeag, the telegram was sent off, and then Strafe and Dekko wanted to see a man called Henry O'Reilly whom we'd met on previous holidays, who organizes mackerel-fishing trips. I waited on my own, picking out postcards in the village shop that sells almost everything, and then I wandered down towards the shore. I knew that they would be having a drink with the boatman because a year had passed since they'd seen him last. They joined me after about twenty minutes, Dekko apologizing but Strafe not seeming to be aware that I'd had to wait because Strafe is not a man who notices little things. It was almost one o'clock when we reached Glencorn Lodge and were told by Mr. Malseed that Cynthia needed looking after.

The hotel, in fact, was in a turmoil. I have never seen anyone as ashen-faced as Mr. Malseed; his wife, in a forget-me-not[7] dress, was limp. It wasn't explained to us immediately what had happened, because in the middle of telling us that Cynthia needed looking after Mr. Malseed was summoned to the telephone. I could see through the half-open door of their little office a glass of whisky or brandy on the desk and Mrs. Malseed's bangled arm reaching out for it. Not for ages did we realize that it all had to do with the lone man whom we'd speculated about the night before.

"He just wanted to talk to me," Cynthia kept repeating hysterically in the hall. "He sat with me by the magnolias."

I made her lie down. Strafe and I stood on either side of her bed as she lay there with her shoes off, her rather unattractively cut plain pink dress crumpled and actually damp from her tears. I wanted to make her take it off and to slip under the bed-clothes in her petticoat but somehow it seemed all wrong, in the circumstances, for Strafe's wife to do anything so intimate in my presence.

"I couldn't stop him," Cynthia said, the rims of her eyes crimson by now, her nose beginning to run again. "From half past ten till well after twelve. He had to talk to someone, he said."

I could sense that Strafe was thinking precisely the same as I was: that the red-haired man had insinuated himself into Cynthia's company by talking about himself and had then put a hand on her knee. Instead of simply standing up and

7. Blue.

going away Cynthia would have stayed where she was, embarrassed or tongue-tied, at any rate unable to cope. And when the moment came she would have turned hysterical. I could picture her screaming in the garden, running across the lawn to the hotel, and then the pandemonium in the hall. I could sense Strafe picturing that also.

"My God, it's terrible," Cynthia said.

"I think she should sleep," I said quietly to Strafe. "Try to sleep, dear," I said to her, but she shook her head, tossing her jumble of hair about on the pillow.

"Milly's right," Strafe urged. "You'll feel much better after a little rest. We'll bring you a cup of tea later on."   60

"My God!" she cried again. "My God, how could I sleep?"

I went away to borrow a couple of mild sleeping pills from Dekko, who is never without them, relying on the things too much in my opinion. He was tidying himself in his room, but found the pills immediately. Strangely enough, Dekko's always sound in a crisis.

I gave them to her with water and she took them without asking what they were. She was in a kind of daze, one moment making a fuss and weeping, the next just peering ahead of her, as if frightened. In a way she was like someone who'd just had a bad nightmare and hadn't yet completely returned to reality. I remarked as much to Strafe while we made our way down to lunch, and he said he quite agreed.

"Poor old Cynth!" Dekko said when we'd all ordered lobster bisque and entrecôte béarnaise.[8] "Poor old sausage."

You could see that the waitress, a new girl this year, was bubbling over with excitement; but Kitty, serving the other half of the dining-room, was grim, which   65
was most unusual. Everyone was talking in hushed tones and when Dekko said, "Poor old Cynth!" a couple of heads were turned in our direction because he can never keep his voice down. The little vases of roses with which Mrs. Malseed must have decorated each table before the fracas had occurred seemed strangely out of place in the atmosphere which had developed.

The waitress had just taken away our soup-plates when Mr. Malseed hurried into the dining-room and came straight to our table. The lobster bisque surprisingly hadn't been quite up to scratch, and in passing I couldn't help wondering if the fuss had caused the kitchen to go to pieces also.

"I wonder if I might have a word, Major Strafe." Mr. Malseed said, and Strafe rose at once and accompanied him from the dining-room. A total silence had fallen, everyone in the dining-room pretending to be intent on eating. I had an odd feeling that we had perhaps got it all wrong, that because we'd been out for our walk when it had happened all the other guests knew more of the details than Strafe and Dekko and I did. I began to wonder if poor Cynthia had been raped.

Afterwards Strafe told us what occurred in the Malseeds' office, how Mrs. Malseed had been sitting there, slumped, as he put it, and how two policemen

---

8. Steak cut from between ribs, with sauce of egg and butter.

had questioned him. "Look, what on earth's all this about!" he had demanded rather sharply.

"It concerns this incident that's taken place, sir," one of the policemen explained in an unhurried voice. "On account of your wife—"

"My wife's lying down. She must not be questioned or in any way disturbed."

"Ach, we'd never do that, sir."

Strafe does a good Co. Antrim brogue and in relating all this to us he couldn't resist making full use of it. The two policemen were in uniform and their natural slowness of intellect was rendered more noticeable by the lugubrious air the tragedy had inspired in the hotel. For tragedy was what it was; after talking to Cynthia for nearly two hours the lone man had walked down to the rocks and been drowned.

When Strafe finished speaking I placed my knife and fork together on my plate, unable to eat another mouthful. The facts appeared to be that the man, having left Cynthia by the magnolias, had clambered down the cliff to a place no one ever went to, on the other side of the hotel from the sands we had walked along to Ardbeag. No one had seen him except Cynthia, who from the cliff-top had apparently witnessed his battering by the treacherous waves. The tide had been coming in, but by the time old Arthur and Mr. Malseed reached the rocks it had begun to turn, leaving behind it the fully dressed corpse. Mr. Malseed's impression was that the man had lost his footing on the seaweed and accidentally stumbled into the depths, for the rocks were so slippery it was difficult to carry the corpse more than a matter of yards. But at least it had been placed out of view, while Mr. Malseed hurried back to the hotel to telephone for assistance. He told Strafe that Cynthia had been most confused, insisting that the man had walked out among the rocks and then into the sea, knowing what he was doing.

Listening to it all, I no longer felt sorry for Cynthia. It was typical of her that she should so sillily have involved us in all this. Why on earth had she sat in the garden with a man of that kind instead of standing up and making a fuss the moment he'd begun to paw her? If she'd acted intelligently the whole unfortunate episode could clearly have been avoided. Since it hadn't, there was no point whatsoever in insisting that the man had committed suicide when at that distance no one could possibly be sure.

"It really does astonish me," I said at the lunch table, unable to prevent myself from breaking our unwritten rule. "Whatever came over her?"

"It can't be good for the hotel," Dekko commented, and I was glad to see Strafe giving him a little glance of irritation.

"It's hardly the point," I said coolly.

"What I meant was, hotels occasionally hush things like this up."

"Well, they haven't this time." It seemed an age since I had waited for them at Ardbeag, since we had been so happily laughing over the effect of Dekko's telegram. He'd included his address in it so that the girl could send a message back, and as we'd returned to the hotel along the seashore there'd been much speculation between the two men about the form this would take.

"I suppose what Cynthia's thinking," Strafe said, "is that after he'd tried something on with her he became depressed."

"Oh, but he could just as easily have lost his footing. He'd have been on edge anyway, worried in case she reported him."

"Dreadful kind of death," Dekko said. His tone suggested that that was that, that the subject should now be closed, and so it was.

After lunch we went to our rooms, as we always do at Glencorn Lodge, to rest for an hour. I took my slacks and blouse off, hoping that Strafe would knock on my door, but he didn't and of course that was understandable. Oddly enough I found myself thinking of Dekko, picturing his long form stretched out in the room called Hydrangea, his beaky face in profile on his pillow. The precise nature of Dekko's relationship with these girls he picks up has always privately intrigued me: was it really possible that somewhere in London there was a girl called Juliet who was prepared to marry him for his not inconsiderable money?

I slept and briefly dreamed. Thrive Major and Warrington P. J. were running the post office in Ardbeag, sending telegrams to everyone they could think of, including Dekko's friend Juliet. Cynthia had been found dead beside the magnolias and people were waiting for Hercule Poirot[9] to arrive. "Promise me you didn't do it," I whispered to Strafe, but when Strafe replied it was to say that Cynthia's body reminded him of a bag of old chicken bones.

Strafe and Dekko and I met for tea in the tea-lounge. Strafe had looked in to see if Cynthia had woken, but apparently she hadn't. The police officers had left the hotel, Dekko said, because he'd noticed their car wasn't parked at the front any more. None of the three of us said, but I think we presumed, that the man's body had been removed from the rocks during the quietness of the afternoon. From where we sat I caught a glimpse of Mrs. Malseed passing quite briskly through the hall, seeming almost herself again. Certainly our holiday would be affected, but it might not be totally ruined. All that remained to hope for was Cynthia's recovery, and then everyone could set about forgetting the unpleasantness. The nicest thing would be if a jolly young couple turned up and occupied the man's room, exorcising the incident, as newcomers would.

The family from France—the two little girls and their parents—were chattering away in the tea-lounge, and an elderly trio who'd arrived that morning were speaking in American accents. The honeymoon couple appeared, looking rather shy, and began to whisper and giggle in a corner. People who occupied the table next to ours in the dining-room, a Wing-Commander Orfell and his wife, from Guildford,[1] nodded and smiled as they passed. Everyone was making an effort, and I knew it would help matters further if Cynthia felt up to a rubber or two before dinner. That life should continue as normally as possible was essential for Glencorn Lodge, the example already set by Mrs. Malseed.

Because of our interrupted lunch I felt quite hungry, and the Malseeds pride themselves on their teas. The chef, Mr. McBride, whom of course we've met,

9. Detective in many of Agatha Christie's murder mysteries.   1. In Surrey, southern England.

has the lightest touch I know with sponge cakes and little currenty scones. I was, in fact, buttering a scone when Strafe said:

"Here she is."

And there indeed she was. By the look of her she had simply pushed herself off her bed and come straight down. Her pink dress was even more crumpled than it had been. She hadn't so much as run a comb through her hair, her face was puffy and unpowdered. For a moment I really thought she was walking in her sleep.

90 Strafe and Dekko stood up. "Feeling better, dear?" Strafe said, but she didn't answer.

"Sit down, Cynth," Dekko urged, pushing back a chair to make room for her.

"He told me a story I can never forget. I've dreamed about it all over again." Cynthia swayed in front of us, not even attempting to sit down. To tell the truth, she sounded inane.

"Story, dear?" Strafe enquired, humouring her.

She said it was the story of two children who had apparently ridden bicycles through the streets of Belfast, out into Co. Antrim. The bicycles were dilapidated, she said; she didn't know if they were stolen or not. She didn't know about the children's homes because the man hadn't spoken of them, but she claimed to know instinctively that they had ridden away from poverty and unhappiness. "From the clatter and the quarrelling," Cynthia said, "Two children who later fell in love."

95 "Horrid old dream," Strafe said. "Horrid for you, dear."

She shook her head, and then sat down. I poured another cup of tea. "I had the oddest dream myself," I said. "Thrive Major was running the post office in Ardbeag."

Strafe smiled and Dekko gave his laugh, but Cynthia didn't in any way acknowledge what I'd said.

"A fragile thing the girl was, with depths of mystery in her wide brown eyes. Red-haired of course he was himself, thin as a rake in those days. Glencorn Lodge was derelict then."

"You've had a bit of a shock, old thing," Dekko said.

100 Strafe agreed, kindly adding, "Look, dear, if the chap actually interfered with you—"

"Why on earth should he do that?" Her voice was shrill in the tea-lounge, edged with a note of hysteria. I glanced at Strafe, who was frowning into his teacup. Dekko began to say something, but broke off before his meaning emerged. Rather more calmly Cynthia said:

"It was summer when they came here. Honeysuckle he described. And mother of thyme.[2] He didn't know the name of either."

No one attempted any kind of reply, not that it was necessary, for Cynthia just continued.

"At school there were the facts of geography and arithmetic. And the legends

2. A low-growing, wide-spreading variety of the aromatic thyme.

of scholars and of heroes, of Queen Maeve and Finn MacCool. There was the coming of St. Patrick[3] to a heathen people. History was full of kings and high-kings, and Silken Thomas and Wolfe Tone, the Flight of the Earls, the Siege of Limerick."[4]

When Cynthia said that, it was impossible not to believe that the unfortunate events of the morning had touched her with some kind of madness. It seemed astonishing that she had walked into the tea-lounge without having combed her hair, and that she'd stood there swaying before sitting down, that out of the blue she had started on about two children. None of it made an iota of sense, and surely she could see that the nasty experience she'd suffered should not be dwelt upon? I offered her the plate of scones, hoping that if she began to eat she would stop talking, but she took no notice of my gesture.

"Look, dear," Strafe said, "there's not one of us who knows what you're talking about."

"I'm talking about a children's story, I'm talking about a girl and a boy who visited this place we visit also. He hadn't been here for years, but he returned last night, making one final effort to understand. And then he walked out into the sea."

She had taken a piece of her dress and was agitatedly crumpling it between the finger and thumb of her left hand. It was dreadful really, having her so grubby-looking. For some odd reason I suddenly thought of her cooking, how she wasn't in the least interested in it or in anything about the house. She certainly hadn't succeeded in making a home for Strafe.

"They rode those worn-out bicycles through a hot afternoon. Can you feel all that? A newly surfaced road, the snap of chippings beneath their tyres, the smell of tar? Dust from a passing car, the city they left behind?"

"Cynthia dear," I said, "drink your tea, and why not have a scone?"

"They swam and sunbathed on the beach you walked along today. They went to a spring for water. There were no magnolias then. There was no garden, no neat little cliff paths to the beach. Surely you can see it clearly?"

"No," Strafe said. "No, we really cannot, dear."

"This place that is an idyll for us was an idyll for them too: the trees, the ferns, the wild roses near the water spring, the very sea and sun they shared. There was a cottage lost in the middle of the woods: they sometimes looked for that. They played a game, a kind of hide and seek. People in a white farmhouse gave them milk."

105

110

---

3. Patrick converted the Irish to Catholicism. *Maeve:* First-century ruler of Connaught who reputedly invaded Ulster and in folk tradition is queen of the fairies. *Finn MacCumhaill:* Third-century chieftain who reputedly possessed gifts of poetry, second sight, and healing.   4. The town of Limerick in southwest Ireland was, in 1791, besieged by troops of King William, and the Irish Army, loyal to the Catholic James II who had been forced off the British throne, was defeated. *Silken Thomas:* Thomas Fitzgerald, tenth Earl of Kildare, rebelled against Henry VIII when he heard his father had been executed, and adorned his helmet and those of his supporters with silken fringe. *Wolfe Tone:* A founder and leader of the United Irishmen, supported religious toleration, separation from England, and the French Revolution and was sentenced to death as a traitor. *The Flight of the Earls:* In 1607 almost a hundred leaders ("Earls") of the North fled rather than serve England and James I, a flight that some believe permanently damaged the Irish cause.

For the second time I offered Cynthia the plate of scones and for the second time she pointedly ignored me. Her cup of tea hadn't been touched. Dekko took a scone and cheerfully said:

115 "All's well that's over."

But Cynthia appeared to have drifted back into a daze, and I wondered again if it could really be possible that the experience had unhinged her. Unable to help myself, I saw her being led away from the hotel, helped into the back of a blue van, something like an ambulance. She was talking about the children again, how they had planned to marry and keep a sweetshop.

"Take it easy, dear," Strafe said, which I followed up by suggesting for the second time that she should make an effort to drink her tea.

"Has it to do with the streets they came from? Or the history they learnt, he from his Christian Brothers, she from her nuns? History is unfinished in this island; long since it has come to a stop in Surrey."

Dekko said, and I really had to hand it to him:

120 "Cynth, we have to put it behind us."

It didn't do any good. Cynthia just went rambling on, speaking again of the girl being taught by nuns, and the boy by Christian Brothers. She began to recite the history they might have learnt, the way she sometimes did when we were driving through an area that had historical connections. "Can you imagine," she embarrassingly asked, "our very favourite places bitter with disaffection, with plotting and revenge? Can you imagine the treacherous murder of Shane O'Neill the Proud?"[5]

Dekko made a little sideways gesture of his head, politely marvelling. Strafe seemed about to say something, but changed his mind. Confusion ran through Irish history, Cynthia said, like convolvulus in a hedgerow. On May 24th, 1487, a boy of ten called Lambert Simnel, brought to Dublin by a priest from Oxford, was declared Edward VI of all England and Ireland, crowned with a golden circlet taken from a statue of the Virgin Mary. On May 24th, 1798, here in Antrim, Presbyterian farmers fought for a common cause with their Catholic labourers.[6] She paused and looked at Strafe. Chaos and contradiction, she informed him, were hidden everywhere beneath nice-sounding names. "The Battle of the Yellow Ford," she suddenly chanted in a sing-song way that sounded thoroughly peculiar, "the Statutes of Kilkenny. The Battle of Glenmama, the Convention of Drumceat.[7] The Act of Settlement, the Renunciation Act. The Act of Union,

---

5. Sixteenth-century leader who tried to take control of Ulster from England (Elizabeth); when the O'Donnells, egged on by the government, defeated Shane (1567), he fled to Scotland, where, though received peacefully, he was murdered.   6. "Edward VI's" rebel forces were defeated by Henry VII and he and the priest were jailed; Antrim was one of the sites of the uprising of the United Irishmen.   7. At the Battle of Yellow Ford, 1598, Hugh O'Neill, nephew of Shane, Earl of Tyrone, in his struggle to prevent the anglicization of Ireland, defeated the English. The statutes, 1366, ordered English (Norman) settlers not to intermarry with the Irish, speak their language, or adopt their customs. At Glenmama, near Dublin, in 999, the Irish defeated the Danes. Dalriada was a kingdom, partly in northeastern Ireland, partly in southwestern Scotland, and in 590 a convention was called at Drumceat County, Londonderry, to see if Scots should give allegiance to the Irish "high king."

the Toleration Act.[8] Just so much history it sounds like now, yet people starved or died while other people watched. A language was lost,[9] a faith forbidden. Famine followed revolt, plantation followed that. But it was people who were struck into the soil of other people's land, not forests of new trees; and it was greed and treachery that spread as a disease among them all. No wonder unease clings to these shreds of history and shots ring out in answer to the mockery of drums. No wonder the air is nervy with suspicion."

There was an extremely awkward silence when she ceased to speak. Dekko nodded, doing his best to be companionable. Strafe nodded also. I simpy examined the pattern of roses on our tea-time china, not knowing what else to do. Eventually Dekko said:

"What an awful lot you know, Cynth!"

"Cynthia's always been interested," Strafe said. "Always had a first-rate memory." 125

"Those children of the streets are part of the battles and the Acts," she went on, seeming quite unaware that her talk was literally almost crazy. "They're part of the blood that flowed around those nice-sounding names." She paused, and for a moment seemed disinclined to continue. Then she said:

"The second time they came here the house was being rebuilt. There were concrete-mixers, and lorries drawn up on the grass, noise and scaffolding everywhere. They watched all through another afternoon and then they went their different ways: their childhood was over, lost with their idyll. He became a dockyard clerk. She went to London, to work in a betting shop."

"My dear," Strafe said very gently, "it's interesting, everything you say, but it really hardly concerns us."

"No, of course not." Quite emphatically Cynthia shook her head, appearing wholly to agree. "They were degenerate, awful creatures. They must have been."

"No one's saying that, my dear." 130

"Their story should have ended there, he in the docklands of Belfast, she recording bets. Their complicated childhood love should just have dissipated, as such love often does. But somehow nothing was as neat as that."

Dekko, in an effort to lighten the conversation, mentioned a boy called Gollsol who'd been at school with Strafe and himself, who'd formed a romantic attachment for the daughter of one of the groundsmen and had later actually married her. There was a silence for a moment, then Cynthia, without emotion, said:

"You none of you care. You sit there not caring that two people are dead."

8. Under the Act of Settlement of 1652, those not friendly to Cromwell's Puritan English government could forfeit part or all of their property. In 1783 the English Parliament recognized Irish independence, rights of Irish courts, and as valid for Ireland only those laws enacted by English king *and* Irish Parliament. Not much later, 1800, the Act of Union united the parliament and kingdoms (thus the United Kingdom or U.K.). Earlier, 1719, the Toleration Act, forced on the Irish Parliament, allowed the Irish freedom to worship and to serve in parish offices if they would swear civil allegiance and renounce "popish," i.e. Roman Catholic, doctrines.   9. The British forbade the Irish to speak or teach their own language and anglicized all place names. *Plantation* (below): the expropriation of Irish land, which was then given to English settlers; it began under Mary I in the 1500s and continued for centuries.

"Two people, Cynthia?" I said.

"For God's sake, I'm telling you!" she cried. "That girl was murdered in a room in Maida Vale."[1]

Although there is something between Strafe and myself, I do try my best to be at peace about it. I go to church and take communion, and I know Strafe occasionally does too, although not as often as perhaps he might. Cynthia has no interest in that side of life, and it rankled with me now to hear her blaspheming so casually, and so casually speaking about death in Maida Vale on top of all this stuff about history and children. Strafe was shaking his head, clearly believing that Cynthia didn't know what she was talking about.

"Cynthia dear," I began, "are you sure you're not muddling something up here? You've been upset, you've had a nightmare: don't you think your imagination, or something you've been reading—"

"Bombs don't go off on their own. Death doesn't just happen to occur in Derry and Belfast, in London and Amsterdam and Dublin, in Berlin and Jerusalem. There are people who are murderers: that is what this children's story is about."

A silence fell, no one knowing what to say. It didn't matter of course because without any prompting Cynthia continued.

"We drink our gin with Angostura bitters, there's lamb or chicken Kiev. Old Kitty's kind to us in the dining-room and old Arthur in the hall. Flowers are everywhere, we have our special table."

"Please let us take you to your room now," Strafe begged, and as he spoke I reached out a hand in friendship and placed it on her arm. "Come on, old thing," Dekko said.

"The limbless are left on the streets, blood spatters the car-parks. *Brits Out* it says on a rockface, but we know it doesn't mean us."

I spoke quietly then, measuring my words, measuring the pause between each so that its effect might be registered. I felt the statement had to be made, whether it was my place to make it or not. I said:

"You are very confused, Cynthia."

The French family left the tea-lounge. The two Dalmatians, Charger and Snooze, ambled in and sniffed and went away again. Kitty came to clear the French family's tea things. I could hear her speaking to the honeymoon couple, saying the weather forecast was good.

"Cynthia," Strafe said, standing up, "we've been very patient with you but this is now becoming silly."

I nodded just a little. "I really think," I softly said, but Cynthia didn't permit me to go on.

"Someone told him about her. Someone mentioned her name, and he couldn't believe it. She sat alone in Maida Vale, putting together the mechanisms of her bombs: this girl who had laughed on the seashore, whom he had loved."

"Cynthia," Strafe began, but he wasn't permitted to continue either. Hopelessly, he just sat down again.

---

1. Section of London with many foreign transients and rooming houses.

"Whenever he heard of bombs exploding he thought of her, and couldn't   150
understand. He wept he said that; her violence haunted him, he said. He couldn't
work, he couldn't sleep at night. His mind filled up with images of her, their
awkward childhood kisses, her fingers working neatly now. He saw her with a
carrier-bag, hurrying it through a crowd, leaving it where it could cause most
death. In front of the mouldering old house that had once been Glencorn Lodge
they'd made a fire and cooked their food. They'd lain for ages on the grass.
They'd cycled home to their city streets."

It suddenly dawned on me that Cynthia was knitting this whole fantasy out
of nothing. It all worked backwards from the moment when she'd had the misfortune to witness the man's death in the sea. A few minutes before he'd been
chatting quite normally to her, he'd probably even mentioned a holiday in his
childhood and some girl there'd been: all of it would have been natural in the
circumstances, possibly even the holiday had taken place at Glencorn. He'd said
good-bye and then unfortunately he'd had his accident. As she watched from the
cliff edge, something had cracked in poor Cynthia's brain, she having always
been a prey to melancholy. I suppose it must be hard having two sons who don't
think much of you, and a marriage and offering you a great deal, bridge and
holidays probably the best part of it. For some odd reason of her own she'd
created her fantasy about a child turning into a terrorist. The violence of the
man's death had clearly filled her imagination with Irish violence, so regularly
seen on television. If we'd been on holiday in Suffolk I wondered how it would
have seemed to the poor creature.

I could feel Strafe and Dekko beginning to put all that together also, beginning to realize that the whole story of the red-haired man and the girl was clearly
Cynthia's invention. "Poor creature," I wanted to say, but did not do so.

"For months he searched for her, pushing his way among the people of
London, the people who were her victims. When he found her she just looked
at him, as if the past hadn't even existed. She didn't smile, as if incapable of
smiling. He wanted to take her away, back to where they came from, but she
didn't reply when he suggested that. Bitterness was like a disease in her, and
when he left her he felt the bitterness in himself."

Again Strafe and Dekko nodded, and I could feel Strafe thinking that there
really was no point in protesting further. All we could hope for was that the end
of the saga was in sight.

"He remained in London, working on the railways. But in the same way as   155
before he was haunted by the person she'd become, and the haunting was more
awful now. He bought a gun from a man he'd been told about and kept it hidden
in a shoe-box in his rented room. Now and again he took it out and looked at it,
then put back. He hated the violence that possessed her, yet he was full of it
himself: he knew he couldn't betray her with anything but death. Humanity had
left both of them when he visited her again in Maida Vale."

To my enormous relief and, I could feel, to Strafe's and Dekko's too, Mr.
and Mrs. Malseed appeared beside us. Like his wife, Mr. Malseed had considerably recovered. He spoke in an even voice, clearly wishing to dispose of the
matter. It was just the diversion we needed.

"I must apologize, Mrs. Strafe," he said. "I cannot say how sorry we are that you were bothered by that man."

"My wife is still a little dicky,[2] Strafe explained, "but after a decent night's rest I think we can say she'll be as right as rain again."

"I only wish, Mrs. Strafe, you had made contact with my wife or myself when he first approached you." There was a spark of irritation in Mr. Malseed's eyes, but his voice was still controlled. "I mean, the unpleasantness you suffered might just have been averted."

"Nothing would have been averted, Mr. Malseed, and certainly not the horror we are left with. Can you see her as the girl she became, seated at a chipped white table, her wires and fuses spread around her? What were her thoughts in that room, Mr. Malseed? What happens in the mind of anyone who wishes to destroy? In a back street he bought his gun for too much money. When did it first occur to him to kill her?"

"We really are a bit at sea," Mr. Malseed replied without the slightest hesitation. He humoured Cynthia by displaying no surprise, by speaking very quietly.

"All I am saying, Mr. Malseed, is that we should root our heads out of the sand and wonder about two people who are beyond the pale."

"My dear," Strafe said, "Mr. Malseed is a busy man."

Still quietly, still perfectly in control of every intonation, without a single glance around the tea-lounge to ascertain where his guests' attention was, Mr. Malseed said:

"There is unrest here, Mrs. Strafe, but we do our best to live with it."

"All I am saying is that perhaps there can be regret when two children end like this."

Mr. Malseed did not reply. His wife did her best to smile away the awkwardness. Strafe murmured privately to Cynthia, no doubt beseeching her to come to her senses. Again I imagined a blue van drawn up in front of Glencorn Lodge, for it was quite understandable now that an imaginative woman should go mad, affected by the ugliness of death. The garbled speculation about the man and the girl, the jumble in the poor thing's mind—a children's story as she called it—all somehow hung together when you realized they didn't have to make any sense whatsoever.

"Murderers are beyond the pale, Mr. Malseed, and England has always had its pales. The one in Ireland began in 1395."[3]

"Dear," I said, "what has happened has nothing whatsoever to do with calling people murderers and placing them beyond some pale or other. You witnessed a most unpleasant accident, dear, and it's only to be expected that you've become just a little lost. The man had a chat with you when you were sitting by the magnolias and then the shock of seeing him slip on the seaweed—"

"He didn't slip on the seaweed," she suddenly screamed. "My God, he didn't slip on the seaweed."

2. Shaky.   3. Richard II visited Ireland 1394–95 to bolster royal authority and (unsuccessfully) to extend English control over lands. The small area around Dublin controlled by England at the time was the "pale," which by extension now refers to areas of British control and influence.

Strafe closed his eyes. The other guests in the tea-lounge had fallen silent ages ago, openly listening. Arthur was standing near the door and was listening also. Kitty was waiting to clear away our tea things, but didn't like to because of what was happening.

"I must request you to take Mrs. Strafe to her room, Major," Mr. Malseed said. "And I must make it clear that we cannot tolerate further upset in Glencorn Lodge."

Strafe reached for her arm, but Cynthia took no notice.

"An Irish joke," she said, and then she stared at Mr. and Mrs. Malseed, her eyes passing over each feature of their faces. She stared at Dekko and Strafe, and last of all at me. She said eventually:

"An Irish joke, an unbecoming tale: of course it can't be true. Ridiculous, that a man returned here. Ridiculous, that he walked again by the seashore and through the woods, hoping to understand where a woman's cruelty had come from."

"This talk is most offensive," Mr. Malseed protested, his calmness slipping just a little. The ashen look that had earlier been in his face returned. I could see he was beside himself with rage. "You are trying to bring something to our doorstep which most certainly does not belong there."

"On your doorstep they talked about a sweetshop: Cadbury's bars and different-flavoured creams, nut-milk toffee, Aero and Crunchie."

"For God's sake pull yourself together," I clearly heard Strafe whispering, and Mrs. Malseed attempted to smile. "Come along now, Mrs. Strafe," she said, making a gesture. "Just to please us, dear. Kitty wants to clear away the dishes. Kitty!" she called out, endeavouring to bring matters down to earth.

Kitty crossed the lounge with her tray and gathered up the cups and saucers. The Malseeds, naturally still anxious, hovered. No one was surprised when Cynthia began all over again, by crazily asking Kitty what she thought of us.

"I think, dear," Mrs. Malseed began, "Kitty's quite busy really."

"Stop this at once," Strafe quietly ordered.

"For fourteen years, Kitty, you've served us with food and cleared away the tea-cups we've drunk from. For fourteen years we've played our bridge and walked about the garden. We've gone for drives, we've bought our tweed, we've bathed as those children did."

"Stop it," Strafe said again, a little louder. Bewildered and getting red in the face, Kitty hastily bundled china on to her tray. I made a sign at Strafe because for some reason I felt that the end was really in sight. I wanted him to retain his patience, but what Cynthia said next was almost unbelievable.

"In Surrey we while away the time, we clip our hedges. On a bridge night there's coffee at nine o'clock, with macaroons or *petits fours*. Last thing of all we watch the late-night News, packing away our cards and scoring-pads, our sharpened pencils. There's been an incident in Armagh, one soldier's had his head shot off, another's run amok. Our lovely Glens of Antrim, we all four think, our coastal drives: we hope that nothing disturbs the peace. We think of Mr. Malseed, still busy in Glencorn Lodge, and Mrs. Malseed finishing her flower-plaques for the rooms of the completed annexe."

175

180

185   "Will you for God's sake shut up?" Strafe suddenly shouted. I could see him struggling with himself, but it didn't do any good. He called Cynthia a bloody spectacle, sitting there talking rubbish. I don't believe she even heard him.

"Through honey-tinted glasses we love you and we love your island, Kitty. We love the lilt of your racy history, we love your earls and heroes. Yet we made a sensible pale here once, as civilized people create a garden, pretty as a picture."

Strafe's outburst had been quite noisy and I could sense him being ashamed of it. He muttered that he was sorry, but Cynthia simply took advantage of his generosity, continuing about a pale.

"Beyond it lie the bleak untouchables, best kept as dots on the horizon, too terrible to contemplate. How can we be blamed if we make neither head nor tail of anything, Kitty, your past and your present, those battles and Acts of Parliament? We people of Surrey: how can we know? Yet I stupidly thought, you see, that the tragedy of two children could at least be understood. He didn't discover where her cruelty had come from because perhaps you never can: evil breeds evil in a mysterious way. That's the story the red-haired stranger passed on to me, the story you huddle away from."

Poor Strafe was pulling at Cynthia, pleading with her, still saying he was sorry.

190   "Mrs. Strafe," Mr. Malseed tried to say, but got no further. To my horror Cynthia abruptly pointed at me.

"That woman," she said, "is my husband's mistress, a fact I am supposed to be unaware of, Kitty."

"My God!" Strafe said.

"My husband is perverted in his sexual desires. His friend, who shared his schooldays, has never quite recovered from that time. I myself am a pathetic creature who has closed her eyes to a husband's infidelity and his mistress's viciousness. I am dragged into the days of Thrive Major and A. D. Cowley-Stubbs: mechanically I smile. I hardly exist, Kitty."

There was a most unpleasant silence, and then Strafe said:

195   "None of that's true. For God's sake, Cynthia," he suddenly shouted, "go and rest yourself."

Cynthia shook her head and continued to address the waitress. She'd had a rest, she told her. "But it didn't do any good, Kitty, because hell has invaded the paradise of Glencorn, as so often it has invaded your island. And we, who have so often brought it, pretend it isn't there. Who cares about children made into murderers?"

Strafe shouted again. "You fleshless ugly bitch!" he cried. "You bloody old fool!" He was on his feet, trying to get her to hers. The blood was thumping in his bronzed face, his eyes had a fury in them I'd never seen before. "Fleshless!" he shouted at her, not caring that so many people were listening. He closed his eyes in misery and in shame again, and I wanted to reach out and take his hand but of course I could not. You could see the Malseeds didn't blame him, you could see them thinking that everything was ruined for us. I wanted to shout at Cynthia too, to batter the silliness out of her, but of course I could not do that. I could feel the tears behind my eyes, and I couldn't help noticing that Dekko's hands were shaking. He's quite sensitive behind his joky manner, and had quite obviously taken to heart her statement that he had never recovered from his schooldays. Nor had it been pleasant, hearing myself described as vicious.

"No one cares," Cynthia said in the same unbalanced way, as if she hadn't just been called ugly and a bitch. "No one cares, and on our journey home we shall all four be silent. Yet is the truth about ourselves at least a beginning? Will we wonder in the end about the hell that frightens us?"

Strafe still looked wretched, his face deliberately turned away from us. Mrs. Malseed gave a little sigh and raised the fingers of her left hand to her cheek, as if something tickled it. Her husband breathed heavily. Dekko seemed on the point of tears.

Cynthia stumbled off, leaving a silence behind her. Before it was broken I knew she was right when she said we would just go home, away from this country we had come to love. And I knew as well that neither here nor at home would she be led to a blue van that was not quite an ambulance. Strafe would stay with her because Strafe is made like that, honourable in his own particular way. I felt a pain where perhaps my heart is, and again I wanted to cry. Why couldn't it have been she who had gone down to the rocks and slipped on the seaweed or just walked into the sea, it didn't matter which? Her awful rigmarole hung about us as the last of the tea things were gathered up—the earls who'd fled, the famine and the people planted. The children were there too, grown up into murdering riff-raff.

200

1981

QUESTIONS

1. How much land *does* a man—or woman—need? What do you mean by "need"?

2. Leila, in "Her First Ball," soon shakes off the gloomy thoughts offered her by her older partner. Is she just an empty-headed girl too shallow to think of serious things, or is she just young and healthy, enjoying life?

3. What does "pale" in the title of the Trevor story mean? How is it significant in the story?

WRITING SUGGESTIONS

1. Compare Hawthorne's and Tolstoy's devils, their disguises, and how they function, and analyze what these figures imply about God and virtue in the two stories.

2. Land works well as a symbol of material wealth and as a symbol of the vanity of human wishes, the inevitable end of life, and therefore of the need for spiritual values. "How Many BMWs Does a Man Need" does not quite make it (but you could try a parody along those lines). Can you find a contemporary symbol that can work the way land does for Tolstoy? If you can, write an imitation or parody, calling it, perhaps, "How Much ——— Does a Person Need?"

3. Rewrite "Her First Ball" using another focus and voice.

7 THE WHOLE TEXT

I feel that discussing story-writing in terms of plot, character,
and theme is like trying to describe the expression on a face by
saying where the eyes, nose, and mouth are.
—FLANNERY O'CONNOR, "Writing Short Stories"

P lot, point of view, character, symbol, and theme are useful concepts. But
they do not really exist as discrete parts or constituents of a finished work.
In "Beyond the Pale," for example, the connection between the private
lives of the vacationing English couples and the Irish "troubles" is both part of
the story's plot and part of its theme; and what the English vacationers do, say,
and think—their contributions to plot and theme—is inextricably related to
their individual characters. Similarly, in "How Much Land Does a Man Need?"
Pahóm's greed is a constituent both of his character and of the story's theme.

Analyzing a story means breaking it down into pieces we can handle. Analyzing may require talking or writing about a story in terms of its "elements,"
but we must remain aware of the arbitrariness of those distinctions and of the
inextricable, organic integrity of the story itself. As you read the stories that
follow in this chapter, apply all that you have learned about the history, the
structure, and the elements of fiction, but be especially alert as to how the elements interact. Notice how after taking it apart in order to analyze it, we can
put the story back together.

JOSEPH CONRAD

The Secret Sharer

I

On my right hand there were lines of fishing-stakes resembling a mysterious
system of half-submerged bamboo fences, incomprehensible in its division of the
domain of tropical fishes, and crazy[1] of aspect as if abandoned for ever by some
nomad tribe of fishermen now gone to the other end of the ocean; for there was
no sign of human habitation as far as the eye could reach. To the left a group of
barren islets, suggesting ruins of stone walls, towers, and blockhouses, had its
foundations set in a blue sea that itself looked solid, so still and stable did it lie

---

1. Irregular, rickety.

below my feet; even the track of light from the westering sun shone smoothly, without that animated glitter which tells of an imperceptible ripple. And when I turned my head to take a parting glance at the tug which had just left us anchored outside the bar, I saw the straight line of the flat shore joined to the stable sea, edge to edge, with a perfect and unmarked closeness, in one leveled floor half brown, half blue under the enormous dome of the sky. Corresponding in their insignificance to the islets of the sea, two small clumps of trees, one on each side of the only fault in the impeccable joint, marked the mouth of the river Meinam[2] we had just left on the first preparatory stage of our homeward journey; and, far back on the inland level, a larger and loftier mass, the grove surrounding the great Paknam pagoda, was the only thing on which the eye could rest from the vain task of exploring the monotonous sweep of the horizon. Here and there gleams as of a few scattered pieces of silver marked the windings of the great river; and on the nearest of them, just within the bar, the tug steaming right into the land became lost to my sight, hull and funnel and masts, as though the impassive earth had swallowed her up without an effort, without a tremor. My eye followed the light cloud of her smoke, now here, now there, above the plain, according to the devious curves of the stream, but always fainter and farther away, till I lost it at last behind the mitre-shaped hill of the great pagoda. And then I was left alone with my ship, anchored at the head of the Gulf of Siam.

She floated at the starting-point of a long journey, very still in an immense stillness, the shadows of her spars flung far to the eastward by the setting sun. At that moment I was alone on her decks. There was not a sound in her—and around us nothing moved, nothing lived, not a canoe on the water, not a bird in the air, not a cloud in the sky. In this breathless pause at the threshold of a long passage we seemed to be measuring our fitness for a long and arduous enterprise, the appointed task of both our existences to be carried out, far from all human eyes, with only sky and sea for spectators and for judges.

There must have been some glare in the air to interfere with one's sight, because it was only just before the sun left us that my roaming eyes made out beyond the highest ridge of the principal islet of the group something which did away with the solemnity of perfect solitude. The tide of darkness flowed on swiftly; and with tropical suddenness a swarm of stars came out above the shadowy earth, while I lingered yet, my hand resting lightly on my ship's rail as if on the shoulder of a trusted friend. But, with all that multitude of celestial bodies staring down at one, the comfort of quiet communion with her was gone for good. And there were also disturbing sounds by this time—voices, footsteps forward; the steward flitted along the main deck, a busily ministering spirit; a hand-bell tinkled urgently under the poop deck. . . .

I found my two officers waiting for me near the supper table, in the lighted cuddy. We sat down at once, and as I helped the chief mate, I said:

"Are you aware that there is a ship anchored inside the islands? I saw her mast-heads above the ridge as the sun went down."

2. The Menan (Chao Phraya) runs through Bangkok, Thailand, into the Gulf of Siam. The Paknam Pagoda stands at the mouth of the river.

He raised sharply his simple face, overcharged by a terrible growth of whisker, and emitted his usual ejaculations, "Bless my soul, sir! You don't say so!"

My second mate was a round-cheeked, silent young man, grave beyond his years, I thought; but as our eyes happened to meet I detected a slight quiver on his lips. I looked down at once. It was not my part to encourage sneering on board my ship. It must be said, too, that I knew very little of my officers. In consequence of certain events of no particular significance, except to myself, I had been appointed to the command only a fortnight before. Neither did I know much of the hands forward. All these people had been together for eighteen months or so, and my position was that of the only stranger on board. I mention this because it has some bearing on what is to follow. But what I felt most was my being a stranger to the ship; and if all the truth must be told, I was somewhat of a stranger to myself. The youngest man on board (barring the second mate), and untried as yet by a position of the fullest responsibility, I was willing to take the adequacy of the others for granted. They had simply to be equal to their tasks; but I wondered how far I should turn out faithful to that ideal conception of one's own personality every man sets up for himself secretly.

Meantime the chief mate, with an almost visible effect of collaboration on the part of his round eyes and frightful whiskers, was trying to evolve a theory of the anchored ship. His dominant trait was to take all things into earnest consideration. He was of a painstaking turn of mind. As he used to say, he "liked to account to himself" for practically everything that came in his way, down to a miserable scorpion he had found in his cabin a week before. The why and the wherefore of that scorpion—how it got on board and came to select his room rather than the pantry (which was a dark place and more what a scorpion would be partial to), and how on earth it managed to drown itself in the inkwell of his writing-desk—had exercised him infinitely. The ship within the islands was much more easily accounted for; and just as we were about to rise from table he made his pronouncement. She was, he doubted not, a ship from home lately arrived. Probably she drew too much water to cross the bar except at the top of spring tides. Therefore she went into that natural harbor to wait for a few days in preference to remaining in an open roadstead.

"That's so," confirmed the second mate suddenly, in his slightly hoarse voice. "She draws over twenty feet. She's the Liverpool ship *Sephora* with a cargo of coal. Hundred and twenty-three days from Cardiff."

We looked at him in surprise.

"The tugboat skipper told me when he come on board for your letters, sir," explained the young man. "He expects to take her up the river the day after tomorrow."

After thus overwhelming us with the extent of his information he slipped out of the cabin. The mate observed regretfully that he "could not account for that young fellow's whims." What prevented him telling us all about it at once, he wanted to know.

I detained him as he was making a move. For the last two days the crew had had plenty of hard work, and the night before they had very little sleep. I felt painfully that I—a stranger—was doing something unusual when I directed him to let all hands turn in without setting an anchor-watch.[3] I proposed to keep on deck myself till one o'clock or thereabouts. I would get the second mate to relieve me at that hour.

"He will turn out the cook and the steward at four," I concluded, "and then give you a call. Of course at the slightest sign of any sort of wind we'll have the hands up and make a start at once."

He concealed his astonishment. "Very well, sir." Outside the cuddy he put his head in the second mate's door to inform him of my unheard-of caprice to take a five hours' anchor-watch on myself. I heard the other raise his voice incredulously—"What? The captain himself?" Then a few more murmurs, a door closed, then another. A few moments later I went on deck.

My strangeness, which had made me sleepless, had prompted that unconventional arrangement, as if I had expected in those solitary hours of the night to get on terms with the ship of which I knew nothing, manned by men of whom I knew very little more. Fast alongside a wharf, littered like any ship in port with a tangle of unrelated things, invaded by unrelated shore people, I had hardly seen her yet properly. Now, as she lay cleared for sea, the stretch of her main deck seemed to me very fine under the stars. Very fine, very roomy for her size, and very inviting. I descended the poop and paced the waist, my mind picturing to myself the coming passage through the Malay Archipelago, down the Indian Ocean, and up the Atlantic. All its phases were familiar enough to me, every characteristic, all the alternatives which were likely to face me on the high seas—everything! . . . except the novel responsibility of command. But I took heart from the reasonable thought that the ship was like other ships, the men like other men, and that the sea was not likely to keep any special surprises expressly for my discomfiture.

Arrived at that comforting conclusion, I bethought myself of a cigar and went below to get it. All was still down there. Everybody at the after end of the ship was sleeping profoundly. I came out again on the quarter-deck, agreeably at ease in my sleeping suit on that warm, breathless night, barefooted, a glowing cigar in my teeth, and, going forward, I was met by the profound silence of the fore end of the ship. Only as I passed the door of the forecastle I heard a deep, quiet, trustful sigh of some sleeper inside. And suddenly I rejoiced in the great security of the sea as compared with the unrest of the land, in my choice of that untempted life presenting no disquieting problems, invested with an elementary moral beauty by the absolute straightforwardness of its appeal and by the singleness of its purpose.

The riding-light[4] in the fore-rigging burned with a clear, untroubled, as if symbolic, flame, confident and bright in the mysterious shades of the night. Passing on my way aft along the other side of the ship, I observed that the rope side-ladder, put over, no doubt, for the master of the tug when he came to fetch away our letters, had not been hauled in as it should have been. I became annoyed

---

3. A detachment of seamen kept on deck while the ship lies at anchor.   4. Special light displayed by ship while ("riding") at anchor.

at this, for exactitude in small matters is the very soul of discipline. Then I reflected that I had myself peremptorily dismissed my officers from duty, and by my own act had prevented the anchor-watch being formally set and things properly attended to. I asked myself whether it was wise ever to interfere with the established routine of duties even from the kindest of motives. My action might have made me appear eccentric. Goodness only knew how that absurdly whiskered mate would "account" for my conduct, and what the whole ship thought of that informality of their new captain. I was vexed with myself.

Not from compunction certainly, but, as it were mechanically, I proceeded to get the ladder in myself. Now a side-ladder of that sort is a light affair and comes in easily, yet my vigorous tug, which should have brought it flying on board, merely recoiled upon my body in a totally unexpected jerk. What the devil! . . . I was so astounded by the immovableness of that ladder that I remained stockstill, trying to account for it to myself like that imbecile mate of mine. In the end, of course, I put my head over the rail.

The side of the ship made an opaque belt of shadow on the darkling glassy shimmer of the sea. But I saw at once something elongated and pale floating very close to the ladder. Before I could form a guess a faint flash of phosphorescent light, which seemed to issue suddenly from the naked body of a man, flickered in the sleeping water with the elusive, silent play of summer lightning in a night sky. With a gasp I saw revealed to my stare a pair of feet, the long legs, a broad livid back immersed right up to the neck in a greenish cadaverous glow. One hand, awash, clutched the bottom rung of the ladder. He was complete but for the head. A headless corpse! The cigar dropped out of my gaping mouth with a tiny plop and a short hiss quite audible in the absolute stillness of all things under heaven. At that I suppose he raised up his face, a dimly pale oval in the shadow of the ship's side. But even then I could only barely make out down there the shape of his black-haired head. However, it was enough for the horrid, frost-bound sensation which had gripped me about the chest to pass off. The moment of vain exclamations was past too. I only climbed on the spare spar and leaned over the rail as far as I could, to bring my eyes nearer to that mystery floating alongside.

As he hung by the ladder, like a resting swimmer, the sea-lightning played about his limbs at every stir; and he appeared in it ghastly, silvery, fish-like. He remained as mute as a fish, too. He made no motion to get out of the water, either. It was inconceivable that he should not attempt to come on board, and strangely troubling to suspect that perhaps he did not want to. And my first words were prompted by just that troubled incertitude.

"What's the matter?" I asked in my ordinary tone, speaking down to the face upturned exactly under mine.

"Cramp," it answered, no louder. Then slightly anxious, "I say, no need to call any one."

"I was not going to," I said.

"Are you alone on deck?"

"Yes."

I had somehow the impression that he was on the point of letting go the

*The opening suggests [?] an
ominous stillness, unsettling
quiet, isolation, profound
loneliness*

ladder to swim away beyond my ken—mysterious as he came. But, for the moment, this being appearing as if he had risen from the bottom of the sea (it was certainly the nearest land to the ship) wanted only to know the time. I told him. And he, down there, tentatively:

"I suppose your captain's turned in?"

"I am sure he isn't," I said.

He seemed to struggle with himself, for I heard something like the low, bitter murmur of doubt. "What's the good?" His next words came out with a hesitating effort.

"Look here, my man. Could you call him out quietly?"

I thought the time had come to declare myself.

"I am the captain."

I heard a "By Jove!" whispered at the level of the water. The phosphorescence flashed in the swirl of the water all about his limbs, his other hand seized the ladder.

"My name's Leggatt."

The voice was calm and resolute. A good voice. The self-possession of that man had somehow induced a corresponding state in myself. It was very quietly that I remarked:

"You must be a good swimmer."

"Yes. I've been in the water practically since nine o'clock. The question for me now is whether I am to let go this ladder and go on swimming till I sink from exhaustion or—to come on board here."

I felt this was no mere formula of desperate speech, but a real alternative in the view of a strong soul. I should have gathered from this that he was young; indeed, it is only the young who are ever confronted by such clear issues. But at the time it was pure intuition on my part. A mysterious communication was established already between us two—in the face of that silent, darkened tropical sea. I was young, too; young enough to make no comment. The man in the water began suddenly to climb up the ladder, and I hastened away from the rail to fetch some clothes.

Before entering the cabin I stood still, listening in the lobby at the foot of the stairs. A faint snore came through the closed door of the chief mate's room. The second mate's door was on the hook, but the darkness in there was absolutely soundless. He, too, was young and could sleep like a stone. Remained the steward, but he was not likely to wake up before he was called. I got a sleeping suit out of my room, and, coming back on deck, saw the naked man from the sea sitting on the main-hatch, glimmering white in the darkness, his elbows on his knees and his head in his hands. In a moment he had concealed his damp body in a sleeping suit of the same gray-stripe pattern as the one I was wearing, and followed me like my double on the poop. Together we moved right aft, barefooted, silent.

"What is it?" I asked in a deadened voice, taking the lighted lamp out of the binnacle, and raising it to his face.

"An ugly business."

He had rather regular features; a good mouth; light eyes under somewhat heavy, dark eyebrows; a smooth, square forehead; no growth on his cheeks; a small, brown mustache, and a well-shaped, round chin. His expression was concentrated, meditative, under the inspecting light of the lamp I held up to his face; such as a man thinking hard in solitude might wear. My sleeping suit was just right for his size. A well-knit young fellow of twenty-five at most. He caught his lower lip with the edge of white, even teeth.

"Yes," I said, replacing the lamp in the binnacle. The warm, heavy tropical night closed upon his head again.

"There's a ship over there," he murmured.

"Yes, I know. The *Sephora*. Did you know of us?"

"Hadn't the slightest idea. I am the mate of her—" He paused and corrected himself. "I should say I *was*."

"Aha! Something wrong?"

"Yes. Very wrong indeed. I've killed a man."

"What do you mean? Just now?"

"No, on the passage. Weeks ago. Thirty-nine south. When I say a man—"

"Fit of temper," I suggested confidently.

The shadowy, dark head, like mine, seemed to nod imperceptibly above the ghostly gray of my sleeping suit. It was, in the night, as though I had been faced by my own reflection in the depths of a sombre and immense mirror.

"A pretty thing to have to own up to for a Conway[5] boy," murmured my double distinctly.

"You're a Conway boy?"

"I am," he said, as if startled. Then, slowly . . . "Perhaps you too . . ."

It was so; but being a couple of years older I had left before he joined. After a quick interchange of dates a silence fell; and I thought suddenly of my absurd mate with his terrific whiskers and the "Bless my soul—you don't say so" type of intellect. My double gave me an inkling of his thoughts by saying:

"My father's a parson in Norfolk. Do you see me before a judge and jury on that charge? For myself I can't see the necessity. There are fellows that an angel from heaven—And I am not that. He was one of those creatures that are just simmering all the time with a silly sort of wickedness. Miserable devils that have no business to live at all. He wouldn't do his duty and wouldn't let anybody else do theirs. But what's the good of talking! You know well enough the sort of ill-conditioned snarling cur . . ."

He appealed to me as if our experiences had been as identical as our clothes. And I knew well enough the pestiferous danger of such a character where there are no means of legal repression. And I knew well enough also that my double there was no homicidal ruffian. I did not think of asking him for details, and he told me the story roughly in brusque, disconnected sentences. I needed no more. I saw it all going on as though I were myself inside that other sleeping suit.

5. The wooden battleship *Conway*, which was used to train young officers for the Royal Navy and merchant service.

"It happened while we were setting a reefed foresail, at dusk. Reefed foresail! You understand the sort of weather. The only sail we had left to keep the ship running; so you may guess what it had been like for days. Anxious sort of job, that. He gave me some of his cursed insolence at the sheet.[6] I tell you I was overdone with this terrific weather that seemed to have no end to it. Terrific, I tell you—and a deep ship. I believe the fellow himself was half crazed with funk. It was no time for gentlemanly reproof, so I turned round and felled him like an ox. He up and at me. We closed just as an awful sea made for the ship. All hands saw it coming and took to the rigging, but I had him by the throat, and went on shaking him like a rat, the men above us yelling. 'Look out! Look out!' Then a crash as if the sky had fallen on my head. They say that for over ten minutes hardly anything was to be seen of the ship—just the three masts and a bit of the forecastle head and of the poop all awash driving along in a smother of foam. It was a miracle that they found us, jammed together behind the forebits. It's clear that I meant business, because I was holding him by the throat still when they picked us up. He was black in the face. It was too much for them. It seems they rushed us aft together, gripped as we were, screaming 'Murder!' like a lot of lunatics, and broke into the cuddy. And the ship running for her life, touch and go all the time, any minute her last in a sea fit to turn your hair gray only a-looking at it. I understand that the skipper, too, started raving like the rest of them. The man had been deprived of sleep for more than a week, and to have this spring on him at the height of a furious gale nearly drove him out of his mind. I wonder they didn't fling me overboard after getting the carcass of their precious shipmate out of my fingers. They had rather a job to separate us, I've been told. A sufficiently fierce story to make an old judge and a respectable jury sit up a bit. The first thing I heard when I came to myself was the maddening howling of that endless gale, and on that the voice of the old man. He was hanging on to my bunk, staring into my face out of his sou'wester.

" 'Mr. Leggatt, you have killed a man. You can act no longer as chief mate of this ship.' "

His care to subdue his voice made it sound monotonous. He rested a hand on the end of the skylight to steady himself with, and all that time did not stir a limb, so far as I could see. "Nice little tale for a quiet tea party," he concluded in the same tone.

One of my hands, too, rested on the end of the skylight; neither did I stir a limb, so far as I knew. We stood less than a foot from each other. It occurred to me that if old "Bless my soul—you don't say so" were to put his head up the companion and catch sight of us, he would think he was seeing double, or imagine himself come upon a scene of weird witchcraft: the strange captain having a quiet confabulation by the wheel with his own gray ghost. I became very much concerned to prevent anything of the sort. I heard the other's soothing undertone:

"My father's a parson in Norfolk," it said. Evidently he had forgotten he had

---

6. Rope or chain attached to lower corner of sail used for shortening or slackening it.

told me this important fact before. Truly a nice little tale.

"You had better slip down into my stateroom now," I said, moving off stealthily. My double followed my movements; our bare feet made no sound; I let him in, closed the door with care, and, after giving a call to the second mate, returned on deck for my relief.

"Not much sign of any wind yet," I remarked when he approached.

"No, sir. Not much," he assented sleepily in his hoarse voice, with just enough deference, no more, and barely suppressing a yawn.

"Well, that's all you have to look out for. You have got your orders."

"Yes, sir."

I paced a turn or two on the poop and saw him take up his position face forward with his elbow in the ratlines of the mizzen-rigging before I went below. The mate's faint snoring was still going on peacefully. The cuddy lamp was burning over the table on which stood a vase with flowers, a polite attention from the ship's provision merchant—the last flowers we should see for the next three months at the very least. Two bunches of bananas hung from the beam symmetrically, one on each side of the rudder-casing. Everything was as before in the ship—except that two of her captain's sleeping suits were simultaneously in use, one motionless in the cuddy, the other keeping very still in the captain's stateroom.

It must be explained here that my cabin had the form of the capital letter L, the door being within the angle and opening into the short part of the letter. A couch was to the left, the bedplace to the right; my writing-desk and the chronometers' table faced the door. But any one opening it, unless he stepped right inside, had no view of what I call the long (or vertical) part of the letter. It contained some lockers surmounted by a bookcase; and a few clothes, a thick jacket or two, caps, oilskin coat, and such-like, hung on hooks. There was at the bottom of that part a door opening into my bathroom, which could be entered also directly from the saloon. But that way was never used.

The mysterious arrival had discovered the advantage of this particular shape. Entering my room, lighted strongly by a big bulkhead lamp swung on gimbals above my writing-desk, I did not see him anywhere till he stepped out quietly from behind the coats hung in the recessed part.

"I heard somebody moving about, and went in there at once," he whispered.

I, too, spoke under my breath.

"Nobody is likely to come in here without knocking and getting permission."

He nodded. His face was thin and the sunburn faded, as though he had been ill. And no wonder. He had been, I heard presently, kept under arrest in his cabin for nearly nine weeks. But there was nothing sickly in his eyes or in his expression. He was not a bit like me, really; yet, as we stood leaning over my bedplace, whispering side by side, with our dark heads together and our backs to the door, anybody bold enough to open it stealthily would have been treated to the uncanny sight of a double captain busy talking in whispers with his other self.

"But all this doesn't tell me how you came to hang on to our sideladder," I

inquired, in the hardly audible murmurs we used, after he had told me something more of the proceedings on board the *Sephora* once the bad weather was
over.

"When we sighted Java Head[7] I had had time to think all those matters out
several times over. I had six weeks of doing nothing else, and with only an hour
or so every evening for a tramp on the quarterdeck."

He whispered, his arms folded on the side of my bedplace, staring through
the open port. And I could imagine perfectly the manner of this thinking out—
a stubborn if not a steadfast operation; something of which I should have been
perfectly incapable.

"I reckoned it would be dark before we closed with the land," he continued,
so low that I had to strain my hearing, near as we were to each other, shoulder
touching shoulder almost. "So I asked to speak to the old man. He always seemed
very sick when he came to see me—as if he could not look me in the face. You
know, that foresail saved the ship. She was too deep to have run long under bare
poles. And it was I that managed to set it for him. Anyway, he came. When I
had him in my cabin—he stood by the door looking at me as if I had the halter
round my neck already—I asked him right away to leave my cabin door unlocked
at night while the ship was going through Sunda Straits. There would be the
Java coast within two or three miles, off Anjer Point. I wanted nothing more.
I've had a prize for swimming my second year in the Conway."

"I can believe it," I breathed out.

"God only knows why they locked me in every night. To see some of their
faces you'd have thought they were afraid I'd go about at night strangling people.
Am I a murdering brute? Do I look it? By Jove! if I had been he wouldn't have
trusted himself like that into my room. You'll say I might have chucked him
aside and bolted out, there and then—it was dark already. Well, no. And for the
same reason I wouldn't think of trying to smash the door. There would have
been a rush to stop me at the noise, and I did not mean to get into a confounded
scrimmage. Somebody else might have got killed—for I would not have broken
out only to get chucked back, and I did not want any more of that work. He
refused, looking more sick than ever. He was afraid of the men, and also of that
old second mate of his who had been sailing with him for years—a gray-headed
old humbug; and his steward, too, had been with him devil knows how long—
seventeen years or more—a dogmatic sort of loafer who hated me like poison,
just because I was the chief mate. No chief mate ever made more than one
voyage in the *Sephora*, you know. Those two old chaps ran the ship. Devil only
knows what the skipper wasn't afraid of (all his nerve went to pieces altogether in
that hellish spell of bad weather we had)—of what the law would do to him—of
his wife, perhaps. Oh yes! she's on board. Though I don't think she would have
meddled. She would have been only too glad to have me out of the ship in any
way. The 'brand of Cain'[8] business, don't you see? That's all right. I was ready

---

7. A famous landmark for clipper ships engaged in the China trade on the western end of Java, the
southern entrance to the Sunda Straits mentioned below; the killing thus took place some 1,500
miles south of the present scene.   8. Genesis 4:14–15.

enough to go off wandering on the face of the earth—and that was price enough to pay for an Abel of that sort. Anyhow, he wouldn't listen to me. 'This thing must take its course. I represent the law here.' He was shaking like a leaf. 'So you won't?' 'No!' 'Then I hope you will be able to sleep on that," I said, and turned my back on him. 'I wonder that *you* can,' cries he, and locks the door.

"Well, after that, I couldn't. Not very well. That was three weeks ago. We have had a slow passage through the Java Sea; drifted about Carimata[9] for ten days. When we anchored here they thought, I suppose, it was all right. The nearest land (and that's five miles) is the ship's destination; the consul would soon set about catching me; and there would have been no object in bolting to these islets there. I don't suppose there's a drop of water on them. I don't know how it was, but tonight that steward, after bringing me my supper, went out to let me eat it, and left the door unlocked. And I ate it—all there was, too. After I had finished I strolled out on the quarterdeck. I don't know that I meant to do anything. A breath of fresh air was all I wanted, I believe. Then a sudden temptation came over me. I kicked off my slippers and was in the water before I had made up my mind fairly. Somebody heard the splash and they raised an awful hullabaloo. 'He's gone! Lower the boats! He's committed suicide! No, he's swimming.' Certainly I was swimming. It's not easy for a swimmer like me to commit suicide by drowning. I landed on the nearest islet before the boat left the ship's side. I heard them pulling about in the dark, hailing, and so on, but after a bit they gave up. Everything quieted down and the anchorage became as still as death. I sat down on a stone and began to think. I felt certain they would start searching for me at daylight. There was no place to hide on those stony things— and if there had been, what would have been the good? But now I was clear of that ship I was not going back. So after a while I took off all my clothes, tied them up in a bundle with a stone inside, and dropped them in the deep water on the outer side of that islet. That was suicide enough for me. Let them think what they liked, but I didn't mean to drown myself. I meant to swim till I sank— but that's not the same thing. I struck out for another of these little islands, and it was from that one that I first saw your riding-light. Something to swim for. I went on easily, and on the way I came upon a flat rock a foot or two above water. In the daytime, I dare say, you might make it out with a glass from your poop. I scrambled up on it and rested myself for a bit. Then I made another start. That last spell must have been over a mile."

His whisper was getting fainter and fainter, and all the time he stared straight out through the porthole, in which there was not even a star to be seen. I had not interrupted him. There was something that made comment impossible, in his narrative, or perhaps in himself; a sort of feeling, a quality, which I can't find a name for. And when he ceased, all I found was a futile whisper, "So you swam for our light?"

"Yes—straight for it. It was something to swim for. I couldn't see any stars low down because the coast was in the way, and I couldn't see the land, either.

85

---

9. The Karimata Islands in the straits between Borneo and Sumatra, some three hundred miles northeast of the Sunda Straits.

The water was like glass. One might have been swimming in a confounded thousand feet deep cistern with no place for scrambling out anywhere; but what I didn't like was the notion of swimming round and round like a crazed bullock before I gave out; and as I didn't mean to go back . . . No. Do you see me being hauled back, stark naked, off one of these little islands by the scruff of the neck and fighting like a wild beast? Somebody would have got killed for certain, and I did not want any of that. So I went on. Then your ladder—"

"Why didn't you hail the ship?" I asked, a little louder.

He touched my shoulder lightly. Lazy footsteps came right over our heads and stopped. The second mate had crossed from the other side of the poop and might have been hanging over the rail, for all we knew.

"He couldn't hear us talking—could he?" My double breathed into my very ear anxiously.

His anxiety was an answer, a sufficient answer, to the question I had put to him. An answer containing all the difficulty of that situation. I closed the port-hole quietly, to make sure. A louder word might have been overheard.

"Who's that?" he whispered then.

"My second mate. But I don't know much more of the fellow than you do."

And I told him a little about myself. I had been appointed to take charge while I least expected anything of the sort, not quite a fortnight ago. I didn't know either the ship or the people. Hadn't had the time in port to look about me or size anybody up. And as to the crew, all they knew was that I was appointed to take the ship home. For the rest, I was almost as much of a stranger on board as himself, I said. And at the moment I felt it most acutely. I felt that it would take very little to make me a suspect person in the eyes of the ship's company.

He had turned about meantime; and we, the two strangers in the ship, faced each other in identical attitudes.

"Your ladder—" he murmured, after a silence. "Who'd have thought of finding a ladder hanging over at night in a ship anchored out here! I felt just then a very unpleasant faintness. After the life I've been leading for nine weeks, anybody would have got out of condition. I wasn't capable of swimming round as far as your rudder-chains. And, lo and behold! there was a ladder to get hold of. After I gripped it I said to myself, 'What's the good?' When I saw a man's head looking over I thought I would swim away presently and leave him shout-ing—in whatever language it was. I didn't mind being looked at. I—I liked it. And then you speaking to me so quietly—as if you had expected me—made me hold on a little longer. It had been a confounded lonely time—I don't mean while swimming. I was glad to talk a little to somebody that didn't belong to the *Sephora*. As to asking for the captain, that was a mere impulse. It could have been no use, with all the ship knowing about me and the other people pretty certain to be round here in the morning. I don't know—I wanted to be seen, to talk with somebody, before I went on. I don't know what I would have said. . . . 'Fine night, isn't it?' or something of the sort."

"Do you think they will be round here presently?" I asked, with some incre-dulity.

"Quite likely," he said faintly.

He looked extremely haggard all of a sudden. His head rolled on his shoulders.

"H'm. We shall see then. Meantime get into that bed," I whispered. "Want help? There."

It was a rather high bedplace with a set of drawers underneath. This amazing swimmer really needed the lift I gave him by seizing his leg. He tumbled in, rolled over on his back, and flung one arm across his eyes. And then, with his face nearly hidden, he must have looked exactly as I used to look in that bed. I gazed upon my other self for a while before drawing across carefully the two green serge curtains which ran on a brass rod. I thought for a moment of pinning them together for greater safety, but I sat down on the couch, and once there I felt unwilling to rise and hunt for a pin. I would do it in a moment. I was extremely tired, in a peculiarly intimate way, by the strain of stealthiness, by the effort of whispering, and the general secrecy of this excitement. It was three o'clock by now, and I had been on my feet since nine, but I was not sleepy; I could not have gone to sleep. I sat there, fagged out, looking at the curtains, trying to clear my mind of the confused sensation of being in two places at once, and greatly bothered by an exasperating knocking in my head. It was a relief to discover suddenly that it was not in my head at all, but on the outside of the door. Before I could collect myself, the words "Come in" were out of my mouth, and the steward entered with a tray, bringing in my morning coffee. I had slept, after all, and I was so frightened that I shouted, "This way! I am here, steward," as though he had been miles away. He put down the tray on the table next the couch and only then said, very quietly, "I can see you are here, sir." I felt him give me a keen look, but I dared not meet his eyes just then. He must have wondered why I had drawn the curtains of my bed before going to sleep on the couch. He went out, hooking the door open as usual.   100

I heard the crew washing decks above me. I knew I would have been told at once if there had been any wind. Calm, I thought, and I was doubly vexed. Indeed, I felt dual more than ever. The steward reappeared suddenly in the doorway. I jumped up from the couch so quickly that he gave a start.

"What do you want here?"

"Close your port, sir—they are washing decks."

"It is closed," I said, reddening.

"Very well, sir." But he did not move from the doorway and returned my   105
stare in an extraordinary, equivocal manner for a time. Then his eyes, wavered, all his expression changed, and in a voice unusually gentle, almost coaxingly.

"May I come in to take the empty cup away, sir?"

"Of course!" I turned my back on him while he popped in and out. Then I unhooked and closed the door and even pushed the bolt. This sort of thing could not go on very long. The cabin was as hot as an oven, too. I took a peep at my double, and discovered that he had not moved; his arm was still over his eyes; but his chest heaved, his hair was wet, his chin glistened with perspiration. I reached over him and opened the port.

"I must show myself on deck," I reflected.

Of course, theoretically, I could do what I liked, with no one to say nay to me within the whole circle of the horizon; but to lock my cabin door and take the key away I did not dare. Directly I put my head out of the companion I saw the group of my two officers, the second mate barefooted, the chief mate in long india-rubber boots, near the break of the poop, and the steward half-way down the poop ladder talking to them eagerly. He happened to catch sight of me and dived, the second ran down on the main deck shouting some order or other, and the chief mate came to meet me, touching his cap.

There was a sort of curiosity in his eye that I did not like. I don't know whether the steward had told them that I was "queer" only, or downright drunk, but I know the man meant to have a good look at me. I watched him coming with a smile which, as he got into point-blank range, took effect and froze his very whiskers. I did not give him time to open his lips.

"Square the yards by lifts and braces before the hands go to breakfast."

It was the first particular order I had given on board that ship; and I stayed on deck to see it executed too. I had felt the need of asserting myself without loss of time. That sneering young cub got taken down a peg or two on that occasion, and I also seized the opportunity of having a good look at the face of every foremast man as they filed past me to go to the after braces. At breakfast time, eating nothing myself, I presided with such frigid dignity that the two mates were only too glad to escape from the cabin as soon as decency permitted; and all the time the dual working of my mind distracted me almost to the point of insanity. I was constantly watching myself, my secret self, as dependent on my actions as my own personality, sleeping in that bed, behind that door which faced me as I sat at the head of the table. It was very much like being mad, only it was worse, because one was aware of it.

I had to shake him for a solid minute, but when at last he opened his eyes it was in the full possession of his senses, with an inquiring look.

"All's well so far," I whispered. "Now you must vanish into the bathroom."

He did so, as noiseless as a ghost, and I then rang for the steward, and facing him boldly, directed him to tidy up my stateroom while I was having my bath— "and be quick about it." As my tone admitted of no excuses, he said, "Yes, sir," and ran off to fetch his dustpan and brushes. I took a bath and did most of my dressing, splashing, and whistling softly for the steward's edification, while the secret sharer of my life stood drawn bolt upright in that little space, his face looking very sunken in daylight, his eyelids lowered under the stern, dark line of his eyebrows drawn together by a slight frown.

When I left him there to go back to my room the steward was finishing dusting. I sent for the mate and engaged him in some insignificant conversation. It was, as it were, trifling with the terrific character of his whiskers; but my object was to give him an opportunity for a good look at my cabin. And then I could at last shut, with a clear conscience, the door of my stateroom and get my double back into the recessed part. There was nothing else for it. He had to sit still on a small folding stool, half smothered by the heavy coats hanging there. We listened to the steward going into the bathroom out of the saloon, filling the water-bottles there, scrubbing the bath, setting things to rights, whisk, bang, clatter— out again into the saloon—turn the key—click. Such was my scheme for keeping my second self invisible. Nothing better could be contrived under the circumstances. And there we sat: I at my writing-desk ready to appear busy with some papers, he behind me, out of sight of the door. It would not have been prudent to talk in daytime; and I could not have stood the excitement of that queer sense of whispering to myself. Now and then, glancing over my shoulder, I saw him far back there, sitting rigidly on the low stool, his bare feet close together, his arms folded, his head hanging on his breast—and perfectly still. Anybody would have taken him for me.

I was fascinated by it myself. Every moment I had to glance over my shoulder. I was looking at him when a voice outside the door said:

"Beg pardon, sir."

"Well!" . . . I kept my eyes on him, and so when the voice outside the door announced, "There's a ship's boat coming our way, sir," I saw him give a start—the first movement he had made for hours. But he did not raise his bowed head.

"All right. Get the ladder over."

I hesitated. Should I whisper something to him? But what? His immobility seemed to have been never disturbed. What could I tell him he did not know already? . . . Finally I went on deck.

II

The skipper of the *Spehora* had a thin, red whisker all round his face, and the sort of complexion that goes with hair of that color; also the particular, rather smeary shade of blue in the eyes. He was not exactly a showy figure; his shoulders were high, his stature but middling—one leg slightly more bandy than the other. He shook hands, looking vaguely around. A spiritless tenacity was his main characteristic, I judged. I behaved with a politeness which seemed to disconcert him. Perhaps he was shy. He mumbled to me as if he were ashamed of what he was saying; gave his name (it was something like Archbold—but at this distance of years I hardly am sure), his ship's name, and a few other particulars of that sort, in the manner of a criminal making a reluctant and doleful confession. He had had terrible weather on the passage out—terrible—terrible—wife aboard, too.

By this time we were seated in the cabin and the steward brought in a tray with a bottle and glasses. "Thanks! No." Never took liquor. Would have some water, though. He drank two tumblerfuls. Terrible thirsty work. Ever since daylight had been exploring the islands round his ship.

"What was that for—fun?" I asked with an appearance of polite interest.

"No!" He sighed. "Painful duty."

As he persisted in his mumbling and I wanted my double to hear every word, I hit upon the notion of informing him that I regretted to say I was hard of hearing.

"Such a young man too!" he nodded, keeping his smeary, blue, unintelligent eyes fastened upon me. "What was the cause of it—some disease?" he inquired, without the least sympathy and as if he thought that, if so, I'd got no more than I deserved.

"Yes; disease," I admitted in a cheerful tone which seemed to shock him.

But my point was gained, because he had to raise his voice to give me his tale. It is not worth while to record that version. It was just over two months since all this had happened, and he had thought so much about it that he seemed completely muddled as to its bearings, but still immensely impressed.

"What would you think of such a thing happening on board your own ship? I've had the *Sephora* for these fifteen years. I am a well-known shipmaster."

He was densely distressed—and perhaps I should have sympathized with him if I had been able to detach my mental vision from the unsuspected sharer of my cabin as though he were my second self. There he was on the other side of the bulkhead, four or five feet from us, no more, as we sat in the saloon. I looked politely at Captain Archbold (if that was his name), but it was the other I saw, in a gray sleeping suit, seated on a low stool, his bare feet close together, his arms folded, and every word said between us falling into the ears of his dark head bowed on his chest.

"I have been at sea now, man and boy, for seven and thirty years, and I've never heard of such a thing happening in an English ship. And that it should be my ship. Wife on board, too."

I was hardly listening to him.

"Don't you think," I said, "that the heavy sea which, you told me, came aboard just then might have killed the man? I have seen the sheer weight of a sea kill a man very neatly, by simply breaking his neck."

"Good God!" he uttered impressively, fixing his smeary blue eyes on me. "The sea! No man killed by the sea ever looked like that." He seemed positively scandalized at my suggestion. And as I gazed at him, certainly not prepared for anything original on his part, he advanced his head close to mine and thrust his tongue out at me so suddenly that I couldn't help starting back.

After scoring over my calmness in this graphic way he nodded wisely. If I had seen the sight, he assured me, I would never forget it as long as I lived. The weather was too bad to give the corpse a proper sea burial. So next day at dawn they took it up on the poop, covering its face with a bit of bunting; he read a short prayer, and then, just as it was, in its oilskins and long boots, they launched it amongst those mountainous seas that seemed ready every moment to swallow up the ship herself and the terrified lives on board of her.

"That reefed foresail saved you," I threw in.

"Under God—it did," he exclaimed fervently. "It was by a special mercy, I firmly believe, that it stood some of those hurricane squalls."

"It was the setting of that sail which—" I began.

"God's own hand in it," he interrupted me. "Nothing less could have done it. I don't mind telling you that I hardly dared give the order. It seemed impossible that we could touch anything without losing it, and then our last hope would have been gone."

The terror of that gale was on him yet. I let him go on for a bit, then said casually—as if returning to a minor subject:

"You were very anxious to give up your mate to the shore people, I believe?"

He was. To the law. His obscure tenacity on that point had in it something incomprehensible and a little awful; something, as it were, mystical, quite apart from his anxiety that he should not be suspected of "countenancing any doings of that sort." Seven and thirty virtuous years at sea, of which over twenty of immaculate command, and the last fifteen in the *Sephora*, seemed to have laid him under some pitiless obligation.

"And you know," he went on, groping shamefacedly amongst his feelings, "I did not engage that young fellow. His people had some interest with my owners. I was in a way forced to take him on. He looked very smart, very gentlemanly, and all that. But do you know—I never liked him, somehow. I am a plain man. You see, he wasn't exactly the sort for the chief mate of a ship like the *Sephora*."

I had become so connected in thoughts and impressions with the secret sharer of my cabin that I felt as if I, personally, were being given to understand that I, too, was not the sort that would have done for the chief mate of a ship like the *Sephora*. I had no doubt of it in my mind.

"Not at all the style of man. You understand," he insisted superfluously, looking hard at me.   145

I smiled urbanely. He seemed at a loss for a while.

"I suppose I must report a suicide."

"Beg pardon?"

"Sui-cide! That's what I'll have to write to my owners directly I get in."

"Unless you manage to recover him before tomorrow," I assented dispassion-   150
ately. . . . "I mean, alive."

He mumbled something which I really did not catch, and I turned my ear to him in a puzzled manner. He fairly bawled:

"The land—I say, the mainland is at least seven miles off my anchorage."

"About that."

My lack of excitement, of curiosity, of surprise, of any sort of pronounced interest, began to arouse his distrust. But except for the felicitous pretense of deafness I had not tried to pretend anything. I had felt utterly incapable of playing the part of ignorance properly, and therefore was afraid to try. It is also certain that he had brought some ready-made suspicions with him, and that he viewed my politeness as a strange and unnatural phenomenon. And yet how else could I have received him? Not heartily! That was impossible for psychological reasons, which I need not state here. My only object was to keep off his inquiries. Surlily? Yes, but surliness might have provoked a point-blank question. From its novelty to him and from its nature, punctilious courtesy was the manner best calculated to restrain the man. But there was the danger of his breaking through my defense bluntly. I could not, I think, have met him by a direct lie, also for psychological (not moral) reasons. If he had only known how afraid I was of his putting my feeling of identity with the other to the test! But, strangely enough (I thought of it only afterward), I believe that he was not a little disconcerted by the reverse side of that weird situation, by something in me that reminded him of the man he was seeking—suggested a mysterious similitude to the young fellow he had distrusted and disliked from the first.

However that might have been the silence was not very prolonged. He took   155
another oblique step.

"I reckon I had no more than a two-mile pull to your ship. Not a bit more."

"And quite enough, too, in this awful heat," I said.

Another pause full of mistrust followed. Necessity, they say, is mother of invention, but fear, too, is not barren of ingenious suggestions. And I was afraid he would ask me point-blank for news of my other self.

"Nice little saloon, isn't it?" I remarked, as if noticing for the first time the way his eyes roamed from one closed door to the other. "And very well fitted out, too. Here, for instance," I continued, reaching over the back of my seat negligently and flinging the door open, "is my bathroom."

160   He made an eager movement, but hardly gave it a glance. I got up, shut the door of the bathroom, and invited him to have a look round, as if I were very proud of my accommodation. He had to rise and be shown round, but he went through the business without any raptures whatever.

"And now we'll have a look at my stateroom," I declared, in a voice as loud as I dared to make it, crossing the cabin to the starboard side with purposely heavy steps.

He followed me in and gazed around. My intelligent double had vanished. I played my part.

"Very convenient—isn't it?"

"Very nice. Very comf . . ." He didn't finish, and went out brusquely as if to escape from some unrighteous wiles of mine. But it was not to be. I had been too frightened not to feel vengeful; I felt I had him on the run, and I meant to keep him on the run. My polite insistence must have had something menacing in it, because he gave in suddenly. And I did not let him off a single item: mates' rooms, pantry, storerooms, the very sail-locker, which was also under the poop— he had to look into them all. When at last I showed him out on the quarter-deck he drew a long, spiritless sigh, and mumbled dismally that he must really be going back to his ship now. I desired my mate, who had joined us, to see to the captain's boat.

165   The man of whiskers gave a blast on the whistle which he used to wear hanging round his neck, and yelled, "*Sephora's* away!" My double down there in my cabin must have heard, and certainly could not feel more relieved than I. Four fellows came running out from somewhere forward and went over the side, while my own men, appearing on deck too, lined the rail. I escorted my visitor to the gangway ceremoniously, and nearly overdid it. He was a tenacious beast. On the very ladder he lingered, and in that unique, guiltily conscientious manner of sticking to the point:

"I say . . . you . . . you don't think that—"

I covered his voice loudly.

"Certainly not. . . . I am delighted. Goodbye."

I had an idea of what he meant to say, and just saved myself by the privilege of defective hearing. He was too shaken generally to insist, but my mate, close witness of that parting, looked mystified and his face took on a thoughtful cast. As I did not want to appear as if I wished to avoid all communication with my officers, he had the opportunity to address me.

170   "Seems a very nice man. His boat's crew told our chaps a very extraordinary

story, if what I am told by the steward is true. I suppose you had it from the captain, sir?"

"Yes. I had a story from the captain."

"A very horrible affair—isn't it, sir?"

"It is."

"Beats all these tales we hear about murders in Yankee ships."

"I don't think it beats them. I don't think it resembles them in the least." 175

"Bless my soul—you don't say so! But of course I've no acquaintance whatever with American ships, not I, so I couldn't go against your knowledge. It's horrible enough for me. . . . But the queerest part is that those fellows seemed to have some idea the man was hidden aboard here. They had really. Did you ever hear of such a thing?"

"Preposterous—isn't it?"

We were walking to and fro athwart the quarter-deck. No one of the crew forward could be seen (the day was Sunday), and the mate pursued:

"There was some little dispute about it. Our chaps took offense. 'As if we would harbor a thing like that,' they said. 'Wouldn't you like to look for him in our coal-hole?' Quite a tiff. But they made it up in the end. I suppose he did drown himself. Don't you, sir?"

"I don't suppose anything."

"You have no doubt in the matter, sir?" 180

"None whatever."

I left him suddenly. I felt I was producing a bad impression, but with my double down there it was most trying to be on deck. And it was almost as trying to be below. Altogether a nerve-trying situation. But on the whole I felt less torn in two when I was with him. There was no one in the whole ship whom I dared take into my confidence. Since the hands had got to know his story, it would have been impossible to pass him off for any one else, and an accidental discovery was to be dreaded now more than ever. . . .

The steward being engaged in laying the table for dinner, we could talk only with our eyes when I first went down. Later in the afternoon we had a cautious try at whispering. The Sunday quietness of the ship was against us; the stillness of air and water around her was against us; the elements, the men were against us—everything was against us in our secret partnership; time itself—for this could not go on for ever. The very trust in Providence was, I supposed, denied to his guilt. Shall I confess that this thought cast me down very much? And as to the chapter of accidents which counts for so much in the book of success, I could only hope that it was closed. For what favorable accident could be expected?

"Did you hear everything?" were my first words as soon as we took up our 185
position side by side, leaning over my bedplace.

He had. And the proof of it was his earnest whisper, "The man told you he hardly dared to give the order."

I understood the reference to be to that saving foresail.

"Yes. He was afraid of it being lost in the setting."

"I assure you he never gave the order. He may think he did, but he never gave it. He stood there with me on the break of the poop after the maintopsail blew away, and whimpered about our last hope—positively whimpered about it and nothing else—and the night coming on! To hear one's skipper go on like that in such weather was enough to drive any fellow out of his mind. It worked me up into a sort of desperation. I just took it into my own hands and went away from him, boiling, and—But what's the use telling you? *You* know! . . . Do you think that if I had not been pretty fierce with them I should have got the men to do anything? Not it! The boss'en[1] perhaps? Perhaps! It wasn't a heavy sea—it was a sea gone mad! I suppose the end of the world will be something like that; and a man may have the heart to see it coming once and be done with it—but to have to face it day after day . . . I don't blame anybody. I was precious little better than the rest. Only—I was an officer of that old coal-wagon, anyhow. . . ."

190

"I quite understand," I conveyed that sincere assurance into his ear. He was out of breath with whispering; I could hear him pant slightly. It was all very simple. The same strung-up force which had given twenty-four men a chance, at least, for their lives had, in a sort of recoil, crushed an unworthy mutinous existence.

But I had no leisure to weigh the merits of the matter—footsteps in the saloon, a heavy knock. "There's enough wind to get under way with, sir." Here was the call of a new claim upon my thoughts and even upon my feelings.

"Turn the hands up," I cried through the door. "I'll be on deck directly."

I was going out to make the acquaintance of my ship. Before I left the cabin our eyes met—the eyes of the only two strangers on board. I pointed to the recessed part where the little camp-stool awaited him and laid my finger on my lips. He made a gesture—somewhat vague—a little mysterious, accompanied by a faint smile, as if of regret.

This is not the place to enlarge upon the sensations of a man who feels for the first time a ship move under his feet to his own independent word. In my case they were not unalloyed. I was not wholly alone with my command; for there was that stranger in my cabin. Or, rather, I was not completely and wholly with her. Part of me was absent. That mental feeling of being in two places at once affected me physically as if the mood of secrecy had penetrated my very soul. Before an hour had elapsed since the ship had begun to move, having occasion to ask the mate (he stood by my side) to take a compass bearing of the Pagoda, I caught myself reaching up to his ear in whispers. I say I caught myself, but enough had escaped to startle the man. I can't describe it otherwise than by saying that he shied. A grave, preoccupied manner, as though he were in possession of some perplexing intelligence, did not leave him henceforth. A little later I moved away from the rail to look at the compass with such a stealthy gait that the helmsman noticed it—and I could not help noticing the unusual roundness of his eyes. These are trifling instances, though it's to no commander's advantage to be suspected of ludicrous eccentricities. But I was also more seriously affected. There are to a seaman certain words, gestures, that should in given conditions come as naturally, as instinctively, as the winking of a menaced

---

1. *Bosun* or *boatswain*, petty officer in charge of deck crew and of rigging.

eye. A certain order should spring on to his lips without thinking; a certain sign should get itself made, so to speak, without reflection. But all unconscious alertness had abandoned me. I had to make an effort of will to recall myself back (from the cabin) to the conditions of the moment. I felt that I was appearing an irresolute commander to those people who were watching me more or less critically.

And, besides, there were the scares. On the second day out, for instance, coming off the deck in the afternoon (I had straw slippers on my bare feet) I stopped at the open pantry door and spoke to the steward. He was doing something there with his back to me. At the sound of my voice he nearly jumped out of his skin, as the saying is, and incidentally broke a cup.

"What on earth's the matter with you?" I asked, astonished.

He was extremely confused. "Beg your pardon, sir. I made sure you were in your cabin."

"You see I wasn't."

"No, sir. I could have sworn I had heard you moving in there not a moment ago. It's most extraordinary . . . very sorry, sir."

I passed on with an inward shudder. I was so identified with my secret double that I did not even mention the fact in those scanty, fearful whispers we exchanged. I suppose he had made some slight noise of some kind or other. It would have been miraculous if he hadn't at one time or another. And yet, haggard as he appeared, he looked always perfectly self-controlled, more than calm—almost invulnerable. On my suggestion he remained almost entirely in the bathroom, which, upon the whole, was the safest place. There could be really no shadow of an excuse for any one ever wanting to go in there, once the steward had done with it. It was a very tiny place. Sometimes he reclined on the floor, his legs bent, his head sustained on one elbow. At others I would find him on the camp-stool, sitting in his gray sleeping suit and with his cropped dark hair like a patient, unmoved convict. At night I would smuggle him into my bedplace, and we would whisper together, with the regular footfalls of the officer of the watch passing and repassing over our heads. It was an infinitely miserable time. It was lucky that some tins of fine preserves were stowed in a locker in my stateroom; hard bread I could always get hold of; and so he lived on stewed chicken, pâté de foie gras, asparagus, cooked oysters, sardines—on all sorts of abominable sham-delicacies out of tins. My early morning coffee he always drank; and it was all I dared do for him in that respect.

Every day there was the horrible maneuvering to go through so that my room and then the bathroom should be done in the usual way. I came to hate the sight of the steward, to abhor the voice of that harmless man. I felt that it was he who would bring on the disaster of discovery. It hung like a sword over our heads.

The fourth day out, I think (we were then working down the east side of the Gulf of Siam, tack for tack,[2] in light winds and smooth water)—the fourth day, I say, of this miserable juggling with the unavoidable, as we sat at our evening

2. By a series of shiftings back and forth of sails.

meal, that man, whose slightest movement I dreaded, after putting down the dishes ran up on deck busily. This could not be dangerous. Presently he came down again; and then it appeared that he had remembered a coat of mine which I had thrown over a rail to dry after having been wetted in a shower which had passed over the ship in the afternoon. Sitting stolidly at the head of the table I became terrified at the sight of the garment on his arm. Of course he made for my door. There was no time to lose.

"Steward!" I thundered. My nerves were so shaken that I could not govern my voice and conceal my agitation. This was the sort of thing that made my terrifically whiskered mate tap his forehead with his forefinger. I had detected him using that gesture while talking on deck with a confidential air to the carpenter. It was too far to hear a word, but I had no doubt that this pantomime could only refer to the strange new captain.

"Yes, sir," the pale-faced steward turned resignedly to me. It was this maddening course of being shouted at, checked without rhyme or reason, arbitrarily chased out of my cabin, suddenly called into it, sent flying out of his pantry on incomprehensible errands, that accounted for the growing wretchedness of his expression.

205 "Where are you going with that coat?"

"To your room, sir."

"Is there another shower coming?"

"I'm sure I don't know, sir. Shall I go up again and see, sir?"

"No! never mind."

210 My object was attained, as of course my other self in there would have heard everything that passed. During this interlude my two officers never raised their eyes off their respective plates; but the lip of that confounded cub, the second mate, quivered visibly.

I expected the steward to hook my coat on and come out at once. He was very slow about it; but I dominated my nervousness sufficiently not to shout after him. Suddenly I became aware (it could be heard plainly enough) that the fellow for some reason or other was opening the door of the bathroom. It was the end. The place was literally not big enough to swing a cat in. My voice died in my throat and I went stony all over. I expected to hear a yell of surprise and terror, and made a movement, but had not the strength to get on my legs. Everything remained still. Had my second self taken the poor wretch by the throat? I don't know what I could have done next moment if I had not seen the steward come out of my room, close the door, and then stand quietly by the sideboard.

"Saved," I thought. "But, no! Lost! Gone! He was gone!"

I laid my knife and fork down and leaned back in my chair. My head swam. After a while, when sufficiently recovered to speak in a steady voice, I instructed my mate to put the ship round at eight o'clock himself.

"I won't come on deck," I went on. "I think I'll turn in, and unless the wind shifts I don't want to be disturbed before midnight. I feel a bit seedy."

215 "You did look middling bad a little while ago," the chief mate remarked without showing any great concern.

They both went out, and I stared at the steward clearing the table. There was nothing to be read on that wretched man's face. But why did he avoid my eyes?

I asked myself. Then I thought I should like to hear the sound of his voice.

"Steward!"

"Sir!" Startled as usual.

"Where did you hang up that coat?"

"In the bathroom, sir." The usual anxious tone. "It's not quite dry yet, sir."   220

For some time longer I sat in the cuddy. Had my double vanished as he had come? But of his coming there was an explanation, whereas his disappearance would be inexplicable. . . . I went slowly into my dark room, shut the door, lighted the lamp, and for a time dared not turn round. When at last I did I saw him standing bolt upright in the narrow recessed part. It would not be true to say I had a shock, but an irresistible doubt of his bodily existence flitted through my mind. Can it be, I asked myself, that he is not visible to other eyes than mine? It was like being haunted. Motionless, with a grave face, he raised his hands slightly at me in a gesture which meant clearly, "Heavens! what a narrow escape!" Narrow indeed. I think I had come creeping quietly as near insanity as any man who has not actually gone over the border. That gesture restrained me, so to speak.

The mate with the terrific whiskers was now putting the ship on the other tack. In the moment of profound silence which follows upon the hands going to their stations I heard on the poop his raised voice: "Hard alee!"[3] and the distant shout of the order repeated on the main deck. The sails, in that light breeze, made but a faint fluttering noise. It ceased. The ship was coming round slowly; I held my breath in the renewed stillness of expectation; one wouldn't have thought that there was a single living soul on her decks. A sudden brisk shout, "Mainsail haul!" broke the spell, and in the noisy cries and rush overhead of the men running away with the main brace we two, down in my cabin, came together in our usual position by the bedplace.

He did not wait for my question. "I heard him fumbling here and just managed to squat myself down in the bath," he whispered to me. "The fellow only opened the door and put his arm in to hang the coat up. All the same. . . ."

"I never thought of that," I whispered back, even more appalled than before at the closeness of the shave, and marveling at that something unyielding in his character which was carrying him through so finely. There was no agitation in his whisper. Whoever was being driven distracted, it was not he. He was sane. And the proof of his sanity was continued when he took up the whispering again.

"It would never do for me to come to life again."   225

It was something that a ghost might have said. But what he was alluding to was his old captain's reluctant admission of the theory of suicide. It would obviously serve his turn—if I had understood at all the view which seemed to govern the unalterable purpose of his action.

"You must maroon me as soon as ever you can get amongst these islands off the Cambodje[4] shore," he went on.

"Maroon you! We are not living in a boy's adventure tale," I protested. His scornful whispering took me up.

"We aren't indeed! There's nothing of a boy's tale in this. But there's nothing

3. Put the helm all the way over to the side away from the wind.   4. Cambodian.

else for it. I want no more. You don't suppose I am afraid of what can be done to me? Prison or gallows or whatever they may please. But you don't see me coming back to explain such things to an old fellow in a wig and twelve respectable tradesmen, do you? What can they know whether I am guilty or not—or of what I am guilty, either? That's my affair. What does the Bible say? 'Driven off the face of the earth.'[5] Very well. I am off the face of the earth now. As I came at night so I shall go."

"Impossible!" I murmured. "You can't."

"Can't? . . . . Not naked like a soul on the Day of Judgment. I shall freeze on to this sleeping suit. The Last Day is not yet—and . . . you have understood thoroughly. Didn't you?"

I felt suddenly ashamed of myself. I may say truly that I understood—and my hesitation in letting that man swim away from my ship's side had been a mere sham sentiment, a sort of cowardice.

"It can't be done now till next night," I breathed out. "The ship is on the offshore tack and the wind may fail us."

"As long as I know that you understand," he whispered. "But of course you do. It's a great satisfaction to have got somebody to understand. You seem to have been there on purpose." And in the same whisper, as if we two whenever we talked had to say things to each other which were not fit for the world to hear, he added, "It's very wonderful."

We remained side by side talking in our secret way—but sometimes silent or just exchanging a whispered word or two at long intervals. And as usual he stared through the port. A breath of wind came now and again into our faces. The ship might have been moored in dock, so gently and on an even keel she slipped through the water, that did not murmur even at our passage, shadowy and silent like a phantom sea.

At midnight I went on deck, and to my mate's great surprise put the ship round on the other tack. His terrible whiskers flitted round me in silent criticism. I certainly should not have done it if it had been only a question of getting out of that sleepy gulf as quickly as possible. I believe he told the second mate, who relieved him, that it was a great want of judgment. The other only yawned. That intolerable cub shuffled about so sleepily and lolled against the rails in such a slack, improper fashion that I came down on him sharply.

"Aren't you properly awake yet?"

"Yes, sir! I am awake."

"Well, then, be good enough to hold yourself as if you were. And keep a look out. If there's any current we'll be closing with some islands long before daylight."

The east side of the gulf is fringed with islands, some solitary, others in groups. On the blue background of the high coast they seem to float on silvery patches of calm water, arid and gray, or dark green and rounded like clumps of evergreen bushes, with the larger ones, a mile or two long, showing the outlines of ridges, ribs of gray rock under the dank mantle of matted leafage. Unknown

5. Genesis 4:14.

to trade, to travel, almost to geography, the manner of life they harbor is an unsolved secret. There must be villages—settlements of fishermen at least—on the largest of them, and some communication with the world is probably kept up by native craft. But all that forenoon, as we headed for them, fanned along by the faintest of breezes, I saw no sign of man or canoe in the field of the telescope I kept on pointing at the scattered group.

At noon I gave no orders for a change of course, and the mate's whiskers became much concerned and seemed to be offering themselves unduly to my notice. At last I said:

"I am going to stand right in. Quite in—as far as I can take her."

The stare of extreme surprise imparted an air of ferocity also to his eyes, and he looked truly terrific for a moment.

"We're not doing well in the middle of the gulf," I continued casually. "I am going to look for the land breezes tonight."

"Bless my soul! Do you mean, sir, in the dark amongst the lot of all them islands and reefs and shoals?"

"Well, if there are any regular land breezes at all on this coast one must get close inshore to find them—mustn't one?"

"Bless my soul!" he exclaimed again under his breath. All that afternoon he wore a dreamy, comtemplative appearance which in him was a mark of perplexity. After dinner I went into my stateroom as if I meant to take some rest. There we two bent our dark heads over a half-unrolled chart lying on my bed.

"There," I said. "It's got to be Koh-ring.[6] I've been looking at it ever since sunrise. It has got two hills and a low point. It must be inhabited. And on the coast opposite there is what looks like the mouth of a biggish river—with some town, no doubt, not far up. It's the best chance for you that I can see."

"Anything. Koh-ring let it be."

He looked thoughtfully at the chart as if surveying chances and distances from a lofty height—and following with his eyes his own figure wandering on the blank land of Cochin-China, and then passing off that piece of paper clean out of sight into uncharted regions. And it was as if the ship had two captains to plan her course for her. I had been so worried and restless running up and down that I had not had the patience to dress that day. I had remained in my sleeping suit, with straw slippers and a soft floppy hat. The closeness of the heat in the gulf had been most oppressive, and the crew were used to see me wandering in that airy attire.

"She will clear the south point as she heads now," I whispered into his ear. "Goodness only knows when, though—but certainly after dark. I'll edge her in to half a mile, as far as I may be able to judge in the dark . . ."

"Be careful," he murmured warningly—and I realized suddenly that all my future, the only future for which I was fit, would perhaps go irretrievably to pieces in any mishap to my first command.

I could not stop a moment longer in the room. I motioned him to get out of

---

6. *Koh* or *Ko* means *island*; there are a large number of islands with that prefix at the head of the Gulf of Siam, but not, apparently, a Koh-ring.

sight and made my way on the poop. That unplayful cub had the watch. I walked up and down for a while thinking things out, then beckoned him over.

"Send a couple of hands to open the two quarter-deck ports," I said mildly.

He actually had the impudence, or else so forgot himself in his wonder at such an incomprehensible order, as to repeat:

"Open the quarter-deck ports! What for, sir?"

"The only reason you need concern yourself about is because I tell you to do so. Have them opened wide and fastened properly."

He reddened and went off, but I believe made some jeering remark to the carpenter as to the sensible practice of ventilating a ship's quarter-deck. I know he popped into the mate's cabin to impart the fact to him, because the whiskers came on deck, as it were by chance, and stole glances at me from below—for signs of lunacy or drunkenness, I suppose.

A little before supper, feeling more restless than ever, I rejoined, for a moment, my second self. And to find him sitting so quietly was surprising, like something against nature, inhuman.

I developed my plan in a hurried whisper.

"I shall stand in as close as I dare and then put her round. I shall presently find means to smuggle you out of here into the sail-locker, which communicates with the lobby. But there is an opening, a sort of square for hauling the sails out, which gives straight on the quarterdeck and which is never closed in fine weather, so as to give air to the sails. When the ship's way is deadened in stays[7] and all the hands are aft at the main braces you shall have a clear road to slip out and get overboard through the open quarter-deck port. I've had them both fastened up. Use a rope's end to lower yourself into the water so as to avoid a splash—you know. It could be heard and cause some beastly complication."

He kept silent for a while, then whispered, "I understand."

"I won't be there to see you go," I began with an effort. "The rest . . . I only hope I have understood too."

"You have. From first to last"—and for the first time there seemed to be a faltering, something strained in his whisper. He caught hold of my arm, but the ringing of the supper bell made me start. He didn't though; he only released his grip.

After supper I didn't come below again till well past eight o'clock. The faint, steady breeze was loaded with dew; and the wet, darkened sails held all there was of propelling power in it. The night, clear and starry, sparkled darkly, and the opaque, lightless patches shifting slowly amongst the low stars were the drifting islets. On the port bow there was a big one more distant and shadowily imposing by the great space of sky it eclipsed.

On opening the door I had a back view of my very own self looking at a chart. He had come out of the recess and was standing near the table.

"Quite dark enough," I whispered.

He stepped back and leaned against my bed with a level, quiet glance. I sat

---

7. When the ship's forward motion is slowed or stopped while its head is being turned toward the wind for the purpose of shifting the sail.

on the couch. We had nothing to say to each other. Over our heads the officer of the watch moved here and there. Then I heard him move quickly. I knew what that meant. He was making for the companion; and presently his voice was outside my door.

"We are drawing in pretty fast, sir. Land looks rather close."

"Very well," I answered. "I am coming on deck directly."

I waited till he was gone out of the cuddy, then rose. My double moved too. The time had come to exchange our last whispers, for neither of us was ever to hear each other's natural voice.

"Look here!" I opened a drawer and took out three sovereigns. "Take this, anyhow. I've got six and I'd give you the lot, only I must keep a little money to buy some fruit and vegetables for the crew from native boats as we go through Sunda Straits."

He shook his head.

"Take it," I urged him, whispering desperately. "No one can tell what . . ."

He smiled and slapped meaningly the only pocket of the sleeping jacket. It was not safe, certainly. But I produced a large old silk handkerchief of mine, and tying the three pieces of gold in a corner, pressed it on him. He was touched, I suppose, because he took it at last and tied it quickly round his waist under the jacket, on his bare skin.

Our eyes met; several seconds elapsed, till, our glances still mingled, I extended my hand and turned the lamp out. Then I passed through the cuddy, leaving the door of my room wide open. . . . "Steward!"

He was still lingering in the pantry in the greatness of his zeal, giving a rub-up to a plated cruet stand the last thing before going to bed. Being careful not to wake up the mate, whose room was opposite, I spoke in an undertone.

He looked round anxiously. "Sir!"

"Can you get me a little hot water from the galley?"

"I am afraid, sir, the galley fire's been out for some time now."

"Go and see."

He fled up the stairs.

"Now," I whispered loudly into the saloon—too loudly, perhaps, but I was afraid I couldn't make a sound. He was by my side in an instant—the double captain slipped past the stairs—through a tiny dark passage . . . a sliding door. We were in the sail-locker, scrambling on our knees over the sails. A sudden thought struck me. I saw myself wandering barefooted, bareheaded, the sun beating on my dark poll. I snatched off my floppy hat and tried hurriedly in the dark to ram it on my other self. He dodged and fended off silently. I wonder what he thought had come to me before he understood and suddenly desisted. Our hands met gropingly, lingered united in a steady, motionless clasp for a second. . . . No word was breathed by either of us when they separated.

I was standing quietly by the pantry door when the steward returned.

"Sorry, sir. Kettle barely warm. Shall I light the spirit-lamp?"

"Never mind."

I came out on deck slowly. It was now a matter of conscience to shave the land as close as possible—for now he must go overboard whenever the ship was

270

275

280

285

put in stays. Must! There could be no going back for him. After a moment I walked over to leeward and my heart flew into my mouth at the nearness of the land on the bow. Under any other circumstances I would not have held on a minute longer. The second mate had followed me anxiously.

I looked on till I felt I could command my voice.

"She will weather," I said then in a quiet tone.

"Are you going to try that, sir?" he stammered out incredulously.

I took no notice of him and raised my tone just enough to be heard by the helmsman.

"Keep her good full."[8]

"Good full, sir."

The wind fanned my cheek, the sails slept, the world was silent. The strain of watching the dark loom of the land grow bigger and denser was too much for me. I had to shut my eyes—because the ship must go closer. She must! The stillness was intolerable. Were we standing still?"

When I opened my eyes the second view started my heart with a thump. The black southern hill of Koh-ring seemed to hang right over the ship like a towering fragment of the everlasting night. On that enormous mass of blackness there was not a gleam to be seen, not a sound to be heard. It was gliding irresistibly towards us and yet seemed already within reach of the hand. I saw the vague figures of the watch grouped in the waist, gazing in awed silence.

"Are you going on, sir?" inquired an unsteady voice at my elbow.

I ignored it. I had to go on.

"Keep her full. Don't check her way. That won't do now," I said warningly.

"I can't see the sails very well," the helmsman answered me, in strange, quavering tones.

Was she close enough? Already she was, I won't say in the shadow of the land, but in the very blackness of it, already swallowed up as it were, gone too close to be recalled, gone from me altogether.

"Give the mate a call," I said to the young man who stood at my elbow as still as death. "And turn all hands up."

My tone had a borrowed loudness reverberated from the height of the land. Several voices cried out together, "We are all on deck, sir."

Then stillness again, with the great shadow gliding closer, towering higher, without a light, without a sound. Such a hush had fallen on the ship that she might have been a bark of the dead floating in slowly under the very gate of Erebus.

"My God! Where are we?"

It was the mate moaning at my elbow. He was thunderstruck, and as it were deprived of the moral support of his whiskers. He clapped his hands and absolutely cried out, "Lost!"

"Be quiet," I said sternly.

He lowered his tone, but I saw the shadowy gesture of his despair. "What are we doing here?"

8. Keep the ship's sails filled with wind.

"Looking for the land wind."

He made as if to tear his hair, and addressed me recklessly.

"She will never get out. You have done it, sir. I knew it'd end in something like this. She will never weather, and you are too close now to stay. She'll drift ashore before she's round. O my God!"

I caught his arm as he was raising it to batter his poor devoted head, and shook it violently.

"She's ashore already," he wailed, trying to tear himself away.

"Is she? . . . Keep good full there!"

"Good full, sir," cried the helmsman in a frightened, thin, childlike voice.

I hadn't let go the mate's arm and went on shaking it. "Ready about,[9] do you hear? You go forward"—shake—"and stop there"—shake—"and hold your noise"—shake—"and see these head-sheets properly overhauled"—shake, shake—shake.

And all the time I dared not look towards the land lest my heart should fail me. I released my grip at last and he ran forward as if fleeing for dear life.

I wondered what my double there in the sail-locker thought of this commotion. He was able to hear everything—and perhaps he was able to understand why, on my conscience, it had to be thus close—no less. My first order "Hard alee!" re-echoed ominously under the towering shadow of Koh-ring as if I had shouted in a mountain gorge. And then I watched the land intently. In that smooth water and light wind it was impossible to feel the ship coming-to.[1] No! I could not feel her. And my second self was making now ready to slip out and lower himself overboard. Perhaps he was gone already. . . ?

The great black mass brooding over our very mast-heads began to pivot away from the ship's side silently. And now I forgot the secret stranger ready to depart, and remembered only that I was a total stranger to the ship. I did not know her. Would she do it? How was she to be handled?

I swung the mainyard and waited helplessly. She was perhaps stopped, and her very fate hung in the balance, with the black mass of Koh-ring like the gate of the everlasting night towering over her taffrail. What would she do now? Had she way on her[2] yet? I stepped to the side swiftly, and on the shadowy water I could see nothing except a faint phosphorescent flash revealing the glassy smoothness of the sleeping surface. It was impossible to tell—and I had not learned yet the feel of my ship. Was she moving? What I needed was something easily seen, a piece of paper, which I could throw overboard and watch. I had nothing on me. To run down for it I didn't dare. There was no time. All at once my strained, yearning stare distinguished a white object floating within a yard of the ship's side—white, on the black water. A phosphorescent flash passed under it. What was that thing? . . . I recognized my own floppy hat. It must have fallen off his head . . . and he didn't bother. Now I had what I wanted—the saving mark for my eyes. But I hardly thought of my other self, now gone from

9. Be ready to shift the sails (tack). The head-sheets, below, are the lines attached to the sails of the forward mast, and to overhaul is to slacken a rope by pulling it in the opposite direction to that used in hoisting a sail and thus loosening the blocks.   1. Coming to a standstill.   2. Was she moving?

In terms of action, the narrator is successful, a hero—Leggatt escapes to life he's chosen, capt. sails on of his ship w/gained confidence

274 ▽ Joseph Conrad

the ship, to be hidden for ever from all friendly faces, to be a fugitive and a vagabond on the earth, with no brand of the curse on his sane forehead to stay a slaying hand . . . too proud to explain.

320 And I watched the hat—the expression of my sudden pity for his mere flesh. It had been meant to save his homeless head from the dangers of the sun. And now—behold—it was saving the ship, by serving me for a mark to help out the ignorance of my strangeness. Ha! It was drifting forward, warning me just in time that the ship had gathered sternway.

ending answer action questions.

"Shift the helm," I said in a low voice to the seaman standing still like a statue.

but it b ept, has passed the test what were the standards he used

The man's eyes glistened wildly in the binnacle light as he jumped round to the other side and spun round the wheel.

I walked to the break of the poop. On the overshadowed deck all hands stood by the forebraces waiting for my order. The stars ahead seemed to be gliding from right to left. And all was so still in the world that I heard the quiet remark, "She's round," passed in a tone of intense relief between two seamen.

"Let go and haul."

325 The foreyards ran round with a great noise, amidst cheery cries. And now the frightful whiskers made themselves heard giving various orders. Already the ship was drawing ahead. And I was alone with her. Nothing! no one in the world should stand now between us, throwing a shadow on the way of silent knowledge and mute affection; the perfect communion of a seaman with his first command.

what was this "ideal" conception of himself

Walking to the taffrail, I was in time to make out, on the very edge of a darkness thrown by a towering black mass like the very gateway of Erebus—yes, I was in time to catch an evanescent glimpse of my white hat left behind to mark the spot where the secret sharer of my cabin and of my thoughts, as though he were my second self, had lowered himself into the water to take his punishment: a free man, a proud swimmer striking out for a new destiny.

darkness or hell

1912

The first paragraph of the story clearly functions as exposition, especially in describing the setting, the place and time of day. Its last sentence suggests something of the situation—the speaker is alone with *his* ship. It also establishes the focus and voice. In the description of the scene in the Gulf of Siam, there are some words that, though appropriate, are not necessarily inevitable. These are words that might not be used by just any narrator or in just any circumstances and so may characterize the speaker or his situation. In the first sentence alone you may notice "mysterious," "incomprehensible," even "crazy," which, though it deals with the physical irregularity of the fences, also suggests the irrational. These words arouse suspense and so further the plot, but they may also suggest something of the theme. And, since another speaker would be likely to see things somewhat differently and use different words, his choices may also characterize the speaker. Some of the details of the paragraph may also be symbolic.

1. How does the second paragraph further advance the description of setting, of situation, of theme? Are any of the details here symbolic or potentially symbolic? The last sentence of this paragraph seems to relate directly to theme, though it may also help characterize the narrator. There are many such sentences in the story—an example might be "And suddenly I rejoiced in the great security of the sea . . ." (par. 17). Collect five or six such sentences and see how they relate not only to theme but to other elements.

2. How does par. 7 characterize the second mate, explain the narrator's situation, and further arouse suspense and further define the theme?

3. How does the description of the episode with the scorpion (par. 8) characterize the chief mate, and, when looked back upon later, further the plot and suspense? How does the chief mate's propensity for logical explanations relate to the theme?

4. How does the "unconventional arrangement" of the narrator-captain's standing the first anchor-watch relate to his character? to the plot? to the theme(s)?

5. When the narrator notices that the rope side-ladder has not been hauled in, he blames himself for having disturbed the ship's routine, "the very soul of discipline," and conjectures about how he will look in the eyes of the officers and crew and how his conduct will be "accounted" for by the chief mate. All this relates to the characters of the two men, the plot or suspense, and the theme. It is just then that "the secret sharer" appears at the very end of that same ladder. Is he, then, in some way symbolic? If so, how? In the light of all that follows, is it good or bad to break the rules? Does following or breaking rules seem to have anything to do with being a captain? Explain.

6. What is the effect of par. 20, in which "something elongated and pale" appears at the bottom of the ladder? How many elements are involved in that description (including the first sentence of the next paragraph)?

7. When Leggatt comes aboard and is dressed in the captain's sleeping suit, he is described as looking like the captain's "double." That, plus Leggatt's arriving from the sea naked, looking like a fish, being phosphorescent and oblong, plus the title of the story, and the narrator's seeing his first command as a test, has led a substantial number of critics and other readers to see these details as Freudian symbols and to see in this story a Freudian, or at least a psychological, theme. Make out the best case you can for such a reading of the story. What happens to the specifics of the situation, the characters, the plot? Which details are symbolic in your version and which are not? Now make out

the best case *against* such a reading. If you are so committed to one position or the other that you cannot see how there can be another side, pair yourself off with someone else in the class who has made the best counter-argument.

8. When Leggatt tells his story there is a shift in the focus and voice. How does this story within a story function in the plot of "The Secret Sharer"? How does it help define the character of Leggatt? How does it relate to the theme of "the double" in the larger story?

9. Why does the captain hide Leggatt rather than turn him in? How do all the elements of the story contribute to your answering this question?

10. The captain of the *Sephora* tells his version of Leggatt's crime, but the narrator says, "It is not worth while to record that version. It was just over two months since all this had happened, and . . . he seemed completely muddled . . ." (par. 128). Yet the narrator is telling his and Leggatt's story at a "distance of years," and there is a bit of Archbold's story in the page that follows. Write a fuller (two- or three-page) version of how the *Sephora* captain would tell the story. How does this shift in focus and voice affect the plot? the characterization of the captain of the *Sephora?* of Leggatt? of the narrator of "The Secret Sharer"? the theme?

11. Archbold believes Leggatt was too gentlemanly to be chief mate of the *Sephora*, and the narrator, so identified now with Leggatt, thinks Archbold would not consider the narrator himself a suitable chief mate (much less captain). How would you analyze this notion in terms of focus? character? symbol? theme?

12. There seems to be a turn in the story after Archbold leaves: ironically, Leggatt seems more of a burden to the narrator, who now seems to see himself in his role as captain: "I was not wholly alone with my command; for there was that stranger in my cabin. . . . Part of me was absent" (par. 194). What is the effect of this feeling of split identity on the plot? How does it relate to focus? The whole story can be read as the initiation of the narrator into leadership or captaincy. How does Leggatt figure in that initiation theme? How does his character relate to it? Is he a symbol? If you think he is, of what is he a symbol? How do the final episode and final two paragraphs of the story relate to this portion of the plot, this view of Leggatt, this theme? Can you imagine this story—the story of a new captain taking over command of a strange ship, with mates not of his own choosing and not of his own "kind," of the strained relations between the new captain and the other officers, of his routine and unroutine orders, of his emotional state, and of his first daring act of seamanship, of all this—without any mention of, or presence of, or story of, a Leggatt, a secret sharer? Write a brief synopsis of such a story. Is there some way in which you

might still call it "The Secret Sharer"? Who has the secret and with whom does he share it?

13. How does the captain's giving Leggatt his hat figure in the plot? What does it suggest about the narrator's character and feelings? Of what, if anything, might it be a symbol?

14. Write a sequel to "The Secret Sharer" about what happens to Leggatt after he leaves the ship, using as much evidence as you can from the elements and details of Conrad's story but with a new focus and voice.

The story that follows is funnier than, but just as serious as, "The Secret Sharer." It is the title story, or chapter, of a work that calls itself a novel but can also be seen as a collection of related but separable stories (indeed, many of the chapters were first published separately as stories). Reading the whole novel or collection may enrich your understanding and enjoyment of the parts but this story is, as you will see, quite wonderful, enjoyable, and understandable by itself. It is a somewhat unfamiliar world you will be entering; though nearer to us in time and space, it is perhaps even stranger than the world of "The Secret Sharer." Stop reading after paragraph 18, look at item 1 below (p. 293), and get your bearings.

LOUISE ERDRICH

Love Medicine

I never really done much with my life, I suppose. I never had a television. Grandma Kashpaw had one inside her apartment at the Senior Citizens, so I used to go there and watch my favorite shows. For a while she used to call me the biggest waste on the reservation and hark back to how she saved me from my own mother, who wanted to tie me in a potato sack and throw me in a slough. Sure, I was grateful to Grandma Kashpaw for saving me like that, for raising me, but gratitude gets old. After a while, stale. I had to stop thanking her. One day I told her I had paid her back in full by staying at her beck and call. I'd do anything for Grandma. She knew that. Besides, I took care of Grandpa like nobody else could, on account of what a handful he'd gotten to be.

But that was nothing. I know the tricks of mind and body inside out without ever having trained for it, because I got the touch. It's a thing you got to be born with. I got secrets in my hands that nobody ever knew to ask. Take Grandma Kashpaw with her tired veins all knotted up in her legs like clumps of blue snails. I take my fingers and I snap them on the knots. The medicine flows out of me. The touch. I run my fingers up the maps of those rivers of veins or I knock very gentle above their hearts or I make a circling motion on their stomachs, and it helps them. They feel much better. Some women pay me five dollars.

I couldn't do the touch for Grandpa, though. He was a hard nut. You know, some people fall right through the hole in their lives. It's invisible, but they come to it after time, never knowing where. There is this woman here, Lulu Lamartine, who always had a thing for Grandpa. She loved him since she was a girl and always said he was a genius. Now she says that his mind got so full it exploded.

How can I doubt that? I know the feeling when your mental power builds up too far. I always used to say that's why the Indians got drunk. Even statistically we're the smartest people on the earth. Anyhow with Grandpa I couldn't hardly believe it, because all my youth he stood out as a hero to me. When he started getting toward second childhood he went through different moods. He would stand in the woods and cry at the top of his shirt. It scared me, scared everyone, Grandma worst of all.

Yet he was so smart—do you believe it?—that he *knew* he was getting foolish.

He said so. He told me that December I failed school and come back on the train to Hoopdance. I didn't have nowhere else to go. He picked me up there and he said it straight out: "I'm getting into my second childhood." And then he said something else I still remember: "I been chosen for it. I couldn't say no." So I figure that a man so smart all his life—tribal chairman and the star of movies and even pictured in the statehouse and on cans of snuff—would know what he's doing by saying yes. I think he was called to second childhood like anybody else gets a call for the priesthood or the army or whatever. So I really did not listen too hard when the doctor said this was some kind of disease old people got eating too much sugar. You just can't tell me that a man who went to Washington and gave them bureaucrats what for could lose his mind from eating too much Milky Way. No, he put second childhood on himself.

Behind those songs he sings out in the middle of Mass, and back of those stories that everybody knows by heart, Grandpa is thinking hard about life. I know the feeling. Sometimes I'll throw up a smokescreen to think behind. I'll hitch up to Winnipeg and play the Space Invaders for six hours, but all the time there and back I will be thinking some fairly deep thoughts that surprise even me, and I'm used to it. As for him, if it was just the thoughts there wouldn't be no problem. Smokescreen is what irritates the social structure, see, and Grandpa has done things that just distract people to the point they want to throw him in the cookie jar where they keep the mentally insane. He's far from that, I know for sure, but even Grandma had trouble keeping her patience once he started sneaking off to Lamartine's place. He's not supposed to have his candy, and Lulu feeds it to him. That's *one* of the reasons why he goes.

Grandma tried to get me to put the touch on Grandpa soon after he began stepping out. I didn't want to, but before Grandma started telling me again what a bad state my bare behind was in when she first took me home, I thought I should at least pretend.

I put my hands on either side of Grandpa's head. You wouldn't look at him and say he was crazy. He's a fine figure of a man, as Lamartine would say, with all his hair and half his teeth, a beak like a hawk, and cheeks like the blades of a hatchet. They put his picture on all the tourist guides to North Dakota and even copied his face for artistic paintings. I guess you could call him a monument all of himself. He started grinning when I put my hands on his templates, and I knew right then he knew how come I touched him. I knew the smokescreen was going to fall.

And I was right: just for a moment it fell.

"Let's pitch whoopee," he said across my shoulder to Grandma.

They don't use that expression much around here anymore, but for damn sure it must have meant something. It got her goat right quick.

She threw my hands off his head herself and stood in front of him, over-matching him pound for pound, and taller too, for she had a growth spurt in middle age while he had shrunk, so now the length and breadth of her surpassed him. She glared up and spoke her piece into his face about how he was off at all hours tomcatting and chasing Lamartine again and making a damn old fool of himself.

"And you got no more whoopee to pitch anymore anyhow!" she yelled at last, surprising me so my jaw just dropped, for us kids all had pretended for so long that those rustling sounds we heard from their side of the room at night never happened. She sure had pretended it, up till now, anyway. I saw that tears were in her eyes. And that's when I saw how much grief and love she felt for him. And it gave me a real shock to the system. You see I thought love got easier over the years so it didn't hurt so bad when it hurt, or feel so good when it felt good. I thought it smoothed out and old people hardly noticed it. I thought it curled up and died, I guess. Now I saw it rear up like a whip and lash.

She loved him. She was jealous. She mourned him like the dead.

And he just smiled into the air, trapped in the seams of his mind.

So I didn't know what to do. I was in a laundry then. They was like parents to me, the way they had took me home and reared me. I could see her point for wanting to get him back the way he was so at least she could argue with him, sleep with him, not be shamed out by Lamartine. She'd always love him. That hit me like a ton of bricks. For one whole day I felt this odd feeling that cramped my hands. When you have the touch, that's where longing gets you. I never loved like that. It made me feel all inspired to see them fight, and I wanted to go out and find a woman who I would love until one of us died or went crazy. But I'm not like that really. From time to time I heal a person all up good inside, however when it comes to the long shot I doubt that I got staying power.

And you need that, staying power, going out to love somebody. I knew this quality was not going to jump on me with no effort. So I turned my thoughts back to Grandma and Grandpa. I felt her side of it with my hands and my tangled guts, and I felt his side of it within the stretch of my mentality. He had gone out to lunch one day and never came back. He was fishing in the middle of Lake Turcot. And there was big thoughts on his line, and he kept throwing them back for even bigger ones that would explain to him, say, the meaning of how we got here and why we have to leave so soon. All in all, I could not see myself treating Grandpa with the touch, bringing him back, when the real part of him had chose to be off thinking somewhere. It was only the rest of him that stayed around causing trouble, after all, and we could handle most of it without any problem.

Besides, it was hard to argue with his reasons for doing some things. Take Holy Mass. I used to go there just every so often, when I got frustrated mostly, because even though I know the Higher Power dwells everyplace, there's something very calming about the cool greenish inside of our mission. Or so I thought, anyway. Grandpa was the one who stripped off my delusions in this matter, for it was he who busted right through what Father Upsala calls the sacred serenity of the place.

We filed in that time. Me and Grandpa. We sat down in our pews. Then the rosary got started up pre-Mass and that's when Grandpa filled up his chest and opened his mouth and belted out them words.

HAIL MARIE FULL OF GRACE.

He had a powerful set of lungs.

And he kept on like that. He did not let up. He hollered and he yelled them prayers, and I guess people was used to him by now, because they only muttered theirs and did not quit and gawk like I did. I was getting red-faced, I admit. I give him the elbow once or twice, but that wasn't nothing to him. He kept on. He shrieked to heaven and he pleaded like a movie actor and he pounded his chest like Tarzan in the Lord I Am Not Worthies. I thought he might hurt himself. Then after a while I guess I got used to it, and that's when I wondered: how come?

So afterwards I out and asked him. "How come? How come you yelled?"

"God don't hear me otherwise," said Grandpa Kashpaw.

I sweat. I broke right into a little cold sweat at my hairline because I knew this was perfectly right and for years not one damn other person had noticed it. God's been going deaf. Since the Old Testament, God's been deafening up on us. I read, see. Besides the dictionary, which I'm constantly in use of, I had this Bible once. I read it. I found there was discrepancies between then and now. It struck me. Here God used to raineth bread from clouds, smite the Phillipines, sling fire down on red-light districts where people got stabbed. He even appeared in person every once in a while. God used to pay attention, is what I'm saying.

Now there's your God in the Old Testament and there is Chippewa Gods as well. Indian Gods, good and bad, like tricky Nanabozho or the water monster, Missepeshu, who lives over in Lake Turcot. That water monster was the last God I ever heard to appear. It had a weakness for young girls and grabbed one of the Blues off her rowboat. She got to shore all right, but only after this monster had its way with her. She's an old lady now. Old Lady Blue. She still won't let her family fish that lake.

Our Gods aren't perfect, is what I'm saying, but at least they come around. They'll do a favor if you ask them right. You don't have to yell. But you do have to know, like I said, how to ask in the right way. That makes problems, because to ask proper was an art that was lost to the Chippewas once the Catholics gained ground. Even now, I have to wonder if Higher Power turned it back, if we got to yell, or if we just don't speak its language.

I looked around me. How else could I explain what all I had seen in my short life—King smashing his fist in things, Gordie drinking himself down to the Bismarck hospitals, or Aunt June left by a white man to wander off in the snow. How else to explain the times my touch don't work, and farther back, to the oldtime Indians who was swept away in the outright germ warfare and dirty-dog killing of the whites. In those times, us Indians was so much kindlier than now.

We took them in.   30

Oh yes, I'm bitter as an old cutworm just thinking of how they done to us and doing still.

So Grandpa Kashpaw just opened my eyes a little there. Was there any sense relying on a God whose ears was stopped? Just like the government? I says then, right off, maybe we got nothing but ourselves. And that's not much, just personally speaking. I know I don't got the cold hard potatoes it takes to understand everything. Still, there's things I'd like to do. For instance, I'd like to help some people like my Grandpa and Grandma Kashpaw get back some happiness within the tail ends of their lives.

I told you once before I couldn't see my way clear to putting the direct touch on Grandpa's mind, and I kept my moral there, but something soon happened to make me think a little bit of mental adjustment wouldn't do him and the rest of us no harm.

It was after we saw him one afternoon in the sunshine courtyard of the Senior Citizens with Lulu Lamartine. Grandpa used to like to dig there. He had his little dandelion fork out, and he was prying up them dandelions right and left while Lamartine watched him.

"He's scratching up the dirt, all right," said Grandma, watching Lamartine   35
watch Grandpa out the window.

Now Lamartine was about half the considerable size of Grandma, but you would never think of sizes anyway. They were different in an even more noticeable way. It was the difference between a house fixed up with paint and picky fence, and a house left to weather away into the soft earth, is what I'm saying. Lamartine was jacked up, latticed, shuttered, and vinyl sided, while Grandma sagged and bulged on her slipped foundations and let her hair go the silver gray of rain-dried lumber. Right now, she eyed the Lamartine's pert flowery dress with such a look it despaired me. I knew what this could lead to with Grandma. Alternating tongue storms and rock-hard silences was hard on a man, even one who didn't notice, like Grandpa. So I went fetching him.

But he was gone when I popped through the little screen door that led out on the courtyard. There was nobody out there either, to point which way they went. Just the dandelion fork quibbling upright in the ground. That gave me an idea. I snookered over to the Lamartine's door and I listened in first, then knocked. But nobody. So I went walking through the lounges and around the card tables. Still nobody. Finally it was my touch that led me to the laundry room. I cracked the door. I went in. There they were. And he was really loving her up good, boy, and she was going hell for leather. Sheets was flapping on the lines above, and washcloths, pillowcases, shirts was also flying through the air, for they was trying to clear out a place for themselves in a high-heaped but shallow laundry cart. The washers and dryers was all on, chock full of quarters, shaking and moaning. I couldn't hear what Grandpa and the Lamartine was billing and cooing, and they couldn't hear me.

I didn't know what to do, so I went inside and shut the door.

The Lamartine wore a big curly light-brown wig. Looked like one of them squeaky little white-people dogs. Poodles they call them. Anyway, that wig is what saved us from the worse. For I could hardly shout and tell them I was in there, no more could I try and grab him. I was trapped where I was. There was nothing I could really do but hold the door shut. I was scared of somebody else upsetting in and really getting an eyeful. Turned out though, in the heat of the clinch, as I was trying to avert my eyes you see, the Lamartine's curly wig jumped off her head. And if you ever been in the midst of something and had a big change like that occur in the someone, you can't help know how it devastates your basic urges. Not only that, but her wig was almost with a life of its own. Grandpa's eyes were bugging at the change already, and swear to God if the thing didn't rear up and pop him in the face like it was going to start something. He scrambled up, Grandpa did, and the Lamartine jumped up after him all addled looking. They just stared at each other, huffing and puffing, with quizzical expression. The surprise seemed to drive all sense completely out of Grandpa's mind.

40 "The letter was what started the fire," he said. "I never would have done it."

"What letter?" said the Lamartine. She was stiff-necked now, and elegant, even bald, like some alien queen. I gave her back the wig. The Lamartine replaced it on her head, and whenever I saw her after that, I couldn't help thinking of her bald, with special powers, as if from another planet.

"That was a close call," I said to Grandpa after she had left.

But I think he had already forgot the incident. He just stood there all quiet and thoughtful. You really wouldn't think he was crazy. He looked like he was just about to say something important, explaining himself. He said something, all right, but it didn't have nothing to do with anything that made sense.

He wondered where the heck he put his dandelion fork. That's when I decided about the mental adjustment.

45 Now what was mostly our problem was not so much that he was not all there, but that what was there of him often hankered after Lamartine. If we could put a stop to that, I thought, we might be getting someplace. But here, see, my touch was of no use. For what could I snap my fingers at to make him faithful to Grandma? Like the quality of staying power, this faithfulness was invisible. I know it's something that you got to acquire, but I never known where from. Maybe there's no rhyme or reason to it, like my getting the touch, and then again maybe it's a kind of magic.

It was Grandma Kashpaw who thought of it in the end. She knows things. Although she will not admit she has a scrap of Indian blood in her, there's no doubt in my mind she's got some Chippewa. How else would you explain the way she'll be sitting there, in front of her TV story, rocking in her armchair and suddenly she turns on me, her brown eyes hard as lake-bed flint.

"Lipsha Morrissey," she'll say, "you went out last night and got drunk."

How did she know that? I'll hardly remember it myself. Then she'll say she just had a feeling or ache in the scar of her hand or a creak in her shoulder. She is constantly being told things by little aggravations in her joints or by her household appliances. One time she told Gordie never to ride with a crazy Lamartine boy. She had seen something in the polished-up tin of her bread toaster. So he didn't. Sure enough, the time came we heard how Lyman and Henry went out of control in their car, ending up in the river. Lyman swam to the top, but Henry never made it.

Thanks to Grandma's toaster, Gordie was probably spared.

Someplace in the blood Grandma Kashpaw knows things. She also remembers things, I found. She keeps things filed away. She's got a memory like them video games that don't forget your score. One reason she remembers so many details about the trouble I gave her in early life is so she can flash back her total when she needs to.

Like now. Take the love medicine. I don't know where she remembered that from. It came tumbling from her mind like an asteroid off the corner of the screen.

Of course she starts out by mentioning the time I had this accident in church and did she leave me there with wet overhalls? No she didn't. And ain't I glad? Yes I am. Now what you want now, Grandma?

But when she mentions them love medicines, I feel my back prickle at the danger. These love medicines is something of an old Chippewa specialty. No other tribe has got them down so well. But love medicines is not for the layman to handle. You don't just go out and get one without paying for it. Before you get one, even, you should go through one hell of a lot of mental condensation. You got to think it over. Choose the right one. You could really mess up your life grinding up the wrong little thing.

So anyhow, I said to Grandma I'd give this love medicine some thought. I knew the best thing was to go ask a specialist like Old Man Pillager, who lives up in a tangle of bush and never shows himself. But the truth is I was afraid of him, like everyone else. He was known for putting the twisted mouth on people, seizing up their hearts. Old Man Pillager was serious business, and I have always thought it best to steer clear of that whenever I could. That's why I took the powers in my own hands. That's why I did what I could.

I put my whole mentality to it, nothing held back. After a while I started to remember things I'd heard gossiped over.

I heard of this person once who carried a charm of seeds that looked like baby pearls. They was attracted to a metal knife, which made them powerful. But I didn't know where them seeds grew. Another love charm I heard about I couldn't go along with, because how was I suppose to catch frogs in the act, which it required. Them little creatures is slippery and fast. And then the powerfullest of all, the most extreme, involved nail clips and such. I wasn't anywhere near asking Grandma to provide me all the little body bits that this last love recipe called for. I went walking around for days just trying to think up something that would work.

Well I got it. If it hadn't been the early fall of the year, I never would have got it. But I was sitting underneath a tree one day down near the school just watching people's feet go by when something tells me, look up! Look up! So I look up, and I see two honkers, Canada geese, the kind with little masks on their faces, a bird what mates for life. I see them flying right over my head naturally preparing to land in some slough on the reservation, which they certainly won't get off of alive.

It hits me, anyway. Them geese, they mate for life. And I think to myself, just what if I went out and got a pair? And just what if I fed some part—say the goose heart—of the female to Grandma and Grandpa ate the other heart? Wouldn't that work? Maybe it's all invisible, and then maybe again it's magic. Love is a stony road. We know that for sure. If it's true that the higher feelings of devotion get lodged in the heart like people say, then we'd be home free. If not, eating goose heart couldn't harm nobody anyway. I thought it was worth my effort, and Grandma Kashpaw thought so, too. She had always known a good idea when she heard one. She borrowed me Grandpa's gun.

So I went out to this particular slough, maybe the exact same slough I never got thrown in by my mother, thanks to Grandma Kashpaw, and I hunched down in a good comfortable pile of rushes. I got my gun loaded up. I ate a few of these soft baloney sandwiches Grandma made me for lunch. And then I waited. The cattails blown back and forth above my head. Them stringy blue herons was spearing up their prey. The thing I know how to do best in this world, the thing I been training for all my life, is to wait. Sitting there and sitting there was no hardship on me. I got to thinking about some funny things that happened. There was this one time that Lulu Lamartine's little blue tweety bird, a paraclete, I guess you'd call it, flown up inside her dress and got lost within there. I recalled her running out into the hallway trying to yell something, shaking. She was doing a right good jig there, cutting the rug for sure, and the thing is it *never* flown out. To this day people speculate where it went. They fear she might perhaps of crushed it in her corsets. It sure hasn't ever yet been seen alive. I thought of funny things for a while, but then I used them up, and strange things that happened started weaseling their way into my mind.

I got to thinking quite naturally of the Lamartine's cousin named Wrist-watch. I never knew what his real name was. They called him Wristwatch because he got his father's broken wristwatch as a young boy when his father passed on. Never in his whole life did Wristwatch take his father's watch off. He didn't care if it worked, although after a while he got sensitive when people asked what time it was, teasing him. He often put it to his ear like he was listening to the tick. But it was broken for good and forever, people said so, at least that's what they thought.

Well I saw Wristwatch smoking in his pickup one afternoon and by nine that evening he was dead.

He died sitting at the Lamartine's table, too. As she told it, Wristwatch had just eaten himself a good-size dinner and she said would he take seconds on the hot dish when he fell over to the floor. They turnt him over. He was gone. But here's the strange thing: when the Senior Citizen's orderly took the pulse he

60

noticed that the wristwatch Wristwatch wore was now working. The moment he died the wristwatch started keeping perfect time. They buried him with the watch still ticking on his arm.

I got to thinking. What if some gravediggers dug up Wristwatch's casket in two hundred years and that watch was still going? I thought what question they would ask and it was this: Whose hand wound it?

I started shaking like a piece of grass at just the thought.

Not to get off the subject or nothing. I was still hunkered in the slough. It was passing late into the afternoon and still no honkers had touched down. Now I don't need to tell you that the waiting did not get to me, it was the chill. The rushes was very soft, but damp. I was getting cold and debating to leave, when they landed. Two geese swimming here and there as big as life, looking deep into each other's little pinhole eyes. Just the ones I was looking for. So I lifted Grandpa's gun to my shoulder and I aimed perfectly, and *blam! Blam!* I delivered two accurate shots. But the thing is, them shots missed. I couldn't hardly believe it. Whether it was that the stock had warped or the barrel got bent someways, I don't quite know, but anyway them geese flown off into the dim sky, and Lipsha Morrissey was left there in the rushes with evening fallen and his two cold hands empty. He had before him just the prospect of another day of bone-cracking chill in them rushes, and the thought of it got him depressed.

Now it isn't my style, in no way, to get depressed.

So I said to myself, Lipsha Morrissey, you're a happy S.O.B. who could be covered up with weeds by now down at the bottom of this slough, but instead you're alive to tell the tale. You might have problems in life, but you still got the touch. You got the power, Lipsha Morrissey. Can't argue that. So put your mind to it and figure out how not to be depressed.

I took my advice. I put my mind to it. But I never saw at the time how my thoughts led me astray toward a tragic outcome none could have known. I ignored all the danger, all the limits, for I was tired of sitting in the slough and my feet were numb. My face was aching. I was chilled, so I played with fire. I told myself love medicine was simple. I told myself the old superstitions was just that— strange beliefs. I told myself to take the ten dollars Mary MacDonald had paid me for putting the touch on her arthritis joint, and the other five I hadn't spent yet from winning bingo last Thursday. I told myself to go down to the Red Owl store.

And here is what I did that made the medicine backfire. I took an evil short-cut. I looked at birds that was dead and froze.

All right. So now I guess you will say, "Slap a malpractice suit on Lipsha Morrissey."

I heard of those suits. I used to think it was a color clothing quack doctors had to wear so you could tell them from the good ones. Now I know better that it's law.

As I walked back from the Red Owl with the rock-hard, heavy turkeys, I argued to myself about malpractice. I thought of faith. I thought to myself that faith could be called belief against the odds and whether or not there's any proof.

How does that sound? I thought how we might have to yell to be heard by Higher Power, but that's not saying it's not *there*. And that is faith for you. It's belief even when the goods don't deliver. Higher Power makes promises we all know they can't back up, but anybody ever go and slap an old malpractice suit on God? Or the U.S. government? No they don't. Faith might be stupid, but it gets us through. So what I'm heading at is this. I finally convinced myself that the real actual power to the love medicine was not the goose heart itself but the faith in the cure.

I didn't believe it, I knew it was wrong, but by then I had waded so far into my lie I was stuck there. And then I went one step further.

The next day, I cleaned the hearts away from the paper packages of gizzards inside the turkeys. Then I wrapped them hearts with a clean hankie and brung them both to get blessed up at the mission. I wanted to get official blessings from the priest, but when Father answered the door to the rectory, wiping his hands on a little towel, I could tell he was a busy man.

"Booshoo,[1] Father," I said. "I got a slight request to make of you this after-noon."

"What is it?" he said.

"Would you bless this package?" I held out the hankie with the hearts tied inside it.

He looked at the package, questioning it.

"It's turkey hearts," I honestly had to reply.

A look of annoyance crossed his face.

"Why don't you bring this matter over to Sister Martin," he said. "I have duties."

And so, although the blessing wouldn't be as powerful, I went over to the Sisters with the package.

I rung the bell, and they brought Sister Martin to the door. I had her as a music teacher, but I was always so shy then. I never talked out loud. Now, I had grown taller than Sister Martin. Looking down, I saw that she was not feeling up to snuff. Brown circles hung under her eyes.

"What's the matter?" she said, not noticing who I was.

"Remember me, Sister?"

She squinted up at me.

"Oh yes," she said after a moment. "I'm sorry, you're the youngest of the Kashpaws. Gordie's brother."

Her face warmed up.

"Lipsha," I said, "that's my name."

"Well, Lipsha," she said, smiling broad at me now, "what can I do for you?"

They always said she was the kindest-hearted of the Sisters up the hill, and she was. She brought me back into their own kitchen and made me take a big yellow wedge of cake and a glass of milk.

"Now tell me," she said, nodding at my package. "What have you got wrapped up so carefully in those handkerchiefs?"

Like before, I answered honestly.

---

1. *Bonjour*, French for "good day."

"Ah," said Sister Martin. "Turkey hearts." She waited.

"I hoped you could bless them."

She waited some more, smiling with her eyes. Kindhearted though she was, I began to sweat. A person could not pull the wool down over Sister Martin. I stumbled through my mind for an explanation, quick, that wouldn't scare her off.

"They're a present," I said, "for Saint Kateri's statue."

"She's not a saint yet."

"I know," I stuttered on, "in the hopes they will crown her."

"Lipsha," she said, "I never heard of such a thing."

So I told her. "Well the truth is," I said, "it's a kind of medicine."

"For what?"

"Love."

"Oh Lipsha," she said after a moment, "you don't need any medicine. I'm sure any girl would like you exactly the way you are."

I just sat there. I felt miserable, caught in my pack of lies.

"Tell you what," she said, seeing how bad I felt, "my blessing won't make any difference anyway. But there is something you can do."

I looked up at her hopeless.

"Just be yourself."

I looked down at my plate. I knew I wasn't much to brag about right then, and I shortly became even less. For as I walked out the door I stuck my fingers in the cup of holy water that was sacred from their touches. I put my fingers in and blessed the hearts, quick, with my own hand.

I went back to Grandma and sat down in her little kitchen at the Senior Citizens. I unwrapped them hearts on the table, and her hard agate eyes went soft. She said she wasn't even going to cook those hearts up but eat them raw so their power would go down strong as possible.

I couldn't hardly watch when she munched hers. Now that's true love. I was worried about how she would get Grandpa to eat his, but she told me she'd think of something and don't worry. So I did not. I was supposed to hide off in her bedroom while she put dinner on a plate for Grandpa and fixed up the heart so he'd eat it. I caught a glint of the plate she was making for him. She put that heart smack on a piece of lettuce like in a restaurant and then attached to it a little heap of boiled peas.

He sat down. I was listening in the next room.

She said, "Why don't you have some mash potato?" So he had some mash potato. Then she gave him a little piece of boiled meat. He ate that. Then she said, "Why you didn't never touch your salad yet. See that heart? I'm feeding you it because the doctor said your blood needs building up."

I couldn't help it, at that point I peeked through a crack in the door.

I saw Grandpa picking at that heart on his plate with a certain look. He didn't look appetized at all, is what I'm saying. I doubted our plan was going to work. Grandma was getting worried, too. She told him one more time, loudly, that he had to eat that heart.

"Swallow it down," she said. "You'll hardly notice it."

He just looked at her straight on. The way he looked at her made me think I was going to see the smokescreen drop a second time, and sure enough it happened.

"What you want me to eat this for so bad?" he asked her uncannily.

Now Grandma knew the jig was up. She knew that he knew she was working medicine. He put his fork down. He rolled the heart around his saucer plate.

"I don't want to eat this," he said to Grandma. "It don't look good."

"Why it's fresh grade-A," she told him. "One hundred percent."

He didn't ask percent what, but his eyes took on an even more warier look.

"Just go on and try it," she said, taking the salt shaker up in her hand. She was getting annoyed. "Not tasty enough? You want me to salt it for you?" She waved the shaker over his plate.

"All right, skinny white girl!" She had got Grandpa mad. Oopsy-daisy, he popped the heart into his mouth. I was about to yawn loudly and come out of the bedroom. I was about ready for this crash of wills to be over, when I saw he was still up to his old tricks. First he rolled it into one side of his cheek. "Mmmmm," he said. Then he rolled it into the other side of his cheek. "Mmmmmmm," again. Then he stuck his tongue out with the heart on it and put it back, and there was no time to react. He had pulled Grandma's leg once too far. Her goat was got. She was so mad she hopped up quick as a wink and slugged him between the shoulderblades to make him swallow.

Only thing is, he choked.

He choked real bad. A person can choke to death. You ever sit down at a restaurant table and up above you there is a list of instructions what to do if something slides down the wrong pipe? It sure makes you chew slow, that's for damn sure. When Grandpa fell off his chair better believe me that little graphic illustrated poster fled into my mind. I jumped out the bedroom. I done everything within my power that I could do to unlodge what was choking him. I squeezed underneath his ribcage. I socked him in the back. I was desperate. But here's the factor of decision: he wasn't choking on the heart alone. There was more to it than that. It was other things that choked him as well. It didn't seem like he wanted to struggle or fight. Death came and tapped his chest, so he went just like that. I'm sorry all through my body at what I done to him with that heart, and there's those who will say Lipsha Morrissey is just excusing himself off the hook by giving song and dance about how Grandpa gave up.

Maybe I can't admit what I did. My touch had gone worthless, that is true. But here is what I seen while he lay in my arms.

You hear a person's life will flash before their eyes when they're in danger. It was him in danger, not me, but it was *his* life come over me. I saw him dying, and it was like someone pulled the shade down in a room. His eyes clouded over and squeezed shut, but just before that I looked in. He was still fishing in the middle of Lake Turcot. Big thoughts was on his line and he had half a case of beer in the boat. He waved at me, grinned, and then the bobber went under.

Grandma had gone out of the room crying for help. I bunched my force up in my hands and I held him. I was so wound up I couldn't even breathe. All the moments he had spent with me, all the times he had hoisted me on his shoulders or pointed into the leaves was concentrated in that moment. Time was flashing back and forth like a pinball machine. Lights blinked and balls hopped and rubber bands chirped, until suddenly I realized the last ball had gone down the drain and there was nothing. I felt his force leaving him, flowing out of Grandpa never to return. I felt his mind weakening. The bobber going under in the lake. And I felt the touch retreat back into the darkness inside my body, from where it came.

One time, long ago, both of us were fishing together. We caught a big old snapper what started towing us around like it was a motor. "This here fishline is pretty damn good," Grandpa said. "Let's keep this turtle on and see where he takes us." So we rode along behind that turtle, watching as from time to time it surfaced. The thing was just about the size of a washtub. It took us all around the lake twice, and as it was traveling, Grandpa said something as a joke. "Lipsha," he said, "we are glad your mother didn't want you because we was always looking for a boy like you who would tow us around the lake." 130

"I ain't no snapper. Snappers is so stupid they stay alive when their head's chopped off," I said.

"That ain't stupidity," said Grandpa. "Their brain's just in their heart, like yours is."

When I looked up, I knew the fuse had blown between my heart and my mind and that a terrible understanding was to be given.

Grandma got back into the room and I saw her stumble. And then she went down too. It was like a house you can't hardly believe has stood so long, through years of record weather, suddenly goes down in the worst yet. It makes sense, is what I'm saying, but you still can't hardly believe it. You think a person you know has got through death and illness and being broke and living on commodity rice will get through anything. Then they fold and you see how fragile were the stones that underpinned them. You see how instantly the ground can shift you thought was solid. You see the stop signs and the yellow dividing markers of roads you traveled and all the instructions you had played according to vanish. You see how all the everyday things you counted on was just a dream you had been having by which you run your whole life. She had been over me, like a sheer overhang of rock dividing Lipsha Morrissey from outer space. And now she went underneath. It was as though the banks gave way on the shores of Lake Turcot, and where Grandpa's passing was just the bobber swallowed under by his biggest thought, her fall was the house and the rock under it sliding after, sending half the lake splashing up to the clouds.

Where there was nothing. 135

You play them games never knowing what you see. When I fell into the dream alongside of both of them I saw that the dominions I had defended myself from anciently was but delusions of the screen. Blips of light. And I was scot-free now, whistling through space.

I don't know how I come back. I don't know from where. They was slapping my face when I arrived back at Senior Citizens and they was oxygenating her. I saw her chest move, almost unwilling. She sighed the way she would when somebody bothered her in the middle of a row of beads she was counting. I think it irritated her to no end that they brought her back. I knew from the way she looked after they took the mask off, she was not going to forgive them disturbing her restful peace. Nor was she forgiving Lipsha Morrissey. She had been stepping out onto the road of death, she told the children later at the funeral. I asked was there any stop signs or dividing markers on that road, but she clamped her lips in a vise the way she always done when she was mad.

Which didn't bother me. I knew when things had cleared out she wouldn't have no choice. I was not going to speculate where the blame was put for Grandpa's death. We was in it together. She had slugged him between the shoulders. My touch had failed him, never to return.

All the blood children and the took-ins, like me, came home from Minneapolis and Chicago, where they had relocated years ago. They stayed with friends on the reservation or with Aurelia or slept on Grandma's floor. They were struck down with grief and bereavement to be sure, every one of them. At the funeral I sat down in the back of the church with Albertine. She had gotten all skinny and ragged haired from cramming all her years of study into two or three. She had decided that to be a nurse was not enough for her so she was going to be a doctor. But the way she was straining her mind didn't look too hopeful. Her eyes were bloodshot from driving and crying. She took my hand. From the back we watched all the children and the mourners as they hunched over their prayers, their hands stuffed full of Kleenex. It was someplace in that long sad service that my vision shifted. I began to see things different, more clear. The family kneeling down turned to rocks in a field. It struck me how strong and reliable grief was, and death. Until the end of time, death would be our rock.

So I had perspective on it all, for death gives you that. All the Kashpaw children had done various things to me in their lives—shared their folks with me, loaned me cash, beat me up in secret—and I decided, because of death, then and there I'd call it quits. If I ever saw King again, I'd shake his hand. Forgiving somebody else made the whole thing easier to bear.

Everybody saw Grandpa off into the next world. And then the Kashpaws had to get back to their jobs, which was numerous and impressive. I had a few beers with them and I went back to Grandma, who had sort of got lost in the shuffle of everybody being sad about Grandpa and glad to see one another.

Zelda had sat beside her the whole time and was sitting with her now. I wanted to talk to Grandma, say how sorry I was, that it wasn't her fault, but only mine. I would have, but Zelda gave me one of her looks of strict warning as if to say, "I'll take care of Grandma. Don't horn in on the women."

If only Zelda knew, I thought, the sad realities would change her. But of course I couldn't tell the dark truth.

It was evening, late. Grandma's light was on underneath a crack in the door. About a week had passed since we buried Grandpa. I knocked first but there wasn't no answer, so I went right in. The door was unlocked. She was there but she didn't notice me at first. Her hands were tied up in her rosary, and her gaze was fully absorbed in the easy chair opposite her, the one that had always been Grandpa's favorite. I stood there, staring with her, at the little green nubs in the cloth and plastic armrest covers and the sad little hair-tonic stain he had made on the white doily where he laid his head. For the life of me I couldn't figure what she was staring at. Thin space. Then she turned.

"He ain't gone yet,' she said.

Remember that chill I luckily didn't get from waiting in the slough? I got it now. I felt it start from the very center of me, where fear hides, waiting to attack. It spiraled outward so that in minutes my fingers and teeth were shaking and clattering. I knew she told the truth. She seen Grandpa. Whether or not he had been there is not the point. She had *seen* him, and that meant anybody else could see him, too. Not only that but, as is usually the case with these here ghosts, he had a certain uneasy reason to come back. And of course Grandma Kashpaw had scanned it out.

I sat down. We sat together on the couch watching his chair out of the corner of our eyes. She had found him sitting in his chair when she walked in the door.

"It's the love medicine, my Lipsha," she said. "It was stronger than we thought. He came back even after death to claim me to his side."

I was afraid. "We shouldn't have tampered with it," I said. She agreed. For a while we sat still. I don't know what she thought, but my head felt screwed on backward. I couldn't accurately consider the situation, so I told Grandma to go to bed. I would sleep on the couch keeping my eye on Grandpa's chair. Maybe he would come back and maybe he wouldn't. I guess I feared the one as much as the other, but I got to thinking, see, as I lay there in darkness, that perhaps even through my terrible mistakes some good might come. If Grandpa did come back, I thought he'd return in his right mind. I could talk with him. I could tell him it was all my fault for playing with power I did not understand. Maybe he'd forgive me and rest in peace. I hoped this. I calmed myself and waited for him all night.

He fooled me though. He knew what I was waiting for, and it wasn't what he was looking to hear. Come dawn I heard a blood-splitting cry from the bedroom and I rushed in there. Grandma turnt the lights on. She was sitting on the edge of the bed and her face looked harsh, pinched-up, gray.

"He was here," she said. "He came and laid down next to me in bed. And he touched me."

Her heart broke down. She cried. His touch was so cold. She laid back in bed after a while, as it was morning, and I went to the couch. As I lay there, falling asleep, I suddenly felt Grandpa's presence and the barrier between us like a swollen river. I felt how I had wronged him. How awful was the place where I had sent him. Behind the wall of death, he'd watched the living eat and cry and get drunk. He was lonesome, but I understood he meant no harm.

"Go back," I said to the dark, afraid and yet full of pity. "You got to be with your own kind now," I said. I felt him retreating, like a sigh, growing less. I felt his spirit as it shrunk back through the walls, the blinds, the brick courtyard of Senior Citizens. "Look up Aunt June," I whispered as he left.

145

150

I slept late the next morning, a good hard sleep allowing the sun to rise and warm the earth. It was past noon when I awoke. There is nothing, to my mind, like a long sleep to make those hard decisions that you neglect under stress of wakefulness. Soon as I woke up that morning, I saw exactly what I'd say to Grandma. I had gotten humble in the past week, not just losing the touch but getting jolted into the understanding that would prey on me from here on out. Your life feels different on you, once you greet death and understand your heart's position. You wear your life like a garment from the mission bundle sale ever after—lightly because you realize you never paid nothing for it, cherishing because you know you won't ever come by such a bargain again. Also you have the feeling someone wore it before you and someone will after. I can't explain that, not yet, but I'm putting my mind to it.

155   "Grandma," I said, "I got to be honest about the love medicine."

She listened. I knew from then on she would be listening to me the way I had listened to her before. I told her about the turkey hearts and how I had them blessed. I told her what I used as love medicine was purely a fake, and then I said to her what my understanding brought me.

"Love medicine ain't what brings him back to you, Grandma. No, it's something else. He loved you over time and distance, but he went off so quick he never got the chance to tell you how he loves you, how he doesn't blame you, how he understands. It's true feeling, not no magic. No supermarket heart could have brung him back."

She looked at me. She was seeing the years and days I had no way of knowing, and she didn't believe me. I could tell this. Yet a look came on her face. It was like the look of mothers drinking sweetness from their children's eyes. It was tenderness.

"Lipsha," she said, "you was always my favorite."

160   She took the beads off the bedpost, where she kept them to say at night, and she told me to put out my hand. When I did this, she shut the beads inside of my fist and held them there a long minute, tight, so my hand hurt. I almost cried when she did this. I don't really know why. Tears shot up behind my eyelids, and yet it was nothing. I didn't understand, except her hand was so strong, squeezing mine.

The earth was full of life and there were dandelions growing out the window, thick as thieves, already seeded, fat as big yellow plungers. She let my hand go. I got up. "I'll go out and dig a few dandelions," I told her.

Outside, the sun was hot and heavy as a hand on my back. I felt it flow down my arms, out my fingers, arrowing through the ends of the fork into the earth. With every root I prized up there was return, as if I was kin to its secret lesson. The touch got stronger as I worked through the grassy afternoon. Uncurling from me like a seed out of the blackness where I was lost, the touch spread. The spiked leaves full of bitter mother's milk. A buried root. A nuisance people dig up and throw in the sun to wither. A globe of frail seeds that's indestructible.

1982

1. In the first dramatized scene, Lipsha, the narrator, at Grandma Kashpaw's request, tries to "put the touch" on Grandpa. By this time, some seventeen or eighteen paragraphs, focus and voice and the setting and situation have been established; you should be getting a good idea of Lipsha's character, and you should be forming some fairly definite expectations about the plot, and, with the help of the title, you should have some glimmers about the developing theme. Write down what you have observed of the structure and elements of the story and what you expect to happen. As you read on, note how your expectations are fulfilled or modified: in what ways are these surprises or changes in expectations related to plot? character? theme? how do they define the world of the fiction? differ from your prior view of the world? To what extent are they convincing?

2. Voice is a dominant element in this story, and it is in large measure through Lipsha's voice that we infer his character. His language is ungrammatical—the story opens with "I never really *done* much . . ." and his narration is full of colloquial phrases like "I don't got"—and his malapropisms (ludicrous misuse of words)—"templates" for "temples," "laundry" for "quandary," and "Phillipines" for "Philistines"—tend to undercut his apparent confidence in his literary skills ("Besides the dictionary, which I'm constantly in use of, I had this Bible once. I read it." [par. 26]). His limitations, skillfully indicated, extend to his somewhat naive view of reality—or causality: for example, his version of why Grandpa has symptoms of senility, his "thoughtful" acceptance of Grandpa's illuminating insight that God is going deaf. These errors, attitudes, and views, however, are endearing and often quite funny. Some of them will turn out, in strange ways, to seem almost wise. His kindness and good nature show through the errors and naivete, and he is capable of insights that, though naive and tender still, are not ludicrous: "I thought love got easier over the years so it didn't hurt so bad when it hurt, or feel so good when it felt good' (par. 14); "From time to time I heal a person all up good inside, however when it comes to the long shot I doubt I got staying power. / And you need that, staying power, going out to love somebody" (par. 18). His voice reveals character and theme, and his character is instrumental in this plot. A challenging topic for a paper might be to show not only how the theme is presented in this story through a character who is not well educated or intellectually profound, but how the character's very limitations contribute meaning and force to that theme.

3. How is "love medicine" related to the plot? to Grandma's and Lipsha's character? to theme? In what way(s) may it be considered a symbol?

4. Lipsha tells the story of Lulu's "tweety bird" that disappeared up her

dress and of Wristwatch, whose broken watch started keeping time after its owner dropped dead. He then says, "Not to get off the subject or nothing" (par. 65). Are these stories off the subject? How do they arouse expectations? How do they function in the plot? What do they tell you of Lipsha's character? of the nature of the people on the reservation? Are they related to the theme? if so, how? When he thinks of Wristwatch's grave being dug up in 200 years, the watch still running, and the diggers asking, "Whose hand wound it?" he says he "started shaking like a piece of grass at just the thought" (par. 64). Is it with awe and fear or with laughter? Do you find it awesome or funny? If there is a difference between how you feel and how you believe Lipsha feels, what is the effect? What is the relationship of this difference to plot, character, voice, and the other elements of the story? How is this episode related to the "subject" he does not mean to be getting off of when the story continues: for example, he says he fires two "accurate" shots at the geese but the shots miss; how does this affect your view of his "reliability" and thus your reading of character? plot? theme? How does it affect your reading of his glance forward, "I never saw at the time how my thoughts led me astray toward a tragic outcome none could have known" (par. 68)? There is a death involved. Is it "tragic"? How do you respond to it? He says he took "an evil shortcut" in practicing love medicine: does that mean that he has discovered that the old beliefs are not "superstitions" or "strange" as he thought at the time?

5. Toward the end of the story, Lipsha tells Grandma that it was not "love medicine" that brought Grandpa's ghost back to her but love itself, not magic but feeling. Grandma looks at him tenderly and says, " 'Lipsha, . . . you was always my favorite' " (par. 159). Explain this passage in terms of the plot (but be sure to remember Lulu); in terms of Lipsha's character; in terms of Grandma's; in terms of theme (and you might even want to think of "love medicine" as symbol).

∨ ∨ ∨

Exploring Contexts

8 THE AUTHOR'S WORK

E ven if it were desirable to read a story as a thing in itself, separate from everything else we had ever read or seen and from everything else the author had written, this is in practice impossible. We can *first* look into Chapman's Homer or Faulkner's fiction only once. After we read a second and then a third story by an author, we recognize the voice and have a sense of familiarity, as we would with a growing acquaintance. Each story is part of the author's entire body of work—the **canon**—which, taken together, forms something like a huge single entity, a vision, a world, a "superwork."

The author's voice and vision soon create in us certain expectations—of action, structure, characterization, world view, language. We come to expect short sentences from Hemingway, long ones from Faulkner, a certain amount of violence from both. We are not surprised if a Conrad story is set in Africa or Asia or aboard ship, but we are surprised if a Faulkner story takes place outside Mississippi (his portion of which, we soon learn, he calls Yoknapatawpha). We expect indirection, irony, and uncertainty (as well as long sentences with lots of commas) from Henry James, so we watch his characters for signs of subtlety or unreliability, and his narrator for careful qualifications and qualifications of qualifications. After reading a significant amount of Faulkner, we will bring our reading of "The Old People" and other stories to our understanding of "blood" in "Barn Burning."

When we find an author's vision attractive or challenging, we naturally want to find out more about it, reading not only the literary works in the canon but the author's nonfictional prose—essays, letters, anything we can find that promises a fuller or clearer view of that unique way of looking at the world.

Such knowledge is helpful—within limits. D. H. Lawrence warned us to trust the tale and not the teller. A statement of beliefs or of intentions is not necessarily the same as what a given work may show or achieve; and, on the other hand, writers often embody in their art what they cannot articulate, what indeed may not be expressible, in discursive prose.

In this chapter we will look closely at the work of two writers, D. H. Lawrence and Flannery O'Connor. We will look both at differences between works by the same writer and at similarities.

The two short stories and brief selections from Lawrence's letters and criticism in this chapter are meant to make you feel more at home (and interested) in Lawrence's world and to raise questions about the relationship of the individual work to an author's work as a whole. Of course, a couple of short stories and a few pages of nonfiction alone cannot adequately represent the career of a writer who was a novelist, poet, critic, and essayist as well as short-story writer, nor can two stories represent the richness and variety of the fifty or more that he published. However, as the stories come from different decades, they do represent somewhat the continuities and changes during his career. "Odour of Chrysanthemums" is characteristically set in the coal-mining region of his native English Midlands, the scene of many of his novels, including three of the most famous, which also span his career—*Sons and Lovers* (1913), *The Rainbow* (1915), and *Lady Chatterly's Lover* (1928). There is no way in so few selections to represent both Lawrence's emphasis on the Midlands and the scope of his settings—his stories take place all over Western Europe, in the Americas, and in Australia. The London setting of "The Rocking-Horse Winner" only faintly indicates Lawrence's growing cosmopolitanism socially as well as geographically. It also suggests, though superficially, his developing interest in the superreal and the mythic—concerns most fully developed in *The Plumed Serpent* (1926) and *The Man Who Died* (1929)—and his movement in content and style away from nineteenth-century notions of realism.

It may be useful to see the first story here (one of Lawrence's very first stories) through the eyes of its first "professional" reader as he remembers the experience. Not long before World War I, a young woman sent to Ford Madox Ford, then editor of *The English Review*, three poems and a short story written by a schoolmaster friend of hers, the then unknown D. H. Lawrence. Ford read the story first and, he recalls, knew immediately that he had a genius on his hands, "a big one." The very title, "Odour of Chrysanthemums," Ford noted, "makes an impact on the mind," indicates that the writer is observant (not many people realize that chrysanthemums have an odor), and sets the dark autumnal tone of the story. From the very first sentence, Ford goes on to say,

. . . you know that this fellow with the power of observation is going to write what-ever he writes about from the inside. The "Number 4" shows that. He will be the sort of fellow who knows that for the sort of people who work about engines, engines have a sort of individuality. He had to give the engine the personality of a number. . . . "With seven full wagons". . . . The "seven" is good. The ordinary careless writer would say "some small wagons." This man knows what he wants. He sees the scene of his story exactly. He has an authoritative mind.

"It appeared round the corner with loud threats of speed." . . . Good writing; slightly, but not *too* arresting. . . . "But the colt that it startled from among the gorse . . . out-distanced it at a canter." Good again. This fellow does not "state." He doesn't say: "It was coming slowly," or—what would have been a little better— "at seven miles an hour." Because even "seven miles an hour" means nothing defi-nite for the untrained mind. It might mean something for a trainer or pedestrian racers. The imaginative writer writes for all humanity; he does not limit his desired readers to specialists. . . . But anyone knows that an engine that makes a great deal of noise and yet cannot overtake a colt at a canter must be a ludicrously ineffective machine. We know then that this fellow knows his job.

. . . . [T]his man knows. He knows how to open a story with a sentence of the right cadence for holding the attention. He knows how to construct a paragraph. He knows the life he is writing about. . . . You can trust him for the rest. . . .

—from "Before the Wars," *Selected Memories, The Bodley Head Ford Madox Ford* (London, 1962), I, 322–323

You will find the same precision of detail suggesting the author's "inside view" in that strange and strangely different story "The Rocking-Horse Winner," in the first description of Paul's riding the horse, for example; in the description of the horse's "lowered face" ("Its red mouth was slightly open, its big eye was wide and glassy-bright" [par. 42]); and in the precise accounting of the races, the odds, the money.

Ford read "Odour of Chrysanthemums" outside the context available to us. He did not know anything of the author and had read nothing else by him. Ford was an excellent editor (as well as writer) and to his credit spotted Law-rence's genius, a genius quite different from his own. Lawrence's mastery of detail made Ford trust him, but what he trusted him for seems to have been knowledge of the "other ninety-nine hundredths" of the population, the work-ing class. An English writer of genius with knowledge of the working class was no doubt rare and notable in those pre-war days, and Lawrence's early works are full of details of the lives of miners and their families. But Lawrence, we now know, considered not class but the man-woman relationship the "great relationship of humanity," all others being subsidiary. Because we know that, know of Lawrence's notoriety for describing sexual relations, know his later works in which sexual relations are the major or basic concern—and perhaps because of the emphasis on sex in our own time—in reading "Odour of Chrysanthemums" we focus our attention less on the picture of the working class than on the strange relationship between the Bateses. The class element is still in the story, but the context of Lawrence's other works and utterances highlights this other human relationship.

Though Ford stressed Lawrence's power of observation in terms of the outside of things, he does say that "this fellow . . . is going to write whatever he writes about from the inside." It is not just Lawrence's powers of observation but his penetration to the inside of his characters' beings, to the shockingly original but convincing motives and feelings he finds there, and his insight into relationships, particularly love relationships, that mark his best work. Unfortunately, there is not space here to represent his more positive, fully developed, and explicit incarnations of man-woman love, found particularly in his novels *Women in Love* (1920) and *Lady Chatterley's Lover*. We can briefly indicate, however, what woman-man love is not in "Odour of Chrysanthemums" and what parent-child love is not in "The Rocking-Horse Winner":

> . . . when her children were present, she always felt the center of her heart go hard. This troubled her, and in her manner she was all the more gentle and anxious for her children, as if she loved them very much. Only she herself knew that at the center of her heart was a hard little place that could not feel love, no, not for anybody. Everybody else said of her: "She is such a good mother. She adores her children." Only she herself, and her children themselves, knew it was not so.
>
> (Par. 1)

In this chapter we have also included two of Flannery O'Connor's stories, both from her posthumous volume, *Everything That Rises Must Converge*, and so representative at least of the final years of her brief career. (She died at thirty-nine, having published some thirty-one stories, two novels, essays, and reviews.) The title story of that final volume is perhaps the more characteristic, for O'Connor frequently turned her piercingly accurate vision on the middle-aged and elderly, especially women, and on the Southern. Both these stories center, as many of her others do, on a sudden revelation of a truth about the self, shedding a new and unflattering light on one's attitudes, behaviors, beliefs. The exposure often involves snobbery, racism, or self-righteousness, often in false religious or falsely humanistic form. The first two are exemplified in "Everything That Rises Must Converge," self-righteousness and the falsely humanistic in "The Lame Shall Enter First." Like Lawrence, O'Connor has a keen eye for realistic detail and for her characters' self-deception. Violence is often in or near the surface of her fiction; as in Faulkner, it is used to shake up the reader and make him or her look beyond the conventional and the ordinary into a kind of truth, often an uncomfortable truth that lies within. Though O'Connor is a deeply religious and serious writer, her stories are replete with irony and wit, and are sometimes downright funny. Indeed, as you will see, she is not above using comic pratfalls seriously.

The central, sometimes obsessive concerns and assumptions that permeate an author's work not only relate the individual stories to each other, mutually illuminating and enriching them, but they also serve as the author's trademark. It is not difficult to recognize or even parody a story by Lawrence or O'Connor.

Embodying these larger concerns and underlying such larger structures as plot, focus, and voice are the basic characteristics of the author's language, such as **diction,** the choice and use of words; sentence structure; **rhetorical tropes,** figures of thought and speech; **imagery;** and **rhythm**—in other words, the author's **style.**

Perhaps because of the uniqueness of style, the vocabulary for discussing stylistic elements is not very precise or accessible. We can broadly characterize diction as **formal** ("The Cask of Amontillado") or **informal** (most of the stories in this collection), and within the broad term **informal** we can identify a level of language that approximates the speech of ordinary people and call it **colloquial** ("My Man Bovanne"). But to characterize precisely an author's diction so that it adequately describes his or her work and marks it off from the works of contemporaries is a very difficult task indeed. We can note Henry James's long sentences, but it is hard to get much definition in the stylistic fingerprint of an author merely by measuring the lengths of sentences or tabulating connectives (though these qualities no doubt do subliminally contribute to the effect of the works on readers and do help them identify an author's work).

Diction and sentence structure contribute to the **tone** of a work, or the implied attitude or stance of the author toward the characters and events, an aspect somewhat analogous to tone of voice. When what is being said and the tone are consistent, it is difficult to separate one from the other; when there seems to be a discrepancy, we have some words that are useful to describe the difference. If the language seems exaggerated, we call it **overstatement.** Sometimes it will be the narrator, sometimes a character, who uses language so intensive or exaggerated that we must read it at a discount, as it were, and judge the speaker's accuracy or honesty in the process. When Julian's mother, in "Everything That Rises Must Converge," says, " 'I've always had a great deal of respect for my colored friends. . . . I'd do anything in the world for them . . .' " (par. 32), we know she is protesting too much, exaggerating, and we see her racism through or underneath her language. When Hazel, in "My Man Bovanne," says that Bovanne "changes the lock on my door when my men friends get messy" (par. 3), we know that "messy" does not quite cover the actions of the men friends. She is indulging in a bit of obvious **understatement**. When a word or expression carries not only its literal meaning, but for the speaker has a different meaning we have an example of **verbal irony**. When Fortunato says, "I shall not die of a cough," Montresor's "True—true" may seem reassuring but we learn later in the story why it is both accurate and ominous. There are also nonverbal forms of irony, the most common of which is **dramatic irony**, in which a character holds a position or has an expectation that is reversed or fulfilled in an unexpected way. Knowing her husband's habit of drinking himself into unconsciousness, Elizabeth Bates expects him to be brought home like a log. How is her expectation fulfilled? She had also said bitterly, "But he needn't come rolling in here in his pit-dirt, for *I* won't wash him," and yet she does. Why is her determination altered? As you read through, or look back over this story, watch for other reversed or unexpectedly fulfilled expectations.

Another, highly emphasized element of style is **imagery**. In its broadest sense imagery includes any sensory detail or evocation in a work. Note how much more imagery in that sense we find in "The Old People" than in, say, "The Zebra Storyteller". Imagery in this broad sense, however, is so prevalent in literature that it would take exhaustive statistics to differentiate styles by counting the number of sensory elements per hundred or thousand words, categorizing the images as primarily visual, tactile, etc. In a more restricted sense imagery refers to figurative language (see Chapter 5 on symbols), particularly that which defines an abstraction or any emotional or psychological state with a sensory comparison. The opening paragraph of "Odour of Chrysanthemums" illustrates the broader definition of imagery, and this passage from later in the same story may represent the figurative sense: "Life with its smoky burning gone from him, had left him apart. . . . In her womb was ice of fear. . . ."

We might say that if an author's vision gives us his or her profile, the style gives us a fingerprint—though the fingerprint is unique and definitive, it is also harder to come by than a glimpse of a profile. Ultimately, however, vision and style are less distinguishable from each other than the profile-fingerprint image suggests. For vision and style, just like history and structure, do more than interact: they are inextricably fused or compounded. Let us look back at the Ford passage. He says this of "the gorse, which still flickered indistinctly in the raw afternoon" (though he misquotes it slightly and rather loosely calls it a phrase):

. . .Good too, distinctly good. This is the just-sufficient observation of Nature that gives you, in a single phrase, landscape, time of day, weather, season.

Is this vision or style? The observation of Nature is clearly vision, but expressing that vision economically, tautly, is style. The two merge.

Whatever else this passage is, it is vintage, typical Lawrence. Perhaps it would take more than just these ten words, but surely in a paragraph or two we know we're in the fictional world that he perceived and that he embodied in his stories, novels, and poems in a language of his own created out of that language we share.

effect of foreshadowing

characterization of Gildilar

THE AUTHOR'S WORK A Glossary

colloquial diction: level of language or vocabulary that is *informal* in that it is the language of ordinary people but tends to imitate or suggest ordinary spoken rather than written language.

diction: choice of words; often generally characterized as *formal, informal,* or *colloquial*; an aspect of *style*

dramatic irony: the unexpected fulfillment or reversal of a character's expectations

formal diction: large, sophisticated, and traditional vocabulary

imagery: broadly thought of, the visual descriptions, or even any sensory impressions generated, in a work, but more narrowly and usually, the figurative language, including *metaphors, similes, analogies* (see *Symbols: A Glossary*, p. 183); an aspect of *style*

informal diction: level of language or vocabulary that characterizes the written language of ordinary people

overstatement: language that is so intense or exaggerated it must be read "at a discount," as meaning less than it literally states

rhetorical tropes: figures of thought or speech; part of *style*

rhythm: the pattern of sound pulsations in the voice as one reads (or as the sound is imagined in the mind); an aspect of *style*

style: the basic characteristics of the language of an author (or an age); while sometimes considered the manner as opposed to the matter, as "ornament," it is now more often seen as organic or fused, with the substance, manner, and matter being as closely related as body and soul; indeed, much recent criticism suggests that there is no "meaning" prior to language, that to think or mean is to think or mean in language itself.

tone: the implied attitude or stance of the author toward the characters and events, somewhat like "tone of voice"

understatement: language that obviously underrates something or portrays it as lesser than it is usually thought to be

verbal irony: a word or expression that carries not only its literal meaning but for the speaker has a different, sometimes even an opposite, meaning

figurative language

motif of light & dark (pattern of imagery)

Theme sound & silence

[handwritten annotations: straightforward chronologically told narrative / conflict starts out as tension of waiting for her husband, but by end conflict changes into more philosophical psychological emotional conflict to come]

D. H. LAWRENCE

Odour of Chrysanthemums

[handwritten: broad / note how the exposition begins w/ 3rd person pt. of view, then gradually narrows to EB's]

I

The small locomotive engine, Number 4, came clanking, stumbling down from Selston with seven full waggons. It appeared round the corner with loud threats of speed, but the colt that it startled from among the gorse, which still flickered indistinctly in the raw afternoon, outdistanced it at a canter. A woman, walking up the railway line to Underwood, drew back into the hedge, held her basket aside, and watched the footplate of the engine advancing. The trucks thumped heavily past, one by one, with slow inevitable movement, as she stood insignificantly trapped between the jolting black waggons and the hedge; then they curved away towards the coppice where the withered oak leaves dropped noiselessly, while the birds, pulling at the scarlet hips beside the track, made off into the dusk that had already crept into the spinney. In the open, the smoke from the engine sank and cleaved to the rough grass. The fields were dreary and forsaken, and in the marshy strip that led to the whimsey, a reedy pit-pond, the fowls had already abandoned their run among the alders, to roost in the tarred fowl-house. The pit-bank loomed up beyond the pond, flames like red sores licking its ashy sides, in the afternoon's stagnant light. Just beyond rose the tapering chimneys and the clumsy black headstocks of Brinsley Colliery. The two wheels were spinning fast up against the sky, and the winding-engine rapped out its little spasms. The miners were being turned up.

The engine whistled as it came into the wide bay of railway lines beside the colliery, where rows of trucks stood in harbour.

Miners, single, trailing and in groups, passed like shadows diverging home. At the edge of the ribbed level of sidings squat a low cottage, three steps down from the cinder track. A large bony vine clutched at the house, as if to claw down the tiled roof. Round the bricked yard grew a few wintry primroses. Beyond, the long garden sloped down to a bush-covered brook course. There were some twiggy apple trees, winter-crack trees, and ragged cabbages. Beside the path hung dishevelled pink chrysanthemums, like pink cloths hung on bushes. A woman came stooping out of the felt-covered fowl-house, half-way down the garden. She closed and padlocked the door, then drew herself erect, having brushed some bits from her white apron.

She was a tall woman of imperious mien, handsome, with definite black eyebrows. Her smooth black hair was parted exactly. For a few moments she stood steadily watching the miners as they passed along the railway: then she turned towards the brook course. Her face was calm and set, her mouth was closed with disillusionment. After a moment she called:

"John!" There was no answer. She waited, and then said distinctly:
"Where are you?"

5

[handwritten margin notes: look at diction; mood/tone set up in 1st ¶; rhetorical tropes; narrows focus; isolation + alienation of marriage]

"Here!" replied a child's sulky voice from among the bushes. The woman looked piercingly through the dusk.

"Are you at that brook?" she asked sternly.

For answer the child showed himself before the raspberry-canes that rose like whips. He was a small, sturdy boy of five. He stood quite still, defiantly.

"Oh!" said the mother, conciliated. "I thought you were down at that wet brook—and you remember what I told you—"

The boy did not move or answer.

"Come, come on in," she said more gently, "it's getting dark. There's your grandfather's engine coming down the line!"

The lad advanced slowly, with resentful, taciturn movement. He was dressed in trousers and waistcoat of cloth that was too thick and hard for the size of the garments. They were evidently cut down from a man's clothes.

As they went slowly towards the house he tore at the ragged wisps of chrysanthemums and dropped the petals in handfuls along the path.

"Don't do that—it does look nasty," said his mother. He refrained, and she, suddenly pitiful, broke off a twig with three or four wan flowers and held them against her face. When mother and son reached the yard her hand hesitated, and instead of laying the flower aside, she pushed it in her apron-band. The mother and son stood at the foot of the three steps looking across the bay of lines at the passing home of the miners. The trundle of the small train was imminent. Suddenly the engine loomed past the house and came to a stop opposite the gate.

The engine-driver, a short man with round grey beard, leaned out of the cab high above the woman.

"Have you got a cup of tea?" he said in a cheery, hearty fashion.

It was her father. She went in, saying she would mash.[1] Directly, she returned.

"I didn't come to see you on Sunday," began the little grey-bearded man.

"I didn't expect you," said his daughter.

The engine-driver winced; then, reassuming his cheery, airy manner, he said:

"Oh, have you heard then? Well, and what do you think———?"

"I think it is soon enough," she replied.

At her brief censure the little man made an impatient gesture, and said coaxingly, yet with dangerous coldness:

"Well, what's a man to do? It's no sort of life for a man of my years, to sit at my own hearth like a stranger. And if I'm going to marry again it may as well be soon as late—what does it matter to anybody?"

The woman did not reply, but turned and went into the house. The man in the engine-cab stood assertive, till she returned with a cup of tea and a piece of bread and butter on a plate. She went up the steps and stood near the footplate of the hissing engine.

"You needn't 'a' brought me bread an' butter," said her father. "But a cup of tea"—he sipped appreciatively—"it's very nice." He sipped for a moment or two,

1. Prepare (tea).

then: "I hear as Walter's got another bout on," he said.

"When hasn't he?" said the woman bitterly.

"I heered tell of him in the 'Lord Nelson'[2] braggin' as he was going to spend that b—— afore he went: half a sovereign[3] that was."

"When?" asked the woman.

"A' Sat'day night—I know that's true."

"Very likely," she laughed bitterly. "He gives me twenty-three shillings."

"Aye, it's a nice thing, when a man can do nothing with his money but make a beast of himself!" said the grey-whiskered man. The woman turned her head away. Her father swallowed the last of his tea and handed her the cup.

"Aye," he sighed, wiping his mouth. "It's a settler, it is——"

He put his hand on the lever. The little engine strained and groaned, and the train rumbled towards the crossing. The woman again looked across the metals. Darkness was settling over the spaces of the railway and trucks: the miners, in grey sombre groups, were still passing home. The winding-engine pulsed hurriedly, with brief pauses. Elizabeth Bates looked at the dreary flow of men, then she went indoors. Her husband did not come.

The kitchen was small and full of firelight; red coals piled glowing up the chimney mouth. All the life of the room seemed in the white, warm hearth and the steel fender reflecting the red fire. The cloth was laid for tea; cups glinted in the shadows. At the back, where the lowest stairs protruded into the room, the boy sat struggling with a knife and a piece of white wood. He was almost hidden in the shadow. It was half-past four. They had but to await the father's coming to begin tea. As the mother watched her son's sullen little struggle with the wood, she saw herself in his silence and pertinacity; she saw the father in her child's indifference to all but himself. She seemed to be occupied by her husband. He had probably gone past his home, slunk past his own door, to drink before he came in, while his dinner spoiled and wasted in waiting. She glanced at the clock, then took the potatoes to strain them in the yard. The garden and fields beyond the brook were closed in uncertain darkness. When she rose with the saucepan, leaving the drain steaming into the night behind her, she saw the yellow lamps were lit along the high road that went up the hill away beyond the space of the railway lines and the field.

Then again she watched the men trooping home, fewer now and fewer.

Indoors the fire was sinking and the room was dark red. The woman put her saucepan on the hob, and set a batter pudding near the mouth of the oven. Then she stood unmoving. Directly, gratefully, came quick young steps to the door. Someone hung on the latch a moment, then a little girl entered and began pulling off her outdoor things, dragging a mass of curls, just ripening from gold to brown, over her eyes with her hat.

Her mother chid her for coming late from school, and said she would have to keep her at home the dark winter days.

---

2. A public house, pub.   **3.** A sovereign was about half a week's wage; there are 20 shillings (see below) to the pound.

40 "Why, mother, it's hardly a bit dark yet. The lamp's not lighted, and my father's not home."

"No, he isn't. But it's a quarter to five! Did you see anything of him?"

The child became serious. She looked at her mother with large, wistful blue eyes.

"No, mother, I've never seen him. Why? Has he come up an' gone past, to Old Brinsley? He hasn't, mother, 'cos I never saw him."

"He'd watch that," said the mother bitterly, "he'd take care as you didn't see him. But you may depend upon it, he's seated in the 'Prince o' Wales.' He wouldn't be this late."

45 The girl looked at her mother piteously.

"Let's have our teas, mother, should we?" said she.

The mother called John to table. She opened the door once more and looked out across the darkness of the lines. All was deserted: she could not hear the winding-engines.

"Perhaps," she said to herself, "he's stopped to get some ripping[4] done."

They sat down to tea. John, at the end of the table near the door, was almost lost in the darkness. Their faces were hidden from each other. The girl crouched against the fender slowly moving a thick piece of bread before the fire. The lad, his face a dusky mark on the shadow, sat watching her who was transfigured in the red glow.

"I do think it's beautiful to look in the fire," said the child.

"Do you?" said her mother. "Why?"

"It's so red, and full of little caves—and it feels so nice, and you can fair smell it."

"It'll want mending directly," replied her mother, "and then if your father comes he'll carry on and say there never is a fire when a man comes home sweating from the pit.—A public-house is always warm enough."

There was silence till the boy said complainingly: "Make haste, our Annie."

55 "Well, I am doing! I can't make the fire do it no faster, can I?"

"She keeps wafflin'[5] it about so's to make 'er slow," grumbled the boy.

"Don't have such an evil imagination, child," replied the mother.

Soon the room was busy in the darkness with the crisp sound of crunching. The mother ate very little. She drank her tea determinedly, and sat thinking. When she rose her anger was evident in the stern unbending of her head. She looked at the pudding in the fender, and broke out:

"It is a scandalous thing as a man can't even come home to his dinner! If it's crozzled[6] up to a cinder I don't see why I should care. Past his very door he goes to get to a public-house, and here I sit with his dinner waiting for him——"

60 She went out. As she dropped piece after piece of coal on the red fire, the shadows fell on the walls, till the room was almost in total darkness.

"I canna see," grumbled the invisible John. In spite of herself, the mother laughed.

---

4. Coal-mining term for taking down the roof of an underground road in order to make it higher.   5. Waving.   6. Shriveled.

"You know the way to your mouth," she said. She set the dustpan outside the door. When she came again like a shadow on the hearth, the lad repeated, complaining sulkily:

"I canna see."

"Good gracious!" cried the mother irritably, "you're as bad as your father if it's a bit dusk!"

Nevertheless she took a paper spill from a sheaf on the mantelpiece and proceeded to light the lamp that hung from the ceiling in the middle of the room. As she reached up, her figure displayed itself just rounding with maternity.

"Oh, mother——!" exclaimed the girl.

"What?" said the woman, suspended in the act of putting the lamp-glass over the flame. The copper reflector shone handsomely on her, as she stood with uplifted arm, turning to face her daughter.

"You've got a flower in your apron!" said the child, in a little rapture at this unusual event.

"Goodness me!" exclaimed the woman, relieved. "One would think the house was afire." She replaced the glass and waited a moment before turning up the wick. A pale shadow was seen floating vaguely on the floor.

"Let me smell!" said the child, still rapturously, coming forward and putting her face to her mother's waist.

"Go along, silly!" said the mother, turning up the lamp. The light revealed their suspense so that the woman felt it almost unbearable. Annie was still bending at her waist. Irritably, the mother took the flowers out from her apron-band.

"Oh, mother—don't take them out!" Annie cried, catching her hand and trying to replace the sprig.

"Such nonsense!" said the mother, turning away. The child put the pale chrysanthemums to her lips, murmuring:

"Don't they smell beautiful!"

Her mother gave a short laugh.

"No," she said, "not to me. It was chrysanthemums when I married him, and chrysanthemums when you were born, and the first time they ever brought him home drunk, he'd got brown chrysanthemums in his button-hole."

She looked at the children. Their eyes and their parted lips were wondering. The mother sat rocking in silence for some time. Then she looked at the clock.

"Twenty minutes to six!" In a tone of fine bitter carelessness she continued: "Eh, he'll not come now till they bring him. There he'll stick! But he needn't come rolling in here in his pit-dirt, for I won't wash him. He can lie on the floor——Eh, what a fool I've been, what a fool! And this is what I came here for, to this dirty hole, rats and all, for him to slink past his very door. Twice last week—he's begun now——"

She silenced herself, and rose to clear the table.

While for an hour or more the children played, subduedly intent, fertile of imagination, united in fear of the mother's wrath, and in dread of their father's home-coming, Mrs. Bates sat in her rocking-chair making a "singlet" of thick cream-coloured flannel, which gave a dull wounded sound as she tore off the grey edge. She worked at her sewing with energy, listening to the children, and her anger wearied itself, lay down to rest, opening its eyes from time to time and steadily watching, its ears raised to listen. Sometimes even her anger quailed and shrank, and the mother suspended her sewing, tracing the footsteps that thudded along the sleepers outside; she would lift her head sharply to bid the children "hush," but she recovered herself in time, and the footsteps went past the gate, and the children were not flung out of their playworld.

But at last Annie sighed, and gave in. She glanced at her waggon of slippers, and loathed the game. She turned plaintively to her mother.

"Mother!"—but she was inarticulate.

John crept out like a frog from under the sofa. His mother glanced up.

"Yes," she said, "just look at those shirtsleeves!"

The boy held them out to survey them, saying nothing. Then somebody called in a hoarse voice away down the line, and suspense bristled in the room, till two people had gone by outside, talking.

"It is time for bed," said the mother.

"My father hasn't come," wailed Annie plaintively. But her mother was primed with courage.

"Never mind. They'll bring him when he does come—like a log." She meant there would be no scene. "And he may sleep on the floor till he wakes himself. I know he'll not go to work tomorrow after this!"

The children had their hands and faces wiped with a flannel.[7] They were very quiet. When they had put on their nightdresses, they said their prayers, the boy mumbling. The mother looked down at them, at the brown silken bush of intertwining curls in the nape of the girl's neck, at the little black head of the lad, and her heart burst with anger at their father who caused all three such distress. The children hid their faces in her skirts for comfort.

When Mrs. Bates came down, the room was strangely empty, with a tension of expectancy. She took up her sewing and stitched for some time without raising her head. Meantime her anger was tinged with fear.

II

The clock struck eight and she rose suddenly, dropping her sewing on her chair. She went to the stairfoot door, opened it, listening. Then she went out, locking the door behind her.

Something scuffled in the yard, and she started though she knew it was only the rats with which the place was overrun. The night was very dark. In the great bay of railway lines, bulked with trucks, there was no trace of light, only away back she could see a few yellow lamps at the pit-top, and the red smear of the burning pit-bank on the night. She hurried along the edge of the track, then, crossing the converging lines, came to the stile by the white gates, whence she emerged on the road. Then the fear which had led her shrank. People were walking up to New Brinsley; she saw the lights in the houses; twenty yards further

7. Washrag.

on were the broad windows of the "Prince of Wales," very warm and bright, and the loud voices of men could be heard distinctly. What a fool she had been to imagine that anything had happened to him! He was merely drinking over there at the "Prince of Wales." She faltered. She had never yet been to fetch him, and she never would go. So she continued her walk towards the long straggling line of houses, standing blank on the highway. She entered a passage between the dwellings.

"Mr. Rigley?—Yes! Did you want him? No, he's not in at this minute."

The raw-boned woman leaned forward from her dark scullery and peered at the other, upon whom fell a dim light through the blind of the kitchen window.

"Is it Mrs. Bates?" she asked in a tone tinged with respect.   95

"Yes. I wondered if your Master was at home. Mine hasn't come yet."

" 'Asn't 'e! Oh, Jack's been 'ome an 'ad 'is dinner an' gone out. 'E's just gone for 'alf an hour afore bedtime. Did you call at the 'Prince of Wales'?"

"No——"

"No, you didn't like——! It's not very nice." The other woman was indulgent. There was an awkward pause. "Jack never said nothink about—about your Mester," she said.

"No!—I expect he's stuck in there!"   100

Elizabeth Bates said this bitterly, and with recklessness. She knew that the woman across the yard was standing at her door listening, but she did not care. As she turned:

"Stop a minute! I'll just go an' ask Jack if 'e knows anythink," said Mrs. Rigley.

"Oh, no—I wouldn't like to put—!"

"Yes, I will, if you will just step inside an' see as th' childer doesn't come downstairs and set theirselves afire."

Elizabeth Bates, murmuring a remonstrance, stepped inside. The other woman   105
apologized for the state of the room.

The kitchen needed apology. There were little frocks and trousers and childish undergarments on the squab[8] and on the floor, and a litter of playthings everywhere. On the black American cloth[9] of the table were pieces of bread and cake, crusts, slops, and a teapot with cold tea.

"Eh, ours is just as bad," said Elizabeth Bates, looking at the woman, not at the house. Mrs. Rigley put a shawl over her head and hurried out, saying:

"I shanna be a minute."

The other sat, noting with faint disapproval the general untidiness of the room. Then she fell to counting the shoes of various sizes scattered over the floor. There were twelve. She sighed and said to herself, "No wonder!"—glancing at the litter. There came the scratching of two pairs of feet on the yard, and the Rigleys entered. Elizabeth Bates rose. Rigley was a big man, with very large bones. His head looked particularly bony. Across his temple was a blue scar, caused by a wound got in the pit, a wound in which the coal-dust remained blue like tattooing.

8. Sofa.   9. Enameled oilcloth.

" 'Asna 'e come whoam yit?" asked the man, without any form of greeting, but with deference and sympathy. "I couldna say wheer he is—'e's non ower theer!"—he jerked his head to signify the "Prince of Wales."

" 'E's 'appen[1] gone up to th' 'Yew,' " said Mrs. Rigley.

There was another pause. Rigley had evidently something to get off his mind: "Ah left 'im finishin' a stint," he began. "Loose-all[2] 'ad bin gone about ten minutes when we com'n away, an' I shouted, 'Are ter comin', Walt?' an' 'e said 'Go on, Ah shanna be but a 'ef a minnit,' so we com'n ter th' bottom, me an' Browers, thinkin' as 'e wor just behint, an' 'ud come up i' th' next bantle[3]——"

He stood perplexed, as if answering a charge of deserting his mate. Elizabeth Bates, now again certain of disaster, hastened to reassure him:

"I expect 'e's gone up to th' 'Yew Tree,' as you say. It's not the first time. I've fretted myself into a fever before now. He'll come home when they carry him."

"Ay, isn't it too bad!" deplored the other woman.

"I'll just step up to Dick's an' see if 'e *is* theer," offered the man, afraid of appearing alarmed, afraid of taking liberties.

"Oh, I wouldn't think of bothering you that far," said Elizabeth Bates, with emphasis, but he knew she was glad of his offer.

As they stumbled up the entry, Elizabeth Bates heard Rigley's wife run across the yard and open her neighbour's door. At this, suddenly all the blood in her body seemed to switch away from her heart.

"Mind!" warned Rigley. "Ah've said many a time as Ah'd fill up them ruts in this entry, sumb'dy 'll be breakin' their legs yit."

She recovered herself and walked quickly along with the miner.

"I don't like leaving the children in bed, and nobody in the house," she said.

"No, you dunna!" he replied courteously. They were soon at the gate of the cottage.

"Well, I shanna be many minnits. Dunna you be frettin' now, 'e'll be all right," said the butty.[4]

"Thank you very much, Mr. Rigley," she replied.

"You're welcome!" he stammered, moving away. "I shanna be many minnits."

The house was quiet. Elizabeth Bates took off her hat and shawl, and rolled back the rug. When she had finished, she sat down. It was a few minutes past nine. She was startled by the rapid chuff of the winding-engine at the pit, and the sharp whirr of the brakes on the rope as it descended. Again she felt the painful sweep of her blood, and she put her hand to her side, saying aloud, "Good gracious!—it's only the nine o'clock deputy going down," rebuking herself.

She sat still, listening. Half an hour of this, and she was wearied out.

"What am I working up like this for?" she said pitiably to herself, "I s'll only be doing myself some damage."

---

1. Perhaps.   2. Signal to quit work and come to the surface.   3. An open seat or car of the lift or elevator that takes the miners to the surface.   4. Buddy, fellow worker.

She took out her sewing again.

At a quarter to ten there were footsteps. One person! She watched for the door to open. It was an elderly woman, in a black bonnet and a black woollen shawl—his mother. She was about sixty years old, pale, with blue eyes, and her face all wrinkled and lamentable. She shut the door and turned to her daughter-in-law peevishly.

"Eh, Lizzie, whatever shall we do, whatever shall we do!" she cried.

Elizabeth drew back a little, sharply.

"What is it, mother?" she said.

The elder woman seated herself on the sofa.

"I don't know, child, I can't tell you!"—she shook her head slowly. Elizabeth sat watching her, anxious and vexed.

"I don't know," replied the grandmother, sighing very deeply. "There's no end to my troubles, there isn't. The things I've gone through, I'm sure it's enough ——!" She wept without wiping her eyes, the tears running.

"But, mother," interrupted Elizabeth, "what do you mean? What is it?"

The grandmother slowly wiped her eyes. The fountains of her tears were stopped by Elizabeth's directness. She wiped her eyes slowly.

"Poor child! Eh, you poor thing!" she moaned. "I don't know what we're going to do, I don't—and you as you are—it's a thing, it is indeed!"

Elizabeth waited.

"Is he dead?" she asked, and at the words her heart swung violently, though she felt a slight flush of shame at the ultimate extravagance of the question. Her words sufficiently frightened the old lady, almost brought her to herself.

"Don't say so, Elizabeth! We'll hope it's not as bad as that; no, may the Lord spare us that, Elizabeth. Jack Rigley came just as I was sittin' down to a glass afore going to bed, an' 'e said, ' 'Appen you'll go down th' line, Mrs. Bates. Walt's had an accident. 'Appen you'll go an' sit wi' 'er till we can get him home.' I hadn't time to ask him a word afore he was gone. An' I put my bonnet on an' come straight down, Lizzie. I thought to myself, 'Eh, that poor blessed child, if anybody should come an' tell her of a sudden, there's no knowin'; what'll 'appen to 'er.' You mustn't let it upset you, Lizzie—or you know what to expect. How long is it, six months—or is it five, Lizzie? Ay!"—the old woman shook her head—"time slips on, it slips on! Ay!"

Elizabeth's thoughts were busy elsewhere. If he was killed—would she be able to manage on the little pension and what she could earn?—she counted up rapidly. If he was hurt—they wouldn't take him to the hospital—how tiresome he would be to nurse!—but perhaps she'd be able to get him away from the drink and his hateful ways. She would—while he was ill. The tears offered to come to her eyes at the picture. But what sentimental luxury was this she was beginning?—She turned to consider the children. At any rate she was absolutely necessary for them. They were her business.

"Ay!" repeated the old woman, "it seems but a week or two since he brought me his first wages. Ay—he was a good lad, Elizabeth, he was, in his way. I don't know why he got to be such a trouble, I don't. He was a happy lad at home, only full of spirits. But there's no mistake he's been a handful of trouble, he has! I hope the Lord'll spare him to mend his ways. I hope so, I hope so. You've had a sight o' trouble with him, Elizabeth, you have indeed. But he was a jolly enough lad wi' me, he was, I can assure you. I don't know how it is. . . ."

The old woman continued to muse aloud, a monotonous irritating sound, while Elizabeth thought concentratedly, startled once, when she heard the winding-engine chuff quickly, and the brakes skirr with a shriek. Then she heard the engine more slowly, and the brakes made no sound. The old woman did not notice. Elizabeth waited in suspense. The mother-in-law talked, with lapses into silence.

"But he wasn't your son, Lizzie, an' it makes a difference. Whatever he was, I remember him when he was little, an' I learned to understand him and to make allowances. You've got to make allowances for them—"

It was half-past ten, and the old woman was saying: "But it's trouble from beginning to end; you're never too old for trouble, never too old for that——" when the gate banged back, and there were heavy feet on the steps.

"I'll go, Lizzie, let me go," cried the old woman, rising. But Elizabeth was at the door. It was a man in pit-clothes.

"They're bringin' 'im, Missis," he said. Elizabeth's heart halted a moment. Then it surged on again, almost suffocating her.

"Is he—is it bad?" she asked.

The man turned away, looking at the darkness:

"The doctor says 'e'd been dead hours. 'E saw 'im i' th' lamp-cabin."

The old woman, who stood just behind Elizabeth, dropped into a chair and folded her hands, crying: "Oh, my boy, my boy!"

"Hush!" said Elizabeth, with a sharp twitch of a frown. "Be still, mother, don't waken th' children: I wouldn't have them down for anything!"

The old woman moaned softly, rocking herself. The man was drawing away. Elizabeth took a step forward.

"How was it?" she asked.

"Well, I couldn't say for sure," the man replied, very ill at ease. " 'E wor finishin' a stint an' th' butties 'ad gone, an' a lot o' stuff come down atop 'n 'im."

"And crushed him?" cried the widow, with a shudder.

"No," said the man, "it fell at th' back of 'im. 'E wor under th' face, an' it niver touched 'im. It shut 'im in. It seems 'e wor smothered."

Elizabeth shrank back. She heard the old woman behind her cry:

"What?—what did 'e say it was?"

The man replied, more loudly: "'E wor smothered!"

Then the old woman wailed aloud, and this relieved Elizabeth.

"Oh, mother," she said, putting her hands on the old woman, "don't waken th' children, don't waken th' children."

She wept a little, unknowing, while the old mother rocked herself and moaned. Elizabeth remembered that they were bringing him home, and she must be ready. "They'll lay him in the parlour," she said to herself, standing a moment pale and perplexed.

Then she lighted a candle and went into the tiny room. The air was cold and damp, but she could not make a fire, there was no fireplace. She set down the candle and looked round. The candlelight glittered on the lustre-glasses,[5] on the two vases that held some of the pink chrysanthemums, and on the dark mahogany. There was a cold, deathly smell of chrysanthemums in the room. Elizabeth stood looking at the flowers. She turned away, and calculated whether there would be room to lay him on the floor, between the couch and the chiffonier. She pushed the chairs aside. There would be room to lay him down and to step round him. Then she fetched the old red tablecloth, and another old cloth, spreading them down to save her bit of carpet. She shivered on leaving the parlour; so, from the dresser-drawer she took a clean shirt and put it at the fire to air. All the time her mother-in-law was rocking herself in the chair and moaning.

"You'll have to move from there, mother," said Elizabeth. "They'll be bringing him in. Come in the rocker."

The old mother rose mechanically, and seated herself by the fire, continuing to lament. Elizabeth went into the pantry for another candle, and there, in the little penthouse[6] under the naked tiles, she heard them coming. She stood still in the pantry doorway, listening. She heard them pass the end of the house, and come awkwardly down the three steps, a jumble of shuffling footsteps and muttering voices. The old woman was silent. The men were in the yard.

Then Elizabeth heard Matthews, the manager of the pit, say: "You go in first, Jim. Mind!"

170

The door came open, and the two women saw a collier backing into the room, holding one end of a stretcher, on which they could see the nailed pitboots of the dead man. The two carriers halted, the man at the head stooping to the lintel of the door.

"Wheer will you have him?" asked the manager, a short, white-bearded man.

Elizabeth roused herself and came from the pantry carrying the unlighted candle.

"In the parlour," she said.

"In there, Jim!" pointed the manager, and the carriers backed round into the tiny room. The coat with which they had covered the body fell off as they awkwardly turned through the two doorways, and the women saw their man, naked to the waist, lying stripped for work. The old woman began to moan in a low voice of horror.

"Lay th' stretcher at th' side," snapped the manager, "an' put 'im on th' cloths. Mind now, mind! Look you now——!"

One of the men had knocked off a vase of chrysanthemums. He stared awkwardly, then they set down the stretcher. Elizabeth did not look at her husband. As soon as she could get in the room, she went and picked up the broken vase and the flowers.

---

5. Glass pendants around the edge of an ornamental vase.   6. Structure, usually with a sloping roof, attached to house.

"Wait a minute!" she said.

The three men waited in silence while she mopped up the water with a duster.

"Eh, what a job, what a job, to be sure!" the manager was saying, rubbing his brow with trouble and perplexity. "Never knew such a thing in my life, never! He'd no business to ha' been left. I never knew such a thing in my life! Fell over him clean as a whistle, an' shut him in. Not four foot of space, there wasn't—yet it scarce bruised him."

He looked down at the dead man, lying prone, half naked, all grimed with coal-dust.

" ' 'Sphyxiated,' the doctor said. It *is* the most terrible job I've ever known. Seems as if it was done o' purpose. Clean over him, an' shut 'im in, like a mouse-trap"—he made a sharp, descending gesture with his hand.

The colliers standing by jerked aside their heads in hopeless comment.

The horror of the thing bristled upon them all.

Then they heard the girl's voice upstairs calling shrilly: "Mother, mother—who is it? Mother, who is it?"

Elizabeth hurried to the foot of the stairs and opened the door:

"Go to sleep!" she commanded sharply. "What are you shouting about? Go to sleep at once—there's nothing——"

Then she began to mount the stairs. They could hear her on the boards, and on the plaster floor of the little bedroom. They could hear her distinctly:

"What's the matter now?—what's the matter with you, silly thing?"—her voice was much agitated, with an unreal gentleness.

"I thought it was some men come," said the plaintive voice of the child. "Has he come?"

"Yes, they've brought him. There's nothing to make a fuss about. Go to sleep now, like a good child."

They could hear her voice in the bedroom, they waited whilst she covered the children under the bedclothes.

"Is he drunk?" asked the girl, timidly, faintly.

"No! No—he's not! He's—he's asleep."

"Is he asleep downstairs?"

"Yes—and don't make a noise."

There was silence for a moment, then the men heard the frightened child again:

"What's that noise?"

"It's nothing, I tell you, what are you bothering for?"

The noise was the grandmother moaning. She was oblivious of everything, sitting on her chair rocking and moaning. The manager put his hand on her arm and bade her "Sh-sh!!"

The old woman opened her eyes and looked at him. She was shocked by this interruption, and seemed to wonder.

"What time is it?"—the plaintive thin voice of the child, sinking back unhappily into sleep, asked this last question.

"Ten o'clock," answered the mother more softly. Then she must have bent down and kissed the children.

Matthews beckoned to the men to come away. They put on their caps, and took up the stretcher. Stepping over the body, they tiptoed out of the house. None of them spoke till they were far from the wakeful children.

When Elizabeth came down she found her mother alone on the parlour floor, leaning over the dead man, the tears dropping on him.

"We must lay him out," the wife said. She put on the kettle, then returning knelt at the feet, and began to unfasten the knotted leather laces. The room was clammy and dim with only one candle, so that she had to bend her face almost to the floor. At last she got off the heavy boots and put them away.

"You must help me now," she whispered to the old woman. Together they stripped the man.

When they arose, saw him lying in the naïve dignity of death, the women stood arrested in fear and respect. For a few moments they remained still, looking down, the old mother whimpering. Elizabeth felt countermanded. She saw him, how utterly inviolable he lay in himself. She had nothing to do with him. She could not accept it. Stooping, she laid her hand on him, in claim. He was still warm, for the mine was hot where he had died. His mother had his face between her hands, and was murmuring incoherently. The old tears fell in succession as drops from wet leaves; the mother was not weeping, merely her tears flowed. Elizabeth embraced the body of her husband, with cheek and lips. She seemed to be listening, inquiring, trying to get some connection. But she could not. She was driven away. He was impregnable.

She rose, went into the kitchen, where she poured warm water into a bowl, brought soap and flannel and a soft towel.

"I must wash him," she said.

Then the old mother rose stiffly, and watched Elizabeth as she carefully washed his face, carefully brushing the big blonde moustache from his mouth with the flannel. She was afraid with a bottomless fear, so she ministered to him. The old woman, jealous, said:

"Let me wipe him!"—and she kneeled on the other side drying slowly as Elizabeth washed, her big black bonnet sometimes brushing the dark head of her daughter. They worked thus in silence for a long time. They never forgot it was death, and the touch of the man's dead body gave them strange emotions, different in each of the women; a great dread possessed them both, the mother felt the lie was given to her womb, she was denied; the wife felt the utter isolation of the human soul, the child within her was a weight apart from her.

At last it was finished. He was a man of handsome body, and his face showed no traces of drink. He was blonde, full-fleshed, with fine limbs. But he was dead.

"Bless him," whispered his mother, looking always at his face, and speaking out of sheer terror. "Dear lad—bless him!" She spoke in a faint sibilant ecstasy of fear and mother love.

Elizabeth sank down again to the floor, and put her face against his neck, and trembled and shuddered. But she had to draw away again. He was dead, and her living flesh had no place against his. A great dread and weariness held her: she was so unavailing. Her life was gone like this.

"White as milk he is, clear as a twelve-month baby, bless him, the darling!" the old mother murmured to herself. "Not a mark on him, clear and clean and white, beautiful as ever a child was made," she murmured with pride. Elizabeth kept her face hidden.

"He went peaceful, Lizzie—peaceful as sleep. Isn't he beautiful, the lamb? Ay—he must ha' made his peace, Lizzie. 'Appen he made it all right, Lizzie, shut in there. He'd have time. He wouldn't look like this if he hadn't made his peace. The lamb, the dear lamb. Eh, but he had a hearty laugh. I loved to hear it. He had the heartiest laugh, Lizzie, as a lad——"

Elizabeth looked up. The man's mouth was fallen back, slightly open under the cover of the moustache. The eyes, half shut, did not show glazed in the obscurity. Life with its smoky burning gone from him, had left him apart and utterly alien to her. And she knew what a stranger he was to her. In her womb was ice of fear, because of this separate stranger with whom she had been living as one flesh. Was this what it all meant—utter, intact separateness, obscured by heat of living? In dread she turned her face away. The fact was too deadly. There had been nothing between them, and yet they had come together, exchanging their nakedness repeatedly. Each time he had taken her, they had been two isolated beings, far apart as now. He was no more responsible than she. The child was like ice in her womb. For as she looked at the dead man, her mind, cold and detached, said clearly: "Who am I? What have I been doing? I have been fighting a husband who did not exist. *He* existed all the time. What wrong have I done? What was that I have been living with? There lies the reality, this man."—And her soul died in her for fear: she knew she had never seen him, he had never seen her, they had met in the dark and had fought in the dark, not knowing whom they met nor whom they fought. And now she saw, and turned silent in seeing. For she had been wrong. She had said he was something he was not; she had felt familiar with him. Whereas he was apart all the while, living as she never lived, feeling as she never felt.

In fear and shame she looked at his naked body, that she had known falsely. And he was the father of her children. Her soul was torn from her body and stood apart. She looked at his naked body and was ashamed, as if she had denied it. After all, it was itself. It seemed awful to her. She looked at his face, and she turned her own face to the wall. For his look was other than hers, his way was not her way. She had denied him what he was—she saw it now. She had refused him as himself.—And this had been her life, and his life.—She was grateful to death, which restored the truth. And she knew she was not dead.

And all the while her heart was bursting with grief and pity for him. What had he suffered? What stretch of horror for this helpless man! She was rigid with agony. She had not been able to help him. He had been cruelly injured, this naked man, this other being, and she could make no reparation. There were the children—but the children belonged to life. This dead man had nothing to do with them. He and she were only channels through which life had flowed to issue in the children. She was a mother—but how awful she knew it now to have

What is marriage? What is the union of a man & woman? What is parenthood? does it unite

The Rocking-Horse Winner ∇ 317

been a wife. And he, dead now, how awful he must have felt it to be a husband. She felt that in her next world he would be a stranger to her. If they met there, in the beyond, they would only be ashamed of what had been before. The children had come, for some mysterious reason, out of both of them. But the children did not unite them. Now he was dead, she knew how eternally he was apart from her, how eternally he had nothing more to do with her. She saw this episode of her life closed. They had denied each other in life. Now he had withdrawn. An anguish came over her. It was finished then: it had become hopeless between them long before he died. Yet he had been her husband. But how little!

"Have you got his shirt, 'Lizabeth?"

Elizabeth turned without answering, though she strove to weep and behave as her mother-in-law expected. But she could not, she was silenced. She went into the kitchen and returned with the garment.

"It is aired," she said, grasping the cotton shirt here and there to try. She was almost ashamed to handle him; what right had she or anyone to lay hands on him; but her touch was humble on his body. It was hard work to clothe him. He was so heavy and inert. A terrible dread gripped her all the while: that he could be so heavy and utterly inert, unresponsive, apart. The horror of the distance between them was almost too much for her—it was so infinite a gap she must look across.

At last it was finished. They covered him with a sheet and left him lying, with his face bound. And she fastened the door of the little parlour, lest the children should see what was lying there. Then, with peace sunk heavy on her heart, she went about making tidy the kitchen. She knew she submitted to life, which was her immediate master. But from death, her ultimate master, she winced with fear and shame.

nothing is really resolved. we know he's dead, but is that the end of the story - what does ending mean?

1914

D. H. LAWRENCE

The Rocking-Horse Winner

opening

There was a woman who was beautiful, who started with all the advantages, yet she had no luck. She married for love, and the love turned to dust. She had bonny children, yet she felt they had been thrust upon her, and she could not love them. They looked at her coldly, as if they were finding fault with her. And hurriedly she felt she must cover up some fault in herself. Yet what it was that she must cover up she never knew. Nevertheless, when her children were present, she always felt the centre of her heart go hard. This troubled her, and in her manner she was all the more gentle and anxious for her children, as if she loved them very much. Only she herself knew that at the centre of her heart was a hard little place that could not feel love, no, not for anybody. Everybody else said of her: "She is such a good mother. She adores her children." Only she

Comparison - how is this different from

herself, and her children themselves, knew it was not so. They read it in each other's eyes.

There were a boy and two little girls. They lived in a pleasant house, with a garden, and they had discreet servants, and felt themselves superior to anyone in the neighbourhood.

Although they lived in style, they felt always an anxiety in the house. There was never enough money. The mother had a small income, and the father had a small income, but not nearly enough for the social position which they had to keep up. The father went in to town to some office. But though he had good prospects, these prospects never materialized. There was always the grinding sense of the shortage of money, though the style was always kept up.

At last the mother said: "I will see if *I* can't make something." But she did not know where to begin. She racked her brains, and tried this thing and the other, but could not find anything successful. The failure made deep lines come into her face. Her children were growing up, they would have to go to school. There must be more money, there must be more money. The father, who was always very handsome and expensive in his tastes, seemed as if he never *would* be able to do anything worth doing. And the mother, who had a great belief in herself, did not succeed any better, and her tastes were just as expensive.

And so the house came to be haunted by the unspoken phrase: *There must be more money! There must be more money!* The children could hear it all the time, though nobody said it aloud. They heard it at Christmas, when the expensive and splendid toys filled the nursery. Behind the shining modern rocking-horse, behind the smart doll's-house, a voice would start whispering: "There *must* be more money! There *must* be more money!" And the children would stop playing, to listen for a moment. They would look into each other's eyes, to see if they had all heard. And each one saw in the eyes of the other two that they too had heard. "There *must* be more money! There *must* be more money!"

It came whispering from the springs of the still-swaying rocking-horse, and even the horse, bending his wooden, champing head, heard it. The big doll, sitting so pink and smirking in her new pram,[1] could hear it quite plainly, and seemed to be smirking all the more self-consciously because of it. The foolish puppy, too, that took the place of the teddy-bear, he was looking so extraordinarily foolish for no other reason but that he heard the secret whisper all over the house: "There *must* be more money!"

Yet nobody ever said it aloud. The whisper was everywhere, and therefore no one spoke it. Just as no one ever says: "We are breathing!" in spite of the fact that breath is coming and going all the time.

"Mother," said the boy Paul one day, "why don't we keep a car of our own? Why do we always use uncle's, or else a taxi?"

"Because we're the poor members of the family," said the mother.

"But why *are* we, mother?"

"Well—I suppose," she said slowly and bitterly, "it's because your father has no luck."

---

1. Baby carriage.

The boy was silent for some time.

"Is luck money, mother?" he asked rather timidly.

"No, Paul. Not quite. It's what causes you to have money."

"Oh!" said Paul vaguely. "I thought when Uncle Oscar said *filthy lucker*, it meant money."

"*Filthy lucre* does mean money," said the mother. "But it's lucre, not luck."

"Oh!" said the boy. "Then what *is* luck, mother?"

"It's what causes you to have money. If you're lucky you have money. That's why it's better to be born lucky than rich. If you're rich, you may lose your money. But if you're lucky, you will always get more money."

"Oh! Will you? And is father not lucky?"

"Very unlucky, I should say," she said bitterly.

The boy watched her with unsure eyes.

"Why?" he asked.

"I don't know. Nobody ever knows why one person is lucky and another unlucky."

"Don't they? Nobody at all? Does *nobody* know?"

"Perhaps God. But He never tells."

"He ought to, then. And aren't you lucky either, mother?"

"I can't be, if I married an unlucky husband."

"But by yourself, aren't you?"

"I used to think I was, before I married. Now I think I am very unlucky indeed."

"Why?"

"Well—never mind! Perhaps I'm not really," she said.

The child looked at her, to see if she meant it. But he saw, by the lines of her mouth, that she was only trying to hide something from him.

"Well, anyhow," he said stoutly, "I'm a lucky person."

"Why?" said his mother, with a sudden laugh.

He stared at her. He didn't even know why he had said it.

"God told me," he asserted, brazening it out.

"I hope He did, dear!" she said, again with a laugh, but rather bitter.

"He did, mother!"

"Excellent!" said the mother, using one of her husband's exclamations.

The boy saw she did not believe him; or, rather, that she paid no attention to his assertion. This angered him somewhat, and made him want to compel her attention.

He went off by himself, vaguely, in a childish way, seeking for the clue to "luck." Absorbed, taking no heed of other people, he went about with a sort of stealth, seeking inwardly for luck. He wanted luck, he wanted it, he wanted it. When the two girls were playing dolls in the nursery, he would sit on his big rocking-horse, charging madly into space, with a frenzy that made the little girls peer at him uneasily. Wildly the horse careered, the waving dark hair of the boy tossed, his eyes had a strange glare in them. The little girls dared not speak to him.

When he had ridden to the end of his mad little journey, he climbed down and stood in front of his rocking-horse, staring fixedly into its lowered face. Its red mouth was slightly open, its big eye was wide and glassy-bright.

"Now!" he would silently command the snorting steed. "Now, take me to where there is luck! Now take me!"

And he would slash the horse on the neck with the little whip he had asked Uncle Oscar for. He *knew* the horse could take him to where there was luck, if only he forced it. So he would mount again, and start on his furious ride, hoping at last to get there. He knew he could get there.

45   "You'll break your horse, Paul!" said the nurse.

"He's always riding like that! I wish he'd leave off!" said his elder sister Joan.

But he only glared down on them in silence. Nurse gave him up. She could make nothing of him. Anyhow he was growing beyond her.

One day his mother and his Uncle Oscar came in when he was on one of his furious rides. He did not speak to them.

"Hallo, you young jockey! Riding a winner?" said his uncle.

50   "Aren't you growing too big for a rocking-horse? You're not a very little boy any longer, you know," said his mother.

But Paul only gave a blue glare from his big, rather close-set eyes. He would speak to nobody when he was in full tilt. His mother watched him with an anxious expression on her face.

At last he suddenly stopped forcing his horse into the mechanical gallop, and slid down.

"Well, I got there!" he announced fiercely, his blue eyes still flaring, and his sturdy long legs straddling apart.

"Where did you get to?" asked his mother.

55   "Where I wanted to go," he flared back at her.

"That's right, son!" said Uncle Oscar. "Don't you stop till you get there. What's the horse's name?"

"He doesn't have a name," said the boy.

"Gets on without all right?" asked the uncle.

"Well, he has different names. He was called Sansovino last week."

60   "Sansovino, eh? Won the Ascot.[2] How did you know his name?"

"He always talks about horse-races with Bassett," said Joan.

The uncle was delighted to find that his small nephew was posted with all the racing news. Bassett, the young gardener, who had been wounded in the left foot in the war[3] and had got his present job through Oscar Cresswell, whose batman he had been, was a perfect blade of the "turf."[4] He lived in the racing events, and the small boy lived with him.

Oscar Cresswell got it all from Bassett.

"Master Paul comes and asks me, so I can't do more than tell him, sir," said

2. A race run at a course of that name in Berkshire. Other races mentioned in the story are Lincoln-shire Handicap, then run at Lincoln Downs; the St. Leger Stakes, run at Doncaster; the Grand National Steeplechase, run at Aintree, the most famous steeplechase in the world; the famous Derby, a mile-and-a-half race for three-year-olds run at Epsom Downs.   3. World War I, 1914–1918.   4. Dashing young horseplayer. *Batman*: British officer's orderly.

Bassett, his face terribly serious, as if he were speaking of religious matters.

"And does he ever put anything on a horse he fancies?"

"Well—I don't want to give him away—he's a young sport, a fine sport, sir. Would you mind asking him himself? He sort of takes a pleasure in it, and perhaps he'd feel I was giving him away, sir, if you don't mind."

Bassett was serious as a church.

The uncle went back to his nephew and took him off for a ride in the car.

"Say, Paul, old man, do you ever put anything on a horse?" the uncle asked.

The boy watched the handsome man closely.

"Why, do you think I oughtn't to?" he parried.

"Not a bit of it! I thought perhaps you might give me a tip for the Lincoln."

The car sped on into the country, going down to Uncle Oscar's place in Hampshire.

"Honour bright?" said the nephew.

"Honour bright, son!" said the uncle.

"Well, then, Daffodil."

"Daffodil! I doubt it, sonny. What about Mirza?"

"I only know the winner," said the boy. "That's Daffodil."

"Daffodil, eh?"

There was a pause. Daffodil was an obscure horse comparatively.

"Uncle!"

"Yes, son?"

"You won't let it go any further, will you? I promised Bassett."

"Bassett be damned, old man! What's he got to do with it?"

"We're partners. We've been partners from the first. Uncle, he lent me my first five shillings, which I lost. I promised him, honour bright, it was only between me and him; only you gave me that ten-shilling note I started winning with, so I thought you were lucky. You won't let it go any further, will you?"

The boy gazed at his uncle from those big, hot, blue eyes, set rather close together. The uncle stirred and laughed uneasily.

"Right you are, son! I'll keep your tip private. Daffodil, eh? How much are you putting on him?"

"All except twenty pounds," said the boy. "I keep that in reserve."

The uncle thought it a good joke.

"You keep twenty pounds in reserve, do you, you young romancer? What are you betting, then?"

"I'm betting three hundred," said the boy, gravely. "But it's between you and me, Uncle Oscar! Honour bright?"

The uncle burst into a roar of laughter.

"It's between you and me all right, you young Nat Gould,"[5] he said, laughing. "But where's your three hundred?"

"Bassett keeps it for me. We're partners."

---

5. Nathaniel Gould (1857–1919) novelist and journalist whose writings in both genres concerned horse-racing.

95 "You are, are you! And what is Bassett putting on Daffodil?"

"He won't go quite as high as I do, I expect. Perhaps he'll go a hundred and fifty."

"What, pennies?" laughed the uncle.

"Pounds," said the child, with a surprised look at his uncle. "Bassett keeps a bigger reserve than I do."

Between wonder and amusement Uncle Oscar was silent. He pursued the matter no further, but he determined to take his nephew with him to the Lincoln races.

100 "Now, son," he said, "I'm putting twenty on Mirza, and I'll put five for you on any horse you fancy. What's your pick?"

"Daffodil, uncle."

"No, not the fiver on Daffodil!"

"I should if it was my own fiver," said the child.

"Good! Good! Right you are! A fiver for me and a fiver for you on Daffodil."

105 The child had never been to a race-meeting before, and his eyes were blue fire. He pursed his mouth tight, and watched. A Frenchman just in front had put his money on Lancelot. Wild with excitement, he flayed his arms up and down, yelling "*Lancelot! Lancelot!*" in his French accent.

Daffodil came in first, Lancelot second, Mirza third. The child, flushed and with eyes blazing, was curiously serene. His uncle brought him four five-pound notes, four to one.

"What am I to do with these?" he cried, waving them before the boy's eyes.

"I suppose we'll talk to Bassett," said the boy. "I expect I have fifteen hundred now; and twenty in reserve; and this twenty."

His uncle studied him for some moments.

110 "Look here, son!" he said. "You're not serious about Bassett and that fifteen hundred, are you?"

"Yes, I am. But it's between you and me, uncle. Honour bright!"

"Honour bright all right, son! But I must talk to Bassett."

"If you'd like to be a partner, uncle, with Bassett and me, we could all be partners. Only, you'd have to promise, honour bright, uncle, not to let it go beyond us three. Bassett and I are lucky, and you must be lucky, because it was your ten shillings I started winning with. . . ."

Uncle Oscar took both Bassett and Paul into Richmond Park for an afternoon, and there they talked.

115 "It's like this, you see, sir," Bassett said. "Master Paul would get me talking about racing events, spinning yarns, you know, sir. And he was always keen on knowing if I'd made or if I'd lost. It's about a year since, now, that I put five shillings on Blush of Dawn for him—and we lost. Then the luck turned, with the ten shillings he had from you, that we put on Singhalese. And since that time, it's been pretty steady, all things considering. What do you say, Master Paul?"

"We're all right when we're sure," said Paul. "It's when we're not quite sure that we go down."

"Oh, but we're careful then," said Bassett.

"But when are you *sure?*" smiled Uncle Oscar.

"It's Master Paul, sir," said Bassett, in a secret, religious voice. "It's as if he had it from heaven. Like Daffodil, now, for the Lincoln. That was as sure as eggs."

"Did you put anything on Daffodil?" asked Oscar Cresswell.

"Yes, sir. I made my bit."

"And my nephew?"

Bassett was obstinately silent, looking at Paul.

"I made twelve hundred, didn't I, Bassett? I told uncle I was putting three hundred on Daffodil."

"That's right," said Bassett, nodding.

"But where's the money?" asked the uncle.

"I keep it safe locked up, sir. Master Paul he can have it any minute he likes to ask for it."

"What, fifteen hundred pounds?"

"And twenty! And *forty*, that is, with the twenty he made on the course."

"It's amazing!" said the uncle.

"If Master Paul offers you to be partners, sir, I would, if I were you; if you'll excuse me," said Bassett.

Oscar Cresswell thought about it.

"I'll see the money," he said.

They drove home again, and sure enough, Bassett came round to the garden-house with fifteen hundred pounds in notes. The twenty pounds reserve was left with Joe Glee, in the Turf Commission deposit.

"You see, it's all right, uncle, when I'm *sure!* Then we go strong, for all we're worth. Don't we, Bassett?"

"We do that, Master Paul"

"And when are you sure?" said the uncle, laughing.

"Oh, well, sometimes I'm *absolutely* sure, like about Daffodil," said the boy; "and sometimes I have an idea; and sometimes I haven't even an idea, have I, Bassett? Then we're careful, because we mostly go down."

"You do, do you! And when you're sure, like about Daffodil, what makes you sure, sonny?"

"Oh, well, I don't know," said the boy uneasily. "I'm sure, you know, uncle; that's all."

"It's as if he had it from heaven, sir," Bassett reiterated.

"I should say so!" said the uncle.

But he became a partner. And when the Leger was coming on, Paul was "sure" about Lively Spark, which was a quite inconsiderable horse. The boy insisted on putting a thousand on the horse, Bassett went for five hundred, and Oscar Cresswell two hundred. Lively Spark came in first, and the betting had been ten to one against him. Paul had made ten thousand.

"You see," he said, "I was absolutely sure of him."

Even Oscar Cresswell had cleared two thousand.

"Look here, son," he said, "this sort of thing makes me nervous."

"It needn't, uncle! Perhaps I shan't be sure again for a long time."

"But what are you going to do with your money?" asked the uncle.

"Of course," said the boy, "I started it for mother. She said she had no luck, because father is unlucky, so I thought if I was lucky, it might stop whispering."

"What might stop whispering?"

"Our house. I *hate* our house for whispering."

"What does it whisper?"

"Why—why"—the boy fidgeted—"why, I don't know. But it's always short of money, you know, uncle."

"I know it, son, I know it."

"You know people send mother writs, don't you, uncle?"

"I'm afraid I do," said the uncle.

"And then the house whispers, like people laughing at you behind your back. It's awful, that is! I thought if I was lucky . . ."

"You might stop it," added the uncle.

The boy watched him with big blue eyes, that had an uncanny cold fire in them, and he said never a word.

"Well, then!" said the uncle. "What are we doing?"

"I shouldn't like mother to know I was lucky," said the boy.

"Why not, son?"

"She'd stop me."

"I don't think she would."

"Oh!"—and the boy writhed in an odd way—"I *don't* want her to know, uncle."

"All right, son! We'll manage it without her knowing."

They managed it very easily. Paul, at the other's suggestion, handed over five thousand pounds to his uncle, who deposited it with the family lawyer, who was then to inform Paul's mother that a relative had put five thousand pounds into his hands, which sum was to be paid out a thousand pounds at a time, on the mother's birthday, for the next five years.

"So she'll have a birthday present of a thousand pounds for five successive years," said Uncle Oscar. "I hope it won't make it all the harder for her later."

Paul's mother had her birthday in November. The house had been "whispering" worse than ever lately, and, even in spite of his luck, Paul could not bear up against it. He was very anxious to see the effect of the birthday letter, telling his mother about the thousand pounds.

When there were no visitors, Paul now took his meals with his parents, as he was beyond the nursery control. His mother went into town nearly every day. She had discovered that she had an odd knack of sketching furs and dress materials, so she worked secretly in the studio of a friend who was the chief "artist" for the leading drapers. She drew the figures of ladies in furs and ladies in silk and sequins for the newspaper advertisements. This young woman artist earned several thousand pounds a year, but Paul's mother only made several hundreds, and she was again dissatisfied. She so wanted to be first in something, and she did not succeed, even in making sketches for drapery advertisements.

She was down to breakfast on the morning of her birthday. Paul watched her face as she read her letters. He knew the lawyer's letter. As his mother read it, her face hardened and became more expressionless. Than a cold, determined look came on her mouth. She hid the letter under the pile of others, and said not a word about it.

"Didn't you have anything nice in the post for your birthday, mother?" said Paul.

"Quite moderately nice," she said, her voice cold and absent.

She went away to town without saying more.

But in the afternoon Uncle Oscar appeared. He said Paul's mother had had   175
a long interview with the lawyer, asking if the whole five thousand could not be advanced at once, as she was in debt.

"What do you think, uncle?" said the boy.

"I leave it to you, son."

"Oh, let her have it, then! We can get some more with the other," said the boy.

"A bird in the hand is worth two in the bush, laddie!" said Uncle Oscar.

"But I'm sure to *know* for the Grand National; or the Lincolnshire; or else   180
the Derby. I'm sure to know for *one* of them," said Paul.

So Uncle Oscar signed the agreement, and Paul's mother touched the whole five thousand. Then something very curious happened. The voices in the house suddenly went mad, like a chorus of frogs on a spring evening. There were certain new furnishings, and Paul had a tutor. He was *really* going to Eton, his father's school, in the following autumn. There were flowers in the winter, and a blossoming of the luxury Paul's mother had been used to. And yet the voices in the house, behind the sprays of mimosa and almond blossom, and from under the piles of iridescent cushions, simply trilled and screamed in a sort of ecstasy: "There *must* be more money! Oh-h-h; there *must* be more money Oh, now, now-w! Now-w-w—there *must* be more money!—more than ever! More than ever!"

It frightened Paul terribly. He studied away at his Latin and Greek with his tutors. But his intense hours were spent with Bassett. The Grand National had gone by: he had not "known," and had lost a hundred pounds. Summer was at hand. He was in agony for the Lincoln. But even for the Lincoln he didn't "know," and he lost fifty pounds. He became wild-eyed and strange, as if something were going to explode in him.

"Let it alone, son! Don't you bother about it!" urged Uncle Oscar. But it was as if the boy couldn't really hear what his uncle was saying.

"I've got to know for the Derby! I've got to know for the Derby!" the child reiterated, his big blue eyes blazing with a sort of madness.

His mother noticed how overwrought he was.   185

"You'd better go to the seaside. Wouldn't you like to go now to the seaside, instead of waiting? I think you'd better," she said, looking down at him anxiously, her heart curiously heavy because of him.

But the child lifted his uncanny blue eyes.

"I couldn't possibly go before the Derby, mother!" he said. "I couldn't possibly!"

"Why not?" she said, her voice becoming heavy when she was opposed.

"Why not? You can still go from the seaside to see the Derby with your Uncle Oscar, if that's what you wish. No need for you to wait here. Besides, I think you care too much about these races. It's a bad sign. My family has been a gambling family, and you won't know till you grow up how much damage it has done. But it has done damage. I shall have to send Bassett away, and ask Uncle Oscar not to talk racing to you, unless you promise to be reasonable about it; go away to the seaside and forget it. You're all nerves!"

"I'll do what you like, mother, so long as you don't send me away till after the Derby," the boy said.

"Send you away from where? Just from this house?"

"Yes," he said, gazing at her.

"Why, you curious child, what makes you care about this house so much, suddenly? I never knew you loved it."

He gazed at her without speaking. He had a secret within a secret, something he had not divulged, even to Bassett or to his Uncle Oscar.

But his mother, after standing undecided and a little bit sullen for some moments, said:

"Very well, then! Don't go to the seaside till after the Derby, if you don't wish it. But promise me you won't let your nerves go to pieces. Promise you won't think so much about horse-racing and events, as you call them!"

"Oh, no," said the boy casually. "I won't think much about them, mother. You needn't worry. I wouldn't worry, mother, if I were you."

"If you were me and I were you," said his mother, "I wonder what we *should* do!"

"But you know you needn't worry, mother, don't you?" the boy repeated.

"I should be awfully glad to know it," she said wearily.

"Oh, well, you *can*, you know. I mean, you *ought* to know you needn't worry," he insisted.

"Ought I? Then I'll see about it," she said.

Paul's secret of secrets was his wooden horse, that which had no name. Since he was emancipated from a nurse and a nursery-governess, he had had his rocking-horse removed to his own bedroom at the top of the house.

"Surely, you're too big for a rocking-horse!" his mother had remonstrated.

"Well, you see, mother, till I can have a *real* horse, I like to have *some* sort of animal about," had been his quaint answer.

"Do you feel he keeps you company?" she laughed.

"Oh, yes! He's very good, he always keeps me company, when I'm there," said Paul.

So the horse, rather shabby, stood in an arrested prance in the boy's bedroom.

The Derby was drawing near, and the boy grew more and more tense. He hardly heard what was spoken to him, he was very frail, and his eyes were really uncanny. His mother had sudden strange seizures of uneasiness about him. Sometimes, for half-an-hour, she would feel a sudden anxiety about him that was almost anguish. She wanted to rush to him at once, and know he was safe.

Two nights before the Derby, she was at a big party in town, when one of her rushes of anxiety about her boy, her first-born, gripped her heart till she could hardly speak. She fought with the feeling, might and main, for she believed in common-sense. But it was too strong. She had to leave the dance and go downstairs to telephone to the country. The children's nursery-governess was terribly surprised and startled at being rung up in the night.

"Are the children all right, Miss Wilmot?"

"Oh, yes, they are quite all right."

"Master Paul? Is he all right?"

"He went to bed as right as a trivet. Shall I run up and look at him?"

"No," said Paul's mother reluctantly. "No! Don't trouble. It's all right. Don't sit up. We shall be home fairly soon." She did not want her son's privacy intruded upon.

"Very good," said the governess.

It was about one o'clock when Paul's mother and father drove up to their house. All was still. Paul's mother went to her room and slipped off her white fur cloak. She had told her maid not to wait up for her. She heard her husband downstairs, mixing a whisky-and-soda.

And then, because of the strange anxiety at her heart, she stole upstairs to her son's room. Noiselessly she went along the upper corridor. Was there a faint noise? What was it?

She stood, with arrested muscles, outside his door, listening. There was a strange, heavy, and yet not loud noise. Her heart stood still. It was a soundless noise, yet rushing and powerful. Something huge, in violent, hushed motion. What was it? What in God's name was it? She ought to know. She felt that she knew the noise. She knew what it was.

Yet she could not place it. She couldn't say what it was. And on and on it went, like a madness.

Softly, frozen with anxiety and fear, she turned the door-handle.

The room was dark. Yet in the space near the window, she heard and saw something plunging to and fro. She gazed in fear and amazement.

Then suddenly she switched on the light, and saw her son, in his green pyjamas, madly surging on the rocking-horse. The blaze of light suddenly lit him up, as he urged the wooden horse, and lit her up, as she stood, blonde, in her dress of pale green and crystal, in the doorway.

"Paul!" she cried. "Whatever are you doing?"

"It's Malabar!" he screamed, in a powerful, strange voice. "It's Malabar!"

His eyes blazed at her for one strange and senseless second, as he ceased urging his wooden horse. Then he fell with a crash to the ground, and she, all her tormented motherhood flooding upon her, rushed to gather him up.

But he was unconscious, and unconscious he remained, with some brain-fever. He talked and tossed, and his mother sat stonily by his side.

"Malabar! It's Malabar! Bassett, Bassett, I *know*! It's Malabar!"

So the child cried, trying to get up and urge the rocking-horse that gave him his inspiration.

"What does he mean by Malabar?" asked the heart-frozen mother.

"I don't know," said the father stonily.

"What does he mean by Malabar?" she asked her brother Oscar.

"It's one of the horses running for the Derby," was the answer.

And, in spite of himself, Oscar Cresswell spoke to Bassett, and himself put a thousand on Malabar: at fourteen to one.

The third day of the illness was critical: they were waiting for a change. The boy, with his rather long, curly hair, was tossing ceaselessly on the pillow. He neither slept nor regained consciousness, and his eyes were like blue stones. His mother sat, feeling her heart had gone, turned actually into a stone.

In the evening, Oscar Cresswell did not come, but Bassett sent a message, saying could he come up for one moment, just one moment? Paul's mother was very angry at the intrusion, but on second thought she agreed. The boy was the same. Perhaps Bassett might bring him to consciousness.

The gardener, a shortish fellow with a little brown moustache, and sharp little brown eyes, tip-toed into the room, touched his imaginary cap to Paul's mother, and stole to the bedside, staring with glittering, smallish eyes, at the tossing, dying child.

"Master Paul!" he whispered. "Master Paul! Malabar came in first all right, a clean win. I did as you told me. You've made over seventy thousand pounds, you have; you've got over eighty thousand. Malabar came in all right, Master Paul."

"Malabar! Malabar! Did I say Malabar, mother? Did I say Malabar? Do you think I'm lucky, mother? I knew Malabar, didn't I? Over eighty thousand pounds! I call that lucky, don't you, mother? Over eighty thousand pounds! I knew, didn't I know I knew! Malabar came in all right. If I ride my horse till I'm sure, then I tell you, Bassett, you can go as high as you like. Did you go for all you were worth, Bassett?"

"I went a thousand on it, Master Paul."

"I never told you, mother, that if I can ride my horse, and *get there*, then I'm absolutely sure—oh absolutely! Mother, did I ever tell you? I *am* lucky!"

"No, you never did," said the mother.

But the boy died in the night.

And even as he lay dead, his mother heard her brother's voice saying to her: "My God, Hester, you're eighty-odd thousand to the good, and a poor devil of a son to the bad. But, poor devil, poor devil, he's best gone out of a life where he rides his rocking-horse to find a winner."

1932

D. H. LAWRENCE

Passages from Essays and Letters

from "Nottingham and the Mining Countryside"

I was born . . . in Eastwood, a mining village of some three thousand souls, about eight miles from Nottingham. . . . It is hilly country. . . . To me it seemed, and still seems, an extremely beautiful countryside, just between the red sandstone and the oak-trees of Nottingham, and the cold limestone, the ash-trees, the stone fences of Derbyshire. To me, as a child and a young man, it was still the old England of the forest and agricultural past; there were no motorcars, the mines were, in a sense, an accident in the landscape, and Robin Hood and his merry men were not very far away.

. . . The people lived almost entirely by instinct, men of my father's age could not really read. And the pit did not mechanize men. . . . My father loved the pit. He was hurt badly, more than once, but he would never stay away. He loved the contact, the intimacy, as men in the war loved the intense male comradeship of the dark days.

Now the colliers had also an instinct for beauty. The colliers' wives had not. The colliers were deeply alive, instinctively. But they had no daytime ambition, and no daytime intellect. They avoided, really, the rational aspect of life. . . . They didn't even care very profoundly about wages. It was the women, naturally, who nagged on this score. . . . The collier went to the pub and drank in order to continue the intimacy with his mates.

. . . Life for him did not consist of facts, but in a flow. Very often he loved his garden. And very often he had a genuine love of the beauty of flowers. . . .

. . . Most women love flowers as possessions, and as trimmings. They can't look at a flower, and wonder a moment, and pass on. If they see a flower that arrests their attention, they must at once pick it, pluck it. Possession! A possession! Something added on to *me*!

from "Love"

. . . the love between a man and a woman . . . is dual. It is the melting into pure communion, and it is the friction of sheer sensuality, both. In pure communion I become whole in love. And in pure, fierce passion of sensuality, I am burned into essentiality. I am driven from the matrix unto sheer separate distinction. I become my single self, inviolable and unique, as the gems were perhaps once driven into themselves out of the confusion of earths. . . .

from "Women Are So Cocksure"

. . . [My mother] was convinced . . . that a man ought not to drink beer. This conviction developed from the fact, naturally, that my father drank beer.

He sometimes drank too much. He sometimes boozed away the money necessary for the young family. When my father came in tipsy, she saw scarlet.

from "Art and Morality"

Apples are always apples! says Vox Populi, Vox Dei.[1]

Sometimes they're sin, sometimes they're a knock on the head, sometimes
they're a bellyache, sometimes they're part of a pie, sometimes they're sauce for
a goose.

What art has got to do, and will go on doing, is to reveal things in their
different relationships. That is to say, you've got to see in the apples the bellyache. Sir Isaac's knock on the cranium, the vast, moist wall through which the
insect bores to lay her eggs in the middle, and the untasted, unknown quality
which Eve saw hanging on a tree.

from "Morality and the Novel"

The business of art is to reveal the relation between man and his circumam-
bient universe, at the living moment. As mankind is always struggling in the
toils of old relationships, art is always ahead of the "times," which themselves
are always far in the rear of the living moment.

When van Gogh paints sunflowers, he reveals, or achieves, the vivid relation
between himself, as man, and the sunflowers, as sunflower, at that quick moment
of time. His painting does not represent the sunflower itself. We shall never
know what the sunflower itself is. And the camera will *visualize* the sunflower
far more perfectly than van Gogh can.

The vision on the canvas is a third thing, utterly intangible and inexplicable,
the offspring of the sunflower itself and van Gogh himself. . . .

. . . The novel is the highest example of subtle interrelatedness that man has
discovered. Everything is true in its own time, place, and circumstance, and
untrue outside of its own place, time, circumstance. If you try to nail anything
down, in the novel, either it kills the novel, or the novel gets up and walks away
with the nail.

. . . Love is a great emotion. But if you set out to write a novel, and you
yourself are in the throes of the great predilection for love, love as the supreme,
the only emotion worth living for, then you will write an immoral novel.

Because *no* emotion is supreme, or exclusively worth living for. *All* emotions
go to the achieving of a living relationship between a human being and the other
human being or creature or thing he becomes purely related to. All emotions,
including love and hate, and rage and tenderness, go to the adjusting of the
oscillating, unestablished balance between two people who amount to anything.

A new relation, a new relatedness hurts somewhat in the attaining; and will
always hurt. So life will always hurt. . . .

1. The voice of the people [is] the voice of God.

Each time we strive to a new relation, with anyone or anything, it is bound to hurt somewhat. Because it means the struggle with and the displacing of old connections, and this is never pleasant. And, moreover, between living things at least, an adjustment means also a fight, for each party, inevitably, must "seek its own" in the other, and be denied. When, in the two parties, each of them seeks his own, her own, absolutely, then it is a fight to the death. And this is true of the thing called "passion."

The great relationship for humanity will always be the relation between man and woman. The relation between man and man, woman and woman, parent and child, will always be subsidiary.

And the relation between man and woman will change forever, and will forever be the new central clue to human life. It is the *relation itself* which is the quick and the central clue to life, not the man, nor the woman, nor the children that result from the relationship, as a contingency.

from "Why the Novel Matters"

We have curious ideas of ourselves. We think of ourselves as a body with a spirit in it, or a body with a soul in it, or a body with a mind in it. . . .

It is a funny sort of superstition. Why should I look at my hand, as it so cleverly writes these words, and decide that it is a mere nothing compared to the mind that directs it? Why should I imagine that there is a *me* which is more *me* than my hand is? Since my hand is absolutely alive, me alive.

And that's what you learn, when you're a novelist. And that's what you are liable *not* to know, if you're a parson, or a philosopher, or a scientist, or a stupid person.

Now I absolutely flatly deny that I am a soul, or a body, or a mind, or an intelligence, or a brain, or a nervous system, or a bunch of glands, or any of the rest of these bits of me. The whole is greater than the part. And therefore, I, who am man alive, am greater than my soul, or spirit, or body, or mind, or consciousness, or anything else that is merely a part of me. I am man a man, and alive. I am man alive, and as long as I can, I intend to go on being man alive.

For this reason I am a novelist. And being a novelist, I consider myself superior to the saint, the scientist, the philosopher, and the poet, who are all great masters of different bits of man alive, but never get the whole thing.

We should ask for no absolutes, or absolute. . . . There is no absolute good, there is nothing absolutely right. All things flow and change, and even change is not absolute. . . .

. . . If the one I love remains unchanged and unchanging, I shall cease to love her. It is only because she changes and startles me into change and defies my inertia, and is herself staggered in her inertia by my changing, that I can continue to love her. If she stayed put, I might as well love the pepper-pot.

In life, there is right and wrong, good and bad, all the time. But what is right in one case is wrong in another. And in the novel you see one man becoming a corpse, because of his so-called goodness, another going dead because of his so-called wickedness. Right and wrong is an instinct: but an instinct of the whole consciousness in a man, bodily, mental, spiritual at once. And only in the novel are *all* things given full play, or at least, they may be given full play, when we realize that life itself, and not inert safety, is the reason for living. For out of the full play of all things emerges the only thing that is anything, the wholeness of a man, the wholeness of a woman, man alive, and live woman.

from *Autobiographical Sketch*

They ask me; "Did you find it very hard to get on and to become a success?" And I have to admit that if I can be said to have got on, and if I can be called a success, then I *did not* find it hard.

I never starved in a garret, nor waited in anguish for the post to bring me an answer from editor or publisher, nor did I struggle in sweat and blood to bring forth mighty works, nor did I ever wake up and find myself famous.

. . . My father was a collier, and only a collier, nothing praise-worthy about him. He wasn't even respectable, in so far as he got drunk rather frequently, never went near a chapel, and was usually rather rude to his little immediate bosses at the pit.

My mother was, I suppose, superior. She came from town, and belonged really to the lower bourgeoisie. She spoke King's English, without an accent, and never in her life could even imitate a sentence of the dialect which my father spoke, and which we children spoke out of doors.

I have *wanted* to feel truly friendly with some, at least, of my fellow-men. Yet I have never quite succeeded. Whether I got on *in* the world is a question; but I certainly don't get on very well *with* the world. And whether I am a worldly success or not I really don't know. But I feel, somehow, not much of a human success.

By which I mean that I don't feel there is any very cordial or fundamental contact between me and society, or me and other people. There is a breach. And my contact is with something that is nonhuman, nonvocal.

[Why?] The answer, as far as I can see, has something to do with class. Class makes a gulf, across which all the best human flow is lost. It is not exactly the triumph of the middle classes that has made the deadness, but the triumph of the middle-class *thing*.

As a man from the working class, I feel that the middle class cut off some of my vital vibration when I am with them. I admit them charming and educated and good people often enough. *But they just stop some part of me from working.* . . .

Then why don't I live with my working people? Because their vibration is limited in another direction. They are narrow, but still fairly deep and passionate, whereas the middle class is broad and shallow and passionless.

I cannot make the transfer from my own class into the middle class. I cannot, not for anything in the world, forfeit my passional consciousness and my old blood-affinity with my fellow-men and the animals and the land, for that other thin, spurious mental conceit which is all that is left of the mental consciousness once it has made itself exclusive.

from the Letters

TO A. W. McLEOD, 26 APRIL 1913

I am so sure that only through a readjustment between men and women, and a making free and healthy of this sex, will she [England] get out of her present atrophy. Oh, Lord, and if I don't "subdue my art to a metaphysic," as somebody very beautifully said of Hardy, I do write because I want folk—English folk—to alter, and have more sense.

TO A. W. McLEOD, 2 JUNE 1914

I think the only re-sourcing of art, revivifying it, is to make it more the joint work of man and woman. I think *the* one thing to do, is for men to have courage to draw nearer to women, expose themselves to them, and be altered by them; and for women to accept and admit men. That is the start—by bringing themselves together, men and women—revealing themselves to each other, gaining great blind knowledge and suffering and joy, which it will take a big further lapse of civilization to exploit and work out. Because the source of all life and knowledge is in man and woman, and the source of all living is in the interchange and the meeting and mingling of these two: man-life and woman-life, man-knowledge and woman-knowledge, man-being and woman-being.

TO J. B. PINKER, 16 DECEMBER 1915

. . . Tell Arnold Bennett[2] that all rules of construction hold good only for novels which are copies of other novels. A book which is not a copy of other books has its own construction, and what he calls faults, he being an old imitator, I call characteristics.

TO ROLF GARDINER, 9 AUGUST 1924

What we need is to smash a few big holes in European suburbanity, let in a little real fresh air.

---

2. An early twentieth-century novelist (1867–1931) whose major works—*The Old Wives' Tale* (1908) and *The Clayhanger Trilogy* (1910–15)—treat the middle classes in the pottery country of the English Midlands in a naturalistic manner (usually criticizing the money-grubbing, social-climbing selfishness of the society). In his later years he more or less turned into a hack, though a clever one, and it is to Bennett as a very popular, successful hack that Lawrence is referring.

To Lady Ottoline Morrell, 5 February 1929

. . . Don't you think it's nonsense when Murry says that my world is not the ordinary man's world and that I am a sort of animal with a sixth sense? Seems to me more likely he's a sort of animal with only four senses—the real sense of touch missing. They all seem determined to make a freak of me—to save their own short-failings, and make them "normal."

FLANNERY O'CONNOR

The Lame Shall Enter First

Sheppard sat on a stool at the bar that divided the kitchen in half, eating his cereal out of the individual pasteboard box it came in. He ate mechanically, his eyes on the child, who was wandering from cabinet to cabinet in the panelled kitchen, collecting the ingredients for his breakfast. He was a stocky blond boy of ten. Sheppard kept his intense blue eyes fixed on him. The boy's future was written in his face. He would be a banker. No, worse. He would operate a small loan company. All he wanted for the child was that he be good and unselfish and neither seemed likely. Sheppard was a young man whose hair was already white. It stood up like a narrow brush halo over his pink sensitive face.

The boy approached the bar with the jar of peanut butter under his arm, a plate with a quarter of a small chocolate cake on it in one hand and the ketchup bottle in the other. He did not appear to notice his father. He climbed up on the stool and began to spread peanut butter on the cake. He had very large round ears that leaned away from his head and seemed to pull his eyes slightly too far apart. His shirt was green but so faded that the cowboy charging across the front of it was only a shadow.

"Norton," Sheppard said, "I saw Rufus Johnson yesterday. Do you know what he was doing?"

The child looked at him with a kind of half attention, his eyes forward but not yet engaged. They were a paler blue than his father's as if they might have faded like the shirt; one of them listed, almost imperceptibly, toward the outer rim.

"He was in an alley," Sheppard said, "and he had his hand in a garbage can. He was trying to get something to eat out of it." He paused to let this soak in. "He was hungry," he finished, and tried to pierce the child's conscience with his gaze.

The boy picked up the piece of chocolate cake and began to gnaw it from one corner.

"Norton," Sheppard said, "do you have any idea what it means to share?"

A flicker of attention. "Some of it's yours," Norton said.

"Some of it's *his*," Sheppard said heavily. It was hopeless. Almost any fault would have been preferable to selfishness—a violent temper, even a tendency to lie.

The child turned the bottle of ketchup upside down and began thumping   10
ketchup onto the cake.

Sheppard's look of pain increased. "You are ten and Rufus Johnson is fourteen," he said. "Yet I'm sure your shirts would fit Rufus." Rufus Johnson was a
boy he had been trying to help at the reformatory for the past year. He had been
released two months ago. "When he was in the reformatory, he looked pretty
good, but when I saw him yesterday, he was skin and bones. He hasn't been
eating cake with peanut butter on it for breakfast."

The child paused. "It's stale," he said. "That's why I have to put stuff on it."

Sheppard turned his face to the window at the end of the bar. The side lawn,
green and even, sloped fifty feet or so down to a small suburban wood. When
his wife was living, they had often eaten outside, even breakfast, on the grass.
He had never noticed then that the child was selfish. "Listen to me," he said,
turning back to him, "look at me and listen."

The boy looked at him. At least his eyes were forward.

"I gave Rufus a key to this house when he left the reformatory—to show my   15
confidence in him and so he would have a place he could come to and feel
welcome any time. He didn't use it, but I think he'll use it now because he's
seen me and he's hungry. And if he doesn't use it, I'm going out and find him
and bring him here. I can't see a child eating out of garbage cans."

The boy frowned. It was dawning upon him that something of his was threatened.

Sheppard's mouth stretched in disgust. "Rufus's father died before he was
born," he said. "His mother is in the state penitentiary. He was raised by his
grandfather in a shack without water or electricity and the old man beat him
every day. How would you like to belong to a family like that?"

"I don't know," the child said lamely.

"Well, you might think about it sometime," Sheppard said.

Sheppard was City Recreational Director. On Saturdays he worked at the   20
reformatory as a counselor, receiving nothing for it but the satisfaction of knowing he was helping boys no one else cared about. Johnson was the most intelligent boy he had worked with and the most deprived.

Norton turned what was left of the cake over as if he no longer wanted it.

"Maybe he won't come," the child said and his eyes brightened slightly.

"Think of everything you have that he doesn't!" Sheppard said. "Suppose
you had to root in garbage cans for food? Suppose you had a huge swollen foot
and one side of you dropped lower than the other when you walked?"

The boy looked blank, obviously unable to imagine such a thing.

"You have a healthy body," Sheppard said, "a good home. You've never   25
been taught anything but the truth. Your daddy gives you everything you need
and want. You don't have a grandfather who beats you. And your mother is not
in the state penitentiary."

The child pushed his plate away. Sheppard groaned aloud.

A knot of flesh appeared below the boy's suddenly distorted mouth. His face
became a mass of lumps with slits for eyes. "If she was in the penitentiary," he
began in a kind of racking bellow, "I could go to seeeeee her." Tears rolled down

his face and the ketchup dribbled on his chin. He looked as if he had been hit in the mouth. He abandoned himself and howled.

Sheppard sat helpless and miserable, like a man lashed by some elemental force of nature. This was not a normal grief. It was all part of his selfishness. She had been dead for over a year and a child's grief should not last so long. "You're going on eleven years old," he said reproachfully.

The child began an agonizing high-pitched heaving noise.

"If you stop thinking about yourself and think what you can do for somebody else," Sheppard said, "then you'll stop missing your mother."

The boy was silent but his shoulders continued to shake. Then his face collapsed and he began to howl again.

"Don't you think I'm lonely without her too?" Sheppard said. "Don't you think I miss her at all? I do, but I'm not sitting around moping. I'm busy helping other people. When do you see me just sitting around thinking about my troubles?"

The boy slumped as if he were exhausted but fresh tears streaked his face.

"What are you going to do today?" Sheppard asked, to get his mind on something else.

The child ran his arm across his eyes. "Sell seeds," he mumbled.

Always selling something. He had four quart jars full of nickels and dimes he had saved and he took them out of his closet every few days and counted them. "What are you selling seeds for?"

"To win a prize."

"What's the prize?"

"A thousand dollars."

"And what would you do if you had a thousand dollars?"

"Keep it," the child said and wiped his nose on his shoulder.

"I feel sure you would," Sheppard said. "Listen," he said and lowered his voice to an almost pleading tone, "suppose by some chance you did win a thousand dollars. Wouldn't you like to spend it on children less fortunate than yourself? Wouldn't you like to give some swings and trapezes to the orphanage? Wouldn't you like to buy poor Rufus Johnson a new shoe?"

The boy began to back away from the bar. Then suddenly he leaned forward and hung with his mouth open over his plate. Sheppard groaned again. Everything came up, the cake, the peanut butter, the ketchup—a limp sweet batter. He hung over it gagging, more came, and he waited with his mouth open over the plate as if he expected his heart to come up next.

"It's all right," Sheppard said, "it's all right. You couldn't help it. Wipe your mouth and go lie down."

The child hung there a moment longer. Then he raised his face and looked blindly at his father.

"Go on," Sheppard said. "Go on and lie down."

The boy pulled up the end of his t-shirt and smeared his mouth with it. Then he climbed down off the stool and wandered out of the kitchen.

Sheppard sat there staring at the puddle of half-digested food. The sour odor reached him and he drew back. His gorge rose. He got up and carried the plate to the sink and turned the water on it and watched grimly as the mess ran down the drain. Johnson's sad thin hand rooted in garbage cans for food while his own child, selfish, unresponsive, greedy, had so much that he threw it up. He cut off the faucet with a thrust of his fist. Johnson had a capacity for real response and had been deprived of everything from birth; Norton was average or below and had had every advantage.

He went back to the bar to finish his breakfast. The cereal was soggy in the cardboard box but he paid no attention to what he was eating. Johnson was worth any amount of effort because he had the potential. He had seen it from the time the boy had limped in for his first interview.

Sheppard's office at the reformatory was a narrow closet with one window and a small table and two chairs in it. He had never been inside a confessional but he thought it must be the same kind of operation he had here, except that he explained, he did not absolve. His credentials were less dubious than a priest's; he had been trained for what he was doing.

When Johnson came in for his first interview, he had been reading over the boy's record—senseless destruction, windows smashed, city trash boxes set afire, tires slashed—the kind of thing he found where boys had been transplanted abruptly from the country to the city as this one had. He came to Johnson's I. Q. score. It was 140. He raised his eyes eagerly.

The boy sat slumped on the edge of his chair, his arms hanging between his thighs. The light from the window fell on his face. His eyes, steel-colored and very still, were trained narrowly forward. His thin dark hair hung in a flat forelock across the side of his forehead, not carelessly like a boy's, but fiercely like an old man's. A kind of fanatic intelligence was palpable in his face.

Sheppard smiled to diminish the distance between them.

The boy's expression did not soften. He leaned back in his chair and lifted a monstrous club foot to his knee. The foot was in a heavy black battered shoe with a sole four or five inches thick. The leather parted from it in one place and the end of an empty sock protruded like a gray tongue from a severed head. The case was clear to Sheppard instantly. His mischief was compensation for the foot.

"Well Rufus," he said, "I see by the record here that you don't have but a year to serve. What do you plan to do when you get out?"

"I don't make no plans," the boy said. His eyes shifted indifferently to something outside the window behind Sheppard in the far distance.

"Maybe you ought to," Sheppard said and smiled.

Johnson continued to gaze beyond him.

"I want to see you make the most of your intelligence," Sheppard said. "What's most important to you? Let's talk about what's important to *you*." His eyes dropped involuntarily to the foot.

"Study it and git your fill," the boy drawled.

Sheppard reddened. The black deformed mass swelled before his eyes. He ignored the remark and the leer the boy was giving him. "Rufus," he said, "you've got into a lot of senseless trouble but I think when you understand why you do these things, you'll be less inclined to do them." He smiled. They had so few friends, saw so few pleasant faces, that half his effectiveness came from nothing more than smiling at them. "There are a lot of things about yourself that I think I can explain to you," he said.

Johnson looked at him stonily. "I ain't asked for no explanation," he said. "I already know why I do what I do."

"Well good!" Sheppard said. "Suppose you tell me what's made you do the things you've done?"

A black sheen appeared in the boy's eyes. "Satan," he said. "He has me in his power."

65   Sheppard looked at him steadily. There was no indication on the boy's face that he had said this to be funny. The line of his thin mouth was set with pride. Sheppard's eyes hardened. He felt a momentary dull despair as if he were faced with some elemental warping of nature that had happened too long ago to be corrected now. This boy's questions about life had been answered by signs nailed on the pine trees: DOES SATAN HAVE YOU IN HIS POWER? REPENT OR BURN IN HELL. JESUS SAVES. He would know the Bible with or without reading it. His despair gave way to outrage. "Rubbish!" he snorted. "We're living in the space age! You're too smart to give me an answer like that."

Johnson's mouth twisted slightly. His look was contemptuous but amused. There was a glint of challenge in his eyes.

Sheppard scrutinized his face. Where there was intelligence anything was possible. He smiled again, a smile that was like an invitation to the boy to come into a school room with all its windows thrown open to the light. "Rufus," he said, "I'm going to arrange for you to have a conference with me once a week. Maybe there's an explanation for your explanation. Maybe I can explain your devil to you."

After that he had talked to Johnson every Saturday for the rest of the year. He talked at random, the kind of talk the boy would never have heard before. He talked a little above him to give him something to reach for. He roamed from simple psychology and the dodges of the human mind to astronomy and the space capsules that were whirling around the earth faster than the speed of sound and would soon encircle the stars. Instinctively he concentrated on the stars. He wanted to give the boy something to reach for besides his neighbor's goods. He wanted to stretch his horizons. He wanted him to *see* the universe, to see that the darkest parts of it could be penetrated. He would have given anything to be able to put a telescope in Johnson's hands.

Johnson said little and what he did say, for the sake of his pride, was in dissent or senseless contradiction, with the clubfoot raised always to his knee like a weapon ready for use, but Sheppard was not deceived. He watched his eyes and every week he saw something in them crumble. From the boy's face, hard but shocked, braced against the light that was ravaging him, he could see that he was hitting dead center.

70   Johnson was free now to live out of garbage cans and rediscover his old ignorance. The injustice of it was infuriating. He had been sent back to the grandfather; the old man's imbecility could only be imagined. Perhaps the boy had by now run away from him. The idea of getting custody of Johnson had occurred to Sheppard before, but the fact of the grandfather had stood in the

way. Nothing excited him so much as thinking what he could do for such a boy. First he would have him fitted for a new orthopedic shoe. His back was thrown out of line every time he took a step. Then he would encourage him in some particular intellectual interest. He thought of the telescope. He could buy a second-hand one and they could set it up in the attic window. He sat for almost ten minutes thinking what he could do if he had Johnson here with him. What was wasted on Norton would cause Johnson to flourish. Yesterday when he had seen him with his hand in the garbage can, he had waved and started forward. Johnson had seen him, paused a split-second, then vanished with the swiftness of a rat, but not before Sheppard had seen his expression change. Something had kindled in the boy's eyes, he was sure of it, some memory of the lost light.

He got up and threw the cereal box in the garbage. Before he left the house, he looked into Norton's room to be sure he was not still sick. The child was sitting cross-legged on his bed. He had emptied the quart jars of change into one large pile in front of him, and was sorting it out by nickels and dimes and quarters.

That afternoon Norton was alone in the house, squatting on the floor of his room arranging packages of flower seeds in rows around himself. Rain slashed against the window panes and rattled in the gutters. The room had grown dark but every few minutes it was lit by silent lightning and the seed packages showed up gaily on the floor. He squatted motionless like a large pale frog in the midst of this potential garden. All at once his eyes became alert. Without warning the rain had stopped. The silence was heavy as if the downpour had been hushed by violence. He remained motionless, only his eyes turning.

Into the silence came the distinct click of a key turning in the front door lock. The sound was a very deliberate one. It drew attention to itself and held it as if it were controlled more by a mind than by a hand. The child leapt up and got into the closet.

The footsteps began to move in the hall. They were deliberate and irregular, a light and then a heavy one, then a silence as if the visitor had paused to listen himself or to examine something. In a minute the kitchen door screeked. The footsteps crossed the kitchen to the refrigerator. The closet wall and the kitchen wall were the same. Norton stood with his ear pressed against it. The refrigerator door opened. There was a prolonged silence.

He took off his shoes and then tiptoed out of the closet and stepped over the seed packages. In the middle of the room, he stopped and remained where he was, rigid. A thin bony-face boy in a wet black suit stood in his door, blocking his escape. His hair was flattened to his skull by the rain. He stood there like an irate drenched crow. His look went through the child like a pin and paralyzed him. Then his eyes began to move over everything in the room—the unmade bed, the dirty curtains on the one large window, a photograph of a wide-faced young woman that stood up in the clutter on top of the dresser.

The child's tongue suddenly went wild. "He's been expecting you, he's going to give you a new shoe because you have to eat out of garbage cans!" he said in a kind of mouse-like shriek.

"I eat out of garbage cans," the boy said slowly with a beady stare, "because I like to eat out of garbage cans. See?"

The child nodded.

"And I got ways of getting my own shoe. See?"

The child nodded, mesmerized.

The boy limped in and sat down on the bed. He arranged a pillow behind him and stretched his short leg out so that the big black shoe rested conspicuously on a fold of the sheet.

Norton's gaze settled on it and remained immobile. The sole was as thick as a brick.

Johnson wiggled it slightly and smiled. "If I kick somebody *once* with this," he said, "it learns them not to mess with me."

The child nodded.

"Go in the kitchen," Johnson said, "and make me a sandwich with some of that rye bread and ham and bring me a glass of milk."

Norton went off like a mechanical toy, pushed in the right direction. He made a large greasy sandwich with ham hanging out the sides of it and poured out a glass of milk. Then he returned to the room with the glass of milk in one hand and the sandwich in the other.

Johnson was leaning back regally against the pillow. "Thanks, waiter," he said and took the sandwich.

Norton stood by the side of the bed, holding the glass.

The boy tore into the sandwich and ate steadily until he finished it. Then he took the glass of milk. He held it with both hands like a child and when he lowered it for breath, there was a rim of milk around his mouth. He handed Norton the empty glass. "Go get me one of them oranges in there, waiter," he said hoarsely.

Norton went to the kitchen and returned with the orange. Johnson peeled it with his fingers and let the peeling drop in the bed. He ate it slowly, spitting the seeds out in front of him. When he finished, he wiped his hands on the sheet and gave Norton a long appraising stare. He appeared to have been softened by the service. "You're his kid all right," he said. "You got the same stupid face."

The child stood there stolidly as if he had not heard.

"He don't know his left hand from his right," Johnson said with a hoarse pleasure in his voice.

The child cast his eyes a little to the side of the boy's face and looked fixedly at the wall.

"Yaketty yaketty yak," Johnson said, "and never says a thing."

The child's upper lip lifted slightly but he didn't say anything.

"Gas," Johnson said. "Gas."

The child's face began to have a wary look of belligerence. He backed away slightly as if he were prepared to retreat instantly. "He's good," he mumbled. "He helps people."

"Good!" Johnson said savagely. He thrust his head forward. "Listen here," he hissed, "I don't care if he's good or not. He ain't *right!*"

Norton looked stunned.

The screen door in the kitchen banged and someone entered. Johnson sat   100
forward instantly. "Is that him?" he said.

"It's the cook," Norton said. "She comes in the afternoon."

Johnson got up and limped into the hall and stood in the kitchen door and
Norton followed him.

The colored girl was at the closet taking off a bright red raincoat. She was a
tall light-yellow girl with a mouth like a large rose that had darkened and wilted.
Her hair was dressed in tiers on top of her head and leaned to the side like the
Tower of Pisa.

Johnson made a noise through his teeth. "Well look at Aunt Jemima," he
said.

The girl paused and trained an insolent gaze on them. They might have   105
been dust on the floor.

"Come on," Johnson said, "let's see what all you got besides a nigger." He
opened the first door to his right in the hall and looked into a pink-tiled bathroom. "A pink can!" he murmured.

He turned a comical face to the child. "Does he sit on that?"

"It's for company," Norton said, "but he sits on it sometimes."

"He ought to empty his head in it," Johnson said.

The door was open to the next room. It was the room Sheppard had slept in   110
since his wife died. An ascetic-looking iron bed stood on the bare floor. A heap
of Little League baseball uniforms was piled in one corner. Papers were scattered
over a large roll-top desk and held down in various places by his pipes. Johnson
stood looking into the room silently. He wrinkled his nose. "Guess who?" he
said.

The door to the next room was closed but Johnson opened it and thrust his
head into the semi-darkness within. The shades were down and the air was close
with a faint scent of perfume in it. There was a wide antique bed and a mammoth dresser whose mirror glinted in the half light. Johnson snapped the light
switch by the door and crossed the room to the mirror and peered into it. A silver
comb and brush lay on the linen runner. He picked up the comb and began to
run it through his hair. He combed it straight down on his forehead. Then he
swept it to the side, Hitler fashion.

"Leave her comb alone!" the child said. He stood in the door, pale and
breathing heavily as if he were watching sacrilege in a holy place.

Johnson put the comb down and picked up the brush and gave his hair a
swipe with it.

"She's dead," the child said.

"I ain't afraid of dead people's things," Johnson said. He opened the top   115
drawer and slid his hand in.

"Take your big fat dirty hands off my mother's clothes!" the child said in a
high suffocated voice.

"Keep your shirt on, sweetheart," Johnson murmured. He pulled up a wrinkled red polka dot blouse and dropped it back. Then he pulled out a green silk
kerchief and whirled it over his head and let it float to the floor. His hand continued to plow deep into the drawer. After a moment it came up gripping a faded

corset with four dangling metal supporters. "Thisyer must be her saddle," he observed.

He lifted it gingerly and shook it. Then he fastened it around his waist and jumped up and down, making the metal supporters dance. He began to snap his fingers and turn his hips from side to side. "Gonter rock, rattle and roll," he sang. "Gonter rock, rattle and roll. Can't please that woman, to save my doggone soul." He began to move around, stamping the good foot down and slinging the heavy one to the side. He danced out the door, past the stricken child and down the hall toward the kitchen.

A half hour later Sheppard came home. He dropped his raincoat on a chair in the hall and came as far as the parlor door and stopped. His face was suddenly transformed. It shone with pleasure. Johnson sat, a dark figure, in a high-backed pink upholstered chair. The wall behind him was lined with books from floor to ceiling. He was reading one. Sheppard's eyes narrowed. It was a volume of the Encyclopedia Britannica. He was so engrossed in it that he did not look up. Sheppard held his breath. This was the perfect setting for the boy. He had to keep him here. He had to manage it somehow.

120   "Rufus!" he said, "it's good to see you boy!" and he bounded forward with his arm outstretched.

Johnson looked up, his face blank. "Oh hello," he said. He ignored the hand as long as he was able but when Sheppard did not withdraw it, he grudgingly shook it.

Sheppard was prepared for this kind of reaction. It was part of Johnson's make-up never to show enthusiasm.

"How are things?" he said. "How's your grandfather treating you?" He sat down on the edge of the sofa.

"He dropped dead," the boy said indifferently.

125   "You don't mean it!" Sheppard cried. He got up and sat down on the coffee table nearer the boy.

"Naw," Johnson said, "he ain't dropped dead. I wisht he had."

"Well where is he?" Sheppard muttered.

"He's gone with a remnant to the hills," Johnson said. "Him and some others. They're going to bury some Bibles in a cave and take two of different kinds of animals and all like that. Like Noah. Only this time it's going to be fire, not flood."

Sheppard's mouth stretched wryly. "I see," he said. Then he said, "In other words the old fool has abandoned you?"

130   "He ain't no fool," the boy said in an indignant tone.

"Has he abandoned you or not?" Sheppard asked impatiently.

The boy shrugged.

"Where's your probation officer?"

"I ain't supposed to keep up with him," Johnson said. "He's supposed to keep up with me."

135   Sheppard laughed. "Wait a minute," he said. He got up and went into the hall and got his raincoat off the chair and took it to the hall closet to hang it up.

He had to give himself time to think, to decide how he could ask the boy so that he would stay. He couldn't force him to stay. It would have to be voluntary. Johnson pretended not to like him. That was only to uphold his pride, but he would have to ask him in such a way that his pride could still be upheld. He opened the closet door and took out a hanger. An old gray winter coat of his wife's still hung there. He pushed it aside but it didn't move. He pulled it open roughly and winced as if he had seen the larva inside a cocoon. Norton stood in it, his face swollen and pale, with a drugged look of misery on it. Sheppard stared at him. Suddenly he was confronted with a possibility. "Get out of there," he said. He caught him by the shoulder and propelled him firmly into the parlor and over to the pink chair where Johnson was sitting with the encyclopedia in his lap. He was going to risk everything in one blow.

"Rufus," he said, "I've got a problem. I need your help."

Johnson looked up suspiciously.

"Listen," Sheppard said, "we need another boy in the house." There was a genuine desperation in his voice. "Norton here has never had to divide anything in his life. He doesn't know what it means to share. And I need somebody to teach him. How about helping me out? Stay here for a while with us, Rufus. I need your help." The excitement in his voice made it thin.

The child suddenly came to life. His face swelled with fury. "He went in her room and used her comb!" he screamed, yanking Sheppard's arm. "He put on her corset and danced with Leola, he . . ."

"Stop this!" Sheppard said sharply. "Is tattling all you're capable of? I'm not asking you for a report on Rufus's conduct. I'm asking you to make him welcome here. Do you understand?

"You see how it is?" he asked, turning to Johnson.

Norton kicked the leg of the pink chair viciously, just missing Johnson's swollen foot. Sheppard yanked him back.

"He said you weren't nothing but gas!" the child shrieked.

A sly look of pleasure crossed Johnson's face.

Sheppard was not put back. These insults were part of the boy's defensive mechanism. "What about it, Rufus?" he said. "Will you stay with us for a while?"

Johnson looked straight in front of him and said nothing. He smiled slightly and appeared to gaze upon some vision of the future that pleased him.

"I don't care," he said and turned a page of the encyclopedia. "I can stand anywhere."

"Wonderful." Sheppard said. "Wonderful."

"He said," the child said in a throaty whisper, "you didn't know your left hand from your right."

There was a silence.

Johnson wet his finger and turned another page of the encyclopedia.

"I have something to say to both of you," Sheppard said in a voice without inflection. His eyes moved from one to the other of them and he spoke slowly as if what he was saying he would say only once and it behooved them to listen. "If it made any difference to me what Rufus thinks of me," he said, "then I wouldn't be asking him here. Rufus is going to help me out and I'm going to help him

140

145

150

out and we're both going to help you out. I'd simply be selfish if I let what Rufus thinks of me interfere with what I can do for Rufus. If I can help a person, all I want is to do it. I'm above and beyond simple pettiness."

Neither of them made a sound. Norton stared at the chair cushion. Johnson peered closer at some fine print in the encyclopedia. Sheppard was looking at the tops of their heads. He smiled. After all, he had won. The boy was staying. He reached out and ruffled Norton's hair and slapped Johnson on the shoulder. "Now you fellows sit here and get acquainted," he said gaily and started toward the door. "I'm going to see what Leola left us for supper."

When he was gone, Johnson raised his head and looked at Norton. The child looked back at him bleakly. "God, kid," Johnson said in a cracked voice, "how do you stand it?" His face was stiff with outrage. "He thinks he's Jesus Christ!"

II

155   Sheppard's attic was a large unfinished room with exposed beams and no electric light. They had set the telescope up on a tripod in one of the dormer windows. It pointed now toward the dark sky where a sliver of moon, as fragile as an egg shell, had just emerged from behind a cloud with a brilliant silver edge. Inside, a kerosene lantern set on a trunk cast their shadows upward and tangled them, wavering slightly, in the joints overhead. Sheppard was sitting on a packing box, looking through the telescope, and Johnson was at his elbow, waiting to get at it. Sheppard had bought it for fifteen dollars two days before at a pawn shop.

"Quit hoggin it," Johnson said.

Sheppard got up and Johnson slid onto the box and put his eye to the instrument.

Sheppard sat down on a straight chair a few feet away. His face was flushed with pleasure. This much of his dream was a reality. Within a week he had made it possible for this boy's vision to pass through a slender channel to the stars. He looked at Johnson's bent back with complete satisfaction. The boy had on one of Norton's plaid shirts and some new khaki trousers he had bought him. The shoe would be ready next week. He had taken him to the brace shop the day after he came and had him fitted for a new shoe. Johnson was as touchy about the foot as if it were a sacred object. His face had been glum while the clerk, a young man with a bright pink bald head, measured the foot with his profane hands. The shoe was going to make the greatest difference in the boy's attitude. Even a child with normal feet was in love with the world after he had got a new pair of shoes. When Norton got a new pair, he walked around for days with his eyes on his feet.

Sheppard glanced across the room at the child. He was sitting on the floor against a trunk, trussed up in a rope he had found and wound around his legs from his ankles to his knees. He appeared so far away that Sheppard might have been looking at him through the wrong end of the telescope. He had had to whip him only once since Johnson had been with them—the first night when Norton had realized that Johnson was going to sleep in his mother's bed. He did not believe in whipping children, particularly in anger. In this case, he had done both and with good results. He had had no more trouble with Norton.

The child hadn't shown any positive generosity toward Johnson but what he couldn't help, he appeared to be resigned to. In the mornings Sheppard sent the two of them to the Y swimming pool, gave them money to get their lunch at the cafeteria and instructed them to meet him in the park in the afternoon to watch his Little League baseball practice. Every afternoon they had arrived at the park, shambling, silent, their faces closed each on his own thoughts as if neither were aware of the other's existence. At least he could be thankful there were no fights.

Norton showed no interest in the telescope. "Don't you want to get up and look through the telescope, Norton?" he said. It irritated him that the child showed no intellectual curiosity whatsoever. "Rufus is going to be way ahead of you."

Norton leaned forward absently and looked at Johnson's back.

Johnson turned around from the instrument. His face had begun to fill out again. The look of outrage had retreated from his hollow cheeks and was shored up now in the caves of his eyes, like a fugitive from Sheppard's kindness. "Don't waste your valuable time, kid," he said. "You seen the moon once, you seen it."

Sheppard was amused by these sudden turns of perversity. The boy resisted whatever he suspected was meant for his improvement and contrived when he was vitally interested in something to leave the impression he was bored. Sheppard was not deceived. Secretly Johnson was learning what he wanted him to learn—that his benefactor was impervious to insult and that there were no cracks in his armor of kindness and patience where a successful shaft could be driven. "Some day you may go to the moon," he said. "In ten years men will probably be making round trips there on schedule. Why you boys may be spacemen. Astronauts!"

"Astro-nuts," Johnson said.

"Nuts or nauts," Sheppard said, "it's perfectly possible that you, Rufus Johnson, will go to the moon."

Something in the depths of Johnson's eyes stirred. All day his humor had been glum. "I ain't going to the moon and get there alive," he said, "and when I die I'm going to hell."

"It's at least possible to get to the moon," Sheppard said dryly. The best way to handle this kind of thing was with gentle ridicule. "We can see it. We know it's there. Nobody has given any reliable evidence there's a hell."

"The Bible has give the evidence," Johnson said darkly, "and if you die and go there you burn forever."

The child leaned forward.

"Whoever says it ain't a hell," Johnson said, "is contradicting Jesus. The dead are judged and the wicked are damned. They weep and gnash their teeth while they burn," he continued, "and it's everlasting darkness."

The child's mouth opened. His eyes appeared to grow hollow.

"Satan runs it," Johnson said.

Norton lurched up and took a hobbled step toward Sheppard. "Is she there?"

he said in a loud voice. "Is she there burning up?" He kicked the rope off his feet. "Is she on fire?"

175   "Oh my God," Sheppard muttered. "No no," he said, "of course she isn't. Rufus is mistaken. Your mother isn't anywhere. She's not unhappy. She just isn't." His lot would have been easier if when his wife died he had told Norton she had gone to heaven and that some day he would see her again, but he could not allow himself to bring him up on a lie.

Norton's face began to twist. A knot formed in his chin.

"Listen," Sheppard said quickly and pulled the child to him, "your mother's spirit lives on in other people and it'll live on in you if you're good and generous like she was."

The child's pale eyes hardened in disbelief.

Sheppard's pity turned to revulsion. The boy would rather she be in hell than nowhere. "Do you understand?" he said. "She doesn't exist." He put his hand on the child's shoulder. "That's all I have to give you," he said in a softer, exasperated tone, "the truth."

180   Instead of howling, the boy wrenched himself away and caught Johnson by the sleeve. "Is she there, Rufus?" he said "Is she there, burning up?"

Johnson's eyes glittered. "Well," he said, "she is if she was evil. Was she a whore?"

"Your mother was not a whore," Sheppard said sharply. He had the sensation of driving a car without brakes. "Now let's have no more of this foolishness. We were talking about the moon."

"Did she believe in Jesus?" Johnson asked.

Norton looked blank. After a second he said, "Yes," as if he saw that this was necessary. "She did," he said. "All the time."

185   "She did not," Sheppard muttered.

"She did all the time," Norton said. "I heard her say she did all the time."

"She's saved," Johnson said.

The child still looked puzzled. "Where?" he said. "Where is she at?"

"On high," Johnson said.

"Where's that?" Norton gasped.

"It's in the sky somewhere," Johnson said, "but you got to be dead to get there. You can't go in no space ship." There was a narrow gleam in his eyes now like a beam holding steady on its target.

"Man's going to the moon," Sheppard said grimly, "is very much like the first fish crawling out of the water onto land billions and billions of years ago. He didn't have an earth suit. He had to grow his adjustments inside. He developed lungs."

"When I'm dead will I go to hell or where she is?" Norton asked.

"Right now you'd go where she is," Johnson said, "but if you live long enough, you'll go to hell."

Sheppard rose abruptly and picked up the lantern. "Close the window, Rufus," he said. "It's time we went to bed."

On the way down the attic stairs he heard Johnson say in a loud whisper behind him, "I'll tell you all about it tomorrow, kid, when Himself has cleared out."

The next day when the boys came to the ball park, he watched them as they came from behind the bleachers and around the edge of the field. Johnson's hand was on Norton's shoulder, his head bent toward the younger boy's ear, and on the child's face there was a look of complete confidence, of dawning light. Sheppard's grimace hardened. This would be Johnson's way of trying to annoy him. But he would not be annoyed. Norton was not bright enough to be damaged much. He gazed at the child's dull absorbed little face. Why try to make him superior? Heaven and hell were for the mediocre, and he was that if he was anything.

The two boys came into the bleachers and sat down about ten feet away, facing him, but neither gave him any sign of recognition. He cast a glance behind him where the Little Leaguers were spread out in the field. Then he started for the bleachers. The hiss of Johnson's voice stopped as he approached.

"What have you fellows been doing today?" he asked genially.

"He's been telling me . . ." Norton started.

Johnson pushed the child in the ribs with his elbow. "We ain't been doing nothing," he said. His face appeared to be covered with a blank glaze but through it a look of complicity was blazoned forth insolently.

Sheppard felt his face grow warm, but he said nothing. A child in a Little League uniform had followed him and was nudging him in the back of the leg with a bat. He turned and put his arm around the boy's neck and went with him back to the game.

That night when he went to the attic to join the boys at the telescope, he found Norton there alone. He was sitting on the packing box, hunched over, looking intently through the instrument. Johnson was not there.

"Where's Rufus?" Sheppard asked.

"I said where's Rufus?" he said louder.

"Gone somewhere," the child said without turning around.

"Gone where?" Sheppard asked.

"He just said he was going somewhere. He said he was fed up looking at stars."

"I see," Sheppard said glumly. He turned and went back down the stairs. He searched the house without finding Johnson. Then he went to the living room and sat down. Yesterday he had been convinced of his success with the boy. Today he faced the possibility that he was failing with him. He had been over-lenient, too concerned to have Johnson like him. He felt a twinge of guilt. What difference did it make if Johnson liked him or not? What was that to him? When the boy came in, they would have a few things understood. As long as you stay here there'll be no going out at night by yourself, do you understand?

I don't have to stay here. It ain't nothing to me staying here.

Oh my God, he thought. He could not bring it to that. He would have to be firm but not make an issue of it. He picked up the evening paper. Kindness and patience were always called for but he had not been firm enough. He sat holding the paper but not reading it. The boy would not respect him unless he showed firmness. The doorbell rang and he went to answer it. He opened it and stepped back, with a pained disappointed face.

A large dour policeman stood on the stoop, holding Johnson by the elbow. At the curb a patrol car waited. Johnson looked very white. His jaw was thrust forward as if to keep from trembling.

"We brought him here first because he raised such a fit," the policeman said, "but now that you've seen him, we're going to take him to the station and ask him a few questions."

"What happened?" Sheppard muttered.

"A house around the corner from here," the policeman said. "A real smash job, dishes broken all over the floor, furniture turned upside down . . ."

"I didn't have a thing to do with it!" Johnson said. "I was walking along minding my own bidnis when this cop came up and grabbed me."

Sheppard looked at the boy grimly. He made no effort to soften his expression.

Johnson flushed. "I was just walking along," he muttered, but with no conviction in his voice.

"Come on, bud," the policeman said.

"You ain't going to let him take me, are you?" Johnson said. "You believe me, don't you?" There was an appeal in his voice that Sheppard had not heard there before.

This was crucial. The boy would have to learn that he could not be protected when he was guilty. "You'll have to go with him, Rufus," he said.

"You're going to let him take me and I tell you I ain't done a thing?" Johnson said shrilly.

Sheppard's face became harder as his sense of injury grew. The boy had failed him even before he had had a chance to give him the shoe. They were to have got it tomorrow. All his regret turned suddenly on the shoe; his irritation at the sight of Johnson doubled.

"You made out like you had all this confidence in me," the boy mumbled.

"I did have," Sheppard said. His face was wooden.

Johnson turned away with the policeman but before he moved, a gleam of pure hatred flashed toward Sheppard from the pits of his eyes.

Sheppard stood in the door and watched them get into the patrol car and drive away. He summoned his compassion. He would go to the station tomorrow and see what he could do about getting him out of trouble. The night in jail would not hurt him and the experience would teach him that he could not treat with impunity someone who had shown him nothing but kindness. Then they would go get the shoe and perhaps after a night in jail it would mean even more to the boy.

The next morning at eight o'clock the police sergeant called and told him he could come pick Johnson up. "We booked a nigger on that charge," he said. "Your boy didn't have nothing to do with it."

Sheppard was at the station in ten minutes, his face hot with shame. Johnson sat slouched on a bench in a drab outer office, reading a police magazine. There was no one else in the room. Sheppard sat down beside him and put his hand tentatively on his shoulder.

The boy glanced up—his lip curled—and back to the magazine.   230

Sheppard felt physically sick. The ugliness of what he had done bore in upon him with a sudden dull intensity. He had failed him at just the point where he might have turned him once and for all in the right direction. "Rufus," he said, "I apologize. I was wrong and you were right. I misjudged you."

The boy continued to read.

"I'm sorry."

The boy wet his finger and turned a page.

Sheppard braced himself. "I was a fool, Rufus," he said.   235

Johnson's mouth slid slightly to the side. He shrugged without raising his head from the magazine.

"Will you forget it, this time?" Sheppard said. "It won't happen again."

The boy looked up. His eyes were bright and unfriendly. "I'll forget it," he said, "but you better remember it." He got up and stalked toward the door. In the middle of the room he turned and jerked his arm at Sheppard and Sheppard jumped up and followed him as if the boy had yanked an invisible leash.

"Your shoe," he said eagerly, "today is the day to get your shoe!" Thank God for the shoe!

But when they went to the brace shop, they found that the shoe had been   240
made two sizes too small and a new one would not be ready for another ten days. Johnson's temper improved at once. The clerk had obviously made a mistake in the measurements but the boy insisted the foot had grown. He left the shop with a pleased expression, as if, in expanding, the foot had acted on some inspiration of its own. Sheppard's face was haggard.

After this he redoubled his efforts. Since Johnson had lost interest in the telescope, he bought a microscope and a box of prepared slides. If he couldn't impress the boy with immensity, he would try the infinitesimal. For two nights Johnson appeared absorbed in the new instrument, then he abruptly lost interest in it, but he seemed content to sit in the living room in the evening and read the encyclopedia. He devoured the encyclopedia as he devoured his dinner, steadily and without dint to his appetite. Each subject appeared to enter his head, be ravaged, and thrown out. Nothing pleased Sheppard more than to see the boy slouched on the sofa, his mouth shut, reading. After they had spent two or three evenings like this, he began to recover his vision. His confidence returned. He knew that some day he would be proud of Johnson.

On Thursday night Sheppard attended a city council meeting. He dropped the boys off at a movie on his way and picked them up on his way back. When they reached home, an automobile with a single red eye above its windshield was waiting in front of the house. Sheppard's lights as he turned into the driveway illuminated two dour faces in the car.

"The cops!" Johnson said. "Some nigger has broke in somewhere and they've come for me again."

"We'll see about that," Sheppard muttered. He stopped the car in the drive-way and switched off the lights. "You boys go in the house and go to bed," he said. "I'll handle this."

245   He got out and strode toward the squad car. He thrust his head in the win-dow. The two policemen were looking at him with silent knowledgeable faces. "A house on the corner of Shelton and Mills," the one in the driver's seat said. "It looks like a train run through it."

"He was in the picture show downtown," Sheppard said. "My boy was with him. He had nothing to do with the other one and he had nothing to do with this one. I'll be responsible."

"If I was you," the one nearest him said, "I wouldn't be responsible for any little bastard like him."

"I said I'd be responsible," Sheppard repeated coldly. "You people made a mistake the last time. Don't make another."

The policemen looked at each other. "It ain't our funeral," the one in the driver's seat said, and turned the key in the ignition.

250   Sheppard went in the house and sat down in the living room in the dark. He did not suspect Johnson and he did not want the boy to think he did. If Johnson thought he suspected him again, he would lose everything. But he wanted to know if his alibi was airtight. He thought of going to Norton's room and asking him if Johnson had left the movie. But that would be worse. Johnson would know what he was doing and would be incensed. He decided to ask Johnson himself. He would be direct. He went over in his mind what he was going to say and then he got up and went to the boy's door.

It was open as if he had been expected but Johnson was in bed. Just enough light came in from the hall for Sheppard to see his shape under the sheet. He came in and stood at the foot of the bed. "They've gone," he said. "I told them you had nothing to do with it and that I'd be responsible."

There was a muttered "Yeah," from the pillow.

Sheppard hesitated. "Rufus," he said, "you didn't leave the movie for any-thing at all, did you?"

"You make out like you got all this confidence in me!" a sudden outraged voice cried, "and you ain't got any! You don't trust me no more now than you did then!" The voice, disembodied, seemed to come more surely from the depths of Johnson than when his face was visible. It was a cry of reproach, edged slightly with contempt.

255   "I do have confidence in you," Sheppard said intensely. "I have every con-fidence in you. I believe in you and I trust you completely."

"You got your eye on me all the time," the voice said sullenly. "When you get through asking me a bunch of questions, you're going across the hall and ask Norton a bunch of them."

"I have no intention of asking Norton anything and never did," Sheppard said gently. "And I don't suspect you at all. You could hardly have got from the picture show downtown and out here to break in a house and back to the picture show in the time you had."

"That's why you believe me!" the boy cried, "—because you think I couldn't have done it."

"No, no!" Sheppard said. "I believe you because I believe you've got the brains and the guts not to get in trouble again. I believe you know yourself well enough now to know that you don't have to do such things. I believe that you can make anything of yourself that you set your mind to."

Johnson sat up. A faint light shone on his forehead but the rest of his face   260
was invisible. "And I could have broke in there if I'd wanted to in the time I had," he said.

"But I know you didn't," Sheppard said. "There's not the least trace of doubt in my mind."

There was a silence. Johnson lay back down. Then the voice, low and hoarse, as if it were being forced out with difficulty, said, "You don't want to steal and smash up things when you've got everything you want already."

Sheppard caught his breath. The boy was thanking him! He was thanking him! There was gratitude in his voice. There was appreciation. He stood there, smiling foolishly in the dark, trying to hold the moment in suspension. Involuntarily he took a step toward the pillow and stretched out his hand and touched Johnson's forehead. It was cold and dry like rusty iron.

"I understand. Good night, son," he said and turned quickly and left the room. He closed the door behind him and stood there, overcome with emotion.

Across the hall Norton's door was open. The child lay on the bed on his side,   265
looking into the light from the hall.

After this, the road with Johnson would be smooth.

Norton sat up and beckoned to him.

He saw the child but after the first instant, he did not let his eyes focus directly on him. He could not go in and talk to Norton without breaking Johnson's trust. He hesitated, but remained where he was a moment as if he saw nothing. Tomorrow was the day they were to go back for the shoe. It would be a climax to the good feeling between them. He turned quickly and went back into his own room.

The child sat for some time looking at the spot where his father had stood. Finally his gaze became aimless and he lay back down.

The next day Johnson was glum and silent as if he were ashamed that he had   270
revealed himself. His eyes had a hooded look. He seemed to have retired within himself and there to be going through some crisis of determination. Sheppard could not get to the brace shop quickly enough. He left Norton at home because he did not want his attention divided. He wanted to be free to observe Johnson's reaction minutely. The boy did not seem pleased or even interested in the prospect of the shoe, but when it became an actuality, certainly then he would be moved.

The brace shop was a small concrete warehouse lined and stacked with the equipment of affliction. Wheel chairs and walkers covered most of the floor. The walls were hung with every kind of crutch and brace. Artificial limbs were stacked on the shelves, legs and arms and hands, claws and hooks, straps and human harnesses and unidentifiable instruments for unnamed deformities. In a small clearing in the middle of the room there was a row of yellow plastic-cushioned chairs and a shoe-fitting stool. Johnson slouched down in one of the chairs and set his foot up on the stool and sat with his eyes on it moodily. What was roughly the toe had broken open again and he had patched it with a piece of canvas; another place he had patched with what appeared to be the tongue of the original shoe. The two sides were laced with twine.

There was an excited flush on Sheppard's face; his heart was beating unnaturally fast.

The clerk appeared from the back of the shop with the new shoe under his arm. "Got her right this time!" he said. He straddled the shoe-fitting stool and held the shoe up, smiling as if he had produced it by magic.

It was a black slick shapeless object, shining hideously. It looked like a blunt weapon, highly polished.

275   Johnson gazed at it darkly.

"With this shoe," the clerk said, "you won't know you're walking. You'll think you're riding!" He bent his bright pink bald head and began gingerly to unlace the twine. He removed the old shoe as if he were skinning an animal still half alive. His expression was strained. The unsheathed mass of foot in the dirty sock made Sheppard feel queasy. He turned his eyes away until the new shoe was on. The clerk laced it up rapidly. "Now stand up and walk around," he said, "and see if that ain't power glide." He winked at Sheppard. "In that shoe," he said, "he won't know he don't have a normal foot."

Sheppard's face was bright with pleasure.

Johnson stood up and walked a few yards away. He walked stiffly with almost no dip in his short side. He stood for a moment, rigid, with his back to them.

"Wonderful!" Sheppard said. "Wonderful." It was as if he had given the boy a new spine.

280   Johnson turned around. His mouth was set in a thin icy line. He came back to the seat and removed the shoe. He put his foot in the old one and began lacing it up.

"You want to take it home and see if it suits you first?" the clerk murmured.

"No," Johnson said. "I ain't going to wear it at all."

"What's wrong with it?" Sheppard said, his voice rising.

"I don't need no new shoe," Johnson said. "And when I do, I got ways of getting my own." His face was stony but there was a glint of triumph in his eyes.

285   "Boy," the clerk said, "is your trouble in your foot or in your head?"

"Go soak your skull," Johnson said. "Your brains are on fire."

The clerk rose glumly but with dignity and asked Sheppard what he wanted done with the shoe, which he dangled dispiritedly by the lace.

Sheppard's face was a dark angry red. He was staring straight in front of him at a leather corset with an artificial arm attached.

The clerk asked him again.

290   "Wrap it up," Sheppard muttered. He turned his eyes to Johnson. "He's not mature enough for it yet," he said. "I had thought he was less of a child."

The boy leered. "You been wrong before," he said.

That night they sat in the living room and read as usual. Sheppard kept himself glumly entrenched behind the Sunday New York *Times*. He wanted to recover his good humor, but every time he thought of the rejected shoe, he felt a new charge of irritation. He did not trust himself even to look at Johnson. He realized that the boy had refused the shoe because he was insecure. Johnson had been frightened by his own gratitude. He didn't know what to make of the new self he was becoming conscious of. He understood that something he had been was threatened and he was facing himself and his possibilities for the first time. He was questioning his identity. Grudgingly, Sheppard felt a slight return of sympathy for the boy. In a few minutes, he lowered his paper and looked at him.

Johnson was sitting on the sofa, gazing over the top of the encyclopedia. His expression was trancelike. He might have been listening to something far away. Sheppard watched him intently but the boy continued to listen, and did not turn his head. The poor kid is lost, Sheppard thought. Here he had sat all evening, sullenly reading the paper, and had not said a word to break the tension. "Rufus," he said.

Johnson continued to sit, stock-still, listening.

"Rufus," Sheppard said in a slow hypnotic voice, "you can be anything in   295
the world you want to be. You can be a scientist or an architect or an engineer or whatever you set your mind to, and whatever you set your mind to be, you can be the best of its kind." He imagined his voice penetrating to the boy in the black caverns of his psyche. Johnson leaned forward but his eyes did not turn. On the street a car door closed. There was a silence. Then a sudden blast from the door bell.

Sheppard jumped up and went to the door and opened it. The same policeman who had come before stood there. The patrol car waited at the curb.

"Lemme see that boy," he said.

Sheppard scowled and stood aside. "He's been here all evening," he said. "I can vouch for it."

The policeman walked into the living room. Johnson appeared engrossed in his book. After a second he looked up with an annoyed expression, like a great man interrupted at his work.

"What was that you were looking at in that kitchen window over on Winter   300
Avenue about a half hour ago, bud?" the policeman asked.

"Stop persecuting this boy!" Sheppard said. "I'll vouch for the fact he was here. I was here with him."

"You heard him," Johnson said. "I been here all the time."

"It ain't everybody makes tracks like you," the policeman said and eyed the clubfoot.

"They couldn't be his tracks," Sheppard growled, infuriated. "He's been here all the time. You're wasting your own time and you're wasting ours." He felt the *ours* seal his solidarity with the boy. "I'm sick of this," he said. "You people are too damn lazy to go out and find whoever is doing these things. You come here automatically."

The policeman ignored this and continued looking through Johnson. His   305
eyes were small and alert in his fleshy face. Finally he turned toward the door.

"We'll get him sooner or later," he said, "with his head in a window and his tail out."

Sheppard followed him to the door and slammed it behind him. His spirits were soaring. This was exactly what he had needed. He returned with an expectant face.

Johnson had put the book down and was sitting there, looking at him slyly. "Thanks," he said.

Sheppard stopped. The boy's expression was predatory. He was openly leering.

"You ain't such a bad liar yourself," he said.

"Liar?" Sheppard murmured. Could the boy have left and come back? He felt himself sicken. Then a rush of anger sent him forward. "Did you leave?" he said furiously. "I didn't see you leave."

The boy only smiled.

"You went up in the attic to see Norton," Sheppard said.

"Naw," Johnson said, "that kid is crazy. He don't want to do nothing but look through that stinking telescope."

"I don't want to hear about Norton," Sheppard said harshly. "Where were you?"

"I was sitting on that pink can by my ownself," Johnson said. "There wasn't no witnesses."

Sheppard took out his handkerchief and wiped his forehead. He managed to smile.

Johnson rolled his eyes. "You don't believe in me," he said. His voice was cracked the way it had been in the dark room two nights before. "You make out like you got all this confidence in me but you ain't got any. When things get hot, you'll fade like the rest of them." The crack became exaggerated, comic. The mockery in it was blatant. "You don't believe in me. You ain't got no confidence," he wailed. "And you ain't any smarter than that cop. All that about tracks—that was a trap. There wasn't any tracks. That whole place is concreted in the back and my feet were dry."

Sheppard slowly put the handkerchief back in his pocket. He dropped down on the sofa and gazed at the rug beneath his feet. The boy's clubfoot was set within the circle of his vision. The pieced-together shoe appeared to grin at him with Johnson's own face. He caught hold of the edge of the sofa cushion and his knuckles turned white. A chill of hatred shook him. He hated the shoe, hated the foot, hated the boy. His face paled. Hatred choked him. He was aghast at himself.

He caught the boy's shoulder and gripped it fiercely as if to keep himself from falling. "Listen," he said, "you looked in that window to embarrass me. That was all you wanted—to shake my resolve to help you, but my resolve isn't shaken. I'm stronger than you are. I'm stronger than you are and I'm going to save you. The good will triumph."

"Not when it ain't true," the boy said. "Not when it ain't right."

"My resolve isn't shaken," Sheppard repeated. "I'm going to save you."

Johnson's look became sly again. "You ain't going to save me," he said.

"You're going to tell me to leave this house. I did those other two jobs too—the first one as well as the one I done when I was supposed to be in the picture show."

"I'm not going to tell you to leave," Sheppard said. His voice was toneless, mechanical. "I'm going to save you."

Johnson thrust his head forward. "Save yourself," he hissed. "Nobody can save me but Jesus."

Sheppard laughed curtly. "You don't deceive me," he said. "I flushed that out of your head in the reformatory. I saved you from that, at least."

The muscles in Johnson's face stiffened. A look of such repulsion hardened on his face that Sheppard drew back. The boy's eyes were like distorting mirrors in which he saw himself made hideous and grotesque. "I'll show you," Johnson whispered. He rose abruptly and started headlong for the door as if he could not get out of Sheppard's sight quick enough, but it was the door to the back hall he went through, not the front door. Sheppard turned on the sofa and looked behind him where the boy had disappeared. He heard the door to his room slam. He was not leaving. The intensity had gone out of Sheppard's eyes. They looked flat and lifeless as if the shock of the boy's revelation were only now reaching the center of his consciousness. "If he would only leave," he murmured. "If he would only leave now of his own accord."

The next morning Johnson appeared at the breakfast table in the grandfather's suit he had come in. Sheppard pretended not to notice but one look told him what he already knew, that he was trapped, that there could be nothing now but a battle of nerves and that Johnson would win it. He wished he had never laid eyes on the boy. The failure of his compassion numbed him. He got out of the house as soon as he could and all day he dreaded to go home in the evening. He had a faint hope that the boy might be gone when he returned. The grandfather's suit might have meant he was leaving. The hope grew in the afternoon. When he came home and opened the front door, his heart was pounding.

He stopped in the hall and looked silently into the living room. His expectant expression faded. His face seemed suddenly as old as his white hair. The two boys were sitting close together on the sofa, reading the same book. Norton's cheek rested against the sleeve of Johnson's black suit. Johnson's finger moved under the lines they were reading. The elder brother and the younger. Sheppard looked woodenly at this scene for almost a minute. Then he walked into the room and took off his coat and dropped it on a chair. Neither boy noticed him. He went on to the kitchen.

Leola left the supper on the stove every afternoon before she left and he put it on the table. His head ached and his nerves were taut. He sat down on the kitchen stool and remained there, sunk in his depression. He wondered if he could infuriate Johnson enough to make him leave of his own accord. Last night what had enraged him was the Jesus business. It might enrage Johnson, but it depressed him. Why not simply tell the boy to go? Admit defeat. The thought of facing Johnson again sickened him. The boy looked at him as if he were the guilty one, as if he were a moral leper. He knew without conceit that he was a good man, that he had nothing to reproach himself with. His feelings about Johnson now were involuntary. He would like to feel compassion for him. He would like to be able to help him. He longed for the time when there would be no one but himself and Norton in the house, when the child's simple selfishness would be all he had to contend with, and his own loneliness.

330   He got up and took three serving dishes off the shelf and took them to the stove. Absently he began pouring the butterbeans and the hash into the dishes. When the food was on the table, he called them in.

They brought the book with them. Norton pushed his place setting around to the same side of the table as Johnson's and moved his chair next to Johnson's chair. They sat down and put the book between them. It was a black book with red edges.

"What's that you're reading?" Sheppard asked, sitting down.

"The Holy Bible," Johnson said.

God give me strength, Sheppard said under his breath.

335   "We lifted it from a ten cent store," Johnson said.

"We?" Sheppard muttered. He turned and glared at Norton. The child's face was bright and there was an excited sheen to his eyes. The change that had come over the boy struck him for the first time. He looked alert. He had on a blue plaid shirt and his eyes were a brighter blue than he had ever seen them before. There was a strange new life in him, the sign of new and more rugged vices. "So now you steal?" he said, glowering. "You haven't learned to be generous but you have learned to steal."

"No he ain't," Johnson said. "I was the one lifted it. He only watched. He can't sully himself. It don't make any difference about me. I'm going to hell anyway."

Sheppard held his tongue.

"Unless," Johnson said, "I repent."

340   "Repent, Rufus," Norton said in a pleading voice. "Repent, hear? You don't want to go to hell."

"Stop talking this nonsense," Sheppard said, looking sharply at the child.

"If I do repent, I'll be a preacher," Johnson said. "If you're going to do it, it's no sense in doing it halfway."

"What are you going to be, Norton," Sheppard asked in a brittle voice, "a preacher too?"

There was a glitter of wild pleasure in the child's eyes. "A space man!" he shouted.

345   "Wonderful," Sheppard said bitterly.

"Those space ships ain't going to do you any good unless you believe in Jesus," Johnson said. He wet his finger and began to leaf through the pages of the Bible. "I'll read you where it says so," he said.

Sheppard leaned forward and said in a low furious voice, "Put that Bible up, Rufus, and eat your dinner."

Johnson continued searching for the passage.

"Put that Bible up!" Sheppard shouted.

350   The boy stopped and looked up. His expression was startled but pleased.

"That book is something for you to hide behind," Sheppard said. "It's for cowards, people who are afraid to stand on their own feet and figure things out for themselves."

Johnson's eyes snapped. He backed his chair a little way from the table. "Satan has you in his power," he said. "Not only me. You too."

Sheppard reached across the table to grab the book but Johnson snatched it and put it in his lap.

Sheppard laughed. "You don't believe in that book and you know you don't believe in it!"

"I believe it!" Johnson said. "You don't know what I believe and what I don't."   355

Sheppard shook his head. "You don't believe it. You're too intelligent."

"I ain't too intelligent," the boy muttered. "You don't know nothing about me. Even if I didn't believe it, it would still be true."

"You don't believe it!" Sheppard said. His face was a taunt.

"I believe it!" Johnson said breathlessly. "I'll show you I believe it!" He opened the book in his lap and tore out a page of it and thrust it into his mouth. He fixed his eyes on Sheppard. His jaws worked furiously and the paper crackled as he chewed it.

"Stop this," Sheppard said in a dry, burnt-out voice. "Stop it."   360

The boy raised the Bible and tore out a page with his teeth and began grinding it in his mouth, his eyes burning.

Sheppard reached across the table and knocked the book out of his hand. "Leave the table," he said coldly.

Johnson swallowed what was in his mouth. His eyes widened as if a vision of splendor were opening up before him. "I've eaten it!" he breathed. "I've eaten it like Ezekiel and it was honey to my mouth!"[1]

"Leave this table," Sheppard said. His hands were clenched beside his plate.

"I've eaten it!" the boy cried. Wonder transformed his face. "I've eaten it like   365
Ezekiel and I don't want none of your food after it nor no more ever."

"Go then," Sheppard said softly. "Go. Go."

The boy rose and picked up the Bible and started toward the hall with it. At the door he paused, a small black figure on the threshold of some dark apocalypse. "The devil has you in his power," he said in a jubilant voice and disappeared.

After supper Sheppard sat in the living room alone. Johnson had left the house but he could not believe that the boy had simply gone. The first feeling of release had passed. He felt dull and cold as at the onset of an illness and dread had settled in him like a fog. Just to leave would be too anticlimactic an end for Johnson's taste; he would return and try to prove something. He might come back a week later and set fire to the place. Nothing seemed too outrageous now.

He picked up the paper and tried to read. In a moment he threw it down and

---

1. Ezekiel 3:1–3. The Lord in a vision told Ezekiel to eat a roll and go speak to the captive Israelites; when he ate "it was in my mouth as honey for sweetness."

got up and went into the hall and listened. He might be hiding in the attic. He went to the attic door and opened it.

370   The lantern was lit, casting a dim light on the stairs. He didn't hear anything. "Norton," he called, "are you up there?" There was no answer. He mounted the narrow stairs to see.

Amid the strange vine-like shadows cast by the lantern, Norton sat with his eye to the telescope. "Norton," Sheppard said, "do you know where Rufus went?"

The child's back was to him. He was sitting hunched, intent, his large ears directly above his shoulders. Suddenly he waved his hand and crouched closer to the telescope as if he could not get near enough to what he saw.

"Norton!" Sheppard said in a loud voice.

The child didn't move.

375   "Norton!" Sheppard shouted.

Norton started. He turned around. There was an unnatural brightness about his eyes. After a moment he seemed to see that it was Sheppard. "I've found her!" he said breathlessly.

"Found who?" Sheppard said.

"Mamma!"

Sheppard steadied himself in the door way. The jungle of shadows around the child thickened.

380   "Come and look!" he cried. He wiped his sweaty face on the tail of his plaid shirt and then put his eye back to the telescope. His back became fixed in a rigid intensity. All at once he waved again.

"Norton," Sheppard said, "you don't see anything in the telescope but star clusters. Now you've had enough of that for one night. You'd better go to bed. Do you know where Rufus is?"

"She's there!" he cried, not turning around from the telescope. "She waved at me!"

"I want you in bed in fifteen minutes," Sheppard said. After a moment he said, "Do you hear me, Norton?"

The child began to wave frantically.

385   "I mean what I say," Sheppard said. "I'm going to call in fifteen minutes and see if you're in bed."

He went down the steps again and returned to the parlor. He went to the front door and cast a cursory glance out. The sky was crowded with the stars he had been fool enough to think Johnson could reach. Somewhere in the small wood behind the house, a bull frog sounded a low hollow note. He went back to his chair and sat a few minutes. He decided to go to bed. He put his hands on the arms of the chair and leaned forward and heard, like the first shrill note of a disaster warning, the siren of a police car, moving slowly into the neighborhood and nearer until it subsided with a moan outside the house.

He felt a cold weight on his shoulders as if an icy cloak had been thrown about him. He went to the door and opened it.

Two policemen were coming up the walk with a dark snarling Johnson between them, handcuffed to each. A reporter jogged alongside and another policeman waited in the patrol car.

"Here's your boy," the dourest of the policemen said. "Didn't I tell you we'd get him?"

Johnson jerked his arm down savagely. "I was waitin for you!" he said. "You wouldn't have got me if I hadn't of wanted to get caught. It was my idea." He was addressing the policemen but leering at Sheppard.

Sheppard looked at him coldly.

"Why did you want to get caught?" the reporter asked, running around to get beside Johnson. "Why did you deliberately want to get caught?"

The question and the sight of Sheppard seemed to throw the boy into a fury. "To show up that big tin Jesus!" he hissed and kicked his leg out at Sheppard. "He thinks he's God. I'd rather be in the reformatory than in his house, I'd rather be in the pen! The Devil has him in his power. He don't know his left hand from his right, he don't have as much sense as his crazy kid!" He paused and then swept on to his fantastic conclusion. "He made suggestions to me!"

Sheppard's face blanched. He caught hold of the door facing.

"Suggestions?" the reporter said eagerly, "what kind of suggestion?"

"Immor'l suggestions!" Johnson said. "What kind of suggestions do you think? But I ain't having none of it, I'm a Christian, I'm . . ."

Sheppard's face was tight with pain. "He knows that's not true," he said in a shaken voice. "He knows he's lying. I did everything I knew how for him. I did more for him than I did for my own child. I hoped to save him and I failed, but it was an honorable failure. I have nothing to reproach myself with. I made no suggestions to him."

"Do you remember the suggestions?" the reporter asked. "Can you tell us exactly what he said?"

"He's a dirty atheist," Johnson said. "He said there wasn't no hell."

"Well, they seen each other now," one of the policemen said with a knowing sigh. "Let's us go."

"Wait," Sheppard said. He came down one step and fixed his eyes on Johnson's eyes in a last desperate effort to save himself. "Tell the truth, Rufus," he said. "You don't want to perpetrate this lie. You're not evil, you're mortally confused. You don't have to make up for that foot, you don't have to . . ."

Johnson hurled himself forward. "Listen at him!" he screamed. "I lie and steal because I'm good at it! My foot don't have a thing to do with it! The lame shall enter first! The halt'll be gathered together. When I get ready to be saved, Jesus'll save me, not that lying stinking atheist, not that . . ."

"That'll be enough out of you," the policeman said and yanked him back. "We just wanted you to see we got him," he said to Sheppard, and the two of them turned around and dragged Johnson away, half turned and screaming back at Sheppard.

"The lame'll carry off the prey!" he screeched, but his voice was muffled inside the car. The reporter scrambled into the front seat with the driver and slammed the door and the siren wailed into the darkness.

Sheppard remained there, bent slightly like a man who has been shot but continues to stand. After a minute he turned and went back in the house and sat down in the chair he had left. He closed his eyes on a picture of Johnson in a circle of reporters at the police station, elaborating his lies. "I have nothing to reproach myself with," he murmured. His every action had been selfless, his one aim had been to save Johnson for some decent kind of service, he had not spared himself, he had sacrificed his reputation, he had done more for Johnson than he had done for his own child. Foulness hung about him like an odor in the air, so close that it seemed to come from his own breath. "I have nothing to reproach myself with," he repeated. His voice sounded dry and harsh. "I did more for him than I did for my own child." He was swept with a sudden panic. He heard the boy's jubilant voice. Satan has you in his power.

"I have nothing to reproach myself with," he began again. "I did more for him than I did for my own child." He heard his voice as if it were the voice of his accuser. He repeated the sentence silently.

Slowly his face drained of color. It became almost gray beneath the white halo of his hair. The sentence echoed in his mind, each syllable like a dull blow. His mouth twisted and he closed his eyes against the revelation. Norton's face rose before him, empty, forlorn, his left eye listing almost imperceptibly toward the outer rim as if it could not bear a full view of grief. His heart constricted with a repulsion for himself so clear and intense that he gasped for breath. He had stuffed his own emptiness with good works like a glutton. He had ignored his own child to feed his vision of himself. He saw the clear-eyed Devil, the sounder of hearts, leering at him from the eyes of Johnson. His image of himself shrivelled until everything was black before him. He sat there paralyzed, aghast.

He saw Norton at the telescope, all back and ears, saw his arm shoot up and wave frantically. A rush of agonizing love for the child rushed over him like a transfusion of life. The little boy's face appeared to him transformed; the image of his salvation; all light. He groaned with joy. He would make everything up to him. He would never let him suffer again. He would be mother and father. He jumped up and ran to his room, to kiss him, to tell him that he loved him, that he would never fail him again.

The light was on in Norton's room but the bed was empty. He turned and dashed up the attic stairs and at the top reeled back like a man on the edge of a pit. The tripod had fallen and the telescope lay on the floor. A few feet over it, the child hung in the jungle of shadows, just below the beam from which he had launched his flight into space.

1965

FLANNERY O'CONNOR

Everything That Rises Must Converge

Her doctor had told Julian's mother that she must lose twenty pounds on account of her blood pressure, so on Wednesday nights Julian had to take her downtown on the bus for a reducing class at the Y. The reducing class was designed for working girls over fifty, who weighed from 165 to 200 pounds. His mother was one of the slimmer ones, but she said ladies did not tell their age or weight. She would not ride the buses by herself at night since they had been integrated, and because the reducing class was one of her few pleasures, necessary for her health, and *free,* she said Julian could at least put himself out to take her, considering all she did for him. Julian did not like to consider all she did for him, but every Wednesday night he braced himself and took her.

She was almost ready to go, standing before the hall mirror, putting on her hat, while he, his hands behind him, appeared pinned to the door frame, waiting like Saint Sebastian for the arrows to begin piercing him.[1] The hat was new and had cost her seven dollars and a half. She kept saying, "Maybe I shouldn't have paid that for it. No, I shouldn't have. I'll take it off and return it tomorrow. I shouldn't have bought it."

Julian raised his eyes to heaven. "Yes, you should have bought it," he said. "Put it on and let's go." It was a hideous hat. A purple velvet flap came down on one side of it and stood up on the other; the rest of it was green and looked like a cushion with the stuffing out. He decided it was less comical than jaunty and pathetic. Everything that gave her pleasure was small and depressed him.

She lifted the hat one more time and set it down slowly on top of her head. Two wings of gray hair protruded on either side of her florid face, but her eyes, sky-blue, were as innocent and untouched by experience as they must have been when she was ten. Were it not that she was a widow who had struggled fiercely to feed and clothe and put him through school and who was supporting him still, "until he got on his feet," she might have been a little girl that he had to take to town.

"It's all right, it's all right," he said. "Let's go." He opened the door himself and started down the walk to get her going. The sky was a dying violet and the houses stood out darkly against it, bulbous liver-colored monstrosities of a uniform ugliness though no two were alike. Since this had been a fashionable neighborhood forty years ago, his mother persisted in thinking they did well to have an apartment in it. Each house had a narrow collar of dirt around it in which sat, usually, a grubby child. Julian walked with his hands in his pockets, his head down and thrust forward and his eyes glazed with the determination to make himself completely numb during the time he would be sacrificed to her pleasure. 5

The door closed and he turned to find the dumpy figure, surmounted by the atrocious hat, coming toward him. "Well," she said, "you only live once and paying a little more for it, I at least won't meet myself coming and going."

"Some day I'll start making money," Julian said gloomily—he knew he never would—"and you can have one of those jokes whenever you take the fit." But first they would move. He visualized a place where the nearest neighbors would be three miles away on either side.

"I think you're doing fine," she said, drawing on her gloves. "You've only been out of school a year. Rome wasn't built in a day."

---

1. Discovered to be a Christian, Sebastian, Roman commander in Milan, was tied to a tree, shot with arrows, and left for dead. (He recovered but reasserted his faith and was clubbed to death.)

She was one of the few members of the Y reducing class who arrived in hat and gloves and who had a son who had been to college. "It takes time," she said, "and the world is in such a mess. This hat looked better on me than any of the others, though when she brought it out I said, 'Take that thing back. I wouldn't have it on my head,' and she said, 'Now wait till you see it on,' and when she put it on me, I said, 'We-ull,' and she said, 'If you ask me, that hat does something for you and you do something for the hat, and besides,' she said, 'with that hat, you won't meet yourself coming and going.' "

Julian thought he could have stood his lot better if she had been selfish, if she had been an old hag who drank and screamed at him. He walked along, saturated in depression, as if in the midst of his martyrdom he had lost his faith. Catching sight of his long, hopeless, irritated face, she stopped suddenly with a grief-stricken look, and pulled back on his arm. "Wait on me," she said. "I'm going back to the house and take this thing off and tomorrow I'm going to return it. I was out of my head. I can pay the gas bill with that seven-fifty."

He caught her arm in a vicious grip. "You are not going to take it back," he said. "I like it."

"Well," she said, "I don't think I ought . . ."

"Shut up and enjoy it," he muttered, more depressed than ever.

"With the world in the mess it's in," she said, "it's a wonder we can enjoy anything. I tell you, the bottom rail is on the top."

Julian sighed.

"Of course," she said, "if you know who are you, you can go anywhere." She said this every time he took her to the reducing class. "Most of them in it are not our kind of people," she said, "but I can be gracious to anybody. I know who I am."

"They don't give a damn for your graciousness," Julian said savagely. "Knowing who you are is good for one generation only. You haven't the foggiest idea where you stand now or who you are."

She stopped and allowed her eyes to flash at him. "I most certainly do know who I am," she said, "and if you don't know who you are, I'm ashamed of you."

"Oh hell," Julian said.

"Your great-grandfather was a former governor of this state," she said. "Your grandfather was a prosperous land-owner. Your grandmother was a Godhigh."

"Will you look around you," he said tensely, "and see where you are now?" and he swept his arm jerkily out to indicate the neighborhood, which the growing darkness at least made less dingy.

"You remain what you are," she said. "Your great-grandfather had a plantation and two hundred slaves."

"There are no more slaves," he said irritably.

"They were better off when they were," she said. He groaned to see that she was off on that topic. She rolled onto it every few days like a train on an open track. He knew every stop, every junction, every swamp along the way, and knew the exact point at which her conclusion would roll majestically into the station: "It's ridiculous. It's simply not realistic. They should rise, yes, but on their own side of the fence."

"Let's skip it," Julian said.

"The ones I feel sorry for," she said, "are the ones that are half white. They're tragic."

"Will you skip it?"

"Suppose we were half white. We would certainly have mixed feelings."

"I have mixed feelings now," he groaned.

"Well let's talk about something pleasant," she said. "I remember going to Grandpa's when I was a little girl. Then the house had double stairways that went up to what was really the second floor—all the cooking was done on the first. I used to like to stay down in the kitchen on account of the way the walls smelled. I would sit with my nose pressed against the plaster and take deep breaths. Actually the place belonged to the Godhighs but your grandfather Chestny paid the mortgage and saved it for them. They were in reduced circumstances," she said, "but reduced or not, they never forgot who they were."

"Doubtless that decayed mansion reminded them," Julian muttered. He never spoke of it without contempt or thought of it without longing. He had seen it once when he was a child before it had been sold. The double stairways had rotted and been torn down. Negroes were living in it. But it remained in his mind as his mother had known it. It appeared in his dreams regularly. He would stand on the wide porch, listening to the rustle of oak leaves, then wander through the high-ceilinged hall into the parlor that opened onto it and gaze at the worn rugs and faded draperies. It occurred to him that it was he, not she, who could have appreciated it. He preferred its threadbare elegance to anything he could name and it was because of it that all the neighborhoods they had lived in had been a torment to him—whereas she had hardly known the difference. She called her insensitivity "being adjustable."

"And I remember the old darky who was my nurse, Caroline. There was no better person in the world. I've always had a great respect for my colored friends," she said. "I'd do anything in the world for them and they'd . . ."

"Will you for God's sake get off that subject?" Julian said. When he got on a bus by himself, he made it a point to sit down beside a Negro, in reparation as it were for his mother's sins.

"You're mighty touchy tonight," she said. "Do you feel all right?"

"Yes I feel all right," he said. "Now lay off."

She pursed her lips. "Well, you certainly are in a vile humor," she observed. "I just won't speak to you at all."

They had reached the bus stop. There was no bus in sight and Julian, his hands still jammed in his pockets and his head thrust forward, scowled down the empty street. The frustration of having to wait on the bus as well as ride on it began to creep up his neck like a hot hand. The presence of his mother was borne in upon him as she gave a pained sigh. He looked at her bleakly. She was holding herself very erect under the preposterous hat, wearing it like a banner of her imaginary dignity. There was in him an evil urge to break her spirit. He suddenly unloosened his tie and pulled it off and put it in his pocket.

She stiffened. "Why must you look like *that* when you take me to town?" she said. "Why must you deliberately embarrass me?"

"If you'll never learn where you are," he said, "you can at least learn where I am."

"You look like a—thug," she said.

"Then I must be one," he murmured.

"I'll just go home," she said. "I will not bother you. If you can't do a little thing like that for me . . ."

Rolling his eyes upward, he put his tie back on. "Restored to my class," he muttered. He thrust his face toward her and hissed, "True culture is in the mind, the *mind*," he said, and tapped his head, "the mind."

"It's in the heart," she said, "and in how you do things and how you do things is because of who you *are*."

"Nobody in the damn bus cares who you are."

"I care who I am," she said icily.

The lighted bus appeared on top of the next hill and as it approached, they moved out into the street to meet it. He put his hand under her elbow and hoisted her up on the creaking step. She entered with a little smile, as if she were going into a drawing room where everyone had been waiting for her. While he put in the tokens, she sat down on one of the broad front seats for three which faced the aisle. A thin woman with protruding teeth and long yellow hair was sitting on the end of it. His mother moved up beside her and left room for Julian beside herself. He sat down and looked at the floor across the aisle where a pair of thin feet in red and white canvas sandals were planted.

His mother immediately began a general conversation meant to attract anyone who felt like talking. "Can it get any hotter?" she said and removed from her purse a folding fan, black with a Japanese scene on it, which she began to flutter before her.

"I reckon it might could," the woman with the protruding teeth said, "but I know for a fact my apartment couldn't get no hotter."

"It must get the afternoon sun," his mother said. She sat forward and looked up and down the bus. It was half filled. Everybody was white. "I see we have the bus to ourselves," she said. Julian cringed.

"For a change," said the woman across the aisle, the owner of the red and white canvas sandals. "I come on one the other day and they were thick as fleas—up front and all through."

"The world is in a mess everywhere," his mother said. "I don't know how we've let it get in this fix."

"What gets my goat is all those boys from good families stealing automobile tires," the woman with the protruding teeth said. "I told my boy, I said you may not be rich but you been raised right and if I ever catch you in any such mess, they can send you on to the reformatory. Be exactly where you belong."

"Training tells," his mother said. "Is your boy in high school?"

"Ninth grade," the woman said.

"My son just finished college last year. He wants to write but he's selling typewriters until he gets started," his mother said.

The woman leaned forward and peered at Julian. He threw her such a malevolent look that she subsided against the seat. On the floor across the aisle there was an abandoned newspaper. He got up and got it and opened it out in front of him. His mother discreetly continued the conversation in a lower tone but the woman across the aisle said in a loud voice, "Well that's nice. Selling typewriters is close to writing. He can go right from one to the other."

"I tell him," his mother said, "that Rome wasn't built in a day."

Behind the newspaper Julian was withdrawing into the inner compartment of his mind where he spent most of his time. This was a kind of mental bubble in which he established himself when he could not bear to be a part of what was going on around him. From it he could see out and judge but in it he was safe from any kind of penetration from without. It was the only place where he felt free of the general idiocy of his fellows. His mother had never entered it but from it he could see her with absolute clarity.

The old lady was clever enough and he thought that if she had started from any of the right premises, more might have been expected of her. She lived according to the laws of her own fantasy world, outside of which he had never seen her set foot. The law of it was to sacrifice herself for him after she had first created the necessity to do so by making a mess of things. If he had permitted her sacrifices, it was only because her lack of foresight had made them necessary. All of her life had been a struggle to act like a Chestny without the Chestny goods, and to give him everything she thought a Chestny ought to have; but since, said she, it was fun to struggle, why complain? And when you had won, as she had won, what fun to look back on the hard times! He could not forgive her that she had enjoyed the struggle and that she thought *she* had won.

What she meant when she said she had won was that she had brought him up successfully and had sent him to college and that he had turned out so well— good looking (her teeth had gone unfilled so that his could be straightened), intelligent (he realized he was too intelligent to be a success), and with a future ahead of him (there was of course no future ahead of him). She excused his gloominess on the grounds that he was still growing up and his radical ideas on his lack of practical experience. She said he didn't yet know a thing about "life," that he hadn't even entered the real world—when already he was as disenchanted with it as a man of fifty.

The further irony of all this was that in spite of her, he had turned out so well. In spite of going to only a third-rate college, he had, on his own initiative, come out with a first-rate education; in spite of growing up dominated by a small mind, he had ended up with a large one; in spite of all her foolish views, he was free of prejudice and unafraid to face facts. Most miraculous of all, instead of being blinded by love for her as she was for him, he had cut himself emotionally free of her and could see her with complete objectivity. He was not dominated by his mother.

The bus stopped with a sudden jerk and shook him from his meditation. A woman from the back lurched forward with little steps and barely escaped falling in his newspaper as she righted herself. She got off and a large Negro got on. Julian kept his paper lowered to watch. It gave him a certain satisfaction to see injustice in daily operation. It confirmed his view that with a few exceptions there was no one worth knowing within a radius of three hundred miles. The

60

Negro was well dressed and carried a briefcase. He looked around and then sat down on the other end of the seat where the woman with the red and white canvas sandals was sitting. He immediately unfolded a newspaper and obscured himself behind it. Julian's mother's elbow at once prodded insistently into his ribs. "Now you see why I won't ride on these buses by myself," she whispered.

The woman with the red and white canvas sandals had risen at the same time the Negro sat down and had gone further back in the bus and taken the seat of the woman who had got off. His mother leaned forward and cast her an approving look.

Julian rose, crossed the aisle, and sat down in the place of the woman with the canvas sandals. From this position, he looked serenely across at his mother. Her face had turned an angry red. He stared at her, making his eyes the eyes of a stranger. He felt his tension suddenly lift as if he had openly declared war on her.

He would have liked to get in conversation with the Negro and to talk with him about art or politics or any subject that would be above the comprehension of those around them, but the man remained entrenched behind his paper. He was either ignoring the change of seating or had never noticed it. There was no way for Julian to convey his sympathy.

His mother kept her eyes fixed reproachfully on his face. The woman with the protruding teeth was looking at him avidly as if he were a type of monster new to her.

"Do you have a light?" he asked the Negro.

Without looking away from his paper, the man reached in his pocket and handed him a packet of matches.

"Thanks," Julian said. For a moment he held the matches foolishly. A NO SMOKING sign looked down upon him from over the door. This alone would not have deterred him; he had no cigarettes. He had quit smoking some months before because he could not afford it. "Sorry," he muttered and handed back the matches. The Negro lowered the paper and gave him an annoyed look. He took the matches and raised the paper again.

His mother continued to gaze at him but she did not take advantage of his momentary discomfort. Her eyes retained their battered look. Her face seemed to be unnaturally red, as if her blood pressure had risen. Julian allowed no glimmer of sympathy to show on his face. Having got the advantage, he wanted desperately to keep it and carry it through. He would have liked to teach her a lesson that would last her a while, but there seemed no way to continue the point. The Negro refused to come out from behind his paper.

Julian folded his arms and looked stolidly before him, facing her but as if he did not see her, as if he had ceased to recognize her existence. He visualized a scene in which, the bus having reached their stop, he would remain in his seat and when she said, "Aren't you going to get off?" he would look at her as a stranger who had rashly addressed him. The corner they got off on was usually deserted, but it was well lighted and it would not hurt her to walk by herself the four blocks to the Y. He decided to wait until the time came and then decide whether or not he would let her get off by herself. He would have to be at the Y at ten to bring her back, but he could leave her wondering if he was going to show up. There was no reason for her to think she could always depend on him.

He retired again into the high-ceilinged room sparsely settled with large pieces of antique furniture. His soul expanded momentarily but then he became aware of his mother across from him and the vision shriveled. He studied her coldly. Her feet in little pumps dangled like a child's and did not quite reach the floor. She was training on him an exaggerated look of reproach. He felt completely detached from her. At that moment he could with pleasure have slapped her as he would have slapped a particularly obnoxious child in his charge.

He began to imagine various unlikely ways by which he could teach her a lesson. He might make friends with some distinguished Negro professor or lawyer and bring him home to spend the evening. He would be entirely justified but her blood pressure would rise to 300. He could not push her to the extent of making her have a stroke, and moreover, he had never been successful at making any Negro friends. He had tried to strike up an acquaintance on the bus with some of the better types, with ones that looked like professors or ministers or lawyers. One morning he had sat down next to a distinguished-looking dark brown man who had answered his questions with a sonorous solemnity but who had turned out to be an undertaker. Another day he had sat down beside a cigar-smoking Negro with a diamond ring on his finger, but after a few stilted pleasantries, the Negro had rung the buzzer and risen, slipping two lottery tickets into Julian's hand as he climbed over him to leave.

He imagined his mother lying desperately ill and his being able to secure only a Negro doctor for her. He toyed with that idea for a few minutes and then dropped it for a momentary vision of himself participating as a sympathizer in a sit-in demonstration. This was possible but he did not linger with it. Instead, he approached the ultimate horror. He brought home a beautiful suspiciously Negroid woman. Prepare yourself, he said. There is nothing you can do about it. This is the woman I've chosen. She's intelligent, dignified, even good, and she's suffered and she hasn't thought it *fun*. Now persecute us, go ahead and persecute us. Drive her out of here, but remember, you're driving me too. His eyes were narrowed and through the indignation he had generated, he saw his mother across the aisle, purple-faced, shrunken to the dwarf-like proportions of her moral nature, sitting like a mummy beneath the ridiculous banner of her hat.

He was tilted out of his fantasy again as the bus stopped. The door opened with a sucking hiss and out of the dark a large, gaily dressed, sullen-looking colored woman got on with a little boy. The child, who might have been four, had on a short plaid suit and a Tyrolean hat with a blue feather in it. Julian hoped that he would sit down beside him and that the woman would push in beside his mother. He could think of no better arrangement.

As she waited for her tokens, the woman was surveying the seating possibilities—he hoped with the idea of sitting where she was least wanted. There was something familiar-looking about her but Julian could not place what it was. She was a giant of a woman. Her face was set not only to meet opposition but to seek it out. The downward tilt of her large lower lip was like a warning sign: DON'T TAMPER WITH ME. Her bulging figure was encased in a green crepe dress and her feet overflowed in red shoes. She had on a hideous hat. A purple velvet flap came down on one side of it and stood up on the other; the rest of it was green and looked like a cushion with the stuffing out. She carried a mammoth red pocketbook that bulged throughout as if it were stuffed with rocks.

To Julian's disappointment, the little boy climbed up on the empty seat beside his mother. His mother lumped all children, black and white, into the common category, "cute," and she thought little Negroes were on the whole cuter than little white children. She smiled at the little boy as he climbed on the seat.

Meanwhile the woman was bearing down upon the empty seat beside Julian. To his annoyance, she squeezed herself into it. He saw his mother's face change as the woman settled herself next to him and he realized with satisfaction that this was more objectionable to her than it was to him. Her face seemed almost gray and there was a look of dull recognition in her eyes, as if suddenly she had sickened at some awful confrontation. Julian saw that it was because she and the woman had, in a sense, swapped sons. Though his mother would not realize the symbolic significance of this, she would feel it. His amusement showed plainly on his face.

The woman next to him muttered something unintelligible to herself. He was conscious of a kind of bristling next to him, a muted growling like that of an angry cat. He could not see anything but the red pocketbook upright on the bulging green thighs. He visualized the woman as she had stood waiting for her tokens—the ponderous figure, rising from the red shoes upward over the solid hips, the mammoth bosom, the haughty face, to the green and purple hat.

His eyes widened.

The vision of the two hats, identical, broke upon him with the radiance of a brilliant sunrise. His face was suddenly lit with joy. He could not believe that Fate had thrust upon his mother such a lesson. He gave a loud chuckle so that she would look at him and see that he saw. She turned her eyes on him slowly. The blue in them seemed to have turned a bruised purple. For a moment he had an uncomfortable sense of her innocence, but it lasted only a second before principle rescued him. Justice entitled him to laugh. His grin hardened until it said to her as plainly as if he were saying aloud: Your punishment exactly fits your pettiness. This should teach you a permanent lesson.

Her eyes shifted to the woman. She seemed unable to bear looking at him and to find the woman preferable. He became conscious again of the bristling presence at his side. The woman was rumbling like a volcano about to become active. His mother's mouth began to twitch slightly at one corner. With a sinking heart, he saw incipient signs of recovery on her face and realized that this was going to strike her suddenly as funny and was going to be no lesson at all. She kept her eyes on the woman and an amused smile came over her face as if the woman were a monkey that had stolen her hat. The little Negro was looking up at her with large fascinated eyes. He had been trying to attract her attention for some time.

"Carver!" the woman said suddenly. "Come heah!"

When he saw that the spotlight was on him at last, Carver drew his feet up and turned himself toward Julian's mother and giggled.

"Carver!" the woman said. "You heah me? Come heah!"

Carver slid down from the seat but remained squatting with his back against the base of it, his head turned slyly around toward Julian's mother, who was smiling at him. The woman reached a hand across the aisle and snatched him to her. He righted himself and hung backwards on her knees, grinning at Julian's mother. "Isn't he cute?" Julian's mother said to the woman with the protruding teeth.

"I reckon he is," the woman said without conviction.

The Negress yanked him upright but he eased out of her grip and shot across the aisle and scrambled, giggling wildly, onto the seat beside his love.

"I think he likes me," Julian's mother said, and smiled at the woman. It was the smile she used when she was being particularly gracious to an inferior. Julian saw everything was lost. The lesson had rolled off her like rain on a roof.

The woman stood up and yanked the little boy off the seat as if she were snatching him from contagion. Julian could feel the rage in her at having no weapon like his mother's smile. She gave the child a sharp slap across his leg. He howled once and then thrust his head into her stomach and kicked his feet against her shins. "Behave," she said vehemently.

The bus stopped and the Negro who had been reading the newspaper got off. The woman moved over and set the little boy down with a thump between herself and Julian. She held him firmly by the knee. In a moment he put his hands in front of his face and peeped at Julian's mother through his fingers.

"I see yoooooooo!" she said and put her hand in front of her face and peeped at him.

The woman slapped his hand down. "Quit yo' foolishness," she said, "before I knock the living Jesus out of you!"

Julian was thankful that the next stop was theirs. He reached up and pulled the cord. The woman reached up and pulled it at the same time. Oh my God, he thought. He had the terrible intuition that when they got off the bus together, his mother would open her purse and give the little boy a nickel. The gesture would be as natural to her as breathing. The bus stopped and the woman got up and lunged to the front, dragging the child, who wished to stay on, after her. Julian and his mother got up and followed. As they neared the door, Julian tried to relieve her of her pocketbook.

"No," she murmured, "I want to give the little boy a nickel."

"No!" Julian hissed. "No!"

She smiled down at the child and opened her bag. The bus door opened and the woman picked him up by the arm and descended with him, hanging at her hip. Once in the street she set him down and shook him.

Julian's mother had to close her purse while she got down the bus step but as soon as her feet were on the ground, she opened it again and began to rummage inside. "I can't find but a penny," she whispered, "but it looks like a new one."

"Don't do it!" Julian said fiercely between his teeth. There was a streetlight on the corner and she hurried to get under it so that she could better see into her pocketbook. The woman was heading off rapidly down the street with the child still hanging backward on her hand.

"Oh little boy!" Julian's mother called and took a few quick steps and caught up with them just beyond the lamppost. "Here's a bright new penny for you," and she held out the coin, which shone bronze in the dim light.

The huge woman turned and for a moment stood, her shoulders lifted and her face frozen with frustrated rage, and stared at Julian's mother. Then all at once she seemed to explode like a piece of machinery that had been given one ounce of pressure too much. Julian saw the black fist swing out with the red pocketbook. He shut his eyes and cringed as he heard the woman shout, "He don't take nobody's pennies!" When he opened his eyes, the woman was disappearing down the street with the little boy staring wide-eyed over her shoulder. Julian's mother was sitting on the sidewalk.

"I told you not to do that," Julian said angrily. "I told you not to do that!"

He stood over her for a minute, gritting his teeth. Her legs were stretched out in front of her and her hat was on her lap. He squatted down and looked her in the face. It was totally expressionless. "You got exactly what you deserved," he said. "Now get up."

105   He picked up her pocketbook and put what had fallen out back in it. He picked the hat up off her lap. The penny caught his eye on the sidewalk and he picked that up and let it drop before her eyes into the purse. Then he stood up and leaned over and held his hands out to pull her up. She remained immobile. He sighed. Rising above them on either side were black apartment buildings, marked with irregular rectangles of light. At the end of the block a man came out of a door and walked off in the opposite direction. "All right," he said, "suppose somebody happens by and wants to know why you're sitting on the sidewalk?"

She took the hand and, breathing hard, pulled heavily up on it and then stood for a moment, swaying slightly as if the spots of light in the darkness were circling around her. Her eyes, shadowed and confused, finally settled on his face. He did not try to conceal his irritation. "I hope this teaches you a lesson," he said. She leaned forward and her eyes raked his face. She seemed trying to determine his identity. Then, as if she found nothing familiar about him, she started off with a headlong movement in the wrong direction.

"Aren't you going on to the Y?" he asked.

"Home," she muttered.

"Well, are we walking?"

110   For answer she kept going. Julian followed along, his hands behind him. He saw no reason to let the lesson she had had go without backing it up with an explanation of its meaning. She might as well be made to understand what had happened to her. "Don't think that was just an uppity Negro woman," he said. "That was the whole colored race which will no longer take your condescending pennies. That was your black double. She can wear the same hat as you, and to be sure," he added gratuitously (because he thought it was funny), "it looked better on her than it did on you. What all this means," he said, "is that the old world is gone. The old manners are obsolete and your graciousness is not worth a damn." He thought bitterly of the house that had been lost for him. "You aren't who you think you are," he said.

She continued to plow ahead, paying no attention to him. Her hair had come undone on one side. She dropped her pocketbook and took no notice. He stooped and picked it up and handed it to her but she did not take it.

"You needn't act as if the world had come to an end," he said, "because it hasn't. From now on you've got to live in a new world and face a few realities for a change. Buck up," he said, "it won't kill you."

She was breathing fast.

"Let's wait on the bus," he said.

"Home," she said thickly. 115

"I hate to see you behave like this," he said. "Just like a child. I should be able to expect more of you." He decided to stop where he was and make her stop and wait for a bus. "I'm not going any farther," he said stopping. "We're going on the bus."

She continued to go on as if she had not heard him. He took a few steps and caught her arm and stopped her. He looked into her face and caught his breath. He was looking into a face he had never seen before. "Tell Grandpa to come get me," she said.

He stared, stricken.

"Tell Caroline to come get me," she said.

Stunned, he let her go and she lurched forward again, walking as if one leg 120 were shorter than the other. A tide of darkness seemed to be sweeping her from him. "Mother!" he cried. "Darling, sweetheart, wait!" Crumpling, she fell to the pavement. He dashed forward and fell at her side, crying, "Mamma, Mamma!" He turned her over. Her face was fiercely distorted. One eye, large and staring, moved slightly to the left as if it had become unmoored. The other remained fixed on him, raked his face again, found nothing and closed.

"Wait here, wait here!" he cried and jumped up and began to run for help toward a cluster of lights he saw in the distance ahead of him. "Help, help!" he shouted, but his voice was thin, scarcely a thread of sound. The lights drifted farther away the faster he ran and his feet moved numbly as if they carried him nowhere. The tide of darkness seemed to sweep him back to her, postponing from moment to moment his entry into the world of guilt and sorrow.

1965

FLANNERY O'CONNOR

Passages from Essays and Letters

from "The Fiction Writer and His Country"

. . . when I look at stories I have written I find that they are, for the most part, about people who are poor, who are afflicted in both mind and body, who have little—or at best a distorted—sense of spiritual purpose, and whose actions do not apparently give the reader a great assurance of the joy of life.

Yet how is this? For I am no disbeliever in spiritual purpose and no vague believer. I see from the standpoint of Christian orthodoxy. This means that for me the meaning of life is centered in our Redemption by Christ and what I see in the world I see in its relation to that.

Some may blame preoccupation with the grotesque on the fact that here we have a Southern writer and that this is just the type of imagination that Southern life fosters. . . . I find it hard to believe that what is observable behavior in one section can be entirely without parallel in another. At least, of late, Southern writers have had the opportunity of pointing out that none of us invented Elvis Presley and that that youth is himself probably less an occasion for concern than his popularity, which is not restricted to the Southern part of the country.

When you can assume that your audience holds the same beliefs you do, you can relax a little and use more normal means of talking to it; when you have to assume that it does not, then you have to make your vision apparent by shock— to the hard of hearing you shout, and for the almost-blind you draw large and startling figures.

from "The Grotesque in Southern Fiction"

All novelists are fundamentally seekers and describers of the real, but the realism of each novelist will depend on his view of the ultimate reaches of reality. . . . If the novelist is in tune with this [modern scientific] spirit, if he believes that actions are predetermined by psychic make-up or the economic situation or some other determinable factor, then he will be concerned above all with an accurate reproduction of the things that most immediately concern man, with the natural forces that he feels control his destiny. . . .

On the other hand, if the writer believes that our life is and will remain essentially mysterious, . . . then what he sees on the surface will be of interest to him only as he can go through it into an experience of mystery itself. . . . [F]or this kind of writer, the meaning of a story does not begin except at a depth where adequate motivation and adequate psychology and the various determinations have been exhausted. Such a writer will be interested in what we don't understand rather than in what we do.

from "The Nature and Aim of Fiction"

. . . The beginning of human knowledge is through the senses, and the fiction writer begins where human perception begins. He appeals through the senses, and you cannot appeal to the senses with abstractions. . . . [F]iction is so very much an incarnational art.

Now the word *symbol* scares a good many people off, just as the word *art* does. They seem to feel that a symbol is some mysterious thing put in arbitrarily by the writer to frighten the common reader—sort of a literary Masonic grip that is only for the initiated. They seem to think that it is a way of saying something that you aren't actually saying, and so . . . they approach it as if it were a problem in algebra. Find x. And when they do find or think they find this abstraction, x, then they go off with an elaborate sense of satisfaction and the notion that they have "understood" the story. . . .

I think for the fiction writer himself, symbols are something he uses simply as a matter of course. You might say that these are details that, while having their essential place in the literal level of the story, operate in depth as well as on the surface, increasing the story in every direction.

People have a habit of saying, "What is the theme of your story?" and they expect you to give them a statement. . . . And when they've got a statement . . . , they go off happy and feel it is no longer necessary to read the story. . . . , but for the fiction writer himself the whole story is the meaning, because it is an experience, not an abstraction.

from "Writing Short Stories"*

. . . A story is a complete dramatic action—and in good stories, the characters are shown through the action and the action is controlled through the characters, and the result of this is meaning that derives from the whole presented experience.

. . . Nothing essential to the main experience can be left out of a short story. All the action has to be satisfactorily accounted for in terms of motivation, and there has to be a beginning, a middle, and an end, though not necessarily in that order.

. . . I prefer to talk about the meaning in a story rather than the theme of a story. People talk about the theme of a story as if the theme were like the string that a sack of chicken feed is tied with. They think that if you can pick out the theme, the way you pick the right thread in the chicken-feed sack, you can rip the story open and feed the chickens. But this is not the way meaning works in fiction.

When you can state the theme of a story, when you can separate it from the story itself, then you can be sure the story is not a very good one. The meaning of a story has to be embodied in it, has to be made concrete in it. A story is a way to say something that can't be said any other way, and it takes every word in the story to say what the meaning is. You tell a story because a statement would be inadequate.

An idiom characterizes a society, and when you ignore the idiom, you are very likely ignoring the whole social fabric that could make a meaningful char-

---

* "The Nature and Aim of Fiction" and "Writing Short Stories" are composites, edited from O'Connor manuscripts by Sally and Robert Fitzgerald in *Mystery and Manners*.

acter. You can't cut characters off from their society and say much about them as individuals. You can't say anything meaningful about the mystery of a personality unless you put that personality in a believable and significant social context.

from "On Her Own Work"

In most English classes the short story has become a kind of literary specimen to be dissected. Every time a story of mine appears in a Freshman anthology, I have a vision of it, with its little organs laid open, like a frog in a bottle.

I realize that a certain amount of this what-is-the-significance has to go on, but I think something has gone wrong in the process when, for so many students, the story becomes simply a problem to be solved, something which you evaporate to get Instant Enlightenment.

A story isn't any good unless it successfully resists paraphrase, unless it hangs on and expands in the mind. Properly, you analyze to enjoy, but it's equally true that to analyze with any discrimination, you have to have enjoyed already, and I think that the best reason to hear a story read is that it should stimulate that primary enjoyment.

I often ask myself what makes a story work, and what makes it hold up as a story, and I have decided that it is probably some action, some gesture of a character that is unlike any other in the story, one which indicates where the real heart of the story lies. This would have to be an action or a gesture which was both totally right and totally unexpected; it would have to be one that was both in character and beyond character; it would have to suggest both the world and eternity. The action or gesture I'm talking about would have to be on the anagogical level, that is, the level which has to do with the Divine life and our participation in it. It would be a gesture that transcended any neat allegory that might have been intended or any pat moral categories a reader could make. It would be a gesture which somehow made contact with mystery.

. . . in my own stories I have found that violence is strangely capable of returning my characters to reality and preparing them to accept their moment of grace . . .

We hear many complaints about the prevalence of violence in modern fiction, and it is always assumed that this violence is a bad thing and meant to be an end in itself. With the serious writer, violence is never an end in itself. It is the extreme situation that best reveals what we are essentially . . .

from "Novelist and Believer"

. . . Great fiction . . . is not simply an imitation of feeling. The good novelist not only finds a symbol for feeling, he finds a symbol and a way of lodging it which tells the intelligent reader whether this feeling is adequate or inadequate, whether it is moral or immoral, whether it is good or evil. And his theology, even in its most remote reaches, will have a direct bearing on this.

. . . The artist penetrates the concrete world in order to find at its depths the image of its source, the image of ultimate reality. This in no way hinders his perception of evil but rather sharpens it, for only when the natural world is seen as good does evil become intelligible as a destructive force and a necessary result of our freedom.

From the Letters

TO A PROFESSOR OF ENGLISH, 28 MARCH 1961

The meaning of a story should go on expanding for the reader the more he thinks about it, but meaning cannot be captured in an interpretation. If teachers are in the habit of approaching a story as if it were a research problem for which any answer is believable so long as it is not obvious, then I think students will never learn to enjoy fiction. Too much interpretation is certainly worse than too little, and where feeling for a story is absent, theory will not supply it.

TO LOUISE AND TOM GOSSETT, 10 APRIL 1961

I have just read a review of my book [The Violent Bear It Away], long and damming [sic], which says it don't give us hope and courage and that all novels should give us hope and courage. I think if the novel is to give us virtue the selection of hope and courage is rather arbitrary—why not charity, peace, patience, joy, benignity, long-suffering and fear of the Lord? Or faith? The fact of the matter is that the modern mind opposes courage to faith. It also demands that the novel provide us with gifts that only religion can give. I don't think the novel can offend against the truth, but I think its truths are more particular than general. But this is a large subject and I ain't no aesthetician.

TO ROSLYN BARNES, 17 JUNE 1961

Can you tell me if the statement: "everything that rises must converge" is a true proposition in physics? I can easily see its moral, historical and evolutionary significance, but I want to know if it is also a correct physical statement.

TO "A", 22 JULY 1961

I had a story that I had written a first draft sort of on and Caroline thought as usual that it wasn't dramatic enough (and she was right) and told me all the things that I tell you when I read one of yours. She did think the structure was good and the situation. All I got to do is write the story. This one is called "The Lame Shall Enter First."

TO "A", 16 SEPTEMBER 1961

The thing I am writing now is surely going to convince Jack [the author John Hawkes] that I am of the Devil's party. It is out of hand right now but I am hoping I can bring it into line. It is a composite of all the eccentricities of my writing and for this reason may not be any good, maybe almost a parody. But what you start, you ought to carry through and if it is no good, I don't have to publish it. I am thinking of changing the title to "The Lame Will Carry Off the Prey."

TO JOHN HAWKES, 28 NOVEMBER 1961

You haven't convinced me that I write with the Devil's will or belong in the romantic tradition and I'm prepared to argue some more with you on this if I can remember where we left off at. I think the reason we can't agree on this is because there is a difference in our two devils. My Devil has a name, a history and a definite plan. His name is Lucifer, he's a fallen angel, his sin is pride, and his aim is the destruction of the Divine plan. Now I judge that your Devil is co-equal to God, not his creature: that pride is his virtue not his sin; and that his aim is not to destroy the Divine plan because there isn't any Divine plan to destroy. My Devil is objective and yours is subjective. You say one becomes "evil" when one leaves the herd. I say that depends entirely on what the herd is doing.

TO "A", 9 DECEMBER 1961

Some friends of mine in Texas wrote me that a friend of theirs went into a bookstore looking for a paperback copy of A Good Man. The clerk said, "We don't have that one but we have another by that author, called The Bear That Ran Away With It. I foresee the trouble I am going to have with "Everything That Rises Must Converge"—"Every Rabbit That Rises Is a Sage."

TO CECIL DAWKINS, 6 SEPTEMBER 1962

About the story ["The Lame Shall Enter First"] I certainly agree that it don't work and have never felt that it did, but in heaven's name where do you get the idea that Sheppard represents Freud? Freud never entered my mind and looking back over it, I can't make him fit now. The story is about a man who thought he was good and thought he was doing good when he wasn't. Freud was a great one, wasn't he, for bringing home to people the fact that they weren't what they thought they were, so if Freud were in this, which he is not, he would certainly be on the other side of the fence from Shepp. The story doesn't work because I don't know, don't sympathize, don't like Mr. Sheppard in the way that I know and like most of my other characters. This is a story, not a statement. I think you ought to look for simpler explanations of why things don't work and not mess around with philosophical ideas where they haven't been intended or don't apply. There's nothing in the story that could possibly suggest that Sheppard represents Freud. This is some theory of which you are possessed. I am wondering if this kind of theorizing could be what is interfering with your getting going on some writing. Don't mix up thought-knowledge with felt-knowledge. If Sheppard represents anything here, it is, as he realizes at the end of the story, the empty man who fills up his emptiness with good works.

TO "A", 3 NOVEMBER 1962

. . . In that story of mine ["The Lame Shall Enter First"] . . . the little boy wouldn't have been looking for his mother if she hadn't been a good one when she was alive. This of course could be debated, but it's nowhere suggested in the story that she wasn't a good one.

TO MARION MONTGOMERY, 16 JUNE 1963

I never wrote and thanked you for innerducing me at Georgia or for the copy of *The Sermon of Introduction*, but I liked them. They made up for my present lack of popularity with the *Atlanta Journal-Constitution* book page, that alert sheet of Sunday criticism. Did you ever see their mention of "Everything That Rises Must Converge"? Unsigned. I suspect somebody from Atlanta U. did it.

TO "A", 1 SEPTEMBER 1963

The topical is poison. I got away with it in "Everything That Rises" but only because I say a plague on everybody's house as far as the race business goes.

QUESTIONS

1. What sensory details do you find in the opening paragraph of "Odour of Chrysanthemums"? later in the story? What expectations are aroused by the opening paragraph? When do you first begin to suspect that Walter Bates is not off drinking somewhere?

2. In what ways might the opening of "The Rocking-Horse Winner" prepare you for the surreal or supernatural events later in the story?

3. If you did not know that "Odour of Chrysanthemums" and "The Rocking-Horse Winner" were by the same author, what internal evidence (elements, views, language within the story) might suggest it? How does "The Rocking-Horse Winner" of 1932 differ from the early story "Odour of Chrysanthemums"?

4. How does Sheppard explain why Norton throws up ("The Lame Shall Enter First," par. 48)? Why do you think he does (other than his putting peanut butter and ketchup on his cake!)?

5 . What internal evidence is there that "The Lame Shall Enter First" and "Everything That Rises Must converge" are by the same author?

WRITING SUGGESTIONS

1. Describe the continuity and the change or development in Lawrence's work, assuming those two stories are typical of that work and time of publication.

2. Briefly retell the story of "Everything That Rises Must Converge" from the point of view, perhaps even in the voice, of the African-American woman who is wearing "THE hat."

3. Compare the function of money in "The Rocking-Horse Winner" and "The Lame Shall Enter First."

9 A KIND: INITIATION

T hemes are useful for grouping stories together for comparison, both to highlight similarities and to reveal differences in history and structure and so to discover the uniqueness of the work. Types of characters—stereotypes—are useful for the same purpose: to show both the common qualities and the unique combination of qualities in a particular character in a story. Though all grouping and classification, used poorly, can blur distinctions and make all members of a group seem the same, when used well they do not blur but bring into focus the individuality of the individual thing or being.

Literary criticism lacks the specific and agreed-on system of classification of biology, so that its terms are not so fixed as *phylum, genus, species*. In general, we use the term **genre** for the largest commonly agreed-on categories: fiction, poetry, drama. When I'm trying to be consistent, I use the term **subgenre** for the divisions of fiction—novel, novella, short story, and so on. A **kind** is a species or subcategory within a subgenre.

There is one kind of short story that is so common that there are those who maintain it is not a kind but is equivalent to the subgenre short story itself. That pervasive kind is the **initiation** story, in which a character—often but not always a child or young person—first learns a significant truth about the universe, reality, society, people, himself or herself. Such a subject tends to dictate the main outlines of the story's action: it begins with the protagonist in a state of innocence or mistaken belief (exposition); it leads up to the moment of illumination or the discovery of the truth (rising action to climax or turning point), and ends usually with some indication of the result of that discovery (falling action to conclusion). This kind is particularly suitable to a short story because it lends itself to brief treatment: the illumination is more or less sudden—there is no need for lengthy development, for multiple scenes or settings, for much time to pass, for too many complications of action or a large cast of characters—yet it can encapsulate a whole life or important segment of a life and wide-ranging, significant themes.

If you've been reading this anthology from the beginning, you have already run into a number of initiation stories, and you may have some idea of what kinds of truths their protagonists discover. Young goodman Brown discovers the universality of evil in human beings. The captain in "The Secret Sharer" discovers that someone very much like him, virtually his double and therefore probably he himself, is not only capable of murder but may, under certain circumstances and in his capacity as a captain or leader, consciously choose murder as the lesser of evils. Leila ("Her First Ball") comes across the truth that youth is fleeting (you cannot say she really learns it, since by the end of that very short story she has forgotten it). We have also seen that one may retreat from the truth physically or psychologically, as does Brown, or remain unchanged or revert to one's former state, as Leila does.

Since to the young all things seem possible—one can be a doctor, novelist, tennis star, saint, and swinger, serially or simultaneously—many of the truths learned in initiation stories have to do with limitation. The girl in "Boys and Girls" learns that she is "only a girl." Fortunately, growing up is not just loss, and there are positive or "happy" initiation stories. The boy in "The Old People" is initiated first into "manhood," and takes his place among "the hunters," and then into a more exclusive, privileged fraternity, that of the owners or, as Faulkner would no doubt prefer it, "custodians" of the land.

Sometimes, the initiation takes place as an unscheduled event, as in "Araby." At other times there is a ritual or **rite of passage**, such as a formal entry into society ("Her First Ball"). What do we usually think of as the purpose of a debut? How does the society intend to induct its new member? As you read "Her First Ball," think about these questions and watch how Leila's debut fulfills its ritual role, how it differs from it, and how it may induct Leila into society more truly than intended. The ritual in "The Old People" is formal, communal, and ceremonial. The formalities of the rite in this story may bring to the surface elements in the pattern that lie beneath the surface in other stories.

By the time you finish this chapter you should have some idea of the variations possible within the initiation story, and as you look back to such stories as "Sonny's Blues," "The Country Husband," "How Much Land Does a Man Need?" "Her First Ball," "Odour of Chrysanthemums," and many of the others, you should have a still better idea of the range of stories in this kind. Adults may be initiated as well as children and adolescents; the truths may be bitter or pleasing, cosmic, social, psychological; the initiates may change forever, retreat, shrug off what they have learned. By seeing all these stories as part of the large group of initiation stories you may the more readily notice the differences in the protagonists, in the learning experience, in the results of the initiation on the protagonists and whether they are permanent or temporary, life-denying or life-enhancing. You may, in other words, have gone a long way toward defining the unique vision of the story, its precise and individual illumination of reality. And that's the function of classification in the first place.

KIND A Glossary

genre: the largest category for classifying literature—fiction, poetry, drama

initiation story: a *kind* of short story in which a character—often but not always a child or young person—first learns a significant, usually life-changing truth about the universe, society, people, himself or herself

kind: a species or subcategory within a *subgenre; initiation stories* are a subcategory of the subgenre short story

rite of passage: a ritual or ceremony marking an individual's passing from one stage or state to a more advance one, or an event in one's life which seems to have such significance; a formal initiation

subgenre: division within the category of a *genre*; novel, novella, and short story are subgenres of the genre fiction

JAMES JOYCE

Araby

North Richmond Street, being blind,[1] was a quiet street except at the hour when the Christian Brothers' School set the boys free. An uninhabited house of two storeys stood at the blind end, detached from its neighbours in a square ground. The other houses of the street, conscious of decent lives within them, gazed at one another with brown imperturbable faces.

The former tenant of our house, a priest, had died in the back drawing-room. Air, musty from having been long enclosed, hung in all the rooms, and the waste room behind the kitchen was littered with old useless papers. Among these I found a few paper-covered books, the pages of which were curled and damp: *The Abbot*, by Walter Scott, *The Devout Communicant* and *The Memoirs of Vidocq*.[2] I liked the last best because its leaves were yellow. The wild garden behind the house contained a central apple tree and a few straggling bushes, under one of which I found the late tenant's rusty bicycle-pump. He had been a very charitable priest; in his will he had left all his money to institutions and the furniture of his house to his sister.

When the short days of winter came, dusk fell before we had well eaten our dinners. When we met in the street the houses had grown sombre. The space of sky above us was the colour of ever-changing violet and towards it the lamps of the street lifted their feeble lanterns. The cold air stung us and we played till our bodies glowed. Our shouts echoed in the silent street. The career of our play brought us through the dark muddy lanes behind the houses, where we ran the gauntlet of the rough tribes from the cottages, to the back doors of the dark dripping gardens where odours arose from the ashpits,[3] to the dark odorous stables where a coachman smoothed and combed the horse or shook music from the buckled harness. When we returned to the street, light from the kitchen windows had filled the areas. If my uncle was seen turning the corner, we hid in the shadow until we had seen him safely housed. Or if Mangan's sister came out on the doorstep to call her brother in to his tea, we watched her from our shadow peer up and down the street. We waited to see whether she would remain or go in and, if she remained, we left our shadow and walked up to Mangan's steps resignedly. She was waiting for us, her figure defined by the light from the half-opened door. Her brother always teased her before he obeyed, and I stood by the railings looking at her. Her dress swung as she moved her body, and the soft rope of her hair tossed from side to side.

Every morning I lay on the floor in the front parlour watching her door. The

---

1. Dead-end street. 2. The 1820 novel by Sir Walter Scott (1771–1834) is a romance about the Catholic Mary Queen of Scots (1542–87), who was beheaded; a Catholic religious tract: *The Devout Communicant: or Pious Meditations and Aspirations for the Three Days Before and Three Days After Receiving the Holy Eucharist* (1813); the "memoirs" were probably *not* written by François Vidocq (1775–1857), a French criminal who became chief of detectives and who died poor and disgraced for his part in a crime that he solved. 3. Where fireplace ashes were dumped.

blind was pulled down to within an inch of the sash so that I could not be seen. When she came out on the doorstep my heart leaped. I ran to the hall, seized my books and followed her. I kept her brown figure always in my eye and, when we came near the point at which our ways diverged, I quickened my pace and passed her. This happened morning after morning. I had never spoken to her, except for a few casual words, and yet her name was like a summons to all my foolish blood.

Her image accompanied me even in places the most hostile to romance. On Saturday evenings when my aunt went marketing I had to go to carry some of the parcels. We walked through the flaring streets, jostled by drunken men and bargaining women, amid the curses of labourers, the shrill litanies of shop-boys who stood on guard by the barrels of pigs' cheeks, the nasal chanting of street-singers, who sang a *come-all-you* about O'Donovan Rossa,[4] or a ballad about the troubles in our native land. These noises converged in a single sensation of life for me: I imagined that I bore my chalice safely through a throng of foes. Her name sprang to my lips at moments in strange prayers and praises which I myself did not understand. My eyes were often full of tears (I could not tell why) and at times a flood from my heart seemed to pour itself out into my bosom. I thought little of the future. I did not know whether I would ever speak to her or not or, if I spoke to her, how I would tell her of my confused adoration. But my body was like a harp and her words and gestures were like fingers running upon the wires.

One evening I went into the back drawing-room in which the priest had died. It was a dark rainy evening and there was no sound in the house. Through one of the broken panes I heard the rain impinge upon the earth, the fine incessant needles of water playing in the sodden beds. Some distant lamp or lighted window gleamed below me. I was thankful that I could see so little. All my senses seemed to desire to veil themselves and, feeling that I was about to slip from them, I pressed the palms of my hands together until they trembled, murmuring: "O love! O love!" many times.

At last she spoke to me. When she addressed the first words to me I was so confused that I did not know what to answer. She asked me was I going to *Araby*.[5] I forgot whether I answered yes or no. It would be a splendid bazaar, she said; she would love to go.

"And why can't you?" I asked.

While she spoke she turned a silver bracelet round and round her wrist. She could not go, she said, because there would be a retreat that week in her convent. Her brother and two other boys were fighting for their caps and I was alone at the railings. She held one of the spikes, bowing her head towards me. The light from the lamp opposite our door caught the white curve of her neck, lit up her hair that rested there and, falling, lit up the hand upon the railing. It fell over one side of her dress and caught the white border of a petticoat, just visible as she stood at ease.

4. Jeremiah O'Donovan (1831–1915) was a militant Irish nationalist who fought on despite terms in prison and banishment. *Come-all-you:* A song, of which there were many, which began "Come, all you Irishmen." 5. A bazaar billed as a "Grand Oriental Fête," Dublin, May 1894.

10

"It's well for you," she said.

"If I go," I said. "I will bring you something."

What innumerable follies laid waste my waking and sleeping thoughts after that evening! I wished to annihilate the tedious intervening days. I chafed against the work of school. At night in my bedroom and by day in the classroom her image came between me and the page I strove to read. The syllables of the word *Araby* were called to me through the silence in which my soul luxuriated and cast an Eastern enchantment over me. I asked for leave to go to the bazaar on Saturday night. My aunt was surprised and hoped it was not some Freemason[6] affair. I answered few questions in class. I watched my master's face pass from amiability to sternness; he hoped I was not beginning to idle. I could not call my wandering thoughts together. I had hardly any patience with the serious work of life which, now that it stood between me and my desire, seemed to me child's play, ugly monotonous child's play.

On Saturday morning I reminded my uncle that I wished to go to the bazaar in the evening. He was fussing at the hallstand, looking for the hat-brush, and answered me curtly:

"Yes, boy, I know."

15

As he was in the hall I could not go into the front parlour and lie at the window. I left the house in bad humour and walked slowly towards the school. The air was pitilessly raw and already my heart misgave me.

When I came home to dinner my uncle had not yet been home. Still it was early. I sat staring at the clock for some time and, when its ticking began to irritate me, I left the room. I mounted the staircase and gained the upper part of the house. The high, cold, empty, gloomy rooms liberated me and I went from room to room singing. From the front window I saw my companions playing below in the street. Their cries reached me weakened and indistinct and, leaning my forehead against the cool glass, I looked over at the dark house where she lived. I may have stood there for an hour, seeing nothing but a brown-clad figure cast by my imagination, touched discreetly by the lamplight at the curved neck, at the hand upon the railings and at the border below the dress.

When I came downstairs again I found Mrs. Mercer sitting at the fire. She was an old, garrulous woman, a pawnbroker's widow, who collected used stamps for some pious purpose. I had to endure the gossip of the tea-table. The meal was prolonged beyond an hour and still my uncle did not come. Mrs. Mercer stood up to go: she was sorry she couldn't wait any longer, but it was after eight o'clock and she did not like to be out late, as the night air was bad for her. When she had gone I began to walk up and down the room, clenching my fists. My aunt said:

"I'm afraid you may put off your bazaar for this night of Our Lord."

At nine o'clock I heard my uncle's latchkey in the hall door. I heard him talking to himself and heard the hallstand rocking when it had received the weight of his overcoat. I could interpret these signs. When he was midway through his dinner I asked him to give me the money to go to the bazaar. He had forgot-ten.

---

6. The Masons, or Freemasons, were considered enemies of the Catholics.

"The people are in bed and after their first sleep now," he said.

I did not smile. My aunt said to him energetically:

"Can't you give him the money and let him go? You've kept him late enough as it is."

My uncle said he was very sorry he had forgotten. He said he believed in the old saying: "All work and no play makes Jack a dull boy." He asked me where I was going and, when I had told him a second time, he asked me did I know *The Arab's Farewell to his Steed.*[7] When I left the kitchen he was about to recite the opening lines of the piece to my aunt.

I held a florin[8] tightly in my hand as I strode down Buckingham Street towards the station. The sight of the streets thronged with buyers and glaring with gas recalled to me the purpose of my journey. I took my seat in a third-class carriage of a deserted train. After an intolerable delay the train moved out of the station slowly. It crept onward among ruinous houses and over the twinkling river. At Westland Row Station a crowd of people pressed to the carriage doors; but the porters moved them back, saying that it was a special train for the bazaar. I remained alone in the bare carriage. In a few minutes the train drew up beside an improvised wooden platform. I passed out on to the road and saw by the lighted dial of a clock that it was ten minutes to ten. In front of me was a large building which displayed the magical name.

I could not find any sixpenny entrance and, fearing that the bazaar would be closed, I passed in quickly through a turnstile, handing a shilling to a weary-looking man. I found myself in a big hall girdled at half its height by a gallery. Nearly all the stalls were closed and the greater part of the hall was in darkness. I recognized a silence like that which pervades a church after a service. I walked into the centre of the bazaar timidly. A few people were gathered about the stalls which were still open. Before a curtain, over which the words *Café Chantant*[9] were written in coloured lamps, two men were counting money on a salver. I listened to the fall of the coins.

Remembering with difficulty why I had come I went over to one of the stalls and examined porcelain vases and flowered tea-sets. At the door of the stall a young lady was talking and laughing with two young gentlemen. I remarked their English accents and listened vaguely to their conversation.

"O, I never said such a thing!"

"O, but you did!"

"O, but I didn't!"

"Didn't she say that?"

"Yes. I heard her."

"O, there's a . . . fib!"

Observing me, the young lady came over and asked me did I wish to buy anything. The tone of her voice was not encouraging; she seemed to have spoken to me out of a sense of duty. I looked humbly at the great jars that stood like eastern guards at either side of the dark entrance to the stall and murmured:

---

7. Or *The Arab's Farewell to His Horse*, sentimental nineteenth-century poem by Caroline Norton. The speaker has sold the horse.   8. Two-shilling piece; thus four times the "sixpenny entrance" fee.   9. Café with music.

"No, thank you."

The young lady changed the position of one of the vases and went back to the two young men. They began to talk of the same subject. Once or twice the young lady glanced at me over her shoulder.

I lingered before her stall, though I knew my stay was useless, to make my interest in her wares seem the more real. Then I turned away slowly and walked down the middle of the bazaar. I allowed the two pennies to fall against the sixpence in my pocket. I heard a voice call from one end of the gallery that the light was out. The upper part of the hall was now completely dark.

Gazing up into the darkness I saw myself as a creature driven and derided by vanity; and my eyes burned with anguish and anger.

1914

ALICE MUNRO

Boys and Girls

My father was a fox farmer. That is, he raised silver foxes, in pens; and in the fall and early winter, when their fur was prime, he killed them and skinned them and sold their pelts to the Hudson's Bay Company or the Montreal Fur Traders. These companies supplied us with heroic calendars to hang, one on each side of the kitchen door. Against a background of cold blue sky and black pine forests and treacherous northern rivers, plumed adventurers planted the flags of England or of France; magnificent savages bent their backs to the portage.

For several weeks before Christmas, my father worked after supper in the cellar of our house. The cellar was white-washed, and lit by a hundred-watt bulb over the worktable. My brother Laird and I sat on the top step and watched. My father removed the pelt inside-out from the body of the fox, which looked surprisingly small, mean and rat-like, deprived of its arrogant weight of fur. The naked, slippery bodies were collected in a sack and buried at the dump. One time the hired man, Henry Bailey, had taken a swipe at me with this sack, saying, "Christmas present!" My mother thought that was not funny. In fact she disliked the whole pelting operation—that was what the killing, skinning, and preparation of the furs was called—and wished it did not have to take place in the house. There was the smell. After the pelt had been stretched inside-out on a long board my father scraped away delicately, removing the little clotted webs of blood vessels, the bubbles of fat; the smell of blood and animal fat, with the strong primitive odour of the fox itself, penetrated all parts of the house. I found it reassuringly seasonal, like the smell of oranges and pine needles.

Henry Bailey suffered from bronchial troubles. He would cough and cough until his narrow face turned scarlet, and his light blue, derisive eyes filled up with tears; then he took the lid off the stove, and, standing well back, shot out a great clot of phlegm—hsss—straight into the heart of the flames. We admired him for this performance and for his ability to make his stomach growl at will,

Major Barbara — "you have learnt something. That always feels at first as if you had lost something"

Boys and Girls ∇ 387

and for his laughter, which was full of high whistlings and gurglings and involved the whole faulty machinery of his chest. It was sometimes hard to tell what he was laughing at, and always possible that it might be us.

After we had been sent to bed we could still smell fox and still hear Henry's laugh, but these things, reminders of the warm, safe, brightly lit downstairs world, seemed lost and diminished, floating on the stale cold air upstairs. We were afraid at night in the winter. We were not afraid of *outside* though this was the time of year when snowdrifts curled around our house like sleeping whales and the wind harassed us all night, coming up from the buried fields, the frozen swamp, with its old bugbear chorus of threats and misery. We were afraid of *inside*, the room where we slept. At this time the upstairs of our house was not finished. A brick chimney went up one wall. In the middle of the floor was a square hole, with a wooden railing around it; that was where the stairs came up. On the other side of the stairwell were the things that nobody had any use for any more—a soldiery roll of linoleum, standing on end, a wicker baby carriage, a fern basket, china jugs and basins with cracks in them, a picture of the Battle of Balaclava,[1] very sad to look at. I had told Laird, as soon as he was old enough to understand such things, that bats and skeletons lived over there; whenever a man escaped from the county jail, twenty miles away, I imagined that he had somehow let himself in the window and was hiding behind the linoleum. But we had rules to keep us safe. When the light was on, we were safe as long as we did not step off the square of worn carpet which defined our bedroom-space; when the light was off no place was safe but the beds themselves. I had to turn out the light kneeling on the end of my bed, and stretching as far as I could to reach the cord.

In the dark we lay on our beds, our narrow life rafts, and fixed our eyes on the faint light coming up the stairwell, and sang songs. Laird sang "Jingle Bells," which he would sing any time, whether it was Christmas or not, and I sang "Danny Boy." I loved the sound of my own voice, frail and supplicating, rising in the dark. We could make out the tall frosted shapes of the windows now, gloomy and white. When I came to the part, *When I am dead, as dead I well may be*—a fit of shivering caused not by the cold sheets but by pleasurable emotion almost silenced me. *You'll kneel and say, an Ave there above me*—What was an Ave? Every day I forgot to find out.

Laird went straight from singing to sleep. I could hear his long, satisfied, bubbly breaths. Now for the time that remained to me, the most perfectly private and perhaps the best time of the whole day, I arranged myself tightly under the covers and went on with one of the stories I was telling myself from night to night. These stories were about myself, when I had grown a little older; they took place in a world that was recognizably mine, yet one that presented opportunities for courage, boldness and self-sacrifice, as mine never did. I rescued people from a bombed building (it discouraged me that the real war had gone on so far away from Jubilee). I shot two rabid wolves who were menacing the schoolyard (the teachers cowered terrified at my back). I rode a fine horse spiritedly down the

5

---

1. An indecisive Crimean War battle fought on October 25, 1854.

main street of Jubilee, acknowledging the townspeople's gratitude for some yet-to-be-worked-out piece of heroism (nobody ever rode a horse there, except King Billy in the Orangemen's Day[2] parade). There was always riding and shooting in these stories, though I had only been on a horse twice—bareback because we did not own a saddle—and the second time I had slid right around and dropped under the horse's feet; it had stepped placidly over me. I really was learning to shoot, but I could not hit anything yet, not even tin cans on fence posts.

Alive, the foxes inhabited a world my father made for them. It was surrounded by a high guard fence, like a medieval town, with a gate that was padlocked at night. Along the streets of this town were ranged large, sturdy pens. Each of them had a real door that a man could go through, a wooden ramp along the wire, for the foxes to run up and down on, and a kennel—something like a clothes chest with airholes—where they slept and stayed in winter and had their young. There were feeding and watering dishes attached to the wire in such a way that they could be emptied and cleaned from the outside. The dishes were made of old tin cans, and the ramps and kennels of odds and ends of old lumber. Everything was tidy and ingenious; my father was tirelessly inventive and his favourite book in the world was Robinson Crusoe.[3] He had fitted a tin drum on a wheelbarrow, for bringing water down to the pens. This was my job in summer, when the foxes had to have water twice a day. Between nine and ten o'clock in the morning, and again after supper, I filled the drum at the pump and trundled it down through the barnyard to the pens, where I parked it, and filled my watering can and went along the streets. Laird came too, with his little cream and green gardening can, filled too full and knocking against his legs and slopping water on his canvas shoes. I had the real watering can, my father's, though I could only carry it three-quarters full.

The foxes all had names, which were printed on a tin plate and hung beside their doors. They were not named when they were born, but when they survived the first year's pelting and were added to the breeding stock. Those my father had named were called names like Prince, Bob, Wally and Betty. Those I had named were called Star or Turk, or Maureen or Diana. Laird named one Maud after a hired girl we had when he was little, one Harold after a boy at school, and one Mexico, he did not say why.

Naming them did not make pets out of them, or anything like it. Nobody but my father ever went into the pens, and he had twice had blood-poisoning from bites. When I was bringing them their water they prowled up and down on the paths they had made inside their pens, barking seldom—they saved that for nighttime, when they might get up a chorus of community frenzy—but always watching me, their eyes burning, clear gold, in their pointed, malevolent faces. They were beautiful for their delicate legs and heavy, aristocratic tails and the

2. The Orange Society is an Irish Protestant group named after William of Orange, who, as King William III of England, defeated the Catholic James II. The Society sponsors an annual procession on July 12 to commemorate the victory of William III at the Battle of the Boyne (1690).   3. Novel (1719) by Daniel Defoe about a man shipwrecked on a desert island; it goes into great detail about his ingenious contraptions.

bright fur sprinkled on dark down their backs—which gave them their name—
but especially for their faces, drawn exquisitely sharp in pure hostility, and their
golden eyes.

Besides carrying water I helped my father when he cut the long grass, and
the lamb's quarter and flowering money-musk, that grew between the pens. He
cut with the scythe and I raked into piles. Then he took a pitchfork and threw
fresh-cut grass all over the top of the pens, to keep the foxes cooler and shade
their coats, which were browned by too much sun. My father did not talk to me
unless it was about the job we were doing. In this he was quite different from my
mother, who, if she was feeling cheerful, would tell me all sorts of things—the
name of a dog she had had when she was a little girl, the names of boys she had
gone out with later on when she was grown up, and what certain dresses of hers
had looked like—she could not imagine now what had become of them. Whatever thoughts and stories my father had were private, and I was shy of him and
would never ask him questions. Nevertheless I worked willingly under his eyes,
and with a feeling of pride. One time a feed salesman came down into the pens
to talk to him and my father said, "Like to have you meet my new hired man."
I turned away and raked furiously, red in the face with pleasure.

"Could of fooled me," said the salesman. "I thought it was only a girl."

After the grass was cut, it seemed suddenly much later in the year. I walked
on stubble in the earlier evening, aware of the reddening skies, the entering
silences, of fall. When I wheeled the tank out of the gate and put the padlock
on, it was almost dark. One night at this time I saw my mother and father
standing talking on the little rise of ground we called the gangway, in front of
the barn. My father had just come from the meathouse; he had his stiff bloody
apron on, and a pail of cut-up meat in his hand.

It was an odd thing to see my mother down at the barn. She did not often
come out of the house unless it was to do something—hang out the wash or dig
potatoes in the garden. She looked out of place, with her bare lumpy legs, not
touched by the sun, her apron still on and damp across the stomach from the
supper dishes. Her hair was tied up in a kerchief, wisps of it falling out. She
would tie her hair up like this in the morning, saying she did not have time to
do it properly, and it would stay tied up all day. It was true, too; she really did
not have time. These days our back porch was piled with baskets of peaches and
grapes and pears, bought in town, and onions and tomatoes and cucumbers
grown at home, all waiting to be made into jelly and jam and preserves, pickles
and chili sauce. In the kitchen there was a fire in the stove all day, jars clinked
in boiling water, sometimes a cheesecloth bag was strung on a pole between two
chairs, straining blue-black grape pulp for jelly. I was given jobs to do and I
would sit at the table peeling peaches that had been soaked in the hot water, or
cutting up onions, my eyes smarting and streaming. As soon as I was done I ran
out of the house, trying to get out of earshot before my mother thought of what
she wanted me to do next. I hated the hot dark kitchen in summer, the green
blinds and the flypapers, the same old oilcloth table and wavy mirror and bumpy
linoleum. My mother was too tired and preoccupied to talk to me, she had no
heart to tell about the Normal School Graduation Dance; sweat trickled over her

10

face and she was always counting under her breath, pointing at jars, dumping cups of sugar. It seemed to me that work in the house was endless, dreary and peculiarly depressing; work done out of doors, and in my father's service, was ritualistically important.

I wheeled the tank up to the barn, where it was kept, and I heard my mother saying, "Wait till Laird gets a little bigger, then you'll have a real help."

What my father said I did not hear. I was pleased by the way he stood listening, politely as he would to a salesman or a stranger, but with an air of wanting to get on with his real work. I felt my mother had no business down here and I wanted him to feel the same way. What did she mean about Laird? He was no help to anybody. Where was he now? Swinging himself sick on the swing, going around in circles, or trying to catch caterpillars. He never once stayed with me till I was finished.

"And then I can use her more in the house," I heard my mother say. She had a dead-quiet, regretful way of talking about me that always made me uneasy. "I just get my back turned and she runs off. It's not like I had a girl in the family at all."

I went and sat on a feed bag in the corner of the barn, not wanting to appear when this conversation was going on. My mother, I felt, was not to be trusted. She was kinder than my father and more easily fooled, but you could not depend on her, and the real reasons for the things she said and did were not to be known. She loved me, and she sat up late at night making a dress of the difficult style I wanted, for me to wear when school started, but she was also my enemy. She was always plotting. She was plotting now to get me to stay in the house more, although she knew I hated it (*because* she knew I hated it) and keep me from working for my father. It seemed to me she would do this simply out of perversity, and to try her power. It did not occur to me that she could be lonely, or jealous. No grown-up could be; they were too fortunate. I sat and kicked my heels monotonously against a feedbag, raising dust, and did not come out till she was gone.

At any rate, I did not expect my father to pay any attention to what she said. Who could imagine Laird doing my work—Laird remembering the padlock and cleaning out the watering-dishes with a leaf on the end of a stick, or even wheeling the tank without it tumbling over? It showed how little my mother knew about the way things really were.

I have forgotten to say what the foxes were fed. My father's bloody apron reminded me. They were fed horsemeat. At this time most farmers still kept horses, and when a horse got too old to work, or broke a leg or got down and would not get up, as they sometimes did, the owner would call my father, and he and Henry went out to the farm in the truck. Usually they shot and butchered the horse there, paying the farmer from five to twelve dollars. If they had already too much meat on hand, they would bring the horse back alive, and keep it for a few days or weeks in our stable, until the meat was needed. After the war the farmers were buying tractors and gradually getting rid of horses altogether, so it sometimes happened that we got a good healthy horse, that there was just no use for any more. If this happened in the winter we might keep the horse in our stable till spring, for we had plenty of hay and if there was a lot of snow—and the plow did not always get our road cleared—it was convenient to be able to go to town with a horse and cutter.[4]

The winter I was eleven years old we had two horses in the stable. We did not know what names they had had before, so we called them Mack and Flora. Mack was an old black workhorse, sooty and indifferent. Flora was a sorrel mare, a driver. We took them both out in the cutter. Mack was slow and easy to handle. Flora was given to fits of violent alarm, veering at cars and even at other horses, but we loved her speed and high-stepping, her general air of gallantry and abandon. On Saturdays we went down to the stable and as soon as we opened the door on its cosy, animal-smelling darkness Flora threw up her head, rolled her eyes, whinnied despairingly and pulled herself through a crisis of nerves on the spot. It was not safe to go into her stall; she would kick.

This winter also I began to hear a great deal more on the theme my mother had sounded when she had been talking in front of the barn. I no longer felt safe. It seemed that in the minds of the people around me there was a steady undercurrent of thought, not to be deflected, on this one subject. The word *girl* had formerly seemed to me innocent and unburdened, like the world *child*; now it appeared that it was no such thing. A girl was not, as I had supposed, simply what I was; it was what I had to become. It was a definition, always touched with emphasis, with reproach and disappointment. Also it was a joke on me. Once Laird and I were fighting, and for the first time ever I had to use all my strength against him; even so, he caught and pinned my arm for a moment, really hurting me. Henry saw this, and laughed, saying, "Oh, that there Laird's gonna show you, one of these days!" Laird was getting a lot bigger. But I was getting bigger too.

My grandmother came to stay with us for a few weeks and I heard other things. "Girls don't slam doors like that." "Girls keep their knees together when they sit down." And worse still, when I asked some questions, "That's none of girls' business." I continued to slam the doors and sit as awkwardly as possible, thinking that by such measures I kept myself free.

When spring came, the horses were let out in the barnyard. Mack stood against the barn wall trying to scratch his neck and haunches, but Flora trotted up and down and reared at the fences, clattering her hooves against the rails. Snow drifts dwindled quickly, revealing the hard grey and brown earth, the familiar rise and fall of the ground, plain and bare after the fantastic landscape of winter. There was a great feeling of opening-out, of release. We just wore rubbers now, over our shoes; our feet felt ridiculously light. One Saturday we went out to the stable and found all the doors open, letting in the unaccustomed sunlight and fresh air. Henry was there, just idling around looking at his collection of calendars which were tacked up behind the stalls in a part of the stable my mother had probably never seen.

"Come to say goodbye to your old friend Mack?" Henry said. "Here, you

4. A small, light sleigh.

give him a taste of oats." He poured some oats into Laird's cupped hands and Laird went to feed Mack. Mack's teeth were in bad shape. He ate very slowly, patiently shifting the oats around in his mouth, trying to find a stump of a molar to grind it on. "Poor old Mack," said Henry mournfully. "When a horse's teeth's gone, he's gone. That's about the way."

25   "Are you going to shoot him today?" I said. Mack and Flora had been in the stable so long I had almost forgotten they were going to be shot.

Henry didn't answer me. Instead he started to sing in a high, trembly, mocking-sorrowful voice, *Oh, there's no more work, for poor Uncle Ned, he's gone where the good darkies go.*[5] Mack's thick, blackish tongue worked diligently at Laird's hand. I went out before the song was ended and sat down on the gangway.

I had never seen them shoot a horse, but I knew where it was done. Last summer Laird and I had come upon a horse's entrails before they were buried. We had thought it was a big black snake, coiled up in the sun. That was around in the field that ran up beside the barn. I thought that if we went inside the barn, and found a wide crack or knothole to look through we would be able to see them do it. It was not something I wanted to see; just the same, if a thing really happened, it was better to see it, and know.

My father came down from the house, carrying the gun.

"What are you doing here?" he said.

30   "Nothing."

"Go on up and play around the house."

He sent Laird out of the stable. I said to Laird, "Do you want to see them shoot Mack?" and without waiting for an answer led him around to the front door of the barn, opened it carefully, and went in. "Be quiet or they'll hear us," I said. We could hear Henry and my father talking in the stable, then the heavy, shuffling steps of Mack being backed out of his stall.

In the loft it was cold and dark. Thin, crisscrossed beams of sunlight fell through the cracks. The hay was low. It was a rolling country, hills and hollows, slipping under our feet. About four feet up was a beam going around the walls. We piled hay up in one corner and I boosted Laird up and hoisted myself. The beam was not very wide; we crept along it with our hands flat on the barn walls. There were plenty of knotholes, and I found one that gave me the view I wanted— a corner of the barnyard, the gate, part of the field. Laird did not have a knothole and began to complain.

I showed him a widened crack between two boards. "Be quiet and wait. If they hear you you'll get us in trouble."

35   My father came in sight carrying the gun. Henry was leading Mack by the halter. He dropped it and took out his cigarette papers and tobacco; he rolled cigarettes for my father and himself. While this was going on Mack nosed around in the old, dead grass along the fence. Then my father opened the gate and they took Mack through. Henry led Mack way from the path to a patch of ground and they talked together, not loud enough for us to hear. Mack again began searching for a mouthful of fresh grass, which was not to be found. My father

---

5. Lines from the Stephen Foster song "Old Uncle Ned."

walked away in a straight line, and stopped short at a distance which seemed to suit him. Henry was walking away from Mack too, but sideways, still negligently holding on to the halter. My father raised the gun and Mack looked up as if he had noticed something and my father shot him.

Mack did not collapse at once but swayed, lurched sideways and fell, first on his side; then he rolled over on his back and, amazingly, kicked his legs for a few seconds in the air. At this Henry laughed, as if Mack had done a trick for him. Laird, who had drawn a long, groaning breath of surprise when the shot was fired, said out loud, "He's not dead." And it seemed to me it might be true. But his legs stopped, he rolled on his side again, his muscles quivered and sank. The two men walked over and looked at him in a businesslike way; they bent down and examined his forehead where the bullet had gone in, and now I saw his blood on the brown grass.

"Now they just skin him and cut him up," I said. "Let's go." My legs were a little shaky and I jumped gratefully down into the hay. "Now you've seen how they shoot a horse," I said in a congratulatory way, as if I had seen it many times before. "Let's see if any barn cat's had kittens in the hay." Laird jumped. He seemed young and obedient again. Suddenly I remembered how, when he was little, I had brought him into the barn and told him to climb the ladder to the top beam. That was in the spring, too, when the hay was low. I had done it out of a need for excitement, a desire for something to happen so that I could tell about it. He was wearing a little bulky brown and white checked coat, made down from one of mine. He went all the way up, just as I told him, and sat down on the top beam with the hay far below him on one side, and the barn floor and some old machinery on the other. Then I ran screaming to my father, "Laird's up on the top beam!" My father came, my mother came, my father went up the ladder talking very quietly and brought Laird down under his arm, at which my mother leaned against the ladder and began to cry. They said to me, "Why weren't you watching him?" but nobody ever knew the truth. Laird did not know enough to tell. But whenever I saw the brown and white checked coat hanging in the closet, or at the bottom of the rag bag, which was where it ended up, I felt a weight in my stomach, the sadness of unexorcized guilt.

I looked at Laird who did not even remember this, and I did not like the look on this thin, winter-pale face. His expression was not frightened or upset, but remote, concentrating. "Listen," I said, in an unusually bright and friendly voice, "you aren't going to tell, are you?"

"No," he said absently.

"Promise."

"Promise," he said. I grabbed the hand behind his back to make sure he was not crossing his fingers. Even so, he might have a nightmare; it might come out that way. I decided I had better work hard to get all thoughts of what he had seen out of his mind—which, it seemed to me, could not hold very many things at a time. I got some money I had saved and that afternoon we went into Jubilee and saw a show, with Judy Canova,[6] at which we both laughed a great deal. After that I thought it would be all right.

40

6. American comedian best known for her yodeling in hillbilly movies of the 1940s.

Two weeks later I knew they were going to shoot Flora. I knew from the night before, when I heard my mother ask if the hay was holding out all right, and my father said, "Well, after to-morrow there'll just be the cow, and we should be able to put her out to grass in another week." So I knew it was Flora's turn in the morning.

This time I didn't think of watching it. That was something to see just one time. I had not thought about it very often since, but sometimes when I was busy, working at school, or standing in front of the mirror combing my hair and wondering if I would be pretty when I grew up, the whole scene would flash into my mind: I would see the easy, practised way my father raised the gun, and hear Henry laughing when Mack kicked his legs in the air. I did not have any great feeling of horror and opposition, such as a city child might have had; I was too used to seeing the death of animals as a necessity by which we lived. Yet I felt a little ashamed, and there was a new wariness, a sense of holding-off, in my attitude to my father and his work.

It was a fine day, and we were going around the yard picking up tree branches that had been torn off in winter storms. This was something we had been told to do, and also we wanted to use them to make a teepee. We heard Flora whinny, and then my father's voice and Henry's shouting, and we ran down to the barn-yard to see what was going on.

The stable door was open. Henry had just brought Flora out, and she had broken away from him. She was running free in the barnyard, from one end to the other. We climbed up on the fence. It was exciting to see her running, whinnying, going up on her hind legs, prancing and threatening like a horse in a Western movie, an unbroken ranch horse, though she was just an old driver, an old sorrel mare. My father and Henry ran after her and tried to grab the dangling halter. They tried to work her into a corner, and they had almost succeeded when she made a run between them, wild-eyed, and disappeared around the corner of the barn. We heard the rails clatter down as she got over the fence, and Henry yelled, "She's into the field now!"

That meant she was in the long L-shaped field that ran up by the house. If she got around the center, heading towards the lane, the gate was open; the truck had been driven into the field this morning. My father shouted to me, because I was on the other side of the fence, nearest the lane, "Go shut the gate!"

I could run very fast. I ran across the garden, past the tree where our swing was hung, and jumped across a ditch into the lane. There was the open gate. She had not got out, I could not see her up on the road; she must have run to the other end of the field. The gate was heavy. I lifted it out of the gravel and carried it across the roadway. I had it half-way across when she came in sight, galloping straight towards me. There was just time to get the chain on. Laird came scrambling through the ditch to help me.

Instead of shutting the gate, I opened it as wide as I could. I did not make any decision to do this, it was just what I did. Flora never slowed down; she galloped straight past me, and Laird jumped up and down, yelling, "Shut it, shut it!" even after it was too late. My father and Henry appeared in the field a moment too late to see what I had done. They only saw Flora heading for the township road. They would think I had not got there in time.

They did not waste any time asking about it. They went back to the barn and got the gun and the knives they used, and put these in the truck; then they turned the truck around and came bouncing up the field toward us. Laird called to them, "Let me go too, let me go too!" and Henry stopped the truck and they took him in. I shut the gate after they were all gone.

I supposed Laird would tell. I wondered what would happen to me. I had never disobeyed my father before, and I could not understand why I had done it. Flora would not really get away. They would catch up with her in the truck. Or if they did not catch her this morning somebody would see her and telephone us this afternoon or tomorrow. There was no wild country here for her to run to, only farms. What was more, my father had paid for her, we needed the meat to feed the foxes, we needed the foxes to make our living. All I had done was make more work for my father who worked hard enough already. And when my father found out about it he was not going to trust me any more; he would know that I was not entirely on his side. I was on Flora's side, and that made me no use to anybody, not even to her. Just the same, I did not regret it; when she came running at me and I held the gate open, that was the only thing I could do.

I went back to the house, and my mother said, "What's all the commotion?" I told her that Flora had kicked down the fence and got away. "Your poor father," she said, "now he'll have to go chasing over the countryside. Well, there isn't any use planning dinner before one." She put up the ironing board. I wanted to tell her, but thought better of it and went upstairs and sat on my bed.

Lately I had been trying to make my part of the room fancy, spreading the bed with old lace curtains, and fixing myself a dressing-table with some leftovers of cretonne for a skirt. I planned to put up some kind of barricade between my bed and Laird's, to keep my section separate from his. In the sunlight, the lace curtains were just dusty rags. We did not sing at night any more. One night when I was singing Laird said, "You sound silly," and I went right on but the next night I did not start. There was not so much need to anyway, we were no longer afraid. We knew it was just old furniture over there, old jumble and confusion. We did not keep to the rules. I still stayed awake after Laird was asleep and told myself stories, but even in these stories something different was happening, mysterious alterations took place. A story might start off in the old way, with a spectacular danger, a fire or wild animals, and for a while I might rescue people; then things would change around, and instead, somebody would be rescuing me. It might be a boy from our class at school, or even Mr. Campbell, our teacher, who tickled girls under the arms. And at this point the story concerned itself at great length with what I looked like—how long my hair was, and what kind of dress I had on; by the time I had these details worked out the real excitement of the story was lost.

It was later than one o'clock when the truck came back. The tarpaulin was over the back, which meant there was meat in it. My mother had to heat dinner up all over again. Henry and my father had changed from their bloody overalls into ordinary working overalls in the barn, and they washed their arms and necks and faces at the sink, and splashed water on their hair and combed it. Laird lifted his arm to show off a streak of blood. "We shot old Flora," he said, "and cut her up in fifty pieces."

"Well I don't want to hear about it," my mother said. "And don't come to my table like that."

My father made him go and wash the blood off.

We sat down and my father said grace and Henry pasted his chewing-gum on the end of his fork, the way he always did; when he took it off he would have us admire the pattern. We began to pass the bowls of steaming, overcooked vegetables. Laird looked across the table at me and said proudly, distinctly, "Anyway it was her fault Flora got away."

"What?" my father said.

"She could of shut the gate and she didn't. She just open' it up and Flora run out."

"Is that right?" my father said.

Everybody at the table was looking at me. I nodded, swallowing food with great difficulty. To my shame, tears flooded my eyes.

My father made a curt sound of disgust. "What did you do that for?"

I did not answer. I put down my fork and waited to be sent from the table, still not looking up.

But this did not happen. For some time nobody said anything, then Laird said matter-of-factly, "She's crying."

"Never mind," my father said. He spoke with resignation, even good humour, the words which absolved and dismissed me for good. "She's only a girl," he said.

I didn't protest that, even in my heart. Maybe it was true.

1968

WILLIAM FAULKNER

The Old People

I

At first there was nothing. There was the faint, cold, steady rain, the gray and constant light of the late November dawn, with the voices of the hounds converging somewhere in it and toward them. Then Sam Fathers, standing just behind the boy as he had been standing when the boy shot his first running rabbit with his first gun and almost with the first load it ever carried, touched his shoulder and he began to shake, not with any cold. Then the buck was there. He did not come into sight; he was just there, looking not like a ghost but as if all of light were condensed in him and he were the source of it, not only moving in it but disseminating it, already running, seen first as you always see the deer, in that split second after he has already seen you, already slanting away in that

We'll be reading 3 Faulkner stories. I want you to be noting similarities of style; theme in each, so by end of semester, you'll be able to write well on Faulkner and what distinguishes him from other writers

first soaring bound, the antlers even in that dim light looking like a small rock-ing-chair balanced on his head.

"Now," Sam Fathers said, "shoot quick, and slow."

The boy did not remember the shot at all. He would live to be eighty, as his father and his father's twin brother and their father in his turn had lived to be, but he would never hear that shot nor remember even the shock of the gun-butt. He didn't even remember what he did with the gun afterward. He was running. Then he was standing over the buck where it lay on the wet earth still in the attitude of speed and not looking at all dead, standing over it shaking and jerking, with Sam Fathers beside him again, extending the knife. "Dont walk up to him in front," Sam said. "If he aint dead, he will cut you all to pieces with his feet. Walk up to him from behind and take him by the horn first, so you can hold his head down until you can jump away. Then slip your other hand down and hook your fingers in his nostrils."

The boy did that—drew the head back and the throat taut and drew Sam Fathers' knife across the throat and Sam stooped and dipped his hands in the hot smoking blood and wiped them back and forth across the boy's face. Then Sam's horn rang in the wet gray woods and again and again; there was a boiling wave of dogs about them, with Tennie's Jim and Boon Hogganbeck whipping them back after each had had a taste of the blood, then the men, the true hunters—Walter Ewell whose rifle never missed, and Major de Spain and old General Compson and the boy's cousin, McCaslin Edmonds, grandson of his father's sister, sixteen years his senior and, since both he and McCaslin were only children and the boy's father had been nearing seventy when he was born, more his brother than his cousin and more his father than either—sitting their horses and looking down at them: at the old man of seventy who had been a negro for two generations now but whose face and bearing were still those of the Chickasaw chief who had been his father; and the white boy of twelve with the prints of the bloody hands on his face, who had nothing to do now but stand straight and not let the trembling show.

"Did he do all right, Sam?" his cousin McCaslin said.

"He done all right," Sam Fathers said.

They were the white boy, marked forever, and the old dark man sired on both sides by savage kings, who had marked him, whose bloody hands had merely formally consecrated him to that which, under the man's tutelage, he had already accepted, humbly and joyfully, with abnegation and with pride too; the hands, the touch, the first worthy blood which he had been found at last worthy to draw, joining him and the man forever, so that the man would continue to live past the boy's seventy years and then eighty years, long after the man himself had entered the earth as chiefs and kings entered it;—the child, not yet a man, whose grandfather had lived in the same country and in almost the same manner as the boy himself would grow up to live, leaving his descendants in the land in his turn as his grandfather had done, and the old man past seventy whose grandfathers had owned the land long before the white men ever saw it and who had vanished from it now with all their kind, what of blood they left behind them running now in another race and for a while even in bondage and now drawing

5

toward the end of its alien and irrevocable course, barren, since Sam Fathers
had no children.

His father was Ikkemotubbe himself, who had named himself Doom. Sam
told the boy about that—how Ikkemotubbe, old Issetibbeha's sister's son, had
run away to New Orleans in his youth and returned seven years later with a
French companion calling himself the Chevalier Soeur-Blonde de Vitry, who
must have been the Ikkemotubbe of his family too and who was already addressing Ikkemotubbe as *Du Homme*[1]—returned, came home again, with his foreign
Aramis[2] and the quadroon slave woman who was to be Sam's mother, and a
gold-laced hat and coat and a wicker wine-hamper containing a litter of month-
old puppies and a gold snuff-box filled with a white powder resembling fine
sugar. And how he was met at the River landing by three or four companions of
his bachelor youth, and while the light of a smoking torch gleamed on the glittering braid of the hat and coat Doom squatted in the mud of the land and took
one of the puppies from the hamper and put a pinch of the white powder on its
tongue and the puppy died before the one who was holding it could cast it away.
And how they returned to the Plantation where Issetibbeha, dead now, had been
succeeded by his son, Doom's fat cousin Moketubbe, and the next day Moketubbe's eight-year-old son died suddenly and that afternoon, in the presence of
Moketubbe and most of the others (the People, Sam Fathers called them) Doom
produced another puppy from the wine-hamper and put a pinch of the white
powder on its tongue and Moketubbe abdicated and Doom became in fact The
Man which his French friend already called him. And how on the day after that,
during the ceremony of accession, Doom pronounced a marriage between the
pregnant quadroon and one of the slave men which he had just inherited (that
was how Sam Fathers got his name, which in Chickasaw had been Had-Two-
Fathers) and two years later sold the man and woman and the child who was his
own son to his white neighbor, Carothers McCaslin.

That was seventy years ago. The Sam Fathers whom the boy knew was already
sixty—a man not tall, squat rather, almost sedentary, flabby-looking though he
actually was not, with hair like a horse's mane which even at seventy showed no
trace of white and a face which showed no age until he smiled, whose only
visible trace of negro blood was a slight dullness of the hair and the fingernails,
and something else which you did notice about the eyes, which you noticed
because it was not always there, only in repose and not always then—something
not in their shape nor pigment but in their expression, and the boy's cousin
McCaslin told him what that was: not the heritage of Ham, not the mark of
servitude but of bondage; the knowledge that for a while that part of his blood
had been the blood of slaves. "Like an old lion or a bear in a cage," McCaslin
said. "He was born in the cage and has been in it all his life; he knows nothing
else. Then he smells something. It might be anything, any breeze blowing past
anything and then into his nostrils. But there for a second was the hot sand or
the cane-brake that he never even saw himself, might not even know if he did

---

1. Mistaken or provincialized French for "The Man," with overtones of nobility.   2. One of
Alexandre Dumas' three musketeers.

see it and probably does know he couldn't hold his own with it if he got back to it. But that's not what he smells then. It was the cage he smelled. He hadn't smelled the cage until that minute. Then the hot sand or the brake blew into his nostrils and blew away, and all he could smell was the cage. That's what makes his eyes look like that."

"Then let him go!" the boy cried. "Let him go!"

His cousin laughed shortly. Then he stopped laughing, making the sound that is. It had never been laughing. "His cage aint McCaslins," he said. "He was a wild man. When he was born, all his blood on both sides, except the little white part, knew things that had been tamed out of our blood so long ago that we have not only forgotten them, we have to live together in herds to protect ourselves from our own sources. He was the direct son not only of a warrior but of a chief. Then he grew up and began to learn things, and all of a sudden one day he found out that he had been betrayed, the blood of the warriors and chiefs had been betrayed. Not by his father," he added quickly. "He probably never held it against old Doom for selling him and his mother into slavery, because he probably believed the damage was already done before then and it was the same warriors' and chiefs' blood in him and Doom both that was betrayed through the black blood which his mother gave him. Not betrayed by the black blood and not wilfully betrayed by his mother, but betrayed by her all the same, who had bequeathed him not only the blood of slaves but even a little of the very blood which had enslaved it; himself his own battleground, the scene of his own vanquishment and the mausoleum of his defeat. His cage aint us," McCaslin said. "Did you ever know anybody yet, even your father and Uncle Buddy, that ever told him to do or not do anything that he ever paid any attention to?"

That was true. The boy first remembered him as sitting in the door of the plantation blacksmith-shop, where he sharpened plow-points and mended tools and even did rough carpenter-work when he was not in the woods. And sometimes, even when the woods had not drawn him, even with the shop cluttered with work which the farm waited on, Sam would sit there, doing nothing at all for half a day or a whole one, and no man, neither the boy's father and twin uncle in their day nor his cousin McCaslin after he became practical though not yet titular master, ever to say to him, "I want this finished by sundown" or "why wasn't this done yesterday?" And once each year, in the late fall, in November, the boy would watch the wagon, the hooped canvas top erected now, being loaded—the food, hams and sausage from the smokehouse, coffee and flour and molasses from the commissary, a whole beef killed just last night for the dogs until there would be meat in camp, the crate containing the dogs themselves, then the bedding, the guns, the horns and lanterns and axes, and his cousin McCaslin and Sam Fathers in their hunting clothes would mount to the seat and with Tennie's Jim sitting on the dog-crate they would drive away to Jefferson, to join Major de Spain and General Compson and Boon Hogganbeck and Walter Ewell and go on into the big bottom of the Tallahatchie where the deer and bear were, to be gone two weeks. But before the wagon was even loaded the boy would find that he could watch no longer. He would go away, running almost, to stand behind the corner where he could not see the wagon and nobody

10

could see him, not crying, holding himself rigid except for the trembling, whispering to himself: "Soon now. Soon now. Just three more years" (or two more or one more) "and I will be ten. Then Cass said I can go."

White man's work, when Sam did work. Because he did nothing else: farmed no alloted acres of his own, as the other ex-slaves of old Carothers McCaslin did, performed no field-work for daily wages as the younger and newer negroes did—and the boy never knew just how that had been settled between Sam and old Carothers, or perhaps with old Carothers' twin sons after him. For, although Sam lived among the negroes, in a cabin among the other cabins in the quarters, and consorted with negroes (what of consorting with anyone Sam did after the boy got big enough to walk alone from the house to the blacksmith-shop and then to carry a gun) and dressed like them and talked like them and even went with them to the negro church now and then, he was still the son of that Chickasaw chief and the negroes knew it. And, it seemed to the boy, not only negroes. Boon Hogganbeck's grandmother had been a Chickasaw woman too, and although the blood had run white since and Boon was a white man, it was not chief's blood. To the boy at least, the difference was apparent immediately you saw Boon and Sam together, and even Boon seemed to know it was there—even Boon, to whom in his tradition it had never occurred that anyone might be better born than himself. A man might be smarter, he admitted that, or richer (luckier, he called it) but not better born. Boon was a mastiff, absolutely faithful, dividing his fidelity equally between Major de Spain and the boy's cousin McCaslin, absolutely dependent for his very bread and dividing that impartially too between Major de Spain and McCaslin, hardy, generous, courageous enough, a slave to all the appetites and almost unratiocinative. In the boy's eyes at least it was Sam Fathers, the negro, who bore himself not only toward his cousin McCaslin and Major de Spain but toward all white men, with gravity and dignity and without servility or recourse to that impenetrable wall of ready and easy mirth which negroes sustain between themselves and white men, bearing himself toward his cousin McCaslin not only as one man to another but as an older man to a younger.

He taught the boy the woods, to hunt, when to shoot and when not to shoot, when to kill and when not to kill, and better, what to do with it afterward. Then he would talk to the boy, the two of them sitting beneath the close fierce stars on a summer hilltop while they waited for the hounds to bring the fox back within hearing, or beside a fire in the November or December woods while the dogs worked out a coon's trail along the creek, or fireless in the pitch dark and heavy dew of April mornings while they squatted beneath a turkey-roost. The boy would never question him; Sam did not react to questions. The boy would just wait and then listen and Sam would begin, talking about the old days and the People whom he had not had time ever to know and so could not remember (he did not remember ever having seen his father's face), and in place of whom the other race into which his blood had run supplied him with no substitute.

And as he talked about those old times and those dead and vanished men of another race from either that the boy knew, gradually to the boy those old times would cease to be old times and would become a part of the boy's present, not only as if they had happened yesterday but as if they were still happening, the men who walked through them actually walking in breath and air and casting an actual shadow on the earth they had not quitted. And more: as if some of them had not happened yet but would occur tomorrow, until at last it would seem to the boy that he himself had not come into existence yet, that none of his race nor the other subject race which his people had brought with them into the land had come here yet; that although it had been his grandfather's and then his father's and uncle's and was now his cousin's and someday would be his own land which he and Sam hunted over, their hold upon it actually was as trivial and without reality as the now faded and archaic script in the chancery book[3] in Jefferson which allocated it to them and that it was he, the boy, who was the guest here and Sam Father's voice the mouthpiece of the host.

Until three years ago there had been two of them, the other a full-blood Chickasaw, in a sense even more incredibly lost than Sam Fathers. He called himself Jobaker, as if it were one word. Nobody knew his history at all. He was a hermit, living in a foul little shack at the forks of the creek five miles from the plantation and about that far from any other habitation. He was a market hunter and fisherman and he consorted with nobody, black or white; no negro would even cross his path and no man dared approach his hut except Sam. And perhaps once a month the boy would find them in Sam's shop—two old men squatting on their heels on the dirt floor, talking in a mixture of negroid English and flat hill dialect and now and then a phrase of that old tongue which as time went on and the boy squatted there too listening, he began to learn. Then Jobaker died. That is, nobody had seen him in some time. Then one morning Sam was missing, nobody, not even the boy, knew when nor where, until that night when some negroes hunting in the creek bottom saw the sudden burst of flame and approached. It was Jobaker's hut, but before they got anywhere near it, someone shot at them from the shadows beyond it. It was Sam who fired, but nobody ever found Jobaker's grave.

The next morning, sitting at breakfast with his cousin, the boy saw Sam pass the dining-room window and he remembered then that never in his life before had he seen Sam nearer the house than the blacksmith-shop. He stopped eating even; he sat there and he and his cousin both heard the voices from beyond the pantry door, then the door opened and Sam entered, carrying his hat in his hand but without knocking as anyone else on the place except a house servant would have done, entered just far enough for the door to close behind him and stood looking at neither of them—the Indian face above the nigger clothes, looking at something over their heads or at something not even in the room.

"I want to go," he said. "I want to go to the Big Bottom to live."

"To live?" the boy's cousin said.

"At Major de Spain's and your camp, where you go to hunt," Sam said. "I could take care of it for you all while you aint there. I will build me a little house in the woods, if you rather I didn't stay in the big one."

"What about Isaac here?" his cousin said. "How will you get away from him?

20

---

3. Public records or archives.

Are you going to take him with you?" But still Sam looked at neither of them, standing just inside the room with that face which showed nothing, which showed that he was an old man only when it smiled.

"I want to go," he said. "Let me go."

"Yes," the cousin said quietly. "Of course. I'll fix it with Major de Spain. You want to go soon?"

"I'm going now," Sam said. He went out. And that was all. The boy was nine then; it seemed perfectly natural that nobody, not even his cousin McCaslin, should argue with Sam. Also, since he was nine now, he could understand that Sam could leave him and their days and nights in the woods together without any wrench. He believed that he and Sam both knew that this was not only temporary but that the exigencies of his maturing, of that for which Sam had been training him all his life some day to dedicate himself, required it. They had settled that one night last summer while they listened to the hounds bringing a fox back up the creek valley; now the boy discerned in that very talk under the h gh, fierce August stars a presage, a warning, of this moment today. "I done taught you all there is of this settled country," Sam said. "You can hunt it good as I can now. You are ready for the Big Bottom now, for bear and deer. Hunter's meat," he said. "Next year you will be ten. You will write your age in two numbers and you will be ready to become a man. Your pa" (Sam always referred to the boy's cousin as his father, establishing even before the boy's orphanhood did that relation between them not of the ward to his guardian and kinsman and chief and head of his blood, but of the child to the man who sired his flesh and his thinking too.) "promised you can go with us then." So the boy could understand Sam's going. But he couldn't understand why now, in March, six months before the moon for hunting.

"If Jobaker's dead like they say," he said, "and Sam hasn't got anybody but us at all kin to him, why does he want to go to the Big Bottom now, when it will be six months before we get there?"

"Maybe that's what he wants," McCaslin said. "Maybe he wants to get away from you a little while."

But that was all right. McCaslin and other grown people often said things like that and he paid no attention to them, just as he paid no attention to Sam saying he wanted to go to the Big Bottom to live. After all, he would have to live there for six months, because there would be no use in going at all if he was going to turn right around and come back. And, as Sam himself had told him, he already knew all about hunting in this settled country that Sam or anybody else could teach him. So it would be all right. Summer, then the bright days after the first frost, then the cold and himself on the wagon with McCaslin this time and the moment would come and he would draw the blood, the big blood which would make him a man, a hunter, and Sam would come back home with them and he too would have outgrown the child's pursuit of rabbits and 'possums. Then he too would make one before the winter fire, talking of the old hunts and the hunts to come as hunters talked.

So Sam departed. He owned so little that he could carry it. He walked. He would neither let McCaslin send him in the wagon, nor take a mule to ride. No one saw him go even. He was just gone one morning, the cabin which had never had very much in it, vacant and empty, the shop in which there never had been very much done, standing idle. Then November came at last, and now the boy made one—himself and his cousin McCaslin and Tennie's Jim, and Major de Spain and General Compson and Walter Ewell and Boon and old Uncle Ash to do the cooking, waiting for them in Jefferson with the other wagon, and the surrey in which he and McCaslin and General Compson and Major de Spain would ride.

Sam was waiting at the camp to meet them. If he was glad to see them, he did not show it. And if, when they broke camp two weeks later to return home, he was sorry to see them go, he did not show that either. Because he did not come back with them. It was only the boy who returned, returning solitary and alone to the settled familiar land, to follow for eleven months the childish business of rabbits and such while he waited to go back, having brought with him, even from his brief first sojourn, an unforgettable sense of the big woods—not a quality dangerous or particularly inimical, but profound, sentient, gigantic and brooding, amid which he had been permitted to go to and fro at will, unscathed, why he knew not, but dwarfed and, until he had drawn honorably blood worthy of being drawn, alien.

Then November, and they would come back. Each morning Sam would take the boy out to the stand allotted him. It would be one of the poorer stands of course, since he was only ten and eleven and twelve and he had never even seen a deer running yet. But they would stand there, Sam a little behind him and without a gun himself, as he had been standing when the boy shot the running rabbit when he was eight years old. They would stand there in the November dawns, and after a while they would hear the dogs. Sometimes the chase would sweep up and past quite close, belling and invisible; once they heard the two heavy reports of Boon Hogganbeck's old gun with which he had never killed anything larger than a squirrel and that sitting, and twice they heard the flat unreverberant clap of Walter Ewell's rifle, following which you did not even wait to hear his horn.

"I'll never get a shot," the boy said. "I'll never kill one."

"Yes you will," Sam said. "You wait. You'll be a hunter. You'll be a man."

But Sam wouldn't come out. They would leave him there. He would come as far as the road where the surrey waited, to take the riding horses back, and that was all. The men would ride the horses and Uncle Ash and Tennie's Jim and the boy would follow in the wagon with Sam, with the camp equipment and the trophies, the meat, the heads, the antlers, the good ones, the wagon winding on among the tremendous gums and cypresses and oaks where no axe save that of the hunter had ever sounded, between the impenetrable walls of cane and brier—the two changing yet constant walls just beyond which the wilderness whose mark he had brought away forever on his spirit even from that first two weeks seemed to lean, stooping a little, watching them and listening, not quite inimical because they were too small, even those such as Walter and Major de Spain and old General Compson who had killed many deer and bear, their sojourn too brief and too harmless to excite to that, but just brooding, secret, tremendous, almost inattentive.

Then they would emerge, they would be out of it, the line as sharp as the demarcation of a doored wall. Suddenly skeleton cotton- and corn-fields would flow away on either hand, gaunt and motionless beneath the gray rain; there would be a house, barns, fences, where the hand of man had clawed for an instant, holding, the wall of the wilderness behind them now, tremendous and still and seemingly impenetrable in the gray and fading light, the very tiny orifice through which they had emerged apparently swallowed up. The surrey would be waiting, his cousin McCaslin and Major de Spain and General Compson and Walter and Boon dismounted beside it. Then Sam would get down from the wagon and mount one of the horses and, with the others on a rope behind him, he would turn back. The boy would watch him for a while against that tall and secret wall, growing smaller and smaller against it, never looking back. Then he would enter it, returning to what the boy believed, and thought that his cousin McCaslin believed, was his loneliness and solitude.

II

35   So the instant came. He pulled trigger and Sam Fathers marked his face with the hot blood which he had spilled and he ceased to be a child and became a hunter and a man. It was the last day. They broke camp that afternoon and went out, his cousin and Major de Spain and General Compson and Boon on the horses, Walter Ewell and the negroes in the wagon with him and Sam and his hide and antlers. There could have been (and were) other trophies in the wagon. But for him they did not exist, just as for all practical purposes he and Sam Fathers were still alone together as they had been that morning. The wagon wound and jolted between the slow and shifting yet constant walls from beyond and above which the wilderness watched them pass, less than inimical now and never to be inimical again since the buck still and forever leaped, the shaking gun-barrels coming constantly and forever steady at last, crashing, and still out of his instant of immortality the buck sprang, forever immortal;—the wagon jolting and bouncing on, the moment of the buck, the shot, Sam Fathers and himself and the blood with which Sam had marked him forever one with the wilderness which had accepted him since Sam said that he had done all right, when suddenly Sam reined back and stopped the wagon and they all heard the unmistakable and unforgettable sound of a deer breaking cover.

Then Boon shouted from beyond the bend of the trail and while they sat motionless in the halted wagon, Walter and the boy already reaching for their guns, Boon came galloping back, flogging his mule with his hat, his face wild and amazed as he shouted down at them. Then the other riders came around the bend, also spurring.

"Get the dogs!" Boon cried. "Get the dogs! If he had a nub on his head, he had fourteen points! Laying right there by the road in that pawpaw[4] thicket! If I'd a knowed he was there, I could have cut his throat with my pocket knife!"

"Maybe that's why he run," Walter said. "He saw you never had your gun." He was already out of the wagon with his rifle. Then the boy was out too with

---

4. Papaw, tree of custard apple family.

his gun, and the other riders came up and Boon got off his mule somehow and was scrabbling and clawing among the duffel in the wagon, still shouting, "Get the dogs! Get the dogs!" And it seemed to the boy too that it would take them forever to decide what to do—the old men in whom the blood ran cold and slow, in whom during the intervening years between them and himself the blood had become a different and colder substance from that which ran in him and even in Boon and Walter.

"What about it, Sam?" Major de Spain said. "Could the dogs bring him back?"

"We wont need the dogs," Sam said. "If he dont hear the dogs behind him, he will circle back in here about sundown to bed." 40

"All right," Major de Spain said. "You boys take the horses. We'll go on out to the road in the wagon and wait there." He and General Compson and McCaslin got into the wagon and Boon and Walter and Sam and the boy mounted the horses and turned back and out of the trail. Sam led them for an hour through the gray and unmarked afternoon whose light was little different from what it had been at dawn and which would become darkness without any graduation between. Then Sam stopped them.

"This is far enough," he said. "He'll be coming upwind, and he dont want to smell the mules." They tied the mounts in a thicket. Sam led them on foot now, unpathed through the markless afternoon, the boy pressing close behind him, the two others, or so it seemed to the boy, on his heels. But they were not. Twice Sam turned his head slightly and spoke back to him across his shoulder, still walking: "You got time. We'll get there fore he does."

So he tried to go slower. He tried deliberately to decelerate the dizzy rushing of time in which the buck which he had not even seen was moving, which it seemed to him must be carrying the buck farther and farther and more and more irretrievably away from them even though there were no dogs behind him now to make him run, even though, according to Sam, he must have completed his circle now and was heading back toward them. They went on; it could have been another hour or twice that or less than half, the boy could not have said. Then they were on a ridge. He had never been in here before and he could not see that it was a ridge. He just knew that the earth had risen slightly because the underbrush had thinned a little, the ground sloping invisibly away toward a dense wall of cane. Sam stopped. "This is it," he said. He spoke to Walter and Boon: "Follow this ridge and you will come to two crossings. You will see the tracks. If he crosses, it will be at one of these three."

Walter looked about for a moment. "I know it," he said. "I've even seen your deer. I was in here last Monday. He aint nothing but a yearling."

"A yearling?" Boon said. He was panting from the walking. His face still looked a little wild. "If the one I saw was any yearling, I'm still in kindergarden." 45

"Then I must have seen a rabbit," Walter said. "I always heard you quit school altogether two years before the first grade."

Boon glared at Walter. "If you dont want to shoot him, get out of the way," he said. "Set down somewhere. By God, I ——"

"Aint nobody going to shoot him standing here," Sam said quietly.

"Sam's right," Walter said. He moved, slanting the worn, silver-colored barrel of his rifle downward to walk with it again. "A little more moving and a little more quiet too. Five miles is still Hogganbeck range, even if we wasn't downwind." They went on. The boy could still hear Boon talking, though presently that ceased too. Then once more he and Sam stood motionless together against a tremendous pin oak in a little thicket, and again there was nothing. There was only the soaring and sombre solitude in the dim light, there was the thin murmur of the faint cold rain which had not ceased all day. Then, as if it had waited for them to find their positions and become still, the wilderness breathed again. It seemed to lean inward above them, above himself and Sam and Walter and Boon in their separate lurking-places, tremendous, attentive, impartial and omniscient, the buck moving in it somewhere, not running yet since he had not been pursued, not frightened yet and never fearsome but just alert also as they were alert, perhaps already circling back, perhaps quite near, perhaps conscious also of the eye of the ancient immortal Umpire. Because he was just twelve then, and that morning something had happened to him: in less than a second he had ceased forever to be the child he was yesterday. Or perhaps that made no difference, perhaps even a city-bred man, let alone a child, could not have understood it; perhaps only a country-bred one could comprehend loving the life he spills. He began to shake again.

"I'm glad it's started now," he whispered. He did not move to speak; only his lips shaped the expiring words: "Then it will be gone when I raise the gun ———"

Nor did Sam. "Hush," he said.

"Is he that near?" the boy whispered. "Do you think ———"

"Hush," Sam said. So he hushed. But he could not stop the shaking. He did not try, because he knew it would go away when he needed the steadiness—had not Sam Fathers already consecrated and absolved him from weakness and regret too?—not from love and pity for all which lived and ran and then ceased to live in a second in the very midst of splendor and speed, but from weakness and regret. So they stood motionless, breathing deep and quiet and steady. If there had been any sun, it would be near to setting now; there was a condensing, a densifying, of what he had thought was the gray and unchanging light until he realised suddenly that it was his own breathing, his heart, his blood—something, all things, and that Sam Fathers had marked him indeed, not as a mere hunter, but with something Sam had had in his turn of his vanished and forgotten people. He stopped breathing then; there was only his heart, his blood, and in the following silence the wilderness ceased to breathe also, leaning, stooping overhead with its breath held, tremendous and impartial and waiting. Then the shaking stopped too, as he had known it would, and he drew back the two heavy hammers of the gun.

Then it had passed. It was over. The solitude did not breathe again yet; it had merely stopped watching him and was looking somewhere else, even turning its back on him, looking on away up the ridge at another point, and the boy knew as well as if he had seen him that the buck had come to the edge of the cane and had either seen or scented them and faded back into it. But the solitude did not breathe again. It should have suspired again then but it did not. It was still facing, watching, what it had been watching and it was not here, not where he and Sam stood; rigid, not breathing himself, he thought, cried *No! No!,* knowing already that it was too late, thinking with the old despair of two and three years ago: *I'll never get a shot.* Then he heard it—the flat single clap of Walter Ewell's rifle which never missed. Then the mellow sound of the horn came down the ridge and something went out of him and he knew then he had never expected to get the shot at all.

"I reckon that's it," he said. "Walter got him." He had raised the gun slightly   55
without knowing it. He lowered it again and had lowered one of the hammers and was already moving out of the thicket when Sam spoke.

"Wait."

"Wait?" the boy cried. And he would remember that—how he turned upon Sam in the truculence of a boy's grief over the missed opportunity, the missed luck. "What for? Dont you hear that horn?"

And he would remember how Sam was standing. Sam had not moved. He was not tall, squat rather and broad, and the boy had been growing fast for the past year or so and there was not much difference between them in height, yet Sam was looking over the boy's head and up the ridge toward the sound of the horn and the boy knew that Sam did not even see him; that Sam knew he was still there beside him but he did not see the boy. Then the boy saw the buck. It was coming down the ridge, as if it were walking out of the very sound of the horn which related its death. It was not running, it was walking, tremendous, unhurried, slanting and tilting its head to pass the antlers through the undergrowth, and the boy standing with Sam beside him now instead of behind him as Sam always stood, and the gun still partly aimed and one of the hammers still cocked.

Then it saw them. And still it did not begin to run. It just stopped for an instant, taller than any man, looking at them; then its muscles suppled, gathered. It did not even alter its course, not fleeing, not even running, just moving with that winged and effortless ease with which deer move, passing within twenty feet of them, its head high and the eye not proud and not haughty but just full and wild and unafraid, and Sam standing beside the boy now, his right arm raised at full length, palm-outward, speaking in that tongue which the boy had learned from listening to him and Joe Baker in the blacksmith shop, while up the ridge Walter Ewell's horn was still blowing them in to a dead buck.

"Oleh, Chief," Sam said. "Grandfather."   60

When they reached Walter, he was standing with his back toward them, quite still, bemused almost, looking down at his feet. He didn't look up at all!

"Come here, Sam," he said quietly. When they reached him he still did not look up, standing above a little spike buck which had still been a fawn last spring. "He was so little I pretty near let him go," Walter said. "But just look at the track he was making. It's pretty near big as a cow's. If there were any more tracks here besides the ones he is laying in, I would swear there was another buck here that I never even saw."

III

It was dark when they reached the road where the surrey waited. It was turning cold, the rain had stopped, and the sky was beginning to blow clear. His cousin and Major de Spain and General Compson had a fire going. "Did you get him?" Major de Spain said.

"Got a good-sized swamp-rabbit with spike horns," Walter said. He slid the little buck down from his mule. The boy's cousin McCaslin looked at it.

"Nobody saw the big one?" he said.

"I dont even believe Boon saw it," Walter said. "He probably jumped somebody's straw cow in that thicket." Boon started cursing, swearing at Walter and at Sam for not getting the dogs in the first place and at the buck and all.

"Never mind," Major de Spain said. "He'll be here for us next fall. Let's get started home."

It was after midnight when they let Walter out at his gate two miles from Jefferson and later still when they took General Compson to his house and then returned to Major de Spain's, where he and McCaslin would spend the rest of the night, since it was still seventeen miles home. It was cold, the sky was clear now; there would be a heavy frost by sunup and the ground was already frozen beneath the horses' feet and the wheels and beneath their own feet as they crossed Major de Spain's yard and entered the house, the warm dark house, feeling their way up the dark stairs until Major de Spain found a candle and lit it, and into the strange room and the big deep bed, the still cold sheets until they began to warm to their bodies and at last the shaking stopped and suddenly he was telling McCaslin about it while McCaslin listened, quietly until he had finished. "You dont believe it," the boy said. "I know you dont ——"

"Why not?" McCaslin said. "Think of all that has happened here, on this earth. All the blood hot and strong for living, pleasuring, that has soaked back into it. For grieving and suffering too, of course, but still getting something out of it for all that, getting a lot out of it, because after all you dont have to continue to bear what you believe is suffering; you can always choose to stop that, put an end to that. And even suffering and grieving is better than nothing; there is only one thing worse than not being alive, and that's shame. But you cant be alive forever, and you always wear out life long before you have exhausted the possibilities of living. And all that must be somewhere; all that could not have been invented and created just to be thrown away. And the earth is shallow; there is not a great deal of it before you come to the rock. And the earth dont want to just keep things, hoard them; it wants to use them again. Look at the seed, the acorns, at what happens even to carrion when you try to bury it: it refuses too, seethes and struggles too until it reaches light and air again, hunting the sun still. And they——" the boy saw his hand in silhouette for a moment against the window beyond which, accustomed to the darkness now, he could see sky where the scoured and icy stars glittered "——they dont want it, need it. Besides, what would it want, itself, knocking around out there, when it never had enough time about the earth as it was, when there is plenty of room about the earth, plenty

of places still unchanged from what they were when the blood used and plea-
sured in them while it was still blood?"

"But we want them," the boy said. "We want them too. There is plenty of   70
room for us and them too."

"That's right," McCaslin said. "Suppose they dont have substance, cant cast
a shadow ——"

"But I saw it!" the boy cried. "I saw him!"

"Steady," McCaslin said. For an instant his hand touched the boy's flank
beneath the covers. "Steady. I know you did. So did I. Sam took me in there
once after I killed my first deer."

1942

QUESTIONS

1. What does the title literally denote in the story "Araby"? What does it
suggest? How do both its denotative and connotative meanings function in the
story?

2. What is the point of view (focus) in "Araby"? Are the words of the story
the boy's? How does the difference between focus and voice define the nature
of the initiation in the story?

3. What is the nature of the initiation in "Boys and Girls"?

4. The phrase "only a girl" appears twice in Alice Munro's story. How do
the contexts differ? How do the implications of the phrase differ on its two
appearances (that is, what does it mean or suggest each time)?

5. What is the point of view or focus of narration in "The Old People"?
Can you rearrange the events directly or indirectly narrated into the story to
their chronological order (that is, their history)? Sam tells Ike about "the People," and "gradually to the boy those old times . . . would become a part of the
boy's present . . . as if they were still happening . . . as if some of them . . .
would occur tomorrow" (par. 15). How does this relate to the handling of the
time element? to the structure of the story? to the theme?

6. What significance do you find in the fact that the initiating act in "Boys
and Girls" is the liberating of an animal, while that in "The Old People" is the
killing of a gentle animal?

WRITING SUGGESTIONS

1. Compare the use of the theme of romance-of-childhood versus realism-of-maturity in "Araby" and "Boys and Girls."

2. Compare or relate the use of "blood" in "The Old People" and "Barn Burning." (You may want to consider the advantages, disadvantages, validity of using one story by an author to explain or expand your reading of another story by that same author.)

10 A MODE: FANTASY

There is a looser and wider-ranging system of literary classification than genres and kinds, one that looks at works (or even parts of works) not as organisms but in terms of **modes,** ways of perceiving or presenting experience. If we call the conventional literary genres poetry, drama, fiction, we call the conventional modes the *poetic* (or *lyric*), the *dramatic,* and the *narrative.* A work that is classified in the subgenre short story, within the genre fiction, may have passages in the poetic mode—passages marked by heightened and highly figurative language, intensification of rhythms and emotions, often focusing on the ideal or spiritual. Gurov standing by the sea or contemplating the nails in the gray fence around Anna's home in "The Lady with the Dog" and the boy wandering through the Dublin streets full of frustration and shame in "Araby" are examples of poetic passages. Some portion of a story, even a whole story, may be in the dramatic mode, like a play, with unmediated or unnarrated dialogue or action. The conversation between Clayton, Julia, and Francis in "The Country Husband" and the one between Julia and Francis that follows seem like scenes from a play; they could be transferred to the stage almost without change. Except for the first and seventh paragraphs (and the latter seems little more than a stage direction), "No One's a Mystery" comes about as close as a short story can to being fully dramatic.

Befitting the looseness of the term, modes do not descend in an orderly way through subheadings, as do genres through subgenres and kinds. **Fantasy,** for example, a literary mode involving the consciously unreal—places, societies, or beings that never existed, do not exist, or do not yet exist, or with qualities that are beyond or counter to the ordinary or commonsensical—can be found in fiction, poetry, or drama.

Fantastic fiction sometimes signals its fictionality immediately or very soon: "Once upon a time . . ." At other times, it goes to some lengths to establish its "reality": many eighteenth-century novels about medieval castles and ghosts (Gothic novels) pretend to be editions of some monk's dusty manuscript, for example. Still other stories, such as "A Very Old Man with Enormous Wings," simply treat the incredible as perfectly natural, if not perfectly common.

Much fantasy has as its aim to stretch or expand our consciousness, our perception and conception of reality. Some stories seek to open us up to possibilities by disorienting us, alternating or mixing the realistic, the fictional, the fantastic in dizzying patterns. "The Garden of Forking Paths" begins realistically, with documentation and an essay-like manner that makes it seem not like a story at all. Then the confession begins, and we recognize that we are in the midst of a common fictional kind, the spy story or thriller. The shift does not bother us too much—it's like the dusty-manuscript device, and the fictional kind we've entered on is so familiar that we're reasonably comfortable. Suddenly the spy story shifts once again, toward fantasy, and just as we're getting used to fantasy, to mysterious Chinese gardens and riddles. The fantasy is used to question whether it is the fantastic that is incredible, or whether our assumption that time is uniform and absolute is merely arbitrary and too restrictive—itself a fantasy. Given eternity, we must admit that everything that might possibly happen *will* happen. So when we make a choice, the choice we did not make but might have made will yet be made; its potential must be realized; it must exist somewhere in the vastness of eternity in a world of events parallel to our own. No wonder, then, when we return to the world of the spy story—which, though fictional, operates within the same notions of uniform, absolute time—it seems credible that the writer of the confession is not concerned with whether he lives or dies, realities that are now "unreal, insignificant."

I don't think what I have told you about "The Garden of Forking Paths" will destroy your interest in the story—indeed, everyone can probably do with a little help in reading this fascinating story for the first time. Its questioning of our assumptions about reality is not too different from what's going on in modern thought. It is precisely because history, psychology, science, philosophy—almost all the intellectual disciplines—have in recent years most urgently called into question our longstanding assumptions about reality that fantasy seems so congenial a mode for us today.

From the middle of the nineteenth century to the middle of ours, the rise of the novel and the rise of realism were assumed to be the same thing, and we looked back on literary history as progress toward the literal, the factual, the ordinary (just as some art historians saw the Renaissance and what followed as demonstrating progress in man's ability to represent things "as they really are"). Long narratives that dwelled on the extraordinary, unusual, bizarre, or supernatural were called **romances,** as opposed to the more realistic **novel.** The early modern short story leaned more heavily toward romance. In the middle of the nineteenth century Poe was perhaps our most widely respected writer, and you can see that "The Cask of Amontillado" is not exactly a story of everyday life. Late in the century, with Maupassant in France (see "The Jewelry") and Chekhov in Russia (see "The Lady with the Dog"), the realistic short story seemed to have caught up with the novel. But already in the nineteenth century "common sense" notions of realism were beginning to give way before the discovery of worlds beyond our unaided senses, observable through microscope and telescope. Darwin, with his notion that species themselves were not fixed but moving and changing in time, made the solid earth under our feet a little less solid. With the rise of psychology, which too was meant to capture more realms for consciousness and science, we became more and more aware that there were realities only dreamed of in our philosophies. When physics, the most advanced and scientific of the sciences, began to tell us that all our knowledge is, if not subjective, at least limited to what the human brain and its instruments can perceive, and is altered by our perception, we were not so sure anymore that reality was what existed "out there" or that we were contained between our hat and boots.

When they first appeared, *Rosemary's Baby* or *The Exorcist* could have had only one ending—a rational explanation for the appearance of the supernatural. Few viewers or readers then would take seriously a work that was not embedded in a world of more or less everyday reality. The supernatural or fantastic in such a world had to be explained away as a dream, hallucination, or other psychological aberration, or as a hoax of some sort, set up to take in the foolish or credulous. Similarly, we would have had to explain away stories like García Márquez's "A Very Old Man with Enormous Wings" and, in "Reading More Fiction," Franz Kafka's "A Hunger Artist" by treating them as allegories. Now we can accept them as symbolic, as experiences that cannot be explained away or reduced to everyday terms, but that exist on their own terms, explaining in fantasy more than we might in our discursive prose, our scientific formulas, graphs, and charts.

The fantasy land of science fiction is usually the future—not so much never-never as never-yet land—which does not necessarily undermine or question conventional reality but projects potential consequences of present knowledge. There are those who maintain that for this very reason it is a mistake to call sci-fi fantasy. Fantasy, they say, involves the incredible or impossible. Science fiction, while it may take place in the future or outside earthly reality, is neither incredible nor impossible but wholly logical, often based on real scientific principles. Others say that's exactly why it's fantasy: historical reality is never predictable, and certainly not by that fantasy called logic.

Science-fiction people are passionate, dedicated, and argumentative, so if it's risky to suggest that science fiction is in the mode of fantasy, it's even riskier to try to define science fiction as a kind, even though everyone will grant that generic definitions are at best only loose approximations. Approximately, **science fiction** is a narrative about events outside the bounds of Earth history, in which science or advanced technology is often centrally important. The term

Earth history allows for both space travel (to imaginary life on real or imaginary planets) in the present and time travel to prehistory. Science and technology in the stories can be merely a plot device or be important as a means of trans-historical travel, or in the operation or perception of that imaginary world, as in "The Eye Altering." I'm sure this loose baggy monster of a definition leaves something out or includes too much, but at least it separates "The Eye Altering" from the other two fantasy stories here, and from "The Rocking-Horse Winner" and, in "Reading More Fiction," from "The Kugelmass Episode" and "A Hunger Artist."

MODE A Glossary

fantasy: a literary mode involving the consciously unreal—places, societies, or beings that never existed, do not exist, or do not yet exist, or with qualities that are beyond or counter to the ordinary, everyday, or commonsensical

mode: a loose system of classifying works or even passages from works of literature according to the way experience is perceived or presented; the conventional modes, then, are the *poetic* (or *lyric*), the *dramatic*, and the *narrative*

novel: a subgenre of fiction; a long, more or less realistic narrative

romance: a narrative mode characterized by the extraordinary, unusual, bizarre, or supernatural; also used to characterize a subgenre of long fiction with these qualities as distinguished from the more realistic *novel*

science fiction: a narrative about events spatially or temporally outside the bounds of earth history in which science or advanced technology is often centrally important

GABRIEL GARCÍA MÁRQUEZ

A Very Old Man with Enormous Wings[1]

A TALE FOR CHILDREN

On the third day of rain they had killed so many crabs inside the house that Pelayo had to cross his drenched courtyard and throw them into the sea, because the newborn child had a temperature all night and they thought it was due to the stench. The world had been sad since Tuesday. Sea and sky were a single ash-gray thing and the sands of the beach, which on March nights glimmered like powdered light, had become a stew of mud and rotten shellfish. The light was so weak at noon that when Pelayo was coming back to the house after throwing away the crabs, it was hard for him to see what it was that was moving and groaning in the rear of the courtyard. He had to go very close to see that it was an old man, a very old man, lying face down in the mud, who, in spite of his tremendous efforts, couldn't get up, impeded by his enormous wings.

Frightened by that nightmare, Pelayo ran to get Elisenda, his wife, who was putting compresses on the sick child, and he took her to the rear of the courtyard. They both looked at the fallen body with mute stupor. He was dressed like a ragpicker. There were only a few faded hairs left on his bald skull and very few teeth in his mouth, and his pitiful condition of a drenched great-grandfather had taken away any sense of grandeur he might have had. His huge buzzard wings, dirty and half-plucked, were forever entangled in the mud. They looked at him so long and so closely that Pelayo and Elisenda very soon overcame their surprise and in the end found him familiar. Then they dared speak to him, and he answered in an incomprehensible dialect with a strong sailor's voice. That was how they skipped over the inconvenience of the wings and quite intelligently concluded that he was a lonely castaway from some foreign ship wrecked by the storm. And yet, they called in a neighbor woman who knew everything about life and death to see him, and all she needed was one look to show them their mistake.

"He's an angel," she told them. "He must have been coming for the child, but the poor fellow is so old that the rain knocked him down."

On the following day everyone knew that a flesh-and-blood angel was held captive in Pelayo's house. Against the judgment of the wise neighbor woman, for whom angels in those times were the fugitive survivors of a celestial conspiracy, they did not have the heart to club him to death. Pelayo watched over him all afternoon from the kitchen, armed with his bailiff's club, and before going to bed he dragged him out of the mud and locked him up with the hens in the wire chicken coop. In the middle of the night, when the rain stopped, Pelayo and Elisenda were still killing crabs. A short time afterward the child woke up without a fever and with a desire to eat. Then they felt magnanimous and decided to

1. Translated by Gregory Rabassa.

put the angel on a raft with fresh water and provisions for three days and leave him to his fate on the high seas. But when they went out into the courtyard with the first light of dawn, they found the whole neighborhood in front of the chicken coop having fun with the angel, without the slightest reverence, tossing him things to eat through the openings in the wire as if he weren't a supernatural creature but a circus animal.

Father Gonzaga arrived before seven o'clock, alarmed at the strange news. By that time onlookers less frivolous than those at dawn had already arrived and they were making all kinds of conjectures concerning the captive's future. The simplest among them thought that he should be named mayor of the world. Others of sterner mind felt that he should be promoted to the rank of five-star general in order to win all wars. Some visionaries hoped that he could be put to stud in order to implant on earth a race of winged wise men who could take charge of the universe. But Father Gonzaga, before becoming a priest, had been a robust woodcutter. Standing by the wire, he reviewed his catechism in an instant and asked them to open the door so that he could take a close look at that pitiful man who looked more like a huge decrepit hen among the fascinated chickens. He was lying in a corner drying his open wings in the sunlight among the fruit peels and breakfast leftovers that the early risers had thrown him. Alien to the impertinences of the world, he only lifted his antiquarian eyes and murmured something in his dialect when Father Gonzaga went into the chicken coop and said good morning to him in Latin. The parish priest had his first suspicion of an imposter when he saw that he did not understand the language of God or know how to greet His ministers. Then he noticed that seen close up he was much too human: he had an unbearable smell of the outdoors, the back side of his wings was strewn with parasites and his main feathers had been mistreated by terrestrial winds, and nothing about him measured up to the proud dignity of angels. Then he came out of the chicken coop and in a brief sermon warned the curious against the risks of being ingenuous. He reminded them that the devil had the bad habit of making use of carnival tricks in order to confuse the unwary. He argued that if wings were not the essential element in determining the difference between a hawk and an airplane, they were even less so in the recognition of angels. Nevertheless, he promised to write a letter to his bishop so that the latter would write to his primate so that the latter would write to the Supreme Pontiff in order to get the final verdict from the highest courts.

His prudence fell on sterile hearts. The news of the captive angel spread with such rapidity that after a few hours the courtyard had the bustle of a marketplace and they had to call in troops with fixed bayonets to disperse the mob that was about to knock the house down. Elisenda, her spine all twisted from sweeping up so much marketplace trash, then got the idea of fencing in the yard and charging five cents admission to see the angel.

The curious came from far away. A traveling carnival arrived with a flying acrobat who buzzed over the crowd several times, but no one paid any attention to him because his wings were not those of an angel but, rather, those of a sidereal bat. The most unfortunate invalids on earth came in search of health: a poor woman who since childhood had been counting her heartbeats and had run out of numbers; a Portuguese man who couldn't sleep because the noise of the stars disturbed him; a sleepwalker who got up at night to undo the things he had done while awake; and many others with less serious ailments. In the midst of that shipwreck disorder that made the earth tremble, Pelayo and Elisenda were happy with fatigue, for in less than a week they had crammed their rooms with money and the line of pilgrims waiting their turn to enter still reached beyond the horizon.

The angel was the only one who took no part in his own act. He spent his time trying to get comfortable in his borrowed nest, befuddled by the hellish heat of the oil lamps and sacramental candles that had been placed along the wire. At first they tried to make him eat some mothballs, which, according to the wisdom of the wise neighbor woman, were the food prescribed for angels. But he turned them down, just as he turned down the papal lunches[2] that the penitents brought him, and they never found out whether it was because he was an angel or because he was an old man that in the end he ate nothing but eggplant mush. His only supernatural virtue seemed to be patience. Especially during the first days, when the hens pecked at him, searching for the stellar parasites that proliferated in his wings, and the cripples pulled out feathers to touch their defective parts with, and even the most merciful threw stones at him, trying to get him to rise so they could see him standing. The only time they succeeded in arousing him was when they burned his side with an iron for branding steers, for he had been motionless for so many hours that they thought he was dead. He awoke with a start, ranting in his hermetic language and with tears in his eyes, and he flapped his wings a couple of times, which brought on a whirlwind of chicken dung and lunar dust and a gale of panic that did not seem to be of this world. Although many thought that his reaction had been one not of rage but of pain, from then on they were careful not to annoy him, because the majority understood that his passivity was not that of a hero taking his ease but that of a cataclysm in repose.

Father Gonzaga held back the crowd's frivolity with formulas of maidservant inspiration while awaiting the arrival of a final judgment on the nature of the captive. But the mail from Rome showed no sense of urgency. They spent their time finding out if the prisoner had a navel, if his dialect had any connection with Aramaic, how many times he could fit on the head of a pin, or whether he wasn't just a Norwegian with wings. Those meager letters might have come and gone until the end of time if a providential event had not put an end to the priest's tribulations.

It so happened that during those days, among so many other carnival attractions, there arrived in town the traveling show of the woman who had been changed into a spider for having disobeyed her parents. The admission to see her was not only less than the admission to see the angel, but people were permitted to ask her all manner of questions about her absurd state and to examine her up and down so that no one would ever doubt the truth of her horror. She was a frightful tarantula the size of a ram and with the head of a sad maiden. What

10

2. Choice, extremely expensive meals.

was most heart-rending, however, was not her outlandish shape but the sincere affliction with which she recounted the details of her misfortune. While still practically a child she had sneaked out of her parents' house to go to a dance, and while she was coming back through the woods after having danced all night without permission, a fearful thunderclap rent the sky in two and through the crack came the lightning bolt of brimstone that changed her into a spider. Her only nourishment came from the meatballs that charitable souls chose to toss into her mouth. A spectacle like that, full of so much human truth and with such a fearful lesson, was bound to defeat without even trying that of a haughty angel who scarcely deigned to look at mortals. Besides, the few miracles attributed to the angel showed a certain mental disorder, like the blind man who didn't recover his sight but grew three new teeth, or the paralytic who didn't get to walk but almost won the lottery, and the leper whose sores sprouted sunflowers. Those consolation miracles, which were more like mocking fun, had already ruined the angel's reputation when the woman who had been changed into a spider finally crushed him completely. That was how Father Gonzaga was cured forever of his insomnia and Pelayo's courtyard went back to being as empty as during the time it had rained for three days and crabs walked through the bedrooms.

The owners of the house had no reason to lament. With the money they saved they built a two-story mansion with balconies and gardens and high netting so that crabs wouldn't get in during the winter, and with iron bars on the windows so that angels wouldn't get in. Pelayo also set up a rabbit warren close to town and gave up his job as bailiff for good, and Elisenda bought some satin pumps with high heels and many dresses of iridescent silk, the kind worn on Sunday by the most desirable women in those times. The chicken coop was the only thing that didn't receive any attention. If they washed it down with creolin[3] and burned tears of myrrh inside it every so often, it was not in homage to the angel but to drive away the dungheap stench that still hung everywhere like a ghost and was turning the new house into an old one. At first, when the child learned to walk, they were careful that he not get too close to the chicken coop. But then they began to lose their fears and got used to the smell, and before the child got his second teeth he'd gone inside the chicken coop to play, where the wires were falling apart. The angel was no less standoffish with him than with other mortals, but he tolerated the most ingenious infamies with the patience of a dog who had no illusions. They both came down with chicken pox at the same time. The doctor who took care of the child couldn't resist the temptation to listen to the angel's heart, and he found so much whistling in the heart and so many sounds in his kidneys that it seemed impossible for him to be alive. What surprised him most, however, was the logic of his wings. They seemed so natural on that completely human organism that he couldn't understand why other men didn't have them too.

When the child began school it had been some time since the sun and rain had caused the collapse of the chicken coop. The angel went dragging himself about here and there like a stray dying man. They would drive him out of the

3. A disinfectant.

bedroom with a broom and a moment later find him in the kitchen. He seemed to be in so many places at the same time that they grew to think that he'd been duplicated, that he was reproducing himself all through the house, and the exasperated and unhinged Elisenda shouted that it was awful living in that hell full of angels. He could scarcely eat and his antiquarian eyes had also become so foggy that he went about bumping into posts. All he had left were the bare cannulae of his last feathers. Pelayo threw a blanket over him and extended him the charity of letting him sleep in the shed, and only then did they notice that he had a temperature at night, and was delirious with the tongue twisters of an old Norwegian. That was one of the few times they became alarmed, for they thought he was going to die and not even the wise neighbor woman had been able to tell them what to do with dead angels.

And yet he not only survived his worst winter, but seemed improved with the first sunny days. He remained motionless for several days in the farthest corner of the courtyard, where no one would see him, and at the beginning of December some large, stiff feathers began to grow on his wings, the feathers of a scarecrow, which looked more like another misfortune of decrepitude. But he must have known the reason for those changes, for he was quite careful that no one should notice them, that no one should hear the sea chanteys that he sometimes sang under the stars. One morning Elisenda was cutting some bunches of onions for lunch when a wind that seemed to come from the high seas blew into the kitchen. Then she went to the window and caught the angel in his first attempts at flight. They were so clumsy that his fingernails opened a furrow in the vegetable patch and he was on the point of knocking the shed down with the ungainly flapping that slipped on the light and couldn't get a grip on the air. But he did manage to gain altitude. Elisenda let out a sign of relief, for herself and for him, when she saw him pass over the last houses, holding himself up in some way with the risky flapping of a senile vulture. She kept watching him even when she was through cutting the onions and she kept on watching until it was no longer possible for her to see him, because then he was no longer an annoyance in her life but an imaginary dot on the horizon of the sea.

1968

URSULA K. LE GUIN

The Eye Altering

Miriam stood at the big window of the infirmary ward and looked out at the view and thought, For twenty-five years I have been standing at this window and looking out at this view. And never once have I seen what I wanted to see.

If I forget thee, O Jerusalem—[1]

1. ". . . let my right hand forget her cunning," Psalm 137:5; the psalm begins, "By the rivers of Babylon, there we sat down, yea, we wept, when we remembered Zion," Zion being both another name for Jerusalem and for the Jewish people.

The pain was forgotten, yes. The hatred and the fear, forgotten. In exile you don't remember the grey days and the black years. You remember the sunlight, the orchards, the white cities. Even when you try to forget it you remember that Jerusalem was golden.

The sky outside the ward window was dulled with haze. Over the low ridge called Ararat[2] the sun was setting; setting slowly, for New Zion had a slower spin than Old Earth, and a twenty-eight-hour day; settling, rather than setting, dully down onto the dull horizon. There were no clouds to gather the colors of sunset. There were seldom any clouds. When the haze thickened there might be a misty, smothering rain; when the haze was thin, as now, it hung high and vague, formless. It never quite cleared. You never saw the color of the sky. You never saw the stars. And through the haze the sun, no, not the sun, but NSC 641 (Class G)[3] burned swollen and vaporous, warty as an orange—remember oranges? the sweet juice on the tongue? the orchards of Haifa?—NSC 641 stared, like a bleary eye. You could stare back at it. No glory of gold to blind you. Two imbeciles staring at each other.

5   Shadows stretched across the valley towards the buildings of the Settlement. In shadows the fields and woods were black; in the light they were brown, purplish, and dark red. Dirty colors, the colors you got when you scrubbed your watercolors too much and the teacher came by and said, You'd better use some fresh water, Mimi, it's getting muddy. Because the teacher had been too kind to say to a ten-year-old, That picture's a total loss, Mimi, throw it away and start fresh.

She had thought of that before—she had thought all her thoughts before, standing at this window—but this time it reminded her of Genya, because of the painting, and she turned to see how he was doing. The shock symptoms were almost gone, his face was no longer so pale and his pulse had steadied. While she held his wrist he sighed a bit and opened his eyes. Lovely eyes he had, grey in the thin face. He had never been much but eyes, poor Genya. Her oldest patient. Twenty-four years he had been her patient, right from the moment of his birth, five pounds, purplish-blue like a fetal rat, a month premature and half dead of cyanosis: the fifth child born on New Zion, the first in Ararat Settlement. A native. A feeble and unpromising native. He hadn't even had the strength, or the sense, to cry at his first breath of this alien air. Sofia's other children had been full-term and healthy, two girls, both married and mothers now, and fat Leon who could hoist a seventy-kilo sack of grain when he was fifteen. Good young colonists, strong stock. But Miriam had always loved Genya, and all the more after her own years of miscarriages and stillbirths, and the last birth, the girl who had lived two hours, whose eyes had been clear grey like Genya's. Babies never have grey eyes, the eyes of the newborn are blue, that was all sentimental rubbish. But how could you ever make sure of what color things were under this damned warty-orange sun? Nothing ever looked right. "So there you are, Gennady Borisovich," she said, "back home, eh?"

---

2. The mountain, in present-day Turkey, where Noah's ark landed after the Flood.   3. I.e., the same kind of star as our sun. NSC 641: The catalogue number of a fictional star.

It had been their joke when he was a child; he had spent so much time in the infirmary that whenever he came in with one of his fevers or fainting spells or gasping asthma he would say, "Here I am, back home, Auntie Doctor. . . ."

"What happened?" he asked.

"You collapsed. Hoeing down in the South Field. Aaron and Tina brought you up here on the tractor. Touch of sunstroke, maybe? You've been doing all right, haven't you?"

He shrugged and nodded.

"Dizzy? Short of breath?"

"On and off."

"Why didn't you come to the clinic?"

"It's no good, Miriam."

Since he was grown he had called her Miriam. She missed "Auntie Doctor." He had grown away from her, these last few years, withdrawn from her into his painting. He had always sketched and painted, but now, all his free time and whatever energy he had left when his Settlement duties were done, he spent in the loft of the generator building where he'd made a kind of studio, grinding colors from rocks and mixing dyes from native plants, making brushes by begging pigtail ends off little girls, and painting—painting on scraps from the lumber mill, on bits of rag, on precious scraps of paper, on smooth slabs of slate from the quarry on Ararat if nothing better was at hand. Painting portraits, scenes of Settlement life, buildings, machinery, still-lifes, plants, landscapes, inner visions. Painting anything, everything. His portraits had been much in demand—people were always kind to Genya and the other sicklies—but lately he had not done any portraits; he had gone in for queer muddy jumbles of forms and lines all in a dark haze, like worlds half created. Nobody liked those paintings, but nobody ever told Genya he was wasting his time. He was a sickly; he was an artist; O.K. Healthy people had no time to be artists. There was too much work to do. But it was good to have an artist. It was human. It was like Earth. Wasn't it?

They were kind to Toby, too, whose stomach troubles were so bad that at sixteen he weighed eighty-four pounds; kind to little Shura, who was just learning to talk at six, and whose eyes wept and wept all day long, even when she was smiling; kind to all their sicklies, the ones whose bodies could not adjust to this alien world, whose stomachs could not digest the native proteins even with the help of the metabolising pills which every colonist must take twice a day every day of his life on New Zion. Hard as life was in the Twenty Settlements, much as they needed every hand to work, they were gentle with their useless ones, their afflicted. In affliction the hand of God is visible. They remembered the words civilisation, humanity. They remembered Jerusalem.

"Genya, my dear, what do you mean, it's no good?"

His quiet voice had frightened her. "It's no good," he had said, smiling. And the grey eyes not clear but veiled, hazy.

"Medicine," he said. "Pills. Cures."

"Of course you know more about medicine than I do," Miriam said. "You're a much better doctor than I am. Or are you giving up? Is that it, Genya? Giving up?" Anger had come upon her so suddenly, from so deep within, from anxiety so long and deeply hidden, that it shook her body and cracked her voice.

"I'm giving up one thing. The metas."

"Metas? Giving them up. What are you talking about?"

"I haven't taken any for two weeks."

The despairing rage swelled in her. She felt her face go hot, so that it felt twice its normal size. "Two weeks! And so, and so, and so you're here! Where did you think you'd end up, you terrible fool? Lucky you're not dead!"

"I haven't been any worse since I stopped taking them, Miriam. Better, this whole last week. Until today. It can't be that. It must have been heatstroke. I forgot to wear a hat. . . . He too flushed faintly, in the eagerness of his pleading, or with shame. It was stupid to work in the fields bareheaded; for all its dull look NSC 641 could hit the unsheltered human head quite as hard as fiery Sol, and Genya was apologetic about his carelessness. "You see, I was feeling fine this morning, really good, I kept right up with the others hoeing. Then I felt a bit dizzy, but I didn't want to stop, it was so good to be able to work right with the others, I never thought about heatstroke."

Miriam found that there were tears in her eyes, and this made her so ultimately and absolutely angry that she couldn't speak at all. She got up off Genya's bed and strode down the ward between the rows of beds, four on one side, four on the other. She strode back and stood staring out the window at the mud-colored shapeless ugly world.

Genya was saying something—"Miriam, honestly, couldn't it be that the metas are worse for me than the native proteins are?"—but she did not listen; the grief and wrath and fear swelled in her and swelled in her, and broke, and she cried out, "Oh, Genya, Genya, how could you? Not you, to give up now, after fighting so long—I can't bear it! I can't bear it!" But she did not cry it out aloud. Not one word of it. Never. She cried out in her mind, and some tears came out and ran down her cheeks, but her back was turned to the patient. She looked through distorting tears at the flat valley and the dull sun and said to them, silent, "I hate you." Then after a while she could turn around and say aloud, "Lie down,"—for he had sat up, distressed by her long silence—"lie down, be quiet. You'll take two metas before dinner. If you need anything, Geza's in the nurse's station." And she walked out.

As she left the infirmary she saw Tina climbing up the back path from the fields, coming to see how Genya was, no doubt. For all his wheezes and fevers Genya had never wanted for girl friends. Tina, and Shoshanna, and Bella, and Rachel, he could have had his pick. But last year when he and Rachel were living together, they had got contraceptives from the clinic regularly, and then they had separated; they hadn't married, though by his age, twenty-four, Settlement kids were married and parents. He hadn't married Rachel, and Miriam knew why. Moral genetics. Bad genes. Shouldn't pass them on to the next generation. Weed out the sicklies. No procreation for him, and therefore no marriage; he couldn't ask Rachel to live barren for the love of him. What the Settlements needed was children, plenty of healthy young natives who, with the help of the meta pills, could survive on this planet.

Rachel hadn't taken up with anybody else. But she was only eighteen. She'd get over it. Marry a boy from another Settlement, most likely, and move away, away from Genya's big grey eyes. It would be best for her. And for him.

No wonder Genya was suicidal! Miriam thought, and put the thought away from her fiercely, wearily. She was very weary. She had meant to go to her room and wash, change her clothes, change her mood, before dinner; but the room was so lonesome with Leonid away at Salem Settlement and not due back for at least another month, she couldn't stand it. She went straight across the dusty central square of the Settlement to the refectory building, and into the Living Room. To get away, clear away, from the windless haze and the grey sky and the ugly sun.

Nobody was in the Living Room but Commander Marca, fast asleep on one of the padded wooden couches, and Reine, reading. The two oldest members of the Settlement. Commander Marca was in fact the oldest person in the world. He had been forty-four when he piloted the Exile Fleet from Old Earth to New Zion; he was seventy now, and very frail. People didn't wear well here. They aged early, died at fifty, sixty. Reine, the biochemist, was forty-five now but looked twenty years older. It's a damned geriatric club, Miriam thought sourly; and it was true that the young, the Zionborn, seldom used the Living Room. They came here to read, as it held the Settlement's library of books and tapes and microfilm, but not many of them read much, or had much time to read. And maybe the April light and the pictures made them a little uneasy. They were such moral, severe, serious young people; there was no leisure in their lives, no beauty in their world; how could they approve of this luxury their elders needed, this one haven, this one place like home. . . .

The Living Room had no windows. Avram, a wizard with anything electrical, had done the indirect lighting, deliberately reproducing the color and quality of sunlight—not NSC 641 light, but sunlight—so that to enter the Living Room was to enter a room in a house on Earth on a warm sunny day of April or early May, to see all things in that clear, clean, lovely light. Avram and several others had worked on the pictures, enlarging colored photos to a meter or so square: scenes of Earth, photographs and paintings brought by the colonists— Venice, the Negev, the domes of the Kremlin, a farm in Portugal, the Dead Sea, Hampstead Heath, a beach in Oregon, a meadow in Poland, cities, forests, mountains, Van Gogh's cypresses, Bierstadt's Rocky Mountains, Monet's water-lilies, Leonardo's blue mysterious caves.[4] Every wall of the room was covered with pictures, dozens of pictures, all the beauty of the Earth. So that the Earth-born could see and remember, so that the Zionborn could see and know.

There had been some discussion about the pictures, twenty years ago when Avram had started putting them up: Was it really wise? Should we look back? And so on. But then Commander Marca had come by on a visit, seen the Living Room of Ararat Settlement, and said, "This is where I'll stay." With every Set-

---

4. I.e., familiar scenes from their homes on earth, including those in the paintings of the Dutch Vincent Van Gogh (1853–90), the German-born American Albert Bierstadt (1830–1902), the French Claude Monet (1840–1926), and the Italian Leonardo da Vinci (1452–1519).

tlement vying to have him, he had chosen Ararat. Because of the pictures of Earth, because of the light of Earth in that room, shining on the green fields, the snowy peaks, the golden forests of autumn, the flight of gulls above the sea, the white and red and rose of waterlilies on blue pools—clear colors, true, pure, the colors of the Earth.

He slept there now, a handsome old man. Outside, in the hard, dull, orange daylight, he would look sick and old, his cheeks veined and muddy. Here you could see what he looked like.

35   Miriam sat down near him, facing her favorite picture, a quiet landscape by Corot, trees over a silvery stream.[5] She was so tired that for once she was willing to just sit, in a mild stupor. Through the stupor, faintly, idly, words came floating. Couldn't it be . . . honestly, couldn't it be that the metas are worse . . . Miriam, honestly, couldn't it be . . .

"Do you think I never thought of that?" she retorted in silence. "Idiot! Do you think I don't know the metas are hard on your guts? Didn't I try fifty different combinations while you were a kid, trying to get rid of the side effects? But it's not as bad as being allergic to the whole damn planet! You know better than the doctor, do you? Don't give me that. You're trying to—" But she broke off the silent dialogue abruptly. Genya was not trying to kill himself. He was not. He would not. He had courage, that one. And brains.

"All right," she said to the quiet young man in her mind. "All right! If you'll stay in the infirmary, under observation—for two weeks, and do exactly what I say—all right, I'll try it!"

Because, said another, even quieter voice deep in her, it doesn't really matter. Whatever you do or don't do, he will die. This year; next year. Two hours; twenty-four years. The sicklies can't adjust to this world. And neither can we, neither can we. We weren't meant to live here, Genya my dear. We weren't made for this world, nor it for us. We were made of Earth, by Earth, to live on Earth, under the blue sky and the golden sun.

The dinner gong began to ring. Going into the refectory she met little Shura. The child carried a bunch of the repulsive blackish-purple native weeds, as a child at home would carry a bunch of white daisies, red poppies picked in the fields. Shura's eyes were teary as usual, but she smiled up at Auntie Doctor. Her lips looked pallid in the red-orange light of sunset through the windows. Everybody's lips looked pallid. Everybody's face looked tired, set, stoical, after the long day's work, as they went into the Settlement dining hall, all together, the three hundred exiles of Ararat on Zion, the eleventh lost tribe.[6]

40   He was doing very well. She had to admit it. "You're doing well," she said, and he, with his grin, "I told you so!"

"It could be because you're not doing anything else," she said, "smart ass."

"Not doing anything? I filed health records for Geza all morning, I played

---

5. I.e., a typical work by French painter Jean-Baptiste-Camille Corot (1796–1875).   6. In popular legend, the ten northern Hebrew tribes captured by the Assyrians in the eighth century B.C. have reappeared at various times and places.

games with Rosie and Moishe for two hours, I've been grinding colors all afternoon—say, I need more mineral oil, can I have another litre? It's a much better pigment vehicle than the vegetable oil."

"Sure. But listen. I have something for you better than that. Little Tel Aviv has got their pulp mill going full time. They sent a truck over yesterday with paper—"

"Paper?"

"Half a ton of it! I took two hundred sheets for you. It's in the office." He was off like a shot, and was into the bundle of paper before she even got there. "Oh, God," he said, holding up a sheet, "beautiful, it's beautiful!" And she thought how often she had heard him say that, "beautiful!" of one drab useful thing or another. He didn't know what beauty was; he'd never seen any. The paper was thick, substantial, greyish, in big sheets, intended to be cut small and used sparingly, of course; but let him have it for his painting. There was little enough else she could give him.

"When you let me out of here," Genya said, hugging the unwieldy bundle with both arms, "I'll go over to Tel Aviv and paint their pulp mill, I'll immortalise their pulp mill!"

"You'd better go lie down."

"No, listen, I promised Moishe I'd beat him at chess. What's wrong with him, anyhow?"

"Rashes, edema."

"He's like me?"

Miriam shrugged. "He was fine till this year. Puberty triggered something. Not unusual with allergic symptoms."

"What is allergy, anyhow?"

"Well, call it a failure of adaptation. Back home, people used to feed babies cows' milk, from bottles. Some of the babies could adapt to it, but some got rashes, breathing trouble, colic. The cow's key didn't fit their metabolic lock. Well, New Zion's protein keys don't fit our locks; so we have to change our metabolism with the metas."

"Would Moishe or I have been an allergic on Earth?"

"I don't know. Prematures often are. Irving, he died, oh, twenty years ago, he was allergic to this terrible list of things on Earth, they should never have let him come, poor thing, he spends his life on Earth half suffocated and comes here and starves to death even on a quadruple dose of metas."

"Aha," said Genya, "you shouldn't have given him metas at all. Just Zion mush."

"Zion mush?" Only one of the native grains yielded enough to be worth harvesting, and it produced a gluey meal which could not be baked.

"I ate three bowls of it for lunch."

"He lies around the hospital all day complaining," Miriam said, "and then stuffs his belly with that slop. How can an artistic soul eat something that tastes like jellied bilge?"

"You feed it to your helpless child patients in your own hospital! I just ate the leftovers."

"Oh, get along with you."

"I am. I want to paint while the sun's still up. On a piece of new paper, a whole piece of new paper. . . ."

It had been a long day at the clinic, but there were no inpatients. She had sent Osip home last night in a cast with a good scolding for being so careless as to tip his tractor over, endangering not only his life but the tractor, which was even harder to replace. And young Moishe had gone back to the children's house, though she didn't like the way his rash kept coming back. And Rosie was over her asthma, and the Commander's heart was doing as well as could be expected; so the ward was empty, except for her permanent inmate of the past two weeks, Genya.

He was sprawled out on his bed under the window, so lax and still that she had a moment of alarm; but his color was good, he breathed evenly, he was simply asleep, deeply asleep, the way people slept after a hard day in the fields, exhausted.

65 He had been painting. He had cleaned up the rags and brushes, he always cleaned up promptly and thoroughly, but the picture stood on his makeshift easel. Usually these days he was secretive about his paintings, hid them, since people had stopped admiring them. The Commander had murmured to her, "What ugly stuff, poor boy!" But she had heard young Moishe, watching Genya paint, say, "How do you do it, Genya, how do you make it so pretty?" and Genya answer, "Beauty's in the eye, Moishe."

Well, that was true, and she went closer to look at the painting in the dull afternoon light. Genya had painted the view out the big window of the ward. Nothing vague and half created this time: realistic, all too realistic. Hideously recognisable. There was the flat ridge of Ararat, the mud-colored trees and fields, the hazy sky, the storage barn and a corner of the school building in the foreground. Her eyes went from the painted scene to the real one. To spend hours, days, painting that! What a waste, what a waste.

It was hard on Genya, it was sad, the way he hid his paintings now, knowing that nobody would want to see them, except maybe a child like Moishe fascinated with the mere skill of the hand, the craftsman's dexterity.

That night as Genya helped her straighten up the injection cabinets—he was a good deal of help around the infirmary these days—she said, "I like the picture you painted today."

"I finished it today," he corrected her. "Damn thing took all week. I'm just beginning to learn to see."

70 "Can I put it up in the Living Room?"

He looked at her across a tray of hypodermic needles, his eyes quiet and a little quizzical. "In the Living Room? But that's all pictures of Home."

"It's time maybe we had some pictures of our new home there."

"A moral gesture, eh? Sure. If you like it."

"I like it very much," she lied blandly.

75 "It isn't bad," he said. "I'll do better, though, when I've learned how to fit myself to the pattern."

"What pattern?"

"Well, you know, you have to look until you *see* the pattern, till it makes sense, and then you have to get that into your hand, too." He made large, vague, shaping gestures with a bottle of absolute alcohol.

"Anybody who asks a painter a question in words deserves what they get, I guess," said Miriam. "Babble, babble. You take the picture over tomorrow and put it up. Artists are so temperamental about where they get their pictures hung, and the lighting. Besides, it's time you were getting out. A little. An hour or two a day. No more."

"Can I eat dinner in the dining hall, then?"

"All right. It'll keep Tina from coming here to keep you from being lonely and eating up all the infirmary rations. That girl eats like a vacuum pump. Listen, if you go out in the middle of the day, will you kindly take the trouble to wear a hat?"

"You think I'm right, then."

"Right?"

"That it was sunstroke."

"That was *my* diagnosis, if you will recall."

"All right: but my addition was that I do better without metas."

"I have no idea. You've got along fine before for weeks, and then poof, down again. Nothing whatever has been proved."

"But a pattern has been established! I've lived a month without metas, and gained six pounds."

"And edema of the head, Mr. Know It All?"

She saw him the next day sitting with Rachel, just before dinnertime, on the slope below the storage barn. Rachel had not come to see him in the infirmary. They sat side by side, very close together, motionless, not talking.

Miriam went on to the Living Room. A half hour there before dinner had become a habit with her lately. It seemed to rest her from the weariness of the day. But the room was less peaceful than usual this evening; the Commander was awake, and talking with Reine and Avram. "Well, where did it come from then?" he was saying in his heavy Italian accent—he had not learned Hebrew till he was forty, in the Transit Camp. "Who put it there?" Then seeing Miriam he greeted her as always with a grand cordiality of voice and gesture. "Ah, Doctor! Please join us, come, solve our mystery for us. You know each picture in this room as well as I do. Where, do you think, and when did we acquire the new one? You see?"

It's Genya's, Miriam was about to say, when she saw the new picture. It wasn't Genya's. It was a painting, all right, a landscape, but a landscape of the Earth: a wide valley, the fields green and green-gold, orchards coming into flower, the sweeping slope of a mountain in the distance, a tower, perhaps a castle or medieval farm building, in the foreground, and over all the pure, subtle, sunlit sky. It was a complex and happy painting, a celebration of the spring, an act of praise.

"How beautiful," she said, her voice catching. "Didn't you put it up, Avram?"

"Me? I can photograph, I can't paint. Look at it, it's no reproduction. Some kind of tempera or oils, see?"

"Somebody brought it from Home. Had it in their baggage," Reine suggested.

95 "For twenty-five years?" said the Commander. "Why? And who? We all know what all the others have!"

"No. I think"—Miriam was confused, and stammered—"I think it's something Genya did. I asked him to put up one of his paintings here. Not this one. How did he do this?"

"Copied from a photograph," Avram suggested.

"No no no no, impossible," old Marca said, outraged. "That is a painting, not a copy! That is a work of art, that was seen, seen with the eyes and the heart!"

With the eyes and the heart.

100 Miriam looked, and she saw. She saw what the light of NSC 641 had hidden from her, what the artificial Earth daylight of the room revealed to her. She saw what Genya saw: the beauty of the world.

"I think it must be in Central France, the Auvergne," Reine was saying wistfully, and the Commander, "Oh no no no, it's near Lake Como, I am certain," and Avram, "Well it looks to me like where I grew up in the Caucasus," when they all turned to look at Miriam. She had made a strange noise, a gasp or laugh or sob. "It's here," she said. "Here. That's Ararat. The mountain. That's the fields, our fields, our trees. That's the corner of the school, that tower. See it? It's here. Zion. It's how Genya sees it. With the eyes and the heart."

"But look, the trees are green, look at the colors, Miriam. It's Earth—"

"Yes! It is Earth. Genya's Earth!"

"But he can't—"

105 "How do we know? How do we know what a child of Zion sees? We can see the picture in this light that's like Home. Take it outside, into the daylight, and you'll see what we always see, the ugly colors, the ugly planet where we're not at home. But he is at home! He is! It's we," Miriam said, laughing in tears, looking at them all, the anxious, tired, elderly faces, "*we* who lack the key. We with our—with our—" she stumbled and leapt at the idea like a horse at a high wall, "with our meta pills!"

They all stared at her.

"With our meta pills, we can survive here, just barely, right? But don't you see, he *lives* here! We were all perfectly adjusted to Earth, too well, we can't fit anywhere else—he wasn't, wouldn't have been; allergic, a misfit—the pattern a little wrong, see? The pattern. But there are many patterns, infinite patterns, he fits this one a little better than we do—"

Avram and the Commander continued to stare. Reine shot an alarmed glance at the picture, but asked gamely, "You're saying that Genya's allergies—"

"Not just Genya! All the sicklies, maybe! For twenty-five years I've been feeding them metas, and they're allergic to *Earth* proteins, the metas just foul them up, they're a different pattern, oh, idiot! Idiot! Oh, my God, he and Rachel can get married. They've got to marry, he should have kids. What about Rachel taking metas while she's pregnant, the foetus. I can work it out, I can work it out. I must call Leonid. And Moishe, thank God! maybe he's another one! Listen, I must go talk to Genya and Rachel, immediately. Excuse me!" She left, a short, grey woman moving like a lightning bolt.

Marca, Avram, and Reine stood staring after her, at each other, and finally back at Genya's painting.

It hung there before them, serene and joyful, full of light.

"I don't understand," said Avram.

"Patterns," Reine said thoughtfully.

"It is very beautiful," said the old Commander of the Exile Fleet. "Only, it makes me homesick."

1982

JORGE LUIS BORGES

The Garden of Forking Paths[1]

FOR *Victoria Ocampo*

On page 22 of Liddell Hart's *History of World War I* you will read that an attack against the Serre-Montauban[2] line by thirteen British divisions (supported by 1,400 artillery pieces), planned for the 24th of July, 1916, had to be postponed until the morning of the 29th. The torrential rains, Captain Liddell Hart comments, caused this delay, an insignificant one, to be sure.

The following statement, dictated, reread and signed by Dr. Yu Tsun, former professor of English at the *Hochschule* at Tsingtao,[3] throws an unsuspected light over the whole affair. The first two pages of the document are missing.

". . . and I hung up the receiver. Immediately afterwards, I recognized the voice that had answered in German. It was that of Captain Richard Madden. Madden's presence in Viktor Runeberg's apartment meant the end of our anxieties and—but this seemed, *or should have seemed,* very secondary to me—also the end of our lives. It meant that Runeberg had been arrested or murdered.[4] Before the sun set on that day, I would encounter the same fate. Madden was implacable. Or rather, he was obliged to be so. An Irishman at the service of

---

1. Translated by Donald A. Yates.   2. Liddell Hart's work is entitled *The Real War, 1914–1918* (1930) and *A History of the World War, 1914–1918* in the enlarged English-language edition (1934). The events of July 1916 do not appear on page 22 in the first and are unlikely to appear so early in any edition. A line between Serre and Montauban forms a defensive position about a hundred miles north-northeast of Paris, north of the Somme River. There is a dizzying mixture of factual references and fiction in this story, the most unlikely often being the factual.   3. The high school in what was the capital of the German colonial enclave in China until the First World War.   4. An hypothesis both hateful and odd, The Prussian spy Hans Rabener, alias Viktor Runeberg, attacked with drawn automatic the bearer of the warrant for his arrest, Captain Richard Madden. The latter, in self-defense, inflicted the wound which brought about Runeberg's death. (Borges's note.)

England, a man accused of laxity and perhaps of treason, how could he fail to seize and be thankful for such a miraculous opportunity: the discovery, capture, maybe even the death of two agents of the German Reich? I went up to my room; absurdly I locked the door and threw myself on my back on the narrow iron cot. Through the window I saw the familiar roofs and the cloud-shaded six o'clock sun. It seemed incredible to me that that day without premonitions or symbols should be the one of my inexorable death. In spite of my dead father, in spite of having been a child in a symmetrical garden of Hai Feng,[5] was I— now—going to die? Then I reflected that everything happens to a man precisely, precisely *now*. Centuries of centuries and only in the present do things happen; countless men in the air, on the face of the earth and the sea, and all that really is happening is happening to me . . . The almost intolerable recollection of Madden's horselike face banished these wanderings. In the midst of my hatred and terror (it means nothing to me now to speak of terror, now that I have mocked Richard Madden, now that my throat yearns for the noose) it occurred to me that that tumultuous and doubtless happy warrior did not suspect that I possessed the Secret. The name of the exact location of the new British artillery park on the River Ancre.[6] A bird streaked across the gray sky and blindly I translated it into an airplane and that airplane into many (against the French sky) annihilating the artillery station with vertical bombs. If only my mouth, before a bullet shattered it, could cry out that secret name so it could be heard in Germany . . . My human voice was very weak. How might I make it carry to the ear of the Chief? To the ear of that sick and hateful man who knew nothing of Runeberg and me save that we were in Staffordshire[7] and who was waiting in vain for our report in his arid office in Berlin, endlessly examining newspapers . . . I said out loud: *I must flee.* I sat up noiselessly, in a useless perfection of silence, as if Madden were already lying in wait for me. Something—perhaps the mere vain ostentation of proving my resources were nil—made me look through my pockets. I found what I knew I would find. The American watch, the nickel chain and the square coin, the key ring with the incriminating useless keys to Runeberg's apartment, the notebook, a letter which I resolved to destroy immediately (and which I did not destroy), a crown, two shillings and a few pence, the red and blue pencil, the handkerchief, the revolver with one bullet. Absurdly, I took it in my hand and weighed it in order to inspire courage within myself. Vaguely I thought that a pistol report can be heard at a great distance. In ten minutes my plan was perfected. The telephone book listed the name of the only person capable of transmitting the message; he lived in a suburb of Fenton, less than a half hour's train ride away.

I am a cowardly man. I say it now, now that I have carried to its end a plan whose perilous nature no one can deny. I know its execution was terrible. I didn't do it for Germany, no. I care nothing for a barbarous country which imposed

---

5. Chinese gardens usually aim for the appearance of nature, so a symmetrical garden would be unusual. Hai Feng seems fictional, as many names here are, but Hai-fang is Chinese for the Vietnamese city of Haiphong and is near the Yunnan province mentioned later.   6. River in northeastern France.   7. County in West Central England.

upon me the abjection of being a spy. Besides, I know of a man from England—a modest man—who for me is no less great than Goethe. I talked with him for scarcely an hour, but during that hour he was Goethe . . . I did it because I sensed that the Chief somehow feared people of my race—for the innumerable ancestors who merge within me. I wanted to prove to him that a yellow man could save his armies. Besides, I had to flee from Captain Madden. His hands and his voice could call at my door at any moment. I dressed silently, bade farewell to myself in the mirror, went downstairs, scrutinized the peaceful street and went out. The station was not far from my home, but I judged it wise to take a cab. I argued that in this way I ran less risk of being recognized; the fact is that in the deserted street I felt myself visible and vulnerable, infinitely so. I remember that I told the cab driver to stop a short distance before the main entrance. I got out with voluntary, almost painful slowness; I was going to the village of Ashgrove but I bought a ticket for a more distant station. The train left within a very few minutes, at eight-fifty. I hurried; the next one would leave at nine-thirty. There was hardly a soul on the platform. I went through the coaches; I remember a few farmers, a woman dressed in mourning, a young boy who was reading with fervor the *Annals* of Tacitus,[8] a wounded and happy soldier. The coaches jerked forward at last. A man whom I recognized ran in vain to the end of the platform. It was Captain Richard Madden. Shattered, trembling, I shrank into the far corner of the seat, away from the dreaded window.

From this broken state I passed into an almost abject felicity. I told myself that the duel had already begun and that I had won the first encounter by frustrating, even if for forty minutes, even if by a stroke of fate, the attack of my adversary. I argued that this slightest of victories foreshadowed a total victory. I argued (no less fallaciously) that my cowardly felicity proved that I was a man capable of carrying out the adventure successfully. From this weakness I took strength that did not abandon me. I foresee that man will resign himself each day to more atrocious undertakings; soon there will be no one but warriors and brigands; I give them this counsel: *The author of an atrocious undertaking ought to imagine that he has already accomplished it, ought to impose upon himself a future as irrevocable as the past.* Thus I proceeded as my eyes of a man already dead registered the elapsing of that day, which was perhaps the last, and the diffusion of the night. The train ran gently along, amid ash trees. It stopped, almost in the middle of the fields. No one announced the name of the station. "Ashgrove?" I asked a few lads on the platform. "Ashgrove," they replied. I got off.

A lamp enlightened the platform but the faces of the boys were in shadow. One questioned me, "Are you going to Dr. Stephen Albert's house?" Without waiting for my answer, another said, "The house is a long way from here, but you won't get lost if you take this road to the left and at every crossroads turn again to your left." I tossed them a coin (my last), descended a few stone steps

5

8. The annals of Cornelius Tacitus (55?–117?) treat the history of Rome from the death of Augustus in 14 to the end of Nero's reign in 68, and the military events of the period.

and started down the solitary road. It went downhill, slowly. It was of elemental earth; overhead the branches were tangled; the low, full moon seemed to accompany me.

For an instant, I thought that Richard Madden in some way had penetrated my desperate plan. Very quickly, I understood that that was impossible. The instructions to turn always to the left reminded me that such was the common procedure for discovering the central point of certain labyrinths. I have some understanding of labyrinths: not for nothing am I the great grandson of that Ts'ui Pên who was governor of Yunnan[9] and who renounced worldly power in order to write a novel that might be even more populous than the *Hung Lu Meng*[1] and to construct a labyrinth in which all men would become lost. Thirteen years he dedicated to these heterogeneous tasks, but the hand of a stranger murdered him—and his novel was incoherent and no one found the labyrinth. Beneath English trees I meditated on that lost maze: I imagined it inviolate and perfect at the secret crest of a mountain; I imagined it erased by rice fields or beneath the water; I imagined it infinite, no longer composed of octagonal kiosks and returning paths, but of rivers and provinces and kingdoms . . . I thought of a labyrinth of labyrinths, of one sinuous spreading labyrinth that would encompass the past and the future and in some way involve the stars. Absorbed in these illusory images, I forgot my destiny of one pursued. I felt myself to be, for an unknown period of time, an abstract perceiver of the world. The vague, living countryside, the moon, the remains of the day worked on me, as well as the slope of the road which eliminated any possibility of weariness. The afternoon was intimate, infinite. The road descended and forked among the now confused meadows. A high-pitched, almost syllabic music approached and receded in the shifting of the wind, dimmed by leaves and distance. I thought that a man can be an enemy of other men, of the moments of other men, but not of a country: not of fireflies, words, gardens, streams of water, sunsets. Thus I arrived before a tall, rusty gate. Between the iron bars I made out a poplar grove and a pavilion. I understood suddenly two things, the first trivial, the second almost unbelievable: the music came from the pavilion, and the music was Chinese. For precisely that reason I had openly accepted it without paying it any heed. I do not remember whether there was a bell or whether I knocked with my hand. The sparkling of the music continued.

From the rear of the house within a lantern approached: a lantern that the trees sometimes striped and sometimes eclipsed, a paper lantern that had the form of a drum and the color of the moon. A tall man bore it. I didn't see his face for the light blinded me. He opened the door and said slowly, in my own language: "I see that the pious Hsi P'êng persists in correcting my solitude. You no doubt wish to see the garden?"

I recognized the name of one of our consuls and I replied, disconcerted, "The garden?"

"The garden of forking paths."

10

9. Southwesternmost of China's eighteen traditional provinces; beautiful but sparsely populated, damp and malarial.   1. *Dream of the Red Chamber*, long semiautobiographical novel by Ts'ao Chan (1715–1763) with more than 430 characters.

Something stirred in my memory and I uttered with incomprehensible certainty, "The garden of my ancestor Ts'ui Pên."

"Your ancestor? Your illustrious ancestor? Come in."

The damp path zigzagged like those of my childhood. We came to a library of Eastern and Western books. I recognized bound in yellow silk several volumes of the Lost Encyclopedia, edited by the Third Emperor of the Luminous Dynasty[2] but never printed. The record on the phonograph revolved next to a bronze phoenix. I also recall a *famille rose*[3] vase and another, many centuries older, of that shade of blue which our craftsmen copied from the potters of Persia . . .

Stephen Albert observed me with a smile. He was, as I have said, very tall, sharp-featured, with gray eyes and a gray beard. He told me that he had been a missionary in Tientsin "before aspiring to become a Sinologist."

We sat down—I on a long, low divan, he with his back to the window and a tall circular clock. I calculated that my pursuer, Richard Madden, could not arrive for at least an hour. My irrevocable determination could wait.

"An astounding fate, that of Ts'ui Pên," Stephen Albert said. "Governor of his native province, learned in astronomy, in astrology and in the tireless interpretation of the canonical books,[4] chess player, famous poet and calligrapher—he abandoned all this in order to compose a book and a maze. He renounced the pleasures of both tyranny and justice, of his populous couch, of his banquets and even of erudition—all to close himself up for thirteen years in the Pavilion of the Limpid Solitude.[5] When he died, his heirs found nothing save chaotic manuscripts. His family, as you may be aware, wished to condemn them to the fire; but his executor—a Taoist or Buddhist monk—insisted on their publication."

"We descendants of Ts'ui Pên," I replied, "continue to curse that monk. Their publication was senseless. The book is an indeterminate heap of contradictory drafts. I examined it once: in the third chapter the hero dies, in the fourth he is alive. As for the other undertaking of Ts'ui Pên, his labyrinth . . ."

"Here is Ts'ui Pên's labyrinth," he said, indicating a tall lacquered desk.

"An ivory labyrinth!" I exclaimed. "A minimum labyrinth."

"A labyrinth of symbols," he corrected. "An invisible labyrinth of time. To me, a barbarous Englishman, has been entrusted the revelation of this diaphanous mystery. After more than a hundred years, the details are irretrievable; but it is not hard to conjecture what happened. Ts'ui Pên must have said once: *I am withdrawing to write a book.* And another time: *I am withdrawing to construct a labyrinth.* Every one imagined two works; to no one did it occur that the book and the maze were one and the same thing. The Pavilion of the Limpid Solitude stood in the center of a garden that was perhaps intricate; that circum-

15

20

2. The "Luminous" Dynasty is the Ming; its third emperor, Yung-lo, reigned 1402–1424. He commissioned a compilation of all significant work done on Chinese history, government, philosophy, geography, etc., which, though incomplete, ran to over 11,000 of the small Chinese volumes—too long to be printed.   3. "Rose family" Chinese porcelain, characterized by rose glaze over the decoration.   4. The Confucian classics which officials had to know thoroughly and apply to contemporary social and political issues.   5. The names of both Ts'ui Pên and the Pavilion seem fictitious.

stance could have suggested to the heirs a physical labyrinth. Ts'ui Pên died; no one in the vast territories that were his came upon the labyrinth; the confusion of the novel suggested to me that *it* was the maze. Two circumstances gave me the correct solution of the problem. One: the curious legend that Ts'ui Pên had planned to create a labyrinth which would be strictly infinite. The other: a fragment of a letter I discovered."

Albert rose. He turned his back on me for a moment; he opened a drawer of the black and gold desk. He faced me and in his hands he held a sheet of paper that had once been crimson, but was now pink and tenuous and cross-sectioned. The fame of Ts'ui Pên as a calligrapher had been justly won. I read, uncomprehendingly and with fervor, these words written with a minute brush by a man of my blood: *I leave to the various futures (not to all) my garden of forking paths.* Wordlessly, I returned the sheet. Albert continued:

"Before unearthing this letter, I had questioned myself about the ways in which a book can be infinite. I could think of nothing other than a cyclic volume, a circular one. A book whose last page was identical with the first, a book which had the possibility of continuing indefinitely. I remembered too that night which is at the middle of the Thousand and One Nights when Scheherazade (through a magical oversight of the copyist) begins to relate word for word the story of the Thousand and One Nights, establishing the risk of coming once again to the night when she must repeat it, and thus on to infinity. I imagined as well a Platonic, hereditary work, transmitted from father to son, in which each new individual adds a chapter or corrects with pious care the pages of his elders. These conjectures diverted me; but none seemed to correspond, not even remotely, to the contradictory chapters of Ts'ui Pên. In the midst of this perplexity, I received from Oxford the manuscript you have examined. I lingered, naturally, on the sentence: *I leave to the various futures (not to all) my garden of forking paths.* Almost instantly, I understood: 'The garden of forking paths' was the chaotic novel; the phrase 'the various futures (not to all)' suggested to me the forking in time, not in space. A broad rereading of the work confirmed the theory. In all fictional works, each time a man is confronted with several alternatives, he chooses one and eliminates the others; in the fiction of Ts'ui Pên, he chooses—simultaneously—all of them. *He creates,* in this way, diverse futures, diverse times which themselves also proliferate and fork. Here, then, is the explanation of the novel's contradictions. Fang, let us say, has a secret; a stranger calls at his door; Fang resolves to kill him. Naturally, there are several possible outcomes: Fang can kill the intruder, the intruder can kill Fang, they both can escape, they both can die, and so forth. In the work of Ts'ui Pên, all possible outcomes occur; each one is the point of departure for other forkings. Sometimes, the paths of this labyrinth converge: for example, you arrive at this house, but in one of the possible pasts you are my enemy, in another, my friend. If you will resign yourself to my incurable pronunciation, we shall read a few pages."

His face, within the vivid circle of the lamplight, was unquestionably that of an old man, but with something unalterable about it, even immortal. He read with slow precision two versions of the same epic chapter. In the first, an army marches to a battle across a lonely mountain; the horror of the rocks and shadows makes the men undervalue their lives and they gain an easy victory. In the second, the same army traverses a palace where a great festival is taking place; the resplendent battle seems to them a continuation of the celebration and they win the victory. I listened with proper veneration to these ancient narratives, perhaps less admirable in themselves than the fact that they had been created by my blood and were being restored to me by a man of a remote empire, in the course of a desperate adventure, on a Western isle. I remember the last words, repeated in each version like a secret commandment: *Thus fought the heroes, tranquil their admirable hearts, violent their swords, resigned to kill and to die.*

From that moment on, I felt about me and within my dark body an invisible, intangible swarming. Not the swarming of the divergent, parallel and finally coalescent armies, but a more inaccessible, more intimate agitation that they in some manner prefigured. Stephen Albert continued:

"I don't believe that your illustrious ancestor played idly with these varia- 25 tions. I don't consider it credible that he would sacrifice thirteen years to the infinite execution of a rhetorical experiment. In your country, the novel is a subsidiary form of literature; in Ts'ui Pên's time it was a despicable form. Ts'ui Pên was a brilliant novelist, but he was also a man of letters who doubtless did not consider himself a mere novelist. The testimony of his contemporaries pro-claims—and his life fully confirms—his metaphysical and mystical interests. Philosophic controversy usurps a good part of the novel. I know that of all prob-lems, none disturbed him so greatly nor worked upon him so much as the abys-mal problem of time. Now then, the latter is the only problem that does not figure in the pages of the *Garden*. He does not even use the word that signifies *time*. How do you explain this voluntary omission?"

I proposed several solutions—all unsatisfactory. We discussed them. Finally, Stephen Albert said to me:

"In a riddle whose answer is chess, what is the only prohibited word?"

I thought a moment and replied, "The word *chess*."

"Precisely," said Albert. "*The Garden of Forking Paths* is an enormous rid-dle, or parable, whose theme is time; this recondite cause prohibits its mention. To omit a word always, to resort to inept metaphors and obvious periphrases, is perhaps the most emphatic way of stressing it. That is the tortuous method pre-ferred, in each of the meanderings of his indefatigable novel, by the oblique Ts'ui Pên. I have compared hundreds of manuscripts, I have corrected the errors that the negligence of the copyists has introduced, I have guessed the plan of this chaos, I have re-established—I believe I have re-established—the primordial organization, I have translated the entire work: it is clear to me that not once does he employ the word 'time.' The explanation is obvious: *The Garden of Forking Paths* is an incomplete, but not false, image of the universe as Ts'ui Pên conceived it. In contrast to Newton and Schopenhauer, your ancestor did not believe in a uniform, absolute time. He believed in an infinite series of times, in a growing, dizzying net of divergent, convergent and parallel times. This network of times which approached one another, forked, broke off, or were unaware of one another for centuries, embraces *all* possibilities of time. We do not exist in the majority of these times; in some you exist, and not I; in others I, and not you; in others, both of us. In the present one, which a favorable fate has granted me, you have arrived at my house; in another, while crossing the garden, you found me dead; in still another, I utter these same words, but I am a mistake, a ghost."

30 "In every one," I pronounced, not without a tremble to my voice, "I am grateful to you and revere you for your re-creation of the garden of Ts'ui Pên."

"Not in all," he murmured with a smile. "Time forks perpetually toward innumerable futures. In one of them I am your enemy."

Once again I felt the swarming sensation of which I have spoken. It seemed to me that the humid garden that surrounded the house was infinitely saturated with invisible persons. Those persons were Albert and I, secret, busy and multiform in other dimensions of time. I raised my eyes and the tenuous nightmare dissolved. In the yellow and black garden there was only one man; but this man was as strong as a statue . . . this man was approaching along the path and he was Captain Richard Madden.

"The future already exists," I replied, "but I am your friend. Could I see the letter again?"

Albert rose. Standing tall, he opened the drawer of the tall desk; for the moment his back was to me. I had readied the revolver. I fired with extreme caution. Albert fell uncomplainingly, immediately. I swear his death was instantaneous—a lightning stroke.

35 The rest is unreal, insignificant. Madden broke in, arrested me. I have been condemned to the gallows. I have won out abominably; I have communicated to Berlin the secret name of the city they must attack. They bombed it yesterday; I read it in the same papers that offered to England the mystery of the learned Sinologist Stephen Albert who was murdered by a stranger, one Yu Tsun. The Chief had deciphered this mystery. He knew my problem was to indicate (through the uproar of the war) the city called Albert, and that I had found no other means to do so than to kill a man of that name. He does not know (no one can know) my innumerable contrition and weariness.

1962

QUESTIONS

1. Is the old man in the García Márquez story a symbol? If so, does he "stand for" something you can name or paraphrase? if he does, what is it? If not, how can he be a symbol? If we do not read this story symbolically, how can we deal with its fantastic elements? take the story as "serious literature"?

2. What humorous elements do you find in "A Very Old Man with Enormous Wings"? How do these function in the story?

3. What is the theme of "The Eye Altering"? How might it be related to all art? to racism? gender differences?

4. Explain in your own words Ts'ui Pên's theory of the universe in "The Garden of Forking Paths." Is this universe "fantasy"? In what ways may this story be considered science fiction?

5. Toward the end of Borges's story "the rest" is said to be "insignificant," though it includes what seem to be important matters like Yu's arrest and condemnation; explain. In what sense is the rest of the rest—the delivery of the message to The Chief—insignificant? Explain the final sentence of the story.

6. What is "the garden of forking paths"?

WRITING SUGGESTIONS

1. Compare the way people or "the public" view the unusual or extraordinary in "A Very Old Man with Enormous Wings" and "A Hunger Artist" and / or the way the stories view people or the public.

2. Compare the views of art and society or art and reality in "The Eye Altering" and one or more of the following: "The Zebra Storyteller," "The Real Thing," "A Hunger Artist."

3. "The garden of forking paths" is an image of the theme (as suggested in question 6 above) but it may also be an image of the path of your expectations as you read through the story. Retrace your anticipations of what would happen next or what things seem to mean when you first read at least the first eight paragraphs of the story.

Evaluating Fiction

To evaluate a work of literature—to determine its worth or quality—is one of the most fundamental, significant, and difficult activities in literary study. It is impossible to dodge such questions as "Is this story good?" "Is it great?" "Is it better than that one? . . . that other one?" "Is it worth reading? studying?" It is equally impossible to answer such questions definitively, for all time and for all readers.

It is, however, usually possible to answer the question, "Do you like this story?" and often possible to answer "Do you like this one more than or less than that other?" Whether you like a story or not when you first read it is therefore probably the proper place to *begin*. But it is a dangerous place to *stop* the process of evaluation. If our appreciation and understanding of literature is to grow, and if we are not content simply to accept without question the authority of "those who know best," we must learn to isolate, analyze, and articulate what it is *we* like about a story and to search out in our minds and experience the reasons *we* like it. We must listen to other readers' responses too, responses that may reinforce our own, may show us things to appreciate in the story that we missed, or may challenge the viability of our reasons, if not that of our responses.

Let us begin by reading a story together. Let's see how we like it, and what we can say about it.

RICHARD CONNELL

The Most Dangerous Game

"Off there to the right—somewhere—is a large island," said Whitney. "It's rather a mystery—"

"What island is it?" Rainsford asked.

The old charts call it 'Ship-Trap Island,' " Whitney replied. "A suggestive name, isn't it? Sailors have a curious dread of the place. I don't know why. Some superstition—"

"Can't see it," remarked Rainsford, trying to peer through the dank tropical night that was palpable as it pressed its thick warm blackness in upon the yacht.

"You've good eyes," said Whitney, with a laugh, "and I've seen you pick off a moose moving in the brown fall bush at four hundred yards, but even you can't see four miles or so through a moonless Caribbean night."

"Nor four yards," admitted Rainsford. "Ugh! It's like moist black velvet."

"It will be light in Rio," promised Whitney. "We should make it in a few days. I hope the jaguar guns have come from Purdey's. We should have some good hunting up the Amazon. Great sport, hunting."

"The best sport in the world," agreed Rainsford.

"For the hunter," amended Whitney. "Not for the jaguar."

"Don't talk rot, Whitney," said Rainsford. "You're a big-game hunter, not a philosopher. Who cares how a jaguar feels?"

"Perhaps the jaguar does," observed Whitney.

"Bah! They've no understanding."

"Even so, I rather think they understand one thing—fear. The fear of pain and the fear of death."

"Nonsense," laughed Rainsford. "This hot weather is making you soft, Whitney. Be a realist. The world is made up of two classes—the hunters and the huntees. Luckily, you and I are hunters. Do you think we've passed that island yet?"

"I can't tell in the dark. I hope so."

"Why? asked Rainsford.

"The place has a reputation—a bad one."

"Cannibals?" suggested Rainsford.

"Hardly. Even cannibals wouldn't live in such a God-forsaken place. But it's gotten into sailor lore; somehow. Didn't you notice that the crew's nerves seemed a bit jumpy today?"

"They were a bit strange, now you mention it. Even Captain Nielsen—"

"Yes, even that tough-minded old Swede, who'd go up to the devil himself and ask him for a light. Those fishy blue eyes held a look I never saw there before. All I could get out of him was: 'This place has an evil name among seafaring men, sir.' Then he said to me, very gravely: 'Don't you feel anything?'— as if the air about us was actually poisonous. Now, you mustn't laugh when I tell you this—I did feel something like a sudden chill.

"There was no breeze. The sea was as flat as a plate-glass window. We were drawing near the island then. What I felt was a—a mental chill; a sort of sudden dread."

"Pure imagination," said Rainsford. "One superstitious sailor can taint the whole ship's company with his fear."

"Maybe. But sometimes I think sailors have an extra sense that tells them when they are in danger. Sometimes I think evil is a tangible thing—with wave lengths, just as sound and light have. An evil place can, so to speak, broadcast vibrations of evil. Anyhow, I'm glad we're getting out of this zone. Well, I think I'll turn in now, Rainsford."

25   "I'm not sleepy," said Rainsford. "I'm going to smoke another pipe up on the after deck."

"Good night, then, Rainsford. See you at breakfast."

"Right. Good night, Whitney."

There was no sound in the night as Rainsford sat there, but the muffled throb of the engine that drove the yacht swiftly through the darkness, and the swish and ripple of the wash of the propeller.

Rainsford, reclining in a steamer chair, indolently puffed on his favorite brier. The sensuous drowsiness of the night was on him. "It's so dark," he thought, "that I could sleep without closing my eyes; the night would be my eyelids—"

30   An abrupt sound startled him. Off to the right he heard it, and his ears, expert in such matters, could not be mistaken. Again he heard the sound, and again. Somewhere, off in the blackness, some one had fired a gun three times.

Rainsford sprang up and moved quickly to the rail, mystified. He strained his eyes in the direction from which the reports had come, but it was like trying to see through a blanket. He leaped upon the rail and balanced himself there, to get greater elevation; his pipe, striking a rope, was knocked from his mouth. He lunged for it; a short, hoarse cry came from his lips as he realized he had reached too far and had lost his balance. The cry was pinched off short as the bloodwarm waters of the Caribbean Sea closed over his head.

He struggled up to the surface and tried to cry out, but the wash from the speeding yacht slapped him in the face and the salt water in his open mouth made him gag and strangle. Desperately he struck out with strong strokes after the receding lights of the yacht, but he stopped before he had swum fifty feet. A certain cool-headedness had come to him; it was not the first time he had been in a tight place. There was a chance that his cries could be heard by some one aboard the yacht, but that chance was slender, and grew more slender as the yacht raced on. He wrestled himself out of his clothes, and shouted with all his power. The lights of the yacht became faint and ever-vanishing fireflies; then they were blotted out entirely by the night.

Rainsford remembered the shots. They had come from the right, and doggedly he swam in that direction, swimming with slow, deliberate strokes, conserving his strength. For a seemingly endless time he fought the sea. He began to count his strokes; he could do possibly a hundred more and then—

Rainsford heard a sound. It came out of the darkness, a high screaming sound, the sound of an animal in an extremity of anguish and terror.

35   He did not recognize the animal that made the sound; he did not try to; with fresh vitality he swam toward the sound. He heard it again; then it was cut short by another noise, crisp, staccato.

"Pistol shot," muttered Rainsford, swimming on.

Ten minutes of determined effort brought another sound to his ears—the most welcome he had ever heard—the muttering and growling of the sea breaking on a rocky shore. He was almost on the rocks before he saw them; on a night less calm he would have been shattered against them. With his remaining strength he dragged himself from the swirling waters. Jagged crags appeared to jut into the opaqueness; he forced himself upward, hand over hand. Gasping, his hands raw, he reached a flat place at the top. Dense jungle came down to the very edge of the cliffs. What perils that tangle of trees and underbrush might hold for him did not concern Rainsford just them. All he knew was that he was safe from his enemy, the sea, and that utter weariness was on him. He flung himself down at the jungle edge and tumbled headlong into the deepest sleep of his life.

When he opened his eyes he knew from the position of the sun that it was late in the afternoon. Sleep had given him new vigor; a sharp hunger was picking at him. He looked about him, almost cheerfully.

"Where there are pistol shots, there are men. Where there are men, there is food," he thought. But what kind of men, he wondered, in so forbidding a place? An unbroken front of snarled and ragged jungle fringed the shore.

He saw no sign of a trail through the closely knit web of weeds and trees; it was easier to go along the shore, and Rainsford floundered along by the water. Not far from where he had landed, he stopped.

40

Some wounded thing, by the evidence a large animal, had thrashed about in the underbrush; the jungle weeds were crushed down and the moss was lacerated; one patch of weeds was stained crimson. A small, glittering object not far away caught Rainsford's eye and he picked it up. It was an empty cartridge.

"A twenty-two," he remarked. "That's odd. It must have been a fairly large animal too. The hunter had his nerve with him to tackle it with a light gun. It's clear that the brute put up a fight. I suppose the first three shots I heard was when the hunter flushed his quarry and wounded it. The last shot was when he trailed it here and finished it."

He examined the ground closely and found what he had hoped to find—the print of hunting boots. They pointed along the cliff in the direction he had been going. Eagerly, he hurried along, now slipping on a rotten log or a loose stone, but making headway; night was beginning to settle down on the island.

Bleak darkness was blacking out the sea and jungle when Rainsford sighted the lights. He came upon them as he turned a crook in the coast line, and his first thought was that he had come upon a village, for there were many lights. But as he forged along he saw to his great astonishment that all the lights were in one enormous building—a lofty structure with pointed towers plunging upward into the gloom. His eyes made out the shadowy outlines of a palatial château; it was set on a high bluff, and on three sides of it cliffs dived down to where the sea licked greedy lips in the shadows.

"Mirage," thought Rainsford. But it was no mirage, he found, when he opened the tall spiked iron gate. The stone steps were real enough; the massive door with a leering gargoyle for a knocker was real enough; yet about it all hung an air of unreality.

45

He lifted the knocker, and it creaked up stiffly, as if it had never before been used. He let it fall, and it startled him with its booming loudness. He thought he heard steps within; the door remained closed. Again Rainsford lifted the heavy knocker, and let it fall. The door opened then, opened as suddenly as if it were on a spring, and Rainsford stood blinking in the river of glaring gold light that poured out. The first thing Rainsford's eyes discerned was the largest man Rainsford had ever seen—a gigantic creature, solidly made and blackbearded to the waist. In his hand the man held a long-barreled revolver, and he was pointing it straight at Rainsford's heart.

Out of the snarl of beard two small eyes regarded Rainsford.

"Don't be alarmed," said Rainsford, with a smile which he hoped was disarming. "I'm no robber. I fell off a yacht. My name is Sanger Rainsford of New York City."

The menacing look in the eyes did not change. The revolver pointed as rigidly as if the giant were a statue. He gave no sign that he understood Rainsford's words, or that he had even heard them. He was dressed in uniform, a black uniform trimmed with gray astrakhan.

50   "I'm Sanger Rainsford of New York," Rainsford began again. "I fell off a yacht. I am hungry."

The man's only answer was to raise with his thumb the hammer of his revolver. Then Rainsford saw the man's free hand go to his forehead in a military salute, and he saw him click his heels together and stand at attention. Another man was coming down the broad marble steps, an erect, slender man in evening clothes. He advanced to Rainsford and held out his hand.

In a cultivated voice marked by a slight accent that gave it added precision and deliberateness, he said: "It is a very great pleasure and honor to welcome Mr. Sanger Rainsford, the celebrated hunter, to my home."

Automatically Rainsford shook the man's hand.

"I've read your book about hunting snow leopards in Tibet, you see" explained the man. "I am General Zaroff."

55   Rainsford's first impression was that the man was singularly handsome; his second was that there was an original, almost bizarre quality about the general's face. He was a tall man past middle age, for his hair was a vivid white; but his thick eyebrows and pointed military mustache were as black as the night from which Rainsford had come. His eyes, too, were black and very bright. He had high cheek bones, a sharp-cut nose, a spare, dark face, the face of a man used to giving orders, the face of an aristocrat. Turning to the giant in uniform, the general made a sign. The giant put away his pistol, saluted, withdrew.

"Ivan is an incredibly strong fellow," remarked the general, "but he has the misfortune to be deaf and dumb. A simple fellow, but, I'm afraid, like all his race, a bit of a savage."

"Is he Russian?"

"He is a Cossack," said the general, and his smile showed red lips and pointed teeth. "So am I."

"Come," he said, "we shouldn't be chatting here. We can talk later. Now you want clothes, food, rest. You shall have them. This is a most restful spot."

60   Ivan had reappeared, and the general spoke to him with lips that moved but gave forth no sound.

"Follow Ivan, if you please, Mr. Rainsford," said the general. "I was about to have my dinner when you came. I'll wait for you. You'll find that my clothes will fit you, I think."

It was to a huge, beam-ceilinged bedroom with a canopied bed big enough for six men that Rainsford followed the silent giant. Ivan laid out an evening suit, and Rainsford, as he put it on, noticed that it came from a London tailor who ordinarily cut and sewed for none below the rank of duke.

The dining room to which Ivan conducted him was in many ways remarkable. There was a medieval magnificence about it; it suggested a baronial hall of feudal times with its oaken panels, its high ceiling, its vast refectory table where twoscore men could sit down to eat. About the hall were the mounted heads of many animals—lions, tigers, elephants, moose, bears; larger or more perfect specimens Rainsford had never seen. At the great table the general was sitting, alone.

"You'll have a cocktail, Mr. Rainsford," he suggested. The cocktail was surpassingly good; and, Rainsford noted, the table appointments were of the finest—the linen, the crystal, the silver, the china.

They were eating *borsch*, the rich, red soup with whipped cream so dear to Russian palates. Half apologetically General Zaroff said: "We do our best to preserve the amenities of civilization here. Please forgive any lapses. We are well off the beaten track, you know. Do you think the champagne has suffered from its long ocean trip?"

"Not in the least," declared Rainsford. He was finding the general a most thoughtful and affable host, a true cosmopolite. But there was one small trait of the general's that made Rainsford uncomfortable. Whenever he looked up from his plate he found the general studying him, appraising him narrowly.

"Perhaps," said General Zaroff, "you were surprised that I recognized your name. You see, I read all books on hunting published in English, French, and Russian. I have but one passion in my life, Mr. Rainsford, and it is the hunt."

"You have some wonderful heads here," said Rainsford as he ate a particularly well cooked filet mignon. "That Cape buffalo is the largest I ever saw."

"Oh, that fellow. Yes, he was a monster."

"Did he charge you?"

"Hurled me against a tree," said the general. "Fractured my skull. But I got the brute."

"I've always thought," said Rainsford, "that the Cape buffalo is the most dangerous of all big game."

For a moment the general did not reply; he was smiling his curious red-lipped smile. Then he said slowly: "No. You are wrong, sir. The Cape buffalo is not the most dangerous big game." He sipped his wine. "Here in my preserve on this island," he said in the same slow tone, "I hunt more dangerous game."

Rainsford expressed his surprise. "Is there big game on this island?"

The general nodded. "The biggest."

"Really?"

"Oh, it isn't here naturally, of course. I have to stock the island."

"What have you imported, general?" Rainsford asked. "Tigers?"

65

70

75

The general smiled. "No," he said. "Hunting tigers ceased to interest me some years ago. I exhausted their possibilities, you see. No thrill left in tigers, no real danger. I live for danger, Mr. Rainsford."

The general took from his pocket a gold cigarette case and offered his guest a long black cigarette with a silver tip; it was perfumed and gave off a smell like incense.

"We will have some capital hunting, you and I," said the general. "I shall be most glad to have your society."

"But what game—" began Rainsford.

"I'll tell you," said the general. "You will be amused, I know. I think I may say, in all modesty, that I have done a rare thing. I have invented a new sensation. May I pour you another glass of port, Mr. Rainsford?"

"Thank you, general."

The general filled both glasses, and said: "God makes some men poets. Some He makes kings, some beggars. Me He made a hunter. My hand was made for the trigger, my father said. He was a very rich man with a quarter of a million acres in the Crimea, and he was an ardent sportsman. When I was only five years old he gave me a little gun, specially made in Moscow for me, to shoot sparrows with. When I shot some of his prize turkeys with it, he did not punish me; he complimented me on my marksmanship. I killed my first bear in the Caucasus when I was ten. My whole life has been one prolonged hunt. I went into the army—it was expected of noblemen's sons—and for a time commanded a division of Cossack cavalry, but my real interest was always the hunt. I have hunted every kind of game in every land. It would be impossible for me to tell you how many animals I have killed."

The general puffed at his cigarette.

"After the debacle in Russia[1] I left the country, for it was imprudent for an officer of the Czar to stay there. Many noble Russians lost everything. I, luckily, had invested heavily in American securities, so I shall never have to open a tea room in Monte Carlo or drive a taxi in Paris. Naturally, I continued to hunt—grizzlies in your Rockies, crocodiles in the Ganges, rhinoceroses in East Africa. It was in Africa that the Cape buffalo hit me and laid me up for six months. As soon as I recovered I started for the Amazon to hunt jaguars, for I had heard they were unusually cunning. They weren't." The Cossack sighed. "They were no match at all for a hunter with his wits about him, and a high-powered rifle. I was bitterly disappointed. I was lying in my tent with a splitting headache one night when a terrible thought pushed its way into my mind. Hunting was beginning to bore me! And hunting, remember, had been my life. I have heard that in America business men often go to pieces when they give up the business that has been their life."

"Yes, that's so," said Rainsford.

The general smiled. "I had no wish to go to pieces," he said. "I must do something. Now, mine is an analytical mind, Mr. Rainsford. Doubtless that is why I enjoy the problems of the chase."

1. The Revolution of 1917, which overthrew the Czar and prepared the way for Communist rule.

"No doubt, General Zaroff."

"So," continued the general, "I asked myself why the hunt no longer fasci- 90
nated me. You are much younger than I am, Mr. Rainsford, and have not
hunted as much, but you perhaps can guess the answer."

"What was it?"

"Simply this: hunting had ceased to be what you call 'a sporting proposition.'
It had become too easy. I always got my quarry. Always. There is no greater bore
than perfection."

The general lit a fresh cigarette.

"No animal had a chance with me any more. That is no boast; it is a math- 95
ematical certainty. The animal had nothing but his legs and his instinct. Instinct
is no match for reason. When I thought of this it was a tragic moment for me, I
can tell you."

Rainsford leaned across the table, absorbed in what his host was saying.

"It came to me as an inspiration what I must do," the general went on.

"And that was?"

The general smiled the quiet smile of one who had faced an obstacle and
surmounted it with success. "I had to invent a new animal to hunt," he said.

"A new animal? You're joking."

"Not at all," said the general. "I never joke about hunting. I needed a new 100
animal. I found one. So I bought this island, built this house, and here I do my
hunting. The island is perfect for my purposes—there are jungles with a maze
of trails in them, hills, swamps—"

"But the animal, General Zaroff?"

"Oh," said the general, "it supplies me with the most exciting hunting in the
world. No other hunting compares with it for an instant. Every day I hunt, and
I never grow bored now, for I have a quarry with which I can match my wits."

Rainsford's bewilderment showed in his face.

"I wanted the ideal animal to hunt," explained the general. "So I said: 'What 105
are the attributes of an ideal quarry?' And the answer was, of course: 'It must
have courage, cunning, and, above all, it must be able to reason.' "

"But no animal can reason," objected Rainsford.

"My dear fellow," said the general, "there is one that can."

"But you can't mean—" gasped Rainsford.

"And why not?"

"I can't believe you are serious, General Zaroff. This is a grisly joke." 110

"Why should I not be serious? I am speaking of hunting."

"Hunting? Good God, General Zaroff, what you speak of is murder."

The general laughed with entire good nature. He regarded Rainsford quiz-
zically. "I refuse to believe that so modern and civilized a young man as you
seem to be harbors romantic ideas about the value of human life. Surely your
experiences in the war—"

"Did not make me condone cold-blooded murder," finished Rainsford stiffly.

Laughter shook the general. "How extraordinarily droll you are!" he said. 115
"One does not expect nowadays to find a young man of the educated class, even
in America, with such a naïve, and, if I may say so, mid-Victorian point of view.

It's like finding a snuff-box in a limousine. Ah, well, doubtless you had Puritan ancestors. So many Americans appear to have had. I'll wager you'll forget your notions when you go hunting with me. You've a genuine new thrill in store for you, Mr. Rainsford."

"Thank you, I'm a hunter, not a murderer."

"Dear me," said the general, quite unruffled, "again that unpleasant word. But I think I can show you that your scruples are quite ill founded."

"Yes?"

"Life is for the strong, to be lived by the strong, and, if need be, taken by the strong. The weak of the world were put here to give the strong pleasure. I am strong. Why should I not use my gift? If I wish to hunt, why should I not? I hunt the scum of the earth—sailors from tramp ships—lascars, blacks, Chinese, whites, mongrels—a thoroughbred horse or hound is worth more than a score of them."

120   "But they are men," said Rainsford hotly.

"Precisely," said the general. "That is why I use them. It gives me pleasure. They can reason, after a fashion. So they are dangerous."

"But where do you get them?"

The general's left eyelid fluttered down in a wink. "This island is called Ship-Trap," he answered. "Sometimes an angry god of the high seas sends them to me. Sometimes, when Providence is not so kind, I help Providence a bit. Come to the window with me."

Rainsford went to the window and looked out toward the sea.

125   "Watch! Out there!" exclaimed the general, pointing into the night. Rainsford's eyes saw only blackness, and then, as the general pressed a button, far out to sea Rainsford saw the flash of lights.

The general chuckled. "They indicate a channel," he said, "where there's none: giant rocks with razor edges crouch like a sea monster with wide-open jaws. They can crush a ship as easily as I crush this nut." He dropped a walnut on the hardwood floor and brought his heel grinding down on it. "Oh, yes," he said, casually, as if in answer to a question, "I have electricity. We try to be civilized here."

"Civilized? And you shoot down men?"

A trace of anger was in the general's black eyes, but it was there for but a second, and he said, in his most pleasant manner: "Dear me, what a righteous young man you are! I assure you I do not do the thing you suggest. That would be barbarous. I treat these visitors with every consideration. They get plenty of good food and exercise. They get into splendid physical condition. You shall see for yourself tomorrow."

"What do you mean?"

130   "We'll visit my training school," smiled the general. "It's in the cellar. I have about a dozen pupils down there now. They're from the Spanish bark San Lucar that had the bad luck to go on the rocks out there. A very inferior lot, I regret to say. Poor specimens and more accustomed to the deck than to the jungle."

He raised his hand, and Ivan, who served as waiter, brought thick Turkish coffee. Rainsford, with an effort, held his tongue in check.

"It's a game, you see," pursued the general blandly. "I suggest to one of them that we go hunting. I give him a supply of food and an excellent hunting knife. I give him three hours' start. I am to follow, armed only with a pistol of the smallest caliber and range. If my quarry eludes me for three whole days, he wins the game. If I find him"—the general smiled—"he loses."

"Suppose he refuses to be hunted?"

"Oh," said the general, "I give him his option, of course. He need not play that game if he doesn't wish to. If he does not wish to hunt, I turn him over to Ivan. Ivan once had the honor of serving as official knouter to the Great White Czar,[2] and he has his own ideas of sport. Invariably, Mr. Rainsford, invariably they choose the hunt."

"And if they win?"

The smile on the general's face widened. "To date I have not lost," he said.

Then he added, hastily: "I don't wish you to think me a braggart, Mr. Rainsford. Many of them afford only the most elementary sort of problem. Occasionally I strike a tartar. One almost did win. I eventually had to use the dogs."

"The dogs?"

"This way, please. I'll show you."

The general steered Rainsford to a window. The lights from the windows sent a flickering illumination that made grotesque patterns on the courtyard below, and Rainsford could see moving about there a dozen or so huge black shapes; as they turned toward him, their eyes glittered greenly.

"A rather good lot, I think," observed the general. "They are let out at seven every night. If anyone should try to get into my house—or out of it—something extremely regrettable would occur to him." He hummed a snatch of song from the Folies Bergère.[3]

"And now," said the general, "I want to show you my new collection of heads. Will you come with me to the library?"

"I hope," said Rainsford, "that you will excuse me tonight, General Zaroff. I'm really not feeling at all well."

"Ah, indeed?" the general inquired solicitously. "Well, I suppose that's only natural, after your long swim. You need a good, restful night's sleep. Tomorrow you'll feel like a new man, I'll wager. Then we'll hunt, eh? I've one rather promising prospect—"

Rainsford was hurrying from the room.

"Sorry you can't go with me tonight," called the general. "I expect rather fair sport—a big, strong black. He looks resourceful—Well, good night, Mr. Rainsford; I hope you have a good night's rest."

The bed was good, and the pajamas of the softest silk, and he was tired in every fiber of his being, but nevertheless Rainsford could not quiet his brain with the opiate of sleep. He lay, eyes wide open. Once he thought he heard stealthy steps in the corridor outside his room. He sought to throw open the door; it would not open. He went to the window and looked out. His room was high up in one of the towers. The lights of the château were out now; and it was dark

2. Probably Nicholas II (1868–1918) who was overthrown by the Revolution and executed; "White" designates those opposed to the Communists, or "Reds."   3. Paris theater and music hall.

and silent, but there was a fragment of sallow moon, and by its wan light he could see, dimly, the courtyard; there, weaving in and out in the pattern of shadow, were black, noiseless forms; the hounds heard him at the window and looked up, expectantly, with their green eyes. Rainsford went back to bed and lay down. By many methods he tried to put himself to sleep. He had achieved a doze when, just as morning began to come, he heard, far off in the jungle, the faint report of a pistol.

General Zaroff did not appear until luncheon. He was dressed faultlessly in the tweeds of a country squire. He was solicitous about the state of Rainsford's health.

"As for me," sighed the general, "I do not feel so well. I am worried, Mr. Rainsford. Last night I detected traces of my old complaint."

150 To Rainsford's questioning glance the general said: "Ennui. Boredom."

Then, taking a second helping of *crêpes suzette*, the general explained: "The hunting was not good last night. The fellow lost his head. He made a straight trail that offered no problems at all. That's the trouble with these sailors; they have dull brains to begin with, and they do not know how to get about in the woods. They do excessively stupid and obvious things. It's most annoying. Will you have another glass of Chablis, Mr. Rainsford?"

"General," said Rainsford firmly, "I wish to leave this island at once."

The general raised his thickets of eyebrows; he seemed hurt. "But, my dear fellow," the general protested, "you've only just come. You've had no hunt-ing—"

"I wish to go today," said Rainsford. He saw the dead black eyes of the general on him, studying him. General Zaroff's face suddenly brightened.

155 He filled Rainsford's glass with venerable Chablis from a dusty bottle.

"Tonight," said the general," we will hunt—you and I."

Rainsford shook his head. "No, general," he said, "I will not hunt."

The general shrugged his shoulders and delicately ate a hothouse grape. "As you wish, my friend," he said. "The choice rests entirely with you. But may I not venture to suggest that you will find my idea of sport more diverting than Ivan's?"

He nodded toward the corner to where the giant stood, scowling, his thick arms crossed on his hogshead of a chest.

160 "You don't mean—" cried Ramsford.

"My dear fellow," said the general, "have I not told you I always mean what I say about hunting? This is really an inspiration. I drink to a foeman worthy of my steel—at last."

The general raised his glass, but Rainsford sat staring at him.

"You'll find this game worth playing," the general said enthusiastically. "Your brain against mine. Your woodcraft against mine. Your strength and stamina against mine. Outdoor chess! And the stake is not without value, eh?"

"And if I win—" began Rainsford huskily.

165 "I'll cheerfully acknowledge myself defeated if I do not find you by midnight of the third day," said General Zaroff. "My sloop will place you on the mainland near a town."

The general read what Rainsford was thinking.

"Oh, you can trust me," said the Cossack. "I will give you my word as a gentleman and a sportsman. Of course you, in turn, must agree to say nothing of your visit here."

"I'll agree to nothing of the kind," said Rainsford.

"Oh," said the general, "in that case—But why discuss that now? Three days hence we can discuss it over a bottle of Veuve Cliquot. [4] unless—"

The general sipped his wine.

Then a businesslike air animated him. "Ivan," he said to Rainsford, "will supply you with hunting clothes, food, a knife. I suggest you wear moccasins; they leave a poorer trail. I suggest too that you avoid the big swamp in the southeast corner of the island. We call it Death Swamp. There's quicksand there. One foolish fellow tried it. The deplorable part of it was that Lazarus followed him. You can imagine my feelings, Mr. Rainsford. I loved Lazarus; he was the finest hound in my pack. Well, I must beg you to excuse me now. I always take a siesta after lunch. You'll hardly have time for a nap, I fear. You'll want to start, no doubt. I shall not follow till dusk. Hunting at night is so much more exciting than by day, don't you think? Au revoir, Mr. Rainsford, au revoir."

General Zaroff, with a deep, courtly bow, strolled from the room.

From another door came Ivan. Under one arm he carried khaki hunting clothes, a haversack of food, a leather sheath containing a long-bladed hunting knife; his right hand rested on a cocked revolver thrust in the crimson sash about his waist. . . .

Rainsford had fought his way through the bush for two hours. "I must keep my nerve. I must keep my nerve," he said through tight teeth.

He had not been entirely clear-headed when the château gates snapped shut behind him. His whole idea at first was to put distance between himself and General Zaroff, and, to this end, he had plunged along, spurred on by the sharp rowels of something very like panic. Now he had got a grip on himself, had stopped, and was taking stock of himself and the situation.

He saw that straight flight was futile; inevitably it would bring him face to face with the sea. He was in a picture with a frame of water, and his operations, clearly, must take place within that frame.

"I'll give him a trail to follow," muttered Rainsford, and he struck off from the rude paths he had been following into the trackless wilderness. He executed a series of intricate loops; he doubled on his trail again and again, recalling all the lore of the fox hunt, and all the dodges of the fox. Night found him leg-weary, with hands and face lashed by the branches, on a thickly wooded ridge. He knew it would be insane to blunder on through the dark, even if he had the strength. His need for rest was imperative and he thought: "I have played the fox, now I must play the cat of the fable. [5] A big tree with a thick trunk and

175

4. A fine champagne; Chablis, above, is a very dry white Burgundy table wine.   5. The fox boasts of his many tricks to elude the hounds; the cat responds he knows only one—to climb the nearest tree—but that this is worth more than all the fox's tricks.

outspread branches was nearby, and, taking care to leave not the slightest mark, he climbed up into the crotch, and stretching out on one of the broad limbs, after a fashion, rested. Rest brought him new confidence and almost a feeling of security. Even so zealous a hunter as General Zaroff could not trace him there, he told himself; only the devil himself could follow that complicated trail through the jungle after dark. But, perhaps, the general was a devil—

An apprehensive night crawled slowly by like a wounded snake, and sleep did not visit Rainsford, although the silence of a dead world was on the jungle. Toward morning when a dingy gray was varnishing the sky, the cry of some startled bird focused Rainsford's attention in that direction. Something was coming through the bush, coming slowly, carefully, coming by the same winding way Rainsford had come. He flattened himself down on the limb, and through a screen of leaves almost as thick as tapestry, he watched. The thing that was approaching was a man.

It was General Zaroff. He made his way along with his eyes fixed in utmost concentration on the ground before him. He paused, almost beneath the tree, dropped to his knees and studied the ground. Rainsford's impulse was to hurl himself down like a panther, but he saw that the general's right hand held something metallic—a small automatic pistol.

180   The hunter shook his head several times, as if he were puzzled. Then he straightened up and took from his case one of his black cigarettes; its pungent incense-like smoke floated up to Rainsford's nostrils.

Rainsford held his breath. The general's eyes had left the ground and were traveling inch by inch up the tree. Rainsford froze there, every muscle tensed for a spring. But the sharp eyes of the hunter stopped before they reached the limb where Rainsford lay; a smile spread over his brown face. Very deliberately he blew a smoke ring into the air; then he turned his back on the tree and walked carelessly away, back along the trail he had come. The swish of the underbrush against his hunting boots grew fainter and fainter.

The pent-up air burst hotly from Rainsford's lungs. His first thought made him feel sick and numb. The general could follow a trail through the woods at night; he could follow an extremely difficult trail; he must have uncanny powers; only by the merest chance had the Cossack failed to see his quarry.

Rainsford's second thought was even more terrible. It sent a shudder of cold horror through his whole being. Why had the general smiled? Why had he turned back?

Rainsford did not want to believe what his reason told him was true, but the truth was as evident as the sun that had by now pushed through the morning mists. The general was playing with him! The general was saving him for another day's sport! The Cossack was the cat; he was the mouse.[6] Then it was that Rainsford knew the full meaning of terror.

185   "I will not lost my nerve. I will not."

He slid down the tree, and struck off again into the woods. His face was set and he forced the machinery of his mind to function. Three hundred yards from

---

6. A cat, sure of his prey, plays with a mouse before killing him.

his hiding place he stopped where a huge dead tree leaned precariously on a smaller, living one. Throwing off his sack of food, Rainsford took his knife from its sheath and began to work with all his energy.

The job was finished at last, and he threw himself down behind a fallen log a hundred feet away. He did not have to wait long. The cat was coming again to play with the mouse.

Following the trail with the sureness of a bloodhound, came General Zaroff. Nothing escaped those searching black eyes, no crushed blade of grass, no bent twig, no mark, no matter how faint, in the moss. So intent was the Cossack on his stalking that he was upon the thing Rainsford had made before he saw it. His foot touched the protruding bough that was the trigger. Even as he touched it, the general sensed his danger and leaped back with the agility of an ape. But he was not quite quick enough; the dead tree, delicately adjusted to rest on the cut living one, crashed down and struck the general a glancing blow on the shoulder as it fell; but for his alertness, he must have been smashed beneath it. He staggered, but he did not fall; nor did he drop his revolver. He stood there, rubbing his injured shoulder, and Rainsford, with fear again gripping his heart, heard the general's mocking laugh ring through the jungle.

"Rainsford," called the general, "if you are within sound of my voice, as I suppose you are, let me congratulate you. Not many men know how to make a Malay man-catcher. Luckily, for me, I too have hunted in Malacca. You are proving interesting, Mr. Rainsford. I am going now to have my wound dressed; it's only a slight one. But I shall be back. I shall be back."

When the general, nursing his bruised shoulder, had gone, Rainsford took up his flight again. It was flight now, a desperate, hopeless flight, that carried him on for some hours. Dusk came, then darkness, and still he pressed on. The ground grew softer under his moccasins; the vegetation grew ranker, denser; insects bit him savagely. Then, as he stepped forward, his foot sank into the ooze. He tried to wrench it back, but the muck sucked viciously at his foot as if it were a giant leech. With a violent effort, he tore his foot loose. He knew where he was now. Death Swamp and its quicksand.

His hands were tight closed as if his nerve were something tangible that someone in the darkness was trying to tear from his grip. The softness of the earth had given him an idea. He stepped back from the quicksand a dozen feet or so and, like some huge prehistoric beaver, he began to dig.

Rainsford had dug himself in in France[7] when a second's delay meant death. That had been a placid pastime compared to his digging now. The pit grew deeper; when it was above his shoulders, he climbed out and from some hard saplings cut stakes and sharpened them to a fine point. These stakes he planted in the bottom of the pit with the points sticking up. With flying fingers he wove a rough carpet of weeds and branches and with it he covered the mouth of the pit. Then, wet with sweat and aching with tiredness, he crouched behind the stump of a lightning-charred tree.

190

7. During World War I he had quickly dug a hole or trench to shelter himself from exploding shells, bullets, etc.

He knew his pursuer was coming; he heard the padding sound of feet on the soft earth, and the night breeze brought him the perfume of the general's ciga-rette. It seemed to Rainsford that the general was coming with unusual swiftness; he was not feeling his way along, foot by foot. Rainsford, crouching there, could not see the general, nor could he see the pit. He lived a year in a minute. Then he felt an impulse to cry aloud with joy, for he heard the sharp crackle of the breaking branches as the cover of the pit gave way; he heard the sharp scream of pain as the pointed stakes found their mark. He leaped up from his place of concealment. Then he cowered back. Three feet from the pit a man was stand-ing, with an electric torch in his hand.

"You've done well, Rainsford," the voice of the general called. "Your Bur-mese tiger pit has claimed one of my best dogs. Again you score. I think, Mr. Rainsford, I'll see what you can do against my whole pack. I'm going home for a rest now. Thank you for a most amusing evening."

At daybreak Rainsford, lying near the swamp, was awakened by a sound that made him know that he had new things to learn about fear. It was a distant sound, faint and wavering, but he knew it. It was the baying of a pack of hounds.

Rainsford knew he could do one of two things. He could stay where he was and wait. That was suicide. He could flee. That was postponing the inevitable. For a moment he stood there, thinking. An idea that held a wild chance came to him, and, tightening his belt, he headed away from the swamp.

The baying of the hounds drew nearer, then still nearer, nearer, ever nearer. On a ridge Rainsford climbed a tree. Down a watercourse, not a quarter of a mile away, he could see the bush moving. Straining his eyes, he saw the lean figure of General Zaroff; just ahead of him Rainsford made out another figure whose wide shoulders surged through the tall jungle weeds; it was the giant Ivan, and he seemed pulled forward by some unseen force; Rainsford knew that Ivan must be holding the pack in leash.

They would be on him any minute now. His mind worked frantically. He thought of a native trick he had learned in Uganda. He slid down the tree. He caught hold of a springy young sapling and to it he fastened his hunting knife, with the blade pointing down the trail; with a bit of wild grapevine he tied back the sapling. Then he ran for his life. The hounds raised their voices as they hit the fresh scent. Rainsford knew now how an animal at bay feels.

He had to stop to get his breath. The baying of the hounds stopped abruptly, and Rainsford's heart stopped too. They must have reached the knife.

He shinnied excitedly up a tree and looked back. His pursuers had stopped. But the hope that was in Rainsford's brain when he climbed died, for he saw in the shallow valley that General Zaroff was still on his feet. But Ivan was not. The knife, driven by the recoil of the springing tree, had not wholly failed.

Rainsford had hardly tumbled to the ground when the pack took up the cry again.

"Nerve, nerve, nerve!" he panted, as he dashed along. A blue gap showed between the trees dead ahead. Ever nearer drew the hounds. Rainsford forced himself on toward that gap. He reached it. It was the shore of the sea. Across a

200

cove he could see the gloomy gray stone of the château. Twenty feet below him the sea rumbled and hissed. Rainsford hesitated. He heard the hounds. Then he leaped far out into the sea. . . .

When the general and his pack reached the place by the sea, the Cossack stopped. For some minutes he stood regarding the blue-green expanse of water. He shrugged his shoulders. Then he sat down, took a drink of brandy from a silver flask, lit a perfumed cigarette, and hummed a bit from "Madame Butterfly."[8]

General Zaroff had an exceedingly good dinner in his great paneled dining hall that evening. With it he had a bottle of Pol Roger and half a bottle of Chambertin.[9] Two slight annoyances kept him from perfect enjoyment. One was the thought that it would be difficult to replace Ivan; the other was that his quarry had escaped him; of course the American hadn't played the game—so thought the general as he tasted his after-dinner liqueur. In his library he read, to soothe himself, from the works of Marcus Aurelius.[1] At ten he went up to his bedroom. He was deliciously tired, he said to himself, as he locked himself in. There was a little moonlight so, before turning on his light, he went to the window and looked down at the courtyard. He could see the great hounds, and he called: "Better luck another time," to them. Then he switched on the light.

A man, who had been hiding in the curtains of the bed, was standing there.

"Rainsford!" screamed the general. "How in God's name did you get here?"

"Swam," said Rainsford. "I found it quicker than walking through the jungle."

The general sucked in his breath and smiled. "I congratulate you," he said. "You have won the game."

Rainsford did not smile. "I am still a beast at bay," he said, in a low, hoarse voice. "Get ready, General Zaroff."

The general made one of his deepest bows. "I see," he said. "Splendid! One of us is to furnish a repast for the hounds. The other will sleep in this very excellent bed. On guard, Rainsford. . . ."

He had never slept in a better bed, Rainsford decided.

1924

A good many readers like "The Most Dangerous Game." In classes I teach it is often a favorite, or even *the* favorite. Yet other readers have urged me to drop this story from the anthology because it is "unworthy," not really Literature. Is this simply ignorance on the one hand or snobbery on the other?

8. Opera (1904) by Giacomo Puccini (1858–1924).   9. Pol Roger is champagne, Chambertin is a highly esteemed red Burgundy wine.   1. Roman emperor (A.D. 161–180), Stoic philosopher, writer, and humanitarian.

Here are two brief papers, somewhat like those a student might write in class, the first supporting "The Most Dangerous Game," the second responding to the first.

Why "The Most Dangerous Game" Is Good Literature

"The Most Dangerous Game" by Richard Connell is exciting. Things happen in it, and you want to read on because you want to find out what will happen next and how it will come out. Too often the things we need to read for class are boring, nothing happens, or, if something does happen, it happens inside somebody's head. But here things happen outside; I mean, there's real action.

Not only is there action, but that action is important, a real life-and-death struggle. This story is not just about whether somebody used the wrong fork or had a good time or didn't have a good time at a party.

The good guy wins, the story ends happily, and when you finish reading it, you feel good about things. Sometimes in class I think only real downers are supposed to be good stories, like life always has to be full of gloom and doom. Now all of us die sooner or later, of course, but that's only the end, a minute or a month or something, and there's all the rest of the time when we're not dead and not really in the process of dying. That's life, and that's what a good story should be about.

"The Most Dangerous Game" is fun to read. Sometimes I think that what are supposed to be the "good" stories are the ones I don't like. But popular stories can be good: there have been several movies made of "The Most Dangerous Game" and several stories adapted from it with just a few things changed. But, I'm told, the world of literature isn't a democracy--you don't vote for what's Literature. When I say I like Stephen King--and I'm sure not the only one, because he sells lots and lots of books--teachers or English majors say wait fifty years and see if his stuff is still around.

Well, "The Most Dangerous Game" is over sixty-five years old, older than at least three-quarters of the stories in this anthology, so it's stood the test of time, whatever that is.

Why "The Most Dangerous Game"
Is Not Good Literature

Though "The Most Dangerous Game" may be "a good read," at least the first time through, and I have nothing against someone reading it or even liking it in its way, I don't think it ought to be in The Norton Introduction to Literature. Being in the anthology gives it a status it does not deserve. It makes it the subject of serious study by college students, and college students ought to be engaged in more challenging and thought-provoking reading material, even if outside of class they are reading Stephen King and the likes of "The Most Dangerous Game."

Though it's true that a life-and-death struggle is important--for the person involved--it has no relevance for us, no outreach: it does not relate to our experience nor does it really illuminate anything about our experience or the way we look at life. I don't mean that a worthy story must have a "message," necessarily, but it should have a "theme," something that explores a significant area of human experience and understanding.

I admit that there is something like suspense in Connell's story, but that is not enough. There's nothing wrong with suspense in itself-- expectations of one sort or another are part of every good work--but here the suspense is manipulated at the price of consistency. Note how we're seeing things from Rainsford's perspective (not through his eyes and mind exactly, not in the first person, but over his shoulder) until near the end when he leaps into the sea. At that point, when we're supposed to want most to know what happens next, there's the more or less artificial suspense added by three dots and a break on the page, and then we're not with Rainsford but Zaroff, just to make us wonder if Rainsford did indeed die. It's a cheap trick. Besides, don't we know from the beginning that in this kind of story the hero never dies, so

isn't the suspense really phony? What's wrong
with stories like this is the unrealistic, wish-
fulfilling way it looks at reality: it tells us
that good guys always finish first; they win
because they're good.

While good guys do sometimes finish first, and
plenty of good stories end happily, more or
less, like "My Man Bovanne," and "The Old People," life is not always like that, and this
victory seems a little too easy.

Finally, Rainsford has no "character"; he's
just a good guy because he's an American and his
life is threatened by a bad guy who's a Russian;
and the bad guy is just a bad guy, with no
redeeming human qualities--it's all about guys
in white hats versus guys in black hats.

These are not polished and conclusive arguments, of course. Had the writer
of the first paper read the response, he might have had more to say. About the
alleged absence of theme in "The Most Dangerous Game," for example:

There is a theme in Connell's story. It is a
very important one, one that you have to think
about, and that some people will agree with,
though it is not a theme that you necessarily
have to agree with in order to appreciate the
story. Notice it is set just after the Russian
Revolution, and Zaroff (the "son of the czar")
is a cruel aristocrat from the czarist regime
who believes in power, believes that might-
makes-right, and believes some people are better

than others and have a right to do what they
will with their "inferiors," even kill them for
pleasure. Rainsford at the beginning is a
hunter/exploiter, never thinking what the "inferior" beast, the hunted, feels like. Having been
put in the place of the hunted he will no doubt
learn to have more reverence for life, more sympathy for the underdog.

The opponent, hearing this contention that there is a significant theme in the story, might well respond that the theme as described is too pat, and that it is presented through too convenient (as well as unbelievable) a situation, too much of a set-up.

This, then, is only one example of the kinds of arguments readers can use to support their judgments. We need to go on from there to consider what we read for ("a good read," "an illumination of human life and experience"), and what we mean by "the reader," the one judging the story to be "good".

Let us assume for the moment that "the readers" can be represented roughly by the people in this class—you, those who agree with you about stories, and those who, though they are more or less like you, do not always agree with you about which stories are good and what makes them good. We said earlier that if our appreciation and understanding of literature is to grow, and if we are not to merely accept what those considered "authorities" say is good or great, we must learn to isolate, analyze, and articulate what *we* like (or dislike) in a story. And, we said, we must listen to those with other responses as they articulate their reasons.

Now for the test. The next story is by a Nobel Laureate and much revered writer, William Faulkner, and this is one of his most admired stories. It has some of the same attractive qualities as "The Most Dangerous Game"—con-flict, action, suspense—but there are those who find it critically flawed. Regardless of which side we are on, we must take seriously both those who have reservations and questions and the author's and the story's established rep-utation. But first, we must read it.

WILLIAM FAULKNER

Barn Burning

The store in which the Justice of the Peace's court was sitting smelled of cheese. The boy, crouched on his nail keg at the back of the crowded room, knew he smelled cheese, and more: from where he sat he could see the ranked shelves close-packed with the solid, squat, dynamic shapes of tin cans whose labels his stomach read, not from the lettering which meant nothing to his mind but from the scarlet devils and the silver curve of fish—this, the cheese which he knew he smelled and the hermetic meat which his intestines believed he smelled coming in intermittent gusts momentary and brief between the other constant one, the smell and sense just a little of fear because mostly of despair and grief, the old fierce pull of blood. He could not see the table where the Justice sat and before which his father and his father's enemy (*our enemy* he thought in that despair; *ourn! mine and hisn both! He's my father!*) stood, but he could hear them, the two of them that is, because his father had said no word yet:

"But what proof have you, Mr. Harris?"

"I told you. The hog got into my corn. I caught it up and sent it back to him. He had no fence that would hold it. I told him so, warned him. The next time I put the hog in my pen. When he came to get it I gave him enough wire to patch up his pen. The next time I put the hog up and kept it. I rode down to his house and saw the wire I gave him still rolled on to the spool in his yard. I told him he could have the hog when he paid me a dollar pound fee. That evening a nigger came with the dollar and got the hog. He was a strange nigger. He said, 'He say to tell you wood and hay kin burn.' I said, 'What?' 'That whut he say to tell you,' the nigger said. 'Wood and hay kin burn.' That night my barn burned. I got the stock out but I lost the barn."

"Where is the nigger? Have you got him?"

"He was a strange nigger, I tell you. I don't know what became of him."

"But that's not proof. Don't you see that's not proof?"

"Get that boy up here. He knows." For a moment the boy thought too that the man meant his older brother until Harris said, "Not him. The little one. The boy," and, crouching, small for his age, small and wiry like his father, in patched and faded jeans even too small for him, with straight, uncombed, brown hair and eyes gray and wild as storm scud, he saw the men between himself and the table part and become a lane of grim faces, at the end of which he saw the Justice, a shabby, collarless, graying man in spectacles, beckoning him. He felt no floor under his bare feet; he seemed to walk beneath the palpable weight of the grim turning faces. His father, stiff in his black Sunday coat donned not for the trial but for the moving, did not even look at him. *He aims for me to lie,* he thought, again with that frantic grief and despair. *And I will have to do hit.*

"What's your name, boy?" the Justice said.

"Colonel Sartoris Snopes," the boy whispered.

"Hey?" the Justice said. "Talk louder. Colonel Sartoris? I reckon anybody

5

10

named for Colonel Sartoris in this country can't help but tell the truth, can they?" The boy said nothing. *Enemy! Enemy!* he thought; for a moment he could not even see, could not see that the Justice's face was kindly nor discern that his voice was troubled when he spoke to the man named Harris: "Do you want me to question this boy?" But he could hear, and during those subsequent long seconds while there was absolutely no sound in the crowded little room save that of quiet and intent breathing it was as if he had swung outward at the end of a grape vine, over a ravine, and at the top of the swing had been caught in a prolonged instant of mesmerized gravity, weightless in time.

"No!" Harris said violently, explosively. "Damnation! Send him out of here!" Now time, the fluid world, rushed beneath him again, the voices coming to him again through the smell of cheese and sealed meat, the fear and despair and the old grief of blood:

"This case is closed. I can't find against you, Snopes, but I can give you advice. Leave this country and don't come back to it."

His father spoke for the first time, his voice cold and harsh, level, without emphasis: "I aim to. I don't figure to stay in a country among people who . . ." he said something unprintable and vile, addressed to no one.

"That'll do," the Justice said. "Take your wagon and get out of this country before dark. Case dismissed."

His father turned, and he followed the stiff black coat, the wiry figure walking a little stiffly from where a Confederate provost's man's[1] musket ball had taken him in the heel on a stolen horse thirty years ago, followed the two backs now, since his older brother had appeared from somewhere in the crowd, no taller than the father but thicker, chewing tobacco steadily, between the two lines of grim-faced men and out of the store and across the worn gallery and down the sagging steps and among the dogs and half-grown boys in the mild May dust, where as he passed a voice hissed:

"Barn burner!"

Again he could not see, whirling; there was a face in a red haze, moonlike, bigger than the full moon, the owner of it half again his size, he leaping in the red haze toward the face, feeling no blow, feeling no shock when his head struck the earth, scrabbling up and leaping again, feeling no blow this time either and tasting no blood, scrabbling up to see the other boy in full flight and himself already leaping into pursuit as his father's hand jerked him back, the harsh, cold voice speaking above him: "Go get in the wagon."

It stood in a grove of locusts and mulberries across the road. His two hulking sisters in their Sunday dresses and his mother and her sister in calico and sunbonnets were already in it, sitting on and among the sorry residue of the dozen and more movings which even the boy could remember—the battered stove, the broken beds and chairs, the clock inlaid with mother-of-pearl, which would not run, stopped at some fourteen minutes past two o'clock of a dead and forgotten day and time, which had been his mother's dowry. She was crying, though when

---

1. Military policeman.

she saw him she drew her sleeve across her face and began to descend from the wagon. "Get back," the father said.

"He's hurt. I got to get some water and wash his . . ."

"Get back in the wagon," his father said. He got in too, over the tail-gate. His father mounted to the seat where the older brother already sat and struck the gaunt mules two savage blows with the peeled willow, but without heat. It was not even sadistic; it was exactly that same quality which in later years would cause his descendants to overrun the engine before putting a motor car into motion, striking and reining back in the same movement. The wagon went on, the store with its quiet crowd of grimly watching men dropped behind; a curve in the road hid it. *Forever* he thought. *Maybe he's done satisfied now, now that he has . . .* stopping himself, not to say it aloud even to himself. His mother's hand touched his shoulder.

"Does hit hurt?" she said.

"Naw," he said. "Hit don't hurt. Lemme be."

"Can't you wipe some of the blood off before hit dries?"

"I'll wash to-night," he said. "Lemme be, I tell you."

The wagon went on. He did not know where they were going. None of them ever did or ever asked, because it was always somewhere, always a house of sorts waiting for them a day or two days or even three days away. Likely his father had already arranged to make a crop on another farm before he . . . Again he had to stop himself. He (the father) always did. There was something about his wolf-like independence and even courage when the advantage was at least neutral which impressed strangers, as if they got from his latent ravening ferocity not so much a sense of dependability as a feeling that his ferocious conviction in the rightness of his own actions would be of advantage to all whose interest lay with his.

That night they camped, in a grove of oaks and beeches where a spring ran. The nights were still cool and they had a fire against it, of a rail lifted from a nearby fence and cut into lengths—a small fire, neat, niggard almost, a shrewd fire; such fires were his father's habit and custom always, even in freezing weather. Older, the boy might have remarked this and wondered why not a big one; why should not a man who had not only seen the waste and extravagance of war, but who had in his blood an inherent voracious prodigality with material not his own, have burned everything in sight? Then he might have gone a step farther and thought that that was the reason: that niggard blaze was the living fruit of nights passed during those four years in the woods hiding from all men, blue or gray,[2] with his strings of horses (captured horses, he called them). And older still, he might have divined the true reason: that the element of fire spoke to some deep mainspring of his father's being, as the element of steel or of powder spoke to other men, as the one weapon for the preservation of integrity, else breath were not worth the breathing, and hence to be regarded with respect and used with discretion.

2. The color of Union and Confederate Civil War (1861–1865) uniforms, respectively.

But he did not think this now and he had seen those same niggard blazes all his life. He merely ate his supper beside it and was already half asleep over his iron plate when his father called him, and once more he followed the stiff back, the stiff and ruthless limp, up the slope and on to the starlit road where, turning, he could see his father against the stars but without face or depth—a shape black, flat, and bloodless as though cut from tin in the iron folds of the frockcoat which had not been made for him, the voice harsh like tin and without heat like tin:

"You were fixing to tell them. You would have told him." He didn't answer. His father struck him with the flat of his hand on the side of the head, hard but without heat, exactly as he had struck the two mules at the store, exactly as he would strike either of them with any stick in order to kill a horse fly, his voice still without heat or anger: "You're getting to be a man. You got to learn. You got to learn to stick to your own blood or you ain't going to have any blood to stick to you. Do you think either of them, any man there this morning, would? Don't you know all they wanted was a chance to get at me because they knew I had them beat? Eh?" Later, twenty years later, he was to tell himself, "If I had said they wanted only truth, justice, he would have hit me again." But now he said nothing. He was not crying. He just stood there. "Answer me," his father said.

"Yes," he whispered. His father turned.

"Get on to bed. We'll be there tomorrow."

Tomorrow they were there. In the early afternoon the wagon stopped before a paintless two-room house identical almost with the dozen others it had stopped before even in the boy's ten years, and again, as on the other dozen occasions, his mother and aunt got down and began to unload the wagon, although his two sisters and his father and brother had not moved.

"Likely hit ain't fitten for hawgs," one of the sisters said.

"Nevertheless, fit it will and you'll hog it and like it," his father said. "Get out of them chairs and help your Ma unload."

The two sisters got down, big, bovine, in a flutter of cheap ribbons; one of them drew from the jumbled wagon bed a battered lantern, the other a worn broom. His father handed the reins to the older son and began to climb stiffly over the wheel. "When they get unloaded, take the team to the barn and feed them." Then he said, and at first the boy thought he was still speaking to his brother: "Come with me."

"Me?" he said.

"Yes," his father said. "You."

"Abner," his mother said. His father paused and looked back—the harsh level stare beneath the shaggy, graying, irascible brows.

"I reckon I'll have a word with the man that aims to begin to-morrow owning me body and soul for the next eight months."

They went back up the road. A week ago—or before last night, that is—he would have asked where they were going, but not now. His father had struck him before last night but never before had he paused afterward to explain why; it was as if the blow and the following calm, outrageous voice still rang, repercussed, divulging nothing to him save the terrible handicap of being young, the

light weight of his few years, just heavy enough to prevent his soaring free of the
world as it seemed to be ordered but not heavy enough to keep him footed solid
in it, to resist it and try to change the course of its events.

Presently he could see the grove of oaks and cedars and the other flowering
trees and shrubs, where the house would be, though not the house yet. They
walked beside a fence massed with honeysuckle and Cherokee roses and came to
a gate swinging open between two brick pillars, and now, beyond a sweep of
drive, he saw the house for the first time and at that instant he forgot his father
and the terror and despair both, and even when he remembered his father again
(who had not stopped) the terror and despair did not return. Because, for all the
twelve movings, they had sojourned until now in a poor country, a land of small
farms and fields and houses, and he had never seen a house like this before. *Hit's
big as a courthouse* he thought quietly, with a surge of peace and joy whose
reason he could not have thought into words, being too young for that: *They are
safe from him. People whose lives are a part of this peace and dignity are beyond
his touch, he no more to them than a buzzing wasp: capable of stinging for a
little moment but that's all; the spell of this peace and dignity rendering even the
barns and stable and cribs which belong to it impervious to the puny flames he
might contrive . . . .* this, the peace and joy, ebbing for an instant as he looked
again at the stiff black back, the stiff and implacable limp of the figure which
was not dwarfed by the house, for the reason that it had never looked big anywhere and which now, against the serene columned backdrop, had more than
ever that impervious quality of something cut ruthlessly from tin, depthless, as
though, sidewise to the sun, it would cast no shadow. Watching him, the boy
remarked the absolutely undeviating course which his father held and saw the
stiff foot come squarely down in a pile of fresh droppings where a horse had stood
in the drive and which his father could have avoided by a simple change of
stride. But it ebbed only for a moment, though he could not have thought this
into words either, walking on in the spell of the house, which he could even
want but without envy, without sorrow, certainly never with that ravening and
jealous rage which unknown to him walked in the ironlike black coat before
him: *Maybe he will feel it too. Maybe it will even change him now from what
maybe he couldn't help but be.*

They crossed the portico. Now he could hear his father's stiff foot as it came
down on the boards with clocklike finality, a sound out of all proportion to the
displacement of the body it bore and which was not dwarfed either by the white
door before it, as though it had attained to a sort of vicious and ravening minimum not to be dwarfed by anything—the flat, wide, black hat, the formal coat
of broadcloth which had once been black but which had now that friction-glazed
greenish cast of the bodies of old house flies, the lifted sleeve which was too
large, the lifted hand like a curled claw. The door opened so promptly that the
boy knew the Negro must have been watching them all the time, an old man
with neat grizzled hair, in a linen jacket, who stood barring the door with his
body, saying, "Wipe yo foots, white man, fo you come in here. Major ain't
home nohow."

"Get out of my way, nigger," his father said, without heat too, flinging the door back and the Negro also and entering, his hat still on his head. And now the boy saw the prints of the stiff foot on the doorjamb and saw them appear on the pale rug behind the machinelike deliberation of the foot which seemed to bear (or transmit) twice the weight which the body compassed. The Negro was shouting "Miss Lula! Miss Lula!" somewhere behind them, then the boy, deluged as though by a warm wave by a suave turn of carpeted stair and a pendant glitter of chandeliers and a mute gleam of gold frames, heard the swift feet and saw her too, a lady—perhaps he had never seen her like before either—in a gray, smooth gown with lace at the throat and an apron tied at the waist and the sleeves turned back, wiping cake or biscuit dough from her hands with a towel as she came up the hall, looking not at his father at all but at the tracks on the blond rug with an expression of incredulous amazement.

"I tried," the Negro cried. "I tole him to . . ."

"Will you please go away?" she said in a shaking voice. "Major de Spain is not at home. Will you please go away?"

His father had not spoken again. He did not speak again. He did not even look at her. He just stood stiff in the center of the rug, in his hat, the shaggy iron-gray brows twitching slightly above the pebble-colored eyes as he appeared to examine the house with brief deliberation. Then with the same deliberation he turned; the boy watched him pivot on the good leg and saw the stiff foot drag round the arc of the turning, leaving a final long and fading smear. His father never looked at it, he never once looked down at the rug. The Negro held the door. It closed behind them, upon the hysteric and indistinguishable womanwail. His father stopped at the top of the steps and scraped his boot clean on the edge of it. At the gate he stopped again. He stood for a moment, planted stiffly on the stiff foot, looking back at the house. "Pretty and white, ain't it?" he said. "That's sweat. Nigger sweat. Maybe it ain't white enough yet to suit him. Maybe he wants to mix some white sweat with it."

Two hours later the boy was chopping wood behind the house within which his mother and aunt and the two sisters (the mother and aunt, not the two girls, he knew that; even at this distance and muffled by walls the flat loud voices of the two girls emanated an incorrigible idle inertia) were setting up the stove to prepare a meal, when he heard the hooves and saw the linen-clad man on a fine sorrel mare, whom he recognized even before he saw the rolled rug in front of the Negro youth following on a fat bay carriage horse—a suffused, angry face vanishing, still at full gallop, beyond the corner of the house where his father and brother were sitting in the two tilted chairs; and a moment later, almost before he could have put the axe down, he heard the hooves again and watched the sorrel mare go back out of the yard, already galloping again. Then his father began to shout one of the sisters' names, who presently emerged backward from the kitchen door dragging the rolled rug along the ground by one end while the other sister walked behind it.

"If you ain't going to tote, go on and set up the wash pot," the first said.

"You, Sarty!" the second shouted. "Set up the wash pot!" His father appeared at the door, framed against that shabbiness, as he had been against that other bland perfection, impervious to either, the mother's anxious face at his shoulder.

"Go on," the father said. "Pick it up." The two sisters stooped, broad, lethargic; stooping, they presented an incredible expanse of pale cloth and a flutter of tawdry ribbons.

"If I thought enough of a rug to have to git hit all the way from France I wouldn't keep hit where folks coming in would have to tromp on hit," the first said. They raised the rug.

"Abner," the mother said. "Let me do it." *why does she always intervene betw. A + kids?*

"You go back and git dinner," his father said. "I'll tend to this."

From the woodpile through the rest of the afternoon the boy watched them, the rug spread flat in the dust beside the bubbling wash-pot, the two sisters stooping over it with that profound and lethargic reluctance, while the father stood over them in turn, implacable and grim, driving them though never raising his voice again. He could smell the harsh homemade lye they were using; he saw his mother come to the door once and look toward them with an expression not anxious now but very like despair; he saw his father turn, and he fell to with the axe and saw from the corner of his eye his father raise from the ground a flattish fragment of field stone and examine it and return to the pot, and this time his mother actually spoke: "Abner. Abner. Please don't. Please, Abner."

Then he was done too. It was dusk; the whippoorwills had already begun. He could smell coffee from the room where they would presently eat the cold food remaining from the mid-afternoon meal, though when he entered the house he realized they were having coffee again probably because there was a fire on the hearth, before which the rug now lay spread over the backs of the two chairs. The tracks of his father's foot were gone. Where they had been were now long, water-cloudy scoriations resembling the sporadic course of a Lilliputian mowing machine.

It still hung there while they ate the cold food and then went to bed, scattered without order or claim up and down the two rooms, his mother in one bed, where his father would later lie, the older brother in the other, himself, the aunt, and the two sisters on pallets on the floor. But his father was not in bed yet. The last thing the boy remembered was the depthless, harsh silhouette of the hat and coat bending over the rug and it seemed to him that he had not even closed his eyes when the silhouette was standing over him, the fire almost dead behind it, the stiff foot prodding him awake. "Catch up the mule," his father said.

When he returned with the mule his father was standing in the black door, the rolled rug over his shoulder. "Ain't you going to ride?" he said.

"No. Give me your foot."

He bent his knee into his father's hand, the wiry, surprising power flowed smoothly, rising, he rising with it, on to the mule's bare back (they had owned a saddle once; the boy could remember it though not when or where) and with the same effortlessness his father swung the rug up in front of him. Now in the starlight they retraced the afternoon's path, up the dusty road rife with honeysuckle, through the gate and up the black tunnel of the drive to the lightless house, where he sat on the mule and felt the rough warp of the rug drag across his thighs and vanish.

"Don't you want me to help?" he whispered. His father did not answer and now he heard again that stiff foot striking the hollow portico with that wooden and clocklike deliberation, that outrageous overstatement of the weight it carried. The rug, hunched, not flung (the boy could tell that even in the darkness) from his father's shoulder struck the angle of wall and floor with a sound unbelievably loud, thunderous, then the foot again, unhurried and enormous; a light came on in the house and the boy sat, tense, breathing steadily and quietly and just a little fast, though the foot itself did not increase its beat at all, descending the steps now; now the boy could see him.

"Don't you want to ride now?" he whispered. "We kin both ride now," the light within the house altering now, flaring up and sinking. *He's coming down the stairs now*, he thought. He had already ridden the mule up beside the horse block; presently his father was up behind him and he doubled the reins over and slashed the mule across the neck, but before the animal could begin to trot the hard, thin arm came round him, the hard, knotted hand jerking the mule back to a walk.

In the first red rays of the sun they were in the lot, putting plow gear on the mules. This time the sorrel mare was in the lot before he heard it at all, the rider collarless and even bareheaded, trembling, speaking in a shaking voice as the woman in the house had done, his father merely looking up once before stooping again to the hame he was buckling, so that the man on the mare spoke to his stooping back:

"You must realize you have ruined that rug. Wasn't there anybody here, any of your women . . ." he ceased, shaking, the boy watching him, the older brother leaning now in the stable door, chewing, blinking slowly and steadily at nothing apparently. "It cost a hundred dollars. But you never had a hundred dollars. You never will. So I'm going to charge you twenty bushels of corn against your crop. I'll add it in your contract and when you come to the commissary you can sign it. That won't keep Mrs. de Spain quiet but maybe it will teach you to wipe your feet off before you enter her house again."

Then he was gone. The boy looked at his father, who still had not spoken or even looked up again, who was now adjusting the logger-head in the hame. "Pap," he said. His father looked at him—the inscrutable face, the shaggy brows beneath which the gray eyes glinted coldly. Suddenly the boy went toward him, fast, stopping as suddenly. "You done the best you could!" he cried. "If he wanted hit done different why didn't he wait and tell you how? He won't git no twenty bushels! He won't git none! We'll gether hit and hide hit! I kin watch . . ."

"Did you put the cutter back in that straight stock like I told you?"

"No, sir," he said.

"Then go do it."

That was Wednesday. During the rest of that week he worked steadily, at what was within his scope and some which was beyond it, with an industry that did not need to be driven nor even commanded twice; he had this from his mother, with the difference that some at least of what he did he liked to do, such as splitting wood with the half-size axe which his mother and aunt had earned, or saved money somehow, to present him with at Christmas. In company with the two older women (and on one afternoon, even one of the sisters), he built pens for the shoat and the cow which were a part of his father's contract with the landlord, and one afternoon, his father being absent, gone somewhere on one of the mules, he went to the field.

They were running a middle buster[3] now, his brother holding the plow straight while he handled the reins, and walking beside the straining mule, the rich black soil shearing cool and damp against his bare ankles, he thought *Maybe this is the end of it. Maybe even that twenty bushels that seems hard to have to pay for just a rug will be a cheap price for him to stop forever and always from being what he used to be*; thinking, dreaming now, so that his brother had to speak sharply to him to mind the mule: *Maybe he even won't collect the twenty bushels. Maybe it will all add up and balance and vanish—corn, rug, fire; the terror and grief, the being pulled two ways like between two teams of horses—gone, done with for ever and ever.*

Then it was Saturday; he looked up from beneath the mule he was harnessing and saw his father in the black coat and hat. "Not that," his father said. "The wagon gear." And then, two hours later, sitting in the wagon bed behind his father and brother on the seat, the wagon accomplished a final curve, and he saw the weathered paintless store with its tattered tobacco- and patent-medicine posters and the tethered wagons and saddle animals below the gallery. He mounted the gnawed steps behind his father and brother, and there again was the lane of quiet, watching faces for the three of them to walk through. He saw the man in spectacles sitting at the plank table and he did not need to be told this was a Justice of the Peace; he sent one glare of fierce, exultant, partisan defiance at the man in collar and cravat now, whom he had seen but twice before in his life, and that on a galloping horse, who now wore on his face an expression not of rage but of amazed unbelief which the boy could not have known was at the incredible circumstance of being sued by one of his own tenants, and came and stood against his father and cried at the Justice: "He ain't done it! He ain't burnt . . ."

"Go back to the wagon," his father said.

"Burnt?" the Justice said. "Do I understand this rug was burned too?"

"Does anybody here claim it was?" his father said. "Go back to the wagon." But he did not, he merely retreated to the rear of the room, crowded as that other had been, but not to sit down this time, instead, to stand pressing among the motionless bodies, listening to the voices:

"And you claim twenty bushels of corn is too high for the damage you did to the rug?"

"He brought the rug to me and said he wanted the tracks washed out of it. I washed the tracks out and took the rug back to him."

"But you didn't carry the rug back to him in the same condition it was in before you made the tracks on it."

His father did not answer, and now for perhaps half a minute there was no sound at all save that of breathing, the faint, steady suspiration of complete and intent listening.

3. A double moldboard plow that throws a ridge of earth both ways.

"You decline to answer that, Mr. Snopes?" Again his father did not answer. "I'm going to find against you, Mr. Snopes. I'm going to find that you were responsible for the injury to Major de Spain's rug and hold you liable for it. But twenty bushels of corn seems a little high for a man in your circumstances to have to pay. Major de Spain claims it cost a hundred dollars. October corn will be worth about fifty cents. I figure that if Major de Spain can stand a ninety-five dollar loss on something he paid cash for, you can stand a five-dollar loss you haven't earned yet. I hold you in damages to Major de Spain to the amount of ten bushels of corn over and above your contract with him, to be paid to him out of your crop at gathering time. Court adjourned."

It had taken no time hardly, the morning was but half begun. He thought they would return home and perhaps back to the field, since they were late, far behind all other farmers. But instead his father passed on behind the wagon, merely indicating with his hand for the older brother to follow with it, and crossed the road toward the blacksmith shop opposite, pressing on after his father, overtaking him, speaking, whispering up at the harsh, calm face beneath the weathered hat: "He won't git no ten bushels neither. He won't git one. We'll . . ." until his father glanced for an instant down at him, the face absolutely calm, the grizzled eyebrows tangled above the cold eyes, the voice almost pleasant, almost gentle:

"You think so? Well, we'll wait till October anyway."

The matter of the wagon—the setting of a spoke or two and the tightening of the tires—did not take long either, the business of the tires accomplished by driving the wagon into the spring branch behind the shop and letting it stand there, the mules nuzzling into the water from time to time, and the boy on the seat with the idle reins, looking up the slope and through the sooty tunnel of the shed where the slow hammer rang and where his father sat on an upended cypress bolt, easily, either talking or listening, still sitting there when the boy brought the dripping wagon up out of the branch and halted it before the door.

"Take them on to the shade and hitch," his father said. He did so and returned. His father and the smith and a third man squatting on his heels inside the door were talking, about crops and animals; the boy, squatting too in the ammoniac dust and hoof-parings and scales of rust, heard his father tell a long and unhurried story out of the time before the birth of the older brother even when he had been a professional horsetrader. And then his father came up beside him where he stood before a tattered last year's circus poster on the other side of the store, gazing rapt and quiet at the scarlet horses, the incredible poisings and convolutions of tulle and tights and the painted leers of comedians, and said, "It's time to eat."

But not at home. Squatting beside his brother against the front wall, he watched his father emerge from the store and produce from a paper sack a segment of cheese and divide it carefully and deliberately into three with his pocket knife and produce crackers from the same sack. They all three squatted on the gallery and ate, slowly, without talking; then in the store again, they drank from a tin dipper tepid water smelling of the cedar bucket and of living beech trees. And still they did not go home. It was a horse lot this time, a tall rail fence upon and along which men stood and sat and out of which one by one horses were led, to be walked and trotted and then cantered back and forth along the road while the slow swapping and buying went on and the sun began to slant westward, they—the three of them—watching and listening, the older brother with his muddy eyes and his steady, inevitable tobacco, the father commenting now and then on certain of the animals, to no one in particular.

It was after sundown when they reached home. They ate supper by lamplight, then, sitting on the doorstep, the boy watched the night fully accomplish, listening to the whippoorwills and the frogs, when he heard his mother's voice: "Abner! No! No! Oh, God. Oh, God. Abner!" and he rose, whirled, and saw the altered light through the door where a candle stub now burned in a bottle neck on the table and his father, still in the hat and coat, at once formal and burlesque as though dressed carefully for some shabby and ceremonial violence, emptying the reservoir of the lamp back into the five-gallon kerosene can from which it had been filled, while the mother tugged at his arm until he shifted the lamp to the other hand and flung her back, not savagely or viciously, just hard, into the wall, her hands flung out against the wall for balance, her mouth open and in her face the same quality of hopeless despair as had been in her voice. Then his father saw him standing in the door.

"Go to the barn and get that can of oil we were oiling the wagon with," he said. The boy did not move. Then he could speak.

"What . . ." he cried. "What are you . . ."

"Go get that oil," his father said. "Go."

Then he was moving, running, outside the house, toward the stable: this the old habit, the old blood which he had not been permitted to choose for himself, which had been bequeathed him willy nilly and which had run for so long (and who knew where, battening on what of outrage and savagery and lust) before it came to him. *I could keep on,* he thought. *I could run on and on and never look back, never need to see his face again. Only I can't. I can't,* the rusted can in his hand now, the liquid splashing in it as he ran back to the house and into it, into the sound of his mother's weeping in the next room, and handed the can to his father.

"Ain't you going to even send a nigger?" he cried. "At least you sent a nigger before!"

This time his father didn't strike him. The hand came even faster than the blow had, the same hand which had set the can on the table with almost excruciating care flashing from the can toward him too quick for him to follow it, gripping him by the back of his shirt and on to tiptoe before he had seen it quit the can, the face stooping at him in breathless and frozen ferocity, the cold, dead voice speaking over him to the older brother, who leaned against the table, chewing with that steady, curious, sidewise motion of cows:

"Empty the can into the big one and go on. I'll catch up with you."

"Better tie him up to the bedpost," the brother said.

"Do like I told you," the father said. Then the boy was moving, his bunched shirt and the hard, bony hand between his shoulder-blades, his toes just touching the floor, across the room and into the other one, past the sisters sitting with

85

spread heavy thighs in the two chairs over the cold hearth, and to where his mother and aunt sat side by side on the bed, the aunt's arms about his mother's shoulders.

"Hold him," the father said. The aunt made a startled movement. "Not you," the father said. "Lennie. Take hold of him. I want to see you do it." His mother took him by the wrist. "You'll hold him better than that. If he gets loose don't you know what he is going to do? He will go up yonder." He jerked his head toward the road. "Maybe I'd better tie him."

95   "I'll hold him," his mother whispered.

"See you do then." Then his father was gone, the stiff foot heavy and measured upon the boards, ceasing at last.

Then he began to struggle. His mother caught him in both arms, he jerking and wrenching at them. He would be stronger in the end, he knew that. But he had no time to wait for it. "Lemme go!" he cried. "I don't want to have to hit you!"

"Let him go!" the aunt said. "If he don't go, before God, I am going up there myself!"

"Don't you see I can't?" his mother cried. "Sarty! Sarty! No! No! Help me, Lizzie!"

100   Then he was free. His aunt grasped at him but it was too late. He whirled, running, his mother stumbled forward on to her knees behind him, crying to the nearer sister: "Catch him, Net! Catch him!" But that was too late too, the sister (the sisters were twins, born at the same time, yet either of them now gave the impression of being, encompassing as much living meat and volume and weight as any other two of the family) not yet having begun to rise from the chair, her head, face, alone merely turned, presenting to him in the flying instant an astonishing expanse of young female features untroubled by any surprise even, wearing only an expression of bovine interest. Then he was out of the room, out of the house, in the mild dust of the starlit road and the heavy rifeness of honeysuckle, the pale ribbon unspooling with terrific slowness under his running feet, reaching the gate at last and turning in, running, his heart and lungs drumming, on up the drive toward the lighted house, the lighted door. He did not knock, he burst in, sobbing for breath, incapable for the moment of speech; he saw the astonished face of the Negro in the linen jacket without knowing when the Negro had appeared.

"De Spain!" he cried, panted. "Where's . . ." then he saw the white man too emerging from a white door down the hall. "Barn!" he cried. "Barn!"

"What?" the white man said. "Barn?"

"Yes!" the boy cried. "Barn!"

"Catch him!" the white man shouted.

105   But it was too late this time too. The Negro grasped his shirt, but the entire sleeve, rotten with washing, carried away, and he was out that door too and in the drive again, and had actually never ceased to run even while he was screaming into the white man's face.

Behind him the white man was shouting, "My horse! Fetch my horse!" and he thought for an instant of cutting across the park and climbing the fence into the road, but he did not know the park nor how high the vine-massed fence might be and he dared not risk it. So he ran on down the drive, blood and breath roaring; presently he was in the road again though he could not see it. He could not hear either: the galloping mare was almost upon him before he heard her, and even then he held his course, as if the very urgency of his wild grief and need must in a moment more find his wings, waiting until the ultimate instant to hurl himself aside and into the weed-choked roadside ditch as the horse thundered past and on, for an instant in furious silhouette against the stars, the tranquil early summer night sky which, even before the shape of the horse and rider vanished, stained abruptly and violently upward: a long, swirling roar incredible and soundless, blotting the stars, and he springing up and into the road again, running again, knowing it was too late yet still running even after he heard the shot and, an instant later, two shots, pausing now without knowing he had ceased to run, crying "Pap! Pap!", running again before he knew he had begun to run, stumbling, tripping over something and scrabbling up again without ceasing to run, looking backward over his shoulder at the glare as he got up, running on among the invisible trees, panting, sobbing, "Father! Father!"

At midnight he was sitting on the crest of a hill. He did not know it was midnight and he did not know how far he had come. But there was no glare behind him now and he sat now, his back toward what he had called home for four days anyhow, his face toward the dark woods which he would enter when breath was strong again, small, shaking steadily in the chill darkness, hugging himself into the remainder of his thin, rotten shirt, the grief and despair now no longer terror and fear but just grief and despair. *Father. My father,* he thought. "He was brave!" he cried suddenly, aloud but not loud, no more than a whisper: "He was! He was in the war! He was in Colonel Sartoris' cav'ry!" not knowing that his father had gone to that war a private in the fine old European sense, wearing no uniform, admitting the authority of and giving fidelity to no man or army or flag, going to war as Malbrouck[4] himself did: for booty—it meant nothing and less than nothing to him if it were enemy booty or his own.

The slow constellations wheeled on. It would be dawn and then sun-up after a while and he would be hungry. But that would be to-morrow and now he was only cold, and walking would cure that. His breathing was easier now and he decided to get up and go on, and then he found that he had been asleep because he knew it was almost dawn, the night almost over. He could tell that from the whippoorwills. They were everywhere now among the dark trees below him, constant and inflectioned and ceaseless, so that, as the instant for giving over to the day birds drew nearer and nearer, there was no interval at all between them. He got up. He was a little stiff, but walking would cure that too as it would the cold, and soon there would be the sun. He went on down the hill, toward the dark woods within which the liquid silver voices of the birds called unceasing— the rapid and urgent beating of the urgent and quiring heart of the late spring night. He did not look back.

1939

---

4. The duke of Marlborough (1650–1722), an English general whose name became distorted as Malbrough and Malbrouch in English and French popular songs celebrating his exploits.

The reservations I hear most often can be summarized as three "charges":

1. Faulkner's style is bad. His sentences are often too long and complicated, vague, unnecessarily wordy and sometimes hard to read.

2. The structure of the story seems almost haphazard: it wanders off the subject or out of focus.

3. The reasons the story gives—and insists upon—for people acting the way they do are unrealistic and shallow.

Can a story with a dubious style, form, theme, and vision of human actions and motives be good, much less great? Should I, must I, like it, or at least recognize its "literary value"?

Let us see a few examples of what those who find the story flawed might isolate, analyze, and articulate. We can begin with Faulkner's awkward and obscure style and pick out an early sentence—the second sentence of the story—as evidence:

> The boy, crouched on his nail keg at the back of the crowded room, knew he smelled cheese, and more: from where he sat he could see the ranked shelves close-packed with the solid, squat, dynamic shapes of tin cans whose labels his stomach read, not from the lettering which meant nothing to his mind but from the scarlet devils and the silver curve of fish—this, the cheese which he knew he smelled and the hermetic meat which his intestines believed he smelled coming in intermittent gusts momentary and brief between the other constant one, the smell and sense just a little of fear because mostly of despair and grief, the old fierce pull of blood.

Even those who do not mind taking some pains in reading will probably acknowledge that this sentence is not immediately clear. The chief problem is how to relate the final phrase "the old fierce pull of blood" to the rest of the sentence, and so to discover what the sentence as a whole means. After a little work, you may decide that what the sentence says is that there is not only the smell of cheese and the imagined smell of canned meat but also the smell of despair and grief and even some smell of fear; and that despair, grief, and fear are in the boy's "blood," that is, inherited, in his genes. We still cannot be sure whether this implies that acquired traits or experiences are hereditary or whether "blood" means something else, and we still cannot be sure whether the smell of fear is imaginary—like the smell of the meat in the cans—or real—like the smell of the cheese (perhaps the smell of the sweat that comes with fear, or the odor some say fear gives off). But even if we have been successful in our unraveling of the meaning, what is the value of a sentence that has to be worked over so much and whose meaning even then is doubtful?

Now as to the matter of form. One reason "The Most Dangerous Game" is just a slick adventure story, some people say, is that everything in it is manipulated to heighten suspense. But if we criticize Connell for shifting focus for his own purposes, what can we say about the shifting of the focus in "Barn Burning"? One such shift occurs when the narrator is explaining why the man who burns other people's barns lights only a small neat fire when it is for his own use:

> Older, the boy might have remarked this and wondered why not a big one; why should not a man who had in his blood an inherent voracious prodigality with material not his own, have burned everything in sight? Then he might have gone a step farther and thought that that was the reason: that niggard blaze was the living fruit of nights passed during those four years in the woods hiding from all men, blue or gray, with his strings of horses (captured horses, he called them). And older still, he might have divined the true reason: that the element of fire spoke to some deep mainspring of his father's being, as the element of steel or of powder spoke to other men, as the one weapon for the preservation of integrity, else breath were not worth the breathing, and hence to be regarded with respect and used with discretion.

Is it okay to shift the focus temporally like this because the purpose of the shift is not "merely" to enhance the suspense but to clarify the meaning, to reveal "the true reason"?

Sometimes the focus shifts to a time outside the story's present, as it does here, but also away from the consciousness of the boy that, like Rainsford's in "The Most Dangerous Game," dominates the rest of the story. When the father climbs aboard the wagon and immediately starts hitting the mules with a willow switch, the narrator comments,

> It was not even sadistic; it was exactly the same quality which in later years would cause his descendants to over-run the engine before putting a motor car into motion, striking and reining back in the same movement.

The time moves backward as well as forward and it always seems to do so in order to clarify or emphasize the meaning or illustrate the concept of "blood"— inborn, inherited habits or feelings. So, when his father tells him to get a can of oil the boy knows will be used to burn still another barn, despite the boy's repugnance at the act, he does it:

> Then he was moving, running, outside the house, toward the stable: this the old habit, the old blood which he had not been permitted to choose for himself, which had been bequeathed him willy nilly and which had run for so long (and who knew where, battening on what of outrage and savagery and lust) before it came to him. *I could keep on*, he thought. *I could run on and on and never look back, never need to see his face again. Only I can't. I can't . . .*

This passage leads us directly into the third reservation or question, that having to do with the story's vision of the springs of human action. Can we accept that such habits, such capacities or incapacities, are bred into the "blood"? Can we even accept that this is a concept that can be taken seriously, even if we cannot accept it? And if a serious concept, where does it lead? to genetic determinism of one kind or another? to justify "class"? to racism?

And, to go back to the earlier passage about the fire: what does it mean that fire can be a "deep mainspring of his father's being, as the element of steel or powder spoke to other men"? And how is it that fire, swords, guns—violence—can be weapons "for the preservation of integrity" without which life is not worth living? What is the "integrity" that the father is so intent on preserving? And what kind of "discretion" does the father show in his use of fire? What makes our acceptance of what this passage seems to say crucial is that it is not embedded in the fiction, as part of the action and thoughts of the characters—the boy, let us say—but it is separated from them by the shift in focus and by the flat statement that we are being given the "true reason"; so it has the authority of the story / author and we either have to believe it or discount the whole vision of the story.

And if we look beneath the surface of these "true reasons" and the "pull of blood" and look at the events of the story itself, we begin to suspect a "hidden agenda," an ideology that determines what the characters are seen to do and why.

Why is it that the boy overcomes or betrays the "pull of blood" only when the "aristocratic" Major de Spain's barn is to be burned? Is the blood of the highborn somehow more valuable than that of the low? (Though a Snopes, the boy's first name is that of the aristocrat Colonel Sartoris.) Is some blood better than others? some loyalties better than others? Or is property a higher good than blood?

The selection of certain key passages or incidents, the analysis and interpretation of the text, can be used to directly confront these critical comments and questions, as well as to explore other, more positive areas of the story and its accomplishment. And the objections themselves can be examined in terms of what unspoken assumptions they make about what makes a story good, and what agendas they hide.

The long second sentence of "Barn Burning" does indeed put extraordinary emphasis on "blood." The concept here embodied in the word "blood" can stand such emphasis, even demands it, for "blood" is one of the forces that are in conflict within the boy. Therefore the sentence, though it may seem difficult, really gives ready access to the meaning of the story by calling attention to one of its key elements. Part of its length, too, consists in magnificent particularizing detail, the kind that convinces you that the author knows what he is talking about, and really "sees" the scene. (See the comments Ford Maddox Ford makes on the first sentence in "Odour of Chrysanthemums"; you can make the same kind of analysis of this sentence.) The density of detail is also necessary in realizing (making real) the boy's sensations. The detail and the focus of the sentence also indicate where the significant action of the story is to take place—that is, inside the boy—and so we are mde to understand and perhaps feel with him. Finally, the move from the smell of cheese to the "smell" of canned meat, to that of fear, is crucial: the smell of cheese is real. The smell of meat is inside the can and though it cannot actually be smelled while the can is intact it is real and is there. So what this suggests is that the boy's sensory imagination does not falsify, it just penetrates into things beyond the immediate present sense perceptions. This gives reality to the smell of despair, grief, fear— not necessarily real to the senses, but really there beneath the surface, real to the imagination. What the sentence does, then, is open up our notions of reality to include not just what the senses tell us, but what the imagination can sense. And since it does so through sensory images that gradually shade off into the imaginative, we are not just told that the imaginative is valid but we are made to feel that this is so. Thus the sentence that seemed unnecessarily long, complex, and difficult turns out to be functional. It does what no short sentence or series of sentences would be likely to manage.

Complexity, even obscurity, is not in all cases "bad"—as the criticism of the sentence seemed to assume. The literary value of language and detail does not necessarily follow rules of usage but questions of function—whether they work to create, reveal, intensify, the meaning and effect of the story.

Before going on to address the issue of the structure or theme of "Barn Burning," it may be appropriate to suggest that it is precisely in this merging of the physical and the imaginative, moral or psychological, that one of the strengths of the story—and of Faulkner—lies. The force that opposes blood, we soon learn, is the boy's sense of right and wrong. His father is accused of maliciously burning down Mr. Harris's barn. The boy knows his father is guilty. But when Harris demands the boy be called before the judge, the boy knows that because his ties to his father are those of "blood," he must lie. When the judge asks if Harris really wants the boy questioned there is a pause. For a boy,

> . . . it was as if he had swung outward at the end of a grape vine, over a ravine, and at the top of the swing had been caught in a prolonged instant of mesmerized gravity, weightless in time.

Most readers would acknowledge the appropriateness of the image both to the feeling of suspense and to the experience of the boy, and the intervention of the image suspends the meaning and imitates the boy's suspense. When Harris says the boy does not have to testify, "the smell of cheese and sealed meat, the fear and despair and the old grief of blood" return to the boy's consciousness. The importance and meaning of fear, despair, and grief in the "blood" is now a little clearer.

Faulkner's complexity, "idiosyncrasies" (what some call "flaws"), and difficulty (sometimes called "obscurity") usually come from this interpenetration of imagination and sensory reality or other things that we usually keep separate, like past and present. Each episode, character, detail, is saturated with the full world of his fiction, and its function seems to be primarily to embody that world rather than to further the plot or make a statement. The present is informed by the past and informs the future. Characters (Major de Spain) and names (Colonel Sartoris) that are minor or casual here are central elsewhere in Faulkner's canon, like actors in a repertory theater. The fiction is all one seamless, interconnected, timeless world. The interpenetration of community and generations is essential to the vision.

This gives both a smaller and larger role to the concept of "blood." "Blood" alone—inherited traits, customs, motives—does not determine behavior, but it is one of the multitude of communal and traditional forces that condition behavior. Though "blood" can explain many acts and impulses, its force does not eliminate free will. The boy does, after all, choose to warn the Major of his father's intention, chooses morality over blood. To claim that it was only Major de Spain's class or property that moved the boy to consider betraying his father is to ignore the fact that the story opens with his being on the verge of doing so in the Harris case. The father's crimes went well beyond the destruction of property; indeed it was the primacy of property over principles in his scheme of values that led him to serve neither North nor South but Mammon (by being a non-partisan horse thief) during the Civil War.

Explaining the function of what may at first have seemed defects does not close the discussion about the merits of a work or the nature and function of literature. The discussion of the value of "Barn Burning" does not necessarily end here.

Until now, we have depersonalized the evaluations, assuming that the pros and cons are intellectual positions that have little or nothing to do with an individual reader, and that the "evidence" is always in the story. But already we have seen that some of the response to Faulkner is ideological, based on social or political values that have little to do with whether the focus shifts or the sentences are too long. We must admit that not all evidence of value is "on the page"; some beauty is in the eyes of the beholder. Let us keep this in mind— that is, be aware of our own responses and try at the same time to account for those responses both in terms of the narrative strategies and in terms of our own prejudices or predispositions.

BHARATI MUKHERJEE

The Management of Grief

A woman I don't know is boiling tea the Indian way in my kitchen. There are a lot of women I don't know in my kitchen, whispering, and moving tactfully. They open doors, rummage through the pantry, and try not to ask me where things are kept. They remind me of when my sons were small, on Mother's Day or when Vikram and I were tired, and they would make big, sloppy omelets. I would lie in bed pretending I didn't hear them.

Dr. Sharma, the treasurer of the Indo-Canada Society, pulls me into the hallway. He wants to know if I am worried about money. His wife, who has just come up from the basement with a tray of empty cups and glasses, scolds him. "Don't bother Mrs. Bhave with mundane details." She looks so monstrously pregnant her baby must be days overdue. I tell her she shouldn't be carrying heavy things. "Shaila," she says, smiling, "this is the fifth." Then she grabs a teenager by his shirttails. He slips his Walkman off his head. He has to be one of her four children, they have the same domed and dented foreheads. "What's the official word now?" she demands. The boy slips the headphones back on. "They're acting evasive, Ma. They're saying it could be an accident or a terrorist bomb."

All morning, the boys have been muttering, Sikh Bomb, Sikh Bomb. The men, not using the word, bow their heads in agreement. Mrs. Sharma touches her forehead at such a word. At least they've stopped talking about space debris and Russian lasers.

Two radios are going in the dining room. They are tuned to different stations. Someone must have brought the radios down from my boys' bedrooms. I haven't gone into their rooms since Kusum came running across the front lawn in her bathrobe. She looked so funny, I was laughing when I opened the door.

The big TV in the den is being whizzed through American networks and cable channels.

"Damn!" some man swears bitterly. "How can these preachers carry on like nothing's happened?" I want to tell him we're not that important. You look at the audience, and at the preacher in his blue robe with his beautiful white hair, the potted palm trees under a blue sky, and you know they care about nothing.

The phone rings and rings. Dr. Sharma's taken charge. "We're with her,"

5

he keeps saying. "Yes, yes, the doctor has given calming pills. Yes, yes, pills are having necessary effect." I wonder if pills alone explain this calm. Not peace, just a deadening quiet. I was always controlled, but never repressed. Sound can reach me, but my body is tensed, ready to scream. I hear their voices all around me. I hear my boys and Vikram cry, "Mommy, Shaila!" and their screams insulate me, like headphones.

The woman boiling water tells her story again and again. "I got the news first. My cousin called from Halifax before six A.M., can you imagine? He'd gotten up for prayers and his son was studying for medical exams and he heard on a rock channel that something had happened to a plane. They said first it had disappeared from the radar, like a giant eraser just reached out. His father called me, so I said to him, what do you mean, 'something bad'? You mean a hijacking? And he said, behn[1], there is no confirmation of anything yet, but check with your neighbors because a lot of them must be on that plane. So I called poor Kusum straightaway. I knew Kusum's husband and daughter were booked to go yesterday."

Kusum lives across the street from me. She and Satish had moved in less than a month ago. They said they needed a bigger place. All these people, the Sharmas and friends from the Indo-Canada Society had been there for the housewarming. Satish and Kusum made homemade tandoori on their big gas grill and even the white neighbors piled their plates high with that luridly red, charred, juicy chicken. Their younger daughter had danced, and even our boys had broken away from the Stanley Cup telecast to put in a reluctant appearance. Everyone took pictures for their albums and for the community newspapers— another of our families had made it big in Toronto—and now I wonder how many of those happy faces are gone. "Why does God give us so much if all along He intends to take it away?" Kusum asks me.

I nod. We sit on carpeted stairs, holding hands like children. "I never once told him that I loved him," I say. I was too much the well brought up woman. I was so well brought up I never felt comfortable calling my husband by his first name.

"It's all right," Kusum says. "He knew. My husband knew. They felt it. Modern young girls have to say it because what they feel is fake."

Kusum's daughter, Pam, runs in with an overnight case. Pam's in her McDonald's uniform. "Mummy! You have to get dressed!" Panic makes her cranky. "A reporter's on his way here."

"Why?"

"You want to talk to him in your bathrobe?" She starts to brush her mother's long hair. She's the daughter who's always in trouble. She dates Canadian boys and hangs out in the mall, shopping for tight sweaters. The younger one, the goody-goody one according to Pam, the one with a voice so sweet that when she sang bhajans[2] for Ethiopian relief even a frugal man like my husband wrote out a hundred dollar check, she was on that plane. She was going to spend July and August with grandparents because Pam wouldn't go. Pam said she'd rather wait-

---

1. "No."   2. Hymns.

ress at McDonald's. "If it's a choice between Bombay and Wonderland, I'm picking Wonderland," she'd said.

"Leave me alone," Kusum yells. "You know what I want to do? If I didn't have to look after you now, I'd hang myself."

Pam's young face goes blotchy with pain. "Thanks," she says, "don't let me stop you."

"Hush," pregnant Mrs. Sharma scolds Pam. "Leave your mother alone. Mr. Sharma will tackle the reporters and fill out the forms. He'll say what has to be said."

Pam stands her ground. "You think I don't know what Mummy's thinking? *Why her?* that's what. That's sick! Mummy wishes my little sister were alive and I were dead."

Kusum's hand in mine is trembly hot. We continue to sit on the stairs.

She calls before she arrives, wondering if there's anything I need. Her name is Judith Templeton and she's an appointee of the provincial government. "Multiculturalism?" I ask, and she says, "partially," but that her mandate is bigger. "I've been told you knew many of the people on the flight," she says. "Perhaps if you'd agree to help us reach the others. . . ?"

She gives me time at least to put on tea water and pick up the mess in the front room. I have a few *samosas*[3] from Kusum's housewarming that I could fry up, but then I think, why prolong this visit?

Judith Templeton is much younger than she sounded. She wears a blue suit with a white blouse and a polka dot tie. Her blond hair is cut short, her only jewelry is pearl drop earrings. Her briefcase is new and expensive looking, a gleaming cordovan leather. She sits with it across her lap. When she looks out the front windows onto the street, her contact lenses seem to float in front of her light blue eyes.

"What sort of help do you want from me?" I ask. She has refused the tea, out of politeness, but I insist, along with some slightly stale biscuits.

"I have no experience," she admits. "That is, I have an MSW and I've worked in liaison with accident victims, but I mean I have no experience with a tragedy of this scale—"

"Who could?" I ask.

"—and with the complications of culture, language, and customs. Someone mentioned that Mrs. Bhave is a pillar—because you've taken it more calmly."

At this, perhaps, I frown, for she reaches forward, almost to take my hand. "I hope you understand my meaning, Mrs. Bhave. There are hundreds of people in Metro directly affected, like you, and some of them speak no English. There are some widows who've never handled money or gone on a bus, and there are old parents who still haven't eaten or gone outside their bedrooms. Some houses and apartments have been looted. Some wives are still hysterical. Some husbands are in shock and profound depression. We want to help, but our hands are tied in so many ways. We have to distribute money to some people, and

3. Fried turnovers filled with meat or vegetable mixtures.

there are legal documents—these things can be done. We have interpreters, but we don't always have the human touch, or maybe the right human touch. We don't want to make mistakes, Mrs. Bhave, and that's why we'd like to ask you to help us."

"More mistakes, you mean," I say.

"Police matters are not in my hands," she answers.

30 "Nothing I can do will make any difference," I say. "We must all grieve in our own way."

"But you are coping very well. All the people said, Mrs. Bhave is the strongest person of all. Perhaps if the others could see you, talk with you, it would help them."

"By the standards of the people you call hysterical, I am behaving very oddly and very badly, Miss Templeton." I want to say to her, *I wish I could scream, starve, walk into Lake Ontario, jump from a bridge.* "They would not see me as a model. I do not see myself as a model."

I am a freak. No one who has ever known me would think of me reacting this way. This terrible calm will not go away.

She asks me if she may call again, after I get back from a long trip that we all must make. "Of course," I say. "Feel free to call, anytime."

35 Four days later, I find Kusum squatting on a rock overlooking a bay in Ireland. It isn't a big rock, but it juts sharply out over water. This is as close as we'll ever get to them. June breezes balloon out her sari and unpin her knee-length hair. She has the bewildered look of a sea creature whom the tides have stranded.

It's been one hundred hours since Kusum came stumbling and screaming across my lawn. Waiting around the hospital, we've heard many stories. The police, the diplomats, they tell us things thinking that we're strong, that knowledge is helpful to the grieving, and maybe it is. Some, I know, prefer ignorance, or their own versions. The plane broke into two, they say. Unconsciousness was instantaneous. No one suffered. My boys must have just finished their breakfasts. They loved eating on planes, they loved the smallness of plates, knives, and forks. Last year they saved the airline salt and pepper shakers. Half an hour more and they would have made it to Heathrow.

Kusum says that we can't escape our fate. She says that all those people— our husbands, my boys, her girl with the nightingale voice, all those Hindus, Christians, Sikhs, Muslims, Parsis, and atheists on that plane—were fated to die together off this beautiful bay. She learned this from a swami in Toronto.

I have my Valium.

Six of us "relatives"—two widows and four widowers—choose to spend the day today by the waters instead of sitting in a hospital room and scanning photographs of the dead. That's what they call us now: relatives. I've looked through twenty-seven photos in two days. They're very kind to us, the Irish are very understanding. Sometimes understanding means freeing a tourist bus for this trip to the bay, so we can pretend to spy our loved ones through the glassiness of waves or in sunspeckled cloud shapes.

I could die here, too, and be content.   40

"What is that, out there?" She's standing and flapping her hands and for a moment I see a head shape bobbing in the waves. She's standing in the water, I, on the boulder. The tide is low, and a round, black, headsized rock has just risen from the waves. She returns, her sari end dripping and ruined and her face is a twisted remnant of hope, the way mine was a hundred hours ago, still laughing but inwardly knowing that nothing but the ultimate tragedy could bring two women together at six o'clock on a Sunday morning. I watch her face sag into blankness.

"That water felt warm, Shaila," she says at length.

"You can't," I say. "We have to wait for our turn to come."

I haven't eaten in four days, haven't brushed my teeth.

"I know," she says. "I tell myself I have no right to grieve. They are in a   45
better place than we are. My swami says I should be thrilled for them. My swami says depression is a sign of our selfishness."

Maybe I'm selfish. Selfishly I break away from Kusum and run, sandals slapping against stones, to the water's edge. What if my boys aren't lying pinned under the debris? What if they aren't stuck a mile below that innocent blue chop? What if, given the strong currents. . . .

Now I've ruined my sari, one of my best. Kusum has joined me, knee-deep in water that feels to me like a swimming pool. I could settle in the water, and my husband would take my hand and the boys would slap water in my face just to see me scream.

"Do you remember what good swimmers my boys were, Kusum?"

"I saw the medals," she says.

One of the widowers, Dr. Ranganathan from Montreal, walks out to us,   50
carrying his shoes in one hand. He's an electrical engineer. Someone at the hotel mentioned his work is famous around the world, something about the place where physics and electricity come together. He has lost a huge family, something indescribable. "With some luck," Dr. Ranganathan suggests to me, " a good swimmer could make it safely to some island. It is quite possible that there may be many, many microscopic islets scattered around."

"You're not just saying that?" I tell Dr. Ranganathan about Vinod, my elder son. Last year he took diving as well.

"It's a parent's duty to hope," he says. "It is foolish to rule out possibilities that have not been tested. I myself have not surrendered hope."

Kusum is sobbing once again. "Dear lady," he says, laying his free hand on her arm, and she calms down.

"Vinod is how old?" he asks me. He's very careful, as we all are. *Is*, not was.

"Fourteen. Yesterday he was fourteen. His father and uncle were going to   55
take him down to the Taj and give him a big birthday party. I couldn't go with them because I couldn't get two weeks off from my stupid job in June." I process bills for a travel agent. June is a big travel month.

Dr. Ranganathan whips the pockets of his suit jacked inside out. Squashed roses, in darkening shades of pink, float on the water. He tore the roses off creepers in somebody's garden. He didn't ask anyone if he could pluck the roses, but now there's been an article about it in the local papers. When you see an Indian person, it says, please give him or her flowers.

"A strong youth of fourteen," he says, "can very likely pull to safety a younger one."

My sons, though four years apart, were very close. Vinod wouldn't let Mithun drown. *Electrical engineering*, I think, foolishly perhaps: this man knows important secrets of the universe, things closed to me. Relief spins me lightheaded. No wonder my boys' photographs haven't turned up in the gallery of photos of the recovered dead. "Such pretty roses," I say.

"My wife loved pink roses. Every Friday I had to bring a bunch home. I used to say, why? After twenty-odd years of marriage you're still needing proof positive of my love?" He has identified his wife and three of his children. Then others from Montreal, the lucky ones, intact families with no survivors. He chuckles as he wades back to shore. Then he swings around to ask me a question. "Mrs. Bhave, you are wanting to throw in some roses for your loved ones? I have two big ones left."

60   But I have other things to float: Vinod's pocket calculator; a half-painted model B-52 for my Mithun. They'd want them on their island. And for my husband? For him I let fall into the calm, glassy waters a poem I wrote in the hospital yesterday. Finally he'll know my feelings for him.

"Don't tumble, the rocks are slippery," Dr. Ranganathan cautions. He holds out a hand for me to grab.

Then it's time to get back on the bus, time to rush back to our waiting posts on hospital benches.

Kusum is one of the lucky ones. The lucky ones flew here, identified in multiplicate their loved ones, then will fly to India with the bodies for proper ceremonies. Satish is one of the few males who surfaced. The photos of faces we saw on the walls in an office at Heathrow and here in the hospital are mostly of women. Women have more body fat, a nun said to me matter-of-factly. They float better.

Today I was stopped by a young sailor on the street. He had loaded bodies, he'd gone into the water when—he checks my face for signs of strength—when the sharks were first spotted. I don't blush, and he breaks down. "It's all right," I say. "Thank you." I had heard about the sharks from Dr. Ranganathan. In his orderly mind, science brings understanding, it holds no terror. It is the shark's duty. For every deer there is a hunter, for every fish a fisherman.

65   The Irish are not shy; they rush to me and give me hugs and some are crying. I cannot imagine reactions like that on the streets of Toronto. Just strangers, and I am touched. Some carry flowers with them and give them to any Indian they see.

After lunch, a policeman I have gotten to know quite well catches hold of me. He says he thinks he has a match for Vinod. I explain what a good swimmer Vinod is.

"You want me with you when you look at photos?" Dr. Ranganathan walks ahead of me into the picture gallery. In these matters, he is a scientist, and I am grateful. It is a new perspective. "They have performed miracles," he says. "We are indebted to them."

The first day or two the policemen showed us relatives only one picture at a time; now they're in a hurry, they're eager to lay out the possibles, and even the probables.

The face on the photo is of a boy much like Vinod; the same intelligent eyes, the same thick brows dipping into a V. But this boy's features, even his cheeks, are puffier, wider, mushier.

"No." My gaze is pulled by other pictures. There are five other boys who   70
look like Vinod.

The nun assigned to console me rubs the first picture with a fingertip. "When they've been in the water for a while, love, they look a little heavier." The bones under the skin are broken, they said on the first day—try to adjust your memories. It's important.

"It's not him. I'm his mother. I'd know."

"I know this one!" Dr. Ranganathan cries out suddenly from the back of the gallery. "And this one!" I think he senses that I don't want to find my boys. "They are the Kutty brothers. They were also from Montreal." I don't mean to be crying. On the contrary, I am ecstatic. My suitcase in the hotel is packed heavy with dry clothes for my boys.

The policeman starts to cry. "I am so sorry, I am so sorry, ma'am. I really thought we had a match."

With the nun ahead of us and the policeman behind, we, the unlucky ones   75
without our children's bodies, file out of the makeshift gallery.

From Ireland most of us go on to India. Kusum and I take the same direct flight to Bombay, so I can help her clear customs quickly. But we have to argue with a man in uniform. He has large boils on his face. The boils swell and glow with sweat as we argue with him. He wants Kusum to wait in line and he refuses to take authority because his boss is on a tea break. But Kusum won't let her coffins out of sight, and I shan't desert her though I know that my parents, elderly and diabetic, must be waiting in a stuffy car in a scorching lot.

"You bastard!" I scream at the man with the popping boils. Other passengers press closer. "You think we're smuggling contraband in those coffins!"

Once upon a time we were well brought up women; we were dutiful wives who kept our heads veiled, our voices shy and sweet.

In India, I become, once again, an only child of rich, ailing parents. Old friends of the family come to pay their respects. Some are Sikh, and inwardly, involuntarily, I cringe. My parents are progressive people; they do not blame communities for a few individuals.

In Canada it is a different story now.   80

"Stay longer," my mother pleads. "Canada is a cold place. Why would you want to be all by yourself?" I stay.

Three months pass. Then another.

"Vikram wouldn't have wanted you to give up things!" they protest. They call my husband by the name he was born with. In Toronto he'd changed to Vik so the men he worked with at his office would find his name as easy as Rod or Chris. "You know, the dead aren't cut off from us!"

My grandmother, the spoiled daughter of a rich *zamindar*[4], shaved her head with rusty razor blades when she was widowed at sixteen. My grandfather died of childhood diabetes when he was nineteen, and she saw herself as the harbinger of bad luck. My mother grew up without parents, raised indifferently by an uncle, while her true mother slept in a hut behind the main estate house and took her food with the servants. She grew up a rationalist. My parents abhor mindless mortification.

85 The zamindar's daughter kept stubborn faith in Vedic rituals; my parents rebelled. I am trapped between two modes of knowledge. At thirty-six, I am too old to start over and too young to give up. Like my husband's spirit, I flutter between worlds.

Courting aphasia, we travel. We travel with our phalanx of servants and poor relatives. To hill stations and to beach resorts. We play contract bridge in dusty gymkhana clubs. We ride stubby ponies up crumbly mountain trails. At tea dances, we let ourselves be twirled twice round the ballroom. We hit the holy spots we hadn't made time for before. In Varanasi, Kalighat, Rishikesh, Hardwar, astrologers and palmists seek me out and for a fee offer me cosmic consolations.

Already the widowers among us are being shown new bride candidates. They cannot resist the call of custom, the authority of their parents and older brothers. They must marry; it is the duty of a man to look after a wife. The new wives will be young widows with children, destitute but of good family. They will make loving wives, but the men will shun them. I've had calls from the men over crackling Indian telephone lines. "Save me," they say, these substantial, educated, successful men of forty. "My parents are arranging a marriage for me." In a month they will have buried one family and returned to Canada with a new bride and partial family.

I am comparatively lucky. No one here thinks of arranging a husband for an unlucky widow.

Then, on the third day of the sixth month into this odyssey, in an abandoned temple in a tiny Himalayan village, as I make my offering of flowers and sweetmeats to the god of a tribe of animists, my husband descends to me. He is squatting next to a scrawny *sadhu* in moth-eaten robes. Vikram wears the vanilla suit he wore the last time I hugged him. The *sadhu* tosses petals on a butter-fed flame, reciting Sanskrit mantras and sweeps his face of flies. My husband takes my hands in his.

90 *You're beautiful,* he starts. Then, *What are you doing here?*

Shall I stay? I ask. He only smiles, but already the image is fading. *You must finish alone what we started together.* No seaweed wreathes his mouth. He speaks

4. Landowner.

too fast just as he used to when we were an envied family in our pink split-level. He is gone.

In the windowless altar room, smoky with joss sticks and clarified butter lamps, a sweaty hand gropes for my blouse. I do not shriek. The *sadhu* arranges his robe. The lamps hiss and sputter out.

When we come out of the temple, my mother says, "Did you feel something weird in there?"

My mother has no patience with ghosts, prophetic dreams, holy men, and cults.

"No," I lie. "Nothing."

But she knows that she's lost me. She knows that in days I shall be leaving.

95

Kusum's put her house up for sale. She wants to live in an ashram in Hardwar. Moving to Hardwar was her swami's idea. Her swami runs two ashrams, the one in Hardwar and another here in Toronto.

"Don't run away," I tell her.

"I'm not running away," she says. "I'm pursuing inner peace. You think you or that Ranganathan fellow are better off?"

Pam's left for California. She wants to do some modelling, she says. She says when she comes into her share of the insurance money she'll open a yoga-cum-aerobics studio in Hollywood. She sends me postcards so naughty I daren't leave them on the coffee table. Her mother has withdrawn from her and the world.

The rest of us don't lose touch, that's the point. Talk is all we have, says Dr. Ranganathan, who has also resisted his relatives and returned to Montreal and to his job, alone. He says, whom better to talk with than other relatives? We've been melted down and recast as a new tribe.

He calls me twice a week from Montreal. Every Wednesday night and every Saturday afternoon. He is changing jobs, going to Ottawa. But Ottawa is over a hundred miles away, and he is forced to drive two hundred and twenty miles a day. He can't bring himself to sell his house. The house is a temple, he says; the king-sized bed in the master bedroom is a shrine. He sleeps on a folding cot. A devotee.

There are still some hysterical relatives. Judith Templeton's list of those needing help and those who've "accepted" is in nearly perfect balance. Acceptance means you speak of your family in the past tense and you make active plans for moving ahead with your life. There are courses at Seneca and Ryerson[5] we could be taking. Her gleaming leather briefcase is full of college catalogues and lists of cultural societies that need our help. She has done impressive work, I tell her.

"In the textbooks on grief management," she replies—I am her confidante, I realize, one of the few whose grief has not sprung bizarre obsessions—"there are stages to pass through: rejection, depression, acceptance, reconstruction." She has compiled a chart and finds that six months after the tragedy, none of us

---

5. Seneca College of Applied Arts and Technology, in Willowdale; Ryerson Polytechnical Institute, Toronto.

still reject reality, but only a handful are reconstructing. "Depressed Acceptance" is the plateau we've reached. Remarriage is a major step in reconstruction (though she's a little surprised, even shocked, over *how* quickly some of the men have taken on new families). Selling one's house and changing jobs and cities is healthy.

105   How do I tell Judith Templeton that my family surrounds me, and that like creatures in epics, they've changed shapes? She sees me as calm and accepting but worries that I have no job, no career. My closest friends are worse off than I. I cannot tell her my days, even my nights, are thrilling.

She asks me to help with families she can't reach at all. An elderly couple in Agincourt whose sons were killed just weeks after they had brought their parents over from a village in Punjab. From their names, I know they are Sikh. Judith Templeton and a translator have visited them twice with offers of money for air fare to Ireland, with bank forms, power-of-attorney forms, but they have refused to sign, or to leave their tiny apartment. Their sons' money is frozen in the bank. Their sons' investment apartments have been trashed by tenants, the furnishings sold off. The parents fear that anything they sign or any money they receive will end the company's or the country's obligations to them. They fear they are selling their sons for two airline tickets to a place they've never seen.

The high-rise apartment is a tower of Indians and West Indians, with a sprinkling of Orientals. The nearest bus stop kiosk is lined with women in saris. Boys practice cricket in the parking lot. Inside the building, even I wince a bit from the ferocity of onion fumes, the distinctive and immediate Indianness of frying *ghee*, but Judith Templeton maintains a steady flow of information. These poor old people are in imminent danger of losing their place and all their services.

I say to her, "They are Sikh. They will not open up to a Hindu woman." And what I want to add is, as much as I try not to, I stiffen now at the sight of beards and turbans. I remember a time when we all trusted each other in this new country, it was only the new country we worried about.

The two rooms are dark and stuffy. The lights are off, and an oil lamp sputters on the coffee table. The bent old lady has let us in, and her husband is wrapping a white turban over his oiled, hip-length hair. She immediately goes to the kitchen, and I hear the most familiar sound of an Indian home, tap water hitting and filling a teapot.

110   They have not paid their utility bills, out of fear and the inability to write a check. The telephone is gone; electricity and gas and water are soon to follow. They have told Judith their sons will provide. They are good boys, and they have always earned and looked after their parents.

We converse a bit in Hindi. They do not ask about the crash and I wonder if I should bring it up. If they think I am here merely as a translator, then they may feel insulted. There are thousands of Punjabi-speakers, Sikhs, in Toronto to do a better job. And so I say to the old lady, "I too have lost my sons, and my husband, in the crash."

Her eyes immediately fill with tears. The man mutters a few words which sound like a blessing. "God provides and God takes away," he says.

I want to say, but only men destroy and give back nothing. "My boys and my husband are not coming back," I say. "We have to understand that."

Now the old woman responds. "But who is to say? Man alone does not decide these things." To this her husband adds his agreement.

Judith asks about the bank papers, the release forms. With a stroke of the pen, they will have a provincial trustee to pay their bills, invest their money, send them a monthly pension.

"Do you know this woman?" I ask them.

The man raises his hand from the table, turns it over and seems to regard each finger separately before he answers. "This young lady is always coming here, we make tea for her and she leaves papers for us to sign." His eyes scan a pile of papers in the corner of the room. "Soon we will be out of tea, then will she go away?"

The old lady adds, "I have asked my neighbors and no one else gets *angrezi*[6] visitors. What have we done?"

"It's her job," I try to explain. "The government is worried. Soon you will have no place to stay, no lights, no gas, no water."

"Government will get its money. Tell her not to worry, we are honorable people."

I try to explain the government wishes to give money, not take. He raises his hand. "Let them take," he says. "We are accustomed to that. That is no problem."

"We are strong people," says the wife. "Tell her that."

"Who needs all this machinery?" demands the husband. "It is unhealthy, the bright lights, the cold air on a hot day, the cold food, the four gas rings. God will provide, not government."

"When our boys return," the mother says. Her husband sucks his teeth. "Enough talk," he says.

Judith breaks in. "Have you convinced them?" The snaps on her cordovan briefcase go off like firecrackers in that quiet apartment. She lays the sheaf of legal papers on the coffee table. "If they can't write their names, an X will do—I've told them that."

Now the old lady has shuffled to the kitchen and soon emerges with a pot of tea and two cups. "I think my bladder will go first on a job like this," Judith says to me, smiling. "If only there was some way of reaching them. Please thank her for the tea. Tell her she's very kind."

I nod in Judith's direction and tell them in Hindi, "She thanks you for the tea. She thinks you are being very hospitable but she doesn't have the slightest idea what it means."

I want to say, humor her. I want to say, my boys and my husband are with me too, more than ever. I look in the old man's eyes and I can read his stubborn, peasant's message: *I have protected this woman as best I can. She is the only person I have left. Give to me or take from me what you will, but I will not sign for it. I will not pretend that I accept.*

In the car, Judith says, "You see what I'm up against? I'm sure they're lovely

6. English, Anglo.

people, but their stubbornness and ignorance are driving me crazy. They think signing a paper is signing their sons' death warrants, don't they?"

130 I am looking out the window. I want to say, *In our culture, it is a parent's duty to hope.*

"Now Shaila, this next woman is a real mess. She cries day and night, and she refuses all medical help. We may have to—"

"—Let me out at the subway," I say.

"I beg your pardon?" I can feel those blue eyes staring at me.

• It would not be like her to disobey. She merely disapproves, and slows at a corner to let me out. Her voice is plaintive. "Is there anything I said? Anything I did?"

135 I could answer her suddenly in a dozen ways, but I choose not to. "Shaila? Let's talk about it," I hear, then slam the door.

A wife and mother begins her new life in a new country, and that life is cut short. Yet her husband tells her: Complete what we have started. We, who stayed out of politics and came halfway around the world to avoid religious and political feuding have been the first in the New World to die from it. I no longer know what we started, nor how to complete it. I write letters to the editors of local papers and to members of Parliament. Now at least they admit it was a bomb. One MP answers back, with sympathy, but with a challenge. You want to make a difference? Work on a campaign. Work on mine. Politicize the Indian voter.

My husband's old lawyer helps me set up a trust. Vikram was a saver and a careful investor. He had saved the boys' boarding school and college fees. I sell the pink house at four times what we paid for it and take a small apartment downtown. I am looking for a charity to support.

We are deep in the Toronto winter, gray skies, icy pavements. I stay indoors, watching television. I have tried to assess my situation, how best to live my life, to complete what we began so many years ago. Kusum has written me from Hardwar that her life is now serene. She has seen Satish and has heard her daughter sing again. Kusum was on a pilgrimage, passing through a village when she heard a young girl's voice, singing one of her daughter's favorite *bhajans*. She followed the music through the squalor of a Himalayan village, to a hut where a young girl, an exact replica of her daughter, was fanning coals under the kitchen fire. When she appeared, the girl cried out, "Ma!" and ran away. What did I think of that?

I think I can only envy her.

140 Pam didn't make it to California, but writes me from Vancouver. She works in a department store, giving make-up hints to Indian and Oriental girls. Dr. Ranganathan has given up his commute, given up his house and job, and accepted an academic position in Texas where no one knows his story and he has vowed not to tell it. He calls me now once a week.

I wait, I listen, and I pray, but Vikram has not returned to me. The voices and the shapes and the nights filled with visions ended abruptly several weeks ago.

I take it as a sign.

One rare, beautiful, sunny day last week, returning from a small errand on Yonge Street, I was walking through the park from the subway to my apartment. I live equidistant from the Ontario Houses of Parliament and the University of Toronto. The day was not cold, but something in the bare trees caught my attention. I looked up from the gravel, into the branches and the clear blue sky beyond. I thought I heard the rustling of larger forms, and I waited a moment for voices. Nothing.

"What?" I asked.

Then as I stood in the path looking north to Queen's Park and west to the university, I heard the voices of my family one last time. *Your time has come,* they said. *Go, be brave.*

I do not know where this voyage I have begun will end. I do not know which direction I will take. I dropped the package on a park bench and started walking.

1988

Let us begin a reader-oriented discussion of this story, by thinking of ourselves first as a general reader reading the opening of this story for the first time:

> A woman I don't know is boiling tea the Indian way in my kitchen. There are a lot of women I don't know in my kitchen, whispering, and moving tactfully. They open doors, rummage through the pantry, and try not to ask me where things are kept. They remind me of when my sons were small, on Mother's Day or when Vikram and I were tired, and they would make big, sloppy omelets. I would lie in bed pretending I didn't hear them.

We are plunged immediately into the mind of an "I" whose identity we do not know, in a setting specified only as in or near a kitchen, and in a situation about which we know nothing. There is no exposition, no explanation. Even the use of the present tense, rather than the more familiar past tense of most stories, tends to thrust us into a narrative present without known precedent or purpose. The uncertainty makes us look at every word and detail for clues: "my kitchen" and "my sons . . . on Mother's Day" soon identifies the narrator as a mature female.

At this point, regardless of whether we find this indirection and uncertainty annoying or engaging (getting us into the story by making us figure out what is going on for ourselves), we may ask a question or two not about the story but about ourselves. The first two stories in this chapter were not only written by men but were almost entirely about men. (No women appear in "The Most Dangerous Game" and the mother, aunt, and daughter in "Barn Burning" are peripheral.) "The Management of Grief" is not only written by a woman but tells the story through the consciousness of a woman, a strong and intelligent woman. On the other hand, this woman is a mother, somewhat older than

145

most college students. The boy in "Barn Burning," though younger than you, is living through a part of life you have already lived through and so know something about first-hand. How much does the age of the central character have to do not just with your understanding, but with your feelings, your affective response to what you are reading?

The name "Vikram" in the first paragraph for many of us suggests little except foreignness, but "Dr. Sharma, the treasurer of the Indo-Canada Society" (par. 2), tells us enough about the cultural setting for the moment. In the ensuing conversation we learn the name of the narrator—Shaila Bhave—and learn that there has been an accident, perhaps a terrorist bombing, which may explain what seems to be the confusion of the opening scene.

The bomb, the next sentence tells us, may have been a Sikh bomb, and in the eighth paragraph we learn that it was a passenger plane that was, or might have been, bombed. What is a Sikh? Why would a Sikh bomb a plane full of people? Does the average American read this story with the same attitudes and emotions as the average Canadian? Indian? Sikh?

This is not to say that an eighteen-year-old male of Polish descent living in Cleveland cannot read this story with strong emotions and with deep sympathy for and understanding of Shaila Bhave and her tragedy. But would his responses be the same in nature and intensity as those of a middle-aged Indian woman living in Toronto or Vancouver?

For Indians, Sikhs, and some Canadians, this incident (which seems to be based on an actual disaster) is also likely to be controversial, even though the story itself does not concentrate on assessing blame or on the political tensions or causes involved. Whether or not a story takes sides, touching on an issue that readers recognize as controversial inevitably affects how those readers evaluate the story. This does not necessarily mean that all Sikhs or all Indians hold one view. People often disagree with their own government's or community's actions—as many Americans did during the Vietnam war. And it is unlikely that most English readers would repudiate "Beyond the Pale" because of its implicit condemnation of certain English attitudes toward the Irish "troubles." The point is not that controversial stories are bad or that considering the politics or ideology of a work in evaluating it is bad. But we need to recognize the ideological or political factor in our assessment, to acknowledge who and where we are, where we are coming from, when we say, "This story is good" or "That story is lousy."

Evaluating a story, then, means reading carefully (and widely), learning as much as we can about the elements of fiction and of narrative strategies, and articulating our analyses; being honest about our own responses and feeling responsible for articulating them as clearly and convincingly as possible; taking our opinions seriously but listening with attention and an open mind to the judgments and reasoning of other readers. It requires as well some examination and knowledge of ourselves, of what in ourselves conditions our responses to fiction, and a willingness to look at what underlies our judgments and how we might learn and grow. Assessing the value of a story is difficult and a firm evaluation elusive in part because it means examining more than words on a page, it means examining so many ideas, beliefs, and feelings we take for granted. It means examining and, to a degree, evaluating our outer world and inner selves.

Reading More Fiction

The Death of Iván Ilyich[1]

I

During an interval in the Melvínski trial in the large building of the Law Courts the members and public prosecutor met in Iván Egórovich Shébek's private room, where the conversation turned on the celebrated Krasóvski case. Fëdor Vasílievich warmly maintained that it was not subject to their jurisdiction, Iván Egórovich maintained the contrary, while Peter Ivánovich, not having entered into the discussion at the start, took no part in it but looked through the *Gazette* which had just been handed in.

"Gentlemen," he said, "Iván Ilyich has died!"

"You don't say!"

"Here read it yourself," replied Peter Ivánovich, handing Fëdor Vasílievich the paper still damp from the press. Surrounded by a black border were the words: "Praskóvya Fëdorovna Goloviná,[2] with profound sorrow, informs relatives and friends of the demise of her beloved husband Iván Ilyich Golovín, Member of the Court of Justice, which occurred on February the 4th of this year 1882. The funeral will take place on Friday at one o'clock in the afternoon."

5   Iván Ilyich had been a colleague of the gentlemen present and was liked by them all. He had been ill for some weeks with an illness said to be incurable. His post had been kept open for him, but there had been conjectures that in case of his death Alexéev might receive his appointment, and that either Vínnikov or Shtábel would succeed Alexéev. So on receiving the news of Iván Ilyich's death

---

1. Translated by Louise and Aylmer Maude.   2. Many Russian family names have masculine and feminine endings, so that Iván's name is *Golovín*, his wife's *Goloviná*. Russian "middle" names are patronymics—the father's name plus an ending that means "son of" or "daughter of": *Fëdorovna* = daughter of Fëdor; *Ilyich* = son of Ilya.

the first thought of each of the gentlemen in that private room was of the changes and promotions it might occasion among themselves or their acquaintances.

"I shall be sure to get Shtábel's place or Vínnikov's," thought Fëdor Vasílievich. "I was promised that long ago, and the promotion means an extra eight hundred rubles[3] a year for me besides the allowance."

"Now I must apply for my brother-in-law's transfer from Kalúga,"[4] thought Peter Ivánovich. "My wife will be very glad, and then she won't be able to say that I never do anything for her relations."

"I thought he would never leave his bed again," said Peter Ivánovich aloud. "It's very sad."

"But what really was the matter with him?"

"The doctors couldn't say—at least they could, but each of them said something different. When last I saw him I thought he was getting better."

"And I haven't been to see him since the holidays. I always meant to go."

"Had he any property?"

"I think his wife had a little—but something quite trifling."

"We shall have to go to see her, but they live so terribly far away."

"Far away from you, you mean. Everything's far away from your place."

"You see, he never can forgive my living on the other side of the river," said Peter Ivánovich, smiling at Shébek. Then, still talking of the distances between different parts of the city, they returned to the Court.

Besides considerations as to the possible transfers and promotions likely to result from Iván Ilyich's death, the mere fact of the death of a near acquaintance aroused, as usual, in all who heard of it the complacent feeling that, "it is he who is dead and not I."

Each one thought or felt, "Well, he's dead but I'm alive!" But the more intimate of Iván Ilyich's acquaintances, his so-called friends, could not help thinking also that they would now have to fulfil the very tiresome demands of propriety by attending the funeral service and paying a visit of condolence to the widow.

Fëdor Vasílievich and Peter Ivánovich had been his nearest acquaintances. Peter Ivánovich had studied law with Iván Ilyich and had considered himself to be under obligations to him.

Having told his wife at dinner-time of Iván Ilyich's death, and of his conjecture that it might be possible to get her brother transferred to their circuit, Peter Ivánovich sacrificed his usual nap, put on his evening clothes, and drove to Iván Ilyich's house.

At the entrance stood a carriage and two cabs. Leaning against the wall in the hall downstairs near the cloak-stand was a coffin-lid covered with cloth of gold, ornamented with gold cord and tassels, that had been polished up with metal powder. Two ladies in black were taking off their fur cloaks. Peter Ivánovich recognized one of them as Iván Ilyich's sister, but the other was a stranger to

---

3. A ruble was then roughly equivalent to a dollar, though its modern purchasing power is difficult to calculate: perhaps four or five dollars per ruble is close enough.   4. City about one hundred miles southwest of Moscow.

him. His colleague Schwartz was just coming downstairs, but on seeing Peter Ivánovich enter he stopped and winked at him, as if to say: "Iván Ilyich has made a mess of things—not like you and me."

Schwartz's face with his Piccadilly whiskers,[5] and his slim figure in evening dress, had as usual an air of elegant solemnity which contrasted with the playfulness of his character and had a special piquancy here, or so it seemed to Peter Ivánovich.

Peter Ivánovich allowed the ladies to precede him and slowly followed them upstairs. Schwartz did not come down but remained where he was, and Peter Ivánovich understood that he wanted to arrange where they should play bridge that evening. The ladies went upstairs to the widow's room, and Schwartz with seriously compressed lips but a playful look in his eyes, indicated by a twist of his eyebrows the room to the right where the body lay.

Peter Ivánovich, like everyone else on such occasions, entered feeling uncertain what he would have to do. All he knew was that at such times it is always safe to cross oneself. But he was not quite sure whether one should make obeisances while doing so. He therefore adopted a middle course. On entering the room he began crossing himself and made a slight movement resembling a bow. At the same time, as far as the motion of his head and arm allowed, he surveyed the room. Two young men—apparently nephews, one of whom was a high-school pupil—were leaving the room, crossing themselves as they did so. An old woman was standing motionless, and a lady with strangely arched eyebrows was saying something to her in a whisper. A vigorous, resolute Church Reader, in a frock-coat, was reading something in a loud voice with an expression that precluded any contradiction. The butler's assistant, Gerásim, stepping lightly in front of Peter Ivánovich, was strewing something on the floor. Noticing this, Peter Ivánovich was immediately aware of a faint odour of a decomposing body.

The last time he had called on Iván Ilyich, Peter Ivánovich had seen Gerásim in the study. Iván Ilyich had been particularly fond of him and he was performing the duty of a sick nurse.

Peter Ivánovich continued to make the sign of the cross slightly inclining his head in an intermediate direction between the coffin, the Reader, and the icons on the table in a corner of the room. Afterwards, when it seemed to him that this movement of his arm in crossing himself had gone on too long, he stopped and began to look at the corpse.

The dead man lay, as dead men always lie, in a specially heavy way, his rigid limbs sunk in the soft cushions of the coffin, with the head forever bowed on the pillow. His yellow waxen brow with bald patches over his sunken temples was thrust up in the way peculiar to the dead, the protruding nose seeming to press on the upper lip. He was much changed and had grown even thinner since Peter Ivánovich had last seen him, but, as is always the case with the dead, his face was handsomer and above all more dignified than when he was alive. The expression on the face said that what was necessary had been accomplished, and accomplished rightly. Besides this there was in that expression a reproach and a

---

5. Sideburns carefully combed out and worn as long as possible, a fashion that died out in the 1880s.

warning to the living. This warning seemed to Peter Ivánovich out of place, or at least not applicable to him. He felt a certain discomfort and so he hurriedly crossed himself once more and turned and went out of the door—too hurriedly and too regardless of propriety, as he himself was aware.

Schwartz was waiting for him in the adjoining room with legs spread wide apart and both hands toying with his top-hat behind his back. The mere sight of that playful, well-groomed, and elegant figure refreshed Peter Ivánovich. He felt that Schwartz was above all these happenings and could not surrender to any depressing influences. His very look said that this incident of a church service for Iván Ilyich could not be a sufficient reason for infringing the order of the session—in other words, that it would certainly not prevent his unwrapping a new pack of cards and shuffling them that evening while a footman placed four fresh candles on the table: in fact, that there was no reason for supposing that this incident would hinder their spending the evening agreeably. Indeed he said this in a whisper as Peter Ivánovich passed him, proposing that they should meet for a game at Fëdor Vasílievich's. But apparently Peter Ivánovich was not destined to play bridge that evening. Praskóvya Fëdorovna (a short, fat woman who despite all efforts to the contrary had continued to broaden steadily from her shoulders downwards and who had the same extraordinary arched eyebrows as the lady who had been standing by the coffin), dressed all in black, her head covered with lace, came out of her own room with some other ladies, conducted them to the room where the dead body lay, and said: "The service will begin immediately. Please go in."

Schwartz, making an indefinite bow, stood still, evidently neither accepting nor declining this invitation. Praskóvya Fëdorovna recognizing Peter Ivánovich, sighed, went close up to him, took his hand, and said: "I know you were a true friend to Iván Ilyich . . ." and looked at him awaiting some suitable response. And Peter Ivánovich knew that, just as it had been the right thing to cross himself in that room, so what he had to do here was to press her hand, sigh, and say, "Believe me . . ." So he did all this and as he did it felt that the desired result had been achieved: that both he and she were touched.

"Come with me. I want to speak to you before it begins," said the widow. "Give me your arm."

Peter Ivánovich gave her his arm and they went to the inner rooms, passing Schwartz who winked at Peter Ivánovich compassionately.

"That does for our bridge! Don't object if we find another player. Perhaps you can cut in when you do escape," said his playful look.

Peter Ivánovich sighed still more deeply and despondently, and Praskóvya Fëdorovna pressed his arm gratefully. When they reached the drawing-room, upholstered in pink cretonne and lighted by a dim lamp, they sat down at the table—she on a sofa and Peter Ivánovich on a low hassock, the springs of which yielded spasmodically under his weight. Praskóvya Fëdorovna had been on the point of warning him to take another seat, but felt that such a warning was out of keeping with her present condition and so changed her mind. As he sat down on the hassock Peter Ivánovich recalled how Iván Ilyich had arranged this room and had consulted him regarding this pink cretonne with green leaves. The whole room was full of furniture and knick-knacks, and on her way to the sofa the lace of the widow's black shawl caught on the carved edge of the table. Peter Ivánovich rose to detach it, and the springs of the hassock, relieved of his weight, rose also and gave him a push. The widow began detaching her shawl herself, and Peter Ivánovich again sat down, suppressing the rebellious springs of the hassock under him. But the widow had not quite freed herself and Peter Ivánovich got up again, and again the hassock rebelled and even creaked. When this was all over she took out a clean cambric handkerchief and began to weep. The episode with the shawl and the struggle with the hassock had cooled Peter Ivánovich's emotions and he sat there with a sullen look on his face. This awkward situation was interrupted by Sokolóv, Iván Ilyich's butler, who came to report that the plot in the cemetery that Praskóvya Fëdorovna had chosen would cost two hundred rubles. She stopped weeping and, looking at Peter Ivánovich with the air of a victim, remarked in French[6] that it was very hard for her. Peter Ivánovich made a silent gesture signifying his full conviction that it must indeed be so.

"Please smoke," she said in a magnanimous yet crushed voice, and turned to discuss with Sokolóv the price of the plot for the grave.

Peter Ivánovich while lighting his cigarette heard her inquiring very circumstantially into the prices of different plots in the cemetery and finally decide which she would take. When that was done she gave instructions about engaging the choir. Sokolóv then left the room.

"I look after everything myself," she told Peter Ivánovich, shifting the albums that lay on the table; and noticing that the table was endangered by his cigarette-ash, she immediately passed him an ashtray, saying as she did so: "I consider it an affectation to say that my grief prevents my attending to practical affairs. On the contrary, if anything can—I won't say console me, but—distract me, it is seeing to everything concerning him." She again took out her handkerchief as if preparing to cry, but suddenly, as if mastering her feeling, she shook herself and began to speak calmly. "But there is something I want to talk to you about."

Peter Ivánovich bowed, keeping control of the springs of the hassock, which immediately began quivering under him.

"He suffered terribly the last few days."

"Did he?" said Peter Ivánovich.

"Oh, terribly! He screamed unceasingly, not for minutes but for hours. For the last three days he screamed incessantly. It was unendurable. I cannot understand how I bore it; you could hear him three rooms off. Oh, what I have suffered!"

"Is it possible that he was conscious all that time?" asked Peter Ivánovich.

"Yes," she whispered. "To the last moment. He took leave of us a quarter of an hour before he died, and asked us to take Vásya[7] away."

The thought of the sufferings of this man he had known so intimately, first as a merry little boy, then as a school-mate, and later as a grown-up colleague, suddenly struck Peter Ivánovich with horror, despite an unpleasant conscious-

---

6. The Russian upper classes commonly spoke French.   7. Nickname for Vasílii, Iván Ilyich's son.

ness of his own and this woman's dissimulation. He again saw that brow, and that nose pressing down on the lip, and felt afraid for himself.

"Three days of frightful suffering and then death! Why, that might suddenly, at any time, happen to me," he thought, and for a moment felt terrified. But— he did not himself know how—the customary reflection at once occurred to him that this had happened to Iván Ilyich and not to him, and that it should not and could not happen to him, and that to think that it could would be yielding to depression which he ought not to do, as Schwartz's expression plainly showed. After which reflection Peter Ivánovich felt reassured, and began to ask with inter- est about the details of Iván Ilyich's death, as though death was an accident natural to Iván Ilyich but certainly not to himself.

After many details of the really dreadful physical sufferings Iván Ilyich had endured (which details he learnt only from the effect those sufferings had pro- duced on Praskóvya Fëdorovna's nerves) the widow apparently found it necessary to get to business.

"Oh, Peter Ivánovich, how hard it is! How terribly, terribly hard!" and she again began to weep.

Peter Ivánovich sighed and waited for her to finish blowing her nose. When she had done so he said, "Believe me . . ." and she again began talking and brought out what was evidently her chief concern with him—namely, to ques- tion him as to how she could obtain a grant of money from the government on the occasion of her husband's death. She made it appear that she was asking Peter Ivánovich's advice about her pension, but he soon saw that she already knew about that to the minutest detail, more even than he did himself. She knew how much could be got out of the government in consequence of her husband's death, but wanted to find out whether she could possibly extract some- thing more. Peter Ivánovich tried to think of some means of doing so, but after reflecting for a while and, out of propriety, condemning the government for its niggardliness, he said he thought that nothing more could be got. Then she sighed and evidently began to devise means of getting rid of her visitor. Noticing this, he put out his cigarette, rose, pressed her hand, and went out into the anteroom.

In the dining-room where the clock stood that Iván Ilyich had liked so much and had bought at an antique shop, Peter Ivánovich met a priest and a few acquaintances who had come to attend the service, and he recognized Iván Ilyich's daughter, a handsome young woman. She was in black and her slim figure appeared slimmer than ever. She had a gloomy, determined, almost angry expression, and bowed to Peter Ivánovich as though he were in some way to blame. Behind her, with the same offended look, stood a wealthy young man, an examining magistrate, whom Peter Ivánovich also knew and who was her fiancé, as he had heard. He bowed mournfully to them and was about to pass into the death-chamber, when from under the stairs appeared the figure of Iván Ilyich's schoolboy son, who was extremely like this father. He seemed a little Iván Ilyich, such as Peter Ivánovich remembered when they studied law together. His tear-stained eyes had in them the look that is seen in the eyes of boys of thirteen or fourteen who are not pure-minded.

When he saw Peter Ivánovich he scowled morosely and shamefacedly. Peter Ivánovich nodded to him and entered the death-chamber. The service began: candles, groans, incense, tears, and sobs. Peter Ivánovich stood looking gloomily down at his feet. He did not look once at the dead man, did not yield to any depressing influence, and was one of the first to leave the room. There was no one in the anteroom, but Gerásim darted out of the dead man's room, rummaged with his strong hands among the fur coats to find Peter Ivánovich's and helped him on with it.

"Well, friend Gerásim," said Peter Ivánovich, so as to say something. "It's a sad affair, isn't it?"

"It's God's will. We shall all come to it some day," said Gerásim, displaying his teeth—the even, white teeth of a healthy peasant—and, like a man in the thick of urgent work, he briskly opened the front door, called the coachman, helped Peter Ivánovich into the sledge, and sprang back to the porch as if in readiness for what he had to do next.

Peter Ivánovich found the fresh air particularly pleasant after the smell of incense, the dead body, and carbolic acid.

"Where to, sir?" asked the coachman.

"It's not too late even now. . . . I'll call round on Fëdor Vasílievich."

He accordingly drove there and found them just finishing the first rubber, so that it was quite convenient for him to cut in.

II

Iván Ilyich's life had been most simple and most ordinary and therefore most terrible.

He had been a member of the Court of Justice, and died at the age of forty-five. His father had been an official who after serving in various ministries and departments in Petersburg[8] had made the sort of career which brings men to positions from which by reason of their long service they cannot be dismissed, though they are obviously unfit to hold any responsible position, and for whom therefore posts are specially created, which though fictitious, carry salaries of from six to ten thousand rubles that are not fictitious, and in receipt of which they live on to a great age.

Such was the Privy Councillor and superfluous member of various superfluous institutions, Ilya Efímovich Golovín.

He had three sons, of whom Iván Ilyich was the second. The eldest son was following in his father's footsteps only in another department, and was already approaching that stage in the service at which a similar sinecure would be reached. The third son was a failure. He had ruined his prospects in a number of positions and was now serving in the railway department. His father and brothers, and still more their wives, not merely disliked meeting him, but avoided remembering his existence unless compelled to do so. His sister had married Baron Greff, a Petersburg official of her father's type. Iván Ilyich was *le phénix de la famille*[9] as

---

8. St. Petersburg (now Leningrad), the capital of Russia (1712–1918) and its cultural and social center.   9. Prodigy of the family.

people said. He was neither as cold and formal as his elder brother nor as wild as the younger, but was a happy mean between them—an intelligent, polished, lively and agreeable man. He had studied with his younger brother at the School of Law, but the latter had failed to complete the course and was expelled when he was in the fifth class. Iván Ilyich finished the course well. Even when he was at the School of Law he was just what he remained for the rest of his life: a capable, cheerful, good-natured, and sociable man, though strict in the fulfilment of what he considered to be his duty: and he considered his duty to be what was so considered by those in authority. Neither as a boy nor as a man was he a toady, but from early youth was by nature attracted to people of high station as a fly is drawn to the light, assimilating their ways and views of life and establishing friendly relations with them. All the enthusiasms of childhood and youth passed without leaving much trace on him; he succumbed to sensuality, to vanity, and latterly among the highest classes to liberalism, but always within limits which his instinct unfailingly indicated to him as correct.

At school he had done things which had formerly seemed to him very horrid and made him feel disgusted with himself when he did them; but when later on he saw that such actions were done by people of good position and that they did not regard them as wrong, he was able not exactly to regard them as right, but to forget about them entirely or not be at all troubled at remembering them.

Having graduated from the School of Law and qualified for the tenth rank of the civil service, and having received money from his father for his equipment, Iván Ilyich ordered himself clothes at Scharmer's, the fashionable tailor, hung a medallion inscribed *respice finem*[1] on his watch-chain, took leave of his professor and the prince who was patron of the school, had a farewell dinner with his comrades at Donon's first-class restaurant, and with his new and fashionable portmanteau, linen, clothes, shaving and other toilet appliances, and a travelling rug, all purchased at the best shops, he set off for one of the provinces where, through his father's influence, he had been attached to the governor as an official for special service.

In the province Iván Ilyich soon arranged as easy and agreeable a position for himself as he had at the School of Law. He performed his official tasks, made his career, and at the same time amused himself pleasantly and decorously. Occasionally he paid official visits to country districts, where he behaved with dignity both to his superiors and inferiors, and performed the duties entrusted to him, which related chiefly to the sectarians,[2] with an exactness and incorruptible honesty of which he could not but feel proud.

In official matters, despite his youth and taste for frivolous gaiety, he was exceedingly reserved, punctilious, and even severe; but in society he was often amusing and witty, and always good-natured, correct in his manner, and *bon enfant*,[3] as the governor and his wife—with whom he was like one of the family—used to say of him.

In the province he had an affair with a lady who made advances to the elegant young lawyer, and there was also a milliner; and there were carousals

---

1. Look to (or consider) the end.   2. A large sect (the "Old Believers") that had broken with the Orthodox church.   3. A good fellow.

with aides-de-camp who visited the district, and after-supper visits to a certain outlying street of doubtful reputation; and there was too some obsequiousness to his chief and even to his chief's wife, but all this was done with such a tone of good breeding that no hard names could be applied to it. It all came under the heading of the French saying: "*Il faut que jeunesse se passe.*"[4] It was all done with clean hands, in clean linen, with French phrases, and above all among people of the best society and consequently with the approval of people of rank.

So Iván Ilyich served for five years and then came a change in his official life. The new and reformed judicial institutions were introduced, and new men were needed. Iván Ilyich became such a new man. He was offered the post of Examining Magistrate, and he accepted it though the post was in another province and obliged him to give up the connexions he had formed and to make new ones. His friends met to give him a send-off; they had a group-photograph taken and presented him with a silver cigarette-case, and he set off to his new post.

As examining magistrate Iván Ilyich was just as *comme il faut* and decorous a man, inspiring general respect and capable of separating his official duties from his private life, as he had been when acting as an official on special service. His duties now as examining magistrate were far more interesting and attractive than before. In his former position it had been pleasant to wear an undress uniform made by Scharmer, and to pass through the crowd of petitioners and officials who were timorously awaiting an audience with the governor, and who envied him as with free and easy gait he went straight into his chief's private room to have a cup of tea and a cigarette with him. But not many people had then been directly dependent on him—only police officials and the sectarians when he went on special missions—and he liked to treat them politely, almost as comrades, as if he were letting them feel that he who had the power to crush them was treating them in this simple, friendly way. There were then but few such people. But now, as an examining magistrate, Iván Ilyich felt that everyone without exception, even the most important and self-satisfied, was in his power, and that he need only write a few words on a sheet of paper with a certain heading, and this or that important, self-satisfied person would be brought before him in the role of an accused person or a witness, and if he did not choose to allow him to sit down, would have to stand before him and answer his questions. Iván Ilyich never abused his power; he tried on the contrary to soften its expression, but the consciousness of it and of the possibility of softening its effect, supplied the chief interest and attraction of his office. In his work itself, especially in his examinations, he very soon acquired a method of eliminating all considerations irrelevant to the legal aspect of the case, and reducing even the most complicated case to a form in which it would be presented on paper only in its externals, completely excluding his personal opinion of the matter, while above all observing every prescribed formality. The work was new and Iván Ilyich was one of the first men to apply the new Code of 1864.[5]

On taking up the post of examining magistrate in a new town, he made new acquaintances and connexions, placed himself on a new footing, and assumed a

---

4. Youth must have its fling. (Translators' note)   5. The emancipation of the serfs in 1861 was followed by a thorough all-round reform of judicial proceedings. (Translators' note)

somewhat different tone. He took up an attitude of rather dignified aloofness towards the provincial authorities, but picked out the best circle of legal gentlemen and wealthy gentry living in the town and assumed a tone of slight dissatisfaction with the government, of moderate liberalism, and of enlightened citizenship. At the same time, without at all altering the elegance of his toilet, he ceased shaving his chin and allowed his beard to grow as it pleased.

Iván Ilyich settled down very pleasantly in this new town. The society there, which inclined towards opposition to the governor, was friendly, his salary was larger, and he began to play *vint* [a form of bridge], which he found added not a little to the pleasure of life, for he had a capacity for cards, played good-humouredly, and calculated rapidly and astutely, so that he usually won.

After living there for two years he met his future wife, Praskóvya Fëdorovna Míkhel, who was the most attractive, clever, and brilliant girl of the set in which he moved, and among other amusements and relaxations from his labours as examining magistrate, Iván Ilyich established light and playful relations with her.

While he had been an official on special service he had been accustomed to dance, but now as an examining magistrate it was exceptional for him to do so. If he danced now, he did it as if to show that though he served under the reformed order of things, and had reached the fifth official rank, yet when it came to dancing he could do it better than most people. So at the end of an evening he sometimes danced with Praskóvya Fëdorovna, and it was chiefly during these dances that he captivated her. She fell in love with him. Iván Ilyich had at first no definite intention of marrying, but when the girl fell in love with him he said to himself: "Really, why shouldn't I marry?"

Praskóvya Fëdorovna came of a good family, was not bad looking, and had some little property. Iván Ilyich might have aspired to a more brilliant match, but even this was good. He had his salary, and she, he hoped, would have an equal income. She was well connected, and was a sweet, pretty, and thoroughly correct young woman. To say that Iván Ilyich married because he fell in love with Praskóvya Fëdorovna and found that she sympathized with his views of life would be as incorrect as to say that he married because his social circle approved of the match. He was swayed by both these considerations: the marriage gave him personal satisfaction, and at the same time it was considered the right thing by the most highly placed of his associates.

So Iván Ilyich got married.

The preparations for marriage and the beginning of married life, with its conjugal caresses, the new furniture, new crockery, and new linen, were very pleasant until his wife became pregnant—so that Iván Ilyich had begun to think that marriage would not impair the easy, agreeable, gay, and always decorous character of his life, approved of by society and regarded by himself as natural, but would even improve it. But from the first months of his wife's pregnancy, something new, unpleasant, depressing, and unseemly, and from which there was no way of escape, unexpectedly showed itself.

His wife, without any reason—*de gaieté de coeur*[6] as Iván Ilyich expressed it

70

6. Wantonly.

to himself—began to disturb the pleasure and propriety of their life. She began to be jealous without any cause, expected him to devote his whole attention to her, found fault with everything, and made coarse and ill-mannered scenes.

At first Iván Ilyich hoped to escape from the unpleasantness of this state of affairs by the same easy and decorous relation to life that had served him heretofore: he tried to ignore his wife's disagreeable moods, continued to live in his usual easy and pleasant way, invited friends to his house for a game of cards, and also tried going out to his club or spending his evenings with friends. But one day his wife began upbraiding him so vigorously, using such coarse words, and continued to abuse him every time he did not fulfil her demands, so resolutely and with such evident determination not to give way till he submitted— that is, till he stayed at home and was bored just as she was—that he became alarmed. He now realized that matrimony—at any rate with Praskóvya Fëdorovna—was not always conducive to the pleasures and amenities of life, but on the contrary often infringed both comfort and propriety, and that he must therefore entrench himself against such infringement. And Iván Ilyich began to seek for means of doing so. His official duties were the one thing that imposed upon Praskóvya Fëdorovna, and by means of his official work and the duties attached to it he began struggling with his wife to secure his own independence.

With the birth of their child, the attempts to feed it and the various failures in doing so, and with the real and imaginary illnesses of mother and child, in which Iván Ilyich's sympathy was demanded but about which he understood nothing, the need of securing for himself an existence outside his family life became still more imperative.

As his wife grew more irritable and exacting and Iván Ilyich transferred the centre of gravity of his life more and more to his official work, so did he grow to like his work better and became more ambitious than before.

Very soon, within a year of his wedding, Iván Ilyich had realized that marriage, though it may add some comforts to life, is in fact a very intricate and difficult affair towards which in order to perform one's duty, that is, to lead a decorous life approved of by society, one must adopt a definite attitude just as towards one's official duties.

And Iván Ilyich evolved such an attitude towards married life. He only required of it those conveniences—dinner at home, housewife, and bed—which it could give him, and above all that propriety of external forms required by public opinion. For the rest he looked for light-hearted pleasure and propriety, and was very thankful when he found them, but if he met with antagonism and querulousness he at once retired into his separate fenced-off world of official duties, where he found satisfaction.

Iván Ilyich was esteemed a good official, and after three years was made Assistant Public Prosecutor. His new duties, their importance, the possibility of indicting and imprisoning anyone he chose, the publicity his speeches received, and the success he had in all these things, made his work still more attractive.

More children came. His wife became more and more querulous and ill-tempered, but the attitude Iván Ilyich had adopted towards his home life rendered him almost impervious to her grumbling.

After seven years' service in that town he was transferred to another province as Public Prosecutor. They moved, but were short of money and his wife did not like the place they moved to. Though the salary was higher the cost of living was greater, besides which two of their children died and family life became still more unpleasant for him.

Praskóvya Fëdorovna blamed her husband for every inconvenience they encountered in their new home. Most of the conversations between husband and wife, especially as to the children's education, led to topics which recalled former disputes, and those disputes were apt to flare up again at any moment. There remained only those rare periods of amorousness which still came to them at times but did not last long. These were islets at which they anchored for a while and then again set out upon that ocean of veiled hostility which showed itself in their aloofness from one another. This aloofness might have grieved Iván Ilyich had he considered that it ought not to exist, but he now regarded the position as normal, and even made it the goal at which he aimed in family life. His aim was to free himself more and more from those unpleasantnesses and to give them a semblance of harmlessness and propriety. He attained this by spending less and less time with his family, and when obliged to be at home he tried to safeguard his position by the presence of outsiders. The chief thing however was that he had his official duties. The whole interest of his life now centered in the official world and that interest absorbed him. The consciousness of his power, being able to ruin anybody he wished to ruin, the importance, even the external dignity of his entry into court, or meetings with his subordinates, his success with superiors and inferiors, and above all his masterly handling of cases, of which he was conscious—all this gave him pleasure and filled his life, together with chats with his colleagues, dinners, and bridge. So that on the whole Iván Ilyich's life continued to flow as he considered it should do—pleasantly and properly.

So things continued for another seven years. His eldest daughter was already sixteen, another child had died, and only one son was left, a schoolboy and a subject of dissensions. Iván Ilyich wanted to put him in the School of Law, but to spite him Praskóvya Fëdorovna entered him at the High School. The daughter had been educated at home and had turned out well: the boy did not learn badly either.

III

So Iván Ilyich lived for seventeen years after his marriage. He was already a Public Prosecutor of long standing, and had declined several proposed transfers while awaiting a more desirable post, when an unanticipated and unpleasant occurrence quite upset the peaceful course of his life. He was expecting to be offered the post of presiding judge in a University town, but Hoppe somehow came to the front and obtained the appointment instead. Iván Ilyich became irritable, reproached Hoppe, and quarrelled both with him and with his immediate superiors—who became colder to him and again passed him over when other appointments were made.

85

This was in 1880, the hardest year of Iván Ilyich's life. It was then that it became evident on the one hand that his salary was insufficient for them to live on, and on the other that he had been forgotten, and not only this, but that what was for him the greatest and most cruel injustice appeared to others a quite ordinary occurrence. Even his father did not consider it his duty to help him. Iván Ilyich felt himself abandoned by everyone, and that they regarded his position with a salary of 3,500 rubles as quite normal and even fortunate. He alone knew that with the consciousness of the injustices done him, with his wife's incessant nagging, and with the debts he had contracted by living beyond his means his position was far from normal.

In order to save money that summer he obtained leave of absence and went with his wife to live in the country at her brother's place.

In the country, without his work, he experienced *ennui* for the first time in his life, and not only *ennui* but intolerable depression, and he decided that it was impossible to go on living like that, and that it was necessary to take energetic measures.

Having passed a sleepless night pacing up and down the veranda, he decided to go to Petersburg and bestir himself, in order to punish those who had failed to appreciate him and to get transferred to another ministry.

Next day, despite many protests from his wife and her brother, he started for Petersburg with the sole object of obtaining a post with a salary of five thousand rubles a year. He was no longer bent on any particular department, or tendency, or kind of activity. All he now wanted was an appointment to another post with a salary of five thousand rubles, either in the administration, in the banks, with the railways, in one of the Empress Márya's Institutions,[7] or even in the customs—but it had to carry with it a salary of five thousand rubles and be in a ministry other than that in which they had failed to appreciate him.

And this quest of Iván Ilyich's was crowned with remarkable and unexpected success. At Kursk an acquaintance of his, F. I. Ilyín, got into the first-class carriage, sat down beside Iván Ilyich, and told him of a telegram just received by the governor of Kursk announcing that a change was about to take place in the ministry: Peter Ivánovich was to be superseded by Iván Semënovich.

The proposed change, apart from its significance for Russia, had a special significance for Iván Ilyich, because by bringing forward a new man, Peter Petróvich, and consequently his friend Zachár Ivánovich, it was highly favourable for Iván Ilyich, since Zachár Ivánovich was a friend and colleague of his.

In Moscow his news was confirmed, and on reaching Petersburg Iván Ilyich found Zachár Ivánovich and received a definite promise of an appointment in his former department of Justice.

A week later he telegraphed to his wife: "Zachár in Miller's place. I shall receive appointment on presentation of report."

Thanks to this change of personnel, Iván Ilyich had unexpectedly obtained an appointment in his former ministry which placed him two stages above his former colleagues besides giving him five thousand rubles salary and three thou-

7. Charitable organization founded nearly a century earlier by the wife of Tsar Paul I.

sand five hundred rubles for expenses connected with his removal.[8] All his ill
humour towards his former enemies and the whole department vanished, and
Iván Ilyich was completely happy.

He returned to the country more cheerful and contented than he had been
for a long time. Praskóvya Fëdorovna also cheered up and a truce was arranged
between them. Iván Ilyich told of how he had been fêted by everybody in Petersburg, how all those who had been his enemies were put to shame and now
fawned on him, how envious they were of his appointment, and how much
everybody in Petersburg had liked him.

Praskóvya Fëdorovna listened to all this and appeared to believe it. She did
not contradict anything, but only made plans for their life in the town to which
they were going. Iván Ilyich saw with delight that these plans were his plans,
that he and his wife agreed, and that, after a stumble, his life was regaining its
due and natural character of pleasant lightheartedness and decorum.

Iván Ilyich had come back for a short time only, for he had to take up his
new duties on the 10th of September. Moreover, he needed time to settle into
the new place, to move all his belongings from the province, and to buy and
order many additional things: in a word, to make such arrangements as he had
resolved on, which were almost exactly what Praskóvya Fëdorovna too had decided
on.

Now that everything had happened so fortunately, and that he and his wife
were at one in their aims and moreover saw so little of one another they got on
together better than they had done since the first years of marriage. Iván Ilyich
had thought of taking his family away with him at once, but the insistence of his
wife's brother and her sister-in-law, who had suddenly become particularly ami-
able and friendly to him and his family, induced him to depart alone.

So he departed, and the cheerful state of mind induced by his success and
by the harmony between his wife and himself, the one intensifying the other,
did not leave him. He found a delightful house, just the thing both he and his
wife had dreamt of. Spacious, lofty reception rooms in the old style, a convenient and dignified study, rooms for his wife and daughter, a study for his son—
it might have been specially built for them. Iván Ilyich himself superintended
the arrangements, chose the wallpapers, supplemented the furniture (preferably
with antiques which he considered particularly *comme il faut*), and supervised
the upholstering. Everything progressed and progressed and approached the ideal
he had set himself: even when things were only half completed they exceeded
his expectations. He saw what a refined and elegant character, free from vulgarity, it would all have when it was ready. On falling asleep he pictured to himself
how the reception-room would look. Looking at the yet unfinished drawing-
room he could see the fireplace, the screen, the what-not, the little chairs dotted
here and there, the dishes and plates on the walls, and the bronzes, as they would
be when everything was in place. He was pleased by the thought of how his wife
and daughter, who shared his taste in this matter, would be impressed by it.
They were certainly not expecting as much. He had been particularly successful

100

8. Moving.

in finding, and buying cheaply, antiques which gave a particularly aristocratic character to the whole place. But in his letters he intentionally understated everything in order to be able to surprise them. All this so absorbed him that his new duties—though he liked his official work—interested him less than he had expected. Sometimes he even had moments of absent-mindedness during the Court Sessions, and would consider whether he should have straight or curved cornices for his curtains. He was so interested in it all that he often did things himself, rearranging the furniture, or rehanging the curtains. Once when mounting a step-ladder to show the upholsterer, who did not understand, how he wanted the hangings draped, he made a false step and slipped, but being a strong and agile man he clung on and only knocked his side against the knob of the window frame. The bruised place was painful but the pain soon passed, and he felt particularly bright and well just then. He wrote: "I feel fifteen years younger." He thought he would have everything ready by September, but it dragged on till mid-October. But the result was charming not only in his eyes but to everyone who saw it.

In reality it was just what is usually seen in the houses of people of moderate means who want to appear rich, and therefore succeed only in resembling others like themselves: there were damasks, dark wood, plants, rugs, and dull and polished bronzes—all the things people of a certain class have in order to resemble other people of that class. His house was so like the others that it would never have been noticed, but to him it all seemed to be quite exceptional. He was very happy when he met his family at the station and brought them to the newly furnished house all lit up, where a footman in a white tie opened the door into the hall decorated with plants, and when they went on into the drawing room and the study uttering exclamations of delight. He conducted them everywhere, drank in their praises eagerly, and beamed with pleasure. At tea that evening, when Praskóvya Fëdorovna among other things asked him about his fall, he laughed, and showed them how he had gone flying and had frightened the upholsterer.

"It's a good thing I'm a bit of an athlete. Another man might have been killed, but I merely knocked myself, just here; it hurts when it's touched, but it's passing off already—it's only a bruise."

So they began living in their new home—in which, as always happens, when they got thoroughly settled in they found they were just one room short—and with the increased income, which as always was just a little (some five hundred rubles) too little, but it was all very nice.

Things went particularly well at first, before everything was finally arranged and while something had still to be done: this thing bought, that thing ordered, another thing moved, and something else adjusted. Though there were some disputes between husband and wife, they were both so well satisfied and had so much to do that it all passed off without any serious quarrels. When nothing was left to arrange it became rather dull and something seemed to be lacking, but they were then making acquaintances, forming habits, and life was growing fuller.

Iván Ilyich spent his mornings at the law court and came home to dinner, and at first he was generally in a good humour, though he occasionally became

irritable just on account of his house. (Every spot on the tablecloth or the uphol-
stery, and every broken window-blind string, irritated him. He had devoted so
much trouble to arranging it all that every disturbance of it distressed him.) But
on the whole his life ran its course as he believed life should do: easily, pleasantly, and decorously.

He got up at nine, drank his coffee, read the paper, and then put on his
undress uniform and went to the law courts. There the harness in which he
worked had already been stretched to fit him and he donned it without a hitch:
petitioners, inquiries at the chancery, the chancery itself, and the sittings public
and administrative. In all this the thing was to exclude everything fresh and vital,
which always disturbs the regular course of official business, and to admit only
official relations with people, and then only on official grounds. A man would
come, for instance, wanting some information. Iván Ilyich, as one in whose
sphere the matter did not lie, would have nothing to do with him: but if the man
had some business with him in his official capacity, something that could be
expressed on officially stamped paper, he would do everything, positively everything he could within the limits of such relations, and in doing so would maintain the semblance of friendly human relations, that is, would observe the courtesies
of life. As soon as the official relations ended, so did everything else. Iván Ilyich
possessed this capacity to separate his real life from the official side of affairs and
not mix the two, in the highest degree, and by long practice and natural aptitude
had brought it to such a pitch that sometimes, in the manner of a virtuoso, he
would even allow himself to let the human and official relations mingle. He let
himself do this just because he felt that he could at any time he chose resume
the strictly official attitude again and drop the human relation. And he did it all
easily, pleasantly, correctly, and even artistically. In the intervals between the
sessions he smoked, drank tea, chatted a little about politics, a little about general
topics, a little about cards, but most of all about official appointments. Tired,
but with the feelings of a virtuoso—one of the first violins who has played his
part in an orchestra with precision—he would return home to find that his wife
and daughter had been out paying calls, or had a visitor, and that his son had
been to school, had done his homework with his tutor, and was duly learning
what is taught at High Schools. Everything was as it should be. After dinner, if
they had no visitors, Iván Ilyich sometimes read a book that was being much
discussed at the time, and in the evening settled down to work, that is, read
official papers, compared the depositions of witnesses, and noted paragraphs of
the Code applying to them. This was neither dull nor amusing. It was dull when
he might have been playing bridge, but if no bridge was available it was at any
rate better than doing nothing or sitting with his wife. Iván Ilyich's chief pleasure
was giving little dinners to which he invited men and women of good social
position, and just as his drawing-room resembled all other drawing-rooms so did
his enjoyable little parties resemble all other such parties.

Once they even gave a dance. Iván Ilyich enjoyed it and everything went off
well, except that it led to a violent quarrel with his wife about the cakes and
sweets. Praskóvya Fëdorovna had made her own plans, but Iván Ilyich insisted
on getting everything from an expensive confectioner and ordered too many

cakes, and the quarrel occurred because some of those cakes were left over and the confectioner's bill came to forty-five rubles. It was a great and disagreeable quarrel. Praskóvya Fëdorovna called him "a fool and an imbecile," and he clutched at his head and made angry allusions to divorce.

But the dance itself had been enjoyable. The best people were there, and Iván Ilyich had danced with Princess Trúfonova, a sister of the distinguished founder of the Society "Bear my Burden."

The pleasures connected with his work were pleasures of ambition; his social pleasures were those of vanity; but Iván Ilyich's greatest pleasure was playing bridge. He acknowledged that whatever disagreeable incident happened in his life, the pleasure that beamed like a ray of light above everything else was to sit down to bridge with good players, not noisy partners, and of course to four-handed bridge (with five players it was annoying to have to stand out, though one pretended not to mind), to play a clever and serious game (when the cards allowed it) and then to have supper and drink a glass of wine. After a game of bridge, especially if he had won a little (to win a large sum was unpleasant), Iván Ilyich went to bed in specially good humour.

So they lived. They formed a circle of acquaintances among the best people and were visited by people of importance and by young folk. In their views as to their acquaintances, husband, wife, and daughter were entirely agreed, and tacitly and unanimously kept at arm's length and shook off the various shabby friends and relations who, with much show of affection, gushed into the drawing-room with its Japanese plates on the walls. Soon these shabby friends ceased to obtrude themselves and only the best people remained in the Golovíns' set.

Young men made up to Lisa, and Petríshchev, an examining magistrate and Dmítri Ivánovich Petríschchev's son and sole heir, began to be so attentive to her that Iván Ilyich had already spoken to Praskóvya Fëdorovna about it, and considered whether they should not arrange a party for them, or get up some private theatricals.

So they lived, and all went well, without change, and life flowed pleasantly.

IV

They were all in good health. It could not be called ill health if Iván Ilyich sometimes said that he had a queer taste in his mouth and felt some discomfort in his left side.

But this discomfort increased and, though not exactly painful, grew into a sense of pressure in his side accompanied by ill humour. And his irritability became worse and worse and began to mar the agreeable, easy, and correct life that had established itself in the Golovín family. Quarrels between husband and wife became more and more frequent, and soon the ease and amenity disappeared and even the decorum was barely maintained. Scenes again became frequent, and very few of those islets remained on which husband and wife could meet without an explosion. Praskóvya Fëdorovna now had good reason to say that her husband's temper was trying. With characteristic exaggeration she said he had always had a dreadful temper, and that it had needed all her good nature to put up with it for twenty years. It was true that now the quarrels were started by him. His bursts of temper always came just before dinner, often just as he began to eat his soup. Sometimes he noticed that a plate or dish was chipped, or the food was not right, or his son put his elbow on the table, or his daughter's hair was not done as he liked it, and for all this he blamed Praskóvya Fëdorovna. At first she retorted and said disagreeable things to him, but once or twice he fell into such a rage at the beginning of dinner that she realized it was due to some physical derangement brought on by taking food, and so she restrained herself and did not answer, but only hurried to get the dinner over. She regarded this self-restraint as highly praiseworthy. Having come to the conclusion that her husband had a dreadful temper and made her life miserable, she began to feel sorry for herself, and the more she pitied herself the more she hated her husband. She began to wish he would die; yet she did not want him to die because then his salary would cease. And this irritated her against him still more. She considered herself dreadfully unhappy just because not even his death could save her, and though she concealed her exasperation, that hidden exasperation of hers increased his irritation also.

After one scene in which Iván Ilyich had been particularly unfair and after which he had said in explanation that he certainly was irritable but that it was due to his not being well, she said that if he was ill it should be attended to, and insisted on his going to see a celebrated doctor.

He went. Everything took place as he had expected and as it always does. There was the usual waiting and the important air assumed by the doctor, with which he was so familiar (resembling that which he himself assumed in court), and the sounding and listening, and the questions which called for answers that were foregone conclusions and were evidently unnecessary, and the look of importance which implied that "if only you put yourself in our hands we will arrange everything—we know indubitably how it has to be done, always in the same way for everybody alike." It was all just as it was in the law courts. The doctor put on just the same air towards him as he himself put on towards an accused person.

The doctor said that so-and-so indicated that there was so-and-so inside the patient, but if the investigation of so-and-so did not confirm this, then he must assume that and that. If he assumed that and that, then . . . and so on. To Iván Ilyich only one question was important: was his case serious or not? But the doctor ignored that inappropriate question. From his point of view it was not the one under consideration, the real question was to decide between a floating kidney, chronic catarrh, or appendicitis. It was not a question of Iván Ilyich's life or death, but one between a floating kidney and appendicitis. And that question the doctor solved brilliantly, as it seemed to Iván Ilyich, in favour of the appendix, with the reservation that should an examination of the urine give fresh indications the matter would be reconsidered. All this was just what Iván Ilyich had himself brilliantly accomplished a thousand times in dealing with men on trial. The doctor summed up just as brilliantly, looking over his spectacles triumphantly and even gaily at the accused. From the doctor's summing up Iván Ilyich concluded that things were bad, but that for the doctor, and perhaps for every-

115

body else, it was a matter of indifference, though for him it was bad. And this conclusion struck him painfully, arousing in him a great feeling of pity for himself and of bitterness towards the doctor's indifference to a matter of such importance.

He said nothing of this, but rose, placed the doctor's fee on the table, and remarked with a sigh: "We sick people probably often put inappropriate questions. But tell me, in general, is this complaint dangerous or not? . . ."

The doctor looked at him sternly over his spectacles with one eye, as if to say: "Prisoner, if you will not keep to the questions put to you, I shall be obliged to have you removed from the court."

"I have already told you what I consider necessary and proper. The analysis may show something more." And the doctor bowed.

Iván Ilyich went out slowly, seated himself disconsolately in his sledge, and drove home. All the way home he was going over what the doctor had said, trying to translate those complicated, obscure, scientific phrases into plain language and find in them an answer to the question: "Is my condition bad? Is it very bad? Or is there as yet nothing much wrong?" And it seemed to him that the meaning of what the doctor had said was it was very bad. Everything in the streets seemed depressing. The cabmen, the houses, the passers-by, and the shops, were dismal. His ache, this dull gnawing ache that never ceased for a moment, seemed to have acquired a new and more serious significance from the doctor's dubious remarks. Iván Ilyich now watched it with a new and oppressive feeling.

He reached home and began to tell his wife about it. She listened, but in the middle of his account his daughter came in with her hat on, ready to go out with her mother. She sat down reluctantly to listen to this tedious story, but could not stand it long, and her mother too did not hear him to the end.

"Well, I am very glad," she said. "Mind now to take your medicine regularly. Give me the prescription and I'll send Gerásim to the chemist's." And she went to get ready to go out.

While she was in the room Iván Ilyich had hardly taken time to breathe, but he sighed deeply when she left it.

"Well," he thought, "perhaps it isn't so bad after all."

He began taking his medicine and following the doctor's directions, which had been altered after the examination of the urine. But then it happened that there was a contradiction between the indications drawn from the examination of the urine and the symptoms that showed themselves. It turned out that what was happening differed from what the doctor had told him, and that he had either forgotten, or blundered, or hidden something from him. He could not, however, be blamed for that, and Iván Ilyich still obeyed his orders implicitly and at first derived some comfort from doing so.

From the time of his visit to the doctor, Iván Ilyich's chief occupation was the exact fulfilment of the doctor's instructions regarding hygiene and the taking of medicine, and the observation of his pain and his excretions. His chief interests came to be people's ailments and people's health. When sickness, deaths, or recoveries were mentioned in his presence, especially when the illness resembled his own, he listened with agitation which he tried to hide, asked questions, and applied what he heard to his own case.

The pain did not grow less, but Iván Ilyich made efforts to force himself to think that he was better. And he could do this so long as nothing agitated him. But as soon as he had any unpleasantness with his wife, any lack of success in his official work, or held bad cards at bridge, he was at once acutely sensible of his disease. He had formerly borne such mischances, hoping soon to adjust what was wrong, to master it and attain success, or make a grand slam. But now every mischance upset him and plunged him into despair. He would say to himself. "There now, just as I was beginning to get better and the medicine had begun to take effect, comes this accursed misfortune, or unpleasantness . . ." And he was furious with the mishap, or with the people who were causing the unpleasantness and killing him, for he felt that this fury was killing him but could not restrain it. One would have thought that it should have been clear to him that this exasperation with circumstances and people aggravated his illness, and that he ought therefore to ignore unpleasant occurrences. But he drew the very opposite conclusion: he said that he needed peace, and he watched for everything that might disturb it and became irritable at the slightest infringement of it. His condition was rendered worse by the fact that he read medical books and consulted doctors. The progress of his disease was so gradual that he could deceive himself when comparing one day with another—the difference was so slight. But when he consulted the doctors it seemed to him that he was getting worse, and even very rapidly. Yet despite this he was continually consulting them.

That month he went to see another celebrity, who told him almost the same as the first had done but put his questions rather differently, and the interview with this celebrity only increased Iván Ilyich's doubts and fears. A friend of a friend of his, a very good doctor, diagnosed his illness again quite differently from the others, and though he predicted recovery, his questions and suppositions bewildered Iván Ilyich still more and increased his doubts. A homeopathist diagnosed the disease in yet another way, and prescribed medicine which Iván Ilyich took secretly for a week. But after a week, not feeling any improvement and having lost confidence both in the former doctor's treatment and in this one's, he became still more despondent. One day a lady acquaintance mentioned a cure effected by a wonder-working icon. Iván Ilyich caught himself listening attentively and beginning to believe that it had occurred. This incident alarmed him. "Has my mind really weakened to such an extent?" he asked himself. "Nonsense! It's all rubbish. I mustn't give way to nervous fears but having chosen a doctor must keep strictly to his treatment. That is what I will do. Now it's all settled. I won't think about it, but will follow the treatment seriously till summer, and then we shall see. From now there must be no more of this wavering!" This was easy to say but impossible to carry out. The pain in his side oppressed him and seemed to grow worse and more incessant, while the taste in his mouth grew stranger and stranger. It seemed to him that his breath had a disgusting smell, and he was conscious of a loss of appetite and strength. There was no deceiving himself: something terrible, new, and more important than anything before in his life, was taking place within him of which he alone was aware. Those about him did not understand or would not understand it, but thought everything in the world was going on as usual. That tormented Iván Ilyich more than anything. He saw that his household, especially his wife and daughter who were in a perfect whirl of visiting, did not understand anything of it and were annoyed that he was so depressed and so exacting, as if he were to blame for it. Though they tried to disguise it he saw that he was an obstacle in their path, and that his wife had adopted a definite line in regard to his illness and kept to it regardless of anything he said or did. Her attitude was this: "You know," she would say to her friends, "Iván Ilyich can't do as other people do, and keep to the treatment prescribed for him. One day he'll take his drops and keep strictly to his diet and go to bed in good time, but the next day unless I watch him he'll suddenly forget his medicine, eat sturgeon—which is forbidden—and sit up playing cards till one o'clock in the morning."

130   "Oh, come, when was that?" Iván Ilyich would ask in vexation. "Only once at Peter Ivánovich's."

"And yesterday with Shébek."

"Well, even if I hadn't stayed up, this pain would have kept me awake."

"Be that as it may you'll never get well like that, but will always make us wretched."

Praskóvya Fédorovna's attitude to Iván Ilyich's illness, as she expressed it both to others and to him, was that it was his own fault and was another of the annoyances he caused her. Iván Ilyich felt that this opinion escaped her involuntarily—but that did not make it easier for him.

135   At the law courts too, Iván Ilyich noticed, or thought he noticed, a strange attitude towards himself. It sometimes seemed to him that people were watching him inquisitively as a man whose place might soon be vacant. Then again, his friends would suddenly begin to chaff him in a friendly way about his low spirits, as if the awful, horrible, and unheard-of thing that was going on within him, incessantly gnawing at him and irresistibly drawing him away, was a very agreeable subject for jests. Schwartz in particular irritated him by his jocularity, vivacity, and *savoir-faire*, which reminded him of what he himself had been ten years ago.

Friends came to make up a set and they sat down to cards. They dealt, bending the new cards to soften them, and he sorted the diamonds in his hand and found he had seven. His partner said "No trumps" and supported him with two diamonds. What more could be wished for? It ought to be jolly and lively. They would make a grand slam. But suddenly Iván Ilyich was conscious of that gnawing pain, that taste in his mouth, and it it seemed ridiculous that in such circumstances he should be pleased to make a grand slam.

He looked at his partner Mikháil Mikháylovich, who rapped the table with his strong hand and instead of snatching up the tricks pushed the cards courteously and indulgently towards Iván Ilyich that he might have the pleasure of gathering them up without the trouble of stretching out his hand for them. "Does he think I am too weak to stretch out my arm?" thought Iván Ilyich, and forgetting what he was doing he over-trumped his partner, missing the grand slam by three tricks. And what was most awful of all was that he saw how upset Mikháil Mikháylovich was about it but did not himself care. And it was dreadful to realize why he did not care.

They all saw that he was suffering, and said: "We can stop if you are tired. Take a rest." Lie down? No, he was not at all tired, and he finished the rubber. All were gloomy and silent. Iván Ilyich felt that he had diffused this gloom over them and could not dispel it. They had supper and went away, and Iván Ilyich was left alone with the consciousness that his life was poisoned and was poisoning the lives of others, and that this poison did not weaken but penetrated more and more deeply into his whole being.

With this consciousness, and with physical pain besides the terror, he must go to bed, often to lie awake the greater part of the night. Next morning he had to get up again, dress, go to the law courts, speak, and write; or if he did not go out, spend at home those twenty-four hours a day each of which was a torture. And he had to live thus all alone on the brink of an abyss, with no one who understood or pitied him.

V

So one month passed and then another. Just before the New Year his brother-in-law came to town and stayed at their house. Iván Ilyich was at the law courts and Praskóvya Fëdorovna had gone shopping. When Iván Ilyich came home and entered his study he found his brother-in-law there—a healthy, florid man—unpacking his portmanteau himself. He raised his head on hearing Iván Ilyich's footsteps and looked up at him for a moment without a word. That stare told Iván everything. His brother-in-law opened his mouth to utter an exclamation of surprise but checked himself, and that action confirmed it all.

"I have changed, eh?"

"Yes, there is a change."

And after that, try as he would to get his brother-in-law to return to the subject of his looks, the latter would say nothing about it. Prakóvya Fëdorovna came home and her brother went out to her. Iván Ilyich locked the door and began to examine himself in the glass, first full face, then in profile. He took up a portrait of himself taken with his wife, and compared it with what he saw in the glass. The change in him was immense. Then he bared his arms to the elbow, looked at them, drew the sleeves down again, sat down on an ottoman, and grew blacker than night.

"No, no, this won't do!" he said to himself, and jumped up, went to the table, took up some law papers and began to read them, but could not continue. He unlocked the door and went into the reception-room. The door leading to the drawing-room was shut. He approached it on tiptoe and listened.

"No, you are exaggerating!" Praskóvya Fëdorovna was saying.

"Exaggerating! Don't you see it? Why, he's a dead man! Look at his eyes—there's no light in them. But what is it that is wrong with him?"

140

145

"No one knows. Nikoláevich [that was another doctor] said something, but I don't know what. And Leshchetítsky [this was the celebrated specialist] said quite the contrary. . ."

Iván Ilyich walked away, went to his own room, lay down and began musing: "The kidney, a floating kidney." He recalled all the doctors had told him of how it detached itself and swayed about. And by an effort of imagination he tried to catch that kidney and arrest it and support it. So little was needed for this, it seemed to him. "No, I'll go to see Peter Ivánovich again." [That was the friend whose friend was a doctor.] He rang, ordered the carriage, and got ready to go.

"Where are you going, *Jean?*"[9] asked his wife, with a specially sad and exceptionally kind look.

This exceptionally kind look irritated him. He looked morosely at her.

"I must go to see Peter Ivánovich."

He went to see Peter Ivánovich, and together they went to see his friend, the doctor. He was in, and Iván Ilyich had a long talk with him.

Reviewing the anatomical and physiological details of what in the doctor's opinion was going on inside him, he understood it all.

There was something, a small thing, in the vermiform appendix. It might all come right. Only stimulate the energy of one organ and check the activity of another, then absorption would take place and everything would come right. He got home rather late for dinner, ate his dinner, and conversed cheerfully, but could not for a long time bring himself to go back to work in his room. At last, however, he went to his study and did what was necessary, but the consciousness that he had put something aside—an important, intimate matter which he would revert to when his work was done—never left him. When he had finished his work he remembered that this intimate matter was the thought of his vermiform appendix. But he did not give himself up to it, and went to the drawing-room for tea. There were callers there, including the examining magistrate who was a desirable match for his daughter, and they were conversing, playing the piano, and singing. Iván Ilyich, as Praskóvya Fëdorovna remarked, spent that evening more cheerfully than usual, but he never for a moment forgot that he had postponed the important matter of the appendix. At eleven o'clock he said goodnight and went to his bedroom. Since his illness he had slept alone in a small room next to his study. He undressed and took up a novel by Zola,[1] but instead of reading it he fell into thought, and in his imagination that desired improvement in the vermiform appendix occurred. There was the absorption and evacuation and the reestablishment of normal activity. "Yes, that's it!" he said to himself. "One need only assist nature, that's all." He remembered his medicine, rose, took it, and lay down on his back watching for the beneficent action of the medicine and for it to lessen the pain. "I need only take it regularly and avoid all injurious influences. I am already feeling better, much better." He began touching his side: it was not painful to the touch. "There, I really don't feel it. It's much better already." He put out the light and turned on his side. . . . "The

---

9. French for *Iván.*   1. The French naturalistic novelist Émile Zola (1840–1902) saw human life as merely a matter of biological and mechanistic functions.

appendix is getting better, absorption is occurring." Suddenly he felt the old, familiar, dull, gnawing pain, stubborn and serious. There was the same familiar loathsome taste in his mouth. His heart sank and he felt dazed. "My God! My God!" he muttered. "Again, again! And it will never cease." And suddenly the matter presented itself in a quite different aspect. "Vermiform appendix! Kidney!" he said to himself. "It's not a question of appendix or kidney, but of life and . . . death. Yes, life was there and now it is going, going and I cannot stop it. Yes. Why deceive myself? Isn't it obvious to everyone but me that I'm dying, and that it's only a question of weeks, days . . . it may happen this moment. There was light and now there is darkness. I was here and now I'm going there! Where?" A chill came over him, his breathing ceased, and he felt only the throbbing of his heart.

"When I am not, what will there be? There will be nothing. Then where shall I be when I am no more? Can this be dying? No, I don't want to!" He jumped up and tried to light the candle, felt for it with trembling hands, dropped candle and candlestick on the floor, and fell back on his pillow.

"What's the use? It makes no difference," he said to himself, staring with wide-open eyes into the darkness. "Death. Yes, death. And none of them know or wish to know it, and they have no pity for me. Now they are playing." (He heard through the door the distant sound of a song and its accompaniment.) "It's all the same to them, but they will die too! Fools! I first, and they later, but it will be the same for them. And now they are merry . . . the beasts!"

Anger choked him and he was agonizingly, unbearably miserable. "It is impossible that all men have been doomed to suffer this awful horror!" He raised himself.

"Something must be wrong. I must calm myself—must think it all over from the beginning." And he again began thinking. "Yes, the beginning of my illness: I knocked my side, but I was still quite well that day and the next. It hurt a little, then rather more. I saw the doctors, then followed despondency and anguish, more doctors, and I drew nearer to the abyss. My strength grew less and I kept coming nearer and nearer, and now I have wasted away and there is no light in my eyes. I think of the appendix—but this is death! I think of mending the appendix, and all the while here is death! Can it really be death!" Again terror seized him and he gasped for breath. He leant down and began feeling for the matches, pressing with his elbow on the stand beside the bed. It was in his way and hurt him, he grew furious with it, pressed on it still harder, and upset it. Breathless and in despair he fell on his back, expecting death to come immediately.

Meanwhile the visitors were leaving. Praskóvya Fëdorovna was seeing them off. She heard something fall and came in.

"What has happened?"

"Nothing. I knocked it over accidentally."

She went out and returned with a candle. He lay there panting heavily, like a man who has run a thousand yards, and stared upwards at her with a fixed look.

"What is it, *Jean*?"

"No . . . o . . . thing. I upset it." ("Why speak of it? She won't understand," he thought.)

And in truth she did not understand. She picked up the stand, lit his candle, and hurried away to see another visitor off. When she came back he still lay on his back, looking upwards.

"What is it? Do you feel worse?"

"Yes."

She shook her head and sat down.

"Do you know, *Jean*, I think we must ask Leshchetítsky to come and see you here."

This meant calling in the famous specialist, regardless of expense. He smiled malignantly and said "No." She remained a little longer and then went up to him and kissed his forehead.

While she was kissing him he hated her from the bottom of his soul and with difficulty refrained from pushing her away.

"Good-night. Please God you'll sleep."

"Yes."

VI

Iván Ilyich saw that he was dying, and he was in continual despair.

In the depth of his heart he knew he was dying, but not only was he not accustomed to the thought, he simply did not and could not grasp it.

The syllogism he had learned from Kiesewetter's *Logic*:[2] "Caius is a man, men are mortal, therefore Caius is mortal," had always seemed to him correct as applied to Caius, but certainly not as applied to himself. That Caius—man in the abstract—was mortal, was perfectly correct, but he was not Caius, not an abstract man, but a creature quite, quite separate from all others. He had been little Ványa, with a mamma and a papa, with Mítya and Volódya, with the toys, a coachman and a nurse, afterwards with Kátenka and with all the joys, griefs, and delights of childhood, boyhood, and youth. What did Caius know of the smell of that striped leather ball Ványa had been so fond of? Had Caius kissed his mother's hand like that, and did the silk of her dress rustle so for Caius? Had he rioted like that at school when the pastry was bad? Had Caius been in love like that? Could Caius preside at a session as he did? "Caius really was mortal, and it was right for him to die; but for me, little Ványa, Iván Ilyich, with all my thoughts and emotions, it's altogether a different matter. It cannot be that I ought to die. That would be too terrible."

Such was his feeling.

"If I had to die like Caius I should have known it was so. An inner voice would have told me so, but there was nothing of the sort in me and I and all my friends felt that our case was quite different from that of Caius. And now here it is!" he said to himself. "It can't be. It's impossible! But here it is. How is this? How is one to understand it?"

2. Karl Kiesewetter (1766–1819), *Outline of Logic According to Kantian Principles* (1796), influential in Russia as basis for school textbooks.

He could not understand it, and tried to drive this false, incorrect, morbid thought away and to replace it by other proper and healthy thoughts. But that thought, and not the thought only but the reality itself, seemed to come and confront him.

And to replace that thought he called up a succession of others, hoping to find in them some support. He tried to get back into the former current of thoughts that had once screened the thought of death from him. But strange to say, all that had formerly shut off, hidden, and destroyed, his consciousness of death, no longer had that effect. Iván Ilyich now spent most of his time in attempting to re-establish that old current. He would say to himself: "I will take up my duties again—after all I used to live by them." And banishing all doubts he would go to the law courts, enter into conversation with his colleagues, and sit carelessly as was his wont, scanning the crowd with a thoughtful look and leaning both his emaciated arms on the arms of his oak chair; bending over as usual to a colleague and drawing his papers nearer he would interchange whispers with him, and then suddenly raising his eyes and sitting erect would pronounce certain words and open the proceedings. But suddenly in the midst of those proceedings the pain in his side, regardless of the stage the proceedings had reached, would begin its own gnawing work. Iván Ilyich would turn his attention to it and try to drive the thought of it away, but without success. *It* would come and stand before him and look at him, and he would be petrified and the light would die out of his eyes, and he would again begin asking himself whether *It* alone was true. And his colleagues and subordinates would see with surprise and distress that he, the brilliant and subtle judge, was becoming confused and making mistakes. He would shake himself, try to pull himself together, manage somehow to bring the sitting to a close, and return home with the sorrowful consciousness that his judicial labours could not as formerly hide from him what he wanted them to hide, and could not deliver him from *It*. And what was worst of all was that *It* drew his attention to itself not in order to make him take some action but only that he should look at *It*, look it straight in the face: look at it without doing anything, suffer inexpressibly.

And to save himself from this condition Iván Ilyich looked for consolations—new screens—and new screens were found and for a while seemed to save him, but then they immediately fell to pieces or rather became transparent, as *It* penetrated them and nothing could veil *It*.

In these latter days he would go into the drawing-room he had arranged—that drawing-room where he had fallen and for the sake of which (how bitterly ridiculous it seemed) he had sacrificed his life—for he knew that his illness originated with that knock. He would enter and see that something had scratched the polished table. He would look for the cause of this and find that it was the bronze ornamentation of an album, that had got bent. He would take up the expensive album which he had lovingly arranged, and feel vexed with his daughter and her friends for their untidiness—for the album was torn here and there and some of the photographs turned upside down. He would put it carefully in order and bend the ornamentation back into position. Then it would occur to him to place all those things in another corner of the room, near the plants. He would call the footman, but his daughter or wife would contradict him, and he would dispute and grow angry. But that was all right, for then he did not think about *It*. *It* was invisible.

But then, when he was moving something himself, his wife would say: "Let the servants do it. You will hurt yourself again." And suddenly *It* would flash through the screen and he would see it. It was just a flash, and he hoped it would disappear, but he would involuntarily pay attention to his side. "It sits there as before, gnawing just the same!" And he could no longer forget *It*, but could distinctly see it looking at him from behind the flowers. "What is it all for?"

"It really is so! I lost my life over that curtain as I might have done when storming a fort. Is that possible? How terrible and how stupid. It can't be true! It can't, but it is."

185   He would go to his study, lie down, and again be alone with *It*: face to face with *It*. And nothing could be done with *It* except to look at it and shudder.

VII

How it happened it is impossible to say because it came about step by step, unnoticed, but in the third month of Iván Ilyich's illness, his wife, his daughter, his son, his acquaintances, the doctors, the servants, and above all he himself, were aware that the whole interest he had for other people was whether he would soon vacate his place, and at last release the living from the discomfort caused by his presence and be himself released from his sufferings.

He slept less and less. He was given opium and hypodermic injections of morphine, but this did not relieve him. The dull depression he experienced in a somnolent condition at first gave him a little relief, but only as something new; afterwards it became as distressing as the pain itself or even more so.

Special foods were prepared for him by the doctors' orders, but all those foods became increasingly distasteful and disgusting to him.

For his excretions also special arrangements had to be made, and this was a torment to him every time—a torment from the uncleanliness, the unseemliness, and the smell, and from knowing that another person had to take part in it.

190   But just through this most unpleasant matter, Iván Ilyich obtained comfort. Gerásim, the butler's young assistant, always came in to carry the things out. Gerásim was a clean, fresh peasant lad, grown stout on town food and always cheerful and bright. At first the sight of him, in his clean Russian peasant costume, engaged on that disgusting task embarrassed Iván Ilyich.

Once when he got up from the commode too weak to draw up his trousers, he dropped into a soft armchair and looked with horror at his bare, enfeebled thighs with the muscles so sharply marked on them.

Gerásim with a firm light tread, his heavy boots emitting a pleasant smell of tar and fresh winter air, came in wearing a clean Hessian apron,[3] the sleeves of his print shirt tucked up over his strong bare young arms; and refraining from looking at his sick master out of consideration for his feelings, and restraining

---

3. Burlap apron.

the joy of life that beamed from his face, he went up to the commode.

"Gerásim!" said Iván Ilyich in a weak voice.

Gerásim started, evidently afraid he might have committed some blunder, and with a rapid movement turned his fresh, kind, simple young face which just showed the first downy sign of a beard.

"Yes, sir?"

"That must be very unpleasant for you. You must forgive me. I am helpless."

"Oh, why, sir," and Gerásim's eyes beamed and he showed his glistening white teeth, "what's a little trouble? It's a case of illness with you, sir."

And his deft strong hands did their accustomed task, and he went out of the room stepping lightly. Five minutes later he as lightly returned.

Iván Ilyich was still sitting in the same position in the armchair.

"Gerásim," he said when the latter had replaced the freshly-washed utensil. "Please come here and help me." Gerásim went up to him. "Lift me up. It is hard for me to get up, and I have sent Dmítri away."

Gerásim went up to him, grasped his master with his strong arms deftly but gently, in the same way that he stepped—lifted him, supported him with one hand, and with the other drew up his trousers and would have set him down again, but Iván Ilyich asked to be led to the sofa. Gerásim, without an effort and without apparent pressure, led him, almost lifting him, to the sofa and placed him on it.

"Thank you. How easily and well you do it all!"

Gerásim smiled again and turned to leave the room. But Iván Ilyich felt his presence such a comfort that he did not want to let him go.

"One thing more, please move up that chair. No, the other one—under my feet. It is easier for me when my feet are raised."

Gerásim brought the chair, set it down gently in place, and raised Iván Ilyich's legs on to it. It seemed to Iván Ilyich that he felt better while Gerásim was holding up his legs.

"It's better when my legs are higher," he said. "Place that cushion under them."

Gerásim did so. He again lifted the legs and placed them, and again Iván Ilyich felt better while Gerásim held his legs. When he set them down Iván Ilyich fancied he felt worse.

"Gerásim," he said. "Are you busy now?"

"Not at all, sir," said Gerásim, who had learnt from the townsfolk how to speak to gentlefolk.

"What have you still to do?"

"What have I to do? I've done everything except chopping the logs for to-morrow."

"Then hold my legs up a bit higher, can you?"

"Of course I can. Why not?" And Gerásim raised his master's legs higher and Iván Ilyich thought that in that position he did not feel any pain at all.

"And how about the logs?"

"Don't trouble about that, sir. There's plenty of time."

Iván Ilyich told Gerásim to sit down and hold his legs, and began to talk to him. And strange to say it seemed to him that he felt better while Gerásim held his legs up.

After that Iván Ilyich would sometimes call Gerásim and get him to hold his legs on his shoulders, and he liked talking to him. Gerásim did it all easily, willingly, simply, and with a good nature that touched Iván Ilyich. Health, strength, and vitality in other people were offensive to him, but Gerásim's strength and vitality did not mortify but soothed him.

What tormented Iván Ilyich most was the deception, the lie, which for some reason they all accepted, that he was not dying but was simply ill, and that he only need keep quiet and undergo a treatment and then something very good would result. He however knew that do what they would nothing would come of it, only still more agonizing suffering and death. This deception tortured him— their not wishing to admit what they all knew and what he knew, but wanting to lie to him concerning his terrible condition, and wishing and forcing him to participate in that lie. Those lies—lies enacted over him on the eve of his death and destined to degrade this awful, solemn act to the level of their visitings, their curtains, their sturgeon for dinner—were a terrible agony for Iván Ilyich. And strangely enough, many times when they were going through their antics over him he had been within a hairbreadth of calling out to them: "Stop lying! You know and I know that I am dying. Then at least stop lying about it!" But he had never had the spirit to do it. The awful, terrible act of his dying was, he could see, reduced by those about him to the level of a casual, unpleasant, and almost indecorous incident (as if someone entered a drawing-room diffusing an unpleasant odour) and this was done by that very decorum which he had served all his life long. He saw that no one felt for him, because no one even wished to grasp his position. Only Gerásim recognized and pitied him. And so Iván Ilyich felt at ease only with him. He felt comforted when Gerásim supported his legs (sometimes all night long) and refused to go to bed, saying: "Don't you worry, Iván Ilyich. I'll get sleep enough later on," or when he suddenly became familiar and exclaimed: "If you weren't sick it would be another matter, but as it is, why should I grudge a little trouble?" Gerásim alone did not lie; everything showed that he alone understood the facts of the case and did not consider it necessary to disguise them, but simply felt sorry for his emaciated and enfeebled master. Once when Iván Ilyich was sending him away he even said straight out: "We shall all of us die, so why should I grudge a little trouble?"—expressing the fact that he did not think his work burdensome, because he was doing it for a dying man and hoped someone would do the same for him when his time came.

Apart from this lying, or because of it, what most tormented Iván Ilyich was that no one pitied him as he wished to be pitied. At certain moments after prolonged suffering he wished most of all (though he would have been ashamed to confess it) for someone to pity him as a sick child is pitied. He longed to be petted and comforted. He knew he was an important functionary, that he had a beard turning grey, and that therefore what he longed for was impossible, but still he longed for it. And in Gerásim's attitude towards him there was something akin to what he wished for, and so that attitude comforted him. Iván Ilyich wanted to weep, wanted to be petted and cried over, and then his colleague

Shébek would come, and instead of weeping and being petted, Iván Ilyich would assume a serious, severe, and profound air, and by force of habit would express his opinion on a decision of the Court of Appeal and would stubbornly insist on that view. This falsity around him and within him did more than anything else to poison his last days.

VIII

It was morning. He knew it was morning because Gerásim had gone, and Peter the footman had come and put out the candles, drawn back one of the curtains, and begun quietly to tidy up. Whether it was morning or evening, Friday or Sunday, made no difference, it was all just the same: the gnawing, unmitigated, agonizing pain, never ceasing for an instant, the consciousness of life inexorably waning but not yet extinguished, the approach of that ever dreaded and hateful Death which was the only reality, and always the same falsity. What were days, weeks, hours, in such a case?

"Will you have some tea, sir?"

"He wants things to be regular, and wishes the gentlefolk to drink tea in the morning," thought Iván Ilyich, and only said "No."

"Wouldn't you like to move onto the sofa, sir?"

"He wants to tidy up the room, and I'm in the way. I am uncleanliness and disorder," he thought, and said only:

"No, leave me alone."

The man went on bustling about. Iván Ilyich stretched out his hand. Peter came up, ready to help.

"What is it, sir?"

"My watch."

Peter took the watch which was close at hand and gave it to his master.

"Half-past eight. Are they up?"

"No sir, except Vladímir Ivánich" (the son) "who has gone to school. Praskóvya Fëdorovna ordered me to wake her if you asked for her. Shall I do so?"

"No, there's no need to." "Perhaps I'd better have some tea," he thought, and added aloud: "Yes, bring me some tea."

Peter went to the door, but Iván Ilyich dreaded being left alone. "How can I keep him here? Oh yes, my medicine." "Peter, give me my medicine." "Why not? Perhaps it may still do me some good." He took a spoonful and swallowed it. "No, it won't help. It's all tomfoolery, all deception," he decided as soon as he became aware of the familiar, sickly, hopeless taste. "No, I can't believe in it any longer. But the pain, why this pain? If it would only cease just for a moment!" And he moaned. Peter turned towards him. "It's all right. Go and fetch me some tea."

Peter went out. Left alone Iván Ilyich groaned not so much with pain, terrible though that was, as from mental anguish. Always and forever the same, always these endless days and nights. If only it would come quicker! If only *what* would come quicker? Death, darkness? . . . No, no! Anything rather than death!

When Peter returned with the tea on a tray, Iván Ilyich stared at him for a

220

225

230

235

time in perplexity, not realizing who and what he was. Peter was disconcerted by that look and his embarrassment brought Iván Ilyich to himself.

"Oh, tea! All right, put it down. Only help me to wash and put on a clean shirt."

And Iván Ilyich began to wash. With pauses for rest, he washed his hands and then his face, cleaned his teeth, brushed his hair, and looked in the glass. He was terrified by what he saw, especially by the limp way in which his hair clung to his pallid forehead.

While his shirt was being changed he knew that he would be still more frightened at the sight of his body, so he avoided looking at it. Finally he was ready. He drew on a dressing-gown, wrapped himself in a plaid, and sat down in the armchair to take his tea. For a moment he felt refreshed, but as soon as he began to drink the tea he was again aware of the same taste, and the pain also returned. He finished it with an effort, and then lay down stretching out his legs, and dismissed Peter.

Always the same. Now a spark of hope flashes up, then a sea of despair rages, and always pain; always pain, always despair, and always the same. When alone he had a dreadful and distressing desire to call someone, but he knew beforehand that with others present it would be still worse. "Another dose of morphine—to lose consciousness. I will tell him, the doctor, that he must think of something else. It's impossible, impossible, to go on like this."

240   An hour and another pass like that. But now there is a ring at the door bell. Perhaps it's the doctor? It is. He comes in fresh, hearty, plump, and cheerful, with that look on his face that seems to say: "There now, you're in a panic about something, but we'll arrange it all for you directly!" The doctor knows this expression is out of place here, but he has put it on once for all and can't take it off—like a man who has put on a frock-coat in the morning to pay a round of calls.

The doctor rubs his hands vigorously and reassuringly.

"Brr! How cold it is! There's such a sharp frost; just let me warm myself!" he says, as if it were only a matter of waiting till he was warm, and then he would put everything right.

"Well now, how are you?"

Iván Ilyich feels that the doctor would like to say: "Well, how are our affairs?" but that even he feels that this would not do, and says instead: "What sort of a night have you had?"

245   Iván Ilyich looks at him as much as to say: "Are you really never ashamed of lying?" But the doctor does not wish to understand this question, and Iván Ilyich says: "Just as terrible as ever. The pain never leaves me and never subsides. If only something . . ."

"Yes, you sick people are always like that. . . . There, now I think I'm warm enough. Even Praskóvya Fëdorovna, who is so particular, could find no fault with my temperature. Well, now I can say good-morning," and the doctor presses his patient's hand.

Then, dropping his former playfulness, he begins with a most serious face to examine the patient, feeling his pulse and taking his temperature, and then begins the sounding and auscultation.

Iván Ilyich knows quite well and definitely that all this is nonsense and pure deception, but when the doctor, getting down on his knee, leans over him, putting his ear first higher then lower, and performs various gymnastic movements over him with a significant expression on his face, Iván Ilyich submits to it all as he used to submit to the speeches of the lawyers, though he knew very well that they were all lying and why they were lying.

The doctor, kneeling on the sofa, is still sounding him when Praskóvya Fëdorovna's silk dress rustles at the door and she is heard scolding Peter for not having let her know of the doctor's arrival.

She comes in, kisses her husband, and at once proceeds to prove that she has been up a long time already, and only owing to a misunderstanding failed to be there when the doctor arrived.

250

Iván Ilyich looks at her, scans her all over, sets against her the whiteness and plumpness and cleanness of her hands and neck, the gloss of her hair, and the sparkle of her vivacious eyes. He hates her with his whole soul. And the thrill of hatred he feels for her makes him suffer from her touch.

Her attitude towards him and his disease is still the same. Just as the doctor had adopted a certain relation to his patient which he could not abandon, so had she formed one towards him—that he was not doing something he ought to do and was himself to blame, and that she reproached him lovingly for this—and she could not now change that attitude.

"You see he doesn't listen to me and doesn't take his medicine at the proper time. And above all he lies in a position that is no doubt bad for him—with his legs up."

She described how he made Gerásim hold his legs up.

The doctor smiled with a contemptuous affability that said: "What's to be done? These sick people do have foolish fancies of that kind, but we must forgive them."

255

When the examination was over the doctor looked at his watch, and then Praskóvya Fëdorovna announced to Iván Ilyich that it was of course as he pleased, but she had sent to-day for a celebrated specialist who would examine him and have a consultation with Michael Danílovich (their regular doctor).

"Please don't raise any objections. I am doing this for my own sake," she said ironically, letting it be felt that she was doing it all for his sake and only said this to leave him no right to refuse. He remained silent, knitting his brows. He felt that he was so surrounded and involved in a mesh of falsity that it was hard to unravel anything.

Everything she did for him was entirely for her own sake, and she told him she was doing for herself what she actually was doing for herself, as if that was so incredible that he must understand the opposite.

At half-past eleven the celebrated specialist arrived. Again the sounding began and the significant conversations in his presence and in other room, about the kidneys and the appendix, and the questions and answers, with such an air of importance that again, instead of the real question of life and death which now alone confronted him, the question arose of the kidney and the appendix which were not behaving as they ought to and would now be attacked by Michael Danílovich and the specialist and forced to amend their ways.

The celebrated specialist took leave of him with a serious though not hopeless look, and in reply to the timid question in Iván Ilyich, with eyes glistening with fear and hope, put to him as to whether there was a chance of recovery, said that he could not vouch for it but there was a possibility. The look of hope with which Iván Ilyich watched the doctor out was so pathetic that Praskóvya Fëdorovna, seeing it, even wept as she left the room to hand the doctor his fee.

The gleam of hope kindled by the doctor's encouragement did not last long. The same room, the same pictures, curtains, wallpaper, medicine bottles, were all there, and the same aching suffering body, and Iván Ilyich began to moan. They gave him a subcutaneous injection and he sank into oblivion.

It was twilight when he came to. They brought him his dinner and he swallowed some beef tea with difficulty, and then everything was the same again and night was coming on.

After dinner, at seven o'clock, Praskóvya Fëdorovna came into the room in evening dress, her full bosom pushed up by her corset, and with traces of powder on her face. She had reminded him in the morning that they were going to the theatre. Sarah Bernhardt was visiting the town and they had a box, which he had insisted on their taking. Now he had forgotten about it and her toilet offended him, but he concealed his vexation when he remembered that he had himself insisted on their securing a box and going because it would be an instructive and aesthetic pleasure for the children.

Praskóvya Fëdorovna came in, self-satisfied but yet with a rather guilty air. She sat down and asked how he was, but, as he saw, only for the sake of asking and not in order to learn about it, knowing that there was nothing to learn—and then went on to what she really wanted to say: that she would not on any account have gone but that the box had been taken and Helen and their daughter were going, as well as Petríshchev (the examining magistrate, their daughter's fiancé) and that it was out of the question to let them go alone; but that she would have much preferred to sit with him for a while; and he must be sure to follow the doctor's orders while she was away.

"Oh, and Fëdor Petróvich" (the fiancé) "would like to come in. May he? And Lisa?"

"All right."

Their daughter came in in full evening dress, her fresh young flesh exposed (making a show of that very flesh which in his own case caused so much suffering), strong, healthy, evidently in love, and impatient with illness, suffering, and death, because they interfered with her happiness.

Fëdor Petróvich came in too, in evening dress, his hair curled *à la Capoul,*[4] a tight stiff collar round his long sinewy neck, an enormous white shirt-front and narrow black trousers tightly stretched over his strong thighs. He had one white glove tightly drawn on, and was holding his opera hat in his hand.

Following him the schoolboy crept in unnoticed, in a new uniform, poor

---

4. With a part in the middle, hair brushed off the sides of the forehead but with two small curls over the middle of the forehead; after Joseph-Amédée-Victor Capoul (1839–1924), French singer and matinee idol.

little fellow, and wearing gloves. Terribly dark shadows showed under his eyes, the meaning of which Iván Ilyich knew well.

His son had always seemed pathetic to him, and now it was dreadful to see the boy's frightened look of pity. It seemed to Iván Ilyich that Vásya was the only one besides Gerásim who understood and pitied him.

They all sat down and again asked how he was. A silence followed. Lisa asked her mother about the opera-glasses, and there was an altercation between mother and daughter as to who had taken them and where they had been put. This occasioned some unpleasantness.

Fëdor Petróvich inquired of Iván Ilyich whether he had ever seen Sarah Bernhardt. Iván Ilyich did not at first catch the question, but then replied: "No, have you seen her before?"

"Yes, in *Adrienne Lecouvreur*."[5]

Praskóvya Fëdorovna mentioned some rôles in which Sarah Bernhardt was particularly good. Her daughter disagreed. Conversation sprang up as to the elegance and realism of her acting—the sort of conversation that is always repeated and is always the same.

In the midst of the conversation Fëdor Petróvich glanced at Iván Ilyich and became silent. The others also looked at him and grew silent. Iván Ilyich was staring with glittering eyes straight before him, evidently indignant with them. This had to be rectified, but it was impossible to do so. The silence had to be broken, but for a time no one dared to break it and they all became afraid that the conventional deception would suddenly become obvious and the truth become plain to all. Lisa was the first to pluck up courage and break that silence, but by trying to hide what everybody was feeling, she betrayed it.

"Well, if we are going it's time to start," she said, looking at her watch, a present from her father, and with a faint and significant smile at Fëdor Petróvich relating to something known only to them. She got up with a rustle of her dress.

They all rose, said good-night, and went away.

When they had gone it seemed to Iván Ilyich that he felt better; the falsity had gone with them. But the pain remained—that same pain and that same fear that made everything monotonously alike, nothing harder and nothing easier. Everything was worse.

Again minute followed minute and hour followed hour. Everything remained the same and there was no cessation. And the inevitable end of it all became more and more terrible.

"Yes, send Gerásim here," he replied to a question Peter asked.

IX

His wife returned late at night. She came in on tiptoe, but he heard her, opened his eyes, and made haste to close them again. She wished to send Gerásim away and to sit with him herself, but he opened his eyes and said: "No, go away."

5. An 1849 play by the prolific and popular French playwright Eugène Scribe (1791–1861), one of Bernhardt's most famous vehicles.

"Are you in great pain?"

"Always the same."

"Take some opium."

285 He agreed and took some. She went away.

Till about three in the morning he was in a state of stupefied misery. It seemed to him that he and his pain were being thrust into a narrow, deep black sack, but though they were pushed further and further in they could not be pushed to the bottom. And this, terrible enough in itself, was accompanied by suffering. He was frightened yet wanted to fall through the sack, he struggled but yet co-operated. And suddenly he broke through, fell, and regained consciousness. Gerásim was sitting at the foot of the bed dozing quietly and patiently, while he himself lay with his emaciated stockinged legs resting on Gerásim's shoulders; the same shaded candle was there and the same unceasing pain.

"Go away, Gerásim," he whispered.

"It's all right, sir. I'll stay a while."

"No. Go away."

290 He removed his legs from Gerásim's shoulders, turned sideways onto his arm, and felt sorry for himself. He only waited till Gerásim had gone into the next room and then restrained himself no longer but wept like a child. He wept on account of his helplessness, his terrible loneliness, the cruelty of man, the cruelty of God, and the absence of God.

"Why hast Thou done all this? Why hast Thou brought me here? Why, dost Thou torment me so terribly?"

He did not expect an answer and yet wept because there was no answer and could be none. The pain again grew more acute, but he did not stir and did not call. He said to himself: "Go on! Strike me! But what is it for? What have I done to Thee? What is it for?"

Then he grew quiet and not only ceased weeping but even held his breath and became all attention. It was as though he were listening not to an audible voice but to a voice of his soul, to the current of thoughts arising within him.

"What is it you want?" was the first clear conception capable of expression in words, that he heard.

295 "What do you want? What do you want?" he repeated to himself.

"What do I want? To live and not to suffer," he answered.

And again he listened with such concentrated attention that even his pain did not distract him.

"To live? How?" asked his inner voice.

"Why, to live as I used to—well and pleasantly."

300 "As you lived before, well and pleasantly?" the voice repeated.

And in imagination he began to recall the moments of his pleasant life. But strange to say none of those best moments of his pleasant life now seemed at all what they had then seemed—none of them except the first recollections of childhood. There, in childhood, there had been something really pleasant with which it would be possible to live if it could return. But the child who had experienced that happiness existed no longer, it was like a reminiscence of somebody else.

As soon as the period began which had produced the present Iván Ilyich, all that had then seemed joys now melted before his sight and turned into something trivial and often nasty.

And the further he departed from childhood and the nearer he came to the present the more worthless and doubtful were the joys. This began with the School of Law. A little that was really good was still found there—there was light-heartedness, friendship, and hope. But in the upper classes there had already been fewer of such good moments. Then during the first years of his official career, when he was in the service of the Governor, some pleasant moments again occurred: they were the memories of love for a woman. Then all became confused and there was still less of what was good; later on again there was still less that was good, and the further he went the less there was. His marriage, a mere accident, then the disenchantment that followed it, his wife's bad breath and the sensuality and hypocrisy: then that deadly official life and those preoccupations about money, a year of it, and two, and ten, and twenty, and always the same thing. And the longer it lasted the more deadly it became. "It is as if I had been going downhill while I imagined I was going up. And that is really what it was. I was going up in public opinion, but to the same extent life was ebbing away from me. And now it is all done and there is only death."

"Then what does it mean? Why? It can't be that life is so senseless and horrible. But if it really has been so horrible and senseless, why must I die and die in agony? There is something wrong!"

"Maybe I did not live as I ought to have done," it suddenly occurred to him. "But how could that be, when I did everything properly?" he replied, and immediately dismissed from his mind this, the sole solution of all the riddles of life and death, as something quite impossible.

"Then what do you want now? To live? Live how? Live as you lived in the law courts when the usher proclaimed 'The judge is coming!' The judge is coming, the judge!" he repeated to himself. "Here he is, the judge. But I am not guilty!" he exclaimed angrily. "What is it for?" And he ceased crying, but turning his face to the wall continued to ponder on the same question: Why, and for what purpose, is there all this horror? But however much he pondered he found no answer. And whenever the thought occurred to him, as it often did, that it all resulted from his not having lived as he ought to have done, he at once recalled the correctness of his whole life, and dismissed so strange an idea.

305

X

Another fortnight passed. Iván Ilyich now no longer left his sofa. He would not lie in bed but lay on the sofa, facing the wall nearly all the time. He suffered ever the same unceasing agonies and in his loneliness pondered always on the same insoluble question: "What is this? Can it be that it is Death?" And the inner voice answered: "Yes, it is Death."

"Why these sufferings?" And the voice answered, "For no reason—they just are so." Beyond and besides this there was nothing.

From the very beginning of his illness, ever since he had first been to see the doctor, Iván Ilyich's life had been divided between two contrary and alternating moods: now it was despair and the expectation of this uncomprehended and terrible death, and now hope and an intently interested observation of the functioning of his organs. Now before his eyes there was only a kidney or an intestine that temporarily evaded its duty, and now only that incomprehensible and dreadful death from which it was impossible to escape.

310

These two states of mind had alternated from the very beginning of his illness, but the further it progressed the more doubtful and fantastic became the conception of the kidney, and the more real the sense of impending death.

He had but to call to mind what he had been three months before and what he was now, to call to mind with what regularity he had been going downhill, for every possibility of hope to be shattered.

Latterly during that loneliness in which he found himself as he lay facing the back of the sofa, a loneliness in the midst of a populous town and surrounded by numerous acquaintances and relations but that yet could not have been more complete anywhere—either at the bottom of the sea or under the earth—during that terrible loneliness Iván Ilyich had lived only in memories of the past. Pictures of his past rose before him one after another. They always began with what was nearest in time and then went back to what was most remote—to his childhood—and rested there. If he thought of the stewed prunes that had been offered him that day, his mind went back to the raw shrivelled French plums of his childhood, their peculiar flavour and the flow of saliva when he sucked their stones, and along with the memory of that taste came a whole series of memories of those days: his nurse, his brother, and their toys. "No, I mustn't think of that. . . . It is too painful," Iván Ilyich said to himself, and brought himself back to the present—to the button on the back of the sofa and the creases in its morocco. "Morocco is expensive, but it does not wear well: there had been a quarrel about it. It was a different kind of quarrel and a different kind of morocco that time when we tore father's portfolio and were punished, and mamma brought us some tarts. . . ." And again his thoughts dwelt on his childhood, and again it was painful and he tried to banish them and fix his mind on something else.

Then again together with that chain of memories another series passed through his mind—of how his illness had progressed and grown worse. There also the further back he looked the more life there had been. There had been more of what was good in life and more of life itself. The two merged together. "Just as the pain went on getting worse and worse, so my life grew worse and worse," he thought. "There is one bright spot there at the back, at the beginning of life, and afterwards all becomes blacker and blacker and proceeds more and more rapidly—in inverse ratio to the square of the distance from death," thought Iván Ilyich. And the example of a stone falling downwards with increasing velocity entered his mind. Life, a series of increasing sufferings, flies further and further towards its end—the most terrible suffering. "I am flying. . . ." He shuddered, shifted himself, and tried to resist, but was already aware that resistance was impossible, and again with eyes weary of gazing but unable to cease seeing what was before them, he stared at the back of the sofa and waited—awaiting that dreadful fall and shock and destruction.

"Resistance is impossible!" he said to himself. "If I could only understand what it is all for! But that too is impossible. An explanation would be possible if it could be said that I have not lived as I ought to. But it is impossible to say that," and he remembered all the legality, correctitude, and propriety of his life. "That at any rate can certainly not be admitted," he thought, and his lips smiled ironically as if someone could see that smile and be taken in by it. "There is no explanation! Agony, death. . . . What for?"

XI

Another two weeks went by in this way and during that fortnight an event occurred that Iván Ilyich and his wife had desired. Petríshchev formally proposed. It happened in the evening. The next day Praskóvya Fëdorovna came into her husband's room considering how best to inform him of it, but that very night there had been a fresh change for the worse in his condition. She found him still lying on the sofa but in a different position. He lay on his back, groaning and staring fixedly straight in front of him.

She began to remind him of his medicines, but he turned his eyes towards her with such a look that she did not finish what she was saying; so great an animosity, to her in particular, did that look express.

"For Christ's sake let me die in peace!" he said.

She would have gone away, but just then their daughter came in and went up to say good morning. He looked at her as he had done at his wife, and in reply to her inquiry about his health said dryly that he would soon free them all of himself. They were both silent and after sitting with him for a while went away.

"Is it our fault?" Lisa said to her mother. "It's as if we were to blame! I am sorry for papa, but why should we be tortured?"

The doctor came at his usual time. Iván Ilyich answered "Yes" and "No," never taking his angry eyes from him, and at last said: "You know you can do nothing for me, so leave me alone."

"We can ease your sufferings."

"You can't even do that. Let me be."

The doctor went into the drawing-room and told Praskóvya Fëdorovna that the case was very serious and that the only resource left was opium to allay her husband's sufferings, which must be terrible.

It was true, as the doctor said, that Iván Ilyich's physical sufferings were terrible, but worse than the physical sufferings were his mental sufferings which were his chief torture.

His mental sufferings were due to the fact that that night, as he looked at Gerásim's sleepy, good-natured face with its prominent cheek-bones, the question suddenly occurred to him: "What if my whole life has really been wrong?"

It occurred to him that what had appeared perfectly impossible before, namely that he had not spent his life as he should have done, might after all be true. It occurred to him that his scarcely perceptible attempts to struggle against what was considered good by the most highly placed people, those scarcely noticeable impulses which he had immediately suppressed, might have been the real thing, and all the rest false. And his professional duties and the whole arrangement of his life and of his family, and all his social and official interests, might all have been false. He tried to defend all those things to himself and suddenly felt the weakness of what he was defending. There was nothing to defend.

"But if that is so," he said to himself, "and I am leaving this life with the consciousness that I have lost all that was given me and it is impossible to rectify it—what then?"

He lay on his back and began to pass his life in review in quite a new way. In the morning when he saw first his footman, then his wife, then his daughter, and then the doctor, their every word and movement confirmed to him the awful truth that had been revealed to him during the night. In them he saw himself—all that for which he had lived—and saw clearly that it was not real at all, but a terrible and huge deception which had hidden both life and death. This consciousness intensified his physical suffering tenfold. He groaned and tossed about, and pulled at his clothing which choked and stifled him. And he hated them on that account.

He was given a large dose of opium and became unconscious, but at noon his sufferings began again. He drove everybody away and tossed from side to side.

30   His wife came to him and said:

"*Jean*, my dear, do this for me. It can't do any harm and often helps. Healthy people often do it."

He opened his eyes wide.

"What? Take communion? Why? It's unnecessary! However . . ."

She began to cry.

35   "Yes, do, my dear. I'll send for our priest. He is such a nice man."

"All right. Very well," he muttered.

When the priest came and heard his confession, Iván Ilyich was softened and seemed to feel a relief from his doubts and consequently from his sufferings, and for a moment there came a ray of hope. He again began to think of the vermiform appendix and the possibility of correcting it. He received the sacrament with tears in his eyes.

When they laid him down again afterwards he felt a moment's ease, and the hope that he might live awoke in him again. He began to think of the operation that had been suggested to him. "To live! I want to live!" he said to himself.

His wife came in to congratulate him after his communion, and when uttering the usual conventional words she added:

40   "You feel better, don't you?"

Without looking at her he said "Yes."

Her dress, her figure, the expression of her face, the tone of her voice, all revealed the same thing. "This is wrong, it is not as it should be. All you have lived for and still live for is falsehood and deception, hiding life and death from you." And as soon as he admitted that thought, his hatred and his agonizing physical suffering again sprang up, and with that suffering a consciousness of the unavoidable, approaching end. And to this was added a new sensation of grinding shooting pain and a feeling of suffocation.

The expression of his face when he uttered that "yes" was dreadful. Having uttered it, he looked her straight in the eyes, turned on his face with a rapidity extraordinary in his weak state and shouted:

"Go away! Go away and leave me alone!"

XII

From that moment the screaming began that continued for three days, and was so terrible that one could not hear it through two closed doors without horror. At the moment he answered his wife he realized that he was lost, that there was no return, that the end had come, the very end, and his doubts were still unsolved and remained doubts.

"Oh! Oh! Oh!" he cried in various intonations. He had begun by screaming "I won't!" and continued screaming on the letter "o."

For three whole days, during which time did not exist for him, he struggled in that black sack into which he was being thrust by an invisible, resistless force. He struggled as a man condemned to death struggles in the hands of the executioner, knowing that he cannot save himself. And every moment he felt that despite all his efforts he was drawing nearer and nearer to what terrified him. He felt that his agony was due to his being thrust into that black hole and still more to his not being able to get right into it. He was hindered from getting into it by his conviction that his life had been a good one. That very justification of his life held him fast and prevented his moving forward, and it caused him most torment of all.

Suddenly some force struck him in the chest and side, making it still harder to breathe, and he fell through the hole and there at the bottom was a light. What had happened to him was like the sensation one sometimes experiences in a railway carriage when one thinks one is going backwards while one is really going forwards and suddenly becomes aware of the real direction.

"Yes, it was all not the right thing," he said to himself, "but that's no matter. It can be done. But what *is* the right thing?" he asked himself, and suddenly grew quiet.

This occurred at the end of the third day, two hours before his death. Just then his schoolboy son had crept softly in and gone up to the bedside. The dying man was still screaming desperately and waving his arms. His hand fell on the boy's head, and the boy caught it, pressed it to his lips, and began to cry.

At that very moment Iván Ilyich fell through and caught sight of the light, and it was revealed to him that though his life had not been what it should have been, this could still be rectified. He asked himself, "What *is* the right thing?" and grew still, listening. Then he felt that someone was kissing his hand. He opened his eyes, looked at his son, and felt sorry for him. His wife came up to him and he glanced at her. She was gazing at him open-mouthed, with undried tears on her nose and cheek and a despairing look on her face. He felt sorry for her too.

"Yes, I am making them wretched," he thought. "They are sorry, but it will be better for them when I die." He wished to say this but had not the strength to utter it. "Besides, why speak? I must act," he thought. With a look at his wife he indicated his son and said: "Take him away . . . sorry for him . . . sorry for you too. . . ." He tried to add, "forgive me," but said "forego" and waved his hand, knowing that He whose understanding mattered would understand.

And suddenly it grew clear to him that what had been oppressing him and would not leave him was all dropping away at once from two sides, from ten sides, and from all sides. He was sorry for them, he must act so as not to hurt them: release them and free himself from these sufferings. "How good and how simple!" he thought. "And the pain?" he asked himself. "What has become of it? Where are you, pain?"

He turned his attention to it.

"Yes, here it is. Well, what of it? Let the pain be."

"And death . . . where is it?"

He sought his former accustomed fear of death and did not find it. "Where is it? What death?" There was no fear because there was no death.

In place of death there was light.

"So that's what it is!" he suddenly exclaimed aloud. "What joy!"

355 To him all this happened in a single instant, and the meaning of that instant did not change. For those present his agony continued for another two hours. Something rattled in his throat, his emaciated body twitched, then the gasping and rattle became less and less frequent.

"It is finished!" said someone near him.

He heard these words and repeated them in his soul.

360 "Death is finished," he said to himself. "It is no more!"

He drew in a breath, stopped in the midst of a sigh, stretched out, and died.

1886

KATE CHOPIN

Beyond the Bayou

The bayou curved like a crescent around the point of land on which La Folle's cabin stood. Between the stream and the hut lay a big abandoned field, where cattle were pastured when the bayou supplied them with enough water. Through the woods that spread back into unknown regions the woman had drawn an imaginary line, and past this circle she never stepped. This was the form of her only mania.

She was now a large, gaunt black woman, past thirty-five. Her real name was Jacqueline, but every one on the plantation called her La Folle,[1] because in childhood she had been frightened literally "out of her senses," and had never wholly regained them.

It was when there had been skirmishing and sharpshooting all day in the

1. The crazy woman.

woods. Evening was near when P'tit Maître,[2] black with powder and crimson with blood, had staggered into the cabin of Jacqueline's mother, his pursuers close at his heels. The sight had stunned her childish reason.

She dwelt alone in her solitary cabin, for the rest of the quarters had long since been removed beyond her sight and knowledge. She had more physical strength than most men, and made her patch of cotton and corn and tobacco like the best of them. But of the world beyond the bayou she had long known nothing, save what her morbid fancy conceived.

People at Bellissime had grown used to her and her way, and they thought nothing of it. Even when "Old Mis' " died, they did not wonder that La Folle had not crossed the bayou, but had stood upon her side of it, wailing and lamenting.   5

P'tit Maître was now the owner of Bellissime. He was a middle-aged man, with a family of beautiful daughters about him, and a little son whom La Folle loved as if he had been her own. She called him Chéri,[3] and so did every one else because she did.

None of the girls had ever been to her what Chéri was. They had each and all loved to be with her, and to listen to her wondrous stories of things that always happened "yonda, beyon' de bayou."

But none of them had stroked her black hand quite as Chéri did, nor rested their heads against her knee so confidingly, nor fallen asleep in her arms as he used to do. For Chéri hardly did such things now, since he had become the proud possessor of a gun, and had had his black curls cut off.

That summer—the summer Chéri gave La Folle two black curls tied with a knot of red ribbon—the water ran so low in the bayou that even the little children at Bellissime were able to cross it on foot, and the cattle were sent to pasture down by the river. La Folle was sorry when they were gone, for she loved these dumb companions well, and liked to feel that they were there, and to hear them browsing by night up to her own inclosure.

It was Saturday afternoon, when the fields were deserted. The men had flocked to a neighboring village to do their week's trading, and the women were occupied with household affairs,—La Folle as well as the others. It was then she mended and washed her handful of clothes, scoured her house, and did her baking.   10

In this last employment she never forgot Chéri. To-day she had fashioned croquignoles[4] of the most fantastic and alluring shapes for him. So when she saw the boy come trudging across the field with his gleaming little new rifle on his shoulder, she called out gayly to him, "Chéri! Chéri!"

But Chéri did not need the summons, for he was coming straight to her. His pockets all bulged out with almonds and raisins and an orange that he had secured for her from the very fine dinner which had been given that day up at his father's house.

He was a sunny-faced youngster of ten. When he had emptied his pockets, La Folle patted his round red cheek, wiped his soiled hands on her apron, and smoothed his hair. Then she watched him as, with his cakes in his hand, he

2. Little Master.   3. Darling.   4. Biscuits.

crossed her strip of cotton back of the cabin, and disappeared into the wood.

He had boasted of the things he was going to do with his gun out there.

15 "You think they got plenty deer in the wood, La Folle?" he had inquired, with the calculating air of an experienced hunter.

"Non, non!" the woman laughed. "Don't you look fo' no deer, Chéri. Dat's too big. But you bring La Folle one good fat squirrel fo' her dinner to-morrow, an' she goin' be satisfi'."

"One squirrel ain't a bite. I'll bring you mo' 'an one, La Folle," he had boasted pompously as he went away.

When the woman, an hour later, heard the report of the boy's rifle close to the wood's edge, she would have thought nothing of it if a sharp cry of distress had not followed the sound.

She withdrew her arms from the tub of suds in which they had been plunged, dried them upon her apron, and as quickly as her trembling limbs would bear her, hurried to the spot whence the ominous report had come.

20 It was as she feared. There she found Chéri stretched upon the ground, with his rifle beside him. He moaned piteously:—

"I'm dead, La Folle! I'm dead! I'm gone!"

"Non, non!" she exclaimed resolutely, as she knelt beside him. "Put you' arm 'roun' La Folle's nake, Chéri. Dat's nuttin'; dat goin' be nuttin'." She lifted him in her powerful arms.

Chéri had carried his gun muzzle-downward. He had stumbled,—he did not know how. He only knew that he had a ball lodged somewhere in his leg, and he thought that his end was at hand. Now, with his head upon the woman's shoulder, he moaned and wept with pain and fright.

"Oh, La Folle! La Folle! it hurt so bad! I can' stan' it, La Folle!"

25 "Don't cry, mon bébé[5] mon bébé, mon Chéri!" the woman spoke soothingly as she covered the ground with long strides. "La Folle goin' mine you; Doctor Bonfils goin' come make mon Chéri well agin."

She had reached the abandoned field. As she crossed it with her precious burden, she looked constantly and restlessly from side to side. A terrible fear was upon her,—the fear of the world beyond the bayou, the morbid and insane dread she had been under since childhood.

When she was at the bayou's edge she stood there, and shouted for help as if a life depended upon it:—

"Oh, P'tit Maître! P'tit Maître! Venez donc! Au secours! Au secours!"[6]

No voice responded. Chéri's hot tears were scalding her neck. She called for each and every one upon the place, and still no answer came.

30 She shouted, she wailed; but whether her voice remained unheard or unheeded, no reply came to her frenzied cries. And all the while Chéri moaned and wept and entreated to be taken home to his mother.

La Folle gave a last despairing look around her. Extreme terror was upon her. She clasped the child close against her breast, where he could feel her heart beat like a muffled hammer. Then shutting her eyes, she ran suddenly down the

5. My baby.   6. Come here! Help! Help!

shallow bank of the bayou, and never stopped till she had climbed the opposite shore.

She stood there quivering an instant as she opened her eyes. Then she plunged into the footpath through the trees.

She spoke no more to Chéri, but muttered constantly, "Bon Dieu, ayez pitié La Folle! Bon Dieu, ayez pitié moi!"[7]

Instinct seemed to guide her. When the pathway spread clear and smooth enough before her, she again closed her eyes tightly against the sight of that unknown and terrifying world.

A child, playing in some weeds, caught sight of her as she neared the quarters. The little one uttered a cry of dismay. 35

"La Folle!" she screamed, in her piercing treble. "La Folle done cross de bayer!"

Quickly the cry passed down the line of cabins.

"Yonda, La Folle done cross de bayou!"

Children, old men, old women, young ones with infants in their arms, flocked to doors and windows to see this awe-inspiring spectacle. Most of them shuddered with superstitious dread of what it might portend. "She totin' Chéri!" some of them shouted.

Some of the more daring gathered about her, and followed at her heels, only to fall back with new terror when she turned her distorted face upon them. Her eyes were bloodshot and the saliva had gathered in a white foam on her black lips. 40

Some one had run ahead of her to where P'tit Maître sat with his family and guests upon the gallery.

"P'tit Maître! La Folle done cross de bayou! Look her! Look her yonda totin' Chéri!" This startling intimation was the first which they had of the woman's approach.

She was now near at hand. She walked with long strides. Her eyes were fixed desperately before her, and she breathed heavily, as a tired ox.

At the foot of the stairway, which she could not have mounted, she laid the boy in his father's arms. Then the world that had looked red to La Folle suddenly turned black,—like that day she had seen powder and blood.

She reeled for an instant. Before a sustaining arm could reach her, she fell heavily to the ground. 45

When La Folle regained consciousness, she was at home again, in her own cabin and upon her own bed. The moon rays, streaming in through the open door and windows, gave what light was needed to the old black mammy who stood at the table concocting a tisane of fragrant herbs. It was very late.

Others who had come, and found that the stupor clung to her, had gone again. P'tit Maître had been there, and with him Doctor Bonfils, who said that La Folle might die.

But death had passed her by. The voice was very clear and steady with which she spoke to Tante[8] Lizette, brewing her tisane there in a corner.

7. Good Lord, have pity on La Folle! Good Lord, have pity on me!   8. Aunt.

"Ef you will give me one good drink tisane, Tante Lizette, I b'lieve I'm goin' sleep, me."

50　　And she did sleep; so soundly, so healthfully, that old Lizette without compunction stole softly away, to creep back through the moonlit fields to her own cabin in the new quarters.

The first touch of the cool gray morning awoke La Folle. She arose, calmly, as if no tempest had shaken and threatened her existence but yesterday.

She donned her new blue cottonade[9] and white apron, for she remembered that this was Sunday. When she had made for herself a cup of strong black coffee, and drunk it with relish, she quitted the cabin and walked across the old familiar field to the bayou's edge again.

She did not stop there as she had always done before, but crossed with a long, steady stride as if she had done this all her life.

When she had made her way through the brush and scrub cottonwood-trees that lined the opposite bank, she found herself upon the border of a field where the white, bursting cotton, with the dew upon it, gleamed for acres and acres like frosted silver in the early dawn.

55　　La Folle drew a long, deep breath as she gazed across the country. She walked slowly and uncertainly, like one who hardly knows how, looking about her as she went.

The cabins, that yesterday had sent a clamor of voices to pursue her, were quiet now. No one was yet astir at Bellissime. Only the birds that darted here and there from hedges were awake, and singing their matins.

When La Folle came to the broad stretch of velvety lawn that surrounded the house, she moved slowly and with delight over the springy turf, that was delicious beneath her tread.

She stopped to find whence came those perfumes that were assailing her senses with memories from a time far gone.

There they were, stealing up to her from the thousand blue violets that peeped out from green, luxuriant beds. There they were, showering down from the big waxen bells of the magnolias far above her head, and from the jessamine clumps around her.

60　　There were roses, too, without number. To right and left palms spread in broad and graceful curves. It all looked like enchantment beneath the sparkling sheen of dew.

When La Folle had slowly and cautiously mounted the many steps that led up to the veranda, she turned to look back at the perilous ascent she had made. Then she caught sight of the river, bending like a silver bow at the foot of Bellissime. Exultation possessed her soul.

La Folle rapped softly upon a door near at hand. Chéri's mother soon cautiously opened it. Quickly and cleverly she dissembled the astonishment she felt at seeing La Folle.

"Ah, La Folle! Is it you, so early?"

"*Oui*,[1] madame. I come ax how my po' li'le Chéri to, 's mo'nin'. "

---

9. Cotton fabric made to resemble wool.　　1. Yes.

"He is feeling easier, thank you, La Folle. Dr. Bonfils says it will be nothing   65
serious. He's sleeping now. Will you come back when he awakes?"

"*Non*, madame. I'm goin' wait yair tell Chéri wake up." La Folle seated
herself upon the topmost step of the veranda.

A look of wonder and deep content crept into her face as she watched for the
first time the sun rise upon the new, the beautiful world beyond the bayou.

1894

CHARLOTTE PERKINS GILMAN

The Yellow Wallpaper

It is very seldom that mere ordinary people like John and myself secure ancestral
halls for the summer.

A colonial mansion, a hereditary estate, I would say a haunted house, and
reach the height of romantic felicity—but that would be asking too much of fate!

Still I will proudly declare that there is something queer about it.

Else, why should it be let so cheaply? And why have stood so long unten-
anted?

John laughs at me, of course, but one expects that in marriage.   5

John is practical in the extreme. He has no patience with faith, an intense
horror of superstition, and he scoffs openly at any talk of things not to be felt and
seen and put down in figures.

John is a physician, and *perhaps*—(I would not say it to a living soul, of
course, but this is dead paper and a great relief to my mind—) *perhaps* that is
one reason I do not get well faster.

You see he does not believe I am sick!

And what can one do?

If a physician of high standing, and one's own husband, assures friends and   10
relatives that there is really nothing the matter with one but temporary nervous
depression—a slight hysterical tendency—what is one to do?

My brother is also a physician, and also of high standing, and he says the
same thing.

So I take phosphates or phosphites—whichever it is, and tonics, and jour-
neys, and air, and exercise, and am absolutely forbidden to "work" until I am
well again.

Personally, I disagree with their ideas.

Personally, I believe that congenial work, with excitement and change, would
do me good.

But what is one to do?   15

I did write for a while in spite of them; but it *does* exhaust me a good deal—
having to be so sly about it, or else meet with heavy opposition.

I sometimes fancy that in my condition if I had less opposition and more
society and stimulus—but John says the very worst thing I can do is to think

about my condition, and I confess it always makes me feel bad.

So I will let it alone and talk about the house.

The most beautiful place! It is quite alone, standing well back from the road, quite three miles from the village. It makes me think of English places that you read about, for there are hedges and walls and gates that lock, and lots of separate little houses for the gardeners and people.

There is a *delicious* garden! I never saw such a garden—large and shady, full of box-bordered paths, and lined with long grape-covered arbors with seats under them.

There were greenhouses, too, but they are all broken now.

There was some legal trouble, I believe, something about the heirs and co-heirs; anyhow, the place has been empty for years.

That spoils my ghostliness, I am afraid, but I don't care—there is something strange about the house—I can feel it.

I even said so to John one moonlight evening, but he said what I felt was a *draught*, and shut the window.

I get unreasonably angry with John sometimes. I'm sure I never used to be so sensitive. I think it is due to this nervous condition.

But John says if I feel so, I shall neglect proper self-control; so I take pains to control myself—before him, at least, and that makes me very tired.

I don't like our room a bit. I wanted one downstairs that opened on the piazza and had roses all over the window, and such pretty old-fashioned chintz hangings! but John would not hear of it.

He said there was only one window and not room for two beds, and no near room for him if he took another.

He is very careful and loving, and hardly lets me stir without special direction.

I have a schedule prescription for each hour in the day; he takes all care from me, and so I feel basely ungrateful not to value it more.

He said we came here solely on my account, that I was to have perfect rest and all the air I could get. "Your exercise depends on your strength, my dear," said he, "and your food somewhat on your appetite; but air you can absorb all the time." So we took the nursery at the top of the house.

It is a big, airy room, the whole floor nearly, with windows that look all ways, and air and sunshine galore. It was nursery first and then playroom and gymnasium, I should judge; for the windows are barred for little children, and there are rings and things in the walls.

The paint and paper look as if a boys' school had used it. It is stripped off—the paper—in great patches all around the head of my bed, about as far as I can reach, and in a great place on the other side of the room low down. I never saw a worse paper in my life.

One of those sprawling flamboyant patterns committing every artistic sin.

It is dull enough to confuse the eye in following, pronounced enough to constantly irritate and provoke study, and when you follow the lame uncertain curves for a little distance they suddenly commit suicide—plunge off at outrageous angles, destroy themselves in unheard of contradictions.

The color is repellant, almost revolting; a smouldering unclean yellow, strangely faded by the slow-turning sunlight.

It is a dull yet lurid orange in some places, a sickly sulphur tint in others.

No wonder the children hated it! I should hate it myself if I had to live in this room long.

There comes John, and I must put this away,—he hates to have me write a word.

We have been here two weeks, and I haven't felt like writing before, since that first day.

I am sitting by the window now, up in this atrocious nursery, and there is nothing to hinder my writing as much as I please, save lack of strength.

John is away all day, and even some nights when his cases are serious.

I am glad my case is not serious!

But these nervous troubles are dreadfully depressing.

John does not know how much I really suffer. He knows there is no *reason* to suffer, and that satisfies him.

Of course it is only nervousness. It does weigh on me so not to do my duty in any way!

I mean to be such a help to John, such a real rest and comfort, and here I am a comparative burden already!

Nobody would believe what an effort it is to do what little I am able,—to dress and entertain, and order things.

It is fortunate Mary is so good with the baby. Such a dear baby!

And yet I *cannot* be with him, it makes me so nervous.

I suppose John never was nervous in his life. He laughs at me so about this wallpaper!

At first he meant to repaper the room, but afterwards he said that I was letting it get the better of me, and that nothing was worse for a nervous patient than to give way to such fancies.

He said that after the wallpaper was changed it would be the heavy bedstead, and then the barred windows, and then that gate at the head of the stairs, and so on.

"You know the place is doing you good," he said, "and really, dear, I don't care to renovate the house just for a three months' rental."

"Then do let us go downstairs," I said, "there are such pretty rooms there."

Then he took me in his arms and called me a blessed little goose, and said he would go down cellar, if I wished, and have it whitewashed into the bargain.

But he is right enough about the beds and windows and things.

It is an airy and comfortable room as any one need wish, and, of course, I would not be so silly as to make him uncomfortable just for a whim.

I'm really getting quite fond of the big room, all but that horrid paper.

Out of one window I can see the garden, those mysterious deep-shaded arbors, the riotous old-fashioned flowers, and bushes and gnarly trees.

Out of another I get a lovely view of the bay and a little private wharf belonging to the estate. There is a beautiful shaded lane that runs down there from the house. I always fancy I see people walking in these numerous paths and arbors, but John has cautioned me not to give way to fancy in the least. He says that with my imaginative power and habit of story-making, a nervous weakness like mine is sure to lead to all manner of excited fancies, and that I ought to use my will and good sense to check the tendency. So I try.

I think sometimes that if I were only well enough to write a little it would relieve the press of ideas and rest me.

But I find I get pretty tired when I try.

It is so discouraging not to have any advice and companionship about my work. When I get really well, John says we will ask Cousin Henry and Julia down for a long visit; but he says he would as soon put fireworks in my pillow-case as to let me have those stimulating people about now.

65   I wish I could get well faster.

But I must not think about that. This paper looks to me as if it *knew* what a vicious influence it had!

There is a recurrent spot where the pattern lolls like a broken neck and two bulbous eyes stare at you upside down.

I get positively angry with the impertinence of it and the everlastingness. Up and down and sideways they crawl, and those absurd, unblinking eyes are every-where. There is one place where two breadths didn't match, and the eyes go all up and down the line, one a little higher than the other.

I never saw so much expression in an inanimate thing before, and we all know how much expression they have! I used to lie awake as a child and get more entertainment and terror out of blank walls and plain furniture than most children could find in a toy-store.

70   I remember what a kindly wink the knobs of our big, old bureau used to have, and there was one chair that always seemed like a strong friend.

I used to feel that if any of the other things looked too fierce I could always hop into that chair and be safe.

The furniture in this room is no worse than inharmonious, however, for we had to bring it all from downstairs. I suppose when this was used as a playroom they had to take the nursery things out, and no wonder! I never saw such ravages as the children have made here.

The wallpaper, as I said before, is torn off in spots, and it sticketh closer than a brother—they must have had perseverance as well as hatred.

Then the floor is scratched and gouged and splintered, the plaster itself is dug out here and there, and this great heavy bed which is all we found in the room, looks as if it had been through the wars.

75   But I don't mind it a bit—only the paper.

There comes John's sister. Such a dear girl as she is, and so careful of me! I must not let her find me writing.

She is a perfect and enthusiastic housekeeper, and hopes for no better profes-sion. I verily believe she thinks it is the writing which made me sick!

But I can write when she is out, and see her a long way off from these windows.

There is one that commands the road, a lovely shaded winding road, and one that just looks off over the country. A lovely country, too, full of great elms and velvet meadows.

This wallpaper has a kind of sub-pattern in a different shade, a particularly irritating one, for you can only see it in certain lights, and not clearly then.

But in the places where it isn't faded and where the sun is just so—I can see a strange, provoking, formless sort of figure, that seems to skulk about behind that silly and conspicuous front design.

There's sister on the stairs!

Well, the Fourth of July is over! The people are all gone and I am tired out. John thought it might do me good to see a little company, so we just had mother and Nellie and the children down for a week.

Of course I didn't do a thing. Jennie sees to everything now.

But it tired me all the same.

John says if I don't pick up faster he shall send me to Weir Mitchell[1] in the fall.

But I don't want to go there at all. I had a friend who was in his hands once, and she says he is just like John and my brother, only more so!

Besides, it is such an undertaking to go so far.

I don't feel as if it was worth while to turn my hand over for anything, and I'm getting dreadfully fretful and querulous.

I cry at nothing, and cry most of the time.

Of course I don't when John is here, or anybody else, but when I am alone.

And I am alone a good deal just now. John is kept in town very often by serious cases, and Jennie is good and lets me alone when I want her to.

So I walk a little in the garden or down that lovely lane, sit on the porch under the roses, and lie down up here a good deal.

I'm getting really fond of the room in spite of the wallpaper. Perhaps *because* of the wallpaper.

It dwells in my mind so!

I lie here on this great immovable bed—it is nailed down, I believe—and follow that pattern about by the hour. It is as good as gymnastics, I assure you. I start, we'll say, at the bottom, down in the corner over there where it has not been touched, and I determine for the thousandth time that I *will* follow that pointless pattern to some sort of conclusion.

I know a little of the principle of design, and I know this thing was not arranged on any laws of radiation, or alternation, or repetition, or symmetry, or anything else that I ever heard of.

It is repeated, of course, by the breadths, but not otherwise.

Looked at in one way each breadth stands alone, the bloated curves and flourishes—a kind of "debased Romanesque" with *delirium tremens*—go waddling up and down in isolated columns of fatuity.

But, on the other hand, they connect diagonally, and the sprawling outlines

---

1. Silas Weir Mitchell (1829–1914), American physician, novelist, and specialist in nerve disorders, popularized the "rest cure."

run off in great slanting waves of optic horror, like a lot of wallowing seaweeds in full chase.

The whole thing goes horizontally, too, at least it seems so, and I exhaust myself in trying to distinguish the order of its going in that direction.

They have used a horizontal breadth for a frieze, and that adds wonderfully to the confusion.

There is one end of the room where it is almost intact, and there, when the crosslights fade and the low sun shines directly upon it, I can almost fancy radiation after all,—the interminable grotesque seem to form around a common center and rush off in headlong plunges of equal distraction.

It makes me tired to follow it. I will take a nap I guess.

105   I don't know why I should write this.

I don't want to.

I don't feel able.

And I know John would think it absurd. But I *must* say what I feel and think in some way—it is such a relief!

But the effort is getting to be greater than the relief.

110   Half the time now I am awfully lazy, and lie down ever so much.

John says I mustn't lose my strength, and has me take cod liver oil and lots of tonics and things, to say nothing of ale and wine and rare meat.

Dear John! He loves me very dearly, and hates to have me sick. I tried to have a real earnest reasonable talk with him the other day, and tell him how I wish he would let me go and make a visit to Cousin Henry and Julia.

But he said I wasn't able to go, nor able to stand it after I got there; and I did not make out a very good case for myself, for I was crying before I had finished.

It is getting to be a great effort for me to think straight. Just this nervous weakness I suppose.

115   And dear John gathered me up in his arms, and just carried me upstairs and laid me on the bed, and sat by me and read to me till it tired my head.

He said I was his darling and his comfort and all he had, and that I must take care of myself for his sake, and keep well.

He says no one but myself can help me out of it, that I must use my will and self-control and not let any silly fancies run away with me.

There's one comfort, the baby is well and happy, and does not have to occupy this nursery with the horrid wallpaper.

If we had not used it, that blessed child would have! What a fortunate escape! Why, I wouldn't have a child of mine, an impressionable little thing, live in such a room for worlds.

120   I never thought of it before, but it is lucky that John kept me here after all, I can stand it so much easier than a baby, you see.

Of course I never mention it to them any more—I am too wise,—but I keep watch of it all the same.

There are things in that paper that nobody knows but me, or ever will.

Behind that outside pattern the dim shapes get clearer every day.

It is always the same shape, only very numerous.

And it is like a woman stooping down and creeping about behind that pat-   125
tern. I don't like it a bit. I wonder—I begin to think—I wish John would take
me away from here!

It is so hard to talk with John about my case, because he is so wise, and
because he loves me so.

But I tried it last night.

It was moonlight. The moon shines in all around just as the sun does.

I hate to see it sometimes, it creeps so slowly, and always comes in by one
window or another.

John was asleep and I hated to waken him, so I kept still and watched the   130
moonlight on that undulating wallpaper till I felt creepy.

The faint figure behind seemed to shake the pattern, just as if she wanted to
get out.

I got up softly and went to feel and see if the paper *did* move, and when I
came back John was awake.

"What is it, little girl?" he said. "Don't go walking about like that—you'll get
cold."

I thought it was a good time to talk, so I told him that I really was not gaining
here, and that I wished he would take me away.

"Why, darling!" said he, "our lease will be up in three weeks, and I can't see   135
how to leave before.

"The repairs are not done at home, and I cannot possibly leave town just
now. Of course if you were in any danger, I could and would, but you really are
better, dear, whether you can see it or not. I am a doctor, dear, and I know.
You are gaining flesh and color, your appetite is better, I feel really much easier
about you."

"I don't weigh a bit more," said I, "nor as much; and my appetite may be
better in the evening when you are here, but it is worse in the morning when
you are away!"

"Bless her little heart!" said he with a big hug, "she shall be as sick as she
pleases! But now let's improve the shining hours by going to sleep, and talk about
it in the morning!"

"And you won't go away?" I asked gloomily.

"Why, how can I, dear? It is only three weeks more and then we will take a   140
nice little trip of a few days while Jennie is getting the house ready. Really dear
you are better!"

"Better in body perhaps—" I began, and stopped short, for he sat up straight
and looked at me with such a stern, reproachful look that I could not say another
word.

"My darling," said he, "I beg of you, for my sake and for our child's sake, as
well as for your own, that you will never for one instant let that idea enter your
mind! There is nothing so dangerous, so fascinating, to a temperament like yours.
It is a false and foolish fancy. Can you not trust me as a physician when I tell
you so?"

So of course I said no more on that score, and we went to sleep before long.

He thought I was asleep first, but I wasn't, and lay there for hours trying to decide whether that front pattern and the back pattern really did move together or separately.

On a pattern like this, by daylight, there is a lack of sequence, a defiance of law, that is a constant irritant to a normal mind.

145 The color is hideous enough, and unreliable enough, and infuriating enough, but the pattern is torturing.

You think you have mastered it, but just as you get well underway in following, it turns a back-somersault and there you are. It slaps you in the face, knocks you down, and tramples upon you. It is like a bad dream.

The outside pattern is a florid arabesque, reminding one of a fungus. If you can imagine a toadstool in joints, an interminable string of toadstools, budding and sprouting in endless convolutions—why, that is something like it.

That is, sometimes!

There is one marked peculiarity about this paper, a thing nobody seems to notice but myself, and that is that it changes as the light changes.

150 When the sun shoots in through the east window—I always watch for that first long, straight ray—it changes so quickly that I never can quite believe it.

That is why I watch it always.

By moonlight—the moon shines in all night when there is a moon—I wouldn't know it was the same paper.

At night in any kind of light, in twilight, candlelight, lamplight, and worst of all by moonlight, it becomes bars! The outside pattern I mean, and the woman behind it is as plain as can be.

I didn't realize for a long time what the thing was that showed behind, that dim sub-pattern, but now I am quite sure it is a woman.

155 By daylight she is subdued, quiet. I fancy it is the pattern that keeps her so still. It is so puzzling. It keeps me quiet by the hour.

I lie down ever so much now. John says it is good for me, and to sleep all I can.

Indeed he started the habit by making me lie down for an hour after each meal.

It is a very bad habit I am convinced, for you see I don't sleep.

And that cultivates deceit, for I don't tell them I'm awake—O no!

160 The fact is I am getting a little afraid of John.

He seems very queer sometimes, and even Jennie has an inexplicable look.

It strikes me occasionally, just as a scientific hypothesis,—that perhaps it is the paper!

I have watched John when he did not know I was looking, and come into the room suddenly on the most innocent excuses, and I've caught him several times *looking at the paper*! And Jennie too. I caught Jennie with her hand on it once.

She didn't know I was in the room, and when I asked her in a quiet, a very quiet voice, with the most restrained manner possible, what she was doing with the paper—she turned around as if she had been caught stealing, and looked quite angry—asked me why I should frighten her so!

Then she said that the paper stained everything it touched, that she had found yellow smooches on all my clothes and John's, and she wished we would be more careful!

Did not that sound innocent? But I know she was studying that pattern, and I am determined that nobody shall find it out but myself!

Life is very much more exciting now than it used to be. You see I have something more to expect, to look forward to, to watch. I really do eat better, and am more quiet than I was.

John is so pleased to see me improve! He laughed a little the other day, and said I seemed to be flourishing in spite of my wallpaper.

I turned it off with a laugh. I had no intention of telling him it was *because* of the wallpaper—he would make fun of me. He might even want to take me away.

I don't want to leave now until I have found it out. There is a week more, and I think that will be enough.

I'm feeling ever so much better! I don't sleep much at night, for it is so interesting to watch developments; but I sleep a good deal in the daytime.

In the daytime it is tiresome and perplexing.

There are always new shoots on the fungus, and new shades of yellow all over it. I cannot keep count of them, though I have tried conscientiously.

It is the strangest yellow, that wallpaper! It makes me think of all the yellow things I ever saw—not beautiful ones like buttercups, but old foul, bad yellow things.

But there is something else about that paper—the smell! I noticed it the moment we came into the room, but with so much air and sun it was not bad. Now we have had a week of fog and rain, and whether the windows are open or not, the smell is here.

It creeps all over the house.

I find it hovering in the dining-room, skulking in the parlor, hiding in the hall, lying in wait for me on the stairs.

It gets into my hair.

Even when I go to ride, if I turn my head suddenly and surprise it—there is that smell!

Such a peculiar odor, too! I have spent hours in trying to analyze it, to find what it smelled like.

It is not bad—at first, and very gentle, but quite the subtlest, most enduring odor I ever met.

In this damp weather it is awful, I wake up in the night and find it hanging over me.

It used to disturb me at first. I thought seriously of burning the house—to reach the smell.

But now I am used to it. The only thing I can think of that it is like is the *color* of the paper! A yellow smell.

185   There is a very funny mark on this wall, low down, near the mopboard. A streak that runs round the room. It goes behind every piece of furniture, except the bed, a long, straight, even *smooch*, as if it had been rubbed over and over.

I wonder how it was done and who did it, and what they did it for. Round and round and round—round and round and round—it makes me dizzy!

I really have discovered something at last.

Through watching so much at night, when it changes so, I have finally found out.

The front pattern *does* move—and no wonder! The woman behind shakes it!

190   Sometimes I think there are a great many women behind, and sometimes only one, and she crawls around fast, and her crawling shakes it all over.

Then in the very bright spots she keeps still, and in the very shady spots she just takes hold of the bars and shakes them hard.

And she is all the time trying to climb through. But nobody could climb through that pattern—it strangles so; I think that is why it has so many heads.

They get through, and then the pattern strangles them off and turns them upside down, and makes their eyes white!

If those heads were covered or taken off it would not be half so bad.

195   I think that woman gets out in the daytime!

And I'll tell you why—privately—I've seen her!

I can see her out of every one of my windows!

It is the same woman, I know, for she is always creeping, and most women do not creep by daylight.

200   I see her in that long shaded lane, creeping up and down. I see her in those dark grape arbors, creeping all around the garden.

I see her on that long road under the trees, creeping along, and when a carriage comes she hides under the blackberry vines.

I don't blame her a bit. It must be very humiliating to be caught creeping by daylight!

I always lock the door when I creep by daylight. I can't do it at night, for I know John would suspect something at once.

And John is so queer now, that I don't want to irritate him. I wish he would take another room! Besides, I don't want anybody to get that woman out at night but myself.

I often wonder if I could see her out of all the windows at once.

205   But, turn as fast as I can, I can only see out of one at one time.

And though I always see her, she *may* be able to creep faster than I can turn!

I have watched her sometimes away off in the open country, creeping as fast as a cloud shadow in a high wind.

If only that top pattern could be gotten off from the under one! I mean to try it, little by little.

I have found out another funny thing, but I shan't tell it this time! It does not do to trust people too much.

There are only two more days to get this paper off, and I believe John is beginning to notice. I don't like the look in his eyes.

And I heard him ask Jennie a lot of professional questions about me. She had a very good report to give.

She said I slept a good deal in the daytime.

John knows I don't sleep very well at night, for all I'm so quiet!

He asked me all sorts of questions, too, and pretended to be very loving and kind.

As if I couldn't see through him!

Still, I don't wonder he acts so, sleeping under this paper for three months.

It only interests me, but I feel sure John and Jennie are secretly affected by it.

Hurrah! This is the last day, but it is enough. John to stay in town over night, and won't be out until this evening.

Jennie wanted to sleep with me—the sly thing! but I told her I should undoubtedly rest better for a night all alone.

That was clever, for really I wasn't alone a bit! As soon as it was moonlight and that poor thing began to crawl and shake the pattern, I got up and ran to help her.

I pulled and she shook, I shook and she pulled, and before morning we had peeled off yards of that paper.

A strip about as high as my head and half around the room.

And then when the sun came and that awful pattern began to laugh at me, I declared I would finish it to-day!

We go away to-morrow, and they are moving all my furniture down again to leave things as they were before.

Jennie looked at the wall in amazement, but I told her merrily that I did it out of pure spite at the vicious thing.

She laughed and said she wouldn't mind doing it herself, but I must not get tired.

How she betrayed herself that time!

But I am here, and no person touches this paper but me,—not *alive*!

She tried to get me out of the room—it was too patent! But I said it was so quiet and empty and clean now that I believed I would lie down again and sleep all I could; and not to wake me even for dinner—I would call when I woke.

So now she is gone, and the servants are gone, and the things are gone, and there is nothing left but that great bedstead nailed down, with the canvas mattress we found on it.

We shall sleep downstairs to-night, and take the boat home to-morrow.

I quite enjoy the room, now it is bare again.

How those children did tear about here!

This bedstead is fairly gnawed!

But I must get to work.

I have locked the door and thrown the key down into the front path.

I don't want to go out, and I don't want to have anybody come in, till John comes.

I want to astonish him.

I've got a rope up here that even Jennie did not find. If that woman does get out, and tries to get away, I can tie her!

But I forgot I could not reach far without anything to stand on!

This bed will *not* move!

I tried to lift and push it until I was lame, and then I got so angry I bit off a little piece at one corner—but it hurt my teeth.

Then I peeled off all the paper I could reach standing on the floor. It sticks horribly and the pattern just enjoys it! All those strangled heads and bulbous eyes and waddling fungus growths just shriek with derision!

I am getting angry enough to do something desperate. To jump out of the window would be admirable exercise, but the bars are too strong even to try.

Besides I wouldn't do it. Of course not. I know well enough that a step like that is improper and might be misconstrued.

I don't like to *look* out of the windows even—there are so many of those creeping women, and they creep so fast.

I wonder if they all come out of that wallpaper as I did?

But I am securely fastened now by my well-hidden rope—you don't get *me* out in the road there!

I suppose I shall have to get back behind the pattern when it comes night, and that is hard!

It is so pleasant to be out in this great room and creep around as I please!

I don't want to go outside. I won't, even if Jennie asks me to.

For outside you have to creep on the ground, and everything is green instead of yellow.

But here I can creep smoothly on the floor, and my shoulder just fits in that long smooch around the wall, so I cannot lose my way.

Why there's John at the door!

It is no use, young man, you can't open it!

How he does call and pound!

Now he's crying for an axe.

It would be a shame to break down that beautiful door!

"John dear!" said I in the gentlest voice, "the key is down by the front steps, under a plantain leaf!"

That silenced him for a few moments.

Then he said—very quietly indeed, "Open the door, my darling!"

"I can't," said I. "The key is down by the front door under a plantain leaf!"

And then I said it again, several times, very gently and slowly, and said it so often that he had to go and see, and he got it of course, and came in. He stopped short by the door.

"What is the matter?" he cried. "For God's sake, what are you doing!"

I kept on creeping just the same, but I looked at him over my shoulder.

"I've got out at last," said I, "in spite of you and Jane? And I've pulled off most of the paper, so you can't put me back!"

Now why should that man have fainted? But he did, and right across my path by the wall, so that I had to creep over him every time!

1892

FRANZ KAFKA

A Hunger Artist[1]

During these last decades the interest in professional fasting has markedly diminished. It used to pay very well to stage such great performances under one's own management, but today that is quite impossible. We live in a different world now. At one time the whole town took a lively interest in the hunger artist; from day to day of his fast the excitement mounted; everybody wanted to see him at least once a day; there were people who bought season tickets for the last few days and sat from morning till night in front of his small barred cage; even in the nighttime there were visiting hours, when the whole effect was heightened by torch flares; on fine days the cage was set out in the open air, and then it was the children's special treat to see the hunger artist; for their elders he was often just a joke that happened to be in fashion, but the children stood open-mouthed, holding each other's hands for greater security, marveling at him as he sat there pallid in black tights, with his ribs sticking out so prominently, not even on a seat but down among straw on the ground, sometimes giving a courteous nod, answering questions with a constrained smile, or perhaps stretching an arm through the bars so that one might feel how thin it was, and then again withdrawing deep into himself, paying no attention to anyone or anything, not even to the all-important striking of the clock that was the only piece of furniture in his cage, but merely staring into vacancy with half shut eyes, now and then taking a sip from a tiny glass of water to moisten his lips.

Besides casual onlookers there were also relays of permanent watchers selected by the public, usually butchers, strangely enough, and it was their task to watch the hunger artist day and night, three of them at a time, in case he should have some secret recourse to nourishment. This was nothing but a formality, instituted to reassure the masses, for the initiates knew well enough that during his fast the artist would never in any circumstances, not even under forcible compulsion, swallow the smallest morsel of food: the honor of his profession forbade it. Not every watcher, of course, was capable of understanding this, there were often groups of night watchers who were very lax in carrying out their duties and deliberately huddled together in a retired corner to play cards with great absorption, obviously intending to give the hunger artist the chance of a little refresh-

1. Translated by Edwin and Willa Muir.

ment, which they supposed he could draw from some private hoard. Nothing annoyed the artist more than such watchers; they made him miserable; they made his fast seem unendurable; sometimes he mastered his feebleness sufficiently to sing during their watch for as long as he could keep going, to show them how unjust their suspicions were. But that was of little use; they only wondered at his cleverness in being able to fill his mouth even while singing. Much more to his taste were the watchers who sat close up to the bars, who were not content with the dim night lighting of the hall but focused him in the full glare of the electric pocket torch given them by the impresario. The harsh light did not trouble him at all, in any case he could never sleep properly, and he could always drowse a little, whatever the light, at any hour, even when the hall was thronged with noisy onlookers. He was quite happy at the prospect of spending a sleepless night with such watchers; he was ready to exchange jokes with them, to tell them stories out of his nomadic life, anything at all to keep them awake and demonstrate to them again that he had no eatables in his cage and that he was fasting as not one of them could fast. But his happiest moment was when the morning came and an enormous breakfast was brought them, at his expense, on which they flung themselves with the keen appetite of healthy men after a weary night of wakefulness. Of course there were people who argued that this breakfast was an unfair attempt to bribe the watchers, but that was going rather too far, and when they were invited to take on a night's vigil without a breakfast, merely for the sake of the cause, they made themselves scarce, although they stuck stubbornly to their suspicions.

Such suspicions, anyhow, were a necessary accompaniment to the profession of fasting. No one could possibly watch the hunger artist continuously, day and night, and so no one could produce first-hand evidence that the fast had really been rigorous and continuous; only the artist himself could know that, he was therefore bound to be the sole completely satisfied spectator of his own fast. Yet for other reasons he was never satisfied; it was not perhaps mere fasting that had brought him to such skeleton thinness that many people had regretfully to keep away from his exhibitions, because the sight of him was too much for them, perhaps it was dissatisfaction with himself that had worn him down. For he alone knew, what no other initiate knew, how easy it was to fast. It was the easiest thing in the world. He made no secret of this, yet people did not believe him, at the best they set him down as modest, most of them, however, thought he was out for publicity or else was some kind of cheat who found it easy to fast because he had discovered a way of making it easy, and then had the impudence to admit the fact, more or less. He had to put up with all that, and in the course of time had got used to it, but his inner dissatisfaction always rankled, and never yet, after any term of fasting—this must be granted to his credit—had he left the cage of his own free will. The longest period of fasting was fixed by his impresario at forty days, beyond that term he was not allowed to go, not even in great cities, and there was good reason for it, too. Experience had proved that for about forty days the interest of the public could be stimulated by a steadily increasing pressure of advertisement, but after that the town began to lose interest, sympathetic support began notably to fall off; there were of course local variations as between one town and another or one country and another, but as a general rule forty days marked the limit. So on the fortieth day the flower-bedecked cage was opened, enthusiastic spectators filled the hall, a military band played, two doctors entered the cage to measure the results of the fast, which were announced through a megaphone, and finally two young ladies appeared, blissful at having been selected for the honor, to help the hunger artist down the few steps leading to a small table on which was spread a carefully chosen invalid repast. And at this very moment the artist always turned stubborn. True, he would entrust his bony arms to the outstretched helping hands of the ladies bending over him, but stand up he would not. Why stop fasting at this particular moment, after forty days of it? He had held out for a long time, an illimitably long time; why stop now, when he was in his best fasting form, or rather, not yet quite in his best fasting form? Why should he be cheated of the fame he would get for fasting longer, for being not only the record hunger artist of all time, which presumably he was already, but for beating his own record by a performance beyond human imagination, since he felt that there were no limits to his capacity for fasting? His public pretended to admire him so much, why should it have so little patience with him; if he could endure fasting longer, why shouldn't the public endure it? Besides, he was tired, he was comfortable sitting in the straw, and now he was supposed to lift himself to his full height and go down to a meal the very thought of which gave him a nausea that only the presence of the ladies kept him from betraying, and even that with an effort. And he looked up into the eyes of the ladies who were apparently so friendly and in reality so cruel, and shook his head, which felt too heavy on its strengthless neck. But then there happened yet again what always happened. The impresario came forward, without a word— for the band made speech impossible—lifted his arms in the air above the artist, as if inviting Heaven to look down upon its creature here in the straw, this suffering martyr, which indeed he was, although in quite another sense; grasped him round the emaciated waist, with exaggerated caution, so that the frail condition he was in might be appreciated; and committed him to the care of the blenching ladies, not without secretly giving him a shaking so that his legs and body tottered and swayed. The artist now submitted completely; his head lolled on his breast as if it had landed there by chance; his body was hollowed out; his legs in a spasm of self-preservation clung close to each other at the knees, yet scraped on the ground as if it were not really solid ground, as if they were only trying to find solid ground; and the whole weight of his body, a feather-weight after all, relapsed onto one of the ladies, who, looking round for help and panting a little—this post of honor was not at all what she had expected it to be— first stretched her neck as far as she could to keep her face at least free from contact with the artist, when finding this impossible, and her more fortunate companion not coming to her aid but merely holding extended on her own trembling hand the little bunch of knucklebones that was the artist's, to the great delight of the spectators burst into tears and had to be replaced by an attendant who had long been stationed in readiness. Then came the food, a little of which the impresario managed to get between the artist's lips, while he sat in a kind of half-fainting trance, to the accompaniment of cheerful patter designed to distract the public's attention from the artist's condition; after that, a toast was drunk to the public, supposedly prompted by a whisper from the artist in the impresario's ear; the band confirmed it with a mighty flourish, the spectators melted away, and no one had any cause to be dissatisfied with the proceedings, no one except the hunger artist himself, he only, as always.

So he lived for many years, with small regular intervals of recuperation, in visible glory, honored by the world, yet in spite of that troubled in spirit, and all the more troubled because no one would take his trouble seriously. What comfort could he possibly need? What more could he possibly wish for? And if some good-natured person, feeling sorry for him, tried to console him by pointing out that his melancholy was probably caused by fasting, it could happen, especially when he had been fasting for some time, that he reacted with an outburst of fury and to the general alarm began to shake the bars of his cage like a wild animal. Yet the impresario had a way of punishing these outbreaks which he rather enjoyed putting into operation. He would apologize publicly for the artist's behavior, which was only to be excused, he admitted, because of the irritability caused by fasting; a condition hardly to be understood by well-fed people; then by natural transition he went on to mention the artist's equally incomprehensible boast that he could fast for much longer than he was doing; he praised the high ambition, the good will, the great self-denial undoubtedly implicit in such a statement; and then quite simply countered it by bringing out photographs, which were also on sale to the public, showing the artist on the fortieth day of a fast lying in bed almost dead from exhaustion. This perversion of the truth, familiar to the artist though it was, always unnerved him afresh and proved too much for him. What was a consequence of the premature ending of his fast was here presented as the cause of it! To fight against this lack of understanding, against a whole world of non-understanding, was impossible. Time and again in good faith he stood by the bars listening to the impresario, but as soon as the photographs appeared he always let go and sank with a groan back on to his straw, and the reassured public could once more come close and gaze at him.

5   A few years later when the witnesses of such scenes called them to mind, they often failed to understand themselves at all. For meanwhile the aforementioned change in public interest had set in; it seemed to happen almost overnight; there may have been profound causes for it, but who was going to bother about that; at any rate the pampered hunger artist suddenly found himself deserted one fine day by the amusement seekers, who went streaming past him to other more favored attractions. For the last time the impresario hurried him over half Europe to discover whether the old interest might still survive here and there; all in vain; everywhere, as if by secret agreement, a positive revulsion from professional fasting was in evidence. Of course it could not really have sprung up so suddenly as all that, and many premonitory symptoms which had not been sufficiently remarked or suppressed during the rush and glitter of success now came retrospectively to mind, but it was now too late to take any countermeasures. Fasting would surely come into fashion again at some future date, yet that was no comfort for those living in the present. What, then, was the hunger artist to do? He had been applauded by thousands in his time and could hardly come down to

showing himself in a street booth at village fairs, and as for adopting another profession, he was not only too old for that but too fanatically devoted to fasting. So he took leave of the impresario, his partner in an unparalleled career, and hired himself to a large circus; in order to spare his own feelings he avoided reading the conditions of his contract.

A large circus with its enormous traffic in replacing and recruiting men, animals and apparatus can always find a use for people at any time, even for a hunger artist, provided of course that he does not ask too much, and in this particular case anyhow it was not only the artist who was taken on but his famous and long-known name as well, indeed considering the peculiar nature of his performance, which was not impaired by advancing age, it could not be objected that here was an artist past his prime, no longer at the height of his professional skill, seeking a refuge in some quiet corner of a circus; on the contrary, the hunger artist averred that he could fast as well as ever, which was entirely credible, he even alleged that if he were allowed to fast as he liked, and this was at once promised him without more ado, he could astound the world by establishing a record never yet achieved, a statement which certainly provoked a smile among the other professionals, since it left out of account the change in public opinion, which the hunger artist in his zeal conveniently forgot.

He had not, however, actually lost his sense of the real situation and took it as a matter of course that he and his cage should be stationed, not in the middle of the ring as a main attraction, but outside, near the animal cages, on a site that was after all easily accessible. Large and gaily painted placards made a frame for the cage and announced what was to be seen inside it. When the public came thronging out in the intervals to see the animals, they could hardly avoid passing the hunger artist's cage and stopping there for a moment, perhaps they might even have stayed longer had not those pressing behind them in the narrow gangway, who did not understand why they should be held up on their way toward the excitements of the menagerie, made it impossible for anyone to stand gazing quietly for any length of time. And that was the reason why the hunger artist, who had of course been looking forward to these visiting hours as the main achievement of his life, began instead to shrink from them. At first he could hardly wait for the intervals; it was exhilarating to watch the crowds come streaming his way, until only too soon—not even the most obstinate self-deception, clung to almost consciously, could hold out against the fact—the conviction was borne in upon him that these people, most of them, to judge from their actions, again and again, without exception, were all on their way to the menagerie. And the first sight of them from the distance remained the best. For when they reached his cage he was at once deafened by the storm of shouting and abuse that arose from the two contending factions, which renewed themselves continuously, of those who wanted to stop and stare at him—he soon began to dislike them more than the others—not out of real interest but only out of obstinate self-assertiveness, and those who wanted to go straight on to the animals. When the first great rush was past, the stragglers came along, and these, whom nothing could have prevented from stopping to look at him as long as they had breath, raced past with long strides, hardly even glancing at him, in their haste to get to the menagerie in time. And all too rarely did it happen that he had a stroke of luck, when some father of a family fetched up before him with his children, pointed a finger at the hunger artist and explained at length what the phenomenon meant, telling stories of earlier years when he himself had watched similar but much more thrilling performances, and the children, still rather uncomprehending, since neither inside nor outside school had they been sufficiently prepared for this lesson—what did they care about fasting?—yet showed by the brightness of their intent eyes that new and better times might be coming. Perhaps, said the hunger artist to himself many a time, things would be a little better if his cage were set not quite so near the menagerie. That made it too easy for people to make their choice, to say nothing of what he suffered from the stench of the menagerie, the animals' restlessness by night, the carrying past of raw lumps of flesh for the beasts of prey, the roaring at feeding times, which depressed him continually. But he did not dare to lodge a complaint with the management; after all, he had the animals to thank for the troops of people who passed his cage, among whom there might always be one here and there to take an interest in him, and who could tell where they might seclude him if he called attention to his existence and thereby to the fact that, strictly speaking, he was only an impediment on the way to the menagerie.

A small impediment, to be sure, one that grew steadily less. People grew familiar with the strange idea that they could be expected, in times like these, to take an interest in a hunger artist, and with this familiarity the verdict went out against him. He might fast as much as he could, and he did so; but nothing could save him now, people passed him by. Just try to explain to anyone the art of fasting! Anyone who has no feeling for it cannot be made to understand it. The fine placards grew dirty and illegible, they were torn down; the little notice board telling the number of fast days achieved, which at first was changed carefully every day, had long stayed at the same figure, for after the first few weeks even this small task seemed pointless to the staff; and so the artist simply fasted on and on, as he had once dreamed of doing, and it was no trouble to him, just as he had always foretold, but no one counted the days, no one, not even the artist himself, knew what records he was already breaking, and his heart grew heavy. And when once in a time some leisurely passer-by stopped, made merry over the old figure on the board and spoke of swindling, that was in its way the stupidest lie ever invented by indifference and inborn malice, since it was not the hunger artist who was cheating; he was working honestly, but the world was cheating him of his reward.

Many more days went by, however, and that too came to an end. An over-seer's eye fell on the cage one day and he asked the attendants why this perfectly good cage should be left standing there unused with dirty straw inside it; nobody knew, until one man, helped out by the notice board, remembered about the hunger artist. They poked into the straw with sticks and found him in it. "Are you still fasting?" asked the overseer. "When on earth do you mean to stop?" "Forgive me, everybody," whispered the hunger artist; only the overseer, who had his ear to the bars, understood him. "Of course," said the overseer, and tapped his forehead with a finger to let the attendants know what state the man was in, "we forgive you." "I always wanted you to admire my fasting," said the hunger artist. "We do admire it," said the overseer, affably. "But you shouldn't admire it," said the hunger artist. "Well, then we don't admire it," said the overseer, "but why shouldn't we admire it?" "Because I have to fast, I can't help it," said the hunger artist. "What a fellow you are," said the overseer, "and why can't you help it?" "Because," said the hunger artist, lifting his head a little and speaking, with his lips pursed, as if for a kiss, right into the overseer's ear, so that no syllable might be lost, "because I couldn't find the food I liked. If I had found it, believe me, I should have made no fuss and stuffed myself like you or anyone else." These were his last words, but in his dimming eyes remained the firm though no longer proud persuasion that he was still continuing to fast.

"Well, clear this out now!" said the overseer, and they buried the hunger artist, straw and all. Into the cage they put a young panther. Even the most insensitive felt it refreshing to see this wild creature leaping around the cage that had so long been dreary. The panther was all right. The food he liked was brought him without hesitation by the attendants; he seemed not even to miss his freedom; his noble body, furnished almost to the bursting point with all that it needed, seemed to carry freedom around with it too; somewhere in his jaws it seemed to lurk; and the joy of life streamed with such ardent passion from his throat that for the onlookers it was not easy to stand the shock of it. But they braced themselves, crowded round the cage, and did not want ever to move away.

1924

KATHERINE ANNE PORTER

The Fig Tree

Old Aunt Nannie had a habit of gripping with her knees to hold Miranda while she brushed her hair or buttoned her dress down the back. When Miranda wriggled, Aunt Nannie squeezed still harder, and Miranda wriggled more, but never enough to get away. Aunt Nannie gathered up Miranda's scalp lock firmly, snapped a rubber band around it, jammed a freshly starched white chambray bonnet over her ears and forehead, fastened the crown to the lock with a large safety pin, and said: "Got to hold you still someways. Here now, don't you take this off your head till the sun go down."

"I didn't want a bonnet, it's too hot, I wanted a hat," said Miranda.

"You not goin' to get a hat, you goin' to get just what you got," said Aunt Nannie in the bossy voice she used for washing and dressing time, "and mo'over some of these days I'm going' to *sew* this bonnet to your topknot. Your daddy says if you get freckles he blame me. Now, you're all ready to set out."

"Where are we going, Aunty?" Miranda could never find out about anything until the last minute. She was always being surprised. Once she went to sleep in her bed with her kitten curled on the pillow purring, and woke up in a stuffy tight bed in a train, hugging a hot-water bottle; and there was Grandmother stretched out beside her in her McLeod tartan dressing-gown, her eyes wide open. Miranda thought something wonderful had happened. "My goodness, Grandmother, where are we going?" And it was only for another trip to El Paso to see Uncle Bill.

Now Tom and Dick were hitched to the carry-all standing outside the gate with boxes and baskets tied on everywhere. Grandmother was walking alone through the house very slowly, taking a last look at everything. Now and then she put something else in the big leather portmoney on her arm until it was pretty bulgy. She carried a long black mohair skirt on her other arm, the one she put on over her other skirt when she rode horseback. Her son Harry, Miranda's father, followed her saying: "I can't see the sense in rushing off to Halifax on five minutes' notice."

Grandmother said, walking on: "It's five hours exactly." Halifax wasn't the name of Grandmother's farm at all, it was Cedar Grove, but Father always called it Halifax. "Hot as Halifax," he would say when he wanted to describe something very hot. Cedar Grove was very hot, but they went there every summer because Grandmother loved it. "I went to Cedar Grove for fifty summers before you were born," she told Miranda, who remembered last summer very well, and the summer before a little. Miranda liked it for watermelons and grasshoppers and the long rows of blooming chinaberry trees where the hounds flattened themselves out and slept. They whined and winked their eyelids and worked their feet and barked faintly in their sleep, and Uncle Jimbilly said it was because dogs always dreamed they were chasing something. In the middle of the day when Miranda looked down over the thick green fields towards the spring she could simply see it being hot: everything blue and sleepy and the mourning doves calling.

"Are we going to Halifax, Aunty?"

"Now just ask your dad if you wanta know so much."

"Are we going to Halifax, Dad?"

Her father twitched her bonnet straight and pulled her hair forward so it would show. "You mustn't get sunburned. No, let it alone. Show the pretty curls. You'll be wading in Whirlypool before supper this evening."

Grandmother said, "Don't say Halifax, child, say Cedar Grove. Call things by their right names."

"Yes, ma'am," said Miranda. Grandmother said again, to her son, "It's five hours, exactly, and your Aunt Eliza has had plenty of time to pack up her telescope, and take my saddle horse. She's been there three hours by now. I imagine she's got the telescope already set up on the hen-house roof. I hope nothing happens."

"You worry too much, Mammy," said her son, trying to conceal his impatience.

"I am not worrying," said Grandmother, shifting her riding skirt to the arm carrying the portmoney. "It will scarcely be any good taking this," she said; "I might in fact as well throw it away for this summer."

"Never mind, Mammy, we'll send to the Black Farm for Pompey, he's a good easy saddler."

"You may ride him yourself," said Grandmother. "I'll never mount Pompey while Fiddler is alive. Fiddler is my horse, and I hate having his mouth spoiled by a careless rider. Eliza never could ride, and she never will. . . ."

Miranda gave a little skip and ran away. So they were going to Cedar Grove. Miranda never got over being surprised at the way grown-up people simply did not seem able to give anyone a straight answer to any question, unless the answer was "No." Then it popped out with no trouble at all. At a little distance, she heard her grandmother say, "Harry, have you seen my riding crop lately?" and her father answered, at least maybe he thought it was an answer, "Now, Mammy, for God's sake let's get this thing over with." That was it, exactly.

Another strange way her father had of talking was calling Grandmother "Mammy." Aunt Jane was Mammy. Sometimes he called Grandmother "Mama," but she wasn't Mama either, she was really Grandmother. Mama was dead. Dead meant gone away forever. Dying was something that happened all the time, to people and everything else. Somebody died, and there was a long string of carriages going at a slow walk over the rocky ridge of the hill towards the river while the bell tolled and tolled, and that person was never seen again by any-body. Kittens and chickens and specially little turkeys died much oftener, and sometimes calves, but hardly ever cows or horses. Lizards on rocks turned into shells, with no lizard inside at all. If caterpillars all curled up and furry didn't move when you poked them with a stick, that meant they were dead—it was a sure sign.

When Miranda found any creature that didn't move or make a noise, or looked somehow different from the live ones, she always buried it in a little grave with flowers on top and a smooth stone at the head. Even grasshoppers. Every-thing dead had to be treated this way. "This way and no other!" Grandmother always said when she was laying down the law about all kinds of things. "It must be done *this* way, and no other!"

Miranda went down the crooked flat-stone walk hopping zigzag between the grass tufts. First there were pomegranate and cape jessamine bushes mixed together; then it got very dark and shady and that was the fig grove. She went to her favorite fig tree where the deep branches bowed down level with her chin, and she could gather figs without having to climb and skin her knees. Grandmother hadn't remembered to take any figs to the country the last time, she said there were plenty of them at Cedar Grove. But the ones at Cedar Grove were big soft greenish white ones, and these at home were black and sugary. It was strange that Grandmother did not seem to notice the difference. The air was sweet among the fig trees, and chickens were always getting out of the run and rushing there to eat the figs off the ground. One mother hen was scurrying around scratching and clucking. She would scratch around a fig lying there in plain sight and cluck to her children as if it was a worm and she had dug it up for them.

"Old smarty," said Miranda, "you're just pretending."

When the little chickens all ran to their mother under Miranda's fig tree, one little chicken did not move. He was spread out on his side with his eyes shut and his mouth open. He was yellow fur in spots and pinfeathers in spots, and

20

the rest of him was naked and sunburned. "Lazy," said Miranda, poking him with her toe. Then she saw that he was dead.

Oh, and in no time at all they'd be setting out for Halifax. Grandmother never went away, she always set out for somewhere. She'd have to hurry like anything to get him buried properly. Back into the house she went on tiptoe hoping not to be seen, for Grandmother always asked: "Where are you going, child? What are you doing? What is that you're carrying? Where did you get it? Who gave you permission?" and after Miranda had explained all that, even if there turned out not to be anything wrong in it, nothing ever seemed so nice any more. Besides it took forever to get away.

Miranda slid open her bureau drawer, third down, left-hand side where her new shoes were still wrapped in tissue paper in a nice white box the right size for a chicken with pinfeathers. She pushed the rustling white folded things and the lavender bags out of the way and trembled a little. Down in front the carry-all wheels screeched and crunched on the gravel, with Old Uncle Jimbilly yelling like a foghorn, "Hiyi, thar, back up, you steeds! Back up thar, you!" and of course, that meant he was turning Tom and Dick around so they would be pointing towards Halifax. They'd be after her, calling and hurrying her, and she wouldn't have time for anything and they wouldn't listen to a word.

25   It wasn't hard work digging a hole with her little spade in the loose dry soil. Miranda wrapped the slimpsy chicken in tissue paper, trying to make it look pretty, laid it in the box carefully, and covered it up with a nice mound, just like people's. She had hardly got it piled up grave shape, kneeling and leaning to smooth it over, when a strange sound came from somewhere, a very sad little crying sound. It said Weep, weep, weep, three times like that slowly, and it seemed to come from the mound of dirt. "My goodness," Miranda asked herself aloud, "what's that?" She pushed her bonnet off her ears and listened hard. "Weep, weep," said the tiny sad voice. And People began calling and urging her, their voices coming nearer. She began to clamor, too.

"Yes, Aunty, wait a minute, Aunty!"

"You come right on here this minute, we're goin'!"

"You *have* to wait, Aunty!"

Her father was coming along the edge of the fig trees. "Hurry up, Baby, you'll get left!"

30   Miranda felt she couldn't bear to be left. She ran all shaking with fright. Her father gave her the annoyed look he always gave her when he said something to upset her and then saw that she was upset. His words were kind but his voice scolded: "Stop getting so excited, Baby, you know we wouldn't leave you for anything." Miranda wanted to talk back: 'Then why did you say so?' but she was still listening for that tiny sound: "Weep, weep." She lagged and pulled backward, looking over her shoulder. but her father hurried her towards the carry-all. But things didn't make sounds if they were dead. They couldn't. That was one of the signs. Oh, but she had heard it.

Her father sat in front and drove, and old Uncle Jimbilly didn't do anything but get down and open gates. Grandmother and Aunt Nannie sat in the back seat, with Miranda between them. She loved setting out somewhere, with everybody smiling and settling down and looking up at the weather, with the horses bouncing and pulling on the reins, the springs jolting and swaying with a creaky noise that made you feel sure you were traveling. That evening she would go wading with Maria and Paul and Uncle Jimbilly, and that very night she would lie out on the grass in her nightgown to cool off, and they would all drink lemonade before going to bed. Sister Maria and Brother Paul would already be burned like muffins because they were sent on ahead the minute school was out. Sister Maria had got freckled and Father was furious. "Keep your bonnet on," he said to Miranda, sternly. "Now remember. I'm not going to have that face ruined, too." But oh, what had made that funny sound? Miranda's ears buzzed and she had a dull round pain in her just under her front ribs. She had to go back and let him out. He'd never get out by himself, all tangled up in tissue paper and that shoebox. He'd never get out without her.

"Grandmother, I've got to go back. Oh, I've *got* to go back!"

Grandmother turned Miranda's face around by the chin and looked at her closely, the way grown folks did. Grandmother's eyes were always the same. They never looked kind or sad or angry or tired or anything. They just looked, blue and still. "What is the matter with you, Miranda, what happened?"

"Oh, I've got to go back—I forg-got something important."

"Stop that silly crying and tell me what you want."   35

Miranda couldn't stop. Her father looked very anxious. "Mammy, maybe the Baby's sick." He reached out his handkerchief to her face. "What's the matter with my honey? Did you eat something?"

Miranda had to stand up to cry as hard as she wanted to. The wheels went grinding round in the road, the carry-all wobbled so that Grandmother had to take her by one arm, and her father by the other. They stared at each other over Miranda's head with a moveless gaze that Miranda had seen often, and their eyes looked exactly alike. Miranda blinked up at them, waiting to see who would win. Then Grandmother's hand fell away, and Miranda was handed over to her father. He gave the reins to Uncle Jimbilly, and lifted her over the top of the seat. She sprawled against his chest and knees as if he were an armchair and stopped crying at once. "We can't go back just for notions," he told her in the reasoning tone he always talked in when Grandmother scolded, and held the muffly handkerchief for her. "Now, blow hard. What did you forget, honey? We'll find another. Was it your doll?"

Miranda hated dolls. She never played with them. She always pulled the wigs off and tied them on the kittens, like hats. The kittens pulled them off instantly. It was fun. She put the doll clothes on the kittens and it took any one of them just half a minute to get them all off again. Kittens had sense. Miranda wailed suddenly, "Oh, I want my doll!" and cried again, trying to drown out the strange little sound, "Weep, weep"—

"Well now, if that's all," said her father comfortably, "there's a raft of dolls at Cedar Grove, and about forty fresh kittens. How'd you like that?"

"Forty?" asked Miranda.   40

"About," said Father.

Old Aunt Nannie leaned and held out her hand. "Look, honey, I toted you some nice black figs."

Her face was wrinkled and black and it looked like a fig upside down with a white ruffled cap. Miranda clenched her eyes tight and shook her head.

"Is that a pretty way to behave when Aunt Nannie offers you something nice?" asked Grandmother in her gentle reminding tone of voice.

45   "No, ma'am," said Miranda meekly. "Thank you, Aunt Nannie." But she did not accept the figs.

Great-Aunt Eliza, half way up a stepladder pitched against the flat-roofed chicken house, was telling Hinry just how to set up her telescope. "For a fellow who never saw or heard of a telescope," Great-Aunt Eliza said to Grandmother, who was really her sister Sophia Jane, "he doesn't do so badly so long as I tell him."

"I do wish you'd stop clambering up stepladders, Eliza," said Grandmother, "at your time of life."

"You're nothing but a nervous wreck, Sophia, I declare. When did you ever know me to get hurt?"

"Even so," said Grandmother tartly, "there is such a thing as appropriate behavior at our time of . . . ."

50   Great-Aunt Eliza seized a fold of her heavy brown pleated skirt with one hand, with the other she grasped the ladder one rung higher and ascended another step. "Now Hinry," she called, "just swing it around facing west and leave it level. I'll fix it the way I want when I'm ready. You can come on down now." She came down then herself, and said to her sister: "So long as you can go bouncing off on that horse of yours, Sophia Jane, I s'pose I can climb ladders. I'm three years younger than you, and *at your time of life* that makes all the difference!"

Grandmother turned pink as the inside of a seashell, the one on her sewing table that had the sound of the sea in it; Miranda knew that she had always been the pretty one, and she was pretty still, but Great-Aunt Eliza was not pretty now and never had been. Miranda, watching and listening—for everything in the world was strange to her and something she had to know about—saw two old women, who were proud of being grandmothers, who spoke to children always as if they knew best about everything and children knew nothing, and they told children all day long to come here, go there, do this, do not do that, and they were always right and children never were except when they did anything they were told right away without a word. And here they were bickering like two little girls at school, or even the way Miranda and her sister Maria bickered and nagged and picked on each other and said things on purpose to hurt each other's feelings. Miranda felt sad and strange and a little frightened. She began edging away.

"Where are you going, Miranda?" asked Grandmother in her everyday voice.

"Just to the house," said Miranda, her heart sinking.

"Wait and walk with us," said Grandmother. She was very thin and pale and had white hair. Beside her, Great-Aunt Eliza loomed like a mountain with her grizzled iron-colored hair like a curly wig, her steel-rimmed spectacles over her snuff-colored eyes, and snuff-colored woollen skirts billowing about her, and her smell of snuff. When she came through the door she quite filled it up. When she sat down the chair disappeared under her, and she seemed to be sitting solidly on herself from her waistband to the floor.

Now with Grandmother sitting across the room rummaging in her work basket and pretending not to see anything, Great-Aunt Eliza took a small brown bottle out of her pocket, opened it, took a pinch of snuff in each nostril, sneezed loudly, wiped her nose with a big white starchy-looking handkerchief, pushed her spectacles up on her forehead, took a little twig chewed into a brush at one end, dipped and twisted it around in the little bottle, and placed it firmly between her teeth. Miranda had heard of this shameful habit in women of the lower classes, but no lady had been known to "dip snuff," and surely not in the family. Yet here was Great-Aunt Eliza, a lady even if not a very pretty one, dipping snuff. Miranda knew how her grandmother felt about it; she stared fascinated at Great-Aunt Eliza until her eyes watered. Great-Aunt Eliza stared back in turn.

"Look here, young one, d'ye s'pose if I gave you a gumdrop you'd get out from underfoot?"

She reached in the other pocket and took out a roundish, rather crushed-looking pink gumdrop with the sugar coating pretty badly crackled. "Now take this, and don't let me lay eyes on you any more today."

Miranda hurried away, clenching the gumdrop in her palm. When she reached the kitchen it was oozing through her fingers. She went to the tap and held her hand under the water and tried to wash off the snuffy smell. After this crime she did not really dare go near Great-Aunt Eliza again soon. "What did you do with that gumdrop so quickly, child?" she could almost hear her asking.

Yet Miranda almost forgot her usual interests, such as kittens and other little animals on the place, pigs, chickens, rabbits, anything at all so it was a baby and would let her pet and feed it, for Great-Aunt Eliza's ways and habits kept Miranda following her about, gazing, or sitting across the dining-table, gazing, for when Great-Aunt Eliza was not on the roof before her telescope, always just before daylight or just after dark, she was walking about with a microscope and a burning glass, peering closely at something she saw on a tree trunk, something she found in the grass; now and then she collected fragments that looked like dried leaves or bits of bark, brought them in the house, spread them out on a sheet of white paper, and sat there, poring, as still as if she were saying her prayers. At table she would dissect a scrap of potato peeling or anything else she might be eating, and sit there, bowed over, saying, "Hum," from time to time. Grandmother, who did not allow the children to bring anything to the table to play with and who forbade them to do anything but eat while they were there, ignored her sister's manners as long as she could, then remarked one day, when Great-Aunt Eliza was humming like a bee to herself over what her microscope had found in a raisin, "Eliza, if it is interesting save it for me to look at after dinner. Or tell me what it is."

"You wouldn't know if I told you," said Great-Aunt Eliza, coolly, putting her microscope away and finishing off her pudding.

When at last, just before they were all going back to town again, Great-Aunt

Eliza invited the children to climb the ladder with her and see the stars through her telescope, they were so awed they looked at each other like strangers, and did not exchange a word. Miranda saw only a great pale flaring disk of cold light, but she knew it was the moon and called out in pure rapture, "Oh, it's like another world!"

"Why, of course, child," said Great-Aunt Eliza, in her growling voice, but kindly, "other worlds, a million other worlds."

"Like this one?" asked Miranda, timidly.

"Nobody knows, child. . . ."

65   "Nobody knows, nobody knows," Miranda sang to a tune in her head, and when the others walked on, she was so dazzled with joy she fell back by herself, walking a little distance behind Great-Aunt Eliza's swinging lantern and her wide-swinging skirts. They took the dewy path through the fig grove, much like the one in town, with the early dew bringing out the sweet smell of the milky leaves. They passed a fig tree with low hanging branches, and Miranda reached up by habit and touched it with her fingers for luck. From the earth beneath her feet came a terrible, faint troubled sound. "Weep weep, weep weep . . ." murmured a little crying voice from the smothering earth, the grave.

Miranda bounded like a startled pony against the back of Great-Aunt Eliza's knees, crying out, 'Oh, oh, oh, wait . . ."

"What on earth's the matter, child?"

Miranda seized the warm snuffly hand held out to her and hung on hard. "Oh, there's something saying 'weep weep' out of the ground!"

Great-Aunt Eliza stooped, put her arm around Miranda and listened carefully, for a moment. "Hear them?" she said. "They're not in the ground at all. They are the first tree frogs, means it's going to rain," she said, "weep weep— hear them?"

70   Miranda took a deep trembling breath and heard them. They were in the trees. They walked on again, Miranda holding Great-Aunt Eliza's hand.

"Just think," said Great-Aunt Eliza, in her most scientific voice, "when tree frogs shed their skins, they pull them off over their heads like little shirts, and they eat them. Can you imagine? They have the prettiest little shapes you ever saw—I'll show you one some time under the microscope."

"Thank you, ma'am," Miranda remembered finally to say through her fog of bliss at hearing the tree frogs sing, "Weep weep . . ."

1944

ERNEST HEMINGWAY

A Clean, Well-Lighted Place

It was late and every one had left the café except an old man who sat in the shadow the leaves of the tree made against the electric light. In the day time the street was dusty, but at night the dew settled the dust and the old man liked to

sit late because he was deaf and now at night it was quiet and he felt the difference. The two waiters inside the café knew that the old man was a little drunk,
and while he was a good client they knew that if he became too drunk he would
leave without paying, so they kept watch on him.

"Last week he tried to commit suicide," one waiter said.

"Why?"

"He was in despair."

"What about?"

"Nothing."

"How do you know it was nothing?"

"He has plenty of money."

They sat together at a table that was close against the wall near the door of
the café and looked at the terrace where the tables were all empty except where
the old man sat in the shadow of the leaves of the tree that moved slightly in the
wind. A girl and a soldier went by in the street. The street light shone on the
brass number on his collar. The girl wore no head covering and hurried beside
him.

"The guard will pick him up," one waiter said.

"What does it matter if he gets what he's after?"

"He had better get off the street now. The guard will get him. They went by
five minutes ago."

The old man sitting in the shadow rapped on his saucer with his glass. The
younger waiter went over to him.

"What do you want?"

The old man looked at him. "Another brandy," he said.

"You'll be drunk," the waiter said. The old man looked at him. The waiter
went away.

"He'll stay all night," he said to his colleague. "I'm sleepy now. I never get
into bed before three o'clock. He should have killed himself last week."

The waiter took the brandy bottle and another saucer from the counter inside
the café and marched out to the old man's table. He put down the saucer and
poured the glass full of brandy.

"You should have killed yourself last week," he said to the deaf man. The
old man motioned with his finger. "A little more," he said. The waiter poured
on into the glass so that the brandy slopped over and ran down the stem into the
top saucer of the pile. "Thank you," the old man said. The waiter took the bottle
back inside the café. He sat down at the table with his colleague again.

"He's drunk now," he said.

"He's drunk every night."

"What did he want to kill himself for?"

"How should I know."

"How did he do it?"

"He hung himself with a rope."

"Who cut him down?"

"His niece."

"Why did they do it?"

"Fear for his soul."

"How much money has he got?"

"He's got plenty."

"He must be eighty years old."

"Anyway I should say he was eighty."

"I wish he would go home. I never get to bed before three o'clock. What kind of hour is that to go to bed?"

"He stays up because he likes it."

"He's lonely. I'm not lonely. I have a wife waiting in bed for me."

"He had a wife once too."

"A wife would be no good to him now."

"You can't tell. He might be better with a wife."

"His niece looks after him. You said she cut him down."

"I know."

"I wouldn't want to be that old. An old man is a nasty thing."

"Not always. This old man is clean. He drinks without spilling. Even now, drunk. Look at him."

"I don't want to look at him. I wish he would go home. He has no regard for those who must work."

The old man looked from his glass across the square, then over at the waiters.

"Another brandy," he said, pointing to his glass. The waiter who was in a hurry came over.

"Finished," he said, speaking with that omission of syntax stupid people employ when talking to drunken people or foreigners. "No more tonight. Close now."

"Another," said the old man.

"No. Finished." The waiter wiped the edge of the table with a towel and shook his head.

The old man stood up, slowly counted the saucers, took a leather coin purse from his pocket and paid for the drinks, leaving half a peseta tip.

The waiter watched him go down the street, a very old man walking unsteadily but with dignity.

"Why didn't you let him stay and drink?" the unhurried waiter asked. They were putting up the shutters. "It is not half-past two."

"I want to go home to bed."

"What is an hour?"

"More to me than to him."

"An hour is the same."

"You talk like an old man yourself. He can buy a bottle and drink at home."

"It's not the same."

"No, it is not," agreed the waiter with a wife. He did not wish to be unjust. He was only in a hurry.

"And you? You have no fear of going home before your usual hour?"

"Are you trying to insult me?"

"No, hombre, only to make a joke."

"No," the waiter who was in a hurry said, rising from pulling down the metal shutters. "I have confidence. I am all confidence."

"You have youth, confidence, and a job," the older waiter said. "You have everything."

"And what do you lack?"

"Everything but work."

"You have everything I have."

"No. I have never had confidence and I am not young."

"Come on. Stop talking nonsense and lock up."

"I am of those who like to stay late at the café," the older waiter said. "With all those who do not want to go to bed. With all those who need a light for the night."

"I want to go home and into bed."

"We are of two different kinds," the older waiter said. He was now dressed to go home. "It is not only a question of youth and confidence although those things are very beautiful. Each night I am reluctant to close up because there may be some one who needs the café."

"Hombre, there are bodegas open all night long."

"You do not understand. This is a clean and pleasant café. It is well lighted. The light is very good and also, now, there are shadows of the leaves."

"Good night," said the younger waiter.

"Good night," the other said. Turning off the electric light he continued the conversation with himself. It is the light of course but it is necessary that the place be clean and pleasant. You do not want music. Certainly you do not want music. Nor can you stand before a bar with dignity although that is all that is provided for these hours. What did he fear? It was not fear or dread. It was a nothing that he knew too well. It was all a nothing and a man was nothing too. It was only that and light was all it needed and a certain cleanness and order. Some lived in it and never felt it but he knew it all was nada y pues nada[1] y nada y pues nada. Our nada who art in nada, nada be thy name thy kingdom nada thy will be nada in nada as it is in nada. Give us this nada our daily nada and nada us our nada as we nada our nadas and nada us not into nada but deliver us from nada; pues nada. Hail nothing full of nothing, nothing is with thee. He smiled and stood before a bar with a shining steam pressure coffee machine.

"What's yours?" asked the barman.

"Nada."

"Otro loco mas,"[2] said the barman and turned away.

"A little cup," said the waiter.

The barman poured it for him.

"The light is very bright and pleasant but the bar is unpolished," the waiter said.

The barman looked at him but did not answer. It was too late at night for conversation.

"You want another copita?" the barman asked.

"No, thank you," said the waiter and went out. He disliked bars and bodegas. A clean, well-lighted café was a very different thing. Now, without thinking

---

1. Nothing and then nothing.   2. One more nutcase.

further, he would go home to his room. He would lie in bed and finally, with daylight, he would go to sleep. After all, he said to himself, it is probably only insomnia. Many must have it.

1933

GRACE PALEY

A Conversation with My Father

My father is eighty-six years old and in bed. His heart, that bloody motor, is equally old and will not do certain jobs any more. It still floods his head with brainy light. But it won't let his legs carry the weight of his body around the house. Despite my metaphors, this muscle failure is not due to his old heart, he says, but to a potassium shortage. Sitting on one pillow, leaning on three, he offers last-minute advice and makes a request.

"I would like you to write a simple story just once more," he says, "the kind de Maupassant wrote, or Chekhov, the kind you used to write. Just recognizable people and then write down what happened to them next."

I say, "Yes, why not? That's possible." I want to please him, though I don't remember writing that way. I *would* like to try to tell such a story, if he means the kind that begins: "There was a woman . . ." followed by plot, the absolute line between two points which I've always despised. Not for literary reasons, but because it takes all hope away. Everyone, real or invented, deserves the open destiny of life.

Finally I thought of a story that had been happening for a couple of years right across the street. I wrote it down, then read it aloud. "Pa," I said, "how about this? Do you mean something like this?"

5
> Once in my time there was a woman and she had a son. They lived nicely, in a small apartment in Manhattan. This boy at about fifteen became a junkie, which is not unusual in our neighborhood. In order to maintain her close friendship with him, she became a junkie too. She said it was part of the youth culture, with which she felt very much at home. After a while, for a number of reasons, the boy gave it all up and left the city and his mother in disgust. Hopeless and alone, she grieved. We all visit her.

"O.K., Pa, that's it," I said, "an unadorned and miserable tale."

"But that's not what I mean," my father said. "You misunderstood me on purpose. You know there's a lot more to it. You know that. You left everything out. Turgenev[1] wouldn't do that. Chekhov wouldn't do that. There are in fact Russian writers you never heard of, you don't have an inkling of, as good as anyone, who can write a plain ordinary story, who would not leave out what you

---

1. Ivan Sergevich Turgenev (1818–1883); his best-known novel, *Fathers and Sons*, deals with the conflict between generations.

have left out. I object not to facts but to people sitting in trees talking senselessly, voices from who knows where . . ."

"Forget that one, Pa, what have I left out now? In this one?"

"Her looks, for instance."

"Oh. Quite handsome, I think. Yes."

"Her hair?"

"Dark, with heavy braids, as though she were a girl or a foreigner."

"What were her parents like, her stock? That she became such a person. It's interesting, you know."

"From out of town. Professional people. The first to be divorced in their county. How's that? Enough?" I asked.

"With you, it's all a joke," he said. "What about the boy's father. Why didn't you mention him? Who was he? Or was the boy born out of wedlock?"

"Yes," I said. "He was born out of wedlock."

"For Godsakes, doesn't anyone in your stories get married? Doesn't anyone have the time to run down to City Hall before they jump into bed?"

"No," I said. "In real life, yes. But in my stories, no."

"Why do you answer me like that?"

"Oh, Pa, this is a simple story about a smart woman who came to N.Y.C. full of interest love trust excitement very up to date, and about her son, what a hard time she had in this world. Married or not, it's of small consequence."

"It is of great consequence," he said.

"O.K.," I said.

"O.K. O.K. yourself," he said, "but listen. I believe you that she's good-looking, but I don't think she was so smart."

"That's true," I said. "Actually that's the trouble with stories. People start out fantastic. You think they're extraordinary, but it turns out as the work goes along, they're just average with a good education. Sometimes the other way around, the person's a kind of dumb innocent, but he outwits you and you can't even think of an ending good enough."

"What do you do then?" he asked. He had been a doctor for a couple of decades and then an artist for a couple of decades and he's still interested in details, craft, technique.

"Well, you just have to let the story lie around till some agreement can be reached between you and the stubborn hero."

"Aren't you talking silly, now?" he asked. "Start again," he said. "It so happens I'm not going out this evening. Tell the story again. See what you can do this time."

"O.K.," I said. "But it's not a five-minute job." Second attempt:

Once, across the street from us, there was a fine handsome woman, our neighbor. She had a son whom she loved because she'd known him since birth (in helpless chubby infancy, and in the wrestling, hugging ages, seven to ten, as well as earlier and later). This boy, when he fell into the fist of adolescence, became a junkie. He was not a hopeless one. He was in fact hopeful, an ideologue and successful converter. With his busy brilliance, he wrote persuasive articles for his high-school newspaper. Seeking a wider audience, using important connections, he drummed into

Lower Manhattan newsstand distribution a periodical called *Oh! Golden Horse!*[2]

In order to keep him from feeling guilty (because guilt is the stony heart of nine tenths of all clinically diagnosed cancers in America today, she said), and because she had always believed in giving bad habits room at home where one could keep an eye on them, she too became a junkie. Her kitchen was famous for a while—a center for intellectual addicts who knew what they were doing. A few felt artistic like Coleridge and others were scientific and revolutionary like Leary.[3] Although she was often high herself, certain good mothering reflexes remained, and she saw to it that there was lots of orange juice around and honey and milk and vitamin pills. However, she never cooked anything but chili, and that no more than once a week. She explained, when we talked to her, seriously, with neighborly concern, that it was her part in the youth culture and she would rather be with the young, it was an honor, than with her own generation.

One week, while nodding[4] through an Antonioni[5] film, this boy was severely jabbed by the elbow of a stern and proselytizing girl, sitting beside him. She offered immediate apricots and nuts for his sugar level, spoke to him sharply, and took him home.

She had heard of him and his work and she herself published, edited, and wrote a competitive journal called *Man Does Live By Bread Alone*. In the organic heat of her continuous presence he could not help but become interested once more in his muscles, his arteries, and nerve connections. In fact he began to love them, treasure them, praise them with funny little songs in *Man Does Live . . .*

> *the fingers of my flesh transcend*
> *my transcendental soul*
> *the tightness in my shoulders end*
> *my teeth have made me whole*

To the mouth of his head (that glory of will and determination) he brought hard apples, nuts, wheat germ, and soybean oil. He said to his old friends, From now on, I guess I'll keep my wits about me. I'm going on the natch. He said he was about to begin a spiritual deep-breathing journey. How about you too, Mom? he asked kindly.

His conversion was so radiant, splendid, that neighborhood kids his age began to say that he had never been a real addict at all, only a journalist along for the smell of the story. The mother tried several times to give up what had become without her son and his friends a lonely habit. This effort only brought it to supportable levels. The boy and his girl took their electronic mimeograph and moved to the bushy edge of another borough. They were very strict. They said they would not see her again until she had been off drugs for sixty days.

At home alone in the evening, weeping, the mother read and reread the seven issues of *Oh! Golden Horse!* They seemed to her as truthful as ever. We often crossed the street to visit and console. But if we mentioned any of our children who were at college or in the hospital or dropouts at home, she would cry out, My baby! My baby! and burst into terrible, face-scarring, time-consuming tears. The End.

---

2. "Horse" is a slang term for heroin.   **3.** Samuel Taylor Coleridge (1772–1834), English Romantic poet, wrote his allegedly unfinished poem *Kubla Khan* in an opium dream. Timothy Leary (b. 1920), American psychologist who promoted the use of psychedelic drugs.   **4.** A slang term referring to the narcotic effect of heroin.   **5.** Michelangelo Antonioni (b. 1912), Italian director (*Blow-Up, Zabriskie Point*).

First my father was silent, then he said, "Number One: You have a nice sense of humor. Number Two: I see you can't tell a plain story. So don't waste time." Then he said sadly, "Number Three: I suppose that means she was alone, she was left like that, his mother. Alone. Probably sick?"

I said, "Yes."

"Poor woman. Poor girl, to be born in a time of fools, to live among fools. The end. The end. You were right to put that down. The end."

I didn't want to argue, but I had to say, "Well, it is not necessarily the end, Pa."

"Yes," he said, "what a tragedy. The end of a person."   40

"No, Pa," I begged him. "It doesn't have to be. She's only about forty. She could be a hundred different things in this world as time goes on. A teacher or a social worker. An ex-junkie! Sometimes it's better than having a master's in education."

"Jokes," he said. "As a writer that's your main trouble. You don't want to recognize it. Tragedy! Plain tragedy! Historical tragedy! No hope. The end."

"Oh, Pa," I said. "She could change."

"In your own life, too, you have to look it in the face." He took a couple of nitroglycerin.[6] "Turn to five," he said, pointing to the dial on the oxygen tank. He inserted the tubes into his nostrils and breathed deep. He closed his eyes and said, "No."

I had promised the family to always let him have the last word when arguing,   45
but in this case I had a different responsibility. That woman lives across the street. She's my knowledge and my invention. I'm sorry for her. I'm not going to leave her there in that house crying. (Actually neither would Life, which unlike me has no pity.)

Therefore: She did change. Of course her son never came home again. But right now, she's the receptionist in a storefront community clinic in the East Village. Most of the customers are young people, some old friends. The head doctor said to her, "If we only had three people in this clinic with your experiences . . ."

"The doctor said that?" My father took the oxygen tubes out of his nostrils and said, "Jokes. Jokes again."

"No, Pa, it could really happen that way, it's a funny world nowadays."

"No," he said. "Truth first. She will slide back. A person must have character. She does not."

"No, Pa," I said. "That's it. She's got a job. Forget it. She's in that storefront   50
working."

"How long will it be?" he asked. "Tragedy! You too. When will you look it in the face?"

1974

___

6. Medicine for certain heart conditions.

WOODY ALLEN

The Kugelmass Episode

Kugelmass, a professor of humanities at City College, was unhappily married for the second time. Daphne Kugelmass was an oaf. He also had two dull sons by his first wife, Flo, and was up to his neck in alimony and child support.

"Did I know it would turn out so badly?" Kugelmass whined to his analyst one day. "Daphne had promise. Who suspected she'd let herself go and well up like a beach ball? Plus she had a few bucks, which is not in itself a healthy reason to marry a person, but it doesn't hurt, with the kind of operating nut[1] I have. You see my point?"

Kugelmass was bald and as hairy as a bear, but he had soul.

"I need to meet a new woman," he went on. "I need to have an affair. I may not look the part, but I'm a man who needs romance. I need softness, I need flirtation. I'm not getting younger, so before it's too late I want to make love in Venice, trade quips at '21,'[2] and exchange coy glances over red wine and candlelight. You see what I'm saying?"

Dr. Mandel shifted in his chair and said, "An affair will solve nothing. You're so unrealistic. Your problems run much deeper."

"And also this affair must be discreet," Kugelmass continued. "I can't afford a second divorce. Daphne would really sock it to me."

"Mr. Kugelmass—"

"But it can't be anyone at City College, because Daphne also works there. Not that anyone on the faculty at C.C.N.Y. is any great shakes, but some of those coeds . . ."

"Mr. Kugelmass—"

"Help me. I had a dream last night. I was skipping through a meadow holding a picnic basket and the basket was marked 'Options.' And then I saw there was a hole in the basket."

"Mr. Kugelmass, the worst thing you could do is act out. You must simply express your feelings here, and together we'll analyze them. You have been in treatment long enough to know there is no overnight cure. After all, I'm an analyst, not a magician."

"Then perhaps what I need is a magician," Kugelmass said, rising from his chair. And with that he terminated his therapy.

A couple of weeks later, while Kugelmass and Daphne were moping around in their apartment one night like two pieces of old furniture, the phone rang.

"I'll get it," Kugelmass said. "Hello."

"Kugelmass?" a voice said, "Kugelmass, this is Persky."

"Who?"

"Persky. Or should I say The Great Persky?"

"Pardon me?"

---

1. Budget, expenses   2. Celebrity nightclub and restaurant.

"I hear you're looking all over town for a magician to bring a little exotica into your life? Yes or no?"

"Sh-h-h," Kugelmass whispered. "Don't hang up. Where are you calling from, Persky?" 20

Early the following afternoon, Kugelmass climbed three flights of stairs in a broken-down apartment house in the Bushwick section of Brooklyn. Peering through the darkness of the hall, he found the door he was looking for and pressed the bell. I'm going to regret this, he thought to himself.

Seconds later, he was greeted by a short, thin, waxy-looking man.

"*You're* Persky the Great?" Kugelmass said.

"The Great Persky. You want a tea?"

"No, I want romance. I want music. I want love and beauty." 25

"But not tea, eh? Amazing. O.K., sit down."

Persky went to the back room, and Kugelmass heard the sounds of boxes and furniture being moved around. Persky reappeared, pushing before him a large object on squeaky roller-skate wheels. He removed some old silk handkerchiefs that were lying on its top and blew away a bit of dust. It was a cheap-looking Chinese cabinet, badly lacquered.

"Persky," Kugelmass said, "what's your scam?"[3]

"Pay attention," Persky said. "This is some beautiful effect. I developed it for a Knights of Pythias[4] date last year, but the booking fell through. Get into the cabinet."

"Why, so you can stick it full of swords or something?" 30

"You see any swords?"

Kugelmass made a face and, grunting, climbed into the cabinet. He couldn't help noticing a couple of ugly rhinestones glued onto the raw plywood just in front of his face. "If this is a joke" he said.

"Some joke. Now, here's the point. If I throw any novel into this cabinet with you, shut the doors, and tap it three times, you will find yourself projected into that book."

Kugelmass made a grimace of disbelief.

"It's the emess,"[5] Persky said. "My hand to God. Not just a novel, either. A 35 short story, a play, a poem. You can meet any of the women created by the world's best writers. Whoever you dreamed of. You could carry on all you like with a real winner. Then when you've had enough you give a yell, and I'll see you're back here in a split second."

"Persky, are you some kind of outpatient?"

"I'm telling you it's on the level," Persky said.

Kugelmass remained skeptical. "What are you telling me—that this cheesy homemade box can take me on a ride like you're describing?"

"For a double sawbuck."[6]

Kugelmass reached for his wallet. "I'll believe this when I see it," he said. 40

Persky tucked the bills in his pants pocket and turned toward his bookcase.

---

3. Scheme, confidence trick.   **4.** Secret fraternal society.   **5.** Truth.   **6.** Twenty dollars.

"So who do you want to meet? Sister Carrie? Hester Prynne? Ophelia? Maybe someone by Saul Bellow? Hey, what about Temple Drake?[7] Although for a man your age she'd be a workout."

"French. I want to have an affair with a French lover."

"Nana?"[8]

"I don't want to have to pay for it."

"What about Natasha in 'War and Peace'?"[9]

"I said French. I know! What about Emma Bovary? That sounds to me perfect."

"You got it, Kugelmass. Give me a holler when you've had enough." Persky tossed in a paperback copy of Flaubert's novel.

"You sure this is safe?" Kugelmass asked as Persky began shutting the cabinet doors.

"Safe. Is anything safe in this crazy world?" Persky rapped three times on the cabinet and then flung open the doors.

Kugelmass was gone. At the same moment, he appeared in the bedroom of Charles and Emma Bovary's house at Yonville.[1] Before him was a beautiful woman, standing alone with her back turned to him as she folded some linen. I can't believe this, thought Kugelmass, staring at the doctor's ravishing wife. This is uncanny. I'm here. It's her.

Emma turned in surprise. "Goodness, you startled me," she said. "Who are you?" She spoke in the same fine English translation as the paperback.

It's simply devastating, he thought. Then, realizing that it was he whom she had addressed, he said, "Excuse me. I'm Sidney Kugelmass. I'm from City College. A professor of humanities. C.C.N.Y.? Uptown. I—oh, boy!"

Emma Bovary smiled flirtatiously and said, "Would you like a drink? A glass of wine, perhaps?"

She is beautiful, Kugelmass thought. What a contrast with the troglodyte who shared his bed! He felt a sudden impulse to take this vision into his arms and tell her she was the kind of woman he had dreamed of all his life.

"Yes, some wine" he said hoarsely. "White. No, red. No, white. Make it white."

"Charles is out for the day," Emma said, her voice full of playful implication.

After the wine, they went for a stroll in the lovely French countryside. "I've always dreamed that some mysterious stranger would appear and rescue me from the monotony of this crass rural existence," Emma said, clasping his hand. They passed a small church. "I love what you have on," she murmured. "I've never seen anything like it around here. It's so . . . so modern."

"It's called a leisure suit," he said romantically. 'It was marked down." Sud-

---

7. Respectively, the fallen heroine of Theodore Dreiser's *Sister Carrie* (1900); the adulterous heroine of Nathaniel Hawthorne's *The Scarlet Letter* (1850); Hamlet's fiancée, who drowns herself; Bellow's heroines are intensely neurotic, sexual, and vindictive; the victim of a bizarre rape in Faulkner's *Sanctuary* (1931), who is also the heroine of his *Requiem for a Nun* (1950).   8. Prostitute-heroine of Émile Zola's *Nana* (1880).   9. Saucy heroine of the novel (1865–1869) by Tolstoy.   1. Town in Normandy, France, where much of Flaubert's novel *Madame Bovary* (1857) is set.

denly he kissed her. For the next hour they reclined under a tree and whispered together and told each other deeply meaningful things with their eyes. Then Kugelmass sat up. He had just remembered he had to meet Daphne at Bloomingdale's.[2] "I must go," he told her. "But don't worry, I'll be back."

"I hope so," Emma said.

He embraced her passionately, and the two walked back to the house. He held Emma's face cupped in his palms, kissed her again, and yelled, "O.K., Persky! I got to be at Bloomingdale's by three-thirty."

There was an audible pop, and Kugelmass was back in Brooklyn.

"So? Did I lie?" Persky asked triumphantly.

"Look, Persky, I'm right now late to meet the ball and chain at Lexington Avenue, but when can I go again? Tomorrow?"

"My pleasure. Just bring a twenty. And don't mention this to anybody."

"Yeah. I'm going to call Rupert Murdoch."[3]

Kugelmass hailed a cab and sped off to the city. His heart danced on point. I am in love, he thought, I am the possessor of a wonderful secret. What he didn't realize was that at this very moment students in various classrooms across the country were saying to their teachers, "Who is this character on page 100? A bald Jew is kissing Madame Bovary?" A teacher in Sioux Falls, South Dakota, sighed and thought, Jesus, these kids, with their pot and acid. What goes through their minds!

Daphne Kugelmass was in the bathroom-accessories department at Bloomingdale's when Kugelmass arrived breathlessly. "Where've you been?" she snapped. "It's four-thirty."

"I got held up in traffic," Kugelmass said.

Kugelmass visited Persky the next day, and in a few minutes was again passed magically to Yonville. Emma couldn't hide her excitement at seeing him. The two spent hours together, laughing and talking about their different backgrounds. Before Kugelmass left, they made love. "My God, I'm doing it with Madame Bovary!" Kugelmass whispered to himself. "Me, who failed freshman English."

As the months passed, Kugelmass saw Persky many times and developed a close and passionate relationship with Emma Bovary. "Make sure and always get me into the book before page 120," Kugelmass said to the magician one day. "I always have to meet her before she hooks up with this Rodolphe character."[4]

"Why?" Persky asked. "You can't beat his time?"

"Beat his time. He's landed gentry. Those guys have nothing better to do than flirt and ride horses. To me, he's one of those faces you see in the pages of *Women's Wear Daily*.[5] With the Helmut Berger[6] hairdo. But to her he's hot stuff."

2. Chic New York department store.   3. Australian newspaper baron, who, in addition to several British papers, owns the New York *Post*, the *Village Voice*, and *New York* magazine.   4. The provincial aristocratic womanizer who seduces Emma, after she has a first romantic, idealistic flirtation with the mooning young Léon (who is mentioned below). The Abbé Bournisien and Binet, mentioned later, are minor characters in the novel.   5. Gossipy New York fashion newspaper. 6. Handsome German actor (b. 1942) who often plays decadent characters (*The Damned*, *Portrait of Dorian Gray*).

"And her husband suspects nothing?"

"He's out of his depth. He's a lackluster little paramedic who's thrown in his lot with a jitterbug. He's ready to go to sleep by ten, and she's putting on her dancing shoes. Oh, well . . . See you later."

75 And once again Kugelmass entered the cabinet and passed instantly to the Bovary estate at Yonville. "How you doing, cupcake?" he said to Emma.

"Oh, Kugelmass," Emma sighed. "What I have to put up with. Last night at dinner, Mr. Personality dropped off to sleep in the middle of the dessert course. I'm pouring my heart out about Maxim's[7] and the ballet, and out of the blue I hear snoring."

"It's O.K., darling. I'm here now," Kugelmass said, embracing her. I've earned this, he thought, smelling Emma's French perfume and burying his nose in her hair. I've suffered enough. I've paid enough analysts. I've searched till I'm weary. She's young and nubile, and I'm here a few pages after Léon and just before Rodolphe. By showing up during the correct chapters, I've got the situation knocked.

Emma, to be sure, was just as happy as Kugelmass. She had been starved for excitement, and his tales of Broadway night life, of fast cars and Hollywood and TV stars, enthralled the young French beauty.

"Tell me again about O.J. Simpson," she implored that evening, as she and Kugelmass strolled past Abbé Bournisien's church.

80 "What can I say? The man is great. He sets all kinds of rushing records. Such moves. They can't touch him."

"And the Academy Awards?" Emma said wistfully. "I'd give anything to win one."

"First you've got to be nominated."

"I know. You explained it. But I'm convinced I can act. Of course, I'd want to take a class or two. With Strasberg[8] maybe. Then, if I had the right agent"—

"We'll see, we'll see. I'll speak to Persky."

85 That night, safely returned to Persky's flat, Kugelmass brought up the idea of having Emma visit him in the big city.

"Let me think about it," Persky said. "Maybe I could work it. Stranger things have happened." Of course, neither of them could think of one.

"Where the hell do you go all the time?" Daphne Kugelmass barked at her husband as he returned home late that evening. "You got a chippie stashed somewhere?"

"Yeah, sure, I'm just the type," Kugelmass said wearily. "I was with Leonard Popkin. We were discussing Socialist agriculture in Poland. You know Popkin. He's a freak on the subject."

"Well, you've been very odd lately," Daphne said. "Distant. Just don't forget about my father's birthday. On Saturday?"

90 "Oh, sure, sure," Kugelmass said, heading for the bathroom.

---

7. Fashionable Paris restaurant.   8. Lee Strasberg's acting school taught the natural acting style known as "The Method" to such stars as Marlon Brando.

"My whole family will be there. We can see the twins. And Cousin Hamish. You should be more polite to Cousin Hamish—he likes you."

"Right, the twins," Kugelmass said, closing the bathroom door and shutting out the sound of his wife's voice. He leaned against it and took a deep breath. In a few hours, he told himself, he would be back in Yonville again, back with his beloved. And this time, if all went well, he would bring Emma back with him.

At three-fifteen the following afternoon, Persky worked his wizardry again. Kugelmass appeared before Emma, smiling and eager. The two spent a few hours at Yonville with Binet and then remounted the Bovary carriage. Following Persky's instructions, they held each other tightly, closed their eyes, and counted to ten. When they opened them, the carriage was just drawing up at the side door of the Plaza Hotel, where Kugelmass had optimistically reserved a suite earlier in the day.

"I love it! It's everything I dreamed it would be," Emma said as she swirled joyously around the bedroom, surveying the city from their window. "There's F.A.O. Schwarz.[9] And there's Central Park, and the Sherry[1] is which one? Oh, there—I see. It's too divine."

On the bed there were boxes from Halston and Saint Laurent.[2] Emma unwrapped a package and held up a pair of black velvet pants against her perfect body.

"The slacks suit is by Ralph Lauren," Kugelmass said. "You'll look like a million bucks in it. Come on, sugar, give us a kiss."

"I've never been so happy!" Emma squealed as she stood before the mirror. "Let's go out on the town. I want to see 'Chorus Line' and the Guggenheim and this Jack Nicholson character you always talk about. Are any of his flicks showing?"

"I cannot get my mind around this," a Stanford professor said. "First a strange character named Kugelmass, and now she's gone from the book. Well, I guess the mark of a classic is that you can reread it a thousand times and always find something new."

The lovers passed a blissful weekend. Kugelmass had told Daphne he would be away at a symposium in Boston and would return Monday. Savoring each moment, he and Emma went to the movies, had dinner in Chinatown, passed two hours at a discothèque, and went to bed with a TV movie. They slept till noon on Sunday, visited SoHo, and ogled celebrities at Elaine's.[3] They had caviar and champagne in their suite on Sunday night and talked until dawn. That morning, in the cab taking them to Persky's apartment, Kugelmass thought, It was hectic, but worth it. I can't bring her here too often, but now and then it will be a charming contrast with Yonville.

At Persky's, Emma climbed into the cabinet, arranged her new boxes of clothes neatly around her, and kissed Kugelmass fondly. "My place next time,"

95

100

9. Well-known toy store.   1. Sherry-Netherland Hotel, also in Central Park area.   2. Famous and expensive fashion designers and couturiers, as is Ralph Lauren, below.   3. SoHo is the center of the contemporary art scene south of Greenwich Village. Elaine's restaurant is frequented by publishing and newspaper notables.

she said with a wink. Persky rapped three times on the cabinet. Nothing happened.

"Hmm," Persky said, scratching his head. He rapped again, but still no magic. "something must be wrong," he mumbled.

"Persky, you're joking!" Kugelmass cried. "How can it not work?"

"Relax, relax. Are you still in the box, Emma?"

"Yes."

105   Persky rapped again—harder this time.

"I'm still here, Persky."

"I know, darling. Sit tight."

"Persky, we *have* to get her back," Kugelmass whispered. "I'm a married man, and I have a class in three hours. I'm not prepared for anything more than a cautious affair at this point."

"I can't understand it," Persky muttered. "It's such a reliable little trick."

110   But he could do nothing. "It's going to take a little while," he said to Kugelmass. "I'm going to have to strip it down. I'll call you later."

Kugelmass bundled Emma into a cab and took her back to the Plaza. He barely made it to his class on time. He was on the phone all day, to Persky and to his mistress. The magician told him it might be several days before he got to the bottom of the trouble.

"How was the symposium?" Daphne asked him that night.

"Fine, fine," he said, lighting the filter end of a cigarette.

"What's wrong? You're as tense as a cat."

115   "Me? Ha, that's a laugh. I'm as calm as a summer night. I'm just going to take a walk." He eased out the door, hailed a cab, and flew to the Plaza.

"This is no good," Emma said. "Charles will miss me."

"Bear with me, sugar," Kugelmass said. He was pale and sweaty. He kissed her again, raced to the elevators, yelled at Persky over a pay phone in the Plaza lobby, and just made it home before midnight.

"According to Popkin, barley prices in Kraków have not been this stable since 1971," he said to Daphne, and smiled wanly as he climbed into bed.

The whole week went by like that. On Friday night, Kugelmass told Daphne there was another symposium he had to catch, this one in Syracuse. He hurried back to the Plaza, but the second weekend there was nothing like the first. "Get me back into the novel or marry me," Emma told Kugelmass. "Meanwhile, I want to get a job or go to class, because watching TV all day is the pits."

120   "Fine. We can use the money," Kugelmass said. "You consume twice your weight in room service."

"I met an Off Broadway producer in Central Park yesterday, and he said I might be right for a project he's doing," Emma said.

"Who is this clown?" Kugelmass asked.

"He's not a clown. He's sensitive and kind and cute. His name's Jeff Something-or-Other, and he's up for a Tony."[4]

---

4. A theater award, comparable to an Oscar.

Later that afternoon, Kugelmass showed up at Persky's drunk.

"Relax," Persky told him. "You'll get a coronary."

"Relax. The man says relax. I've got a fictional character stashed in a hotel room, and I think my wife is having me tailed by a private shamus."

"O.K., O.K. We know there's a problem." Persky crawled under the cabinet and started banging on something with a large wrench.

"I'm like a wild animal," Kugelmass went on. "I'm sneaking around town, and Emma and I have had it up to here with each other. Not to mention a hotel tab that reads like the defense budget."

"So what should I do? This is the world of magic," Persky said. "It's all nuance."

"Nuance, my foot. I'm pouring Dom Pérignon and black eggs[5] into this little mouse, plus her wardrobe, plus she's enrolled at the Neighborhood Playhouse and suddenly needs professional photos. Also, Persky, Professor Fivish Kopkind, who teaches Comp Lit and who has always been jealous of me, has identified me as the sporadically appearing character in the Flaubert book. He's threatened to go to Daphne. I see ruin and alimony jail. For adultery with Madame Bovary, my wife will reduce me to beggary."

"What do you want me to say? I'm working on it night and day. As far as your personal anxiety goes, that I can't help you with. I'm a magician, not an analyst."

By Sunday afternoon, Emma had locked herself in the bathroom and refused to respond to Kugelmass's entreaties. Kugelmass stared out the window at the Wollman Rink[6] and contemplated suicide. Too bad this is a low floor, he thought, or I'd do it right now. Maybe if I ran away to Europe and started life over . . . Maybe I could sell the *International Herald Tribune*, like those young girls used to.[7]

The phone rang. Kugelmass lifted it to his ear mechanically.

"Bring her over," Persky said. "I think I got the bugs out of it."

Kugelmass's heart leaped. "You're serious?" he said. "You got it licked?"

"It was something in the transmission. Go figure."

"Persky, you're a genius. We'll be there in a minute. Less than a minute."

Again the lovers hurried to the magician's apartment, and again Emma Bovary climbed into the cabinet with her boxes. This time there was no kiss. Persky shut the doors, took a deep breath, and tapped the box three times. There was the reassuring popping noise, and when Persky peered inside, the box was empty. Madame Bovary was back in her novel. Kugelmass heaved a great sigh of relief and pumped the magician's hand.

"It's over," he said. "I learned my lesson. I'll never cheat again, I swear it." He pumped Persky's hand again and made a mental note to sent him a necktie.

Three weeks later, at the end of a beautiful spring afternoon, Persky answered his doorbell. It was Kugelmass, with a sheepish expression on his face.

---

5. An especially fine champagne and caviar.   6. Skating rink in Central Park.   7. This was what some American dropouts of the 1950s did; Jean Seberg portrayed one in the 1959 film *Breathless*.

"O.K., Kugelmass," the magician said. "Where to this time?"

"It's just this once," Kugelmass said. "The weather is so lovely, and I'm not getting any younger. Listen, you've read 'Portnoy's Complaint'? Remember The Monkey?"[8]

"The price is now twenty-five dollars, because the cost of living is up, but I'll start you off with one freebie, due to all the trouble I caused you."

"You're good people," Kugelmass said, combing his few remaining hairs as he climbed into the cabinet again. "This'll work all right?"

"I hope. But I haven't tried it much since all that unpleasantness."

"Sex and romance," Kugelmass said from inside the box. "What we go through for a pretty face."

Persky tossed in a copy of "Portnoy's Complaint" and rapped three times on the box. This time, instead of a popping noise there was a dull explosion, followed by a series of crackling noises and a shower of sparks. Persky leaped back, was seized by a heart attack, and dropped dead. The cabinet burst into flames, and eventually the entire house burned down.

Kugelmass, unaware of this catastrophe, had his own problems. He had not been thrust into "Portnoy's Complaint," or into any other novel, for that matter. He had been projected into an old textbook, "Remedial Spanish" and was running for his life over a barren, rocky terrain as the word *"tener"* ("to have")—a large and hairy irregular verb—raced after him on its spindly legs.

p. 1977

LUISA VALENZUELA

The Redtown Chronicles[1]

I. LITTLEHERB

He arrived in this no-man's town shouldering his bundle. He was tired of towns that belonged to someone, to the others.

The first thing he did was write his name on a rock: one way among many to assert himself and avenge himself on stones. They had made him suffer enough—stones, that is—especially when thrown in his face by unknown hands. The stones' fault? No, of course not. But stone he was familiar with and could avenge himself on confidently, whereas the hand that does the throwing is always anonymous. There are too many anonymous hands in the world, though few shameless enough to throw stones at him, who is usually so unobtrusive.

In this town, luckily, no hands, no feet, nothing human; only red sand, red stone; a town indistinguishable from the mountains and abandoned for years.

"Hello," was the first thing he said to the town in general, but most particu-

---

8. The leading character in Philip Roth's 1969 novel, The Monkey is less romantic than Flaubert's Emma Bovary and more sexually carefree and . . . experimental.   1. Translated by Christopher Leland

larly to one house there on the left, which appeared the coziest. Or at least, the most intact: walls of red stone, the color of the earth, and an absolute, spacious rooflessness that allowed him to see stars in a new, nonmetaphorical way. He dragged his bundle into that new home and settled in. He unrolled his sleeping bag and pulled out his little burner and pot, his gourd and his sipper.

Stingily preparing his maté, he said to himself: "Here I am." And he had never been so much there as in this town that belonged to no one, that was his alone.

The maté had a different flavor, though it was made with the herb from the towns where they had stoned him. He had little left. Littleherb, he called himself, which sounded much sweeter to him than his old name, now abandoned forever on that rock on the outskirts of town.

Stripped of his name, with only Littleherb to cover him, he felt much better—relieved, more in tune with the air of the town. He put more wood on the fire he had built, making a huge blaze inside the house, and he was glad there was neither roof nor door nor anything else combustible around.

Next morning he made a trip through the town, taking possession of places by putting up signs. With that in mind, he had not burned the wood that seemed most likely to be useful, planks on which he could write (for example) "Sheriff's Office" or "Hotel," "Church" or "Town Hall."

But the following day, the sun's first rays hadn't even waked him when the Indians, come down from the highlands, did. He saw them, a stain of color on the red town in their ponchos with geometric designs. To speak with him, they respectfully removed their hats.

"Pardon us, sir, but you can't build a fire here. There can be no life in this town."

"Why not?" he asked, astonished.

And they replied: "Because this is a dead town."

And he had to accept that, whether he liked it or not, because they refused to say anymore and, turning away, left him with that gentle advice that was almost a threat.

"Dead town, my ass," he said to himself. He mumbled a number of other things as he went from door to door nailing up his signs with growing enthusiasm, as if he were resuscitating the town. The noise of hammering made the adobe ring in a new way, and the old walls waggled like the tail of a grateful dog. Later, with the houses marked—posted—it was as if there were people around. "Bakery"—just imagine, there among the rocks—"General Store." "Saloon." "Jail" he never put up, it was too painful for him.

Littleherb went into each building—some almost completely in ruins—and went through a private ritual: "Do come in, ma'am," he would say to a passing breeze, "we have the best merchandise in these parts. What was it you were looking for?"

Dead town. Ha! He, Littleherb, knew it wasn't Deadtown. No! Redtown. Vital, radiant there in the sunshine. A little dry, true. Like the skin of a snake, which was the only animal he had seen during his long wanderings through the town. Not a bird. Not an ant. Nothing. So much the better, he said to himself, no need to worry about spiders crawling into his sleeping bag. But it wasn't very pleasant to find himself like that, with no company at all. A nothing town with nobody in it, only a tiny stream that ran some distance away, without even a fish in the water.

Littleherb was counting on the Indians to help him get a bit of food, but after that first day, they did not come down again. Occasionally, at night, Littleherb thought he heard their voices descending from on high: "Dead town! Dead town!" But they did not venture into the valley.

And Littleherb, involved in reviving the town, didn't notice how he was beginning to resemble it: red and dry. Red from the dust that settled into his pores; dry from that unforgiving sun. Poor Littleherb. He was Hardly-any-herb these days. Just stubble. Still and all, he continued drinking his maté, each time a little weaker, and thus passed days that seemed years to him, as he learned to be happy for long periods. He finally came to know how to lean quietly against an adobe wall and allow happiness slowly to infuse him. Happy while he contemplated the distinct tones of the red mountains or when he put up new and fantastic signs: "Dreameria," "Rainbow Shop," "Bordello de luxe," "Pink Corner." Happy as he wandered down those deserted desert streets. He didn't even hear the shouts of "dead town" that those up above cast down on him, or he thought they cast down. Shouts, after all, don't hurt, do they? Not like the stones he had been pelted with when he passed through living towns with his angelic, irritating air.

He wandered through the red town posting signs, and one night he slept in the town hall, and the next in the general store, the bordello, or the bakery. Happy each night, happy in his days of sign-posting, a happiness ever more solid, even if he was running out of paint.

20   Just as the last of his supplies were tap-dancing on the bottom of the basket he carried, he reached the far edge of town and found himself before a vast field sown with crosses. With all his accumulated happiness, he wrote "Cemetery" and sat down to wait. Peacefully.

II. Littleherb and the Infidels

Afterward came the time when the Indians tried to save Littleherb. They succeeded only in prolonging his life a bit, a few years at most, not much reckoned against the mountains.

Littleherb did not thank them, letting resignation lick the wounds of his soul. (Stupid Indians. Completely acculturated, having forgotten the secrets of their race, not knowing what constitutes the final self-realization, the ultimate, most profound surrender.)

They had been watching him from above, and only deigned to go down to him when they saw him fall after two days of standing guard at the old cemetery. Up to then, he had remained erect, casting shade like a tree. They went to rescue him even though they did not approve of his way of disturbing the peace of Deadtown—little signs all over the place! For what? Signs they couldn't read, but which nonetheless restored its proper name to each building, putting each in its place. Now nobody would forget. They, at least, would not forget, and to better remember—to better recount it all to coming generations—they descended a second time to Deadtown to bear the man to the heights, to those windy plateaus where their grandparents had settled.

The stranger was brought up unconscious, not much of a burden to carry up the craggy slope. It was like rescuing a stray sheep, a lost animal, and returning it to the heights.

When he first opened his eyes, Littleherb saw an eagle fly by and said to himself: "I'm dead. If there's something alive, it must mean I'm dead, because in this town there is absolutely nothing."

When he heard voices, he hadn't the slightest doubt, and when he was asked, "What is your name?" he replied, "Littleherb," since that was how he wanted to figure in the register of souls.

The name Littleherb sounded familiar to the Indians, and they decided this fellow with the kind eyes must be one of them, in spite of his beard. They gave him something to eat—an activity Littleherb had almost forgotten—and bathed him, more to get the stink of Deadtown off him than to clean him up.

After this, they took him to the shrine of Fewfleas, and Littleherb had no choice but to fall in love with the young shaman. She was like that: she had dazzling eyes. Dozens of lynx eyes, cleverly preserved, were arranged in an arc over her altar. The eyes formed a halo around Fewfleas, and Littleherb couldn't help but love her for her eyes.

When he was a bit fatter and somewhat recuperated, they were married most intimately, blessed by the winds.

The tenderness of Littleherb—who had achieved happiness and now needed nothing more—made Fewfleas forget some of her divinity and transformed her into the best of wives, two facts that cost her many subjects.

Within Littleherb, meanwhile, guilt began to blossom, growing and growing there high in the mountains till it reached the point that guilt almost sent him tumbling down the slope, back to Deadtown.

He took to spending long hours on the lip of the chasm, looking toward where Deadtown, Redtown, *His*town stood. But it was impossible, at that distance, to make it out. Because of its color and materials, it vanished into the landscape. Finally, as his own eyes were insufficient, he brought out to the cliff's edge the arc of lynx eyes from the altar of Fewfleas.

At night, the eyes served as tiny reflectors, and it was as if the invisible town was lit by thousands of fireflies. So Littleherb could locate exactly where he had christened every house.

Fewfleas, good wife to the end, came to fetch him when it got too late, and for a while would stand in wonder at the fireflies of the town. But only for a while. It seemed unwise to openly applaud other people's miracles.

Fewfleas wasn't the only one to wonder at the tiny, green lights that the lynx eyes seemed to project over Deadtown. Little by little, the whole tribe knew about the miracle and ended up clumped around Littleherb on the edge of the mountain.

Sometimes they had to forcefully restrain Littleherb, who wanted to launch himself head over heels to return to that peaceful felicity he had known in his adobe town. But more than the hands of the Indians, the voice of Fewfleas held him there, when she called him from their hut at that hour of a different joy, a moveable one.

While restraining Littleherb, the tribe embraced him, and finally came to worship him. That was the way Littleherb was: he awakened passions without wanting to, like the hatred of those people who had thrown stones at him.

Passions come and go. As it turned out, the Indians up above came to adore him as a god from the regions of light. And he himself began to believe that his ascension had not been in vain and that, in some yet unknowable way, he ought to return to the infidels what they had forgotten down in Redtown.

III. The Second Founding of Redtown

The Indians eventually took Littleherb for an oracle. Fewfleas dictated the words in his ear, and all he had to do was repeat them with great feeling, appending to each prophecy: "Happiness lies below in Redtown, Belletown, Towntown."

40

Fewfleas pinched him subtly to make him shut up, afraid the others might discover the subterfuge, now that the only thing her husband wanted, sickened by the highland winds, was to descend. But everyone looked upon him goggle-eyed, and thanks to the lights of Deadtown, they were even inclined to believe his words. He did work, it must be admitted, a certain number of miraculous cures by the laying on of hands, and he gave good counsel to the confused. In the end, one fine day, the Indians decided to undertake the journey down, bearing him along in a litter crowned with the halo of lynx eyes. First went the goats, as if opening up the road, then the pigs and the first men, single file, carrying cages of chickens. Admittedly, there was wisdom in all this: the animals knew how to choose the best path. It was not an easy descent. Surely not, hanging from the rocks! But still they went, singing and playing the flute from stone to stone, sometimes slipping right to the edge of the abyss.

They arrived at the end of an exhausting day's travel. After looking around a bit, they understood the mystery of the celebrated fireflies—nothing more than the sparkling, on moonlit nights, of the phosphorescent paint Littleherb had happened to use to make the signs. But the Indians chose not to investigate further, to leave things as they were.

They did, however, worship the rock on the outskirts of town. There, boldly writ, was what they intuited to be Littleherb's secret name. In a gesture of real affection, he took a piece of coal and added, "And Fewfleas," and drew a heart with an arrow, which the Indians interpreted as a sign of good omen. They entered the town singing so loudly that the adobe walls began to tremble. Finally, on one particularly high note, the walls tumbled down thunderously in an ugly cloud of dust.

At first panic reigned, but then the collapse gave rise to considerable mirth. Littleherb was the only one who failed to see much comedy in it: his poor town reduced to rubble. And when the children began to play war with shards of adobe, he feared getting a piece in the face as in other, unfortunate times. But no, there were no attacks here where everyone adored him, and after a while, he decided to see the positive side of the disaster: that no-place town had been his alone; the new town they would build would be of stone, more resilient.

They chose the most appropriate color of stone for each house—red for the distinguished, pinkest for those of pleasure. The house of Littleherb and Fewfleas was nearly crimson and Fewfleas began to recover her various dignities, even the arc of eyes. Littleherb ceded them to her with no regrets, as she had once ceded them to him. And he found much more to his liking the role of living god than that of miracle worker.

He took to sitting in the afternoons on the rock inscribed with his old name. Gazing west, he could recapture bits of that happiness he had known before.

He still played—perfectly, constantly—the part of a god, so deeply had he imbibed the idea. It wasn't for nothing that he had been born, suffered, and thought, and had come to the point of giving up there by the cemetery. He never returned there, and didn't much want to. His rock was enough. And he really did seem a god, sitting on that stone cross-legged, a soft wind or the cry of a bird rustling his beard. He had such wise eyes. He knew so many things, though he never spoke them.

A select member of the tribe had the honor of handing him his maté, made with aromatic herbs. Sometimes the sipper clogged, and as he sipped it made little noises that everyone marveled at. But the greatest marvel occurred the day he decided to teach them all to read, and at last they could decipher the meaning of those signs they revered as relics.

Veneration reached its peak when the entire tribe finally read effortlessly. That was indeed a glorious day for everyone, except for Littleherb. From then on, he had to write ever more complicated texts. The Indians loudly demanded new reading material, and complained bitterly when it wasn't to their liking. For more than a year, Littleherb wrote tirelessly while the others went about their simple labors—tilling the earth, tending the animals, or bartering with distant tribes.

Poor Littleherb! He didn't even have time to watch the rebirth of his old Deadtown, his beloved Redtown, so tightly did writing hem him in. Till the day arrived when he had written for the Indians their entire history and that of their town and, feeling himself fulfilled, he resigned from his task.

He forever renounced being a living god and lapsed into the comfortable role of priest-consort. It's the kind of life we all envy now, as we spend our days writing him stories. Like this one.

1987

BOBBIE ANN MASON

Shiloh

Leroy Moffitt's wife, Norma Jean, is working on her pectorals. She lifts three-pound dumbbells to warm up, then progresses to a twenty-pound barbell. Standing with her legs apart, she reminds Leroy of Wonder Woman.

"I'd give anything if I could just get these muscles to where they're real hard," says Norma Jean. "Feel this arm. It's not as hard as the other one."

"That's cause you're right-handed," says Leroy, dodging as she swings the barbell in an arc.

"Do you think so?"

"Sure."

Leroy is a truckdriver. He injured his leg in a highway accident four months ago, and his physical therapy, which involves weights and a pulley, prompted Norma Jean to try building herself up. Now she is attending a body-building class. Leroy has been collecting temporary disability since his tractor-trailer jack-knifed in Missouri, badly twisting his left leg in its socket. He has a steel pin in his hip. He will probably not be able to drive his rig again. It sits in the backyard, like a gigantic bird that has flown home to roost. Leroy has been home in Kentucky for three months, and his leg is almost healed, but the accident frightened him and he does not want to drive any more long hauls. He is not sure what to do next. In the meantime, he makes things from craft kits. He started by building a miniature log cabin from notched Popsicle sticks. He varnished it and placed it on the TV set, where it remains. It reminds him of a rustic Nativity scene. Then he tried string art (sailing ships on black velvet), a macramé owl kit, a snap-together B-17 Flying Fortress,[1] and a lamp made out of a model truck, with a light fixture screwed in the top of the cab. At first the kits were diversions, something to kill time, but now he is thinking about building a full-scale log house from a kit. It would be considerably cheaper than building a regular house, and besides, Leroy has grown to appreciate how things are put together. He has begun to realize that in all the years he was on the road he never took time to examine anything. He was always flying past scenery.

"They won't let you build a log cabin in any of the new subdivisions," Norma Jean tells him.

"They will if I tell them it's for you," he says, teasing her. Ever since they were married, he has promised Norma Jean he would build her a new home one day. They have always rented, and the house they live in is small and nondescript. It does not even feel like a home, Leroy realizes now.

Norma Jean works at the Rexall drugstore, and she has acquired an amazing amount of information about cosmetics. When she explains to Leroy the three stages of complexion care, involving creams, toners, and moisturizers, he thinks happily of other petroleum products—axle grease, diesel fuel. This is a connec-

---

1. World-War II bomber.

tion between him and Norma Jean. Since he has been home, he has felt unusually tender about his wife and guilty over his long absences. But he can't tell what she feels about him. Norma Jean has never complained about his traveling; she has never made hurt remarks, like calling his truck a "widow-maker." He is reasonably certain she has been faithful to him, but he wishes she would celebrate his permanent homecoming more happily. Norma Jean is often startled to find Leroy at home, and he thinks she seems a little disappointed about it. Perhaps he reminds her too much of the early days of their marriage, before he went on the road. They had a child who died as an infant, years ago. They never speak about their memories of Randy, which have almost faded, but now that Leroy is home all the time, they sometimes feel awkward around each other, and Leroy wonders if one of them should mention the child. He has the feeling that they are waking up out of a dream together—that they must create a new marriage, start afresh. They are lucky they are still married. Leroy has read that for most people losing a child destroys the marriage—or else he heard this on *Donahue*. He can't always remember where he learns things anymore.

At Christmas, Leroy bought an electric organ for Norma Jean. She used to play the piano when she was in high school. "It don't leave you," she told him once. "It's like riding a bicycle." 10

The new instrument had so many keys and buttons that she was bewildered by it at first. She touched the keys tentatively, pushed some buttons, then pecked out "Chopsticks." It came out in an amplified fox-trot rhythm, with marimba sounds.

"It's an orchestra!" she cried.

The organ had a pecan-look finish and eighteen preset chords, with optional flute, violin, trumpet, clarinet, and banjo accompaniments. Norma Jean mastered the organ almost immediately. At first she played Christmas songs. Then she bought *The Sixties Songbook* and learned every tune in it, adding variations to each with the rows of brightly colored buttons.

"I didn't like these old songs back then," she said. "But I have this crazy feeling I missed something."

"You didn't miss a thing," said Leroy. 15

Leroy likes to lie on the couch and smoke a joint and listen to Norma Jean play "Can't Take My Eyes Off You" and "I'll Be Back."[2] He is back again. After fifteen years on the road, he is finally settling down with the woman he loves. She is still pretty. Her skin is flawless. Her frosted curls resemble pencil trimmings.

Now that Leroy has come home to stay, he notices how much the town has changed. Subdivisions are spreading across western Kentucky like an oil slick. The sign at the edge of town says "Pop: 11,500"—only seven hundred more than it said twenty years before. Leroy can't figure out who is living in all the new houses. The farmers who used to gather around the courthouse square on Saturday afternoons to play checkers and spit tobacco juice have gone. It has been

2. 1960s hit songs.

years since Leroy has thought about the farmers, and they have disappeared without his noticing.

Leroy meets a kid named Stevie Hamilton in the parking lot at the new shopping center. While they pretend to be strangers meeting over a stalled car, Stevie tosses an ounce of marijuana under the front seat of Leroy's car. Stevie is wearing orange jogging shoes and a T-shirt that says CHATTAHOOCHEE SUPER-RAT. His father is a prominent doctor who lives in one of the expensive subdivisons in a new white-columned brick house that looks like a funeral parlor. In the phone book under his name there is a separate number, with the listing "Teenagers."

"Where do you get this stuff?" asks Leroy. "From your pappy!"

20 "That's for me to know and you to find out," Stevie says. He is slit-eyed and skinny.

"What else you got?"

"What you interested in?'

"Nothing special. Just wondered."

Leroy used to take speed on the road. Now he has to go slowly. He needs to be mellow. He leans back against the car and says, "I'm aiming to build me a log house, soon as I get time. My wife, though, I don't think she likes the idea."

25 "Well, let me know when you want me again," Stevie says. He has a cigarette in his cupped palm, as though sheltering it from the wind. He takes a long drag, then stomps it on the asphalt and slouches away.

Stevie's father was two years ahead of Leroy in high school. Leroy is thirty-four. He married Norma Jean when they were both eighteen, and their child Randy was born a few months later, but he died at the age of four months and three days. He would be about Stevie's age now. Norma Jean and Leroy were at the drive-in, watching a double feature (*Dr. Strangelove* and *Lover Come Back*),[3] and the baby was sleeping in the back seat. When the first movie ended, the baby was dead. It was the sudden infant death syndrome. Leroy remembers handing Randy to a nurse at the emergency room, as though he were offering her a large doll as a present. A dead baby feels like a sack of flour. "It just happens sometimes," said the doctor, in what Leroy always recalls as a nonchalant tone. Leroy can hardly remember the child anymore, but he still sees vividly a scene from *Dr. Strangelove* in which the President of the United States was talking in a folksy voice on the hot line to the Soviet premier about the bomber accidentally headed toward Russia. He was in the War Room, and the world map was lit up. Leroy remembers Norma Jean catatonically beside him in the hospital and himself thinking: Who is this strange girl? He had forgotten who she was. Now scientists are saying that crib death is caused by a virus. Nobody knows anything, Leroy thinks. The answers are always changing.

When Leroy gets home from the shopping center, Norma Jean's mother, Mabel Beasley, is there. Until this year, Leroy has not realized how much time she spends with Norma Jean. When she visits, she inspects the closets and then

---

3. A 1963 satire on nuclear war and a 1961 Rock Hudson–Doris Day romantic comedy satirizing the advertising business.

the plants, informing Norma Jean when a plant is droopy or yellow. Mabel calls the plants "flowers," although there are never any blooms. She always notices if Norma Jean's laundry is piling up. Mabel is a short, overweight woman whose tight, brown-dyed curls look more like a wig than the actual wig she sometimes wears. Today she has brought Norma Jean an off-white dust ruffle she made for the bed; Mabel works in a custom-upholstery shop.

"This is the tenth one I made this year," Mabel says. "I got started and couldn't stop."

"It's real pretty," says Norma Jean.

"Now we can hide things under the bed," says Leroy, who gets along with his mother-in-law primarily by joking with her. Mabel has never really forgiven him for disgracing her by getting Norma Jean pregnant. When the baby died, she said that fate was mocking her.

"What's that thing?" Mabel says to Leroy in a loud voice, pointing to a tangle of yarn on a piece of canvas.

Leroy holds it up for Mabel to see. "It's my needlepoint," he explains. "This is a *Star Trek* pillow cover."

"That's what a woman would do," says Mabel. "Great day in the morning!"

"All the big football players on TV do it," he says.

"Why, Leroy, you're always trying to fool me. I don't believe you for one minute. You don't know what to do with yourself—that's the whole trouble. Sewing!"

"I'm aiming to build us a log house," says Leroy. "Soon as my plans come."

"Like *heck* you are," says Norma Jean. She takes Leroy's needlepoint and shoves it into a drawer. "You have to find a job first. Nobody can afford to build now anyway."

Mabel straightens her girdle and says, "I still think before you get tied down y'all ought to take a little run to Shiloh."

"One of these days, Mama," Norma Jean says impatiently.

Mabel is talking about Shiloh, Tennessee. For the past few years, she has been urging Leroy and Norma Jean to visit the Civil War battleground there.[4] Mabel went there on her honeymoon—the only real trip she ever took. Her husband died of a perforated ulcer when Norma Jean was ten, but Mabel, who was accepted into the United Daughters of the Confederacy in 1975, is still preoccupied with going back to Shiloh.

"I've been to kingdom come and back in that truck out yonder," Leroy says to Mabel, "but we never yet set foot in that battleground. Ain't that something? How did I miss it?"

"It's not even that far," Mabel says.

After Mabel leaves, Norma Jean reads to Leroy from a list she has made. "Thing you could do," she announces. "You could get a job as a guard at Union Carbide, where they'd let you set on a stool. You could get on at the lumberyard.

4. Where, in April 1862, more than 23,000 troops of the North and South, one-quarter of those who fought there, died. This was the first real indication of how bitter and bloody the war was to be. General Ulysses S. Grant, when reinforcements arrived, drove the Confederate forces, which had gained an initial victory by a surprise attack, back to their base in Corinth, Mississippi.

You could do a little carpenter work, if you want to build so bad. You could—"

"I can't do something where I'd have to stand up all day."

45   "You ought to try standing up all day behind a cosmetics counter. It's amazing that I have strong feet, coming from two parents that never had strong feet at all." At the moment Norma Jean is holding on to the kitchen counter, raising her knees one at a time as she talks. She is wearing two-pound ankle weights.

"Don't worry," says Leroy. "I'll do something."

"You could truck calves to slaughter for somebody. You wouldn't have to drive any big old truck for that."

"I'm going to build you this house," says Leroy. "I want to make you a real home."

"I don't want to live in any log cabin."

50   "It's not a cabin. It's a house."

"I don't care. It looks like a cabin."

"You and me together could lift those logs. It's just like lifting weights."

Norma Jean doesn't answer. Under her breath, she is counting. Now she is marching through the kitchen. She is doing goose steps.

Before his accident, when Leroy came home he used to stay in the house with Norma Jean, watching TV in bed and playing cards. She would cook fried chicken, picnic ham, chocolate pie—all his favorites. Now he is home alone much of the time. In the mornings, Norma Jean disappears, leaving a cooling place in the bed. She eats a cereal called Body Buddies, and she leaves the bowl on the table, with soggy tan balls floating in a milk puddle. He sees things about Norma Jean that he never realized before. When she chops onions, she stares off into a corner, as if she can't bear to look. She puts on her house slippers almost precisely at nine o'clock every evening and nudges her jogging shoes under the couch. She saves bread heels for the birds. Leroy watches the birds at the feeder. He notices the peculiar way goldfinches fly past the window. They close their wings, then fall, then spread their wings to catch and lift themselves. He wonders if they close their eyes when they fall. Norma Jean closes her eyes when they are in bed. She wants the lights turned out. Even then, he is sure she closes her eyes.

55   He goes for long drives around town. He tends to drive a car rather carelessly. Power steering and an automatic shift make a car feel so small and inconsequential that his body is hardly involved in the driving process. His injured leg stretches out comfortably. Once or twice he has almost hit something, but even the prospect of an accident seems minor in a car. He cruises the new subdivisions, feeling like a criminal rehearsing for a robbery. Norma Jean is probably right about a log house being inappropriate here in the new subdivisions. All the houses look grand and complicated. They depress him.

One day when Leroy comes home from a drive he finds Norma Jean in tears. She is in the kitchen making a potato and mushroom-soup casserole, with grated-cheese topping. She is crying because her mother caught her smoking.

"I didn't hear her coming. I was standing here puffing away pretty as you please," Norma Jean says, wiping her eyes.

"I knew it would happen sooner or later," says Leroy, putting his arm around her.

"She don't know the meaning of the word 'knock,' " says Norma Jean. "It's a wonder she hadn't caught me years ago."

"Think of it this way," Leroy says. "What if she caught me with a joint?"   60

"You better not let her!" Norma Jean shrieks. "I'm warning you, Leroy Moffitt!"

"I'm just kidding. Here, play me a tune. That'll help you relax."

Norma Jean puts the casserole in the oven and sets the timer. Then she plays a ragtime tune, with horns and banjo, as Leroy lights up a joint and lies on the couch, laughing to himself about Mabel's catching him at it. He thinks of Stevie Hamilton—a doctor's son pushing grass. Everything is funny. The whole town seems crazy and small. He is reminded of Virgil Mathis, a boastful policeman Leroy used to shoot pool with. Virgil recently led a drug bust in a back room at a bowling alley, where he seized ten thousand dollars' worth of marijuana. The newspaper had a picture of him holding up the bags of grass and grinning widely. Right now, Leroy can imagine Virgil breaking down the door and arresting him with a lungful of smoke. Virgil would probably have been alerted to the scene because of all the racket Norma Jean is making. Now she sounds like a hard-rock band. Norma Jean is terrific. When she switches to a latin-rhythm version of "Sunshine Superman," Leroy hums along. Norma Jean's foot goes up and down, up and down.

"Well, what do you think?" Leroy says, when Norma Jean pauses to search through her music.

"What do I think about what?"   65

His mind has gone blank. Then he says, "I'll sell my rig and build us a house." That wasn't what he wanted to say. He wanted to know what she thought—what she *really* thought—about them.

"Don't start in on that again," says Norma Jean. She begins playing "Who'll Be the Next in Line?"

Leroy used to tell hitchhikers his whole life story—about his travels, his hometown, the baby. He would end with a question: "Well, what do you think?" It was just a rhetorical question. In time, he had the feeling that he'd been telling the same story over and over to the same hitchhikers. He quit talking to hitchhikers when he realized how his voice sounded—whining and self-pitying, like some teenage-tragedy song. Now Leroy has the sudden impulse to tell Norma Jean about himself, as if he had just met her. They have known each other so long they have forgotten a lot about each other. They could become reacquainted. But when the oven timer goes off and she runs to the kitchen, he forgets why he wants to do this.

The next day, Mabel drops by. It is Saturday and Norma Jean is cleaning. Leroy is studying the plans of his log house, which have finally come in the mail. He has them spread out on the table—big sheets of stiff blue paper, with diagrams and numbers printed in white. While Norma Jean runs the vacuum, Mabel drinks coffee. She sets her coffee cup on a blueprint.

70 "I'm just waiting for time to pass," she says to Leroy, drumming her fingers on the table.

As soon as Norma Jean switches off the vacuum, Mabel says in a loud voice, "Did you hear about the datsun dog that killed the baby?"

Norma Jean says, "The word is 'dachshund.' "

"They put the dog on trial. It chewed the baby's legs off. The mother was in the next room all the time." She raises her voice. "They thought it was neglect."

Norma Jean is holding her ears. Leroy manages to open the refrigerator and get some Diet Pepsi to offer Mabel. Mabel still has some coffee and she waves away the Pepsi.

75 "Datsuns are like that," Mabel says. "They're jealous dogs. They'll tear a place to pieces if you don't keep an eye on them."

"You better watch out what you're saying, Mabel," says Leroy.

"Well, facts is facts."

Leroy looks out the window at his rig. It is like a huge piece of furniture gathering dust in the backyard. Pretty soon it will be an antique. He hears the vacuum cleaner. Norma Jean seems to be cleaning the living room rug again.

Later, she says to Leroy, "She just said that about the baby because she caught me smoking. She's trying to pay me back."

80 "What are you talking about?" Leroy says, nervously shuffling blueprints.

"You know good and well," Norma Jean says. She is sitting in a kitchen chair with her feet up and her arms wrapped around her knees. She looks small and helpless. She says, "The very idea, her bringing up a subject like that! Saying it was neglect."

"She didn't mean that," Leroy says.

"She might not have *thought* she meant it. She always says things like that. You don't know how she goes on."

"But she didn't really mean it. She was just talking."

85 Leroy opens a king-sized bottle of beer and pours it into two glasses, dividing it carefully. He hands a glass to Norma Jean and she takes it from him mechanically. For a long time, they sit by the kitchen window watching the birds at the feeder.

Something is happening. Norma Jean is going to night school. She has graduated from her six-week body-building course and now she is taking an adult-education course in composition at Paducah Community College. She spends her evenings outlining paragraphs.

"First you have a topic sentence," she explains to Leroy. "Then you divide it up. Your secondary topic has to be connected to your primary topic."

To Leroy, this sounds intimidating. "I never was any good in English," he says.

"It makes a lot of sense."

90 "What are you doing this for, anyhow?"

She shrugs. "It's something to do." She stands up and lifts her dumbbells a few times.

"Driving a rig, nobody cared about my English."

"I'm not criticizing your English."

Norma Jean used to say, "If I lose ten minutes' sleep, I just drag all day." Now she stays up late, writing compositions. She got a B on her first paper—a how-to theme on soup-based casseroles. Recently Norma Jean has been cooking unusual foods—tacos, lasagna, Bombay chicken. She doesn't play the organ anymore, though her second paper was called "Why Music Is Important to Me." She sits at the kitchen table, concentrating on her outlines, while Leroy plays with his log house plans, practicing with a set of Lincoln Logs. The thought of getting a truckload of notched, numbered logs scares him, and he wants to be prepared. As he and Norma Jean work together at the kitchen table, Leroy has the hopeful thought that they are sharing something, but he knows he is a fool to think this. Norma Jean is miles away. He knows he is going to lose her. Like Mabel, he is just waiting for time to pass.

One day, Mabel is there before Norma Jean gets home from work, and Leroy   95
finds himself confiding in her. Mabel, he realizes, must know Norma Jean better than he does.

"I don't know what's got into that girl," Mabel says. "She used to go to bed with the chickens. Now you say she's up all hours. Plus her a-smoking. I like to died."

"I want to make her this beautiful home," Leroy says, indicating the Lincoln Logs. "I don't think she even wants it. Maybe she was happier with me gone."

"She don't know what to make of you, coming home like this."

"Is that it?"

Mabel takes the roof off his Lincoln Log cabin. "You couldn't get *me* in a   100
log cabin," she says. "I was raised in one. It's no picnic, let me tell you."

"They're different now," says Leroy.

"I tell you what," Mabel says, smiling oddly at Leroy.

"What?"

"Take her on down to Shiloh. Y'all need to get out together, stir a little. Her brain's all balled up over them books."

Leroy can see traces of Norma Jean's features in her mother's face. Mabel's   105
face has the texture of crinkled cotton, but suddenly she looks pretty. It occurs to Leroy that Mabel has been hinting all along that she wants them to take her with them to Shiloh.

"Let's all go to Shiloh," he says. "You and me and her. Come Sunday."

Mabel throws up her hands in protest. "Oh, no, not me. Young folks want to be by theirselves."

When Norma Jean comes in with groceries, Leroy says excitedly, "Your mama here's been dying to go to Shiloh for thirty-five years. It's about time we went, don't you think?"

"I'm not going to butt in on anybody's second honeymoon," Mabel says.

"Who's going on a honeymoon, for Christ's sake?" Norma Jean says loudly.   110

"I never raised no daughter of mine to talk that-a-way," Mabel says.

"You ain't seen nothing yet," says Norma Jean. She starts putting away boxes and cans, slamming cabinet doors.

"There's a log cabin at Shiloh." Mabel says, "It was there during the battle. There's bullet holes in it."

"When are you going to *shut up* about Shiloh, Mama?" asks Norma Jean.

115 "I always thought Shiloh was the prettiest place, so full of history," Mabel goes on. "I just hoped y'all could see it once before I die, so you could tell me about it." Later, she whispers to Leroy, "You do what I said. A little change is what she needs."

"Your name means 'the king,' " Norma Jean says to Leroy that evening. He is trying to get her to go to Shiloh, and she is reading a book about another century.
"Well, I reckon I ought to be right proud."
"I guess so."
"Am I still king around here?"
120 Norma Jean flexes her biceps and feels them for hardness. "I'm not fooling around with anybody, if that's what you mean," she says.
"Would you tell me if you were?"
"I don't know."
"What does *your* name mean?"
"It was Marilyn Monroe's real name."
125 "No kidding!"
"Norma comes from the Normans. They were invaders," she says. She closes her book and looks hard at Leroy. "I'll go to Shiloh with you if you'll stop staring at me."

On Sunday, Norma Jean packs a picnic and they go to Shiloh. To Leroy's relief, Mabel says she does not want to come with them. Norma Jean drives, and Leroy, sitting beside her, feels like some boring hitchhiker she has picked up. He tries some conversation, but she answers him in monosyllables. At Shiloh, she drives aimlessly through the park, past bluffs and trails and steep ravines. Shiloh is an immense place, and Leroy cannot see it as a battleground. It is not what he expected. He thought it would look like a golf course. Monuments are everywhere, showing through the thick clusters of trees. Norma Jean passes the log cabin Mabel mentioned. It is surrounded by tourists looking for bullet holes.
"That's not the kind of log house I've got in mind," says Leroy apologetically.
"I know *that*."
130 "This is a pretty place. Your mama was right."
"It's O.K.," says Norma Jean. "Well, we've seen it. I hope she's satisfied."
They burst out laughing together.
At the park museum, a movie on Shiloh is shown every half hour, but they decide that they don't want to see it. They buy a souvenir Confederate flag for Mabel, and then they find a picnic spot near the cemetery. Norma Jean has brought a picnic cooler, with pimiento sandwiches, soft drinks, and Yodels. Leroy eats a sandwich and then smokes a joint, hiding it behind the picnic cooler. Norma Jean has quit smoking altogether. She is picking cake crumbs from the cellophane wrapper, like a fussy bird.
Leroy says, "So the boys in gray ended up in Corinth. The Union soldiers zapped 'em finally. April 7, 1862."
135 They both know that he doesn't know any history. He is just talking about

some of the historical plaques they have read. He feels awkward, like a boy on a date with an older girl. They are still just making conversation.

"Corinth is where Mama eloped to," says Norma Jean.

They sit in silence and stare at the cemetery for the Union dead and, beyond, at a tall cluster of trees. Campers are parked nearby, bumper to bumper, and small children in bright clothing are cavorting and squealing. Norma Jean wads up the cake wrapper and squeezes it tightly in her hand. Without looking at Leroy, she says, "I want to leave you."

Leroy takes a bottle of Coke out of the cooler and flips off the cap. He holds the bottle poised near his mouth but cannot remember to take a drink. Finally he says, "No, you don't."

"Yes, I do."

"I won't let you." 140

"You can't stop me."

"Don't do me that way."

Leroy knows Norma Jean will have her own way. "Didn't I promise to be home from now on?" he says.

"In some ways, a woman prefers a man who wanders," says Norma Jean. "That sounds crazy, I know."

"You're not crazy." 145

Leroy remembers to drink from his Coke. Then he says, "Yes, you *are* crazy. You and me could start all over again. Right back at the beginning."

"We *have* started all over again," says Norma Jean. "And this is how it turned out."

"What did I do wrong?"

"Nothing."

"Is this one of those women's lib things?" Leroy asks. 150

"Don't be funny."

The cemetery, a green slope dotted with white markers, looks like a subdivision site. Leroy is trying to comprehend that his marriage is breaking up, but for some reason he is wondering about white slabs in a graveyard.

"Everything was fine till Mama caught me smoking," says Norma Jean, standing up. "That set something off."

"What are you talking about?"

"She won't leave me alone—*you* won't leave me alone." Norma Jean seems 155 to be crying, but she is looking away from him. "I feel eighteen again. I can't face that all over again." She starts walking away. "No, it *wasn't* fine. I don't know what I'm saying. Forget it."

Leroy takes a lungful of smoke and closes his eyes as Norma Jean's words sink in. He tries to focus on the fact that thirty-five hundred soldiers died on the grounds around him. He can only think of that war as a board game with plastic soldiers. Leroy almost smiles, as he compares the Confederates' daring attack on the Union camps and Virgil Mathis's raid on the bowling alley. General Grant, drunk and furious, shoved the Southerners back to Corinth, where Mabel and Jet Beasley were married years later, when Mabel was still thin and good-looking. The next day, Mabel and Jet visited the battleground, and then Norma Jean was born, and then she married Leroy and they had a baby, which they lost, and now Leroy and Norma Jean are here at the same battleground. Leroy knows he is leaving out a lot. He is leaving out the insides of history. History was always just names and dates to him. It occurs to him that building a house out of logs is similarly empty—too simple. And the real inner workings of a marriage, like most of history, have escaped him. Now he sees that building a log house is the dumbest idea he could have had. It was clumsy of him to think Norma Jean would want a log house. It was a crazy idea. He'll have to think of something else, quickly. He will wad the blueprints into tight balls and fling them into the lake. Then he'll get moving again. He opens his eyes. Norma Jean has moved away and is walking through the cemetery, following a serpentine brick path.

Leroy gets up to follow his wife, but his good leg is asleep and his bad leg still hurts him. Norma Jean is far away, walking rapidly toward the bluff by the river, and he tries to hobble toward her. Some children run past him, screaming noisily. Norma Jean has reached the bluff, and she is looking out over the Tennessee River. Now she turns toward Leroy and waves her arms. Is she beckoning to him? She seems to be doing an exercise for her chest muscles. The sky is unusually pale—the color of the dust ruffle Mabel made for their bed.

1982

RICHARD FORD

Great Falls

This is not a happy story. I warn you.

My father was a man named Jack Russell, and when I was a young boy in my early teens, we lived with my mother in a house to the east of Great Falls, Montana, near the small town of Highwood and the Highwood Mountains and the Missouri River. It is a flat, treeless benchland there, all of it used for wheat farming, though my father was never a farmer, but was brought up near Tacoma, Washington, in a family that worked for Boeing.

He—my father—had been an Air Force sergeant and had taken his discharge in Great Falls. And instead of going home to Tacoma, where my mother wanted to go, he had taken a civilian's job with the Air Force, working on planes, which was what he liked to do. And he had rented the house out of town from a farmer who did not want it left standing empty.

The house itself is gone now—I have been to the spot. But the double row of Russian olive trees and two of the outbuildings are still standing in the milkweeds. It was a plain, two-story house with a porch on the front and no place for the cars. At the time, I rode the school bus to Great Falls every morning, and my father drove in while my mother stayed home.

5   My mother was a tall pretty woman, thin, with black hair and slightly sharp features that made her seem to smile when she wasn't smiling. She had grown up in Wallace, Idaho, and gone to college a year in Spokane, then moved out

to the coast, which is where she met Jack Russell. She was two years older than he was, and married him, she said to me, because he was young and wonderful looking, and because she thought they could leave the sticks and see the world together—which I suppose they did for a while. That was the life she wanted, even before she knew much about wanting anything else or about the future.

When my father wasn't working on airplanes, he was going hunting or fishing, two things he could do as well as anyone. He had learned to fish, he said, in Iceland, and to hunt ducks up on the DEW line—stations he had visited in the Air Force. And during the time of this—it was 1960—he began to take me with him on what he called his "expeditions." I thought even then, with as little as I knew, that these were opportunities other boys would dream of having but probably never would. And I don't think that I was wrong in that.

It is a true thing that my father did not know limits. In the spring, when we would go east to the Judith River Basin and camp up on the banks, he would catch a hundred fish in a weekend, and sometimes more than that. It was all he did from morning until night, and it was never hard for him. He used yellow corn kernels stacked onto a #4 snelled hook, and he would rattle this rig-up along the bottom of a deep pool below a split-shot sinker, and catch fish. And most of the time, because he knew the Judith River and knew how to feel his bait down deep, he would catch fish of good size.

It was the same with ducks, the other thing he liked. When the northern birds were down, usually by mid-October, he would take me and we would build a cattail and wheatstraw blind on one of the tule ponds or sloughs he knew about down the Missouri, where the water was shallow enough to wade. We would set out his decoys to the leeward side of our blind, and he would sprinkle corn on a hunger-line from the decoys to where we were. In the evenings when he came home from the base, we would go and sit out in the blind until the roosting fights came and put down among the decoys—there was never calling involved. And after a while, sometimes it would be an hour and full dark, the ducks would find the corn, and the whole raft of them—sixty, sometimes—would swim in to us. At the moment he judged they were close enough, my father would say to me, "Shine, Jackie," and I would stand and shine a seal-beam car light out onto the pond, and he would stand up beside me and shoot all the ducks that were there, on the water if he could, but flying and getting up as well. He owned a Model 11 Remington with a long-tube magazine that would hold ten shells, and with that many, and shooting straight over the surface rather than down onto it, he could kill or wound thirty ducks in twenty seconds' time. I remember distinctly the report of that gun and the flash of it over the water into the dark air, one shot after another, not even so fast, but measured in a way to hit as many as he could.

What my father did with the ducks he killed, and the fish, too, was sell them. It was against the law then to sell wild game, and it is against the law now. And though he kept some for us, most he would take—his fish laid on ice, or his ducks still wet and bagged in the burlap corn sacks—down to the Great Northern Hotel, which was still open then on Second Street in Great Falls, and sell them to the Negro caterer who bought them for his wealthy customers and for the dining car passengers who came through. We would drive in my father's Plymouth to the back of the hotel—always this was after dark—to a concrete loading ramp and lighted door that were close enough to the yards that I could sometimes see passenger trains waiting at the station, their car lights yellow and warm inside, the passengers dressed in suits, all bound for someplace far away from Montana—Milwaukee or Chicago or New York City, unimaginable places to me, a boy fourteen years old, with my father in the cold dark selling illegal game.

10   The caterer was a tall, stooped-back man in a white jacket, who my father called "Professor Ducks" or "Professor Fish," and the Professor referred to my father as "Sarge." He paid a quarter per pound for trout, a dime for whitefish, a dollar for a mallard duck, two for a speckle or a blue goose, and four dollars for a Canada. I have been with my father when he took away a hundred dollars for fish he'd caught and, in the fall, more than that for ducks and geese. When he had sold game in that way, we would drive out 10th Avenue and stop at a bar called The Mermaid which was by the air base, and he would drink with some friends he knew there, and they would laugh about hunting and fishing while I played pinball and wasted money in the jukebox.

It was on such a night as this that the unhappy things came about. It was in late October. I remember the time because Halloween had not been yet, and in the windows of the houses that I passed every day on the bus to Great Falls, people had put pumpkin lanterns, and set scarecrows in their yards in chairs.

My father and I had been shooting ducks in a slough on the Smith River, upstream from where it enters on the Missouri. He had killed thirty ducks, and we'd driven them down to the Great Northern and sold them there, though my father had kept two back in his corn sack. And when we had driven away, he suddenly said, "Jackie, let's us go back home tonight. Who cares about those hard-dicks at The Mermaid. I'll cook these ducks on the grill. We'll do something different tonight." He smiled at me in an odd way. This was not a thing he usually said, or the way he usually talked. He liked The Mermaid, and my mother—as far as I knew—didn't mind it if he went there.

"That sounds good," I said.

"We'll surprise your mother," he said. "We'll make her happy."

15   We drove out past the air base on Highway 87, past where there were planes taking off into the night. The darkness was dotted by the green and red beacons, and the tower light swept the sky and trapped planes as they disappeared over the flat landscape toward Canada or Alaska and the Pacific.

"Boy-oh-boy," my father said—just out of the dark. I looked at him and his eyes were narrow, and he seemed to be thinking about something. "You know, Jackie" he said, "your mother said something to me once I've never forgotten. She said, 'Nobody dies of a broken heart.' This was somewhat before you were born. We were living down in Texas and we'd had some big blow-up, and that was the idea she had. I don't know why." He shook his head.

He ran his hand under the seat, found a half-pint bottle of whiskey, and held it up to the lights of the car behind us to see what there was left of it. He unscrewed the cap and took a drink, then held the bottle out to me. "Have a drink, son," he said. "Something oughta be good in life." And I felt that something was wrong. Not because of the whiskey, which I had drunk before and he had reason to know about, but because of some sound in his voice, something I didn't recognize and did not know the importance of, though I was certain it was important.

I took a drink and gave the bottle back to him, holding the whiskey in my mouth until it stopped burning and I could swallow it a little at a time. When we turned out the road to Highwood, the lights of Great Falls sank below the horizon, and I could see the small white lights of farms, burning at wide distances in the dark.

"What do you worry about, Jackie," my father said. "Do you worry about girls? Do you worry about your future sex life? Is that some of it?" He glanced at me, then back at the road.

"I don't worry about that," I said. 20

"Well, what then?" my father said. "What else is there?"

"I worry if you're going to die before I do," I said, though I hated saying that, "or if Mother is. That worries me."

"It'd be a miracle if we didn't," my father said, with the half-pint held in the same hand he held the steering wheel. I had seen him drive that way before. "Things pass too fast in your life, Jackie. Don't worry about that. If I were you, I'd worry we might not." He smiled at me, and it was not the worried, nervous smile from before, but a smile that meant he was pleased. And I don't remember him ever smiling at me that way again.

We drove on out behind the town of Highwood and onto the flat field roads toward our house. I could see, out on the prairie, a moving light where the farmer who rented our house to us was disking his field for winter wheat. "He's waited too late with that business," my father said and took a drink, then threw the bottle right out the window. "He'll lose that," he said, "the cold'll kill it." I did not answer him, but what I thought was that my father knew nothing about farming, and if he was right it would be an accident. He knew about planes and hunting game, and that seemed all to me.

"I want to respect your privacy," he said then, for no reason at all that I 25 understood. I am not even certain he said it, only that it is in my memory that way. I don't know what he was thinking of. Just words. But I said to him, I remember well, "It's all right. Thank you."

We did not go straight out the Geraldine Road to our house. Instead my father went down another mile and turned, went a mile and turned back again so that we came home from the other direction. "I want to stop and listen now," he said. "The geese should be in the stubble." We stopped and he cut the lights and engine, and we opened the car windows and listened. It was eight o'clock at night and it was getting colder, though it was dry. But I could hear nothing, just the sound of air moving lightly through the cut field, and not a goose sound. Though I could smell the whiskey on my father's breath and on mine, could hear the motor ticking, could hear him breathe, hear the sound we made sitting side by side on the car seat, our clothes, our feet, almost our hearts beating. And I could see out in the night the yellow lights of our house, shining through the olive trees south of us like a ship on the sea. "I hear them, by God," my father said, his head stuck out the window. "But they're high up. They won't stop here now, Jackie. They're high flyers, those boys. Long gone geese."

There was a car parked off the road, down the line of wind-break trees, beside a steel thresher the farmer had left there to rust. You could see moonlight off the taillight chrome. It was a Pontiac, a two-door hard-top. My father said nothing about it and I didn't either, though I think now for different reasons.

The floodlight was on over the side door of our house and lights were on inside, upstairs and down. My mother had a pumpkin on the front porch, and the wind chime she had hung by the door was tinkling. My dog, Major, came out of the quonset shed and stood in the car lights when we drove up.

"Let's see what's happening here," my father said, opening the door and stepping out quickly. He looked at me inside the car, and his eyes were wide and his mouth drawn tight.

30 We walked in the side door and up the basement steps into the kitchen, and a man was standing there—a man I had never seen before, a young man with blond hair, who might've been twenty or twenty-five. He was tall and was wearing a short-sleeved shirt and beige slacks with pleats. He was on the other side of the breakfast table, his fingertips just touching the wooden tabletop. His blue eyes were on my father, who was dressed in hunting clothes.

"Hello," my father said.

"Hello," the young man said, and nothing else. And for some reason I looked at his arms, which were long and pale. They looked like a young man's arms, like my arms. His short sleeves had each been neatly rolled up, and I could see the bottom of a small green tattoo edging out from underneath. There was a glass of whiskey on the table, but no bottle.

"What's your name?" my father said, standing in the kitchen under the bright ceiling light. He sounded like he might be going to laugh.

"Woody," the young man said and cleared his throat. He looked at me, then he touched the glass of whiskey, just the rim of the glass. He wasn't nervous, I could tell that. He did not seem to be afraid of anything.

35 "Woody," my father said and looked at the glass of whiskey. He looked at me, then sighed and shook his head. "Where's Mrs. Russell, Woody? I guess you aren't robbing my house, are you?"

Woody smiled. "No," he said. "Upstairs. I think she went upstairs."

"Good," my father said, "that's a good place." And he walked straight out of the room, but came back and stood in the doorway. "Jackie, you and Woody step outside and wait on me. Just stay there and I'll come out." He looked at Woody then in a way I would not have liked him to look at me, a look that meant he was studying Woody. "I guess that's your car," he said.

"That Pontiac." Woody nodded.

"Okay. Right," my father said. Then he went out again and up the stairs. At that moment the phone started to ring in the living room, and I heard my mother say, "Who's that?" And my father say, "It's me. It's Jack." And I decided I wouldn't go answer the phone. Woody looked at me, and I understood he wasn't sure what to do. Run, maybe. But he didn't have run in him. Though I thought he would probably do what I said if I would say it.

"Let's just go outside," I said.

And he said, "All right."

Woody and I walked outside and stood in the light of the floodlamp above the side door. I had on my wool jacket, but Woody was cold and stood with his hands in him pockets, and his arms bare, moving from foot to foot. Inside, the phone was ringing again. Once I looked up and saw my mother come to the window and look down at Woody and me. Woody didn't look up or see her, but I did. I waved at her, and she waved back at me and smiled. She was wearing a powder-blue dress. In another minute the phone stopped ringing.

Woody took a cigarette out of his shirt pocket and lit it. Smoke shot through his nose into the cold air, and he sniffed, looked around the ground and threw his match on the gravel. His blond hair was combed backwards and neat on the sides, and I could smell his aftershave on him, a sweet, lemon smell. And for the first time I noticed his shoes. They were twotones, black with white tops and black laces. They stuck out below his baggy pants and were long and polished and shiny, as if he had been planning on a big occasion. They looked like shoes some country singer would wear, or a salesman. He was handsome, but only like someone you would see beside you in a dime store and not notice again.

"I like it out here," Woody said, his head down, looking at his shoes. "Nothing to bother you. I bet you'd see Chicago if the world was flat. The Great Plains commence here."

"I don't know," I said.

Woody looked up at me, cupping his smoke with one hand. "Do you play football?"

"No," I said. I thought about asking him something about my mother. But I had no idea what it would be.

"I *have* been drinking," Woody said, "but I'm not drunk now."

The wind rose then, and from behind the house I could hear Major bark once from far away, and I could smell the irrigation ditch, hear it hiss in the field. It ran down from Highwood Creek to the Missouri, twenty miles away. It was nothing Woody knew about, nothing he could hear or smell. He knew nothing about anything that was here. I heard my father say the words, "That's a real joke," from inside the house, then the sound of a drawer being opened and shut, and a door closing. Then nothing else.

Woody turned and looked into the dark toward where the glow of Great Falls rose on the horizon, and we both could see the flashing lights of a plane lowering to land there. "I once passed my brother in the Los Angeles airport and didn't even recognize him," Woody said, staring into the night. "He recognized *me*, though. He said, 'Hey, bro, are you mad at me, or what?' I wasn't mad at him. We both had to laugh."

Woody turned and looked at the house. His hands were still in his pockets, his cigarette clenched between his teeth, his arms taut. They were, I saw, bigger, stronger arms than I had thought. A vein went down the front of each of them.

40

45

50

I wondered what Woody knew that I didn't. Not about my mother—I didn't know anything about that and didn't want to—but about a lot of things, about the life out in the dark, about coming out here, about airports, even about me. He and I were not so far apart in age, I knew that. But Woody was one thing, and I was another. And I wondered how I would ever get to be like him, since it didn't necessarily seem so bad a thing to be.

"Did you know your mother was married before?" Woody said.

"Yes," I said. "I knew that."

"It happens to all of them, now," he said. "They can't wait to get divorced."

55   Woody dropped his cigarette into the gravel and toed it out with his black-and-white shoe. He looked up at me and smiled the way he had inside the house, a smile that said he knew something he wouldn't tell, a smile to make you feel bad because you weren't Woody and never could be.

It was then that my father came out of the house. He still had on his plaid hunting coat and his wool cap, but his face was as white as snow, as white as I have ever seen a human being's face to be. It was odd. I had the feeling that he might've fallen inside, because he looked roughed up, as though he had hurt himself somehow.

My mother came out the door behind him and stood in the floodlight at the top of the steps. She was wearing the powder-blue dress I'd seen through the window, a dress I had never seen her wear before, though she was also wearing a car coat and carrying a suitcase. She looked at me and shook her head in a way that only I was supposed to notice, as if it was not a good idea to talk now.

My father had his hands in his pockets, and he walked right up to Woody. He did not even look at me. "What do you do for a living?" he said, and he was very close to Woody. His coat was close enough to touch Woody's shirt.

60   "I'm in the Air Force," Woody said. He looked at me and then at my father. He could tell my father was excited.

"Is this your day off, then?" my father said. He moved even closer to Woody, his hands still in his pockets. He pushed Woody with his chest, and Woody seemed willing to let my father push him.

"No," he said, shaking his head.

I looked at my mother. She was just standing, watching. It was as if someone had given her an order, and she was obeying it. She did not smile at me, though I thought she was thinking about me, which made me feel strange.

"What's the matter with you?" my father said into Woody's face, right into his face—his voice tight, as if it had gotten hard for him to talk. "Whatever in the world is the matter with you? Don't you understand something?" My father took a revolver pistol out of his coat and put it up under Woody's chin, into the soft pocket behind the bone, so that Woody's whole face rose, but his arms stayed at his sides, his hands open. "I don't know what to do with you," my father said. "I don't have any idea what to do with you. I just don't." Though I thought that what he wanted to do was hold Woody there just like that until something important took place, or until he could simply forget about all this.

65   My father pulled the hammer back on the pistol and raised it tighter under Woody's chin, breathing into Woody's face—my mother in the light with her

suitcase, watching them, and me watching them. A half a minute must've gone by.

And then my mother said, "Jack, let's stop now. Let's just stop."

My father stared into Woody's face as if he wanted Woody to consider doing something—moving or turning around or anything on his own to stop this—that my father would then put a stop to. My father's eyes grew narrowed, and his teeth were gritted together, his lips snarling up to resemble a smile. "You're crazy, aren't you?" he said. "You're a goddamned crazy man. Are you in love with her, too? Are you, crazy man? Are you? Do you say you love her? Say you love her! Say you love her so I can blow your fucking brains in the sky."

"All right," Woody said. "No. It's all right."

"He doesn't love me, Jack. For God's sake," my mother said. She seemed so calm. She shook her head at me again. I do not think she thought my father would shoot Woody. And I don't think Woody thought so. Nobody did, I think, except my father himself. But I think he did, and was trying to find out how to.

My father turned suddenly and glared at my mother, his eyes shiny and moving, but with the gun still on Woody's skin. I think he was afraid, afraid he was doing this wrong and could mess all of it up and make matters worse without accomplishing anything.

"You're leaving," he yelled at her. "That's why you're packed. Get out. Go on."

"Jackie has to be at school in the morning," my mother said in just her normal voice. And without another word to any one of us, she walked out of the floodlamp light carrying her bag, turned the corner at the front porch steps and disappeared toward the olive trees that ran in rows back into the wheat.

My father looked back at me where I was standing in the gravel, as if he expected to see me go with my mother toward Woody's car. But I hadn't thought about that—though later I would. Later I would think I should have gone with her, and that things between them might've been different. But that isn't how it happened.

"You're sure you're going to get away now, aren't you, mister?" my father said into Woody's face. He was crazy himself, then. Anyone would've been. Everything must have seemed out of hand to him.

"I'd like to," Woody said. "I'd like to get away from here."

"And I'd like to think of some way to hurt you," my father said and blinked his eyes. "I feel helpless about it." We all heard the door to Woody's car close in the dark. "Do you think that I'm a fool?" my father said.

"No," Woody said. "I don't think that."

"Do you think you're important?"

"No," Woody said. "I'm not."

My father blinked again. He seemed to be becoming someone else at that moment, someone I didn't know. "Where are you from?"

And Woody closed his eyes. He breathed in, then out, a long sigh. I was as if this was somehow the hardest part, something he hadn't expected to be asked to say.

"Chicago," Woody said. "A suburb of there."

70

75

80

"Are your parents alive?" my father said, all the time with his blue magnum pistol pushed under Woody's chin.

"Yes," Woody said. "Yessir."

85 "That's too bad," my father said. "Too bad they have to know what you are. I'm sure you stopped meaning anything to them a long time ago. I'm sure they both wish you were dead. You didn't know that. But I know it. I can't help them out, though. Somebody else'll have to kill you. I don't want to have to think about you anymore. I guess that's it."

My father brought the gun down to his side and stood looking at Woody. He did not back away, just stood, waiting for what I don't know to happen. Woody stood a moment, then he cut his eyes at me uncomfortably. And I know that I looked down. That's all I could do. Though I remember wondering if Woody's heart was broken and what any of this meant to him. Not to me, or my mother, or my father. But to him, since he seemed to be the one left out somehow, the one who would be lonely soon, the one who had done something he would someday wish he hadn't and would have no one to tell him that it was all right, that they forgave him, that these things happen in the world.

Woody took a step back, looked at my father and at me again as if he intended to speak, then stepped aside and walked away toward the front of our house, where the wind chime made a noise in the new cold air.

My father looked at me, his big pistol in his hand. "Does this seem stupid to you?" he said. "All this? Yelling and threatening and going nuts? I wouldn't blame you if it did. You shouldn't even see this. I'm sorry. I don't know what to do now."

"It'll be all right," I said. And I walked out to the road. Woody's car started up behind the olive trees. I stood and watched it back out, its red taillights clouded by exhaust. I could see their two heads inside, with the headlights shining behind them. When they got into the road, Woody touched his brakes, and for a moment I could see that they were talking, their heads turned toward each other, nodding. Woody's head and my mother's. They sat that way for a few seconds, then drove slowly off. And I wondered what they had to say to each other, something important enough that they had to stop right at that moment and say it. Did she say, *I love you?* Did she say, *This is not what I expected to happen?* Did she say, *This is what I've wanted all along?* and did he say, *I'm sorry for all this,* or *I'm glad,* or *None of this matters to me?* These are not the kinds of things you can know if you were not there. And I was not there and did not want to be. It did not seem like I should be there. I heard the door slam when my father went inside, and I turned back from the road where I could still see their taillights disappearing, and went back into the house where I was to be alone with my father.

90 Things seldom end in one event. In the morning I went to school on the bus as usual, and my father drove in to the air base in his car. We had not said very much about all that had happened. Harsh words, in a sense, are all alike. You can make them up yourself and be right. I think we both believed that we were in a fog we couldn't see through yet, though in a while, maybe not even a long while, we would see lights and know something.

In my third-period class that day a messenger brought a note for me that said I was excused from school at noon, and I should meet my mother at a motel down 10th Avenue South—a place not so far from my school—and we would eat lunch together.

It was a gray day in Great Falls that day. The leaves were off the trees and the mountains to the east of town were obscured by a low sky. The night before had been cold and clear, but today it seemed as if it would rain. It was the beginning of winter in earnest. In a few days there would be snow everywhere.

The motel where my mother was staying was called the Tropicana, and was beside the city golf course. There was a neon parrot on the sign out front, and the cabins made a U shape behind a little white office building. Only a couple of cars were parked in front of cabins, and no car was in front of my mother's cabin. I wondered if Woody would be here, or if he was at the air base. I wondered if my father would see him there, and what they would say.

I walked back to cabin 9. The door was open, though a DO NOT DISTURB sign was hung on the knob outside. I looked through the screen and saw my mother sitting on the bed alone. The television was on, but she was looking at me. She was wearing the powder-blue dress she had had on the night before. She was smiling at me, and I liked the way she looked at that moment, through the screen, in shadows. Her features did not seem as sharp as they had before. She looked comfortable where she was, and I felt like we were going to get along, no matter what had happened, and that I wasn't mad at her—that I had never been mad at her.

She sat forward and turned the television off. "Come in, Jackie," she said, and I opened the screen door and came inside. "It's the height of grandeur in here, isn't it?" My mother looked around the room. Her suitcase was open on the floor by the bathroom door, which I could see through and out the window onto the golf course, where three men were playing under the milky sky. "Privacy can be a burden, sometimes," she said, and reached down and put on her highheeled shoes. "I didn't sleep very well last night, did you?"

"No," I said, though I had slept all night. I wanted to ask her where Woody was, but it occurred to me at that moment that he was gone now and wouldn't be back, that she wasn't thinking in terms of him and didn't care where he was or ever would be.

"I'd like a nice compliment from you," she said. "Do you have one of those to spend?"

"Yes," I said. "I'm glad to see you."

"That's a nice one," she said and nodded. She had both her shoes on now. "Would you like to go have lunch? We can walk across the street to the cafeteria. You can get hot food."

"No" I said. "I'm not really hungry now."

"That's okay," she said and smiled at me again. And, as I said before, I liked the way she looked. She looked pretty in a way I didn't remember seeing her, as if something that had had a hold on her had let her go, and she could be different about things. Even about me.

"Sometimes, you know," she said, "I'll think about something I did. Just anything. Years ago in Idaho, or last week, even. And it's as if I'd read it. Like a story. Isn't that strange?"

"Yes," I said. And it did seem strange to me because I was certain then what the difference was between what had happened and what hadn't, and knew I always would be.

"Sometimes," she said, and she folded her hands in her lap and stared out the little side window of her cabin at the parking lot and the curving row of other cabins. "Sometimes I even have a moment when I completely forget what life's like. Just altogether." She smiled. "That's not so bad, finally. Maybe it's a disease I have. Do you think I'm just sick and I'll get well?"

105   "No. I don't know," I said. "Maybe. I hope so." I looked out the bathroom window and saw the three men walking down the golf course fairway carrying golf clubs.

"I'm not very good at sharing things right now," my mother said. "I'm sorry." She cleared her throat, and then she didn't say anything for almost a minute while I stood there. "I *will* answer anything you'd like me to answer, though. Just ask me anything, and I'll answer it the truth, whether I want to or not. Okay? I will. You don't even have to trust me. That's not a big issue with us. We're both grown-ups now."

And I said, "Were you ever married before?"

My mother looked at me strangely. Her eyes got small, and for a moment she looked the way I was used to seeing her—sharp-faced, her mouth set and taut. "No," she said. "Who told you that? That isn't true. I never was. Did Jack say that to you? Did your father say that? That's an awful thing to say. I haven't been that bad."

"He didn't say that," I said.

110   "Oh, of course he did," my mother said. "He doesn't know just to let things go when they're bad enough."

"I wanted to know that," I said. "I just thought about it. It doesn't matter."

"No, it doesn't," my mother said. "I could've been married eight times. I'm just sorry he said that to you. He's not generous sometimes."

"He didn't say that," I said. But I'd said it enough, and I didn't care if she believed me or didn't. It was true that trust was not a big issue between us then. And in any event, I know now that the whole truth of anything is an idea that stops existing finally.

"Is that all you want to know, then?" my mother said. She seemed mad, but not at me, I didn't think. Just at things in general. And I sympathized with her. "Your life's your own business, Jackie," she said. "Sometimes it scares you to death it's so much your own business. You just want to run."

115   "I guess so," I said.

"I'd like a less domestic life, is all." She looked at me, but I didn't say anything. I didn't see what she meant by that, though I knew there was nothing I could say to change the way her life would be from then on. And I kept quiet.

In a while we walked across 10th Avenue and ate lunch in the cafeteria. When she paid for the meal I saw that she had my father's silver-dollar money clip in her purse and that there was money in it. And I understood that he had been to see her already that day, and no one cared if I knew it. We were all of us on our own in this.

When we walked out onto the street, it was colder and the wind was blowing. Car exhausts were invisible and some drivers had their lights on, though it was only two o'clock in the afternoon. My mother had called a taxi, and we stood and waited for it. I didn't know where she was going, but I wasn't going with her.

"Your father won't let me come back," she said, standing on the curb. It was just a fact to her, not that she hoped I would talk to him or stand up for her or take her part. But I did wish then that I had never let her go the night before. Things can be fixed by staying; but to go out into the night and not come back hazards life, and everything can get out of hand.

My mother's taxi came. She kissed me and hugged me very hard, then got inside the cab in her powder-blue dress and high heels and her car coat. I smelled her perfume on my cheeks as I stood watching her. "I used to be afraid of more things than I am now," she said, looking up at me, and smiled. "I've got a knot in my stomach, of all things." And she closed the cab door, waved at me, and rode away.

I walked back toward my school. I thought I could take the bus home if I got there by three. I walked a long way down 10th Avenue to Second Street, beside the Missouri River, then over to town. I walked by the Great Northern Hotel, where my father had sold ducks and geese and fish of all kinds. There were no passenger trains in the yard and the loading dock looked small. Garbage cans were lined along the edge of it, and the door was closed and locked.

As I walked toward school I thought to myself that my life had turned suddenly, and that I might not know exactly how or which way for possibly a long time. Maybe, in fact, I might never know. It was a thing that happened to you— I knew that—and it had happened to me in this way now. And as I walked on up the cold street that afternoon in Great Falls, the questions I asked myself were these: why wouldn't my father let my mother come back? Why would Woody stand in the cold with me outside my house and risk being killed? Why would he say my mother had been married before, if she hadn't been? And my mother herself—why would she do what she did? In five years my father had gone off to Ely, Nevada, to ride out the oil strike there, and been killed by accident. And in the years since then I have seen my mother from time to time—in one place or another, with one man or other—and I can say, at least, that we know each other. But I have never known the answer to these questions, have never asked anyone their answers. Though possibly it—the answer—is simple: it is just low-life, some coldness in us all, some helplessness that causes us to misunderstand life when it is pure and plain, makes our existence seem like a border between two nothings, and makes us no more or less than animals who meet on the road—watchful, unforgiving, without patience or desire.

1987

JAMAICA KINCAID

Girl

Wash the white clothes on Monday and put them on the stone heap; wash the color clothes on Tuesday and put them on the clothesline to dry; don't walk barehead in the hot sun; cook pumpkin fritters in very hot sweet oil; soak your little cloths right after you take them off; when buying cotton to make yourself a nice blouse, be sure that it doesn't have gum on it, because that way it won't hold up well after a wash; soak salt fish overnight before you cook it; is it true that you sing benna[1] in Sunday school?; always eat your food in such a way that it won't turn someone else's stomach; on Sundays try to walk like a lady and not like the slut you are so bent on becoming; don't sing benna in Sunday school; you mustn't speak to wharf-rat boys, not even to give directions; don't eat fruits on the street—flies will follow you; *but I don't sing benna on Sundays at all and never in Sunday school*; this is how to sew on a button; this is how to make a buttonhole for the button you have just sewed on; this is how to hem a dress when you see the hem coming down and so to prevent yourself from looking like the slut I know you are so bent on becoming; this is how you iron your father's khaki shirt so that it doesn't have a crease; this is how you iron your father's khaki pants so that they don't have a crease; this is how you grow okra— far from the house, because okra tree harbors red ants; when you are growing dasheen, make sure it gets plenty of water or else it makes your throat itch when you are eating it; this is how you sweep a corner; this is how you sweep a whole house; this is how you sweep a yard; this is how you smile to someone you don't like too much; this is how you smile to someone you don't like at all; this is how you smile to someone you like completely; this is how you set a table for tea; this is how you set a table for dinner; this is how you set a table for dinner with an important guest; this is how you set a table for lunch; this is how you set a table for breakfast; this is how to behave in the presence of men who don't know you very well, and this way they won't recognize immediately the slut I have warned you against becoming; be sure to wash every day, even if it is with your own spit; don't squat down to play marbles—you are not a boy, you know; don't pick people's flowers—you might catch something; don't throw stones at blackbirds, because it might not be a blackbird at all; this is how to make a bread pudding; this is how to make doukona;[2] this is how to make pepper pot; this is how to make a good medicine for a cold; this is how to make a good medicine to throw away a child before it even becomes a child; this is how to catch a fish; this is how to throw back a fish you don't like, and that way something bad won't fall on you; this is how to bully a man; this is how a man bullies you; this is how to love a man, and if this doesn't work there are other ways, and if they don't work don't feel too bad about giving up; this is how to spit up in the air if you feel like

1. Sing popular music, calypso.   2. A spicy pudding, often made from plantain and wrapped in a plantain or banana leaf.

it, and this is how to move quick so that it doesn't fall on you; this is how to make ends meet; always squeeze bread to make sure it's fresh; *but what if the baker won't let me feel the bread?*; you mean to say that after all you are really going to be the kind of woman who the baker won't let near the bread?

1983

WRITING ABOUT FICTION

Writing About
Fiction

INTRODUCTION

Writing about literature ought to be easier than writing about anything else. When you write about painting, for example, you have to translate shapes and colors and textures into words. When you write about music, you have to translate various aspects and combinations of sounds into words. When you write about that complex, mysterious, fleeting thing called "reality" or "life," you have an even more difficult task. Worst of all, perhaps, is trying to put into words all that is going on at any given moment inside your particular and unique self. So you ought to be relieved to know that you are going to write—that is, use words—about fiction—again, words.

But writing about fiction will not be easy if you haven't learned to *read* fiction, for in order to write about anything you have to know that something rather well. Helping you to learn to read fiction is what the rest of this book is about; this chapter is about the writing. (But, as you will see, you cannot fully separate the writing from the reading.)

Another thing keeps writing about fiction from being easy: writing itself is not easy. Writing well requires a variety of language skills—a good working vocabulary, for example—and a sense of ordering your ideas, of how to link one idea or statement to another, of what to put in and what to leave out. Worse, writing is not a finite or definite skill or art; you never really "know how to write," you just learn how to write a little better about a little more. These very words you are reading have been written and revised several times, even though your editors have had a good many years in which to practice.

REPRESENTING THE LITERARY TEXT

Copying

If writing about literature is using words about words, what words should you use? Since most writers work very hard to get each word exactly right and in exactly the right order, there are no better words to use in discussing what the literature is about than those of the literary work itself. Faced with writing about a story, then, you could just write the story over again, word for word:

> Once upon a time there was a Siamese cat who pretended to be a lion and spoke inappropriate Zebraic . . .

and so on until the end. Copying texts was useful in medieval monasteries, but nowadays, what with printing, word processors, and Fax machines, it would not seem to be very useful. Besides, if you try to copy a text, you will probably find that spelling or punctuation errors, reversed word order, missing or added or just different words seem mysteriously to appear. Still, it's a good exercise for teaching yourself accuracy and attention to detail, and you will probably discover things about the text you are copying that you would be unlikely to notice otherwise. Early in a fiction course, particularly, copying can serve as a useful step in the direction of learning how to read and write about fiction; later, being able to copy a passage accurately will help when you want to quote a passage to illustrate or prove a point you are making. But copying is not, in itself, writing *about* fiction.

Reading aloud, a variation of copying, may be a more original and interpretive exercise than copying itself, since by tone, emphasis, and pace you are clarifying the text or indicating the way you understand the text. But it, too, is not *writing* about fiction, and you will not long be satisfied with merely repeating someone else's words. You will have perceptions, responses, and ideas that you will want to express for yourself about what you are reading. And having something to say and wanting to say or write it is the first and most significant step in learning to write about fiction.

Paraphrase

If you look away from the text for a while and then write the same material but in your own words, you are writing a **paraphrase.**

For example, let's try to paraphrase the first sentence of Jane Austen's *Pride and Prejudice:* "It is a truth universally acknowledged that a single man in possession of a good fortune, must be in want of a wife." We can start by making "It is a truth" a little less formal: *It's true that,* perhaps. Now "universally acknowledged": *everybody acknowledges,* or, a little more loosely, *everybody agrees.* Now we may choose to drop the whole first clause and begin, *Everybody agrees that* "a single man"—*a bachelor*—"in possession of a good fortune"—*rich*—"must be in want of a wife"—*wants a wife.* Or is it *needs a wife?* Okay, *Everybody agrees that a rich bachelor needs* (or *wants*) *a wife.* You can see that the process of paraphrase is something like that of translation. We are translating Austen's nineteenth-century formal English prose into twentieth-century informal American prose.

But what good is that? First of all, it enables us to test whether we really understand what we are reading. Second, certain elements of the text become clearer: we may see now that Austen's sentence is meant to be ironic or humorous, and we now understand the two possible meanings of "in want of." Third, we can check our paraphrase with those of others, our classmates' versions, for example, to compare our understanding of the passage with theirs. Finally, we have learned how dependent fiction is upon words. A paraphrase, no matter how precise, can render only an approximate equivalent of the meaning of a text—how *good* Austen's sentence is, how *flat* our paraphrase.

Paraphrasing, like copying, is not in itself an entirely satisfactory way of writing about fiction, but, like copying, it can be a useful tool when you write about fiction in other ways. In trying to explain or clarify a literary text for someone, to illustrate a point you are making about that text, or to remind your readers of or to acquaint them with a text or passage you will at times want to paraphrase. Unlike an exact copy, a paraphrase, being in your own words, adds something of yours to the text or passage—your emphasis, your perspective, your understanding.

Summary

Paraphrase follows faithfully the outlines of the text. But if you stand back far enough from the text so as not to see its specific words or smaller details and put down briefly in your own words what you believe the work is about, you will have a summary. How briefly? Well, you could summarize the story of the whole long play *Hamlet*, for example, in a single sentence: "A young man, seeking to avenge the murder of his father by his uncle, kills his uncle, but he himself and others die in the process." Has *too* much been left out? What do you feel it essential to add? Let's try again: "In Denmark, many centuries ago, a young prince avenged the murder of his father, the king, by his uncle, who had usurped the throne, but the prince himself was killed as were others, and a well-led foreign army had no trouble successfully invading the decayed and troubled state." A classmate may have written this summary: "From the ghost of his murdered father a young prince learns that his uncle, who has married the prince's mother, much to the young man's shame and disgust, is the father's murderer, and he plots revenge, feigning madness, acting erratically—even to insulting the woman he loves—and, though gaining his revenge, causes the suicide of his beloved and the deaths of others and, finally, of himself."

The last two, though accurate enough, sound like two different plays, don't they? To summarize means to select and emphasize and so to interpret: that is, not to replicate the text in miniature, as a reduced photograph might replicate the original, but while reducing it to change the angle of vision and even the filter, to represent the essentials as the reader or summarizer sees them. When you write a summary you should try to be as objective as possible; nevertheless, your summary will reflect not only the literary text but also your own understanding and attitudes. There's nothing wrong with your fingerprints or "mindprints" appearing on the summary, so long as you recognize that in summarizing you are doing more than copying, paraphrasing, or merely reflecting the literary text. You might learn something about both literature and yourself by comparing your summaries of, say, three or four short stories with summaries of the same works by several of your classmates. Try to measure the refraction of the text as it passes through the lens of each student's mind. You might then write a composite summary that would include all that any one reader felt important. You might try the same exercise again on different texts. Has the practice made you more careful? More inclusive? Is there a greater degree of uniformity or inclusiveness in your summaries?

A good summary can be a form of literary criticism. Though you will seldom be called upon merely to summarize a work, a good deal of writing about fiction requires that at some point or other you do summarize—a whole work, a particular incident or chapter or scene. But beware: a mere summary, no matter how accurate, will seldom satisfy the demand for a critical essay.

REPLYING TO THE TEXT

Imitation and Parody

While paraphrase is something like translation—a faithful following of the original text but in different words—and summary is the faithful, but inevitably interpretive, reduction of the matter, there is another kind of writing about fiction that faithfully follows the manner or matter or both of a literary text, but that does so for different ends. It's called **imitation.**

Art students learn to paint by copying the Old Masters; "writing from models," was for many generations the way students were taught to write. Many serious works are, in one way or another, imitations: *The Aeneid*, for example, may be said to be an imitation of *The Odyssey*, and, in a very different way, so might James Joyce's *Ulysses*. You too may be able to learn a good deal about writing—and reading—by trying your hand at an imitation.

But how would *you* go about writing an imitation? You first analyze the original—that is, break it down into its characteristics or qualities—and decide just what you want to preserve in your version. Sometimes you can poke fun at a work by imitating it but at the same time exaggerating its style or prominent characteristics, or placing it in an inappropriate context; that kind of imitation, a kind that is still popular, is called a **parody.** The list of qualities and the model might be much the same for a serious imitation and for a parody, only in a parody you can exaggerate a little—or a lot. To parody the style of Henry James, around the time of "The Real Thing," you could imitate or, if possible, exaggerate his long, halting, rather roundabout and somewhat obscure sentences, full of phrases interrupting other phrases or clauses, of understatement, reticence, and indirection. You might also parody this subtle, probing style and its air of questioning and mystery by applying it to a ludicrously trivial, unsuitable subject. In Max Beerbohm's "The Mote in the Middle Distance" two Jamesian children awaken on Christmas morning and are tempted to look in their Christmas stocking; Beerbohm begins:

> It was with the sense of a, for him, very memorable something that he peered now into the immediate future, and tried, not without compunction, to take that period up where he had, prospectively, left it. But just where the deuce *had* he left it? The consciousness of dubiety was, for our friend, not, this morning, quite yet clean-cut

enough to outline the figures on what she had called his "horizon," between which and himself the twilight was indeed of a quality somewhat intimidating.

In order to write a good imitation or parody you must read and re-read the original very carefully, examine it, and identify just those elements and qualities that go to make it up and be itself. You may or may not greatly admire a work you wish to parody, but parody itself is fun to do and fun to read. In either case, such close attention to how a professional piece of writing is put together and how its parts function together along with your effort to reproduce the effects are sure to help you understand the process of writing and improve your own ability to write about fiction knowledgeably.

Re-creation and Reply

Sometimes a story will seem so partial, biased, or unrealistic that it will stimulate a response. Such a response may involve a shift in perspective: it may tell the same story as the original but from a different angle, not only giving a different view of the same events and people but also adding details that the original focus ignored or could not perceive. In *Jane Eyre*, for example, Bertha Mason Rochester is the hero's bestial, mad wife, whom he has locked away upstairs and whose existence, when it comes to light, prevents for a time our heroine, our Jane, from marrying her heart's desire; Bertha is, in effect, the villainess. In *Wide Sargasso Sea*, Jean Rhys not only gives Bertha's side of Charlotte Brontë's story but tells us more details about Bertha's earlier life: poor Bertha was more sinned against than sinning, it turns out.

We may respond to a work whose view seems partial or distorted by shifting the perspective in time as well as in space. Are Francis Weed's marital and other problems solved by his recognition, at the end of "The Country Husband," that life in the suburbs can be, in its own way, as adventurous as more romantic kinds of existence? What will happen to him next spring? On his fortieth birthday? As he lies dying?

You may have noticed that while retorts can often be witty, they are also serious. Usually they say not merely, "That's not how the story went," but "That's not what life is really like." We must always read fiction initially with the aim of understanding it and taking it at its highest value (rather than reducing it and quibbling). We must try to "hear" what it is saying and not impose our own notions of reality prematurely upon a work but if possible learn from it and broaden our own views. We must finally, however, read it critically as well, asking, "Is this the way things *really* are?" or, more generously, "If I were standing over there, where the story (author, character) is, would things really look that way?"

Perhaps the most familiar kind of literary re-creation or reply is the **adaptation,** especially that of fiction into film. (Among the stories in this anthology that have been made into feature-length films are "The Most Dangerous Game," "An Occurrence at Owl Creek Bridge," "The Lady with the Dog," and "The Rocking-Horse Winner.") In adaptation, the rather contradictory demands of faithfulness to the original and appropriateness to the new medium can teach us a great deal about both the content and the medium of the original. It is unlikely you will have the opportunity in this course to make a film based on a story but you can still try your hand at adapting a work or piece of a work to a new medium. You might want to turn "The Cask of Amontillado" into verse (probably as a dramatic monologue) or write a short story called *Hamlet* or a one-act play called "Young Goodman Brown." It is quite likely that you will learn not only about the nature of the original work but also something of the nature of the medium in which you are trying to work.

EXPLAINING THE TEXT

Description

To give an account of the form of a work or passage rather than merely a brief version of its content or plot you may wish to write a **description.** Summaries tend to concentrate on subject and plot, whereas descriptions may concentrate on the narrative structure, point of view, or imagery, though descriptions of stories almost inevitably involve content.

In addition to describing the narrative structure or focus and voice of a short story, you might also describe the diction (word choice), the sentence structure, the amount of description of the characters or landscape, and so on.

Analysis

Like copying, paraphrase, and summary, a description of a work or passage rarely stands alone as a piece of writing about fiction. It is, instead, a tool, a means of supporting a point or opinion. Even the description we have given above borders on **analysis.** To analyze is to break something down into its parts to discover what they are, and, usually, how they function in and relate to the whole. Even a lengthy description of each of the scenes in "The Country Husband" would not in itself constitute an analysis, for you would also have to indicate how each contributes to our understanding of the story as a whole. You might ask yourself what the connection might be between the airplane incident and Francis's crush on Anne Murchison, and from that question you might go on to ask how all the other scenes relate to each other. Perhaps the last sentence of your description—about Francis's state of mind—might be a clue. But, back to the airplane incident. How about a paper called:

```
To Begin at the Beginning . . ."

In John Cheever's story "The Country Hus-
band," Francis Weed, a married man with three
```

children, falls in love with the young girl who
baby-sits his children. His marriage almost
breaks up, he goes to a psychiatrist, takes up
woodworking, and, at the end, is happy in his
conventional, suburban life.

This sort of story, that of a middle-aged
married man becoming infatuated with a young
girl, is not unusual. What is unusual here is
the embedding of this story amid other scenes
and details that seem to have no obvious connection with the "love affair." For example, the
story begins not with man-meets-girl but with
the protagonist's being on a plane that nearly
crashes. That incident is introduced with the
words, "To begin at the beginning, the airplane
from Minneapolis . . ." Why is this the beginning?

If a beginning is something that generates
the events that follow, this does not seem the
true beginning, for it does not seem to cause
what follows. Indeed, what follows is that no
one wants to listen when Francis tries to tell
them about his "brush with death." His friend
and fellow-commuter Trace Bearden does not
respond and just picks up his newspaper as
usual. When Francis gets home his first sentence
about the flight is interrupted by a fight among
the kids, and the squabble continues all through
dinner.

That's the last we hear of the airplane incident, which is supposed to be the beginning of

this whole story. The next night Francis and his wife go out to dinner and he recognizes the new French maid as a woman he saw being punished in Normandy just after the war--she had collaborated with the Nazis. This not only has nothing much to do with the plane incident, it does not seem to have much to do with what follows: he takes the young baby sitter home. She cries on his shoulder, he comforts her, and then, "At the steps, she freed her hand and then turned and kissed him swiftly (par. 29)." Shouldn't the story begin where it really begins, when he comes home, "Expecting to see Mrs. Heninlein, the old lady who usually stayed with the children . . . [and] was surprised when a young [beautiful] girl opened the door . . ." (par. 15)?

Why not omit the first two episodes? Let us look at what they have in common, and then see if we can connect them to the central episodes of the story.

The first is a brush with death--not something that happens every day to someone living in the American suburbs. The second seems to have a little to do with death, since it is about World War II and its consequences, but it is not exactly death that connects the two. What is it? The extraordinary, the significant, the newsworthy, the unusual, perhaps even the adventurous. These events clash with the routine, the dullness of Francis's everyday life.

Between the first two episodes he goes into
the garden, where all the usual things were
going on in the neighborhood, but Francis's (and
thus the reader's) attention is focused on the
neighbor's dog Jupiter who "was an anomaly . . .
his high spirits were out of place in Shady Hill
(par. 10)." High spirits, adventure, even mischief, the break with routine and orderliness.
Francis is prepared for his adventure, his mischief.

The story centers on the conflict between the
domestic and orderly--and dull--and the adventurous, romantic--and foolish. The beginning is
the first event that shakes Francis out of his
routine . . .

And the paper could go on, connecting the scenes, especially those not
directly related to the "romance," bringing in the setting (to enhance the other
side of the coin, the suburban routine), and even the focus, balancing analytical statements with textual evidence and evidence with generalizing, analytical
statements.

Interpretation

Principles and Procedures

If you have been reading carefully, you may have noticed what looks like a
catch: to turn description into analysis, you must relate what you are describing
to the theme, the overall effect and meaning of the work of fiction. But how do
you know what the theme is? If analysis relates the part to the whole, how can
you know the "whole" before you have analyzed each part? But then, how can
you analyze each part—relating it to the whole—if you don't know what that
whole is?

Interpretation, or the expression of your understanding of a literary work and its meaning, involves an initial general impression that is then supported and, often, modified by analysis of the particulars. It involves looking at the whole, the part, the whole, the part, the whole, the part, in a series of approximations and adjustments. (Note, in particular, that you must keep your mind open for modifications or changes rather than forcing your analysis to confirm your first impressions.)

This procedure should in turn suggest something of the nature and even the form of the critical essay, or essay of interpretation. The essay should present the overall theme and support that generalization with close analyses of the major elements of the text (or, in some essays, an analysis of one significant element)—showing how one or more of such elements as plot, character, or voice reinforce, define, or modify the theme of the story. Often the conclusion of such an essay will be a fuller, more refined statement of the theme.

Both the definition of and the procedures for interpreting a work suggest that a literary text is unified, probably around a theme, a meaning and effect. In interpreting, you therefore keep asking of each element or detail, "How does it fit? How does it contribute to *the* theme or whole?" In most instances, especially when you are writing on shorter works, if you dig hard and deep enough, you will find a satisfactory interpretation or central theme. Even after you have done your best, however, you must hold your "reading" or interpretation as a hypothesis rather than a final truth. Your experience of reading criticism has probably already shown you that more than one reading of a literary work is possible and that no reading exhausts the meaning and totality of a work. Nonetheless, you must begin reading a literary text as if it were going to make a central statement and create a single effect, no matter how complex. You must try as conscientiously as you can to "make sense" of the work, to analyze it, show how its elements work together. In analyzing elements, you kept your initial sense of the whole as hypothesis and did not try to force evidence to fit your first impression. So, too, you must hold your interpretation as a hypothesis even in its final stages, even at the end. It is, you must be sure, the fullest and best "reading" of the text you are capable of at this time, with the evidence and knowledge you have at this moment; but only that. In other words, an interpretation is "only an opinion." But just as your political and other opinions are not lightly held but are what you really feel and believe based on all you know and have experienced and all you have thought and felt, so your opinion or interpretation of a literary work should be as responsible as you can make it. Your opinions are a measure of your knowledge, intelligence, and sensibility. They should not be lightly changed but neither should they be obstinately and inflexibly held.

Reading and Theme Making

Because you need a sense of the whole text before you can analyze it, analysis and interpretation would seem to be possible only after repeated readings. Though obvious, logical, and partially true, this may not be *entirely* true. In reading, we actually anticipate theme or meaning much as we anticipate what will happen next. Often this anticipation or expectation of theme or effect begins with reading the first words of a story—or even before, in reading the title. "Beyond the Pale"suggests not only the location of the story in Ireland to those who know the history of that country, but also suggests conduct that is unacceptable, outside civilized feelings or behavior. Here, indeed, for those not too familiar with Ireland, the thematic implications of the title are clearer than its suggestion of the setting or situation.

Such anticipation of theme and effect, projecting and modifying understanding and response, continues as you read. When you read the first four words of "The Zebra Storyteller"—"Once upon a time . . ."—the strange title is to some extent explained and the kind of story you are about to read and its relation to everyday reality has been established. The title and the first short section of "The Most Dangerous Game" arouse expectations of the supernatural, the frightening, the adventurous, creating suspense: "What will happen next?" we ask as we read the first few paragraphs. The brief conversation about hunting, toward the end of that section, not only educates our expectations but also generates a moral and thematic question: "Are there really two animal classes—the hunters and the hunted—and does being lucky enough to be among the hunters justify insensitivity toward the feelings of the hunted?" While the question may recede from the foreground of our attention for a while, it has nonetheless been raised. It is, in addition, reinforced by the break on the page, which forces us to pause and, even if but momentarily, reflect. It comes forward again when General Zaroff introduces the subject of hunting. At these two points, at least, a thematic hypothesis based on hunters and hunted begins forming, however faintly, in our minds. That is enough to give us grounds—even as we read the story for the first time—for an analysis of elements and their relationship to our very tentatively formulated theme, and perhaps for beginning to modify or modulate our articulation of that theme. Many details in the story indicate that there is a political coloring to the theme: Zaroff is a Cossack—a people noted for fierceness—and is, or was, a Czarist general; he keeps a giant Cossack servant who was an official flogger under the Czar; he refers to the Revolution of 1917 in Russia as a "debacle"; he is clearly a racist. We may want to alter "hunter" and "hunted" in our first version of the antici-pated theme to something broader—"strong" and "weak," perhaps, or "privileged" and "underprivileged," or we may need fuller definitions of the implications of the terms "hunter" and "hunted."

Just as we have more than one expectation of what may happen next as we read a story, so we may have more than one expectation of what it is going to be "about" in the more general sense: as we read along we have expectations or hypotheses of meaning, and so we consciously or unconsciously try to fit together the pieces of elements of what we are reading into a pattern of significance. By the end of our first reading we should have a fairly well-defined sense of what the story is "about," what it means, even how some of the elements have worked together to produce that meaning and effect. Indeed, isn't this the way we read when we are not reading for a class or performance? Don't most people read most stories only once? And don't we usually think we have understood what we have read? Shouldn't we be able to read a very short story in class just once and immediately write an interpretive paper based on that first reading?

This is not to say that we cannot understand more about a work by repeated re-readings, or that there is some virtue or purity of response in the naive first reading that is lost in closer study. Our first "reading" —"reading" in the sense of both "casting our eye over" and "interpretation"—is almost certain to be modified or refined by re-reading: if nothing else, we know from the beginning what the most dangerous game is, and that the behavior of the English couples from "beyond the pale" is crass, insensitive, unacceptable. The theme or meaning is likely to be modulated by later readings, the way the elements function in defining or embodying meaning is likely to be clearer; the effect of the second reading is certain to be different from that of the first. It may be instructive to re-read several times the short work we interpreted in class after a single reading, write a new interpretive essay, and see how our understanding has been changed and enriched by subsequent readings.

Opinions, Right and Wrong

Just as each of our separate readings is different, so naturally one reader's fullest and "final" reading, interpretation, or opinion will differ somewhat from another's. Seldom will readers agree entirely with any full statement of the theme of a literary text. Nor is one of these interpretations entirely "right" and all the others necessarily "wrong." For no thematic summary, no analysis or interpretation, no matter how full, can exhaust the affective or intellectual significance of a major literary text. There are various approximate readings of varying degrees of acceptability, various competent or "good" readings, not just one single "right" reading.

Anyone who has heard two accomplished musicians faithfully perform the same work, playing all the "same" notes; or anyone who has seen two performances of *Hamlet*, will recognize how "interpretations" can be both correct and different. You might try to get hold of several recordings of one or more of Hamlet's soliloquies—by John Barrymore, Sir John Gielgud, Richard Burton, Sir Lawrence Olivier, for example—and notice how each of these actors lends to identical passages his own emphasis, pacing, tone, color, his own effect, and so, ultimately, his own meaning. These actors reading the identical words are, in effect, "copying," not paraphrasing or putting Shakespeare's Elizabethan poetry into modern American prose, not "interpreting" as we have defined it, or putting his play into their own words. If merely performing or reading the words aloud generates significant differences in interpretation, it is no wonder that when you write an interpretive essay about literature, when you give your conception of the meaning and effect of the literary text in your own words, your interpretation will differ from other interpretations, even when each of the different interpretations is competent and "correct."

Any communication, even a work of literature, is refracted by the recipient, and, in one sense, it is not complete until it is received, just as, in a sense, a musical score is not "music" until it is played. Philip Roth reported, not too long ago, how perturbed he was by what the critics and other readers said of his first novel—that was not at all what he intended, what the novel really was, he thought at first. But then he realized that once he had had his say in the novel, it was "out there," and each reader had to understand it within the limits and range of his or her own perspectives and literary and life experiences. His novel, once in print, was no longer merely "his," and rightly so.

That quite different interpretations may be "correct" is not to say, with Alice's Humpty-Dumpty, that a word or a work "means just what I choose it to mean." Though there may not be one "right" reading, some readings are more appropriate and convincing than others and some readings are demonstrably wrong.

What would you say about this reading of *Hamlet?*

The play is about the hero's sexual love for his mother. He sees his father's "ghost" because he feels guilty, somehow responsible for his father's death, more than likely because he had often wished his father dead. To free himself from this feeling of guilt, he imagines that he sees his father's ghost and that the ghost tells him that his uncle murdered his father. He focuses upon his uncle because he is fiercely jealous that it is his uncle not himself who has replaced his father in his mother's bed. He so resents his mother's choice of so unworthy a mate, he attributes it not to love but to mere lust, clearly a projection of his own lust for his mother, which he calls love. His mother's lust so disgusts him that he hates all women now, even Ophelia. When his father was alive he could be fond of Ophelia, for his sexual feeling for his mother was deflected by his father-the-king's powerful presence. Now, however, he must alienate Ophelia not only because of his new hatred of women but because he has a chance of winning his mother, especially if he can get rid of Claudius, his uncle.

Such a reading explains more or less convincingly certain details in the play, but it wrenches some out of context and it leaves a good deal out and a good deal unexplained: why, for example, do others see the ghost of Hamlet's father if it is just a figment of his imagination? What are Horatio and Fortinbras and the political elements doing in the play? *If* you accept certain Freudian premises about human psychology and see life in Freudian terms; *if* you see literary texts as the *author's* psychic fantasy stimulating your own psychic fantasies and believe that interpretation of *Hamlet* is not merely a reading of the play itself but an analysis of Shakespeare's psyche, you will find this reading convincing. You will perhaps explain away some of the details of the play that do not seem to fit your Freudian reading as a cover-up, an attempt by Shakespeare to disguise the true but hidden meaning of his dramatic fantasy from others—and from himself. Such a reading is probably neither right nor wrong but only a way of interpreting *Hamlet* based on certain assumptions about psychology and about the way literature *means* and so it would be "right" or acceptable to those who share those assumptions.

Suppose one of your ingenious classmates were to argue that the real subject of *Hamlet* is that the hero has tuberculosis. This would explain, your classmate would say, the hero's moodiness, his pretended madness that sometimes seems real, his rejection of Ophelia (he wouldn't want their children to suffer from the disease), his father's ghost (he, too, died of consumption), his anger at his uncle (who carries the disease, of course) for marrying Hamlet's mother, and so on. Your classmate might even argue that the text of the play is flawed, that it was just copied down during a performance by someone in the audience or was printed from an actor's imperfect copy. Therefore, "O that this too too *solid flesh*" should read "*sullied flesh*," as many scholars have argued (and might not "sullied flesh" suggest tuberculosis?). And, therefore, isn't it quite possible that the most famous soliloquy in the play really began or was meant to begin, "TB or not TB"? "No way!" we'd say. We would be reasonably sure that this is not just "not proved" but just plain *wrong*. It might be interesting and illuminating to rebut that reading in a paper of your own and to notice what kinds of evidence you bring to bear on an interpretive argument.

Reader and Text

If it is difficult to say exactly what a piece of literature *says*, it is usually not because it is vague or meanin*gless* but because it is too specific and meanin*gful* to paraphrase satisfactorily in any language other than its own. Since no two human beings are identical and no two people can inhabit the same space at the same time, no two people can see exactly the same reality from the same angle and vantage point. Most of us get around this awkward truth by saying that we see—or by only actually seeing—what we are "supposed" to see, a generalized, common-sense approximation of reality. We are all, in effect, like Polonius in the third act of *Hamlet*, who sees in a cloud a camel, a weasel, a whale—whatever Hamlet tells him he sees.

Some individuals struggle to see things as fully and clearly as possible from their own unique vantage point and to communicate to others their particular—even peculiar—vision. But here too we are individuated, for though we speak of our "common language," we each speak a unique language, made up of "dialects" that are not only regional and ethnic but also conditioned by our age group, our profession, our education, travel, reading—all our experiences. Yet if we want to express our unique vision to others who have different visions and different "languages" we must find some medium that is both true to ourselves and understandable to others.

There is for these individuals—these writers of literature—a constant tug-of-war between the uniqueness of their individual visions and the generalizing nature of language. The battle does not always result in sheer loss, however. Often, in the very struggle to get their own perceptions into language, writers sharpen those perceptions or discover what they themselves did not know when they began to write. You have probably made similar discoveries some time or other in the process of writing a letter or an assigned paper. But writers also find that what they have written does not perfectly embody what they meant it to, just as you perhaps have found that your finished papers have been not quite so brilliant as your original idea.

"Understanding" is not a passive reception of a text but an active reaching out from our own experiences toward the text. At least at first we need to do so by meeting the author on the ground of a common or general language and set of conventions—things that everybody "knows." The first task of the reader, therefore, is to get not to the author's intention, but to the general statement that the work itself makes—that is, its theme or thesis. After a few readings we can usually make a stab at articulating the theme of most works. What a work says in the way of a general theme, however, is not necessarily its full or ultimate meaning; otherwise we would read theme summaries and not stories. The theme is the meaning accessible to all through close reading of the text and common to all, but a literary text is not all statement. There are often cloudy areas in the text where we cannot be sure what is **implication,** the suggestion of the text, and what is our **inference,** or interpretation, of the text. Why does Doris Lessing's Judith prefer having a tomcat put to death to having him neutered but does not suggest that the female kitten who has been ruined for procreation be put death? Does this suggest that males, including human males, exist only to fertilize eggs, but that females have other functions as well? Or, at least, that this is what Judith believes? Does this give us more insight into Judith's life, her singleness, her refusal to marry the Greek professor, her ultimate flight from Luigi? The story does not *say* this, but many readers will find this inference convincing. If accepted, this changes the meaning of the story to some degree. Still, it need not be accepted; the story does not, will never say. The meaning of the story for the reader who is convinced will differ from the meaning for the reader who is not convinced.

The full meaning of a work for you is not only in its stated theme, one that everyone can agree on, but in the meaning you derive by bringing together that generalized theme, the precise language of the text, and your own applicable experiences—including reading experience—and imagination. That "meaning" is not the total meaning of the work, not what the author originally perceived and "meant to say"; it is the vision of the author as embodied in the work *and re-viewed from your own angle of vision.*

Your role in producing a meaning from the text does not free you, please note, from paying very close attention to the precise language of the text, the words and their meanings, their order, the syntax of the sentences, and even such mundane details as punctuation. You cannot impose a meaning on the text, no matter how sincerely and intensely you feel it, in defiance of the rules of grammar and the nature of the language.

Still, the reader must be an artist too, trying to experience the reality of the work as the author experienced reality, and with the same reverence and sense of responsibility for the original. To write about fiction you must try to embody your reading experience—or interpretation—of the work in language. Alas, writing about fiction, using words about words, is not as easy as it sounded at first. But it is more exciting, giving you a chance to see with another's eyes, to explore another's perceptions or experiences, and to explore and more fully understand your own in the process, thus expanding the horizon of your experience, perception, consciousness.

When some rich works of literature, like *Hamlet,* seem to have more than one meaning or no entirely satisfactory meaning or universally agreed upon single theme, it is not that they are not saying something, and saying something very specific, but that what they are saying is too specific, and complex, and profound, and true, perhaps, to be generalized or paraphrased in a few dozen words. The literary work is meaning*ful*—that is, full of meaning or meanings; but it is the reader who produces each particular meaning from the work, using the work itself, the language of the community and of the work, and his or her own language, experience, and imagination.

As readers trying to understand the unique perception and language of the author, we must translate the text as best we can into terms we can understand for ourselves. We try not to reduce the text to our own earlier, limited understanding but to stretch our minds and feelings toward its vision.

An interpretation, then, is not a clarification of what the writer "was trying to say"; it is a process that itself says, in effect, "The way I am trying to understand this story is . . . ."

It might help to keep in mind that a story is somewhat like a musical score and that you, the reader, are the performer. The "notes," the words of the story, are always the same, but no two "performances" are identical: you may choose to "play" faster or slower, emphasize this or that. And in a story there are always the equivalent of "grace notes," what some critics call "gaps," where the reader not only can but must fill in what the story leaves out. Sometimes it is difficult to tell what is *in* the story and what you as a reader add, extract, or interpret. The most obvious example of this is **implication,** something that is suggested, or, to put it more strongly and accurately, something that though it is not said (explicit) must be understood or filled in by the reader. That which is implied, then, is not in the story but must be put in. Surely you have to put the indentation on the second pillow together with the color of the hair in order to understand the final paragraph of "A Rose for Emily":

> Then we noticed that in the second pillow was the indentation of a head. One of us lifted something from it, and leaning forward, that faint and invisible dust dry and acrid in the nostrils, we saw a long strand of iron-gray hair.

Some would say that implication is just a brief or single instance of interpretation, that there is a single meaning in or implied in a story and that if you put it all together, fill in all the gaps "correctly," the "real" meaning will emerge. Others argue, however, that this assumes that there is a single meaning, that stories are just vehicles to carry that meaning, and that this is to undervalue the richness and complexity of literature and to make rational, paraphrasable statements more important than the literary incarnation of experience and vision.

Though we may read every word of a story, just as a performer plays every note, when we "understand" the work we select and fill in and reshape based on our own life and reading experiences—and that is why no two readings are ever exactly alike.

CRITICAL APPROACHES

The way you read and talk about a literary text depends on your assumptions, usually unconscious or unarticulated, about what a work of literature is, what is it supposed to do, and what makes it good. Literary critics, however, often define their assumptions about literature and the proper way to go about reading it and writing about it. The results are critical theories or critical approaches. Looking at a few of these, you may recognize some of your own assumptions, see new and exciting ways of looking at literature, or, at the very least, become aware of your own critical premises and prejudices.

Objectivism

We might begin by asking just what, quite literally, a work of literature *is*. There are critics who think of it as a fixed and freestanding object made up of words on a page. It is "freestanding" in that it has no connection on the one hand with the author or his or her intention or life, nor, on the other hand, with the historical or cultural context of the author or the reader. These we might call **objectivist** critics; they believe that a text is an independent object, free from the subjectivity of author and reader.

Formalism

Among the objectivist critics are the **formalists.** One common formalist conception is that a work is **autotelic,** that is, complete in itself, written for its own sake, and unified by its form—that which makes it a work of art. Content is less important than form. Literature involves a special kind of language that sets it apart from merely utilitarian writing; the formal strategies that organize and animate that language valorize literature and give it a special, almost religious character.

NEW CRITICISM   One group of formalists, the **New Critics,** dominated literary criticism in the middle of the 20th century, and New Criticism remains an important influence today. Their critical practice is to demonstrate formal unity by showing how every part of a work—every word, every image, every element—contributes to a central unifying theme. Because the details of the work relate to a theme or idea, they are generally treated as *symbolic*, as figurative or allegorical, representations of that central, unifying idea. The kind of unity thus demonstrated, in which every part is related to the whole and the whole is reflected in each part, is called **organic unity.** The New Critics differentiate organic unity from (and much prefer it to) **mechanical unity,** the external, preconceived structure or rules that do not arise from the individuality of the work but from the type or genre. New Critical analysis, or **explication of the text,** is especially effective in the critical reading of lyric poetry. It has become so universally accepted as *at least the first step* in the understanding of literature that it is almost everywhere the critical approach taught in introductory literature courses. It is, indeed, the basic approach of the "Understanding the Text" sections in *The Norton Introduction to Fiction*.

The New Critics' focus on theme or meaning as well as form means that for them literature is **referential:** it points to something outside itself, things in the real, external world or in human experience—a tree, a sound wave, love. The New Critics, in general, do not question the reality of the phenomenal world or the ability of language to represent it.

Structuralism

For many formalists, however, literature is not referential. The words in a story, poem, or play no longer point outward to the things, people, or world they are supposed to denote, as they might do in ordinary, "nonliterary" discourse, but point inward to each other and to the formal system they create. The critic still focuses on interrelatedness but is less concerned with "meaning"; words are treated not as symbols with meaning but like numbers; poetry is likened to mathematics or music.

Structuralism focuses on the text as an independent aesthetic object and also tends to detach literature from history and social and political implications, but much more than New Criticism, structuralism emphasizes systematic analysis, aspiring to make literary criticism a branch of scientific inquiry. It sees every literary work as a separate "system" and seeks to discover the principles or general laws that govern the interaction of parts within the system. Structuralism has its roots in modern linguistic theory; it looks especially to the work of Ferdinand de Saussure (1857–1913), the founder of structural linguistics early in the 20th century. Structuralism in criticism did not, however, flourish internationally until the early 1960s when a combination of space-age preoccupation with science and cold-war fear of implication led to a view of literature as intellectually challenging yet socially and politically noncontroversial.

Although based on linguistic theory, structuralism tries to extend newly discovered principles about language to other aspects of literature. Drawing on the **semiotic** principle that a vast and intricate system of signs enables human beings to communicate through language, structuralism asks readers to consider the way that other kinds of sign systems within a work—structures all—combine to produce meaning. Language and its characteristic habits are important to structuralists, but it is not enough to consider any single part of a work or any single kind of sign—linguistic or otherwise—within it. Structuralism aspires to elucidate the meaning of a work of literature by seeing the way all of its parts work relationally toward some wholeness of structure and meaning. Like formalism, it shows little interest in the creative process as such and has virtually no interest in authors, their intentions, or the circumstances or contexts of creation. It takes texts to represent interactions of words and ideas apart from individual human identities or socio-political commitments, and concentrates its analytical attention on what can be said about how different elements or processes in a text operate in relation to one another. Structuralists are less likely than formalists to concentrate their attention on some single all-explaining characteristic of literature (such as Cleanth Brooks's "tension" or William Empson's "ambiguity") and its practitioners are less likely to privilege a particular text for its revelation or authority. Structuralism may be seen as a sort of secular equivalent of formalism; it is less mysterious and authoritarian, and it has both the advantage and disadvantage of seeming to be less arbitrary and more "objectively" reliable. But in some ways it seems to promise too much for method and "objectivity," and by the 1970s its insights into the ways of language were already beginning to be used against it to attack the certitudes it appeared to promise and to emphasize instead the uncertainties and indeterminateness of texts.

Post-structuralism

Post-structuralism is the broad term used to designate the several directions of literary criticism that, while depending crucially on the insights of science-based theory, attack the very idea that any kind of certitude can exist about the meaning, understandability, or sharability of texts. Post-structuralists, disturbed at the optimism of positivist philosophy in suggesting that the world is knowable and explainable, ultimately doubt the possibility of certainties of any kind, and they see language as especially elusive and unfaithful. Much of post-structuralism involves undoing; the best-known variety of post-structuralism, **deconstruction,** suggests as much in its very name.

DECONSTRUCTION   Deconstruction takes the observations of structuralism to their logical conclusion, arguing that the elaborate web of semiotic differentiations created by the principle of difference in language means that no text can ultimately have any stable, definite, or discoverable meaning.

For the deconstructionist, language consists just in black marks on a page that repeat or differ from each other and the reader is the only author, one who can find whatever can be found in, or be made to appear in, those detached, isolated marks. The deconstructionist conception of literature is thus very broad—almost any writing will do. While this may seem "subjective," in that the critical reader has great freedom, it is the object—the black marks on the blank page—that is the sole subject/object of intention/attention.

As practiced by its most famous proponent, the French philosopher Jacques Derrida (b. 1930), deconstruction endeavors to trace the way texts challenge or cancel their explicit meanings and wrestle themselves into stasis or neutrality. Many deconstructionists have strong radical political commitments (it is possible to argue that the radical counterculture of the 1960s and especially the political events in Paris of 1968 are the crucial context for understanding the origins of deconstructionism), but the retreat from meaning and denial of clear signification that characterizes deconstruction also has affinities with formalism and structuralism, particularly as deconstruction is practiced by American critics. Rather than emphasizing form over content, however, deconstruction tries to deny the possibility of content and places value instead on verbal play as a characteristic outlet of a fertile, adroit, and supple human mind. Like structuralism, it lives almost completely in a self-referential verbal world rather than a world in which texts represent some larger or other reality, but unlike structuralism it denies that the verbal world adds up to anything coherent, consistent, or meaningful in itself. Deconstruction also influences other varieties of post-structuralism with different kinds of interests in history and ideology. Michel Foucault (1926–1984), Julia Kristeva (b. 1941), and Jacques Lacan (1901–1981)—though their disciplinary interests are in social history, feminist philosophy, and psychoanalysis, respectively, all come out of deconstructionist assumptions and carry the indeterminacies of post-structuralism (and of postmodernism more generally) into kinds of literary criticism with interests fundamentally different from those of structuralism.

Subjectivism

Opposed to objectivism is what might be called **subjectivism.** This loose term can be used to embrace many forms of psychological and self-, subject-, or reader-centered criticism.

Psychological Criticism

The assumption is that literature is the expression of the author's psyche, often his or her unconscious, and, like dreams, needs to be interpreted.

FREUDIAN CRITICISM   The dominant school is the **Freudian,** based on the work of Sigmund Freud (1856–1939). Many of its practitioners assert that the meaning of a literary work does not lie on its surface but in the psyche (some would even claim, in the neuroses) of the author. The value of the work, then, lies in how powerfully and convincingly it expresses the author's unconscious and how universal the psychological elements are. A well-known Freudian reading of *Hamlet*, for example, insists that Hamlet is upset because he is jealous of his uncle, for he, *like all male children*, unconsciously wants to go to bed with his mother. The ghost, in such a reading, is a figment of Hamlet's unconscious desire; his madness is not just acting but is the result of this frustrated desire; his cruelly gross mistreatment of Ophelia is a deflection of his disgust at his mother's being "lecherous," "unfaithful" in her love for him. A Freudian critic may assume then that Hamlet is suffering from an Oedipus complex, a Freudian term for the desire of the son for his mother, its name derived from the Greek myth that is the basis of Sophocles' play *Oedipus the King*.

Some Freudian critics stress the author's psyche and find *Hamlet* the expression of Shakespeare's own Oedipus complex. Others stress the effect on the reader, the work having a purgative or cleansing effect by expressing in socially and morally acceptable ways unconscious desires that would be unacceptable if expressed directly.

LACANIAN CRITICISM   As it absorbs the indeterminacies of post-structuralism under the influence of thinkers such as Jacques Lacan, psychological criticism has become increasingly complex. Accepting the Oedipal paradigm and the unconscious as the realm of repressed desire, Lacanian psychology (and the critical theory that depends from that psychology) conflates these concepts with the deconstructionist emphasis on language as expressing absence—you use a word to represent an absent object but you cannot make it present. The word, then, like the unconscious desire, is something that cannot be fulfilled. Language, reaching out with one word after the other, striving for but never reaching its object, is the arena of desire.

JUNGIAN CRITICISM   Just as a Freudian assumes that human psyches have similar histories and structures, the **Jungian** critic assumes that we all share a universal or **collective unconscious** (as well as having a racial and individual unconscious). According to Carl Gustav Jung (1875–1961) and his followers, in the collective and in our individual unconscious are universal images, patterns, and forms of human experiences or **archetypes.** These archetypes can never be known directly, but they surface in art in an imperfect, shadowy way, taking the form of **archetypal images**—the snake with its tail in its mouth, rebirth, mother, the double, the descent into Hell. To get a sense of the archetype beneath the archetypal images or shadows in the characters, plot, language, and images of a work, to bring these together in an archetypal interpretation, is the function of the Jungian critic. He is guided by his belief that there is a central myth common to all literature. Just as, for the Freudian literary critic, the "family romance," out of which the Oedipus story comes, is central, so the Jungian assumes there is a **monomyth** that underlies the archetypal images and gives a clue as to how they can be related to suggest the archetypes themselves. The myth is that of the quest. In that all-encompassing myth the hero struggles to free himself (the gender of the pronoun is specific and significant) from the Great Mother, to become a separate, self-sufficient being who is then rewarded by union with his ideal other, the feminine *anima*.

Phenomenological Criticism

Another kind of subjectivist criticism is **phenomenology,** especially as it is practiced by **critics of consciousness.** They consider all the writings of an author—laundry lists and letters as well as lyrics—as the expression of his or her mindset or way of looking at reality. Such a critic looks for repeated or obsessive use of certain key words, incidents, patterns, and angles of vision, and maps out thereby the inner world of the writer.

Reader-response Criticism

The formalists focus on the text. Though the psychological critics focus most frequently on the author, their assumptions about the similarity or universality of the human mind make them consider as well the role of the reader. There is another approach that, though not psychological in the usual sense of the word, also focuses on the reception of the text, on **reader response.** The conventional notion of reading is that a writer or speaker has an "idea," **encodes** it—that is, turns it into words—and the reader or listener decodes it, deriving, when successful, the writer/speaker's "idea." What the reader-response critic assumes, however, is that such equivalency between sender and receiver is impossible. The literary **work** therefore does *not* exist on the page; that is only the **text.** The text becomes a work only when it is read, just as a score becomes music only when it is played. And just as every musical performance, even of exactly the same notes, is somewhat different, a different "interpretation," so no two readers read or perform exactly the same work from identical texts. Besides the individual differences of readers, space is made for different readings or interpretations by **gaps** in a text itself. Some of these are temporary— such as the withholding of the name of the murderer until the end—and are closed by the text sooner or later, though each reader will in the meantime fill them differently. But others are permanent, and can never be filled with certainty; the result is a degree of uncertainty or **indeterminacy** in the text.

The reader-response critic's focus on the reading process is especially useful in the study of long works such as novels. The critic follows the text sequentially, observing what **expectations** are being aroused, how they are being satisfied or modified, how the reader recapitulates "evidence" from the portion of the text he has read to project forward a **configuration,** a tentative assumption of what the work as a whole will be and mean once it is done. The expectations are in part built by the text and in part by the repertoire of the reader, the reader's reading experience and social and cultural knowledge.

Historical Criticism

Dialogism

Another critical approach that gives a significant role to the reader and is particularly useful for long fiction is **dialogism,** largely identified with the work of Mikhail Bakhtin (1895–1975). The dialogic critic bases the study of language and literature on the individual utterance, taking into account the specific time, the place, the speaker, and the listener or reader. Such critics thus see language as a continuous dialogue, each utterance being a reply to what has gone before. Even thought, which they define as inner speech, is a dialogue between utterances that you have taken in. Even your own language (and thus thought) is itself dialogic, for it is made up of the dialogue in which you are engaged, that which you have heard from parents and peers, teachers and television, all kinds of social and professional discourse and reading. Indeed, you speak many "languages"—those of your ethnic, social, economic, national, professional, gender, and other identities. Your individual language consists in the combination of those languages. The literary form in which the dialogic is most interesting, complex, and significant is the novel, for there you have the languages not only of the characters (as you do in drama), but also that of a mediator or narrator and passages of description or analysis or information that seem to come from other voices—newspapers, whaling manuals, legal cases, and so on. Because the world is growing more interrelated and we have multiple voices rather than one dominant voice or language, the novel has become the most appropriate form for the representation of that world.

Because the dialogic sees utterances, including literary utterances or works, as specific to a time and place, one of its dimensions, unlike formalist, structuralist, or psychological criticism, is *historical*. Nineteenth-century **historical criticism** took the obvious fact that a work is created in a specific historical and cultural context and that the author is a member of that context and treated literature as a product of the culture. Formalists and others emphasizing the **aesthetic** value of literature saw this as reducing the literary work to the status of a mere historical document and the abandonment of literary study to history. The dialogic critic sees the work in relation to its host context, a part of the dialogue of the culture. The work in turn helps to create the context for other utterances, literary and otherwise. Some even consider dialogic criticism a form of sociological criticism.

SOCIOLOGICAL CRITICISM   More recently, as the scientists from psychology to physics recognized the role of the perceiver in perception, historians realized that they were not only discovering and looking at facts but were finding what they were looking for, selecting facts to fit preconceived views or interpretations. Literary historians or historical critics began to see literature not as a mere passive product of "history" but a contributor and even creator of history. An early form of this kind of historicism was **sociological criticism,** in which literature is seen as one aspect of the larger processes of history, especially those processes involving people acting in social groups or as members of social institutions or movements. Much sociological criticism uses literary texts to illustrate social attitudes and tendencies—and therefore has been strongly resisted by formalists, structuralists, and other "objectivist" critics as not being properly literary—but sociological criticism also attempts to relate what happens in texts to social events and patterns and is as concerned about the effects of texts on human events as about the effects of historical events on texts. Sociological criticism assumes that the most significant aspects of human beings are social and that the most important functions of literature thus involve the way that literature both portrays and influences human interactions. Much sociological criticism centers its attention on contemporary life and texts, seeking to affect both societal directions and literary ones in the present, but some sociological criticism is historical, concerned with differences in different times and places and anxious to interpret directions of literature in terms of historical emphases and patterns.

MARXIST CRITICISM   The most insistent and vigorous historicism through most of the 20th century has been **Marxism,** based on the work of Karl Marx (1818–1883). Marxist criticism, like other historical critical methods in the 19th century, treated literature as a passive product of the culture, specifically of the economic aspect, and therefore of class warfare. Economics, the underlying cause of history, was thus the *base,* and culture, including literature and the other arts, the *superstructure.* The literary works of a period would, then, properly viewed from the Marxist perspective, reveal the state of the struggle between classes in the historical place and moment.

Marxist critics, however, early on recognized the role of perception. They insisted that all use of language, including literary and critical language, is **ideological,** that is, that it derives from and expresses preconceived ideas, particularly economic or class values. Criticism is thus not just the product of the culture but part of the discourse or "conversation" that is what we call history. Formalism and even the extreme apolitical position of **aestheticism,** "art for art's sake," by placing art in a realm above the grubbiness of everyday life— above such mundane things as politics and money—removes art from having any importance in that life. This "bourgeois mystification of art" tends to support the class in power. Marxism has traditionally been sensitive to and articulate about power politics in both life and literature, and both its social and literary analysis has often been based on an explicit or implicit political agenda, though many Marxist critics are motivated more by theoretical than practical aims. In recent years, especially in the wake of post-structuralism and the psychoanalytical criticism of the 70s and 80s, Marxist criticism has become increasingly theoretical and less doctrinaire politically. Critics such as Raymond Williams, Fredric Jameson, Terry Eagleton, Pierre Macherey, Walter Benjamin, and Louis Althusser have gained wide audiences among readers with a variety of political and literary commitments. Over the course of the century, it has been Marxism that has most often and most consistently raised referential and historical issues about literature, and those readers who have been interested in the interactive relationship between literature and life have most often turned for their guidance on such issues to Marxist analysts, whether or not they share their philosophical or political assumptions. In the past decade, however, two other critical schools with strong commitments to historical and cultural issues have become very powerful intellectually and have attracted many practitioners and adherents. These two, feminism and new historicism, have (along with Marxism and, in its way, dialogism) turned critical attention powerfully toward historical and representational issues, and since the mid-1980s they have set the dominant directions in literary criticism.

FEMINIST CRITICISM Like Marxist criticism, feminist criticism derives from firm political and ideological commitments and insists that literature both reflects and influences human behavior in the larger world. Feminist criticism often, too, has practical and political aims. Strongly conscious that most of recorded history has given grossly disproportionate attention to the interests, thoughts, and actions of men, feminist thought endeavors both to extend contemporary attention to distinctively female concerns, ideas, and accomplishments and to recover the largely unrecorded and unknown history of women in earlier times. Not all directions of feminist criticism are historical; feminism has, in fact, taken many different directions and forms in recent years, and it has many different concerns. French feminist criticism, for example, has been deeply influenced by psychoanalysis, especially Lacanian psychoanalysis, and by French post-structuralist emphasis on language. Beyond their common aim of explicating and furthering specifically female interests, feminist critics may differ substantially in their assumptions and emphases. Like Marxism, feminism draws creatively on various other approaches and theories for its several methodologies. The most common historical directions of American feminism in particular involve the recovery of neglected or forgotten texts written by women in earlier times, the redrawing of literary values to include forms of writing (letters and autobiography, for example) that women were able to create when more public and accepted forms were denied to them, the discovery of the roles (positive and negative) that reading played in the lives and consciousnesses of women when they were unable to pursue more "active" and "public" courses, and the sorting out of cultural values implicit in the way women are represented in the texts of particular times and places.

New Historicism

New historicism has less obvious ideological commitments than Marxism or feminism, but it shares their interest in the investigation of how power is distributed and used in different cultures. Drawing on the insights of modern anthropology (and especially on the work of Clifford Geertz), new historicism wishes to isolate the fundamental values in texts and cultures, and it regards texts both as evidence of basic cultural patterns and as forces in cultural and social change. Many of the most influential practitioners of the new historicism come out of the ranks of Marxism and feminism, and new historicists are usually knowledgeable about most varieties of literary theory. Like Marxists and feminists, they are anxious to uncover the ideological commitments in texts, and they care deeply about historical and cultural difference and the way texts represent it. But personal commitments and specific political agendas usually are less important—at least explicitly—to new historicists, and one of the main contentions between feminists and new historicists—or between Marxists and new historicists—involves disagreement about the role that one's own politics should play in the practice of criticism. Many observers regard new historicism as politically to the left in its analysis of traditional cultural values, but critics on the left are suspicious of new historicism, especially of its reluctance to state its premises openly, and they generally regard its assumptions as conservative. Whatever its fundamental political commitments, however (or whether its commitments can be fairly described as having a consistent and specifiable bias), new historicism is far more interested than any other literary approach in social groups generally ignored by literary historians, and it refuses to privilege "literature" over other printed, oral, or material texts. "Popular literature" often gets major attention in the work of new historicists, who see all texts in a culture as somehow expressive of its values and directions and thus as equally useful in determining the larger intellectual, epistemological, and ethical system of which any text is a part. Texts here are thus seen as less specifically individual and distinctive than in most objectivist criticisms, and although new historicists are sometimes interested in the psychology of authors or readers their main concern is with the prevailing tendencies shared across a culture and thus shared across all kinds of texts, whatever their class status, literary value, or political aim.

Pluralism

These classifications are not pigeonholes, and you will notice that many of the approaches overlap: many feminists, especially French feminist critics, are Lacanian or post-structuralist as well, while British feminists often lean toward sociological, especially Marxist, criticism; dialogic critics accept many of the starting points and methods of reader-response and sociological critics, and so on. These crossovers or combinations are generally enriching; they cause problems only when the critic seems to be operating out of contradictory assumptions.

There is a lively debate among critics and theorists at present involving the question of whether readers should bring together the insights and methods of different schools (practitioners of the mixing of methods are usually called **pluralists**) or whether they should commit themselves wholeheartedly to a single system. Pluralists contend that they make use of promising insights or methods wherever they find them and argue that putting together the values of different approaches leads to a more fair and balanced view of texts and their uses. Opponents—those who insist on a consistency of ideological commitment— argue that pluralists are simply unwilling to state or admit their real commitments, and that any mixing of methods leads to confusion, uncertainty, and inconsistency rather than fairness. Readers, conscious or not of their assumptions and their methods, make this basic choice—to follow one lead or many— and the kind of reading they do and the conclusions they come to depend not only on this basic choice but many others suggested by the dominant strands of recent criticism that have been described here. Not all critics are aware of their assumptions, methodologies, or values, and some would even deny that they begin with any particular assumptions or biases, but is is often useful, especially to readers newly learning to practice literary criticism, to sort out their own beliefs carefully and see exactly what kind of difference it makes in the way they read literature and ask questions of it.

Further Reading on Critical Approaches

For good introductions to the issues discussed here, see the following books from which we have drawn in our discussion and definitions:

Robert Alter, *The Pleasures of Reading in an Ideological Age*, New York, 1989

Jonathan Culler, *The Pursuit of Signs*, London, 1981

Jonathan Culler, *On Deconstruction*, London, 1983

Robert Con Davis and Ronald Schleifer, *Contemporary Literary Criticism*, 2d ed., New York, 1989

Mary Eagleton (ed.), *Feminist Literary Theory: A Reader*, Oxford, 1986

Terry Eagleton, *Literary Theory: An Introduction*, Minneapolis, 1983

Nannerl Keohane, Michelle Z. Rosaldo, and Barbara C. Gelpi (eds.), *Feminist Theory: A Critique of Ideology*, Chicago, 1982

Dominick LaCapra, *History and Criticism*, Ithaca, N.Y., 1985

Frank Lentricchia, *After the New Criticism*, Chicago, 1980

Frank Lentricchia and Thomas Mclaughlin (eds.), *Critical Terms for Literary Study*, Chicago, 1990

Richard Macksey and Eugenio Donato (eds.), *The Structuralist Controversy: The Languages of Criticism and the Sciences of Man*, Baltimore, 1972

Toril Moi, *Sexual-Textual Politics*, New York, 1985

Jean Piaget (translated by Chanihan Maschler), *Structuralism*, New York, 1970

Tzvetan Todorov, *Mikhail Bakhtin: The Dialogic Principle*, Minneapolis, 1984

DECIDING WHAT TO WRITE ABOUT

Having Something to Say

Deciding what to write about—what approach to use, which questions to ask—seems like the first step in the process of writing a paper about a work of fiction. It isn't. Before that, you have to have confidence that you have something to say. If you are a beginner at this kind of writing, you are likely to have deep doubts about that. Developing confidence is not, at the beginning, easy. You may feel as if you can *never* begin and want to put off the paper forever, or you may want to plunge in fast and get it over with. Either of these approaches, though common and tempting, is a mistake: the best way is to begin preparing for the paper as soon as possible—the moment you know you have one to write—but not to hurry into the writing itself.

The first step is to get close enough to the work to feel comfortable with it. Before you can tell anyone else about what you have read—and writing about fiction is just another form of talking about fiction, although a more formal and organized one—you need to "know" the work, to have a sure sense of what the work itself is like, how its parts function, what ideas it expresses, how it creates particular effects, how it makes you feel. And the only way you will get to know the work is to spend time with it, reading it carefully and thoughtfully and turning it over in your mind. There is no substitute for reading, several times and with care, the work you are going to write about *before* you pick up a pen and prepare to write. And let your reading be the *work itself*, not something *about* that work, at least at first; later, your instructor may steer you to back-ground materials or to critical readings about the work, but at first you should encounter the work alone and become aware of your own private responses to the work.

Begin, then, by reading, several times, the work you are going to write about. The first time, read it straight through at one sitting: read slowly, paus-ing at its natural divisions—between paragraphs, or sections, or chapters, or at the ends of scenes—to consider how you are responding to the work. Later, when your knowledge of the work is more nearly complete and when you have the "feel" of the whole, you can compare your early responses with your more considered thoughts about the work, in effect "correcting" your first impres-sions in whatever way seems necessary on the basis of new and better knowledge. But if you are non-committal at first, refusing to notice what you think and feel, you will have nothing to correct, and you may cut yourself off from the most direct routes of response. Feelings are not always reliable—about literature any more than about people—but they are always the first point of contact with a literary work: you feel before you think. Try to start with your mind open, as if it were a blank sheet of paper ready to receive an impression from what you read.

When you have finished a first reading, think about your first impressions. Think about how the story began, how it gained your interest, how its conflicts and issues were resolved, how it ended, how it made you feel from beginning to end. Write down any phrases or events that you remember especially vividly, anything you are afraid you might forget. Look back at any parts that puzzled you at first. Write down in one sentence what you think the story is about. Then read the story again, this time much more slowly, making notes as you go on any passages that seem especially significant and pausing over any features or passages that puzzle you. Then write a longer statement—three or four sentences—summarizing the story and suggesting more fully what it seems to be about. Try to write the kind of summary described above on pages 659–660.

Stop. Do something else for a while, something as different as possible—see a movie, do math problems, ride a bicycle, listen to music, have a meal, take a nap, mow the lawn, build a loft. Do NOT do some other reading you have been meaning to do. When you go back to the story and finish reading it for the third time—rapidly and straight through—write down in a sentence the most important thing you would want to tell someone else who was about to read the story for the first time: not just whether you liked it or not, but what exactly you liked, how the whole story seems to have worked.

Now you are ready to choose a topic.

Choosing a Topic

Once you are ready to choose a topic, the chances are that you have already—quietly and unconsciously—chosen one. The clue is in the last statement you wrote. The desire to tell someone about a work of fiction is a wonderful place to begin. Good papers almost always grow out of a desire to communicate. Desire is not enough, of course—the substance (and most of the work, sentence by sentence) is still ahead of you; but desire will get you started. Chances are that what you wrote down as the one thing you most wanted to say is close to the heart of the central issue in the work you are going to write about. Your statement will become, perhaps, in somewhat revised form, your thesis.

The next step is to convert your personal feelings and desire to communicate into something communicable—into an "objective" statement about the work, a statement that will mean something to someone else. Again, you may already be further along than you realize. Look at the "summary" you wrote after your second reading. The summary will probably sound factual, objective, and general about the work; the personal statement you wrote after the third reading will be more emotional, subjective, and particular about some aspect of the work. In combining the two successfully lies the key to a good paper: what you need to do is to write persuasively an elaboration and explanation of the last statement so that your reader comes to share the "objective" view of the whole work that your summary expresses. The summary you have written will, in short, be implicit in the whole essay; your total essay will suggest to your reader the wholeness of the work you are writing about, but it will do so by focusing its attention on some particular aspect of the work—on a part that leads to, or suggests, or represents the whole. What you want to do is build an essay on the basis of your first statement, taking a firm hold on the handle you have found. The summary is your limit and guide: it reminds you of where you will come out. Any good topic ultimately leads back to the crucial perceptions involved in a summary. Ultimately, any good writing about literature leads to a full and resonant sense of the central thrust of the work, but the most effective way to find that center is by discovering a pathway that particularly interests you. The best writing about fiction presents a clear—and well-argued—thesis about a work or works and presents it from the perspective of personal, individual perception. But the thesis should clarify the central thrust of the work, helping it to open itself up to readers more completely and more satisfyingly.

Topics often suggest themselves after a second or third reading, simply because one feature or problem stands out so prominently that it almost demands to be talked about. What is real in "The Real Thing"? Will the love between Gurov and the lady with the dog last? Sometimes you may be lucky: your instructor may *assign* a topic instead of asking you to choose your own. At first glance, that may not seem like a good break: it often feels confining to follow specific directions or to have to operate within limits and rules prescribed by someone else. The advantage is that it may save a lot of time and prevent floundering around. If your instructor assigns a topic, it is almost certain to be one that will work, one that has a payoff if you approach it creatively and without too much resentment at being directed so closely and precisely. It is time-consuming, even when you have tentatively picked a topic, to think through its implications and be sure it works. And an instructor's directions, especially if they are detailed and call attention to particular questions or passages, may aid greatly in helping you focus on particular issues or in leading you to evidence crucial to the topic.

Or one of these questions and titles might suit or might suggest a similar topic of interest to you:

1. A Plotless Story about Plot: Grace Paley's "A Conversation with My Father"?
2. The Selection and Ordering of the Scenes in "The Country Husband"
3. What does the voice in "Love Medicine" contribute to the story's structure, tone, and effect?
4. Who Am I? The Nature of the Narrator in "Our Friend Judith"
5. The Self-Characterization of Montresor in "The Cask of Amontillado"
6. Sonny's Brother's Character
7. Symbolic Cats and Symbolic Hats? "Our Friend Judith" and "Everything that Rises Must Converge"
8. The Image and Import of the Sea in "The Lady with the Dog"
9. "Only a Girl": The Theme of "Boys and Girls"
10. What is the theme of "The Rocking-Horse Winner," and how does it relate to the title of the story?

If your instructor does *not* give you a topic, if the list is not helpful, and if no topic suggests itself to you after you have read a particular work three or four times, you may sometimes have to settle for the kind of topic that will—more or less—be safe for any literary work. Some topics are almost all-purpose. You can always analyze devices of characterization in a story, showing how descriptive detail, dialogue, and the reactions of other people in the story combine to present a particular character and evoke the reader's response to him or her, for example. Such "fall-back" topics are, however, best used only as last resorts, when your instincts have failed you in a particular instance. When choice is free, a more lively and committed paper is likely to begin from a particular insight or question, something that grabs you and makes you want to say something, or solve a problem, or formulate a thesis. The best papers are usually very personal in origin; even when a topic is set by the assignment, the best papers come from a sense of having personally found an answer to a significant question. To turn a promising idea into a good paper, however, personal responses usually need to be supported by a considerable mass of evidence; the process often resembles the testing of "evidence" in a laboratory or the formulation of hypotheses and arguments in a law case—and they will usually need to go through repeated written revisions that will sharpen and refine them.

Considering Your Audience

Thinking of your paper as an argument or an explanation will also help with one of the most sensitive issues in writing about literature. The issue: To whom are you writing? Who is your audience? The obvious answer is, your instructor, but in an important sense, that is the wrong answer. It is wrong because, although it could literally be true that your instructor will be the only person (besides you) who will ever read your paper, your object in writing about literature is to learn to write for an audience of peers, people a lot like yourself who are sensible, pretty well educated, and need to have something (in this case a literary work) explained to them so that they will be able to understand it more fully. Picture your ideal reader as someone about your own age and with about the same educational background. Assume that the person is intelligent and has some idea of what literature is like and how it works, but that he or she has just read this particular literary work for the first time and has not yet had a chance to think about it carefully. Don't be insulting and explain the obvious, but don't assume either that your reader has noticed and considered every detail. The object is to inform and convince your reader, not to try to impress.

Should you, then, altogether ignore the obvious fact that it is an instructor—probably with a master's degree or Ph.D. in literature—who is your actual reader? Not altogether: you don't want to get so carried away with speaking to people of your own age and interests that you slip into slang, or feel the need to explain what a stanza is, or leave an allusion to a rock star unexplained, and you do want to learn from the kind of advice your instructor has given in class or from comments he or she may have made on other papers you have written. But don't become preoccupied with the idea that you are writing for someone in "authority" or someone you need to please. Most of all, don't think of yourself as writing for a captive audience, for a reader who *has* to read what you write. It is not always easy to know exactly who your audience is or how interested your readers may be, so you have to make the most of every single word. It is your job to get the reader's attention. And you will have to do it subtly, making conscious assumptions about what your reader already knows and what he or she can readily understand. You cannot, as in a conversation, watch the facial expressions, the eyes, the gestures of your audience and improvise. The tone of your paper should be serious and straightforward and its attitude respectful toward the reader, as well as toward the literary work. But its approach and vocabulary, while formal enough for academic writing, should be readily understandable by someone with your own background and reading experience. And it should be lively enough to interest someone like you. Try to imagine, as your ideal reader, the person in your class whom you most respect. Write to get, and hold, that person's serious attention. Try to communicate, try to teach.

FROM TOPIC TO ROUGH DRAFT

Writing about literature is very much like talking about literature. But there is one important difference. When we talk, we organize as we go—trying to get a handle, experimenting, working toward an understanding. And the early stages of preparing a paper—the notetaking, the outlining, the rough drafts—are much like that. A "finished" paper, however, has the uncertainties and tentativeness worked out and presents an argument that moves carefully and compellingly toward a conclusion. How does one get from here to there?

Once you have decided on a topic, the process of planning is fairly straightforward, but it can be time consuming and (often) frustrating. There are three basic steps in the planning process: first you gather the evidence, then you sort it into order, and (finally) you develop it into a convincing argument. The easiest way is to take these steps one by one.

Gathering Evidence

The first step involves accumulating evidence that supports the statement you have decided to make about your topic (that is, your thesis), and that takes you back (yet once more) to the text. But before you read the text again, look over the notes you have already made in the margin of that text or on separate pieces of paper. Which of them have something to do with the topic you have now defined? Which of them will be useful to you in making your main point? Which ones can you now set aside as irrelevant to the topic you have decided on?

Reading over the notes you have already made is a good preparation for re-reading the work again, for this time as you read it (at least the fourth time you will have read it) you will be looking at it in a new and quite specific way, looking for all the things in it that relate to the topic you have decided on. This time you will, in effect, be flagging everything—words, phrases, structural devices, changes of tone, anything—that bears upon your topic. As you read—very slowly and single-mindedly, with your topic always in mind—keep your pen constantly poised to mark useful points. Be ready to say something about the points as you come upon them; it's a good idea to write down, immediately, any sentences that occur to you as you re-read this time. Some of these sentences will turn out to be useful when you actually begin to write your paper. Some will be incorporated in your paper; but some will not: you will find that a lot of the notes you take, like a lot of the footage shot in making a film, will end up on the cutting room floor.

No one can tell you exactly how to take notes. Good notetaking is a highly individualized skill; precisely what notes you will need to take and how will depend on the particulars of the paper you are about to write. Ultimately, you will develop a style that is right for you, but some general guidelines may be useful. Here are five hints toward successful notetaking.

1. Keep your topic and your thesis about your topic constantly in mind as you re-read and take notes. Mark all passages in the work that bear on your topic, and for each one write on a note card a single sentence that describes how the passage relates to your topic and thesis. Indicate, for each passage, the specific location in the text by page or paragraph number.

2. Keep re-reading and taking notes until one of five things happens:

a. You get too tired and lose your concentration. (If that happens, stop and then start again when you are rested, preferably the next day.)

b. You stop finding relevant passages or perceive a noticeable drying up of your ideas. (Again, time to pause; give the work at least one more reading later when your mind is fresh and see whether the juices start anew. If they don't, you may be ready to outline and write.)

c. You begin to find yourself annotating every single sentence or line, and the evidence all begins to run together into a single blob. (Stop and sort out your thesis again, simplifying and narrowing it so that you don't try to include everything. Then go back to your notetaking and discriminate more carefully between what actually is important to your thesis and what only relates at some distance.)

d. You become impatient with your notetaking and can't wait to get started writing. (Start writing. Use scrap paper, and be prepared to go back to systematic notetaking if your ideas or your energy fade. The chances are that the prose passages you write this way will find a place in your paper, but they may not belong exactly where you think they do when you first write them down.)

e. You find that there is insufficient evidence for your thesis, that the evidence points in another direction, or that the evidence contradicts your thesis. (Revise your topic to reflect the evidence, and begin re-reading once more.)

3. When you think you have finished your notetaking, read all your note cards over slowly, one by one, and jot down any further ideas as they occur to you, each one on a separate note card. (Sometimes it will seem as if note cards beget note cards. Too much is better than too little at the notetaking stage: you can always discard them before the final draft. Don't worry if you seem to have too many notes and too much material. But later, when you boil down to essentials, you will have to be ruthless with yourself and omit some of your favorite ideas.)

4. Transfer all of your notes to pieces of paper—or note cards—that are all the same size, one note on each. It is easier to sort them this way when you get ready to organize and outline. If you like to write notes in the margin of your text (or on the backs of envelopes, or on dinner napkins, or shirtsleeves), systematically transfer every note to uniform sheets of paper or cards before you begin to outline. Having everything easily recorded on sortable cards that can be moved from one pile to another makes organizing easier later, especially when you change your mind (as you will) and decide to move a point from one part of your paper to another. Index cards—either 3 × 5, if you write small and make economical notes, or 4 × 6, if you need more space—are ideal for notetaking and sorting.

5. When you think you are done taking notes (because you are out of ideas, or out of time, or getting beyond a manageable number of pieces of evidence), read through the whole pile one more time, again letting any new ideas—or ideas that take on a fresh look because you combine them in a new way—spawn new sentences for new note cards.

How many times should you read a story before you stop taking notes? There is no right answer. If you have read the work three times before settling on a topic, two more readings may do. But it could take several more. Common sense, endurance, and deadlines will all have an effect on how many re-readings you do. Let your conscience, your judgment, and your clock be your guides.

Organizing Your Notes

The notes you have taken will become, in the next few hours, almost the whole content of your paper. The task remaining is to give that content the form and shape that will make it appealing and persuasive. But it is not an easy task: the best content in the world isn't worth much if it isn't effectively presented. The key to the task is getting all your ideas into the right order, that is, into a sequence that will allow them to argue your thesis most persuasively.

In order to put your notes into a proper order, you will need (ironically) to get a little distance from your notes. (The key to good planning and writing— and to many other pursuits—is in knowing when to back away and get some perspective.) Set your notes aside, but not too far away. On a fresh sheet of paper, write down all the major points you want to be sure to make. Write them down randomly, as they occur to you. Now read quickly through your pack of note cards and add to your list any important points you have left out. Then decide which ideas should go first, which should go second, and so on.

Putting your points in order is something of a guess at this point. You may well want to re-order them before you begin to write—or later when you are writing a first (or even later) draft. But make your best guess. The easiest way to try out an order is to take your random list and put a 1 in front of the point you will probably begin with, a 2 before the probable second point, and so on. Then copy the list, in numerical order, onto a clean sheet of paper, revising (if you need to) as you go. Do not be surprised if later you have to revise your list further. Your next task is to match up your note cards (and the examples they contain) with the points on your outline.

Putting things in a particular order is a spatial problem, and by having your notes on cards or pieces of paper of a uniform size you can do much of your organizing physically. Do your sorting on a large table or sit in the middle of the floor. Prepare a title card for each point in your outline, writing on it the point and its probable place in your paper, then line them up on the table or floor in order before you begin writing.

Two-thirds of this exercise is quite easy: most examples and ideas you have written down will match quite easily with a particular point. But some cards will resist classification. Some cards will seem to belong in two or more places; others will not seem to belong at all. If a card seems to belong to more than one point, put it in the pile with the lowest number (but write on it the number or numbers of other possible locations). If, for example, a card might belong in point 2 but could also belong in point 6 or 9, put it in the pile of 2's and write "maybe 6 or 9" on the card; if you don't use it in writing about point 2 move it to pile 6; if you don't use it in 6, move it to 9. Remember that you will work your way through the piles in numerical order, so that you have a safety system for notes that don't seem to belong where you first thought but that still belong somewhere in your paper. Move them to a possible later point, or put them in a special pile (marked "?" or "use in revised draft") and, once you have completed a first draft on your paper, go through this pile, carefully looking for places in your paper where these ideas may belong. Almost never will everything fit neatly into your first draft. If everything does seem to fit exactly as you had originally planned, you have either done an incredible job of planning and guessing about the organization of your paper, or you are forcing things into inappropriate places.

Don't be surprised if you have a large number of leftover note cards, that is, cards whose ideas you haven't yet used, after you have written your first draft. You will probably find places for many of these ideas later, but some just won't fit and won't be needed for the paper you ultimately write, no matter how good the ideas are. No paper will do everything it could do. Writing a paper is a *human* project; it has limits.

Before you actually start writing, you may want to develop a more elaborate outline, incorporating your examples and including topic sentences for each paragraph, or you may wish to work from your sketchy outline and the accompanying packs of cards. Do the more detailed outline if it seems right to you, but don't delay the writing too long. You are probably ready right now, and any exercises you invent to delay writing are probably just excuses.

Developing an Argument

Once you have decided on your major points and assembled your evidence, you have to decide how you are going to present your argument and how you are going to present *yourself.* What you say is, of course, more important than how you say it, but your manner of presentation can make a world of difference. Putting your evidence together effectively—in a coherent and logical order so that your readers' curiosities and questions are answered systematically and fully—is half the task in developing a persuasive argument. The other half involves your choice of a voice and tone that will make readers want to read on—and make them favorably disposed toward what you say.

The tone of your paper is the basis of your relationship with your reader. "I will be just *me,*" you may say, "and write naturally." But writing is not a "natural" act, any more than swinging a tennis racket, carrying a football, or dancing a pirouette. The "me" you choose to present is only one of several possible me's; you will project a certain mood, a certain attitude toward your subject, a certain confidence. How do you want your readers to feel about you and your argument? Being too positive can make your readers fell stupid and inadequate and can turn them into defensive, resistant readers who will rebel at your every point. Friendship with your reader is better than an adversary relationship. Sounding like a nice person who is talking reasonably and sensibly is not enough if in fact you don't make sense or have nothing to say, but the purpose of the tone you choose is to make your reader receptive to your content, not hostile. The rest of the job depends on the argument itself.

It has been said that all good papers should be organized in the same way:

1. Tell 'em what you're going to tell 'em.
2. Tell 'em.
3. Tell 'em what you told 'em.

That description fits—in pretty general terms—the most common kind of organization, which includes an introduction, a body of argument, and a conclusion, but if it is followed too simplistically it can lead to a paper that sounds simple-minded. The beginning does need to introduce the subject, sort out the essential issues, and suggest what your perspective will be, and the conclusion does need to sum up what you have said in the main part of your paper, but the first paragraph shouldn't give *everything* away, nor should the final one simply repeat what is already clear. Lead into your subject clearly but with a little subtlety; arrange your main points in the most effective manner you can think of, building a logical argument and supporting your general points with clear textual evidence, concisely phrased and presented, and at the end show *how* your argument has added up—don't just *say* that it did.

There are, of course, other ways to organize than the basic Tell-3 method, but the imagination and originality that can be exercised in a straightforward Tell-3 paper are practically unlimited.

Writing the First Draft

It is now time to set pen to paper. No one can help you much now for a while. The main thing is to get started right with a clear first sentence that expresses your sense of direction and arrests the attention of your readers. (If you can't think of a good first sentence, don't pause over it too long. Write down a paraphrase of what you want it to say—something like the statement you wrote down after your third reading—and go on to start writing about your main points. Your "first" sentence may sometimes be the last one you will write.) And then you inch along, word by word and sentence by sentence, as you follow your outline from one paragraph to another. Keep at it. Struggle. Stare into space. Bite your pen when you feel like it. Get up and stride about the room. Scratch your head. Sharpen a pencil. Run your fingers through your hair. Groan. Snap your fingers. Pray. But keep writing.

It is often frustrating as you search for the right word or struggle to decide how the next sentence begins, but it is satisfying when you get it right. Stay with it until you complete a draft you think you can live with. Write "The End" at the bottom and set it aside. Breathe a sigh of relief.

And try not to think about the revisions you will do tomorrow.

FROM ROUGH DRAFT TO COMPLETED PAPER

Revising

This final stage of the process is the most important of all, and it is the easiest one to mismanage. There is a world of difference between a bunch of ideas that present a decent interpretation of a work of literature and a cogent, coherent, persuasive essay that will stir your readers to a nod of agreement and shared pleasure in a moment of insight. If you haven't done good literary analysis and sorted out your insights earlier, nothing you do at this stage will help much, but if what you have done so far is satisfactory, this is the stage that can turn your paper into something special.

The important thing is not to allow yourself to be too easily satisfied. If you have struggled with earlier stages, it may be tempting to think you are finished when you have put a period to the last sentence in your first draft. It will often feel as if you are done: you may feel drained, tired of the subject, anxious to get on to other things, such as sleep or food or friends or another project. And it *is* a good idea to take a break once you've finished a draft and let what you have done settle for a few hours, preferably overnight. (The Roman poet and critic Horace suggested putting a draft aside for nine years, but most instructors won't wait that long.) Re-reading it "cold" may be discouraging, though: all those sentences that felt so good when you wrote them often seem flat and stale, or even worthless, when a little time has elapsed. The biggest struggle in moving from a first draft to a second one is to keep from throwing what you have written into a wastebasket—or to keep from throwing up on top of it. Resist. It will get better, but not without your help.

It may take *several* more drafts to produce your best work. Often it is tempting to cut corners—to smooth out a troublesome paragraph by obscuring the issue or by omitting the difficult point altogether instead of confronting it, or to ask a roommate or friend for help in figuring out what is wrong with a particular passage. But you will learn more in the long run—and probably do better in the short run as well—if you make yourself struggle a bit. When a particular word or phrase you have used turns out to be imprecise, or misleading, or ambiguous, search until you find the *right* word or phrase. (At the least put a big X in the margin so that you will come back and fix it later.) If a paragraph is incomplete or poorly organized, fill it out or reorganize it. If a transition from one point to another does not work, look again at your outline and see if another way of ordering your points would help. *Never* decide that the problem can best be solved by hoping that your reader will not notice. The satisfaction of finally solving the problem will build your confidence and sooner or later make your writing easier and better.

Reviewing Your Work and Revising Again

Precisely how you move from one draft to another is up to you and will properly depend on the ways you work best; the key is to find all the things that bother you (and that *should* bother you) and then gradually correct them, moving toward a better paper with each succeeding draft. Here are some things to watch for.

Thesis and central thrust: Is it clear what your main point is? Do you state it clearly, effectively, and early? Do you make clear what the work is about? Are you fair to the spirit and emphasis of the work? Do you make clear the relationship between your thesis and the central thrust of the work? Do you explain *how* the work creates its effect rather than just asserting it?

Organization: Does your paper move logically from beginning to end? Does your first paragraph set up the main issue you are going to discuss and suggest the direction of your discussion? Do your paragraphs follow each other in a coherent and logical order? Does the first sentence of each paragraph accurately suggest what that paragraph will contain? Does your final paragraph draw a conclusion that follows from the body of your paper? Do you resolve the issues you say you resolve?

Use of evidence: Do you use enough examples? Too many? Does each example prove what you say it does? Do you explain each example fully enough? Are the examples sufficiently varied? Are any of them labored, or over-explained, or made to bear more weight than they can stand? Have you left out any examples useful to your thesis? Do you include any gratuitous ones just because you like them? Have you achieved a good balance between examples and generalizations?

Tone: How does your voice sound in the paper? Confident? Arrogant? Boastful? Does it show off too much? Is it too timid or self-effacing? Do you ever sound smug? Too tentative? Too dogmatic? Would a neutral reader be put off by any of your assertions? By your way of arguing? By your choice of examples? By the language you use?

Sentences: Does each sentence read clearly and crisply? Have you rethought and rewritten any sentences you can't explain? Is the first sentence of your paper a strong, clear one likely to gain the interest of a neutral reader? Is the first sentence of each paragraph an especially vigorous one? Are your sentences varied enough? Do you avoid the passive voice and "there is/there are" sentences?

Word Choice: Have you used any words whose meaning you are not sure of? In any cases in which you were not sure of what word to use, did you stay with the problem until you found the exact word? Do your metaphors and figures of speech make literal sense? Are all the idioms used correctly? Is your terminology correct? Are your key words always used to mean *exactly* the same thing? Have you avoided sounding repetitive by varying your sentences rather than using several different terms to mean precisely the same thing?

Conciseness: Have you eliminated all the padding you put in when you didn't think your paper would be long enough? Have you gone through your paper, sentence by sentence, to eliminate all the unnecessary words and phrases? Have you looked for sentences (or even paragraphs) that essentially repeat what you have already said—and eliminated all repetition? Have you checked for multiple examples and pared down to the best and most vivid ones? Have you got rid of all inflated phrasing calculated to impress readers? Have you eliminated all roundabout phrases and rewritten long, complicated, or confusing sentences into shorter, clearer ones? Are you convinced that you have trimmed every possible bit of excess and that you cannot say what you have to say any more economically?

Mechanics: Have you checked the syntax in each *separate* sentence? Have you checked the spelling of any words that you are not sure of or that look funny? Have you examined each sentence separately for punctuation? Have you checked every quotation word by word against the original? Have you given proper credit for all material—written or oral—that you have borrowed from others? Have you followed the directions your instructor gave you for citations, footnotes, and form?

The most effective way to revise in the final stages is to read through your paper looking for one problem at a time, that is, to go through it once looking at paragraphing, another time looking at individual sentences, still another for word choice or problems of grammar. It is almost impossible to check too many things too often—although you can get so absorbed with little things that you overlook larger matters. With practice, you will learn to watch carefully for the kinds of mistakes you are most prone to. Everyone has individual weaknesses and flaws. Here are some of the most common temptations that beginning writers fall for:

1. Haste. (Don't start too late, or finish too soon after you begin.)
2. Pretentiousness. (Don't use words you don't understand, tackle problems that are too big for you, or write sentences you can't explain; it is more important to make sense than to make a big, empty impression.)
3. Boredom. (The quickest way to bore others is to be bored yourself. If you think your paper will be a drag, you are probably right. It is hard to fake interest in something you can't get excited about; keep at it until you find a spark.)
4. Randomness. (Don't try to string together half a dozen unrelated ideas or insights and con yourself into thinking that you have written a paper.)
5. Imprecision. (Don't settle for approximation, either in words or ideas; something that is 50 percent right is also 50 percent wrong.)
6. Universalism. (Don't try to be a philosopher and make grand statements about life; stick to what is in the story you are writing about.)
7. Vagueness. (Don't settle for a general "sense" of the work you are talking about; get it detailed, get it right.)
8. Wandering. (Don't lose track of your subject or the work that you are talking about.)
9. Sloppiness. (Don't sabotage all your hard work on analysis and writing by failing to notice misspelled words, grammatical mistakes, misquotations, incorrect citations or references, or typographical errors. Little oversights make readers suspicious.)
10. Impatience. (Don't be too anxious to get done. Enjoy the experience; savor the process. Have fun watching yourself learn.)

Being flexible—being willing to rethink your ideas and reorder your argument as you go—is crucial to success in writing, especially in writing about fiction. You will find different (and better) ways to express your ideas and feelings as you struggle with revisions, and you will also find that—in the course of analyzing the work, preparing to write, writing, and rewriting—your response to the work itself will have grown and shifted somewhat. Part of the reason is that you will have become more knowledgeable as a result of the time and effort you have spent, and you will have a more subtle understanding of the work. But part of the reason will also be that the work itself will not be exactly the same. Just as a work is a little different for every reader, it is also a little different with every successive reading by the *same* reader, and what you will be capturing in your words is some of the subtlety of the work, its capacity to produce effects that are alive and that are therefore always changing just slightly. You need not, therefore, feel that you must say the final word about the work you are writing about—but you do want to say whatever word you have to say in the best possible way.

You can turn all this into a full-time job, of course, but you needn't. It is hard work, and at first the learning seems slow and the payoff questionable. A basketball novice watching the magic of Magic Johnson may find it hard to see the point of practicing lay-ups, but even creative geniuses have to go through those awful moments of sitting down and putting pen to paper (and then crossing out and rewriting again and again). But that's the way you learn to make it seem easy. Art is mostly craft, and craft means methodical work.

It *will* come more easily with practice. But you needn't aspire to professional writing to take pleasure in what you accomplish. Learning to write well about fiction will help you with all sorts of tasks, some of them having little to do with writing. Writing trains the mind, creates habits, teaches you procedures that will have all kinds of long-range effects that you may not immediately recognize or be able to predict. And ultimately it is very satisfying, even if it is not easy, to be able to stand back and say, "That is mine. Those are my words. I know what I'm talking about. I understand, and I can make someone else understand."

One final bit of advice: do not follow, too rigidly or too closely, anyone's advice, including ours. We have suggested some general strategies and listed some common pitfalls. But writing is a very personal experience, and you will have talents (and faults) that are a little different from anyone else's. Learn to play to your own strengths and avoid the weaknesses that you are especially prone to. Pay attention to your instructor's comments; learn from your own mistakes.

A SUMMARY OF THE PROCESS

Here, briefly, is a summary, step by step, of the stages we have suggested you move through in preparing a paper about fiction.

Stage One: Deciding what to write about

- Read the work straight through, thoughtfully. Make notes at the end on any points that caught your special attention.
- Read the work again more slowly, pausing to think through all the parts you don't understand. When you finish, write a three- or four-sentence summary.
- Read the work again, carefully but quite quickly. Decide what you feel most strongly about in the work, and write down the one thing you would most want to explain to a friend about how the story works, or (if the work still puzzles you) the one question you would most like to be able to answer.
- Decide how the statement you made at the end of your third reading relates to the summary you wrote down after the second reading.
- Write a one-paragraph "promise" of what your paper is going to argue.

Stage Two: Planning your paper

- Read the work at least twice more and make notes on anything that relates to your thesis.
- Read through all your notes so far, and for each write a sentence articulating how it relates to your thesis.
- Transfer all your notes to note cards of uniform size.
- Read through all your notes again and record any new observations or ideas on additional note cards.
- Set aside your note cards for the moment, and make a brief outline of the major points you intend to make.
- Sort the note cards into piles corresponding to the major points in your outline. Sort the cards in each separate pile into the most likely order of their use in the paper.
- Make a more detailed outline (including the most significant examples) from your pile of note cards on each point.

- Reconsider your order of presentation and make any necessary adjustments.
- Begin writing.

Stage Three: Rewriting

- Go over your writing, word by word, sentence by sentence, and paragraph by paragraph, in draft after draft until your writing is worthy of the ideas you want to express.

Stage Four: Final preparation

- Type or word-process. Chances are that your instructor does not have a degree in hieroglyphics.
- Proofread. Who wants to read a paper you did not care enough about to read yourself?
- Proofread again. Find your mistakes before someone else does.
- Read it one more time.
- Keep your fingers crossed.

A SAMPLE PAPER

The essay that follows was written by a student in his first year at Emory University. We are grateful to Geoffrey Clement for his kind permission to reprint his paper here.

The Struggle to Surface
in the Water of "Sonny's Blues"

Geoffrey Clement

In "Sonny's Blues," James Baldwin employs water as a symbol that enables him to concentrate more clearly on the lack of and the crucial need for a real sense of communication among members of society. As Baldwin captures the intensity of Sonny's and his brother's struggles to understand their situation, he vividly depicts a society that seeks to swallow up the souls of its inhabitants and gradually to drown them spiritually. Thus, Baldwin illustrates quite clearly his sense of the hopelessness in man's plight. In portraying the struggle of street life in Harlem, he uses water in its opposite forms--frozen water and boiling water-- and toward the end of the story, as Sonny's and his brother's revelations help to resolve the conflict, the water becomes calm.

Initially, and as a result of Sonny's arrest, Sonny's brother gradually realizes that he has not fulfilled his promise and that his feelings of love for his brother have certainly gone unexpressed, if indeed they exist. As a result, he feels physically the coldness that has permeated his emotional life: "It was a special kind of ice. It kept melting, sending trickles of ice water all up and down my veins, but it never got less. Sometimes it hardened and seemed to expand . . ." (par. 2). So the ice represents his guilt and his fears, both of which will lessen little. Although he learns to adapt to these feelings, they occasionally resurface. Upon Sonny's return from prison, for example, his brother thinks, "and thank God she [his wife] was there, for I was filled with that icy dread again. Everything I did seemed awkward to me, and everything I said sounded freighted with hidden meaning. . . . I was dying to hear him tell me he was safe." (par. 76) In addition to this guilt, Sonny's brother experiences much of the same emotional turmoil that Sonny has endured. In this passage in particular, he is seeking reassurance that there is a way to survive their imprisonment without having to feel the pain Sonny felt. Baldwin not only uses ice to show the brother's disappointment in his failures as a brother but also to point to the brother's own struggle for security, identity, and communication.

As Sonny's brother begins to realize that within him there has grown a heart hardened and haunted by the cold darkness of Harlem's

streets, he also begins to recognize many of the
realities that his brother has faced and that he
too must eventually face. Sonny's brother is
spiritually walking through "the vivid, killing
streets of our childhood. These streets hadn't
changed, though housing projects jutted up out
of them now like rocks in the middle of a boiling sea." (par. 73) Here, Baldwin paints an
almost hellish picture of pain and suffering, of
emotional torment and fears, and of spiritual
drowning and isolation, all of which slowly
become real in the mind of Sonny's brother. He
begins to feel for the first time in his life
the depth of his denial of his brother. Tragi-
cally, he finds that when he is ready to reach
out to help Sonny, he cannot, for he is even
more lost and confused than Sonny himself. Sonny's brother wants desperately to save Sonny
from the inevitable struggle, yet he learns from
Sonny that "the storm inside" (par. 217) will
pass over only with the constant expression of
love. Clearly, the process of revelation is a
very dramatic one, since Sonny's brother comes
to understand Sonny's need for a giving, communicating, responsible relationship, a commitment
filled with careful listening, compassion, and
understanding. Sonny does not believe he can
make his brother understand his experiences with
drugs: "I can never tell you. I was all by
myself at the bottom of something, and I thought
I'd die if I couldn't get away from it and yet,

all the same, I knew that everything I was doing
was just locking me in with it" (par. 220). Once
his brother grasps the importance of listening
with love and understanding, however, Sonny is
finally able to reach out.

Toward the end of the story, the ice and the
boiling sea come together, and there is peace;
Sonny is able to reach out, and he starts to
swim in the calmer water. Now, he finds freedom
in expressing his struggles through his music,
while at the same time alerting his audience to
the lessons he has learned. Creole "wanted Sonny
to leave the shoreline and strike out for the
deep water. He was Sonny's witness that deep
water and drowning were not the same thing"
(par. 234). As Sonny ventures further and further into his own understanding of life's struggles, he tries, his brother tells us, "to find
new ways to make us listen. For, while the tale
of how we suffer, and how we are delighted, and
how we may triumph is never new, it always must
be heard. . . . it's the only light we've got in
all this darkness" (par. 238). In a powerful
way, Sonny taught the audience to listen: "Freedom lurked around us and I understood, at last,
that he could help us be free if we would listen, that we would never be free until we did"
(par. 240). The boiling rage of the streets and
the coldness within his heart are reconciled as
the brother finally witnesses "Sonny's world"
(par. 231). Finally, he recognizes that Sonny

has found the strength of knowing that he has discovered in music the outlet through which he can express himself and warn others of his mistakes. He sends up to the bandstand not water, not ice, but Scotch and milk. Sonny sips it in a sort of communion and puts it back on top of the piano, where "it glowed and shook about . . . [his] head like the very cup of trembling" (par. 241).

Thoughout his story, Baldwin stresses the lack of companionship to try to manipulate the reader's emotions. Playing on the contrasts between forms of water, he draws parallels to the theme of emotional conflict within the minds of Sonny and his brother. While the sea is calmer toward the end, there is still a sense of rage, because only in the expression of his struggle is Sonny able to find meaning, satisfaction, and forgiveness for his brother. The streets, society's common ground, still try to isolate its members as each person individually struggles to reach the surface. But if the struggler can find a listening helper, which Sonny finds in his brother, then he will reach the surface and breathe the fulfilling breath of love. The cup of trembling will be taken out of the struggler's hands, the Bible tells us, and will be put "into the hands of them that afflict thee" (p. 300n.). Light gracefully touches and penetrates the surface of the water, and the cup of trembling is still.

BIOGRAPHICAL SKETCHES

WOODY ALLEN (b. 1935)

A native of Brooklyn, Allen Stewart Konigsberg is a comedian, actor, playwright, screenwriter, writer, and director. He began his career in 1952, when he joined the National Broadcasting Corporation as a staff writer. His screenplays began with *What's New Pussycat?* (1965) and include a number of critically acclaimed films in which he was also actor and director, his latest being *Crimes and Misdemeanors* (1989). He has also written several Broadway plays. His books *Getting Even* (1971), *Without Feathers* (1975), and *Side Effects* (1980), primarily composed of essays and sketches previously published in *The New Yorker*, take a humorous look at the modern American city dweller and at such concerns as death, God, and sex. Allen has won several Academy Awards for his films; "The Kugelmass Episode" won the annual O. Henry Award as the best story of 1978.

MARGARET ATWOOD (b. 1939)

Atwood spent her first eleven years in sparsely populated areas of northern Ontario and Quebec, where her father worked as an entomologist. After her education at the University of Toronto and Harvard, she held various jobs in Canada, America, England, and Italy. Atwood published her first poem when she was just nineteen, and she has won numerous prizes for her poetry as well as her fiction, which has become increasingly political over the years. Her novels include *The Edible Woman* (1969), *Surfacing* (1972), *Lady Oracle* (1976), *Life Before Man* (1979), *Bodily Harm* (1982), *The Handmaid's Tale* (1985), and *Cat's Eye* (1988). Many of her stories have been collected in *Dancing Girls and Other Stories* (1978), *Murder in the Dark* (1983), and *Bluebeard's Egg* (1983).

JAMES BALDWIN (1924–1987)

Baldwin was for some time perhaps the leading literary spokesman for black Americans. Born in Harlem, long a resident of France, he first attracted critical attention with two extraordinary novels, *Go Tell It on the Mountain* (1953) and *Giovanni's Room* (1956), which dealt, somewhat autobiographically, with religious awakening (Baldwin was a minister at fourteen but later left his church) and the anguish of being black and homosexual in a white and heterosexual society. Baldwin was also a dramatist and an outstanding essayist, his best-known nonfiction prose being *Notes of a Native Son* (1955), *Nobody Knows My Name* (1961), and *The Fire Next Time* (1963), aimed at unraveling the repressive myths of white society and at healing the disastrous estrangement he found in the lives of black people in America. His stories are collected in *Going to Meet the Man* (1965), from which "Sonny's Blues" is taken.

TONI CADE BAMBARA (b. 1939)

Born in New York City, Bambara grew up in Harlem and Bedford-Stuyvesant, two of its poorest neighborhoods. She began writing while still a child. After graduating from Queens College, she worked at various jobs while studying for her M.A. at the City College of

New York, writing fiction all the while in "the predawn in-betweens." Bambara began to publish her stories in 1962. She has also been a dancer, teacher, editor, and critic, and has worked in psychiatric and drug therapy, youth organizing, and settlement houses. Her work includes two anthologies, *The Black Woman* (1970) and *Stories for Black Folks* (1971), and two collections of stories, *Gorilla My Love* (1972) and *The Sea Birds Are Still Alive* (1977). She has also written a novel, *The Salt Eaters* (1980).

ANN BEATTIE (b. 1947)

Beattie grew up in the Washington suburb of Chevy Chase, Maryland. She received a B.A. from American University and went on to the University of Connecticut as a graduate student in English literature. Beattie's first published story, "A Rose for Judy Garland's Casket," appeared in 1972, and after many rejections she began publishing in *The New Yorker* shortly thereafter. Beattie's stories have made her a spokesperson for a generation that came of age in the sixties as they adapt to or are baffled and worn out by the oncoming years. Many of them have been collected in *Distortions* (1976), *Secrets and Surprises* (1979), *Jacklighting* (1981), *The Burning House* (1982), and *Where You'll Find Me* (1986). Her novels are *Chilly Scenes of Winter* (1976), *Falling in Place* (1980), *Love Always* (1985), and *Picturing Will* (1990).

AMBROSE BIERCE (1842–1914?)

The tenth child of a poor Ohio family, Bierce rose during the Civil War to the rank of major, was twice wounded and cited fifteen times for bravery. He stayed in the army for a time after the war, then was a journalist in California and London, where his boisterous Western mannerisms and savage wit made him a celebrity and earned him the name "Bitter Bierce." He published *Tales of Soldiers and Civilians* (later called *In the Midst of Life*) (1891) and another volume of short stories, *Can Such Things Be?* (1893). The death of his two sons in 1889 and 1901, along with his divorce in 1891, might well have led him to Mexico, where he reportedly rode with Pancho Villa's revolutionaries. He disappeared and is presumed to have died there. Bierce is well known as the author of *The Cynic's Wordbook* (later called *The Devil's Dictionary*) (1906), but his short stories are his finest achievement.

JORGE LUIS BORGES (1899–1986)

A fifth-generation Argentinian, Borges moved with his family to Europe in 1914 and remained there until 1921, associating himself with avant-garde literary groups. Until the 1930s he was primarily a poet and a leader in *Ultraismo*, a literary movement based on Imagism and Surrealism, but he turned to prose—both fiction and essays—as his varied intellectual interests came together to suggest new forms. A vastly erudite man who directed the Biblioteca Nacional until the dictator Juan Peron for political reasons demoted him to the rank of chicken inspector, Borges created a "literature about literature"; his brief narratives and essays are often miniature encyclopedias of literary history and theory. His works available in English include *Labyrinths* (1962), *Ficciones* (1962), *Dreamtigers* (1964), *The Book of Imaginary Beings* (1969), *The Aleph and Other Stories* (1970), *Dr. Brodie's Report* (1972), and *The Book of Sand* (1979). He lost his sight in 1955.

JOHN CHEEVER (1912–1982)

Cheever was born in Quincy, Massachusetts. His formal education ended when he was expelled from Thayer Academy at the age of seventeen; thereafter he devoted himself completely to fiction writing, except for brief interludes of teaching at Barnard College and the University of Iowa, and script-writing for television. Cheever published his first story when he was sixteen, and until his first novel, *The Wapshot Chronicle*, won the National Book Award in 1958, he was known primarily as a superb and prolific writer of short stories. Built around a strong moral core and tinged with melancholy nostalgia for the past, they form a running commentary on the tensions, manners, and crippled aspirations of urban and suburban life. Many have won awards, including the O. Henry Award in 1956 for "The Country Husband." *The Stories of John Cheever* (1978) won the Pulitzer Prize.

ANTON CHEKHOV (1860–1904)

Son of a serf, Chekhov became a physician and author of a handful of classic plays and of hundreds of stories which changed the course of both genres. His first published work (1880) was written, it was said, to earn enough money to buy his mother a pie for her birthday. His first story collection, *The Tales of Melpomene*, was published in 1884, the year he completed his medical studies and went into practice in Moscow; the lung disease from which he was increasingly to suffer had already appeared the year before. The newly founded Moscow Art Company assured his success as a dramatist when it performed *The Sea Gull* in 1898 (a play that had failed two years earlier), *Uncle Vanya* the next year, *Three Sisters* in 1901, and *The Cherry Orchard* in 1904, the year of his death at a German health resort. Around the turn of the century his collected works appeared in ten volumes. He was diffident about the immense success of his works, thinking they would scarcely outlive him, and despite that success he never forgot his own early poverty and struggle for education—and the plight of those who had not been able to escape such conditions.

KATE CHOPIN (1851–1904)

The St. Louis–born Kate O'Flaherty married Oscar Chopin in 1879 and moved first to New Orleans, then to a Louisiana plantation, then, after her husband's death from swamp fever, back to St. Louis, where she began to fashion a literary career out of her experience of Louisiana life. When she was nearly forty years old she published her first novel, *At Fault* (1890). Her two volumes of short stories, *Bayou Folk* (1894) and *A Night in Acadie* (1897), were for a long time dismissed as mere tales of "local color." Recent attention to her last work, a short novel *The Awakening* (1899), which treats sex and marriage from a woman's point of view, has sparked renewed interest in and reassessment of her works.

RICHARD CONNELL (1893–1949)

Connell, like Ernest Hemingway, began his writing career as a journalist. At the age of sixteen, he was city editor of his native *Poughkeepsie News-Press*; later he was editor of both the *Crimson* and the *Lampoon* at Harvard, from which he graduated in 1915. After World War I, he left his New York job as an advertising editor to become a freelance writer, traveling to Paris and London and finally settling in Beverly Hills, California. His works include volumes of short stories—*Apes and Angels* (1924), *The Sin of Monsieur Pettipon* (1925), *Variety* (1925), and *Ironies* (1930)—and novels: *Mad Lover* (1927), *Murder at Sea* (1929), *Playboy* (1936), and *What Ho!* (1937).

JOSEPH CONRAD (1857–1924)

Jozeph Teodor Konrad Nalecz Korzeniowski was born in Berdyczew, Polish Ukraine. At five he accompanied his parents into exile in northern Russia and later near Kiev; he was left an orphan at eleven. Before he was seventeen he was off to Marseille, making several trips to the West Indies as an apprentice seaman. After some veiled troubles in France, involving gambling debts and an apparent suicide attempt, he sailed on a British ship, landed in England in 1878, and spent the next sixteen years in the British merchant service, rising to master in 1886, the year he became a British subject. In 1890, he worked on a boat that sailed up the Congo, the inspiration for *Heart of Darkness* (1899). He began writing in 1889 but did not publish his first novel, *Almayer's Folly*, until 1896. Though a successful writer, he was not truly popular or financially independent until the publication of *Chance* in 1912–13. Among his major novels are *The Nigger of the "Narcissus"* (1897), *Lord Jim* (1900), *Nostromo* (1904), *Under Western Eyes* (1910), and *Victory* (1915). His short-story collections include *Tales of Unrest* (1898), *Typhoon and Other Stories* (1903), *'Twixt Land and Sea* (1912), from which "The Secret Sharer" is taken, and *Within the Tides: Tales* (1915).

LOUISE ERDRICH (b. 1954)

Born in Little Falls, Minnesota, of German-American and Chippewa descent, Erdrich grew up in Wahpeton, North Dakota, as a member of the Turtle Mountain Band of Chippewa, and attended Dartmouth College. After graduation, she returned to teach in North Dakota's Poetry in the Schools Program. She received an M.A. in creative writing from Johns Hopkins University in 1979. In the same year, *Jacklight*, a collection of poetry, was published. Her novels are *Love Medicine* (1984), *The Beet Queen* (1986), and *Tracks* (1988). *Love Medicine*, which has been praised as a landmark work in its depiction of the lives of contemporary Native Americans, was the winner of the National Book Critics' Circle Award for fiction.

WILLIAM FAULKNER (1897–1962)

Faulkner spent almost his entire life in his native state of Mississippi. He left high school without graduating, joined the Royal Canadian Air Force in 1918, and in the mid-1920s lived briefly in New Orleans, where he was encouraged by Sherwood Anderson. He then spent a few miserable months as a clerk in a New York bookstore, published a collection of poems, *The Marble Faun*, in 1924, and took a long walking tour of Europe in 1925. In later years he made several visits to Hollywood, writing a screenplay for *The Big Sleep*, among others, and spent his last years in Charlottesville, Virginia. With the publication of *Sartoris* in 1929, Faulkner began a cycle of works interrelated by his fictional Yoknapatawpha County and the reappearance of characters or families from work to work. These include *As I Lay Dying* (1930), *Light in August* (1932), *Absalom, Absalom!* (1936), *The Unvanquished* (1939), *The Hamlet* (1940), and *Go Down, Moses* (1942), in which "The Old People" appears. His short fiction can be found in *The Collected Stories of William Faulkner* (1950). He received the Nobel Prize for Literature in 1950.

RICHARD FORD (b. 1944)

Ford was born in Jackson, Mississippi, attended Michigan State University, and received an M.F.A. in creative writing from the University of California. Since that time he has been awarded a Guggenheim Foundation fellowship and lived in western Montana, New York, Mississippi, and currently New Orleans. His first novel, *A Piece of My Heart*, was published in 1976. He has published three more novels, *The Ultimate Good Luck* (1981), *The Sportswriter* (1986), and *Wildlife* (1990), and a volume of short stories, *Rock Springs* (1987).

GABRIEL GARCÍA MÁRQUEZ (b. 1928)

Born in Aracataca, a remote town in Magdalena province near the Caribbean coast of Colombia, García Márquez studied law at the University of Bogotá and then worked as a journalist in Latin America, Europe, and the United States. In 1967 he took up permanent residence in Barcelona, Spain. His first published book, *Leaf Storm* (1955, translated 1972), in which "A Very Old Man with Enormous Wings" appears, is set in the fictional small town of Macondo, based on the myths and legends of his childhood home. His most famous novel, *One Hundred Years of Solitude* (1967, translated 1970) presents six generations of one family in Macondo, fusing magic, reality, fable, and fantasy in a way which also allows the town to serve as a microcosm of many of the social, political, and economic problems of Latin America. Among his works are *The Autumn of the Patriarch* (1975, translated 1976), *Innocent Eréndira and Other Stories* (1972, translated 1978), *Chronicle of a Death Foretold* (1981, translated 1982), and *Love in the Time of Cholera* (1987, translated 1988). Garcia Márquez won the Nobel Prize for Literature in 1982.

CHARLOTTE PERKINS GILMAN (1860–1935)

Charlotte Anna Perkins was born in Hartford, Connecticut. After a painful, lonely childhood and several years supporting herself as a governess, art teacher, and designer of greeting cards, Charlotte Perkins married the artist Charles Stetson. Following several extended periods of depression, she was put by her husband into the hands of Dr. S. Weir Mitchell, who "sent me home with the solemn advice to 'live as domestic a life as . . . possible,' to 'have but two hours' intellectual life a day,' and 'never to touch pen, brush, or pencil again' as long as I lived." Three months of this, ending "near the borderline of utter mortal ruin," became the inspiration for "The Yellow Wallpaper." In 1900 she married George Houghton Gilman, having divorced Stetson in 1892. Her nonfiction works, which placed her at the center of the early women's movement, include *Women and Economics* (1898) and *Man-Made World* (1911). She also wrote several utopian novels, including *Moving the Mountain* (1911) and *Herland* (1915).

NADINE GORDIMER (b. 1923)

Gordimer was born in a gold-mining town in South Africa and has lived all her life in that country, exploring, through her writing, the effects of apartheid in all its forms with intelligence and acute sensitivity. Her novels include *The Lying Days* (1953), *A World of Strangers* (1958), *A Guest of Honor* (1970), *The Conservationist* (1975), *Burger's Daughter* (1979), and *A Sport of Nature* (1987). Among her short-story collections are *Six Feet of the Country* (1956), *Friday's Footprint and Other Stories* (1960), and *A Soldier's Embrace.* (1980). Her *Selected Stories* were published in 1976. For Gordimer, "a short story *occurs,* in the most imaginative sense. To write one is to express from a situation in the exterior or interior world the life-giving drop . . . that will spread an intensity on the page; burn a hole in it."

NATHANIEL HAWTHORNE (1804–1864)

Hawthorne was born in Salem, Massachusetts, a descendent of Puritan immigrants; one ancestor had been a judge in the Salem witchcraft trials. Educated at Bowdoin College, he was agonizingly slow in winning acclaim for his work, and supported himself from time to time in government service—working in the custom houses of Boston and Salem and serving as the United States consul in Liverpool. His early collections of stories, *Twice-Told Tales* (1837) and *Mosses from an Old Manse* (1846), in which "Young Goodman Brown" appears, did not sell well, and it was not until the publication in 1850 of his most famous novel, *The Scarlet Letter,* that his fame spread beyond a discerning few. His other novels include *The House of the Seven Gables* (1851) and *The Blithedale Romance* (1852).

ERNEST HEMINGWAY (1899–1961)

Born in Oak Park, Illinois, Hemingway was first a reporter, then an ambulance-service volunteer in France and infantryman in Italy in 1918, when he was wounded and decorated for valor. After the war and more reporting, he settled for a time in Paris, where he knew Gertrude Stein and Ezra Pound, among others. From 1925 to 1935 he published two volumes of stories, *In Our Time* (1925) and *Death in the Afternoon* (1932), and two major novels, *The Sun Also Rises* (1926) and *A Farewell to Arms* (1929), which established his international reputation. Hemingway helped the Loyalists in the Spanish Civil War, the subject of *For Whom the Bell Tolls* (1940), served as a war correspondent in the Second World War, and from 1950 to 1962 lived in Cuba. *The Old Man and the Sea* was published in 1952, winning a Pulitzer Prize. Hemingway was awarded the Nobel Prize for Literature in 1954. He committed suicide in 1961.

SPENCER HOLST (b. 1926)

Well known in the literary underground, Holst has published his short stories and poetry in numerous periodicals such as *Mademoiselle* and *Oui*. He has translated the work of German poet Vera Lachmann and published several volumes of his own writing, including two volumes of short stories, *Language of Cats and Other Stories* (1971) and *Spencer Holst Stories* (1976), a collection of imaginative and humorous fables which play with reality and fantasy.

HENRY JAMES (1843–1916)

Son of a writer and religious philosopher, brother of the philosopher William James, Henry James was born in New York and entered Harvard Law School in 1862, after private study, art school, and study and residence abroad. Thereafter his American home was in Cambridge, Massachusetts, but he lived in England from 1876 until his death forty years later, having become a British subject in 1915. James's fiction often centers on the confrontation of Americans with Europe or Europeans; he treats the two as moral or value systems as much as geographical entities. His practice and theory of fiction, set forth mainly in the prefaces to his novels, dominated fiction criticism for generations. Among his works are *The American* (1877), *Daisy Miller* (1879), *Portrait of a Lady* (1881), *The Turn of the Screw* (1898), *The Wings of the Dove* (1902), *The Ambassadors* (1903), and *The Golden Bowl* (1904).

JAMES JOYCE (1882–1941)

In 1902, after graduating from University College, Dublin, Joyce left his native city for Paris, only to return in April 1903 to teach school. In the spring of 1904 he lived at the Martello Tower, Sandycove, a site made famous by his great novel, *Ulysses* (1921). In October 1904 he eloped with Nora Barnacle and left Ireland again, this time for Trieste where he taught English for the Berlitz school. Though he lived abroad the rest of his life, that first abortive trip proved symbolic: in his fiction the expatriate could never leave Dublin. Joyce had more than his share of difficulties with publication and censorship. His volume of short stories, *Dubliners* (in which "Araby" appears), completed in 1905, was not published until 1914. His *Portrait of the Artist as a Young Man*, dated "Dublin 1904, Trieste 1914," appeared first in America, in 1916. *Ulysses* was banned for a dozen years in the United States and as long or longer elsewhere. Though he published a play, *Exiles*, and poetry, the three works mentioned and the monumental, experimental, and puzzling *Finnegans Wake* (1939) are the basis of his reputation.

FRANZ KAFKA (1883–1924)

Born in Prague of a middle-class Jewish family, Kafka earned a doctorate in law from the German University in that city and held an inconspicuous position in the civil service for many years. Emotionally and physically ill for the last seven or eight years of his short life, he died of tuberculosis in Vienna, never having married (though he was twice engaged to the same woman and lived with an actress in Berlin for some time before he died) and not having published his three major novels, *The Trial* (1925), *The Castle* (1926), and *Amerika* (1927). Indeed, he ordered his friend Max Brod to destroy them and other works he had left in manuscript. Fortunately, Brod did not, and not long after his death, Kafka's work was world famous and widely influential. His stories in English translation can be found in *The Great Wall of China* (1933), *The Penal Colony* (1948), and *The Complete Stories* (1976).

JAMAICA KINCAID (b. 1949)

Born in St. John's, Antigua (an island in the West Indies north of Guadeloupe), Jamaica Kincaid now lives in New York, where she is a staff writer for the *New Yorker*. She is the author of a volume of short stories, *At the Bottom of the River* (1984), and two novels, *Annie John* (1985) and *Lucy* (1990). Although Kincaid left her native island as a teenager, a deeply-felt—and richly-evocative—sense of place pervades her work.

D. H. LAWRENCE (1885–1930)

Son of a coal miner and a middle-class schoolteacher, Lawrence won a scholarship to Nottingham High School at thirteen but had to leave a few years later when his elder brother died. He worked for a surgical appliance manufacturer, attended Nottingham College, and taught school in Croyden, near London. In 1911, when his first novel, *The White Peacock*, was published, he left teaching to devote his time to writing, though it was not until the publication of *Sons and Lovers* (1913) that he was established as a major literary figure. In 1912 he eloped to the Continent with Frieda von Richthofen, and in 1914, after her divorce, they were married. During World War I, both his novels and the fact that his wife was German gave him trouble: *The Rainbow* was published in September 1915 and suppressed in November. In November 1919 the Lawrences left England and their years of wandering began: first Italy, then Ceylon and Australia, Mexico and New Mexico, then back to England and Italy. *Women in Love* was published in New York in 1920, and *Lady Chatterley's Lover*, his most sexually explicit and controversial novel, eight years later. Through it all he suffered from tuberculosis, the disease from which he finally died, in France. Lawrence's stories are available in a three-volume edition, first published in 1961.

URSULA K. LE GUIN (b. 1929)

A writer of short stories, poetry, science fiction novels, novels of fantasy, and works increasingly difficult to categorize, Le Guin was born in Berkeley, California, and educated at Radcliffe and Columbia. She studied in Paris and taught creative writing before his first novel, *Rocannon's World*, was published in 1964. Since then, she has gone on to publish, among others, *The Left Hand of Darkness* (1969), which won the Hugo and Nebula Awards; *The Lathe of Heaven* (1970); *The Farthest Shore* (1973), winner of the National Book Award; *The Dispossessed* (1974); *Malafrena* (1979); *The Eye of the Heron* (1983); *Always Coming Home* (1985) and *Tehanu* (1990). Her volumes of short fiction include *The Wind's Twelve Quarters* (1975), *Orsinian Tales* (1976), and *The Compass Rose* (1982). She has also published a volume of essays, *The Language of the Night:*

Essays on Fantasy and Science Fiction, which appeared in 1979. She says of her books, "I write science fiction because that is what publishers call my books. Left to myself, I should call them novels."

DORIS LESSING (b. 1919)

Born in Persia, Lessing lived for twenty-five years in Southern Rhodesia (now Zimbabwe) before moving to England, where soon thereafter her first novel, *The Grass Is Singing* (1950), was published. She has since published voluminously. Her books include *The Golden Notebook* (1962), the five Martha Quest novels, *Children of Violence*, published between 1952 and 1969, *Briefing for a Descent into Hell* (1971), *The Summer Before the Dark* (1973), and *The Good Terrorist* (1985). She has also published eight volumes of short fiction, including *A Man and Two Women* (1963) and *The Memoirs of a Survivor* (1975), and has written plays, television plays, poetry, and essays. Her work is known for its range and variety, some of it set in Africa, a significant portion of it political (she was once a Communist), much of it examining inner lives of women in modern society, and some of it lately reflecting her interest in extrasensory perception. Several of Lessing's recent novels, beginning with *Shikasta* (1979), are part of a visionary, futuristic work called *Canopus in Argos: Archives.*

KATHERINE MANSFIELD (1888–1923)

Born in New Zealand, Mansfield studied music at Queen's College, London, and was an accomplished cellist. She published three major volumes of short stories during her short life: *Bliss* (1920), which established her reputation, *The Garden Party* (1922), and *The Dove's Nest* (1923). With John Middleton Murry and D. H. Lawrence she founded an influential literary review, *The Signature*. She died of tuberculosis in France, and a final volume of stories, *Something Childish* (1924), appeared shortly after her death. Her *Collected Stories* were published in 1945.

BOBBIE ANN MASON (b. 1940)

Mason, who grew up on a farm near Mayfield, Kentucky, has written for *Movie Stars, Movie Life,* and *T.V. Star Parade. The New Yorker* published her first story in 1980. Since then, she has been awarded a Guggenheim Foundation fellowship, has had stories in *Best American Short Stories* in 1981 and 1983, and won the Pushcart Prize for fiction in 1983. *Shiloh and Other Stories* (1982), her first collection, won the Ernest Hemingway Foundation Award. She has also written a novel, *In Country* (1985), a short novel, *Spence and Lila* (1988), and a second collection of stories, *Love Life* (1989). "The people I write about," she says "either want to get away from home, get away from town, see the world, or they want to stay home, and they're afraid to leave, so they accommodate . . . I'm interested in that tension between longing to stay and longing to go."

GUY DE MAUPASSANT (1850–1893)

Born Henri René Albert in Normandy, France, at sixteen Maupassant was expelled from a Rouen seminary and finished his education in a public high school. After serving in the Franco-Prussian War, he was for ten years a government clerk in Paris. A protégé of Flaubert, during the 1880s he published some three hundred stories, a half-dozen novels, and plays. The short stories, which appeared regularly in popular periodicals, sampled military and peasant life, the decadent world of politics and journalism, prostitution, the supernatural, and the hypocrisies of solid citizens. With Chekhov, he may be said to have created the modern short story; his reliance on plot, plot twists, and sometimes heavy irony became facile in the hands of his followers and has somewhat diminished his own reputation the past quarter-century and more. His life ended somewhat like one of his own stories: he died in an asylum, of syphilis. His novels include *Une Vie* (*A Life*, 1883), *Bel Ami* (*Handsome Friend*, 1885), and *Pierre et Jean* (1888). His stories are most readily available in his *Collected Works*.

BHARATI MUKHERJEE (b. 1940)

Brought up in an upper-class Bengali family of the Brahmin caste, Mukherjee attended private schools in India, London, and Switzerland before a business disaster wiped out the family fortune. She won a scholarship in 1961 to the University of Iowa Writer's Workshop, and has since lived with her husband (also a writer) and two children in Canada, India, and the United States, supporting herself through teaching and other jobs, and writing in the small hours of the morning. In 1971 her critically acclaimed first novel, *The Tiger's Daughter*, appeared; her other novels are *Wife* (1975) and *Jasmine* (1989). Mukherjee's short fiction collections are *Darkness* (1985), stories of South Asian immigrants, and *The Middleman* (1988), which includes characters and voices from various countries and social strata: "Mine is not minimalism, which strips away, but compression, which reflects many layers of meaning."

ALICE MUNRO (b. 1931)

Munro grew up on a farm near Lake Huron in Ontario and attended the University of Western Ontario, where she began publishing short stories. Much of her fiction grows out of her childhood memories of rural family life: "I write about places where your roots are and most people don't live that kind of life anymore at all." Her first book, a collection of stories entitled *Dance of the Happy Shades* (1968) in which "Boys and Girls" appears, won a Governor General's Award. Munro has written a novel, *Lives of Girls and Women* (1971), and five other short-story collections, *Something I've Been Meaning to Tell You* (1974), *Who Do You Think You Are?* (1978, published in the United States as *The Beggar Maid* in 1979), *The Moons of Jupiter* (1983), *The Progress of Love* (1986), and *Friend of My Youth* (1990).

FLANNERY O'CONNOR (1925–1964)

O'Connor was born in Savannah, Georgia, studied at the Georgia State College for Women, and won a fellowship to the Writer's Workshop of the University of Iowa, where she received an M.F.A. degree. Her first novel, *Wise Blood*, was published in 1952, and her first collection of stories, *A Good Man Is Hard to Find*, in 1955. She was able to complete only one more novel, *The Violent Bear It Away* (1960), and a second collection of stories, *Everything That Rises Must Converge* (1965), before dying of an incurable illness in Milledgeville, Georgia. Her reputation has grown steadily since her untimely death. A collection of letters, edited by Sally Fitzgerald under the title *The Habit of Being*, appeared in 1979.

GRACE PALEY (b. 1922)

A native New Yorker, Paley studied at Hunter College and New York University. She currently teaches literature at Sarah Lawrence College and gives frequent readings from her work. Her short stories have appeared in leading magazines as well as in three collections, *The Little Disturbances of Man* (1959), *Enormous Changes at the Last Minute* (1974), and *Later the Same Day* (1985). Though few, her stories have been admired for their stylistic liveliness and for their fusion of sardonic observation with spare, expressive form.

EDGAR ALLAN POE (1809–1849)

Poe's actor father deserted his wife and son when Edgar was less than a year old. His mother died before he was three, and he and his younger sister were separated and taken into different families. The Allans (who gave Poe his middle name) moved, in 1815, to England, where Edgar had his early schooling. He studied briefly at the University of Virginia and in 1827 paid to have a volume of poems published in Boston (his birthplace); a second volume appeared in 1829 in Baltimore (where he was to die twenty years later). Having served for two years in the army, he was appointed to West Point in 1830 but apparently managed to have himself expelled within the year for cutting classes. Living in Baltimore with his grandmother, aunt, and cousin Virginia (whom he married in 1835 when she was thirteen), Poe began to attract critical attention but made very little money. For the twelve years of his bizarre marriage, he wrote, worked as journalist and editor, and drank. Not long after his wife died in 1847 he seemed to be straightening himself out when, on election day—October 3—he was found semiconscious near a polling place and died four days later without fully regaining consciousness. It is testimony to the continuing fame of his works that they need not be named here.

KATHERINE ANNE PORTER (1890–1980)

Porter was born Callie Russell Porter in Indian Creek, Texas. Her writing career was remarkable for its brilliance as well as its brevity. Her first volume, *Flowering Judas* (1930), was made up of stories that appeared in magazines in the previous decade. Her last (except for her *Collected Stories*, 1965, which included only earlier works) was *The Leaning Tower* (1944). She published a book of essays *The Days Before* (1952), and one long novel, *Ship of Fools* (1962), twenty-five years in the making, but is at her best in shorter forms, where her concision and precision of diction and style enable her brilliantly to capture a character, a culture, or chaos. A warning about reading "The Fig Tree" or her other stories: "Reviewers are much mistaken," she said, "when they insist on identifying me with any and every woman that appears in my stories. . . . I am a considerably more complicated person than they. They were not writers."

MORDECAI RICHLER (b. 1931)

Richler was born in Montreal, the son of working-class Jewish parents; *The Street* (1975) is a loosely autobiographical depiction of his childhood. Richler attended Sir George Williams University for two years and worked as a freelance writer in Paris and London from 1952, returning to live in his native Quebec only in 1980. His writing is varied and includes short stories, essays, screenplays, and novels. His *Cocksure* (1968) and *St. Urbain's Horseman* (1971) won the Governor General's Award, and his own screen adaptation of his novel *The Apprenticeship of Duddy Kravitz* (1959) was nominated for an Academy Award in 1974. His novels include *Joshua Then and Now* (1980) and *Solomon Gursky Was Here* (1990).

ELIZABETH TALLENT (b. 1954)

Tallent studied anthropology at the University of Illinois before turning to writing. Best known for her stories, she has won the Pushcart Prize and has had work published in *The New Yorker*, the *Paris Review*, *Esquire*, and *Grand Street*. Although she makes her home in Santa Fe, New Mexico, she teaches at the University of California at Davis in the winter and the University of Iowa in the summer. Her published books include the story collections *In Constant Flight* (1983) and *Time with Children* (1987), and the novel *Museum Pieces* (1985).

AMY TAN (b. 1952)

Tan was born in Oakland, California, just two and a half years after her parents immigrated there from China. She has worked as a consultant to programs for disabled children and as a freelance writer. In 1987 she visited China for the first time—"As soon as my feet touched China, I became Chinese"—and returned to write her first book, *The Joy Luck Club* (1989).

LEO TOLSTOY (1828–1910)

Tolstoy's life would have made a fitting subject for one of his novels. Born into a noble Russian family, orphaned before he was ten, he studied Oriental languages, then law, then settled on the family estate where he tried to improve the lot of his serfs though they treated him with suspicion. He served in the army, returned home to found a school, married, and wrote two monumental novels, his masterpieces *War and Peace* (1863–69) and *Anna Karenina* (1873–76). But he wasn't satisfied; he found his life, in his own words, "absurd . . . a stupid and spiteful joke," and was converted, first to his national religion, then to a kind of "primitive" Christianity. He opposed the military, capital punishment, persecution of the Jews; he gave up alcohol, meat, and as much of his property as his family would allow. In the end he fled from home—where his wife was trying to have him declared incompetent—intending to enter a monastery, but died in a railway station en route. His works, after his conversion, include *The Death of Iván Ilyich* (1886), "How Much Land Does a Man Need," and many other stories, parables, and novels.

WILLIAM TREVOR (b. 1928)

Born William Coxin in County Cork, Ireland, Trevor moved to Devon, England, in 1960. He was been a teacher—chiefly in England but including a stint in Armagh, Northern Ireland, 1950–52—advertising copywriter, sculptor, novelist—his novels include *The Old Boys* (1964), *Lovers of Their Time* (1979), *Other People's Worlds* (1980), and *Fools of Fortune* (1983)—and short-story writer. Many of his stories have been adapted for BBC radio. His volumes of short stories include *The Day We Got Drunk on Cake* (1972), *Angels at the Ritz* (1975), and *Beyond the Pale* (1982); *The Stories of William Trevor* was published in 1983. Trevor was named Commander, Order of the British Empire, in 1979.

LUISA VALENZUELA (b. 1938)

Valenzuela grew up in the thriving literary atmosphere of Buenos Aires, Argentina (her mother was a novelist and friend of Jorge Luis Borges). After attending the University of Buenos Aires, she began writing for magazines and newspapers, traveling widely in the United States, Europe, and Latin America. Her first story collection, *Hay que sonreir* (1966), was published in the United States as *Clara* (1979). Another collection, *Strange Things Happen Here* (1976, translated 1979), reflected some of the horrors of the military regime of the late 1970s. In 1979, Valenzuela moved to New York, where she now lives. She has published another novel, *The Lizard's Tale* (1983), and three collections of stories, *Other Weapons* (1985), *He Who Searches* (1987), and *Open Door* (1988).

INDEX OF AUTHORS

INDEX OF TITLES